Praise for Elizabeth Bear's
Hammered

"*Hammered* is a very exciting, very polished, very impressive debut novel." —Mike Resnick

"Gritty, insightful, and daring—Elizabeth Bear is a talent to watch." —David Brin, author of the Uplift novels and *Kil'n People*

"A gritty and painstakingly well-informed peek inside a future we'd all better hope we don't get, liberally seasoned with VR delights and enigmatically weird alien artifacts. Genevieve Casey is a pleasingly original female lead, fully equipped with the emotional life so often lacking in military SF yet tough and full of noir attitude; old enough by a couple of decades to know better but conflicted enough to engage with the sleazy dynamics of her situation regardless. Out of this basic contrast, Elizabeth Bear builds her future nightmare tale with style and conviction and a constant return to the twists of the human heart." —Richard Morgan, author of *Altered Carbon*

"*Hammered* has it all. Drug wars, hired guns, corporate skullduggery, and bleeding-edge AI, all rolled into one of the best first novels I've seen in I don't know how long. This is the real dope!" —Chris Moriarty, author of *Spin State*

"Bear devotes admirable attention to the physical and mental challenges that radical augmentation would likely entail, and *Hammered* certainly establishes Bear as a writer with intriguing potential." —*F&SF*

"With Jenny Casey, author Elizabeth Bear delivers a kick-butt fighter who could easily hold her own against Kristine Smith's Jani Killian or Elizabeth Moon's Heris Serrano.... What Bear has done in *Hammered* is create a world that is all too plausible, one wracked by environmental devastation and political chaos. Through Jenny Casey's eyes, she conducts a tour of this society's darker corners, offering an unnerving peek into a future humankind would be wise to avoid." —SciFi.com

"*Hammered* is a tough, gritty novel sure to appeal to fans of Elizabeth Moon and David Weber.... In Jenny Casey, Bear has created an admirably Chandler-esque character, street-smart and battle-scarred, tough talking and quick on the trigger.... Bear shuttles effortlessly back and forth across time to weave her disparate cast of characters together in a tightly plotted page-turner. The noir universe she creates is as hard-edged as the people who inhabit it. The dialogue and descriptions are suitably spartan, but every one of her characters has their own recognizable voice. It takes no effort at all to imagine *Hammered* on the big screen." —*SFRevu*

"A sobering projection of unchecked current social, political, and environmental trends...Although a careless reader might be lulled by the presence of drugs, the hard-edged narration, and the run-down setting of the opening scene into thinking this novel is dystopian or even cyberpunk in nature, such expectations are quickly undercut by Bear.... Without giving too much away, it can be said that the underlying theme of Bear's novel is *salvage*, in all its senses.... Indeed, every character in *Hammered*, even the villainous, have their own powerful motives for their actions; and conversely, the hands of the 'good' characters are never entirely clean, and they make fearful moral bargains and compromises simply because they can't see any better way to do what they must. They all try to salvage what they can...[which] embodies the novel's central theme of how what we would choose to preserve and what we wish to discard are sometimes inextricable."
—*Green Man Reviews*

"[An] enjoyable dystopian thriller...The nicest thing about this novel is the rich characters....It's a roller-coaster of a good thriller, too....Elizabeth Bear has carved herself out a fantastic little world with this first novel. Long may it continue." —*SF Crow's Nest*

"*Hammered* is a well-written debut, and Bear's deft treatment of the characters and their relationships pushed the book up to keeper level....I would gladly hand it over to anyone who would appreciate a broader spectrum of strong female characters to choose from, particularly in the realm of speculative fiction." —*Broad Universe*

"An enthralling roller-coaster ride through a dark and possible near future." —*Starlog*

"Bear has done a bang-up job re-arranging a few squares of the here-and-now into a future that's guaranteed to raise the blood pressure of readers in the present. Sure, we all want heart-pounding suspense, and Bear offers that in spades. But she also provides the kind of pressurizing prescience that doesn't exactly see the future so much as it re-paints the most unpleasant parts of the present into a portrait of a world that knows and loathes itself all too well." —*Agony Column*

"[Bear] does it like a juggler who is also a magician." —Matthew Cheney, *Mumpsimus*

"Packed with a colorful panoply of characters, a memorable and likeable anti-heroine, and plenty of action and intrigue, *Hammered* is a superbly written novel that combines high tech, military-industrial politics, and complex morality. There is much to look forward to in new writer Elizabeth Bear." —Karin Lowachee, Campbell Award–nominated author of *Warchild*

"Even in scenes where there is no violent action, or even much physical action at all, the thoughts and emotions of Ms. Bear's characters, as well as the dynamic tensions of their relationships, create an impression of feverish activity going on below the surface and liable to erupt into plain view at any moment.... The language is terse and vivid, punctuated by ironic asides whose casual brutality—sometimes amusing, sometimes shocking—speaks volumes about these people and their world.... This is a superior piece of work by a writer of enviable talents. I look forward to reading more!" —Paul Witcover, author of *Waking Beauty*

"*Hammered* is one helluva good novel! Elizabeth Bear writes tight and tough and tender about grittily real people caught up in a highly inventive story of a wild and wooly tomorrow that grabs the reader from the get-go and will not let go. Excitement, intrigue, intelligence—and a sense of wonder, too! Who could ask for anything more?" —James Stevens-Arce, author of *Soulsaver*, Best First Novel 2000 (*Denver Rocky Mountain News*)

"In this promising debut novel, Elizabeth Bear deftly weaves thought-provoking ideas into an entertaining and tight narrative." —Dena Landon, author of *Shapeshifter's Quest*

Praise for *Scardown*

"Bear deftly creates believable characters who walk into your heart and mind easily.... [Her] prose is easy on the mind's ears, her dialogue generally crisp and lifelike."
—Scifi.com

"*Scardown* is a wonderfully written book, and should be a prerequisite for anyone who wants to write intrigue. Although it doesn't reinvent the cyberpunk genre with radically new science or philosophy, it uses the established conventions to tell a thoroughly engaging story, and tell it with a high degree of skill. It's engaging brain candy with surprising emotional insights—and some cool gun fights—and you won't be able to put it down." —*Reflection's Edge*

"For all the widescreen fireworks and exotic tech, it is also a tale in which friendships and familial relationships drive as much of the action as enmity, paranoia and Machiavellian scheming.... Here there be nifty Ideas about natural and artificial intelligences; satisfyingly convoluted conspiracies; interestingly loose-limbed and unconventional interpersonal relationships; and some pretty good jokes.... I will simply warn the tenderhearted that Bad Things great and small will indeed be allowed to happen, but that those who come through the other side will have exhibited that combination of toughness and humanity that makes Bear one of the most welcome writers to come over the horizon lately." —*Locus*

Praise for *Worldwired*

"Elizabeth Bear...has forged a peculiar and powerful path with her tripartite novel. By sheer force of will and great writing, Bear has pulled off a rather remarkable feat without drawing attention to that feat. That is, beyond the attention you get when you nab a John W. Campbell Award...What we didn't expect was that she'd manage to sort of re-invent the novel and re-invigorate the science fiction series...[A] rip-roaring tale of detection, adventure, aliens, conspiracy and much more told in carefully turned prose with well-developed characters." —*Agony Column*

"Elizabeth Bear is simply magisterial. She asserts firm control of her characters, her setting, and her research (for the novels). She creates flourishes of style and excitement; not one time does this novel bore its characters or readers.... It really is a fine thing to see a writer mature as well and as successfully as Elizabeth has—and in only her third published book. I can pay her the ultimate compliment a reader can make a writer: I will purchase and read each of her books. Yes, I trust her insights and talent that much.... Run, do not walk, to your nearest bookseller, buy this book, and then sit back and enjoy." —Las Vegas SF Society

"Most of *Worldwired* is about attempts to find common ground—whether within a broken family, between countries on the brink of war, or with aliens so truly alien that humans may not be able to communicate. Bear excels at breaking world-altering political acts and military coups into personal ambitions, compromises, and politicians who are neither gods nor monsters.... *Worldwired* is a thinking person's book, almost more like a chess match than a traditional narrative.... Hardcore science fiction fans—especially those who read David Brin and Larry Niven—won't want to miss it." —*Reflection's Edge*

"The language is taut, the characters deep and the scenes positively crackle with energy. Not to mention that this is real science fiction, with rescues from crippled starships and exploration of mysterious alien artifacts and international diplomatic brinksmanship between spacefaring powers China and Canada. Yes, Canada!" —James Patrick Kelly, author of *Strange but Not a Stranger* and *Think Like a Dinosaur*

"This final volume really rounds out the series and brings it to an enjoyable end.... *Worldwired* shifts between multiple characters very well, giving us many viewpoints on the complex future Bear has imagined. The politics of a world wracked by global warming and world wars is believable and often electric as the premiers of China and Canada face off against each other. The alien tech is refreshingly alien and overall it feels like we're somewhere very much fully realized.... An enjoyable, thoughtful and above all fun trio of books. Elizabeth Bear's work is definitely worth sampling but you probably won't want to stop with just the one book." —*SF Crow's Nest*

"A compelling story... Bear has plotted the global geopolitics of the next sixty years with considerable depth and aplomb." —*Strange Horizons*

Praise for *Carnival*

"Enjoyable, thought-provoking... Like the best of speculative fiction, Bear has created a fascinating and complete universe that blends high-tech gadgetry with Old World adventure and political collusion." —*Publishers Weekly*

Also by Elizabeth Bear

UNDERTOW

Elizabeth Bear

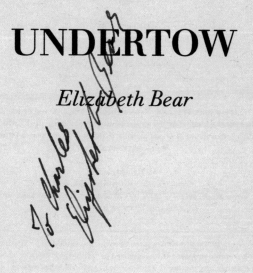

BANTAM BOOKS

UNDERTOW

A Bantam Spectra Book / August 2007

Published by Bantam Dell
A Division of Random House, Inc.
New York, New York

This is a work of fiction. Names, characters, places, and incidents
either are the product of the author's imagination or are used fictitiously.
Any resemblance to actual persons, living or dead, events, or locales
is entirely coincidental.

Bantam Books, the rooster colophon, Spectra, and the portrayal of a
boxed "s" are trademarks of Random House, Inc.

ISBN 978-0-553-58905-4

Printed in the United States of America
Published simultaneously in Canada

www.bantamdell.com

OPM 10 9 8 7 6 5 4 3 2

This book is for Sarah and Allen Monette

Acknowledgments

The author would like to thank her first readers, especially Jaime Voss, Kat Allen, Leah Bobet, Amanda Downum, Chelsea Polk, and Sarah Monette (all of whom really ought to be demanding boxes of cookies at least by now); her agent, Jenn Jackson (who provides her own cookies, which are much better than the author's in any case); her editor, Anne Groell, and copy editor, Faren Bachelis, and the rest of the Bantam Spectra team; and enough other people that the orchestra would be playing her off before she got halfway down the list.

And of course the readers, without whom this wouldn't be any fun at all.

1

THE MORNING AFTER HE KILLED EUGENE SHAPIRO, ANDRÉ Deschênes woke early. Before his headset warble ended, he rolled from the bed and landed palms-down on the deck of his bedroom. He slept in loose white trousers; nudity implied vulnerability. The raw breeze through the long windows above his bed roughened his shoulders, scalp, and nape. A clap punctuated each push-up, and he followed the set with five sun salutations to warm up and release his muscles.

He dressed and skinned and was out the door in minutes.

His footfalls chased him through the leaden morning. Roaches and rats scattered before him: humanity's companions all the way to the stars. The air was thick with the promise of rain; André's skin steamed before he'd run five hundred meters. The tide was in, the streets riding high on the pilings, and though he ran through a commercial zone, his filters held. Just one pop-ad penetrated, and he squelched it with an eye-flick.

In André's neighborhood, the streets were wood slat, floating piers independent of the houses and shops moored to them. They echoed under his running shoes, a hollow *thump-thump-thump* still unadulterated by other sounds.

He might have been the only one awake in all of Novo Haven. If he lived on Bayside, he would have seen the fishing boats and tenders sliding gulfward with the first light of morning. But from here, only thin channels of bay were visible between the floating streets and under the bridges, and the dinghies and scooters and small boats were still moored by the various steps that led up to street level. He passed more shops than houses; above them on the flat-decked, seaworthy cruisers were second-floor apartments with lifts or spiral walk-ups, but the lower levels had shuttered windows suitable for opening to catch sunlight and the attention of passersby. Ladders and gangplanks ran down to the water, where small craft waited and taxi drivers read the news and drank their coffee.

André ran by greengrocers and tackle shops, a geomancer's, an interface outlet, two brothels, a fixit shop for headsets and other implants, a skin-and-fashion store, a corner clinic, a beautician's parlor, and a Chinese restaurant. The bakery on Seagrove wasn't open yet, but good smells emanated from the back, and the clang of pans on counters rattled through the screen door.

He almost tripped crossing up onto the sidewalk beside the 400 "barge"—actually, a twenty-meter cruiser ringed with boardwalks and lashed to pilings. The barge was lower in the water than code permitted, and loosely moored. The sidewalk dipped alarmingly when his weight hit it, but he skipped a step and kept running. More cooking smells now, the distant sound of engines, lights flicking off over doorways as the landward sky paled gold. Someone ran on ahead, a woman with golden skin and black hair clubbed at the nape of her neck, her small breasts bouncing in a crimson sport top. He magnified her, recognized her, and decided she was a good enough reason to run faster. But she turned to port, down Amaryllis, between the white-and-pastel apartment blocks, and his road lay straight on. He didn't want to look too eager.

He wasn't jogging now but running, hard out, breath whistling between his teeth in misty streamers. His heels hit staccato, the street rocking under his stride. He counted breaths, pulling his elbows back each time his arms pumped, feeling the pivot and snap of each foot as it landed, as it left the slats again.

Running was good. Mornings were good. The wet air scraped his throat, chilled his lungs as he sucked it in, shoved it out again. Running hard, running cold, running over the water as the sun warmed the roof peaks and the streets began to hum.

His route was a circle. Or a ragged ungeometric circuit, which brought him panting back down Seagrove just as the bakery's armored shutters glided up, revealing the cheery blues and yellows of an interior bathed in full-spectrum light. Awnings, also automated, fanned out to shade the street. The light off the water would be brutal when the sun got past the rooflines. The fortune-teller next door wouldn't open until after lunchtime, but his awnings rolled out as well. A public service.

André let his pace drop to a trot, a jog, a stumbling amble. Sweat, and perhaps some condensation, slid down his chilled face, stung his eyes, and scattered off his nose. He slapped his biceps and thighs to get some heat into the skin, which felt like wax fruit. He set his status as unavailable when he ran—he liked the morning clean—but only an idiot would completely drop connex. So it was uncomplicated to check the price of bread on his headset. Citywide, it was a bit lower than the Seagrove bakery broadcast, but this was fresh and here and it smelled good. He transferred credit as he was walking up; one of the bakers, wearing a tall white hat and a skin that made blue and gold sparkles in the depths of her irises, handed him a warm semipermeable bag over the window ledge. "Thanks, Jacinta," he said. She winked at him, that eye flashing for an instant, brilliant gold.

André wasn't wearing a cosmetic himself, so he contented himself with a grin. He wiped sweat on his bare arm, flicked the droplets over the channel, and watched the ripples as some lurking fish disappointed themselves on the mouthfuls.

Jacinta tapped a golden loaf steaming gently on a cutting board. It made a hollow sound. The scent rose sweetly. "Want a slice?"

It smelled of cinnamon and raisins. "Can't eat until I wash," he said. "But thank you."

Back at his house—the 1100 barge of Redbridge—he walked through the security field, which recognized the hard code access in his headset and let him in without so much as a tingle. He dropped off the loaf of rye, showered, depilated his scalp, trimmed his beard, and dressed. The sharp suit of gold-shot scarlet was Earth silk with an autofit. He inspected his image as rebroadcast into the headset, activated his stock ticker, chat boxes, news scroll, and the standard informational detritus of his daily connex. His cousin Maryanne thought he was weird to leave it off in the morning—she probably reached for her connex the way her great-great-grandfather would have reached for his glasses—but the run with nobody in his head kept him centered. He thought of it as moving meditation, one brief chance to arrive at silence before swimming into the currents of the day.

He patted his house on the door to let it know he was leaving, stepped into his work shoes, picked up his walking stick, and went.

It was early yet, and André was his own boss. But there were messages to be answered, and he had rules about bringing work home.

It took him longer to walk in than he'd anticipated, and not because he strode through morning traffic now. Halfway down Fairview, when the shakes from exertion had finally settled out of his calves, an attention signal pinged at the corner of his field. His heart skipped painfully when he caught the ident.

He slowed, turned as if watching a bird dip-glide across the water. He crossed wavering slats and balanced by the rail, the red blooms of a genemod geranium brushing his ankle. The woman who walked toward him through the crowd wore saffron: flowing trousers and an ankle-length open tunic over a white, square-necked blouse. Gold and citrine sparkled along the hollow of her throat; her hair was as sleek and black as it had been when he saw her running, but now it fell forward, framing her cheekbones and chin.

"M~ Zhou," he said, as she hooked the right-side locks behind her ear. "How kind of you to see me in person."

"Let's walk," she answered, taking his elbow and turning him with her fingertips, so he fell into step alongside her. They walked in silence along the awning-shaded street until he cleared his throat and glanced at her sidelong.

"Are we drawing out the anticipation, mambo?"

"Oh, very funny." There were more geraniums, their red as bright as snapping banners. The shopkeepers along this stretch had interplanted the stainless-steel city beautification buckets with kleenexplant and paperwhites, and the sweet aromas mingled with the sharp herbal note of the geranium.

Which made André sneeze. He filtered them out.

"Actually, it was a serious question. You must have thought about my offer." Or she'd not have come to find him, even if she had noticed him giving chase that morning.

"I wonder why you think you want to conjure."

Not an unexpected question, but he gave it a show of consideration. "Why I think I want it? Or why I do want it?"

"That's a question I can't answer for you." Her fingers had gone from resting lightly on the bone of his elbow to threading through the crook. He permitted her to steer him.

The crowds thinned as they walked, but the second wave would emerge soon—those who did not choose to separate their home and work lives but who telepresenced, and who came out for their daily bread and fish and produce after the rush had faded. Or those who worked on other planets, and could do as well sitting in a café under a parasol, uplinked lag-free through a quantum connection, as they could in an overpriced office on Bayside, where you paid for the view and walked sixty barges to the nearest coffee shop because the rents were so high.

"Croissant?" Ziyi Zhou asked him, gesturing to an open-air café with a few lingering customers.

"Maryanne will kill me if I don't eat at the office," André said, excusing himself with a one-shouldered shrug. M~ Zhou was holding his right arm. He rubbed at his beard with the left hand. "But I'd love to buy you a cup of coffee."

She stepped back, but not before she squeezed his arm. "You're good at that."

"Dodging questions?"

A good try, but she gave him not even a quirk of smile back. "Establishing a claim on people."

He shrugged again, acknowledgment this time, and spread his hands. He had to squint at M~ Zhou through the sunlight. Fat biting flies zoomed overhead, hunting in pairs; he swatted them away backhanded. Somewhere back there was a reptile brain that never quite trusted technology. She did smile this time. "Does that mean you're ready to answer the question now, André?"

"I can't imagine an answer that isn't something you've already heard a thousand times, M~ Zhou. Should I tell you that it's because I applied to Rim's Exigency Corps for training as a coincidence engineer when I was twenty, and the god-botherers wouldn't take me? That I never wanted to be anything else? That I grew up on the idea of the corps as the people who were going to save the universe? It's all quite embarrassing when you try to put it into words."

"So you're a romantic?"

He crossed his arms and felt the sun on his shoulders. The biters came back around, but this time zoomed off in pursuit of someone wearing a blue-lavender sunblouse before they got within swatting range. "I have to be."

Eyes wide, she looked up at him. "Would you hand a child a loaded gun, André?"

"Depending on the child——"

"——exactly. Depending on the child. Maybe one in a thousand, you could trust to do more good than harm with such a thing. So prove to me that you're that one in a thousand."

He hadn't expected it to be easy. "A virtuous life by example isn't enough?"

She snorted. "I know what you do. You have your own ways of influencing the future, M~ Deschênes."

A retreat from the first name. Calculated, like everything else about her. "It's a living. And that concerns you? Because I do adhere to certain ethical standards."

The twist of her mouth told him everything he needed to know. There was no point in arguing situational ethics in a society in which skinning, data mining, and routine privacy invasions were a matter of course.

André dated an archinformist. Personally, he thought what he did was more ethical. He just *killed* people. Cricket took apart their lives, everything they might have backed up, relegated to hard memory, recorded on their headsets or in the data holds. Only wet memory was safe from her and her data-mining fellows, both those who worked for Rim and Core—— the Rim and Core of the Earth-settled territories, not the rim and core of the galaxy, though to judge by popular entertainment broadcasts a lot of people didn't know the difference——and those who went freelance.

And without people like her, without the absolute knowledge of the stuff of people's lives, the kinds of manipulations conjures like Ziyi Zhou and licensed coincidence engineers performed would be impossible.

Never mind skinning your boss into an anteater, or secretly holocording the girl in the next cube so you could take her home and do whatever you wanted to her avatar... Compared to what M~ Zhou did in running people's lives for them, determining their fates, André's professional modus operandi of a quick, untelegraphed, painless death was as humane as it got.

For one thing, if his subjects ever so much as knew he was coming, he had erred badly. He didn't take cruelty jobs. And an encounter with him was the best most of his subjects could have hoped for.

If he came looking for somebody, they'd earned the visit.

It was a more honest trade than conjure, he thought bitterly. How dare Zhou hold that over him?

But there was no way to say that, not when he was asking her to teach him. Because he knew what the next question would be, then—a reiteration. *So if you think it's wrong, why do you want to do it?*

And he knew the answer, too. Not just passion, though the passion was there, and he would have sold himself to Core to get it and taken their damned destiny lock, let himself be chained to their service forever. But something else, the thing he was scared of losing. And yes, he was aware of the conflict implicit in that as well, though he wouldn't call it—quite—hypocrisy.

Maybe *bargaining*.

What André wanted was control. And self-defense, of course, but to pretend that was all of it would be self-deception. He gave her the second half.

"I want to be able to take care of myself," he said. "I'll run up on people who have the mojo working for them. Who've paid somebody like you or Jean Gris or one of the others"—one of the lessers, because every other conjure in Novo Haven, hell, every other conjure on Greene's World, was lesser than Ziyi Zhou or Jean

Kroc, who they called Jean Gris—"or who've sold themselves to Rim for the protection. And I need a little mojo of my own."

"And it's that simple for you?"

He shrugged. Omitting wasn't *really* lying.

It was enough to make her nod a little. But the razor lines beside her eyes didn't soften, and it wasn't just a squint into the sun. "Fine," she said. "But I *am* in a precarious position." As an unlicensed conjure, she meant. It wasn't illegal to know how to do it. But it was illegal to try, or to own the necessary equipment. "And you do work for Rim, and for Charter Trade."

"I'm not going to sell you to Jefferson Greene, Ziyi."

She turned so that her shoulder was to him, her back to the sun. Their shadows stretched ahead on the decking as she started forward. He hurried two steps and caught her. "That's not why I'm concerned. As I said: maybe one in a thousand children can handle the responsibility that comes with that gun."

"I already carry one of those."

"Was that a threat, André?"

As if that would get him anywhere. "It was a plea for lenience. As you very well know. Are you trying to see if you can pick a fight with me?"

The arch of her eyebrows confirmed it. "My situation is complicated by another issue. Of those thousand children, maybe five of them can actually *operate* this gun with professional skill."

"Everybody gets lucky once in a while."

"You can teach most people to carry a tune, but one in a thousand is born to be a singer."

He stopped. She walked three steps more before she did likewise. She didn't turn back to him. "So it's no, then?"

I'm sorry, André, he prayed for. *Maybe if you could prove to me I can trust you—*

But what he got was a flat shake of her head, the glossy blunt-cut ends of her hair whisking over golden-yellow-clad shoulders. "You're not a child I can hand a gun, André. I hope...I hope this won't prejudice our relationship."

"If you mean," he said, "am I likely to respond in a manner you might regret? M~ Zhou, I don't bring my work home."

She glanced over her shoulder and gave him a tight little smile and a nod. "Good then, that's settled. Come talk to me if you need some work done. Or send Cricket."

"I will," he answered, and watched as she walked on, until the crowd swallowed her. When she passed out of sight he turned and knotted his hands on the rail, leaning over the channel. Fish flocked to his shadow, hopeful of crumbs, wary of an opportunistic seabird that swung around to see if any would pass too high. "Shit," he said, and kicked the upright with the instep of his shoe.

A passing businessman chuckled under his breath and rolled a sympathetic eye. André caught it and rolled one back, and they shared a rueful grin for a moment before the businessman was past him.

Women.

What are you gonna do?

But women might be the answer, too. He composed a message to Cricket, thought about it, and added a paragraph on either end. Her connex was down; either she was sleeping, blocking, or busy. So he sent it headmail rather than instant message.

She'd get it the next time she checked in. One of the

interesting things about Cricket was that Cricket knew *everyone*.

In the meantime, another one of his messages was from a man named Timothy Closs. And that one might mean a paycheck, if everything played out right.

Coincidence made Timothy Closs tired.

And it was only due to an awkward coincidence that there was more than a minimal loss of life when the barge exploded. It blew up between twelve and thirteen, the darkest time of the morning, when neither diurnal humans nor crepuscular ranids tended to be awake. The recruitment barge should have been empty except for a night watchman, who was scheduled to be on deck when it exploded—and if he had been where he was supposed to be, he would have lived.

But the evening crew had stayed behind for some impromptu overtime. The sort where "working late" was a euphemism that even the most naive spouse would be unlikely to believe, given a good whiff of the miscreant's breath. So there were four men aboard, in the control cabin.

The rear of the barge would have been empty, too, had not one of the native affairs coordinators, insomniac and behind a deadline, also been working ridiculously late. Uneuphemistically, in her case.

She'd been in the interview room, open to the water and astern of almost everything—a sealed bathyspheric bubble accessible only via an airlock or the warm waters of Novo Haven Bay. But what exactly she was doing there three hours after midnight was a question that Closs knew would probably never be answered.

Cold, freak chance: there wouldn't be enough recov-

ered of Lisa Anne Angley for a decent burial. Let alone
any possibility of recovering her hard memory. The
Bose-Einstein condensate processor and solid-state core
of her headset were so much particulate in the sea air
Closs breathed.

His sunrise came on like war. Recovery teams were
already moving over the wreckage, illuminated under
the glare of sodium-vapor lights. The gray dawn
couldn't compete.

Closs watched from the deck of a Charter Trade
cruiser a half-kilometer off, shoulders squared in a
smart-fabric wind-cheater. The day should heat up
later, but for now the morning was cold, and suppres-
sant foam dotting the water had quenched the floating
fires.

Technically speaking, Closs didn't have to be here.
He curled his gloved hands on the rail, steel conduct-
ing heat from his palms. Technically speaking, he'd
probably get a better view of the proceedings on the
screen wall of his office.

But technicalities weren't going to boost shattered
morale the way having an officer on scene would. An
officer of the corporation, rather than a real officer,
these days, but Closs still had enough sense to stay the
hell out of the incident commander's way. And it
didn't hurt to show up and look interested and confident. It was good when the team was comfortable with
the boss, knew how to respond around him, knew that
the chain of command was strong. It saved on time and
precision lost to panicked errors when one wandered
down from the ivory tower and startled those who
weren't accustomed to one's majestic propinquity.

His headset plinked, the reserved code for his staff
archinformist, Maurice Sadowski.

"Hello, Maurice." There was visual. He must be calling from a desk.

"Hello, Major." Maurice was fortyish, square-jawed, his hair ponytailed at the nape of the neck. He wore a lightcoil spiraled through the rim of his left ear, but he'd deactivated it in observance of the tragedy. It shone dull bronze. He picked at it with a thumbnail, frowning. "Nobody's claimed responsibility."

"Well, the forensic team says the night watch was fucking around belowdecks, so anybody could have sailed up and tossed a grenade. But that isn't what happened."

"The bomb was placed?"

Closs leaned his elbows on the rail and steepled his fingers. Maurice's translucent image floated before him, projected into his brain because that was a less complex feat than projecting it onto his retinas. "The blast originated in the engine compartment," Closs said. "There wasn't any bomb."

"Mechanical failure?"

"Anything's possible," Closs said. "The barge was serviced three weeks ago."

Maurice flinched. "Freak accident," he said. "A freak accident that somebody engineered."

"Yeah," Closs said. "I think we've got an unlicensed conjure on our hands."

It wasn't earth, the stuff Cricket Earl Murphy spaded through, that gritted under her fingernails and left damp brown patches on the knees of her trousers. It wasn't earth that she scratched clawed fingers into, raked up moist and crumbling, black as the void between stars and redolent of rotting. It wasn't earth; Earth was on the other side of a long irrevocable relativistic slide, her old life receding like a missed train station.

It wasn't *earth*. But people used the word anyway.

Cricket found it—alien was an ironic word, when she was already on another planet—but alien to work so with her hands, unskinned and unconnected, only sensing the texture of the soil with her fingertips. At home, she gardened, but she did it with all her skins and augments intact. She could zoom in to examine the fine grains of sand among the loam, check chemical composition, gather data effortlessly.

Here, in Lucienne's garden, she did not use connex. She felt, and smelled, and cocked her head to listen to the sound the grains made when she rubbed them together. A different kind of parsing, almost medieval.

She was getting the hang of it. But she still couldn't quite get used to it.

It was almost pointless to compost such soil as this, but she didn't let that stop her, folding the crumbled dark mixture into earth that was no lighter, aerating the soil, laying it down in soft beds, ready for the hungry roots. She never would have done this in her old life, deep in the chaotic, elegant Core. Where houseplants were tended by hired gardeners or service bots, and were lacy froths of greenery or slick broad-leaved, jade-colored exotics, orchids hung with flowers that looked like they would bruise in a strong breath—things that were toxic to gnawing children and unwary pets.

Not tomatoes, leeks, ramps, radishes. Not maize, red and white and golden, single kernels pushed down in their mounds with a thumb, the hole closed and scattered round with bean and squash seeds. Not marigolds, just as effective against the native pests of Greene's World as they were against those of Earth, and which Cricket was planting now, seating each one in its carefully dug hole amid the vegetables, a scatter of compost under the roots. She pressed each one into place with the side of her thumbs and smiled. Not much in the way of tomatoes, but the early peas were almost ready, their billowing pink and white flowers faded. She should pick some now, while they were sweet.

As if reading her mind—which might, in fairness, have been possible if both of them hadn't had their headsets and connex shut down—Lucienne came out of the minifab with a bucket in her hand. It was Lucienne's garden, though not Lucienne's house. Or, more precisely, Lucienne stayed there. But the house belonged to her lover, Jean.

The garden, however, he stayed out of, except for purposes of rambling through—and, when they were ripe, picking the occasional tomato. It was Lucienne's, and Lucienne shared it with Cricket.

And that was pretty good.

Lucienne crouched beside Cricket and held out a damp rag. "Is that the last of the marigolds?"

Cricket, wiping her hands, nodded. "It should be all in."

"Good." Lucienne Spivak rattled the bucket as she rose to her feet. "Let's take some back out again."

Lucienne was a tall, curvy sort of woman, the skin of her brown thighs slightly dimpled below the ragged hems of her white shorts. She wore real cloth, old-fashioned, which was a side effect of living with Jean as well. He liked to talk about mature technologies, the redundancy and robustness of biological systems over technological ones. *A human being is more than just a biomechanical machine.*

Cricket was never exactly sure if she believed him, or if all the world really was predetermined, and consciousness some cruel joke of the wide ironic universe. Jean had to disagree: he was a conjure man, and changing the future was his livelihood. But Cricket knew a fair number of scientists who would swear that even the measurable statistical effects of coincidence engineering meant nothing about free will, because the act of the engineering and its outcomes had already been determined.

Of course, as far as Cricket was concerned, it didn't make any real difference. You were still stuck not knowing one way or the other until it happened, and even if it didn't matter what you did, when the anxiety hit, it sure felt like it.

She picked up the watering can and watered the last marigold, then stood, pushing herself off her knees flat-handed. Lucienne caught her under the elbow and gave her a boost. Lucienne's thick, dark-brown braid fell over her shoulder, banging Cricket on the ear. Lucienne's first name was French and her last name was Ukrainian, but she herself looked Indian or Pakistani. And Cricket still had to keep reminding herself that none of that mattered on the Rim, where there were no nationalities.

Or rather, there were. There were the *important* nationalities. Like, Rim company man, and alien, and colonial, and Coreworlder, and criminal. By which the Rim meant people like Lucienne. Revolutionaries, Greens, fair-trade activists, native-rights agitators.

But not like Cricket. No matter what Cricket had done in her other life.

Though if Lucienne kept asking, you never knew. She might become a criminal again. Of a better sort, this time.

They moved along the row of peas in stooped, companionable silence. Pods pattered into the bucket, first a thin layer and then handfuls. Some plants still held sprays of blossom among the nearly ripe legumes and their curling tendrils. Cricket snapped one off and tucked it into her thin creepery hair; Lucienne, laughing silently, copied. The flowers were baby-pink, breath-white. They smelled so sweet that Cricket kept looking around for the lilies.

"Did you know your boyfriend sent a message to Jean?" Bluntly, without games or preamble. That was Lucienne.

Cricket, on the other hand, was a liar. But maybe not to Lucienne. Well, not often. "André's not my boyfriend."

"So you knew, in other words."

She nodded. She slipped her hand among the leaves, found a spray of round, firm pods. They cracked off the stems when she twisted them. The surfaces were not quite as smooth as they looked, and stuck to her fingers slightly when she shook them off into the pail. "You're not granting me any great revelations."

"Do you think—"

Cricket shook her head. "He told me, actually. And I—"

Lucienne pressed both fists into the small of her back, the bucket swinging against her hip. She arched, stretched, stooped again. "He wanted you to put in a word for him, did he?"

Cricket shook her head. "I wouldn't trust him. He's not like you. Not an idealist."

"I trust you."

"And I sleep with him, so he must be okay?" When Lucienne looked up, Cricket was smiling at her, worrying the string out of a pea pod with her thumbnail. "You realize that doesn't follow."

"No," Lucienne said. "Anyway, whatever you think

of André, I wish *you'd* come with us. At least to meet them."

Us meant Lucienne and Jean. Them...

Them was a temptation. Cricket dropped the pod in the pail and reached for another one. "The froggies."

Lucienne glanced over her shoulder, as if somebody could possibly be listening. "Tonight. Stay to dinner; come out after." She shook the bucket. "Damned if we don't have enough peas."

Some men stop believing in love as they grow older. Some simply stop expecting it to find them.

Jean Kroc had never succumbed to the first failing, though the second had seemed likely. Whether he had any use for the emotion himself had remained an open question, one complicated because the image of happy domesticity did not fit the role of conjure he portrayed. Which was an odd thing; if people came to you for happiness, wouldn't they expect you to be able to provide happiness for yourself?

Which had always been the sorcerer's secret. Knowledge might be power. But power was a long walk from joy.

But today, there was Lucienne standing beside him, her elbow brushing his elbow, her long almost-black hair braided thick as his wrist down her back, with her high cheekbones and her almond eyes and the beauty mark in the corner of her mouth, looking like Durga come to life, without the tiger. And so, as Jean helped Lucienne shuck peas in the kitchen, and Lucienne's slight, riverine friend Cricket boiled the salted water, the settled domesticity of the scene amused him.

It might have been four hundred years before, some randomly selected afternoon in the first century B.G.

The kitchen was gas and electric, no smart appliances, no adaptive fab. He lived off the grid, Jean Kroc did. Lucienne teased that if he could sink a well, or if the river water were halfway safe, he'd haul buckets rather than palm a tap.

It was a pleasant kind of teasing, though; keeping the house unconnexed served her as well as him. The lives lived within it were safe from registry in any data hold, which was a necessary thing for anybody who wanted to keep a secret. Cricket's research skills were proof enough of that. Jean had seen her generate a complete list of a Rim associate manager's sex partners, accurate—by Cricket's estimate—to 95 percent, simply by hacking her security monitor. Which had still been registered to one of sixty-four thousand factory presets.

Elapsed time, thirty-five seconds.

However, it also meant that when a hum of motors was followed by the crunch of footsteps up the clamshell path—Greene's World bivalves, not real Earth clams, but people, Jean included, were sloppy about terminology—he couldn't snap on a smart perimeter with a headset command and have six methods of disposal at his fingertips. Black security was illegal, which wouldn't stop anybody who thought he needed it.

Which was why everything Jean would have killed to protect, other than himself and Lucienne, was fifteen miles away.

He slicked a thumbnail up the inside of the pod he still held, let the peas drop into the bowl and roll down the little pyramid there while their green musk rose, then cast the husk aside. It turned over in midair, sideslipping, and landed in the stained white sink. Jean wiped his hands on a towel and thumbed a keypad hung on his belt.

He didn't use connex, but that didn't mean he didn't have screens. The big one on the wall by the window lit up, showing a speedboat moored at the end of his rickety parawood dock. The boat was a four-seater, ivory and rust in Rim Company livery.

"Corps?" Lucienne asked softly, cracking open another pod with her nails.

The piping below the gunwales was jade-colored, for the Greene's World Charter Trade Corporation. Not the Exigency Corps. Salt stains curling along the boat's bone-colored flanks gave the incongruous appearance of medieval embroidery. A woman in a Rimmer sunshade, her clipped hair blue, sat in the back, bent over with one finger pressed to her ear and the expression of somebody in heavy connex. Two men were tromping up the white path to the door. "Local," Jean answered, and watched Lucienne's shoulders pull back.

Cricket gave a quick twist of her neck to stare at him sideways, lids wide enough that white rings stood around her water-brown irises. "You sure?"

He took the slotted spoon from her hand. "You have some reason to be scared of the Corps? Turn the stove off; I don't think this will take too long."

She did what he said, silently, and went to sit on the creaking wicker sofa while he and Lucienne went to the door. He timed it just right; the Rimmer had started to knock when he pulled the door open.

Jean granted the medium-brown, medium-height man who leaned back so suddenly a certain amount of credit. He didn't fall over and he recovered himself fast. "Jean Kroc?"

"I am he."

The Rimmer glanced over Jean's shoulder. His own backup stood at the bottom of the steps, off to the port, covering both his partner and the door. "And is this M~ Spivak?"

"M~ Spivak can speak for herself," Lucienne said. She didn't step forward out of the shadows, however.

The Rimmer cleared his throat. "I'm David Kountché," he said. "My identification—"

Which was connex, of course, and Officer Kountché colored under his café-au-lait complexion when he realized the reason for Jean's slight, incurious smile. He dug into his hip bag and came up with a warrant card, holoplastic, chipped at one edge, with his retinal print and image indelibly recorded on the surface. He was, Jean reassessed, a Dayvid with a y.

"If you'd like to come in, you have to take your shoes off," Jean said, handing back the warrant card.

"I'm sorry?"

"No shoes in the house," Lucienne said. She pushed past Jean and came out under the awning. Kountché stepped back to give her room, without seeming to realize that he'd handed her control of the situation. Lucienne continued, "And unless you have a warrant, I'll have to ask you both to power down. Jean has a religious objection to connex in his home. Do you want me to come out instead?"

"We didn't say it was you we needed to speak to, ma'am," the Rimmer said. Jean could not fault him on politeness, anyway. Which wasn't as rare a trait as you might expect, in cops.

"No, but you talked around me, so I guessed. Coming in or staying out? And who might your partner be?"

Officer Kountché cleared his throat. And, gamely, sat down on the plascrete steps and touched open the tabs on his shoes. "Officer Garnet Spencer, ma'am," he said, and Officer Spencer tapped his sunshade just below the speckled band. Lucienne was too much of a lady to show it publicly, but Jean Kroc echoed her concealed wince. Somebody's mother had watched too many romances.

"Delighted to meet you, Officer Spencer." He looked a bit like a boiled fruit: his eyebrows made pale swipes in the redness of his face. Lucienne pointed to his feet. "There's tea inside, or I can bring you a lemonade on the porch."

After trading one quick look—backed, no doubt, by connex—Officer Kountché finished pulling his shoes off and powered down. Officer Spencer opted for the hospitality of the front stoop, and Jean brought him a lemonade while Lucienne led the other one inside. When Jean returned to the living room—the kitchen was more an alcove off the side than a separate space—Cricket had taken herself back out to the garden and Officer Kountché was perched uncomfortably on the edge of a wicker slouch chair, maintaining a stiff spine as if in defiance of the urgings of the household goods. Lucienne had turned the burner back on under Cricket's teakettle, and was measuring leaves into a pot. "Whatever questions you wanted to ask me," she said, "you can ask in front of Jean."

The officer looked uncomfortable, but folded his hands over his knee. "Where were you last night, M~ Spivak?"

"Please. Call me Lucienne."

"You don't stand on ceremony?"

"I don't stand on much," she answered. "Occasionally, my principles. Sugar, Officer?"

"Sugar, please. And answer the question. Please."

Lucienne frowned, as if measuring spoonfuls of white crystals into the cup was an unwonted effort. "I was here."

"You can confirm?"

She shrugged. "No connex," she said. "I live here. I wasn't anywhere else."

Officer Kountché glanced at Jean, who leaned, arms folded, beside the door. "I'll testify to that," Jean answered.

"M~ Kroc," the officer asked, "what's your means of support?"

"I'm a prospector," Jean answered. "And I consult."

"No work in the, ah, service industry?"

Jean just smiled. "Not what I would call it, no. Does that have any bearing on your investigation of my partner?"

"Now, M~ Kroc," Kountché said, apparently having recovered himself, "I'm sure I never said your partner was under investigation."

The smile Lucienne gave Kountché was almost as plastic as the one she got back. "Jean," she said, "there's nothing here you need to defend me from."

He unfolded his arms and said nothing. She turned back to face the counter and poured the tea. She served him and offered a cup to Jean, who waved it away with the back of his hand, then poured for herself. A delaying action, and a few moments later she ensconced herself across from him, her mug cradled between her hands. "So," the officer said, "you can't prove where you were last night?"

Whatever floated in the depths of her tea must have been extraordinarily interesting. She dipped a finger into the steaming surface and bit the resulting droplet from the tip. "Can you prove I was somewhere else?"

"What's your relationship with the ELF?"

"The Extee Lib Foundation? I give them money. I volunteer in the front office. It's a perfectly legal and registered charity. Officer."

"Blowing up a native worker recruitment station is a charitable function?"

"Is *that* what exploded last night?" Lucienne leaned forward, between her knees, to set her cup down on the plascrete not far from the edge of the braided rug. "You think I had something to do with that?"

"I'm not suggesting any such thing." He sipped his tea. If he was a hunting dog, Jean thought, his ears would be pricked up. "*Do* you know anything about it?"

"No connex, remember?"

He shook his head, as if it was a little hard for him to understand the implications. No instant news, no instant messages. No instantaneous communication with people on other planets, halfway across the galaxy.

No constant hum of commercials in the back of your brain. No hacked perceptions, showing you a woman in a red dress and heels when she was wearing a pantsuit and thongs, and weighed fifteen pounds worth of muscle less than the image projected into your brain.

No connex. Alone with the silence inside your own brain.

Not too long ago, of course, it would have been alien to Lucienne, too. But she'd adapted, as Jean had expected she would. If nothing else, it gave you time to think.

"You'll answer questions under a lie sensor, if necessary?"

Lucienne smiled. "If you subpoena my cooperation. I know my rights, Officer."

The answering tip of his head was tight. "Are you certain you don't wish to call your solicitor now?"

"Why should I?" she said. "I've nothing to hide."

2

JEAN LIKED THAT CRICKET STAYED ON AFTER THE RIMMERS departed, all three together. The one who'd waited on the stoop had left his untouched lemonade on the corner of the plascrete, all the ice melted and condensation rolling down the sides.

"As if you'd poison a Rimmer," Lucienne said disdainfully, while Cricket was bringing the remains of dinner out to her beloved compost pile. Lucienne dumped the glass in the sink and scrubbed it out by hand. She racked it and dried her hands on a towel, while Jean pressed his palms to her shoulders to feel her muscles slide. She leaned on the touch, letting him support her.

"He bugged the chair," Jean murmured against the black hawser of her braid. "Want to give him an earful after your friend leaves?"

She tossed the towel across the edge of the sink. "As if you haven't already disabled it."

He couldn't shrug and rub her shoulders at the same

time, so he settled for a kiss on the nape of her neck. Still brown, this skin, but paler, and vulnerable-seeming, nonetheless. "He can't prove a thing. Breathe out."

She obeyed, and breathed in, too, then repeated the process more slowly, with concentrated care. "If he could, he'd have us both in custody. It might be time to step back for a bit. We're not outraged doomsayers, and I refuse to be herded. Either by Rimmer visits, or by Closs's threats to assay settled wetlands for mining potential, and hang the treaty. We're not doing the froggies any good if we wind up inmates at a seaweed farm."

"We're not doing ourselves any good either." He stepped back and let his hands fall away. "There's always legal challenges."

"If we could afford better lawyers."

He nibbled his thumb, turning away from the window, through which the setting sun glared, flashing off spectacles that always drew a double-take when he was introduced to someone new. "I'll see what I can do. About Cricket—"

"Yes. We can trust her."

He licked his lips, put his shadow between them so he could see her expression when she turned. The line between her eyebrows was deeper, but the curl of her lips was wry.

"She doesn't want to be a part of our revolution, Luce," he said.

"But where she goes, Deschênes follows."

He didn't have a ready answer, so Lucienne continued, shading her eyes so *she* could look straight at *him*. "I'll take her to see the ranids tonight. If that doesn't shift her, nothing will."

André walked home two hours later than he usually did. The traffic in the streets had fallen off; his meeting had stretched through the afternoon rush. A face-to-face meeting. One of the reasons André kept office hours—kept an office at all—was that his business wasn't always best handled via connex.

Cricket still hadn't answered his call about Jean Kroc, which was for the best. He'd have more work for her if she did call. Cricket charged high, even as archinformists went, but she was worth every demark. And if she didn't call, André would just have to get a head start on the information himself. Because his meeting had been with Timothy Closs, a Rim Company VP who reported directly to Jefferson Greene, the titular head of the Greene's World Charter Trade Corporation.

And Charter Trade had contacted André because it was looking for a speedy resolution.

André wasn't a nice man, and he didn't do a nice job. But he also understood that it wasn't that different from jobs that had been necessary, spurned, and not very nice since the first web-footed amphibian crawled from the primal ooze and set up shop to sell dirt to other amphibians from farther downriver. It was a living, and he didn't play politics, and he didn't execute grudges. He stuck to what passed for the ethical rules of his profession, and Charter Trade left him alone except for when it needed him.

And on Colonial Charter steadings like Greene's World, the Rimmers were the law—and had been for the last 250 years, since A.G. 75 or so, though Greene's World itself was not that old. And the only court of appeals was the Earth-centered, teeming worlds of the Core. Which relied on trade from the ever-expanding halo of the Rim to keep it fed and housed and enjoying an increasing standard of living. A lot of people came to the Rim because they couldn't live in the Core anymore, for one reason or another.

Frontiers had always been a sort of social pressure valve.

Really, in the end, André just saved Charter Trade the money it would have spent documenting a kangaroo trial. And as for the family of the accused, he saved them some embarrassment.

The sort of people he needed to talk to tonight didn't do business over connex either. They also weren't the sort to hang out in pool halls, Italian restaurants, or drinking establishments, adding a little stereotypical color to the place. But Nouel Huc did have an affection for a particular raucous dinner theater on Seagrove—West Seagrove, a much more upscale neighborhood than André's. Not that that would be a problem, since André was dressed for the office.

He strolled past tall, white-faced, balconied cruisers that smiled around their storm shutters. The air was cooling as the red sun sank, the breeze lifting the day's last sweat from his neck. The barges here were more solidly lashed, partially because people took more trouble with it and partially because Bayside was the windward edge of Novo Haven, and caught the storms blowing in off the gulf, most of which were not nearly bad enough to scatter the city for. But they could pitch and rub the barges, and the worst damage didn't come from the wind, under those circumstances, but from the hulls crushing the sidewalks. Bumpers and braces could only do so much.

The awnings were rolled in for afternoon, letting the last light of day reach the blue and green and goldenrod doors, filter in the parlor windows. If André hadn't known where he was going, he could have picked out the Zheleznyj Tigr from the residences on either side. It was on the 8100 barge, and the velvet ropes leading to the door set it apart, as did the attendant standing by. She was shapely and very pale, her white-blond hair clubbed at the nape of her neck, and she wore a red velvet tailcoat and a tall black hat. She smiled at André as she opened the door, plated heels clicking cheerfully. He answered her crisp bow with a playful one of his own, just to see her pale skin blush.

She must spend a fortune on sunblock.

Inside, candles and wall sconces flickered, dusting dark wood and more red velvet with erratic light. Somebody was playing a neono, not loudly enough to be heard in the street. Not yet. André cocked his head at the music and glanced slowly around. Empty booths, a few occupied, the glossy tabletops mostly innocent yet of glasses.

Nouel Huc sat alone. That was by no means uncommon, but neither was it de rigueur. He was a broad Asian-looking man whose frown lines made him seem brooding, and a little cruel, though he was neither of those things. Women, André imagined, found the contrast irresistible.

It couldn't have been Nouel's *looks*.

André made some noise coming up, though Nouel certainly expected him; he'd IMed a query before he left his office, and gotten the nod to come down. Nouel was tangled up with a woman who lived on Yap, and sometimes when he seemed to be alone, he was actually quite distracted.

But this time, Nouel pushed the chair opposite out with his foot; André dropped into it lightly and reached for the order pad. "What's the play tonight?"

"*Zaire*," Nouel said. "Voltaire. Will you stay for it?"

"I could be convinced," André answered, pulling up reviews, a synopsis, and clips on his headset. "Do you know the special?"

Nouel made a broad gesture with a heavily ringed

hand. Jewels caught the candlelight, their flash and sparkle enhanced by Nouel's skins. André knew at least two rings were external hard memory, easily exchanged or discarded, while one housed a cutting laser. "I haven't ordered."

"Oh." André downloaded the specials, IMed them to Nouel via a direct-read. "There's shiro," he said, as if Nouel would not have noticed it. A local-world, deepsea, heavy-bodied whitefish. Most of it was exported to the Core to feed the sushi market as a welcome replacement for Earth's own extinct stocks of albacore and escolar.

Nouel smacked his lips. "A bottle of wine?"

"I am at your disposal," André answered, and pushed the order pad to Nouel. Nouel must have livelinked it, because André didn't see him touch a key. André was buying, of course. It was part of the honorarium one paid Nouel in exchange for his information.

"Oh, I don't think I'll dispose of you just yet." He tipped his thumb to the stage. "Not until I hear your opinion of the play. They run a repertory here, you know. It's rare to get something genuinely new."

André did know, but it would have been rude to mention it. He nodded, instead, and thumbed through the drug list. Expensive alcohol, opiates, tailored drugs. Nothing unexpected. He settled on a brandy and also ordered a gin and ice for Nouel, as his was rattling in the glass.

Nouel nodded thanks, and their drinks arrived a moment later. Nothing had yet replaced the live waiter; expert systems did not maintain an adequate standard of customer service, and people liked to be smiled at. He stirred his ice with the glass rod and said, "Was this just a social call, André?"

"If it were, would I be plying you with alcohol?"

Nouel laughed, head down and shoulders back, almost spilling his drink. He wasn't an archinformist, but he employed them. Nouel was a broker. And sometimes he could find out things that weren't in a data hold. "Ask. Before the fish comes; I hate to talk when I could be eating."

"Lucienne Spivak," André said.

A long whistle like the call of trains since time immemorial rose over the tinkling neono. You got the Bayside view here, and with it the sound of lighters landing day and night, ferrying cargo and—more rarely—personnel up to the orbital transfer station. You didn't build a matter transfer station on a habitable planet.

Just in case.

Nouel stopped with his drink tipped to his lips. He looked at it thoughtfully, took a sip anyway, and set it down precisely in its own ring of condensation. "What's it worth to you?"

"Three hundred," André replied, a flat inflexible offer.

"Make them pay you hazard," Nouel said. "If you haven't shaken hands on it already. How fast do you need it?"

Closs wanted the job done as fast as safely possible. He had told André he had intelligence that Spivak was going to receive damaging information from a source inside Rim, and that he needed her removed before she could pass it on.

"Fastest. Who is she?" André waved his brandy snifter under his nose, wafting the aroma from the glass. "Other than the presumed head of GreenWorld, now that Tavish is dead."

"She stays out in the bayou."

"She's a frog-kisser. It's not unheard of."

"No," Nouel said, as the cold hors d'oeuvre arrived. "The issue is who she stays with." With the pricker-tipped tongs, Nouel selected a slick sea-fruit and tossed it into his mouth. It burst with an audible pop. "An old swamp-crawling conjure man."

"No. *No!*" André laughed in disbelief, rocking his head from side to side. Fate was gaming with him.

"Yes. Better make sure nobody can connect it to you, if it comes off." Nouel's eyes twinkled—literally, a programmed effect of his skin. "I wouldn't want Jean Gris knowing I was the man who killed his piece of tail."

It wasn't that Cricket had never been in the delta before. Because of course she had. She'd been on hover-boats and a transport; she'd been upriver as far as Romeo. She'd even taken a swamp hike in hip waders with a horticulturist and gotten a six-hour crash course in the native wildflowers of Greene's World. The part she had found most charming was the discovery that all sorts of names she was familiar with from Earth plants had been recycled shamelessly, for flowers that often bore only a passing resemblance to any Terran plant. She'd seen swamp iris—which on Greene's World was a deep green-streaked bronze—and moon-flower, and orioleplant (named after a bird, not even a vegetable), and dozens of other native ornamentals. And the invasive garden species, from Earth and Babel and wherever else people had gone and found things that were pretty. Importing live seed was supposed to be illegal. But unlike chordate animals, plants survived matter transfer fine, and it wasn't as if anybody enforced the regulations.

So she'd done all that, got the mud between her toes,

felt halfway grounded on her new planet. New being a decade and a half now.

But she'd never been in the bayou at night, with the three lumpy moons and the sharply spherical silver disk of the transport station swinging by overhead and the reeds casting razory shadows across the silvered water. The smallest moon, sulfur-stained Flash, actually moved fast enough for its transit across the larger white-gold moon called Arthur to be noticeable to the unaided eye. Com kept running stories that Rim planned to bump it out a few thousand kilometers because it might be sliding down the sky fast enough to be a threat one of these years.

Lucienne urged her over spongy ground carpeted in flat dense green, a high-intensity minilight shone low, to illuminate only the path before their feet. "They're not fond of bright lights in darkness," she whispered. "Their eyes don't adjust as fast as ours."

Cricket matched Lucienne's tone. "Are we taking a boat?"

"No, it's just up along the bank." And then Lucienne giggled. "Why are we whispering?"

"So as not to disturb the ranids?"

"They can't hear you."

Cricket stumbled. Lucienne, behind her, caught her elbow and held her up. "Can't hear me? They're not *deaf*."

"No—" Lucienne's gesture set the light in her hands to wavering wildly. "They respond to a different set of frequencies, and their hearing in air is not that great. They'd just hear, I dunno, rumbling and squeaks. Like we just hear them croaking."

"So how will they know to meet us? How will we talk to them?"

"You'll see," Lucienne said, patting a capacious cargo pocket on her thigh. "Patience."

Cricket was ready to swallow her tongue. Ranids shouldn't be that exciting. She'd seen them working on the drill platforms in the distance, seen them—occasionally—scudding effortlessly through the crystalline bay. She'd watched documentaries, of course. And the popular dramas sometimes had ranids in them: real ones or—more often—holograms.

That wasn't the same as talking to a real alien while crouched in a swamp by moonlight.

"Hold still," Lucienne said, and Cricket paused midstep. "You can put your foot down."

The trace of a laugh in Lucienne's voice made Cricket smile, too. Wet earth molded to her foot as her weight came down on it. She could feel the cool moisture rising from the mud even through her flexible sole. The sawtooth-edged leaves of the reeds that weren't all that much like real reeds whispered in the darkness, leaving Cricket with the urge to whisper back. Living up to her name, she thought, and her smile broadened until it pulled at her cheeks.

Lucienne turned off the light.

Cricket managed not to yelp, but she couldn't hold back a flinch. The bayou had already been huge and tangled where it stretched beyond the reach of the flashlight: slumbering softly, but infinitely old and sharp-witted. Now, before Cricket's eyes adjusted, the sounds and scents seemed to rush at her with the darkness. She breathed deep, fixing the black-earth scent of vegetable rot at the bottom of her lungs, so she smelled it again, warmer, as her breath came back.

Insects sawed and droned, and creatures large enough to support vocal cords made more complex noises. Something crashed, and something screamed;

she didn't know if it was a mating fight or the sound of something becoming another something's dinner. She tried to force her eyes to adapt faster.

The moonlight was shifting. One set of shadows, the faintest, seemed to twist about her as she watched, as if someone meant to wind her legs with ribbons. That was Flash, and it would cross the sky again two and a half times before sunrise. Arthur took a more stately route, as befitted the farthest satellite, and cast steady steel-blue shadows. Subtractive mixing—still counterintuitive to Cricket after thirty-four years in which the light from the sky had only been one color at a time—turned the intersecting shadows black.

The third moon, Alice, was a grayish wraithlike shape with low albedo, smaller, closer, and faster than Arthur but larger and slower than Flash. It cast no appreciable light unless it was alone in the sky, and even then, only enough to guess at the motion of a hand. If the person waving it was light-skinned.

If the Greene's World tide charts hadn't been in databases, they would have run to volumes.

"What are we waiting for?" Cricket finally whispered.

"Not waiting." Lucienne touched her shoulder, and Cricket noticed herself shivering. The moist still air was also cool. "Looking. There, off to port."

Cricket turned her head and squinted. A patch of moonlight—no. Brighter than moonlight. And a greeny-yellow that neither Arthur nor Flash reflected. Bioluminescence? "Algae?"

"Froggies," Lucienne said. "They're expecting us. Come on."

A narrow path led through the reeds, invisible from the green riverbank. Cricket reached out and swiped across the glowing patch as they walked past it, flattened

reeds crunching softly underfoot. Water seeped between
the aligned stems, but they kept the mud beneath from
greasing her way down the bank.

Her fingertip glowed citrine-yellow when she
turned her hand over. "They use marking paint?"

"Something like that." Lucienne had taken the
lead, for which Cricket was just as grateful, in the dark.
She clutched reeds to steady herself, leaving lumines-
cent smears behind. "Stop here."

Cricket had already halted. She could see the
moonlit channel gleaming beyond Lucienne, its surface like oiled black opal. Cricket watched while
Lucienne flipped her braid behind one broad shoulder
and crouched easily in the mud. Whatever had been in
her pocket was in her right hand now; it looked like a
wand with green and yellow lights glowing on the
handle.

She slid it into the water and thumbed a control.

Cricket neither heard nor felt a thing, but the lights
rippled encouragingly, and Lucienne seemed satisfied
as she pulled the wand up and whipped an arc of droplets off the tip.

"And now?"

"We wait. Some patient researcher you are."
Lucienne reached back and patted her on the ankle.
Cricket sighed and squatted down, resting her elbows
on her knees, trying to trap some warmth between her
belly and her thighs. "Oh. When they come—don't
make direct eye contact. And don't touch them. It
breaks their mucous coating."

Cricket was prepared for a long, cold wait, but her
expectation was mercifully disappointed. The water
rippled and bulged, and one-two-three domed arrow-
shaped heads emerged, arrayed in an uneven wedge.
They bobbed, as if their owners floated free in the wa-

ter, though Cricket couldn't imagine it was very deep. But they slid to the bank smoothly, and she stood up and moved back as Lucienne scooted aside to give them room.

Cricket heard herself breathing, loud as if she stood in an echo chamber. Only one of the ranids emerged from the water—a greeny-black shape with a pale mottled belly. Its arms were long, almost as long as its spindly legs, and it had spidery, webbed, opposable digits on all four limbs. It wasn't quite as tall as Cricket, standing, which wasn't very tall at all. It hunched forward enough, head stretching out on a neck that would collapse into the body for swimming, so that she saw pale mottles that would be butter- or cream-colored in sunlight. "We have to give them names," Lucienne said over her shoulder. "Their names for themselves are a little beyond us. Cricket, this is Caetei. Caetei, this is Cricket." When Lucienne addressed the froggie directly, she overpronounced, as if speaking to a child or a lip-reader.

The ranid wore a sort of web belt, farther up its midsection than a human waist would be, above the great angular hip bones that canted it forward in such an awkward and unbalanced fashion. It flexed its legs, not quite sinking down into a high-kneed crouch, and supported itself on one hand while it unclipped a perfectly normal—if waterproofed—child's slate from a carabiner. It settled further, a tapered cone between the high flexed knees, and began to type.

"And do they have names for us?" Cricket asked, coming forward. She pressed her shoulder against Lucienne's rounded biceps, soaking up radiant warmth.

"If they do, they never tell us." Lucienne accepted the slate from Caetei and read it quickly, angling the face so Cricket could see the backlit screen.—*Plsd. U R cmng 2 hlp us?*

Inelegant, but efficient. Cricket glanced at Lucienne. Lucienne shrugged. "You can type on the slate, connex to the slate and IM, or speak directly. Caetei reads lips. Not all ranids do."

Cricket handed the slate back, the tips of the ranid's spatulate fingers brushing the side of her hand. There must be claws retracted in the cool slippery flesh, because something scratched her like a burr. "Pleased to meet you, too," she answered, a great swelling of disbelief making her wish she could shake her head and pace in circles until it sank in what she was doing here. "Lucienne thought I should come and talk to you. To help make up my mind."

The ranid's head settled back against its shoulders. It bobbed slightly and typed again. While it worked, Lucienne patted Cricket on the elbow. "You're doing fine."

The slate came back. —*Wld U C wht Rim ds 2 my sibs?*

"It's not pretty," Lucienne cautioned.

Cricket nodded. "I will see."

Caetei splashed the water with one foot. The other two bobbing ranid heads emerged from the water, and neither of these two wore web belts or carried Rim equipment. One wore the seashell and seawrack vest and girdle affected by the unacculturated ranids. It was decorative, woven of tropical colors and light-catching stones, and also served to display the prowess of the ranid that wore it. Not only did the vests create drag, impeding the owner, but the best vests belonged to far-swimmers, who had traveled great distances along the surface currents, and visited many islands and become exoparents on many shores. A sensible custom, one that encouraged both the reproduction of the strongest and the wide spread of biological diversity.

This particular far-swimmer also wore a Charter Trade harpoon gun. Which was *not* something any native was supposed to have. *Tetra,* Caetei typed, and the ranid head-bobbed. Lucienne bowed, a human equivalent, and Cricket copied her. This, she guessed, would be the bodyguard.

And nothing like a tame froggie at all. Caetei had a distinct, moist, amphibian aroma. Tetra—or its harness—smelled of tide pools and heaped seaweed and broken shells.

When Tetra turned to help the third ranid from the water, though, Cricket gasped. She hadn't been able to see, when it swam partially submerged, but this froggie was disfigured. It was obviously blind in one eye, a great white scar carved down the side of its face and across the shoulder, its left arm ending below the shoulder in a knobby lump. It listed as it struggled up the bank, so Cricket suspected spinal or brain damage.

"This is Parrot. It survived an industrial accident," Lucienne said, because Caetei had stopped typing. "And Rim sometimes provides medical care to site workers—it's one of the things they trade for coolie labor"—the distaste in her voice when she said *coolie* was acid enough to sting—"but of course if you can't work they don't treat you."

"God," Cricket said, or shaped, anyway. She wasn't sure she got any breath through the word.

Not that that mattered to the ranids. Caetei reached out and brushed her bare leg, with just fingertip pads, and looked up quizzically. She glanced down. "Yes," Cricket said. "Thank you. Please tell it—" *Tell it I'm sorry.*

But the dismissive flicking gesture of Caetei's hand needed no translation. Like scattering water on the ocean. The mutilated ranid would not understand.

"Thank you." Lucienne to the rescue. She swept her hand to her mouth to direct Caetei's attention. "If you don't need more, Caetei, thank you and Tetra and Parrot. Thank you very much."

Caetei patted Cricket's calf once more quickly, and the three ranids slipped back into the brackish channel. For a moment, Cricket saw the lights of Caetei's slate dimmed by the muddy channel, and then they were gone, along with the ranids.

"Medical care?" Cricket asked, when the wonder had blown off her enough to allow her to talk. "They work for what any Core or Rim citizen gets as a birthright?"

"It's one of the things they earn. They're not citizens."

"It's exploitation."

"That is," Lucienne said gently, "what I have been telling you. You're not...shocked?"

"No." She wished she was. She wished she had the innocence left to be shocked. "But I am outraged."

"Good." Lucienne paused, still looking out over the water. Flash already almost touched the top of the reeds in the west. "I meant you to be."

Cricket let the silence handle that one. "I still don't know if I have the guts to get involved. What else do they—what else does Charter Trade barter to the ranids?"

"They protect their sacred sites, for one thing. There are places in the deep bayou and salt marsh that the ranids hold holy. And, maybe the biggest thing..." She shrugged. "Stories."

"Stories?" Cricket heard herself, and lowered her voice. "Like, once upon a time?"

"It's their whole culture. They talk. When they get out in the deep ocean, *halfway around the world* they can talk. Don't underestimate what new information is worth to them."

Cricket twisted her hands together. She was getting a little annoyed with feeling abashed. "I'm sorry," she said. "I don't mean to sound like an idiot."

"Not an idiot," Lucienne said. She flicked her flashlight on and shone it up the reedy path. Cricket, taking a hint, scrambled up. "Not even ignorant, really. But nobody talks about this stuff."

"Because we don't want to know?"

"Something like that," Lucienne said. "Come on. I'll run you home."

"I can get there myself. Just drop me at the ferry stop—"

"Don't worry about it." As they emerged from the reeds atop the grassy bank, the night was cool and still. Exactly as they had left it, except the angle of the light had changed. "I was going out anyway. I have to meet somebody around midnight."

Raindrops pattered on the surface, the sound echoing softly through the sheltered backwater where Gourami slept and kept se treasures. Se lived in a humen-built cottage that bobbed amid rows of sixteens of similar bubbles, all on automatic moorings so that they were held more or less taut no matter how the tide changed.

Gourami rested on one of the broad comfortable shelves that projected from the walls just below water level, spading a protein-enriched algae broth from a shallow bowl and watching larger-than-life images flicker on the wall. The splashing wavelets were warm; the heat in se sleeping bench was on. Humen toys were very pleasant.

Se was watching a humen drama—they had drama, just like plays except they made them permanent so one could *watch* again and again, not just *tell* them— and the squiggles across the bottom of the image meant their words. So se was practicing, in addition to being entertained. Which was good. The humen liked it if one did more than one thing at a time, though Gourami thought they would be wiser to care if one did it well.

But that was humen.

They built good houses, anyway.

And someone was scratching by the door of Gourami's. Se set the half-empty bowl on a higher shelf, where water would not slop into it (imagine trying to keep water out of food! Imagine eating food served warm!) and slid through the opening in the ring-shaped shelf, dropping toward the bottom of the house and the underwater door. There was a hatch to the roof as well, for emergencies and sunbathing, reached by an ascending spiral of shelves, and some houses had a second underwater exit. But those were houses for families—endoparents with broods, or exogroups, or sometimes both at the same time where there was a lasting attachment.

Gourami's place was only one bubble. As se swam under the encircling shelf of the primary living space, the flickering light of the drama provided enough glow to see by. Se'd reverse it when se came back up, if guilt won over irritation. It wasn't very good. But it was a story, and se winced at self's irresponsibility in letting it run itself out unregarded.

Still. Still. Se could always reverse it. It wasn't sac-rilege, not like missing part of a play, which was ephemeral and would only continue to exist as long as there was somebody to remember it, somebody who could tell it if the need arose.

The gate was shot; se hadn't planned on going out until morning and the last thing se needed was a pod of snakewhites wandering in an unbarred door in the middle of the night. Se churruped, the swelling sur-face of se throat vibrating into the water. Beyond the gate, someone's pale belly reflected the moving light. The other churruped back.

Caetei was a relative, one of Gourami's endosibs. They were kin by water rather than gametes, but some said that was the strongest bond.

Caetei also worked for Rim.

Gourami slipped the gate and let se kick inside. —*I wouldn't expect you to still be awake.*

Caetei shot upward with a powerful flexion of legs. Se voice echoed oddly for a moment as se hauled self from full submersion to a comfortably damp perch on the ledge. —*I knew you would be.*

Gourami was a night-swimmer, a noon-sleeper by preference. As everybody in three rows knew, from the flicker of stories on se walls late into the night. Se heaved onto the ledge and stood to stretch, palms sticky flat against the arched roof of the house for bal-ance. Bubble-shaped was not just sturdy and pleasant; it was safest in a storm.—*I was watching a story.* But of course, Caetei was already transfixed by the flicker. Se understood humen very well, better maybe than Gourami. Se hunched forward, half-crouched, and tilted side to side as if to improve perception of the huge humen figures imbedded in Gourami's house-wall.

—*Will you restart?*

—*I watched this one before,* Gourami lied. Too much exposure to humen, not to care about a drama. It's just a story, se wanted to say. It is recorded. It will remember itself, like the stories the Other Ones took with them, when they left. But se didn't, and was glad when se noticed the set of Caetei's shoulders, which suggested something along the lines of: Oh. But I haven't.

Se didn't actually make the noises, though, so Gourami could pretend se had been looking away. Se did not want to watch the bad movie again.

Se did not even particularly want to watch the ending.

But se did, and when it flicked dark and the walls took up a mellow sun-colored glow to compensate for the lost illumination of the movie, se shifted se hips on the ledge. A few spans closer to Caetei was enough to press on se attention. Caetei blinked wide high-set eyes and shuddered, shaking out of the memorizy trance. —*You can have the code,* Gourami said. —*I won't watch it again.*

Caetei ducked in thanks and acknowledgment; Gourami made a sweeping, paddling gesture with se handfingers. Away from the mouth, not toward. —*Nothing to thank me for.*

Se sank down in the warm water and let it flow up between the ridges of se hips. Se legs stretched long, toefingers dangling over the edge of the ledge. Not a position to take in open water, when toefingers looked like food to many swimmers.

Comfortable, though.

—*You were just coming to visit? Would you care for some soup?* There was plenty of broth, and Gourami could thicken it with seaweed for a meal. But Caetei's posture did not suggest hunger, and se answered with the same paddling motion Gourami had used.

—*I need to ask you to take an action.* Caetei hesitated, delicately. Gourami warbled quiet encouragement twice before se would continue. —*The thing the humen have green-band sibs drilling for on the shelf.*

The thing that wasn't petroleum. Which Gourami knew because Gourami had been liaison between the persons assigned to the drill and the humen assay team. And the assay team had tended to talk freely in front of persons, as some humen did. As if Gourami couldn't lip-read perfectly well.

Gourami did not know what was *tanglestone,* or *omelite* either. Se did not understand humen excitement over *forking* and *incomplete forking.* But se understood that the humen were not drilling for oil. No matter what they told the persons at work, and the humen inspectors who came to the drill.

—*It was a mistake to talk about it.* Because it was a *secret,* se had realized too late. And secrets were the opposite of stories. Se could lose se position from talking, se own comfortable existence, and se contribution to bandweal. —*I can't tell you any more.*

—*I know a human who can help. If we bring it evidence stories. There might be other ways to protect the greatparents than begging Rim.*

There might be. Gourami folded in on self, wrapping arms around flexed legs, and put se face between fleshy thighs. Se was moist and warm and comfortable, and shuddered anyway, as if attempting to shiver loose a parasite. Too much risk. Too much risk to the greatparents, to bandweal. To self.

The status quo was not so terrible. And se did not see it being better, for persons or for the greatparents of

thousand-year memory, to start a revolution. Caetei
never said so much, would not. But Gourami had
no doubts as to what se endosib intended as an outcome.

—*I won't risk the greatparents,* se said, lurching upright and leaning forward. Se caught Caetei's eye and
held it, forcing a lock to be certain Caetei understood.
Will not. What the humen could do to us—

The whirring, melodious croak died at the back of
se throat, se throatpouch still expanded. Se looked
down, accidentally releasing Caetei.

Because they could. Gourami watched their stories,
both the history and the inventions. The magnitude
of the destruction that humen could wreak was in-
conceivable, if they grew wrathful. —*No.* Gourami
said. —*No, I will not talk to your humen. I have greatparents to protect. I have egglings to think of. I cannot
contribute to a war.* Se whirring had risen to operatic
levels, echoing under the domed roof of se house until
it boomed like a mating call.

Se fixed Caetei an acidic glance and modulated se
voice, as Caetei ducked to avoid being gazelocked again.
Gourami continued, —*And you should not either. You
memorizy, I see you. If you think of being a greatparent,
you must put others first.*

Caetei knew that. Of course, and Caetei rose up on
shaky legs, wincing apologetically. —*I will show myself out.*

—*I am not angry.* But Gourami was, upset at least,
worried, and they both could smell it in the water,
see it in the flush that surrounded paling mottles. —*Please come back when you want to talk
about something else.*

There. That was better.

—*I will come back*, Caetei answered, and slipped into the ring pool.

Gourami waited until the gate thumped before turning back to se dinner. The broth had long gone cold.

3

OVER THE YEARS, ANDRÉ HAD COME TO ACCEPT THAT HIS luck was often ridiculous, but he hadn't expected a shot at filling the contract his first night out. He folded his forearms over the handlebars of his wet-dry scoot and let it bob, lights dark, on the moonlit water of the bay. The floor pushed his feet as it yawed. He hid behind the faring so his head wouldn't silhouette on the horizon. The craft was low-profile; without the brightness of the sky or of Novo Haven's lights behind him, André was nothing more than a blacker patch on the water.

About that luck, he thought, watching Lucienne Spivak and her guest come chattering down the floating dock. Ridiculous wasn't the half of it. Epic, maybe. Operatic. *Farcical*. Because even by moonlight, with his lowlight adapt kicked up, he recognized the woman walking alongside Spivak, leaning into her so that their shoulders brushed, ducking down as they shook their heads over some joke funny enough that André could hear their laughter across the water.

"You know," he murmured under his breath, "you couldn't make this shit up."

He wasn't going to kill anybody in front of his girl-friend. Some things were beyond the call of duty, and it would be difficult to make it look like an accident if Spivak suddenly went down clutching her throat. *And* he wasn't in a hurry. Impatient men often didn't do well in André's line of work. *Luck will only get you so far.* Even ridiculous luck—

With his lowlight, he could make out the hunched shape of a minifab at the top of the dock, a white shell path leading up to it. The residence itself was in a shel-tered inlet that a high tide would turn into an island, not quite up the bayou—as Nouel had suggested—but on a channel and away from the open bay. A paraman-grove swamp cut sight lines to the city, and the ap-proach path of descending lighters lay directly over the house, which explained why this wasn't more pop-ular property. That, and the inconvenience of being an hour and a half by scoot or boat from the city.

He'd wait for Cricket to leave, and then he'd slip close enough to get an overview of the location. It would be better if he could catch Spivak away from home, but it didn't hurt to know the turf. He'd have to be careful, though; Jean Kroc's house was a homestead, no plans on record, and he had no idea what sort of se-curity devices the conjure man might use. Anything from tiger pits to tracking lasers were possible, and it would be embarrassing to take a load of buckshot in the fundament.

André folded his arms and waited, listening to the women laugh. The breeze across the water was cool, carrying a taint of the heady sweetness from the parasitic flowers that swathed the paramangrove limbs. The scent carried over miles, and right now it told André that the wind was offshore. Which was also helpful to him; even if Kroc had a sniffer or a smart guard dog, it wouldn't pick up André's scent.

Yep. Luck was wonderful.

Pity he couldn't talk any conjure on Greene's World into helping him train it.

He wondered if he should have turned down this job. Closs would just have found somebody else, of course. Somebody who might botch it, or somebody who might be the kind of sadistic bastard who got his kinks out in his work.

He shifted on the hard seat of the scooter, pretending resignation as if he could convince himself. No matter how much of a hurry Closs was in, it wasn't as if André had to kill anybody *tonight*.

Except it didn't look like Cricket was leaving alone. She climbed into the passenger chair of the waiting flashboat and Spivak followed, settling in the pilot's seat. If she was just running Cricket down to the ferry, about fifteen minutes, then—

—André might not need the research after all. More luck, that he hadn't mentioned it to Cricket.

It could have put a strain on the relationship.

The engine of the flashboat was faster and louder than the caterpillar drive on the scoot. André waited until his prey was in motion before powering up. His scoot was dark gray, and the topcoat had a gloss-or-matte option that got a lot of work on night jobs. With the lowlight, he didn't need the running lights.

He concentrated very hard, thinking of Spivak dropping Cricket off at the ferry landing just the other side of the paramangrove swamp and turning back for home, maybe a little careless and tired. He couldn't

take a blacked-out scoot into the city; if he didn't get
run down by a barge, he'd get pulled over by traffic en-
forcement—and Cricket might recognize him or the
vehicle under conditions of more light. The ideal, of
course, would be for her to drop off Cricket, turn
around, head home, and run into engine trouble.
Unfortunately, André didn't think his untrained mojo
was enough to pull off that set of coincidences, but he
held the thought anyway, sharp and fine, visualizing in
detail.

Such things happened, after all. More often than
anyone admitted. His own childhood was a kind of an-
ecdotal proof.

But Spivak guided the flashboat toward the lights of
Novo Haven. The universe wasn't listening. Or somebody else's free will was getting in the way again. Just
plain inconvenient.

She opened quite a gap as she headed inward—his
craft wasn't as speedy—but André wasn't worried.
It shouldn't matter, as long as he could spot her running lights and the silhouette of her boat across open
water.

Traffic was light at first, and there were no street—
or channel—lights on the outskirts, other than the occasional door or dock lamp. But the traffic regs ensured
that Spivak couldn't just flash off and leave his slower
vehicle behind. André flicked on his running lights to
be legal, made up some of the distance, and slotted his
scoot in behind a water taxi two vehicles back from
Spivak and Cricket.

He didn't even need to follow that closely. It was obvious pretty quickly that they were going to Cricket's
new flat. André hadn't been there yet, but he had the
address, and it was a neighborhood he knew.

He stuck close anyway, though, the tactile rubber of

the scoot's handlebars molding his palms, the engine
softly vibrating his calves. He pulled a hooded sweater
on one arm at a time—keeping his eye on traffic—and
slipped on eye protection. Too dark for dark glass in the
goggles, but they changed the line of his face a little.
He skinned the beard off, which wouldn't help if neither woman was running connex, but he knew Cricket
at least usually kept her skins live. She hypertexted like
a mad thing in conversation, her agile brain tending to
shoot off in six unrelated directions at once.

The scoot was a quiet little craft, and André was
glad of that as he ducked it out of the traffic stream
one bridge shy of Cricket's flat and diagonally across
the channel. They unloaded quickly—a small favor
from fate—and Cricket gave Spivak a one-armed hug
as she climbed past her before turning away. André
crushed a pang of conscience. He'd be there to console
her.

It might even bring them closer together. Cricket
had this unnerving tendency to flit just out of reach, as
if she were covered in something slick and transparent. You could brush against her surface, but there was
never any way to get a grip.

A minute later, Spivak finished fussing with her
safety belts and pulled away from the landing. Headed
in the opposite direction, not back across the side channel where André lay in wait. He twisted the throttle
and sent the scoot forward, pulling into traffic
smoothly to avoid attracting attention.

Now his heart thumped his breastbone. The crackle
of tension spidered up his back to grab across his shoulder blades, and his stomach seemed to sway in his gut
like a ballast bag of wet sand. His skin crawled taut
across his thighs and groin; nausea chased bitterness
up the back of his throat.

This was it.

The luck was running now.

It was ninety minutes before he got his shot. Spivak
stayed in the city, visited a tavern André didn't follow
her into—it was on a decommissioned ferry, moored
along the east side of Broadbrook, and there was no
way off it that wasn't immediately obvious—and returned to her flashboat after less that forty-five minutes. It might have been the meet, but his job wasn't to
stop the meet, or identify the other party. He didn't do
that sort of thing.

Afterward, she headed west, out of the city on
Bayside. Not back the way they had come, but this was
a shorter way and she could always cut across the shipping lanes for a nearly direct route back to Kroc's
house—a shortcut that would be ideal for André's purposes. Not only did lighters kick up a hell of a splash
when they touched down—a splash that could turn
over a small craft—but big ships sometimes didn't notice little boats, and accidents could happen.

André didn't like to smile over his work; it seemed
disrespectful. But it was hard to keep this one down:
maybe prayer was good for something.

He should have stuck to his demand to be paid a
bonus for a twenty-four-hour closure.

The only potential problem was the top speed of his
scoot. If Spivak raced home, there was no way he could
keep up. But if she was cutting the lanes, she'd want to
proceed cautiously, with one eye on the sky. That
would be better.

And it seemed to be her plan. André hung back almost a half-kilometer, trailing Spivak until they were
well clear of Novo Haven. The submerged lights of the

shipping lanes glowed beneath the surface of the bay, but there was no real danger of being caught against them; they were meant to be seen from above. Only one lighter splashed down during the transect, and that one well off to the south and gently enough that by the time the wake reached André, he cut across it diagonally and noticed only what the skip and lurch did in his already nervous belly. The night was calm, still warmer than he'd expected, and the breeze from landward had faded off, leaving a few late-traveling sailboats motoring along the placid surface with their white sails hanging slack. Spivak, charting a stately progress, seemed inclined to enjoy the night. André had no problem with letting her do it. It was a point of honor with him that his targets never even knew they were in danger. Necessity did not have to be cruel.

Around the middle of the landing field, he goosed it. The caterpillar drive wasn't fast, but it was fast enough if Spivak didn't hear him coming, and quiet enough that she shouldn't. He set the autocruise, looped his hard memory, and—keeping one eye on the sky and the other on his quarry—began to assemble his weapon.

In most cases, André killed with a long-barreled sniping weapon, a combination rifle brand-named Locutor A.G. 351, for the year the design had been introduced. It adapted to either caseless standard ammunition—jacketed projectiles fired by a chemical accelerant—or crystalline slivers of hemorragine fired by compressed air, which dissolved in the victim's blood, causing symptoms of a cerebral aneurysm, then broke down into innocuous organic compounds within the day.

That was what he would be using tonight. He

preferred a bullet; it killed instantly if you did it right, whereas the hemorragine left the victim sometimes as long as 120 seconds to feel fear. And that was ugly and cruel.

The other issue with the damned things was that they didn't fly far, and a fairly light cross-breeze could deflect them. He'd have to be within a hundred meters, and he wouldn't get more than a couple of shots. People tended to notice when someone pointed a rifle at them and fired poisoned needles at the back of their heads.

He'd put one needle into her back, wait for her to go down, approach with caution, and download her hard memory for Closs—as instructed, just to be sure. Then he'd capsize her boat, lose the body someplace where it shouldn't be recovered for at least a day (long enough for the hemorragine to break down, and for her hard memory to wipe), and pretend, in the morning, to be shocked when he heard the news.

The scoot purred forward. André extended the telescope rest and slid the weapon-mount onto the peg. He squinted through the sight, focusing down through the scope because only an idiot would connex this—though idiots did—and took a sighting.

Lucienne Spivak was sitting upright in the pilot's chair, her braid whipping behind her, her shoulders square and facing him. Easy. The only way he could miss was a divine intervention.

He measured his breathing, matched it to the regular rise and fall of the swells, tugged his glove off with his teeth, slid his finger under the trigger guard. He waited for the moment, the moment when his breath would pause naturally just as the scoot topped one of the gentle waves.

The moment came. He squeezed the trigger. A jet of cool grease-scented air stroked his cheek.

There was no sound.

The sun wasn't up yet when someone hammered on Cricket's door frame. No doorbell, no chime of connex and the name of the importunate visitor, just the thumping of fist on paramangrove paneling.

"Oh, fuck," Cricket murmured, twisting her legs into the cool air. She slept nude; she dragged the robe she kept on the bedpost over chilled skin and stumbled barefoot across a morphing rug that this morning was off-white and shaggily looped. Her toes curled as she stepped onto the decking, as if she could somehow protect the tender instep of her foot from the crawling chill. "Fuck, who is it?"

"Kroc," came the voice from the other side of the door, which answered the question of why he was knocking. No connex to ring her chimes. His voice shivered, high and sharp, almost shrill. "Is Lucienne with you?"

"Shit," Cricket said, and palmed the lock plate faster than she should have. "She left me around one hundred and one. She was going to get a drink and go home."

"She didn't make it," Kroc said, unnecessarily, because sometimes it was better making a noise. He ducked under her arm into the flat, and she locked up behind him. "Check your messages. If she sent anything—"

It would have been to Cricket, because Jean was not connected. She tightened her robe and scrubbed her eyes on the sleeve. "One second."

She dropped her connex at night, except for the flat

security and a couple of emergency codes. If it had been really important, Lucienne would have spared the couple of extra keystrokes and sent to one of those.

But there were messages waiting. The one from André, which she hadn't answered. One or two from connex acquaintances, people she knew from online groups. And one from Lucienne.

She looked at Jean, so he would know. His face paled under his stubble, but he didn't speak.

Cricket opened the message.

And would have fallen if Jean had not caught her.

It was a sense-dump, night water and darkness, the smell of lubricant and the texture of the flashboat's controls in her hands, all subsumed by a hypodermic stab to the left of her spine, the building pressure of a migraine like the handle of a knife pressed to her eye. She gasped but couldn't make her diaphragm work. Jean's hands on her shoulders guided her back, cushioning her until she slumped against a chair. The robe was everywhere, he must be getting an eyeful, but he caught her under the chin and made her look into his eyes. "You need EMS."

"No," Cricket said, a shrill spasming whine. She couldn't lift her hand to push at him, so she thumped the heel on the deck for emphasis. She felt him jump. "No doctor. Just . . . a minute."

Dying. Cricket— no, Lucienne was dying. Lucienne knew she was dying, and she knew why. And there was no time to explain.

So she showed.

The file was encoded, and Cricket's breath came back into her with a rush as the flood of numbers washed away the swelling pain in her head. Lucienne had swamped her connex, a massive core-dump—

Corrupt. Corrupt. Corrupt.

"Shit!" The word of the day, apparently. Cricket scrambled to save, to back up, to dump what Lucienne had sent her into a protected hold. Cricket was an arch-informist. She had better security protocols than most governments. And she knew how to sling data, and how to repair it—

She went after it, the bones in Jean's wrists creaking as she clenched her hands. But the file was incomplete. And a nonholographic transmission, so what she had was a chunk of data, but not the sort of chunk that could give you a fuzzy picture of the whole. This was a linear string. Though Cricket was pretty sure she could find the key, because Lucienne would have wanted her—or Jean—to crack the code, she only had part of it.

And now was not the time for trying to patch out a crack on what she had. Not when Jean was leaning over her, moving his hands inside her slackening grip to tug her dressing gown shut over her breasts, breathing so shallowly that listening to him made *her* lungs hurt.

She let her hands loosen. He touched her shoulder and sat back. "Jean," she said. She opened her eyes. His, water-colored behind his rimless glasses, looked back.

He sighed, short and sharp. "No."

She put a hand down and picked herself off the floor. She'd bruised her shoulders on the chair. When she extended her hand to pull Jean off his knees, the stretch of muscle made her wince. "I—"

"It's not your fault." Abruptly, preemptive.

"It had to be André."

"It's still not your fault." He straightened, fist pressed into his side like a runner with a stitch. "His responsibility. Did she . . . send you anything else?"

"Part of a file." She swallowed. "It was coded. The connex cut off."

"Shit." With exactly the same inflection she'd said it, too. Her smile hurt more than frowning had. He opened his mouth, looked at her, shut it.

She couldn't stand the look on his face, the wary softness of it. Jean Gris should never look so unguarded. "You're not even going to recite the stupid parable about the snake at me, are you?"

He snorted, a pained laugh that didn't open his mouth. "No." And then a pause. "He's got the knack, doesn't he?"

"Could he have got past what you hung on Lucienne if he didn't?"

Untrained, unassisted. Jean shook his head. Cricket's heart twisted in her chest.

Nobody'd ever loved her like that. "Do you think you can—" *...save him...fix him.* She didn't even know the word she wanted.

Jean shrugged. Not a dismissal. A *maybe*. Even now. "I've known men as bad, turned out better." Jean's brand of revenge didn't run to murder. "Once you send me that file, I'll let you out of it. I know you didn't want to be involved."

"In what you and Lucienne were doing?"

He nodded. Even here, it didn't pay to be too specific.

"Actually," Cricket said, balling her hands in the pockets of her robe, "I was kind of changing my mind."

Sitting at the kitchen table, they drank a great deal of tea. Cricket hunched over her mug, sipping distractedly, while Jean filled and refilled it. "So tell me about

André," he said, when her fingers were no longer clenched so tightly on the cup that they whitened at the edges.

Her eyes were red, the lid-edges slick inside the lashes when she looked up. "What do you need?"

"Why does he want to conjure so bad?" She opened her mouth a little too fast, and Jean held up his hand. "Not the facile answer, please. You're an archinformist"—she laughed—"don't tell me you didn't pull his records back to first grade before you got involved with him."

The corner of her mouth quirked. Touché. "He'd never tell you. He's got a sister he can't stand. Left home in his teens, after his older brother got killed in a gang fight and he didn't pass evaluation for Exigency Corps training."

"So he wanted to be a god-botherer. He's got the talent—"

"His mother was a conjure." She pushed the cup away with her fingertips. Jean felt it scrape through the table and lifted his hands. "His sister is, too. He doesn't talk about them. I can only speculate..."

"So? Speculate."

She snatched the teacup and drained it. "I think he blames his mom for... He had a brother. A year older. Honoré. A tough boy, ran with a bad crowd. And whether their mom could actually conjure or not, she couldn't keep Honoré home."

"Or André from running with him." Jean lifted the pot. She held her hand over her cup.

"Or keep Honoré alive," Cricket said. "André got pretty badly beaten up around the same time. I think he blames his mother and sister for, you know." She waved at the ceiling.

"Not keeping Honoré alive?"

"Sure. So he tried to get into the Corps, and they wouldn't take him because of his family background. And he wants nothing to do with Zoë—she's his sister. She's a conjure, too."

"Any good?"

Cricket shrugged. "Are any of them? I mean, other than you?"

"There's a few," Jean allowed. He cleared his throat. "So André grew up a killer instead."

Changing her mind, Cricket reached for the teapot after all. "So it would seem."

The morning was hotter, humid, and bright. André was intent enough on his interface that he jumped when Maryanne bumped the door open with her hip, though he didn't look up until she set a tin tray on the steel edge of his desk. The napkin-covered outline of an antique revolver lay beside the coffeepot, the china cup, and a doughnut on the gold-rimmed plate.

Wordlessly, stiff-backed, Maryanne turned on a pointed shoe and left him staring at the thing. He reached out and brushed the napkin aside, then checked the load. One bullet.

Maryanne let the door snap shut behind her audibly. She had to give it an extra little push to get that click, and André read the message in it. Maryanne was his cousin, as well as his employee. Normally, she kept her opinions to herself, and her work for him met both their needs. He got to give something back to his family, and in return got help he could trust.

But Maryanne lived with André's older sister, Zoë, a charlatan conjurer like their mother, and—

There were family differences. Leave it at that.

He set the revolver aside. There was a real paper envelope underneath, his name in actual handwriting, actual ink. *M~ A. Deschênes.*

Shit, he thought. And also, *at last.*

This was more usually a graduation test, as he understood it. A message as plain as the gun: you are playing in the big leagues now. He spun the cylinder, closing his eyes while he listened to it whir, picturing the chamber with the single cartridge dropping to the bottom, away from the hammer, pausing there as the cylinder ratcheted to a halt.

If Kroc knew about Spivak, the weapon was bait. The fix was in, this was no test, and accepting the challenge would mean his death. If Kroc didn't know—if Cricket had spoken to him about André—then this was André's chance. He might be able to affect the spin of the cylinder. He might just—get lucky.

Unlike the cat in the box, he did *not* know if he was dead.

The gun might be archaic, but the antitampering lock was not. The diamond-tipped drill *zinged* into metal as the cylinder stopped. The weapon shuddered as the bolt slipped home, a delicate warble alerting him to the activation of the transmitter. Kroc would know if he cheated.

The question being asked had a yes or no answer. Did he want to conjure enough to die for it?

André slid the room-temperature barrel into his mouth, tasting gun oil, sleek and unpleasantly aromatic. He pictured *misfire*. He pictured a misaligned chamber, a hammer bent enough to miss contacting the primer. A revolver was a primitive machine, an effective machine. Not much could go wrong.

He was dead or he wasn't. A closed box. *About time,* he thought, and opened his eyes for one long look at the screen across from his desk, the one that showed the endless blue expanse of bay, the contrail of another lighter towing its string-of-pearls cargo pods toward the spaceport after splashdown. Up and down, up and down, never getting anywhere.

The wake hit; his office rose and dropped, the stylus rolling across his interface stopped by the lip on the desk.

His finger convulsed.

It was the best damned coffee André had ever tasted.

He gulped the first cup in three painful, searing swallows, then poured another and soaked broken bites of doughnut. It was a ritual, a discipline, and he didn't pick up the envelope until he'd tossed back the crumb-laden dregs and poured himself a third cup, oily and black. By then, his hands were shaking too badly to drink and *machismo* was satisfied, so he set it aside and picked up the envelope in its stead.

Hand-addressed, as he'd noticed. The writing was smooth and controlled, not jerky the way most people's was when they were forced to use archaic tools. He knew before he opened it that the note inside, like the envelope, would be real paper, dead trees and cloth fiber, rather than epaper. There would be no data trail.

André read over the address and the invitation and drank his third cup of coffee while memorizing both. Wet memory, not hard.

No etrails.

The fourth cup of coffee was the last one in the pot. It steamed thickly into the humid air while André tapped the last few droplets free and then unscrewed the element from the bottom of the pot. It wasn't hot enough to glow when he laid the insulated cap down on the tray, but it was hot enough to blacken paper, and—when he bent forward and blew softly on the thin ember—to set it brilliantly aflame.

The invitation burned the envelope, and both scorched André's fingertips before he dropped them in the recycler and poured half the last cup of coffee on top. What remained was bitter, and there were grounds in it. André could afford the real, imported bean. Not a stunning expense—coffee went through a transmitter just fine—but supplies were limited and that made it a not insignificant one.

He savored those last swallows. Then he stood, and set the cup aside on the painted tin tray, and summoned his weapons and his coat. He walked past Maryanne on his way out; she caught his wrist so he turned and met her gaze. She shook her head so her earrings rattled on her earpiece, lips pressed tight, conservative bleached dreadlocks caught back in a bun.

"Thank God," she said, and squeezed tight enough to leave nail cuts in his flesh before he pulled back. The half-moon marks blanched, then reddened on pale gold skin inside his wrist—so much lighter than his scarred knuckles, than the back of his arm.

"Nothing to do with God," he answered, and patted her on the shoulder, feeling her bones shift as she shrugged, before he moved away.

"I'm glad you survived Kroc's invitation, André. And by the way, I quit." She smoothed her hair, and then invoked the unholy, the name of André's sister. "I have to live with Zoë."

André parked his scoot in front of Jean Kroc's minifab and paused at the bottom of the floating dock, looking around. He wasn't surprised to see Cricket sitting spread-kneed on the second step, shucking peas into a bucket set between her sandals. She looked up when he crunched up the seashell-and-broken-plascrete path.

She never changed. Her eyes were still the brown of weak tea or swamp water, and you could see the flecks in them when you got close enough, like loam or bits of leaf. She was skinny and not too tall, blue veins visible under the skin of her throat. Her fine black hair rat-tailed in the humid heat.

She stood up, bucket swinging, colander full of peas set aside on the steps. "Jean's waiting for you."

"You know," André said, before he pocketed his shades, wiped the sweat off his temples, and stole a kiss, "you can buy those."

"Taste better if you grow them yourself," she answered, and grabbed a fistful of beard to kiss him back. Her shoulders were tense under the light-colored blouse, though, and her back hunched as if she fought the urge to cringe.

He didn't withdraw until she'd smoothed one hand across his bald scarred scalp. "Oh, I have time to do that search for you tomorrow if you still need it."

"No," he said, shifting his weight. "I took care of it myself."

A tight smile and a small nod. "Power down, André. No devices inside."

He blinked. "All I've got is a headset. You know——"

"Power *down*." She bent over enough to pick up the colander and balanced it inside the bucket, and André didn't brush against those promising haunches. This time. "Nothing that happens in Jean's house enters a data hold."

She swung the bucket into his hand. He took it

reflexively, then watched her ass sway up the steps. She paused with her hand on the door, eyebrows raised as she glanced over her shoulder. He sighed and rolled his eyes skyward, where a sticky haze did nothing to cut the heat, and toggled his headset off.

The world went flat. Isotherms, stock ticker, weather report, chat group, reality skins dropped off his display, leaving his head and his vision curiously empty. Even in the mornings, when he ran, he wasn't this naked.

As if it were a security blanket, he kept the sense augment on. Not even Jean could complain about that. "You want my hardware, baby?"

"No," said Cricket. "Jean Gris isn't worried about your guns."

The body was tangled in the cables, halfway down.

And every time Gourami let the nictitating membranes flicker across se eyes, se remembered. So Gourami tapped the slate on the bar beside se cup to summon another glass of poison, and drew webbed fingery feet up in the rung of the humen-type stool where they wouldn't get stepped on, balancing awkwardly with knees drawn up to either side of se shoulders.

Gourami was the only person in the tavern. Not that persons were forbidden to enter humen taverns, but generally they kept to themselves, slept wet, stayed low. The contractors didn't like it if the persons caused trouble. And a lot of humen didn't care to take the time to understand, to parse a slate or study hand gestures.

But the people's bars weren't open yet; everybody

was still on shift. And Gourami had badly, badly needed a drink.

Because the body had been tangled in the cables, halfway down, and none of the humen on the tender had been particularly concerned. They'd given Gourami the rest of the day off when se'd brought it up—all limp dangling and waterlogged mammal flesh. But what se'd seen cutting across the green water toward the anchor platform wasn't a humen hearse or ambulance, but a black-windowed limousine—

The bartender slid a clean glass of cold green tea across the bar and retrieved the dirty one. It wasn't as poisonous to people's physiology as alcohol, but had enough of a sting to make one woozy—a pleasant recreational toxin rather than a life-threatening one.

The humen had brought all sorts of interesting things.

Including disrespect for their dead.

Gourami nursed the tea, cupping the humen-shaped drinking vessel between spidery handfingers, the webs tucked together so they wouldn't cling to the glass. Se rolled the fluid around se mouth, pushing it back and forth through the same fluted cartilaginous plates used for straining water weed and insects from the marshes, if one did not have soup.

It made gums and tongue and palate numb.

Se swallowed and became aware of a shadow darkening the sun-warmth that dappled se back. Gourami disentangled handfingers from the glass and turned, nictitating for a better view. A human stood there, tall and male, by the ringlets of fur on his face. He dropped his hand on Gourami's shoulder, the dry mammal warmth chafing through se protective mucous gloss.

Gourami pulled back automatically.

—*Stand up*, the human mouthed. *Stand up, frog.*

Lips moved, breath brushed across Gourami's face. Se heard nothing but squeaks and rumbles, and could not have duplicated them to save se life. The frequency of humen voices was all wrong. But se could lipread much humen speech from se job as liaison. And humen body language, too, after a fashion.

Se was in grave trouble.

Gourami could have run; could have fought, exploded off the bar stool and barreled through the big human that stood making exaggerated lip movements and calling se "Froggie." The humen who weren't contractors always said they couldn't tell one person from another.

Except the human was making eye contact, was making physical contact, and while Gourami knew that humen did that to intimidate, between the tea and the endorphins released by the kinesthetic signals, se was too relaxed to initiate violent movement.

—*Stand up!* The human shaped again, and then made some other short noises and tossed his head, shaking shaggy mud-brown fur out in every direction. Then he reached for Gourami's slate, grabbing with frustration.

But Gourami did not wish to relinquish it, and so, with the eye and hand contact broken, stood.

The human stepped back a pace, fumbling at his belt. But then Gourami wobbled—standing at full extension required balance, and after ... several ... helpings of poison, se had little left—and sank back.

Se toefingers curled on the hard dry floor, contracting automatically to protect the delicate webs, but still seeking purchase. The bar rose on the swell of a taxiing lighter. Gourami could have run, again, but still fumbled with the slate, hoping to explain or to obtain an explanation of the human's odd behavior, when the human managed to slip the shocker from his belt and touch it to the base of Gourami's skull, above the retracted neck, behind the ear membrane.

Nobody intervened. It was a humen bar.

4

IF CRICKET HAD A MAN, IT WOULD BE ANDRÉ DESCHÊNES. But she didn't. And after last night, she was doubly glad. She hadn't wanted a man before and she didn't want one now. They had both been happier with the sort of halfway state in which—*things*—stood, the one where nobody owned either one of them.

And now there was Lucienne.

She knew what he'd say if she asked him. It was business, and he didn't talk about business.

She wondered if she would ever forgive him. Even if Jean was right. She wondered if she would ever *want* to forgive. So she let her fingertips brush his palm when she relieved him of the bucket, and smiled back when he smiled, white teeth flashing in the dim, damp entrylock of the minifab, and felt mostly like she'd swallowed ice. There was more plascrete underfoot, badly poured so her sandals scuffed on the ripples, and the bolts holding the structure's shell to the slab around the margin protruded enough to tear careless toenails off. No smart matter here, no computronium, nothing electronic at all.

André blinked heavily in the darkness, his eyes adjusting without the help from his headset. Cricket nibbled her lip to stop the frown, even if he probably wouldn't have seen it, and walked past him to the inner door. She knew her way around in the dark.

The main room of the minifab had a galley kitchen in the back corner, just where your line of sight would land as you came in the lock. The walls had a curious texture under the paint that hid the extruded surface. Somebody—Jean Kroc, as far as Cricket knew—had papered over them in layers, tearing the sheets into ragged bits, so the edges left abstract patterns under saturated blues and greens and oranges and yellows. The colors were bold but not glaring, and the overall effect was sunny, reinforced by braided rag rugs softening the plum-colored plascrete floor.

In addition to the warm decor, the room was full of light. Jean had torched curved windows in the minifab shell and fixed clear poly over them expediently, by cutting the sheets larger than the windows and running a torch around the edges so the bubbled scars made a weld. With Cricket's help, Lucienne had sunk hooks and hung curtains across the scorched bits; it looked pretty good.

"Shoes," Cricket said, once there was enough light for André to see his feet. She toed out of her sandals and kicked them back into the entry. After a moment, André copied her, though she noticed him craning his neck as if searching for signs of either Jean or a flicker stage-set of a conjure man's workshop.

He caught her looking, and tipped his head. "I was expecting—"

"—stuffed alligators," Cricket agreed. "Lucienne gave them all to Planetary Relief. Have a seat, André. I'll get the tea."

"Where's Kroc?" He did as she said, though, and settled his long body into a blue-cushioned basket chair that creaked under his weight. When he leaned forward to lock his hand around his wrist, hugging his knees, his red brocade fogjacket strained over muscular shoulders. He'd shut down the autofit, too.

She kissed the top of his head as she went past, a calculated reward for following orders, and made sure she held the muddy bottom of the bucket clear of both the upholstery and his clothes. "He'll be inside in a minute," she said, as she dropped the bucket in the sink. "He knows you're here."

The plumbing was old-fashioned, too. She had to turn a knob to pull water from the pipes. She slid a copper kettle under the stream and started the gas fire while it filled. Water droplets sizzled when she set the kettle on the burner.

She stretched on tiptoe over the stove to pull down pottery cups—teal and rose, cheerful and antiquated as everything else in the 'fab—and let them clink on the tile counter. The silence that followed lasted until the water boiled, and then André cleared his throat again.

"Did you put a word in for me, Cricket?"

She turned off the stove and came back to him, balancing two cups in hands damp from washing the dirt and pea-pod strings from under her nails. She slid André one cup and plumped down on a cushion on the floor, elevating her own mug until she was settled so it wouldn't spill. "Who else would have done it?"

"Good." He sipped the tea. "Glad I can count on you."

Cricket smiled around the rim of her cup. She had

loved how André could never quite meet her eyes when she glanced up at him through her lashes. It made her feel powerful. Now it made her feel lied to. "You should come by more often," she said. "You haven't seen where I sleep now."

"I thought you might be with Kroc, too."

"I haven't got a man," she said. And might have said more, but she heard slapping footsteps beyond the door beside the galley and twisted where she sat to catch Jean Kroc's eye as he entered. He was barefoot, his rinsed toes leaving damp pad-prints on the plascrete. He dried his hands on his shorts and smiled. He was a ropy, sallow, middle-aged man whose round spectacles sat unevenly on crooked ears, half-concealing slight epicanthic folds that gave his eyes an Earthasian cast. Cricket knew one of his grandmothers had been Korean, and that was probably also where he got the high forehead that shone with sweat on either side of a widow's peak. A short grizzled beard softened his gaunt cheeks and the worn line of his jaw, but that wasn't why they called him *Jean Gray*.

He half-nodded to Cricket and André, then fetched another mug down from over the stove. Jean Kroc wasn't as tall or as broad as André, but he didn't have to stand on tiptoe to reach as Cricket did. "You lived," he said with his back to Cricket and André both. "Good, that's good."

"I lived," André answered. He finished his tea in three gulps; it was still hot enough that steam came out with his breath when he continued. "So, Jean Gris. Who is it that you would like for me to kill?"

Gourami woke dry and aching. The surface se lay on was spongy without being soft, a kind of foam mat like

the ones the humen used under their offspring's climbing apparatus. The adults mostly seemed landbound,
but the offspring were as light and agile as mossglid-
ers, without the vestigial wings—

Gourami curled handfingers over eyes and squinched
them tight, trying to chase out random thoughts for
something a little more presently useful. Se neck hurt,
fizzing pain like a chemical burn, and se remembered
the shocker and the hand on the shoulder. Se flinched,
and then gingerly slid fingers around the back of se
skull in order to check the burn.

The flesh felt crusted and cracked, two finger-pad-
size sores that were moist in the middle but dry at the
edges. Se dabbed skin mucous over the wounds and the
pain eased at once, leaving only lingering tenderness
and a ringing in se skull like the vibrations from an
outboard motor.

Se sat upright, blinking in the darkness. If se eyes
had been going to adapt, they would have by now,
which meant there was very little light. And se slate
was missing, along with the web-rig, rigging kit, and
passcode stick.

No way to call for help.

Se rolled belly-down, pressing soft-tacky skin to the
mat, and laid jaw to floor. Bone conduction might tell
more—like whether the structure in which se was
trapped was a floating one or rested on land.

Se held a breath, and listened.

Waves. Waves slapping against the hull, and the
thrum of engines attenuated by water. And voices,
people voices, which could be carrying ten or a dozen
humen miles. They spoke of commonplaces: work and
egglings, food and education. Gourami's handfingers
twitched toward them spastically.

Se pushed up, unmolding from the mat. The mat was

bad; it was not helpful. Se could not send signals ringing through the water by tapping on the decking, for example, even if se had something with which to tap.

The wounds itched. Se resealed them and set about exploring the prison in a crouch, sweeping long arms through the darkness, feeling for obstacles. Se touched nothing. Gourami clicked tongue against palate to generate saliva, and dragged each webbed hand across the tongue in turn. Sticky saliva adhered to the webs, mingling in strings with the mucous; se chafed the palms and fingerpads together, licking dry eyes in concentration. The chemical reaction was fast and a moment later se palms began to glow with blue-green bioluminescence.

Se lifted glowing hands in the darkness. As long as se didn't look at them directly, the light was enough for dark-adapted eyes to see.

The prison was small. There was a metal door in one wall, and the bulkheads were all metal, too. Gourami couldn't make out the color by biolume, and anyway the humen would see it differently. Their eyesight was shifted into the infrared; they could see as colors wavelengths that Gourami perceived only as heat.

Metal. The walls were metal. Which meant that the flooring under the padding was probably metal, too.

Well, that was something, then.

Se plumped down on the padded floor with knees lifted on either side of se head, smoothed more mucous—glowing now—over the wounds, extended claws from toefingers, and dug hard into the tough membrane of the mat, peeling it back.

Jefferson Greene sat back and amused himself by contemplating the humors and nature of his second-in-

command. Timothy Closs did not think of himself a
nice man, or even a particularly good one, but if
pressed he would call himself honest. He believed in
hard work, deserved rewards, and a refined form of
Social Darwinism, though he didn't actually identify it
as such.

He was currently furious almost beyond the capacity for rational thought, and Jefferson could tell because he was sitting quietly, all of his usual intent
energy focused on the backs of his hands as if he could
bore through skin and bones and the desktop interface
and the decking below, and sink the whole damned office cruiser into Novo Haven Bay.

He could have been checking his tickers, instant
messages, voicemail. But Jefferson knew he wasn't, because his eyes were perfectly still, his lips compressed,
his fingers motionless—not shivering with nearly im-
perceptible commands.

Jefferson sat still for five minutes, thirty-two seconds, timed on his head's-up, and listened to Closs
think. He managed not to sigh when Closs lifted his
head, but the truth was that he'd been close to resort-
ing to a pharmaceutical drip.

The expression on Closs's face provided no relief,
just a clarifying rush of adrenaline. Jefferson sank his
nails into the arms of his chair. "This is bad."

Closs nodded with sarcastic slowness and got up out
of his chair. He was a smallish man, fit in middle age,
still military in his bearing though his hair was ash
gray at the temples. "We're going to have to kill it," he
said.

Jefferson shuddered. He'd been hoping for a softer
solution, or at least a calming euphemism. "Major"—
Closs was still *the Major*, though he hadn't seen military service in twenty standard years his body-time.

Which came out to 150 or so nonrelativistic since he'd become attached to the Colonial Rim Company, Greene's World, and associated territories—"there's got to be another way."

Jefferson wasn't the Greene that Greene's World was named after, but rather the grandson of the famous explorer. Those were big shoes to fill: by Novo Haven standards, the biggest. He forced himself to meet Closs's gaze when Closs turned to stare at him.

"Your position here rests on keeping the stream of omelite coming. No tanglestone, no Slide. No Slide, no connex. No Rim, no Core, no nothing, except a scatter of planets hundreds of years of travel time apart. Nobody's going to let the Roman Empire fall, Jefferson, because you didn't have the balls to do what you have to do. Make no mistake, this is your balls-up. If you'd just let the frog *go,* there would have been nothing to explain except a drowning. Now that you've *grabbed* the poor creature, what did you expect us to do with it?"

Closs paced back and forth in front of the curved windows overlooking the bay, the spaceport, and the sparse ranks of drill platforms marching out to sea beyond. Jefferson relaxed slightly: a pacing Closs was a Closs with a plan. "Not only have you given it a better story to tell and a reason to tell it," Closs continued, "but if it can ever prove it was detained, you've validated its word. I already have ranid terrorism to contend with, reformers and Greens picketing my drill platforms, omelite and petroleum quotas to meet—"

"It's a fucking ranid," Jefferson replied, fiddling his ring, not bothering to rise. Omelite was a proprietary secret; as far as most of the galaxy was concerned, there were no natural sources of entangled pairs. The primary mission of the Greene's World Charter Trade

Company was classified. "It doesn't even know the *word* tanglestone, much less what it's mining. And it brought up the body. There hasn't been time for the hard memory to dump yet, and Security will download whatever's in there."

"Which at best will prove her a criminal."

"And at worst will prove somebody killed her, and maybe uncork the thing you wanted her dealt with to cork in the first place. Can we talk about how close we are to a native uprising right this second, Tim?"

Closs lifted an eyebrow at him, and for a moment Jefferson thought he'd won the round. None of his employees gave him half the trouble Closs did. But then, Closs wasn't exactly an employee, though he controlled a smaller percentage of the Greene's World Rim Charter Trade Company than Jefferson did. Jefferson cleared his throat. "I thought we could question it, find out how much it knew."

"More now than it did this morning, that's for damned sure."

Jefferson took a breath. Losing his temper with Closs wouldn't get him anything either, except Closs's scorn. "Who the hell is it going to talk to? The local media?"

Which was Rim-owned. Like Security. And easier, in general, to control. There were idealists in Security. Far more of them, ironically, than in Com. A good thing there was no chance of it getting in touch with Earth; the press *there* liked to bring down governments.

Closs shook his head. He put his back to the glass and folded his hands. "It'll have to be killed."

Jefferson clambered from his chair, finally, to face Closs on his feet. "I hope you don't think——"

"Don't worry," Closs answered, turning back to his

desk, giving Jefferson his shoulder with an air of final-
ity that both relieved and infuriated. "I wouldn't ask.
You figure out what we're going to do about getting
whatever was in Spivak's hard memory away from
Security, would you?"

"I know who to assign," Jefferson said, thinking of
Dayvid Kountché. Who was both ambitious and dis-
creet.

"You mistake me, André." Jean Kroc leaned against
the counter with a mug cupped in his right hand and
the still-hot kettle by his left. Half-moons of dirt darkened his fingernails, and he bowed his face over the
steam, breathing deeply with closed eyes. "More tea?"

André got up and brought his cup to Kroc. The tea-
making involved Kroc dumping the old teabag in the
sink, fishing a new one from the box, and adding it to
the cup in advance of water—which he reheated to
boiling before he poured. It was like watching a medieval alchemist at work.

"You don't want someone killed?" André asked. Just
to be clear, because sometimes people didn't want to
come right out and say it. "Then what did you want
me for?"

Kroc returned the pottery cup to him and gestured
him back to the padded wicker chair. "I heard you
were lucky," Kroc said, picking up his own mug again.
"You proved it today. I also heard you wanted to learn
the mojo, sing gris gris. You want to be a conjure man,
André Deschênes? Bend the world to your will?"

"You make it sound like magic," André answered.

Kroc's eyes were a flat pale color under his gray-
laced brows. His spectacles caught the light in level re-
flections when he turned his face toward the window,

but then he'd look back at André directly and André would almost feel his gaze, like a pin scratched over his skin. It was peculiarly intense, focusing; he wondered if there was something in the tea, something his wetware couldn't have caught because he'd powered down.

There were easier ways to kill him. Though, who knew what a conjure man thought an initiation was supposed to look like?

If that was what this was.

André set his mug on the glass-topped wicker table.

"It's not magic." Kroc spoke suddenly, breaking the stretched silence, dismissing the comment with a flip of his hand. "It's not luck either, though luck helps prove you can be taught. What it is"—he grinned, showing tea-stained teeth, and tapped the side of his nose with a finger—"is a useful manipulation of the observer effect. So you can change the world if you just think at it right."

Kroc drank his tea; André folded his hands in his lap. Cricket crossed the 'fab silently and settled onto the wicker lounge, drawing her bare feet up under her ass and curling into the corner like a cat.

"That's why some people are so spectacularly *unlucky*, too, isn't it?" Kroc asked, glancing sideways to fix his gaze on her.

"Hmm?" She raised her eyes dreamily. André recognized the role. No one ever saw the real Cricket Earl Murphy. Nobody even knew her real name. "Oh, right, Jean. Yes, I'd say you're right." She didn't smile, studying André over her tea.

André smiled. "So you can teach what I want to learn. How do I earn the teaching, M~ Kroc, if you don't want me for my skills?"

"I didn't say that." Kroc moved now, finally, crossing

the rugs to sit on the floor beside Cricket's lounge. He folded his legs and settled straight down. "I'd like to put you on retainer, as it were."

André had already set his cup down, so he had nothing to divest himself of when he stood. "I don't take open contracts," he said. "I know what I'm doing when I'm going in. That's not negotiable."

But Kroc didn't hasten to his feet or hurry to smooth things over. He emptied his hands and laced his fingers together. "M~ Deschênes," Jean Kroc said, tipping his head back to look André in the face, "did you know that the model of wet-dry scoot you use has a small, but deadly, history of explosion following a hydrogen leak? No? Three instances, I think, on the five worlds where they're in service. Freak accidents happen."

André's fingertips grew cold. "You're *not* claiming responsibility for those."

"André—" Cricket said. She bit her lip, though, and gestured to Kroc, who appeared to be waiting politely for her comment. He shrugged and continued.

"Of course not. Nor would I be responsible, you see, if there were a similar freak accident here in Novo Haven. But the point I'm making is that I certainly don't need your assistance to *kill* people. If I wanted to engage in such a problematic undertaking."

"So what do you want?" André didn't sit, but he didn't step away from the chair either.

"Information."

"I don't talk about my clients."

"That's all right," Jean Kroc said. "I don't care about your clients. But I care about the Colonial Rim Company—are they hiring out their wet work now?— and I know you have ways of finding things out."

Cricket leaned forward, her lower lip still pinched

between her teeth. She was staring at André, willing him toward some decision, some course of action, but she didn't speak.

André looked from her water-brown eyes to Kroc's flat blue-gray ones. He sat down in the wicker chair, and let it creak under his weight. He could refuse to answer—as good as an admission that he'd worked for Rim, and a violation of confidentiality in itself—but there was a threat in what Kroc was saying. *He can't know about Spivak. If he knew about Spivak, I'd be dead.*

Wouldn't he?

God-botherers were licensed and controlled for good reason. Unchecked coincidence could break *planets* apart—and had nearly done so on Patience.

He had other sources of information. But—

"I can't make these promises."

"I will never ask you to do what you find…unethical," Jean said. "A handshake contract. You can walk away any time."

André picked up the tea again, blew across it, drank. Something to steady his hands. An elaborate game of cat and mouse? He swallowed the fluid: sweet, warm, full-bodied.

How badly did he want this?

Cricket was looking at him, a little smile curving the corners of her mouth. She was not the sort of woman who would lay down an ultimatum. She was not the sort of woman who said, "Either you change or I go." She was the sort of woman who watched until she didn't like what she saw anymore, and *then* she went. No games, not with somebody like her. No manipulation.

"Teach me," André said.

Kroc smiled. "I hope you don't have anywhere to be for the next few hours."

Gourami in se captivity could not see the swift failure of the equatorial twilight. But se felt it in the shift of the air, the humidity, the coolness from the ventilation ducts—and knew the wait would now not be long. It must not be long; se was drying, laid long on the floor, lungs heaving with the effort of respiring when the skin was too parched to exchange gases.

Se closed se eyes to concentrate on the work of staying alive, thinking, *they will be coming*. As night fell, clouds would coalesce over the mining platforms, in air saturated by steam from the seawater used to cool the drills. They would spread, water first precipitating from the atmosphere into visible vapor and then precipitating in truth, falling in fat warm blobs to the accompaniment of crackling thunder. It was good, a good omen; Gourami did not think that the humen's wet eyes—sonar, especially—would work well with ripples of sound-interference everywhere.

The rescuers came at sunset. Gourami did not hear them, did not know they had arrived until there was a hiss and sizzle in the darkness, the reek of scorching insulation. Se nictitated when the light spilled through the opening crack, but it still took moments to adapt. Se blinked, dazzled, and pressed hand-pads to eyes until pupils could contract.

After a moment, the pressure of light eased and se could no longer see hand bones. Se pushed up to stand, licking eyes over nictitating membranes. In the doorway stood a hand of people, all four of them naked of identifying patches, wearing only belts of canvas strapping from which to hang their tools. They carried no

slates, no locators; nothing that might be used to identify them. Gourami could not tell if they were coolies
or savages, even, to use the humen terms. But the light
behind wasn't bright enough to silhouette, and when
the smallest person turned sideways Gourami could
see skin dyed an even, artificial green to hide the mottles.

The smallest person made the scrape and click of
Gourami's own-name, with a question-trill. The smallest person was Caetei.

—*Here,* Gourami answered, staggering forward. Se
did not add the croak-trill-scrape of the smallest person's own-name. The aliens might recognize se real
name if they listened through their devices.

Caetei wrapped handfingers around Gourami's
wrist and pulled se forward. Se had been dry too long;
se felt dizzy, cracked, and se mucous was pasty. But the
grasp gave se strength, and se answered Caetei's unspo-
ken command. Triggered by the touch, endorphins
helped. Gourami was docile, and Caetei's desire was
that se follow.

Se would follow until se flippers wore to nubs.

There were humen here and there in the corridors,
on the deck, each one trussed and glaring. Gourami
waddled past, moving only because Caetei pulled se
and se must do what touch commanded. The unmot-
tled green backs were curiously anonymous. Unless
their owners spoke, Gourami could not identify
them—though the long one might be Tetra, egg-mate
of one of Gourami's exoparents, related by blood
rather than by water.

That one cross-wired a final door lock, and the little
party came out in starlight on a battered-looking barge
that was quite at odds with the gleaming modern interior. There were more persons here, two hands of

them, and while Gourami leaned on Caetei, the rangy
person passed the tool se had used to cross-wire the
door into se toefingers and used its waterproofed handle to pound on the deck.

From other hatchways, persons scrambled, some of
them hopping on all fours in their haste. Some were
pear-shaped, their pouches full of seawater and nutri-
tion for egglings still too small and presentient to swim
free. Three hands, five—Gourami, dizzy, could not
count them as Caetei dragged se toward the railing.
Some of the persons dragged bound humen, lowered
dinghies over the sides of the barge. They all moved
with great haste, efficiently, in teams.

Se could not clamber over; se feet would not lift
high enough to hook the bottom railing. But Caetei insisted, leaning in to make eye contact, and from that
demand Gourami drew the strength to climb.

Still, if it had not been for Caetei's hands curled
under Gourami's armpits, lifting, se would have ended
slumped, halfway over the rail. Caetei wrapped bony
fingers around Gourami's ankles. Se crouched and
heaved, lifting with the powerful muscles of thigh
and haunch. Gourami slithered overboard, bruising
pelvis and knees on the rail. And then se was falling,
uncontrolled, tumbling, and then the warm water
smacked se hard along the left side, bruising webs
between reaching toefingers, stinging the outflung
arm. A pop as a handfinger dislocated, pain that
coiled se arm like jelly-colony sting. Se shocked alert,
wet now, warm in the shallow water of the bay. Se
gasped, wetting throat and sinuses, skin prickling
as toxins and foreign matter adhered to drying mucous washed away. The burn-wound seared, dazzled,
numbed.

Se was wet again.

Se breathed deep, oxygenating, feeling mottles flush and go violet. The itching tightness eased. Mucous flowed freely, rehydrated, and Gourami croaked in relieved pleasure as Caetei and the disguised others began to splash into the bay. —*Hurry*, Caetei thrummed into the water. —*We must be away when the barge sinks.*

Se words caressed Gourami's flanks. —*Sinks?*

—*Hippolytae mined it with a boring charge. It will sink; we must be clear. Can you swim?*

Gourami's damaged handfinger delivered a nauseous spike of pain when se tried to paddle, and so se tucked arms to chest and kicked experimentally. Se glided forward, water sluicing along a streamlined form. The course was unpredictable, with only one hand to steer with, but speed was not impaired.

—*I can swim*, Gourami answered. —*Caetei—*

—*Then swim*, the other interrupted. —*Talk when we're away from the bomb.*

—*But what about the humen on the barge?* Se'd seen some lowered into the rubber boats. But had they all gotten off? Would the boats withstand a nearby explosion? They drowned in water, humen. Faster, much faster, than Gourami would drown in either water or dry air. They could not skin-breathe; they had not even rudimentary gills.

Se made a small sound of protest. Caetei did not answer, though se must have felt the noise. Gourami kicked, feeling green bodies stirring the water alongside, and held peace.

For now.

Later, there would be words. Words with a human Gourami thought se could trust. Because if the humen slew their own and gave no respect to the passing, then that was ill. But if they hurt or killed persons, and persons hurt or killed humen—

—then that was war.

Red light slicked Jean Kroc's windows before those inside felt the shock or heard the explosion. André was moving before he had time to hope it was ridiculous, cold tea scattering from the mug he kicked over, his foot just missing the remains of supper on his plate. He clotheslined Cricket as she lurched to her feet. She folded around his arm and he twisted, pressing her into his chest. He fell underneath her, rolled to cover her with his body, tucking her face against his throat. She shoved his chest with both hands. "Oaf!"

André pressed her down.

Kroc rose from his chair. Wiry, a little bowlegged, most of his weight rested on the outside edges of his feet. "It's not close enough," he said; the floor lurched up and thumped André in the knees and elbows on the fourth syllable. Cricket grunted against his chest. He lifted his chest and hips; she wriggled free, palm on his shoulder, elbow pressing his upper arm, and eeled away.

The atmospheric shock wave hit a moment later, the poly groaning as André's ears popped, the sound a thud like a crushed drum. Cricket had one knee down, one palm flat. She squeaked like something stepped-on and clapped her hands to the sides of her head. André knelt, staring at Kroc. "It could have been a nuke."

"My eyes haven't melted." Kroc slipped his hands under Cricket's armpits and pulled her to her feet, then scrubbed palms and fingers on his shorts. He walked to the window, padding over rag rug and plascrete. The red glare of the explosion had faded, but firelight limned Kroc's cheek and temple as he pressed his face to the window.

"Lighter crash?"

"Looks like a barge exploded on the bay," Kroc said. "It's burning to the water." He put his back to it. "Hell of a thing. You know, there was just one the other night. Getting to be a habit."

André pushed to a crouch. His back protested. He'd skinned a knee. "Cricket, you all right?"

Her lip curled, but whatever she'd been about to say, she thought better of it and looked down. "Thanks," she said. "Although if it had been a nuke, it wouldn't have helped."

André shrugged around his grin. "You don't think I'm radiation-proof?" He turned to Kroc, caught a glimpse of the tiny, burning shape a mile or so out on the water. "Shit—"

A thumping sound was rescue craft, their lights playing over the water. There couldn't have been much warning. André expected fruitless sweeps, perhaps doll-small figures sliding in harness to pluck bodies from the water. But as he watched they dropped rescue harnesses, hauled up kicking women or men.

It was strange, seeing it all through a chunk of clear plastic, barely augmented, unskinned. It was flat, without hyperlinks. He couldn't zoom. He couldn't access histories or burn context.

Just what was out there, reality primitive as an oil painting. Even with the augments, he hadn't seen the world this way since his teens. Since he got out of his mom's house and started making some real money.

And this was how Kroc lived all the time?

André wet his lips with his tongue. He didn't know quite what he'd say, but he thought he'd find out when it got out of his mouth.

Whatever it was going to be, he never heard it; there was a thumping at the door and he startled. Kroc brushed past him, one hand steadying André's shoulder, and strode to the door. "I'm not feeding anybody else," Cricket called over the noise of the kettle boiling.

The entry was dark. André couldn't see what security measures Kroc took, but it was a minute before he opened the door. When he did, he jerked it abruptly. What André saw past him was not human, with its teardrop-shaped body, thick indistinguishable neck smoothing to sloped shoulders, and thick-thighed, crooked legs. The ranid steadied itself on the doorframe, the other knobby forelimb akimbo and firelight lending unnaturally green skin a mucilaginous shine. It crouched between its knees, eyes tilted up at Kroc, and darted hand-gestures this way and that. It wore only a woven belt, no slate and no pass-tags. Not an employee of Rim, then. A wild froggie, a savage. André tensed, though he couldn't make out a weapon.

Kroc stepped back. "André," he said without turning his head, "go home."

André glanced over his shoulder at Cricket. She did not look up from her fussing by the cooker. "By water, now?"

The scooter had a shallow draft, and there wouldn't be that broad of a cordon around the fire. He wanted an excuse to stay and see what happened next.

"I'll call you," Kroc said. "Please, go now." He raised his voice. "Cricket, you, too."

She came out drying her hands. She sat down on the floor without a word and started pulling on her shoes.

André offered her a lift, and she took it. Took him home with her, too, and what with one thing and another, it was an hour and a half before he remembered

to power up and connex, and morning before he
checked his messages.

Gourami hunkered, wet, amid waterplant and reed in
the brackish water where the delta ran into the bay. Se
croaked low in frustration—an anonymous noise in
the dark—and dipped under again so only bulging
eyes and comma-shaped nostrils would show. Se mottles were not dyed into green anonymity, as the com-
mandos' had been, but even humen technology would
not single se out so hidden.

In the dark nearby, other persons moved, thrummed
through swelled throats, quiet reassuring conversation.
Gourami filtered water, swallowed plankton and waterweed. As it too often did in the bay now, the food
had an acrid tang. Se ate farmed on the job and at
home—

Se could not go home. Se had no home. No position
now. Reinvention or death.

Because the body had been tangled in the cables,
halfway down. And when Gourami had tugged it free,
had brought it up, none of the humen had cared. Had
honored the dead. Se knew its name; it had been a
friend of some of the other persons. And the mate of
this one they came to talk to now, because the humen
mated like animals, with their pair-bonds and their
closed little families.

Se thought somebody should have sung for it. Even
if it was an animal. And even if, though se had not yet
worked out the logic behind it, it was the dead animal's
fault that Gourami could not go home.

There were footsteps through the marsh. Some humen, booted, and a person's, too. Ripples in the water
stroked Gourami's skin. The person at se left hand sang

low, and a song answered. Tetra had returned. With the human Gourami had heard, and the rest said, could be trusted. The mate of the human who had become the body in the cables.

The rest. The rest were revolutionaries. The persons who had come to rescue se were rebels. They had destroyed the humen ship. And Caetei was one of them.

Gourami sank into calming mud and water, nostrils sealing as se submerged. The human needed a light to walk in the dark. It bobbed, reed-cut, reflecting splinters off the water. Gourami let a thin stream of silver slip from se nostrils. Handfingers brushed a still-sore shoulder; se leaned into Caetei's touch, allowed Caetei to lead. The light clicked off as they came forward, as if the human knew it would hurt a person's dark-adapted eyes.

Se slipped up the bank beside Caetei. Tetra's palms luminesced faintly, enough to guide them. The human stank in the dark, of poison—which the humen drank as if they breathed it—and of fire-charred humen food and chemicals. It—he, it was a he, by the flat chest and the bristles on its face—did not reach out for Gourami, who folded se hurt hand to chest and waited.

Instead, he hunkered on his heels in the dark, a humen approximation of a person's rest-pose, and extended the back of one arm. Something glimmered there. Gourami crouched, too, knees higher than the half-seated human's head, and bent to see what he offered.

A slate. There was a slate on his wrist, and it made words when he made those burbling humen noises.

—*I am Jean,* the machine wrote. —*Tetra says they call you Gourami. Can you tell me what you've seen?*

Gourami was not a very good storyteller. But a not-very-good storyteller by a person's standards was an

exceptional one, as humen went. And se was an experienced liaison.

With a ripping sound, se tugged the gripping fabric
loose and pulled the waterproof slate from the human's arm. With the tips of se handfingers, ignoring
the hurt in the one, se keyed: —*the body was tangled in
the cables, halfway down.*

5

CLOSS'S VIEW OF THE EXPLOSION WAS BETTER THAN HE would have preferred. His office had real windows, shatterproof laminate rated to blast level seven with a reality-skin interleaf that he habitually shut down. Closs wasn't a Naturalist; he wore a headset and augments like any sensible man. But he found no wisdom in relying too heavily on technological crutches.

Better to get the benefit when you needed it, and deal with reality the rest of the time. Not useful to forget that others were skinning their reality tunnels, that their perceptions were modified to suit their preferences.

Even if it would have been soothing, once in a while, to skin Jefferson Greene with a pink-and-black-spotted pig. *Oink.*

So he watched the real fire burn, across the water, while windowpanes alongside his primary view overlaid close-up, replay, feeds from the rescue choppers and the divers' masks. The barge's own connex had not dropped when the explosion hit, which told Closs—and his Rim security agents, who would not be sleeping tonight—that any feed they'd gotten off the ship itself was useless, a patch-loop.

They'd been hacked.

Closs dragged his fingertips down the image of the burning vessel. "Connect," he said, command-pitch. "Rim Corporation, Paris head office, code one four seven H."

It would be just after ten in the morning in Paris. He'd been waiting until *she* would be there, leisurely breakfast seen to, a second cup of coffee cooling on her desk. It did not do to hurry the vice president.

She was stirring cream into a china cup when her image resolved. Her hair fell across her forehead, razor-cut, brushing the architectural precision of one dark eyebrow. When she looked up, setting her chased silver spoon down on the saucer with a delicate click, he was caught by the flecks of darker color in her eyes. She was fashionably thin, the line of her jaw sharp as the detail on a porcelain horse, the tendons in her throat vanishing under the ivory silk collar of her suit. "M~ Morrow..." Closs began.

"Major," she replied. "I've seen the feed. I hope you're not calling to justify yourself to me."

"I'm afraid the error is beyond justification."

She lifted her cup and sipped, steam caressing her cheek. She took her time about it, which was more a statement of her willingness to waste Closs's time than of any unconcern about the cost of the call. The Slide was cheap—instantaneous transmission of matter or data over any distance.

Matter, or data. As long as it wasn't alive. Transportation of *personnel* between worlds was complex and costly, and travelers must contend with relativistic effects. But transportation of *goods* only required a matter transfer. This was the same technology at its base as the specialty of the Exigency Corps: probability manipulation. But a much safer manifestation, at that, without the risk of unforeseen coincidental fallout.

Unfortunately, this process could not be used on living creatures. You could certainly put a person in one side of a matter transmitter, but you did not get a living person back out the other end. Any organism complex enough—conscious enough—to have a concept of *I* could not Slide alive.

This was because—Closs did not entirely understand the science—the Slide was a quantum device, relying on the uncertainty principle to work. But a self-aware cargo counted as an observer.

In Schrödinger's famous thought-experiment, the *cat* knows whether it's alive or it is dead.

M~ Morrow swallowed twice, her larynx making shadows under the pale skin of her throat. "This won't affect your delivery schedule?"

"For petroleum?"

She set her cup down, dabbed her lip, and shrugged. "Greene's World is not the only source of base materials for manufacturing. It's the omelite I'm concerned with."

Closs considered his answer. Tanglestone's existence and its sole source were closely held. And unlike the Slide, whose inexpensive operation it made possible, it was *not* cheap. Just cheaper than *manufacturing* entangled pairs. Whether it was a natural substance, or some relic of a prior advanced civilization, no one had determined. Teams of Corpsmen were at work on it, but

unless somebody higher than Closs had sealed the results, the god-botherers had nothing.

"You understand, Vice President, that we are still
having issues with native uprisings and with human
abolitionists who think we're interfering with the
ranid culture. Such as it is."

She waited, stroking the gold-painted thumb rest
atop the handle of her cup.

Closs folded his hands behind his back. "We also
have labor unions that are unhappy with the use of
ranids in any job that could be handled by human
divers."

M~ Morrow nodded. "I appreciate the challenges,
Major. However——"

"The quota," he said, "will be met."

She let her fretting hand slide to the desk. "I need
you to exceed it."

"Vice President?"

Her head turned slightly, as if she lifted her eyes to
a wall screen or a skin. Her fingers moved across the
desktop; Closs recognized the gesture as a pass through
a virtual three-dimensional interface. "What I am
about to tell you, Major, is not to leave your office."

"What about Greene?"

"No one," she said. A fine arrogant dodge of the
chain of command, ignoring the fact that Greene was
the CEO of Charter Trade, the titular head of Rim on-
planet. She slid her cup aside and leaned forward on
her elbows. "Major, what do you know about artificial
intelligence and the Slide?"

He closed his teeth on a snide comment and counted
three. Backward. "Practically?"

"Theoretically."

"Theoretically," he said, "an intelligence that was

neither organic nor self-aware might be Slid. But it's practically irrelevant because—"

"—strong A.I. is still fifteen years in the future, just as it has been for the last three hundred years." She wet her lips, a gesture of nervousness he had not seen her make before. Her fingertips blanched as she steepled her hands.

"But?"

"But we may have run up against somebody who *has* found it. Or something that looks a hell of a lot like it. Unless they're running their ships by remote control, which is of course possible. And whatever they are, they're aggressive, Timothy."

He could have asked, *What did we lose?* He could have asked, *Where did they hit us? How far from Earth? How close to the Core?* But it wasn't his need to know, anymore. It wasn't his war to fight. And of course it didn't matter where they were now, or how far from Earth, if they could Slide.

"If they're not...conscious," he said, quietly, "then they can't conjure, can they?"

Her nose wrinkled at the crude term for probability manipulation, but she nodded. "Omelite," she said. And then answered a question he would not have chosen to ask, her little pat on the head to keep him well behaved. "They attacked shipping near Greene's World, Timothy. Once is not much of a sample, but I think it's you they're gunning for."

He swallowed. "I'll get you everything I can."

André's executary had tagged the message from Timothy Closs as highest priority, but he didn't answer it immediately. Instead he cleaned his teeth and used Cricket's elutrior. She was out of bed when he emerged, the covers shaking themselves tidy as she un-snarled her hair. The static wand first made it writhe, then stand straight out, crackling. Another tap and a touch to the control and strands drifted over her shoulders, briefly silken. It would cord into locks again by lunchtime, he thought, fondly.

He stored the image of her fixing her hair in hard memory, so he could take the file out and replay it later, and kissed her on the head. "Tonight, where are you?"

"Working," she answered. She touched her headset access port—a nervous gesture, the controls were all neuroelectrochemical—and smiled with one corner of her mouth. André's reactivated skin put a warmth in her complexion. Pretty girl. "I've seven hours of data mining to get through, more if I'm not lucky enough to hit the information in the usual lodes."

"Blink me," he said, and showed himself out.

On the gently pitching deck, he leaned against the rail and watched a pump glide up and down atop a distant mining platform. His skins adapted to the glare off the water, the weave of his fogjacket opening to catch the breeze as sun warmed his shoulders. He paled the jacket's color to ivory and watched ripples break against the barge's hull.

He preferred his messages transcribed; he could read more quickly and with greater retention than he could listen.

> M~ Deschênes:
>
> Please contact me regarding a possible extension of our previous contract, if you are interested. Something of an unusual case. It might prove a challenge.
>
> —Closs

André cleared the message and used a subroutine to overwrite the sectors, a precaution he never skimped on. Especially for innocuous messages. He knew how Cricket earned her bread, and she knew what he did as well and they had a tacit agreement not to ask. But not all the synthesists, archinformists, or net miners on the Rim were his lovers. And though he trusted Cricket Earl Murphy as much as he trusted anyone, only a fool baited temptation.

Any business Closs had to offer wasn't the sort of thing best discussed on a broadcast channel. Especially when André wasn't certain he'd be able to avoid a conflict of interest. He inspected his scoot, wincing in self-consciousness when he located not so much as a loose wire, and dropped into the saddle. He could have walked; Cricket's float hooked up to a sidewalk, and there was a bridge across the canal that would lead him downtown, through the maze of barges and waterways that made up the floating city of Novo Haven. But he'd have to come back for his scoot then.

Meanwhile, the major would be expecting him.

Later, sitting on Jean Gris's crude wicker couch, Cricket Earl Murphy reviewed her few remaining articles of faith. For example, she believed that if one must keep secrets, it was best if they happened to be incredible. Melodrama was good, especially when it involved spies, forgotten royalty, or the downfall of governments. Outrageous scandals were more survivable than petty ones; a truly lurid tale could only improve one's reputation, unless it involved allegations of rape (squalid), insider trading (pathetic), or cannibalism (still beyond the pale).

Petty moral failures led to disgrace only because

they had no scope. It was too easy for the opprobrious
to condemn their own small criminal hypocrisies when
they recognized them in another. An adultery, a financial manipulation, the poisoning of a spouse: anybody
could compass such crimes. And because they could
imagine them, they could defend against them.

A truly outrageous crime provoked disbelief—*such
things only happen in melodramas*—and then, after,
awe.

If you must steal, swipe a planet.

As a consequence of this philosophy, Cricket very
rarely lied. Her secrets, while plentiful, were the sort
that people did not inquire after. She was safe—safe
here, especially, here on the Rim, on Greene's World, a
corner of the settled galaxy that could not be less interesting to the Core, to anybody with money, to the
woman she had been.

The Core never thought about the Rim if it could
help it, except to set pulp holodrama there. As far as
civilization was concerned, the Rim had nothing to offer except wilderness, Iron Age aliens—the ones that
had advanced that far—and a romantic but generally
nasty and unsafe frontier. And, of course, the bounty of
limitless natural resources to exploit and fortunes to be
made. With the added benefit that any personal problems one left behind on Earth would very probably be
dead by the time one landed on Greene's World,
Xanadu, or Yap.

And she kept telling herself that, right up to the
moment Jean Gris steepled his gnawed fingertips and
said, "It'd be the biggest scandal since Moon Morrow
resigned."

Cricket's shoulders tautened. She kept her eyes wide
and innocent, and did not even allow the name to echo
in her mind. Superstitiously, as if Jean were the wizard

the ignorant painted him. As if he could read her thoughts.

She wondered, even should she say it outright, if he would ever believe her. "Moon who?"

The crease deepened over his broken nose, shadows rough along his bristled jaw. His eyes caught the light as his head tilted. "Morrow. She was the Earth Unified government's minister of colonization during the first Downham administration. She resigned under a cloud about fifteen Standard ago. Took the fall for an anti-matter test station failure at Patience. Do you recall *that*?"

Of course she did. The destroyed space station, the devastated biosphere of the planet below, the frozen corpses floating in orbit—where there *was* anything to recover. The disaster had been caused by a failed Exigency Corps engineering operation. Morrow, it came out later, had pushed the god-botherers to augment the chance of success for the experimental power station beyond any margin of safety.

There was still debate as to whether the plant's design was flawed, or whether the Corps interference caused a localized probability storm.

Twenty thousand, two hundred and thirteen dead. Unsurprisingly, almost no surviving wounded.

Oh, yes. Cricket recalled.

She could close her eyes and see the corona of wreckage around the devastated station. She could close her eyes, and imagine she felt the thirty seconds of hard vacuum that was all you got to feel before you died. Eyeballs freezing, capillaries bursting. Thirty seconds was a long, long time.

"Oh, *her*. I'd forgotten her name."

Jean watched her carefully, long enough to make her worry, and then licked his lips and said, "Went to work for Core, I think, after the jail sentence, and hasn't been heard from since. She dropped out of sight completely."

"And you think she has something to do with Lucienne's being killed?" Sidetrack, play dumb. Look confused. "Was it something the ranid said?"

Not too confused, however. More's the pity; Jean knew she wasn't stupid.

The ranid that had found Lucienne's body was hunkered comfortably in the reedy mud upriver, according to Jean, and Cricket had no reason not to believe him. It was a more comfortable topic than Moon Morrow.

"No," Jean said. "I think if she's not still working for Core, she's relativistic under an assumed name, and our grandchildren will hear from her when time and scandal have forgotten her. Or she's melting into an unmarked grave." Jean let his fingers slide together, interlock. "It's seventeen years body-time from Earth. At least a hundred, nonrelativistic—" he looked up, blinked his watery eyes. "But you know that, don't you?" Cricket had never quite lost her North American accent. "Or you could be seeing how much line you can feed me before you set the hook, chérie."

She smiled.

He caught her fingers sideways and gave them a squeeze. "What did you learn?"

"I'm still looking for the key to what Lucienne managed to mail me. I'll find that—" She rubbed at the corners of her eyes with the other hand, feeling incredibly tired. "I wish we knew who she was meeting. I wish we had the rest of the file—"

"Do we know what Rim did with the body?"

"If they didn't resink it?"

Jean gave her the raised eyebrow. She took her hand back, stood up, wishing she wasn't at Jean's house so she could check status on the half-dozen searches, bots, and ferrets she had running that didn't require her constant attention—and the compiler trying to resolve the fragment of Lucienne's deathbed message into something parseable. She wanted to walk away from Kroc, so she went to make tea, wondering if the tomatoes had ripened enough overnight to give her an excuse to walk out to the truck garden and pick some. Better than growing them in tubs on her deck, that was for sure. She liked the dirt under her fingernails.

He said, "No, they wouldn't have made sure it got snagged in the cables if they didn't want it found."

"But did they want it found so soon?"

"What do you mean?"

Right. Jean didn't know a damned thing about wetware, hard memory, or any of it. "Her hard memory would decay in something like twenty to thirty hours. Any data in her head would be irretrievable at that point. We know she was sending me something—"

"The other half might still be queued."

"It probably is," Cricket said, glancing at him. "We can't obtain her body before we lose that data to bit-rot."

Jean pressed the side of his hand to his mouth. From the way the muscle in his jaw worked, he was chewing the flesh near his thumb. "What if they downloaded her?"

Cricket shrugged, sliding the pot onto the stove. Cold water slopped over the enamel surface and wet her hand. "Whatever they killed her to keep her from bringing back to you might be in the file. Which would be in a Charter Trade data hold. Blasted Rimmers."

Jean's nose had been broken once and he'd never gotten it fixed. His breath whistled on the outflow. "You still think it was André, Cricket?"

If she bit her cheek hard enough, she could keep her eyes from stinging. "The common factor linking all of my unhappy romances is me."

"Is that an answer?"

"It's what you get. I don't ask those things. I think it must have been——"

"I don't have to use him."

The water steamed, not yet bubbling. She threw tea bags into mugs. "Use him," she said. "I knew it was on fire when I lay down on it."

"Why?"

"Why did I know he was on fire?"

"No," Jean said, very patiently. Silently he'd come up behind her; she saw his reflection in the cooktop before he laid his hand on her arm. "Why did you pick him?"

The water boiled. She wrapped the handle in a terry rag and lifted the kettle off the heat. "Because," she said, roughly, "he could beat up my dad."

"Excuse me?"

"Bad men," Cricket said. "Bad men, the badder the better. And they don't come badder than André Deschênes. He's so bad he can be sweet as ice cream every second, and nobody forgets for any one of those seconds that he's the baddest man in the room. That's what I like. Men who could beat up my dad. They make me feel safe." She lifted her chin and set the kettle down. "I know it's crazy. It's why I don't let any of them get too close. Because I know what they are."

She shook her head, shook Jean's hand off, and—turning—warded him back with a cup of hot tea. "Anyway, that doesn't matter. I think . . . I think they wanted it to look like an accident. Or like she ran afoul of a ranid sect. Some of the savages still kill humans in the marsh, you know."

"Some humans."

She didn't need to turn around to know he was smiling. Jean Kroc—whatever his real name was, and she didn't ask that either—went into the marsh with impunity. Lucienne had, too. "Discredit the labor rights movement," she continued, as if he had not interrupted. "Maybe something more complicated, but that'll do for a surface motive."

"If they wanted the body found, why grab the person that found it?"

She shrugged. "Somebody made a mistake? The frog saw something it shouldn't have? The body was supposed to be found by a human and not a ranid? It was found too soon? Could be a lot of reasons." The water hissed. She poured. "If there's information out there, I'll find it."

If the information was connex anywhere. But that went without saying.

She had learned a lot about net mining in fifteen years. She was good at it, knew roots and routes to old caches and layered backups and coredumps and virtual lockers from two hundred years ago. She had old ciphers and she had archives and she had backdoors into current data holds, too.

The more old information one could find in the warrens of connex, the more uncharted paths one knew from point A to point Q, the more *new* information one could get to that one wasn't supposed to know about. And sometimes the old records were useful in themselves. For historical reasons, or—in a relativistic galaxy—sometimes for more present ones.

Cricket had never actually had to blackmail anyone. Not since she became an archinformist, anyway.

"You always do," Jean said, bringing the tea that Cricket thought was still too hot to drink to his mouth.

It was why he needed her. He might conjure, and she would bet he had the illegal coincidence engines to do it with. But he wouldn't swallow wire, or live with it in his head.

She tapped fingers on the edge of her mug. "Do you think they'll let a ranid person testify in a Core court?"

"Well, they would if they were a tech species. Of course, if they were a tech species, we wouldn't be here, would we?"

Cricket hated him for a moment, hated the falseness of his pale, open gaze. "Like they'd let it make a difference."

"They?"

"Core," she said. And then qualified, "Charter Trade. They'd find a way around the law, even if the ranids had spaceflight, if there were something on Greene's World that they wanted." There was; she knew it, and she suspected Jean did, too. "They don't care where the luxuries come from, or who suffers to pay the way."

Jean looked down. She wondered if she had shamed him. "Find out, won't we? I need you to step up your efforts regarding Closs and his cronies."

There were a half-dozen stupid questions she could have asked, most of them the kind of contentless noises people made to reassure themselves that communication was taking place. If Jean didn't think, or at least hope, that Closs was involved in something dirty enough to bring him down, he wouldn't have asked her to keep looking. And Cricket knew the sorts of things that people who should know better got up to.

She drank off her tea. She'd been right; it was hot enough to break sweat across her forehead, and she mopped her face with her sleeve after she put the mug in the sink. "I'll ask André to come see you when I blink him tonight. I'm going to go look at the vegetables."

Jean laid a hand inside her elbow as she stepped past him. "What are you doing on a lump of mud like this, Cricket?"

"Instead of gnawing imported bonbons in the Core? Connex doesn't take time, Jean. I can live anywhere. It's cheaper to do it here." Practically guileless, she smiled into his eyes.

"And here I was hoping that maybe you killed a man."

She winked and drew her arm away. "Nothing so romantic, I'm afraid."

André's clients usually came to him, though for Rim he made exceptions. He still didn't like to be seen entering their barge, however, so he skinned in the bathroom of a coffee shop (after he ordered a mug he would not drink) and walked into reception resembling himself only casually. Of course he flagged as altered in anyone's headset, but cosmetic skins were more common than not.

Reception chipped him, verified that he was expected, and locked on a wristlet to guide him up. He didn't need it—he knew where Timothy Closs worked—but Security would have its little games and this would get him past most of them.

Its plaintive beeping led him on.

Closs got up from the desk to greet him. One thing about Timothy; the ceremonies he stood on were all politeness. He extended his right hand, gave André's larger but not much darker one a clasp, and handed

him a drink without asking. "Good job last night,
André."

André took the seat Closs gestured him into and set
the stubby glass on the arm. "Thank you, Major. I hope
there's not a problem." He would prefer not to talk
about old business under any circumstances. Like a leaf
upon the water: let the current slide it by.

"Not with your work," Closs replied, returning to
his chair. Perched on the edge of it, he gave the impression of someone still in motion. A compact brown
man in a navy and white suit, he seemed—to André—
condensed. "No, it's another problem entirely. One of
the board made an unfortunate decision, and it's left us
a loose end."

"This all sounds very euphemistic."

"To put it mildly." Speaking quickly, Closs outlined
the problem: the scheduling conflict that had led to a
ranid liaison discovering the body ahead of time, the
site team's errors in recovery, Jefferson Greene's overreaction.

"He's given it something to talk about," André said,
understanding.

Closs knuckled his eye and nodded. "It gets worse.
The witness was liberated last night."

"The explosion."

"Unfortunately. We think it's been taken by a ranid
anticolonialist faction. You can appreciate the implications."

"If they can get anyone to listen to them."

"Connex is free," Closs said. "There are humans on
this planet who would be all too happy to foster a scandal, if it affected Rim. The savages aren't the only
Greens in the galaxy. Or the only enemies of Rim."

"True enough." But André's hand gesture said,
What do you want me to do about it?

Closs put his hands on the desk. "We want you to cover the contract, André. At something more than your ordinary fee."

Jean Kroc poled his skiff upriver.

He could have used his motors, sure, and the caterpillars weren't even too noisy. But the birds could hear them, and the ranids, and it never hurt to show a little courtesy. Besides, there were enough powered craft on Greene's to affect the natives' long-distance communications. Like Earth's cetaceans, the ranids took advantage of the sound-conducting properties of water to hold conversations with friends and relatives they might never have swum side by side with. The advent of mechanized transportation had been unkind to their culture, their art, their discourse, and their science.

And in any case, there was something to be said for slipping over the brown water in the heat of afternoon, his shirt rubbing sweat from his shoulders as he threaded the channels of the delta. Four-winged insects so like an Earth darning-needle that they bore the same common name slipped over the water, leaving chains of ripples like the paths of skipped stones. With a quicksilver twist one rocketed upward, the drone of straining wings rising in pitch. It clutched something that twisted in muscular panic; Jean winced, but it was just a fish or a tadpole——too small for an eggling, and anyway no endoparent would let an infant out of its pouch. Fat drops of water scattered, and the darning-needle settled on the flat prow of Jean's skiff to sever its dinner's spine with a scissoring bite.

He could not *actually* hear the crunching.

Green reeds rose up around him, reflected smoothly

in flat water. Their heads nodded, heavy with pollen in feather-duster flowers. A red flannel rag off to port marked his channel. It was an odd-numbered rag and the knot was at the top; he turned away from it.

Even Jean Kroc needed a little aide-mémoire to find his way around the bayou.

The yellow sun rode behind haze, swarms of no-see-ums zooming among the tassels. Greene's World was better than Earth that way; about half of the local biting insectoid life had no use for mammal blood. The leeches, however, weren't so particular. And the ragweed equivalents could have choked an elephant.

The air felt primitive. The rich scent of fermenting vegetation bubbled from beneath the water, and Jean's salt stung his cracked lip and his eyes, dried itchy among his stubble. Even to the profusion of alien flowers—mauve and white silverling with its feet wet and its belled heads shaded beneath taller plants, parasitic cutthroat weed threading from reed to reed, its waxy paraorchids dripping treacle-sweet beads of sap with which to trap small unwary creatures—the New Nile Delta could have been Earth in the Upper Cretaceous. Jean could imagine a *Dryptosaurus* slipping along the shallow waterways, barely ruffling a leaf in passing— eyeing him like the also-extinct tiger from between concealing reeds.

His hands sweated inside his fingerless gloves as he dragged the pole from the sucking mud of the channel bed and swung it forward. The strain caught him first along the biceps and across the shoulders, and as he leaned into the push, he felt it in his chest, triceps, latissimus dorsi, hamstrings, calves. He tugged the pole again, let the momentum of the skiff draw it from the bottom, swung it up. The name of the game was control. He glanced over his shoulder, as if a dinosaur might in fact be considering him for its supper, and almost missed the blue rag with the knot tied downward that marked the next turn.

He poled toward this one, moving farther from the New Nile's dredged main channel and closer to the paramangroves that made a thunderhead darkness off to the east when he got a glimpse at them up a channel that headed in that direction.

The sun stood another hand higher and he was picking up ranid chatter on the underwater microphones when he slid the skiff underneath a moldy thermocamouflage netting strung between paramangroves. He moored the skiff against the aerial roots of the nearest tree, drove the pole in deep to wedge it, and tied that off as well. The tender water-brown skin of the roots was polished shiny where he stepped; he frowned when he noticed. Time to move the mooring.

Or maybe he should bring André here, and move afterward. Once a site was contaminated there was no point in rushing to burn another if the first could still be used in the short term. And he was more concerned with satellite imaging than with some bayou boy or mud-puppy skipper tripping over his facility. There were ways to ensure that that would remain unlikely.

The paramangroves grew knotted together, branches interlaced like the fan vaults of a cathedral, roots like the tentacles of angry octopods. Jean Kroc skipped along them all but silently, rubber soles tacky enough that his feet did not skid from the algae-hung bark. Animals zipped about his head. The Greene's World "birds" were awfully birdy, as such things went, though they tended to beaks fenced in whiskery feathers. The air under the paramangroves was a soup of insects; easier to sweep them up en masse than grab just one or two.

The door in the trunk was hard to see. Jean found the nub that fit just between his thumb and forefinger and pressed his palm through the holographic bark. Not even a fog; just an image. But you had to know where to touch, and in the dim green light beneath the leaves like broad-palmed hands, huddled into the gap between umbrella branches and spreading roots, on one big tree of a million, it was unlikely that it would be stumbled upon. And Jean could make it more unlikely as he chose.

The plate beneath was warm and smooth. It recognized Jean's palm and depressed slightly, soundlessly into the trunk. The door eased open—popped up and slid aside—and Jean Kroc stepped within, entering the lair of a mad scientist.

The room was somewhat smaller than the diameter of the great tree, carved from deadwood only. One worn swivel chair commanded the scuffed floor, the upholstery patched with tape. Around it, granting just enough room for his knees, was a series of pitted panels topped by an eclectic assortment of display and interface hardware—holographic projectors, screen monitors, an old 3-D hand-interface that looked like the ears of a theremin and operated on more or less the same principles. There were also three keyboards and a holoface; none of them matched.

In addition to the marks of hand-welding evident where sheet steel had been bent and fixed together, the slots through which readouts protruded were more often taped to fit than cut. The chamber was barely big enough for two if one was standing. Or willing to perch on the commode, tucked into a cutout niche, because the chamber did not have corners. The control panels followed the arc of the hollowed-out paramangrove, the tree's weakened structure reinforced by the plascrete sealant bonding the external wall.

He'd moved his home plenty in the last thirty years: apartments, minifabs, a clamshell hut on stilts in the bayou for a while. *This* was eternal. This was what he couldn't afford to rebuild, and so he hid it well, changed his routes, came here erratically, and rarely showed the way to anyone. Cricket didn't know how to find this place, though she had to suspect it existed. The bayou and the mangrove stand themselves were protection, as they shifted and rechanneled and never twice looked the same.

Lucienne knew it, though, and how to find it. Somebody had to, in case something happened to Jean.

Jean gave it a moment to power up, using stored solar from concealed panels and fuel cells buried far enough underwater that they shouldn't emit to space. A planet was a big place for complete sat-coverage on a colonial corporation's budget.

It all seemed to be humming. He dusted the moss stains from his hands and closed the door, sealing himself into the blue-lit coolness of the most illegal thing on Greene's World.

Vengeance wasn't his metier. But he was here to make some black magic happen.

A little red flannel bag, that weren't nothing.

6

"HOW DO YOU GO ABOUT FINDING ONE NAKED AMPHIBIAN on a whole muddy goddamn world?" André shook his head like a dog shaking off water. "It's not as if I can go around DNA-typing every frog I meet. And the insurgents use disguises, don't they? If I were your ranid, Tim, frankly I'd dig in deep in the swamp and go seven kinds of native. You don't need me; you need a good old boy from back in the delta."

"We can make sure you find the ranid," Closs answered. He wasn't pacing. Instead, he stood before his wide windows, hands folded, watching the light glint off the water. The bay lay pellucid beyond the polarized display glass, water limpid enough that André could make out shells and stones on the pale sand bottom. The water might run down the New Nile muddy and rich, but most of its sediment dropped out in the broad wandering delta, and what flowed into the sea was almost polished.

Beyond the zone of riverine admixture, where the brackish water clouded, in good weather the bay was clear as quartz. The sleek pewter outline of a long-necked animal glided past, sunning itself just below the surface. André caught a glimpse of its creamy belly and snaggle teeth as it banked down and away, curving in sudden pursuit. A nessie. They usually haunted deeper water and avoided industry, as shy as they were toothy, but this one looked young. And there were bigger predators in the deeps.

"If you can find the ranid, then I don't see why you'd be willing to pay my fee."

"You misapprehend me." Closs turned around, beckoned André with two curving fingers. André stood, leaving behind his untouched glass. When he was an arm's length away, Closs continued. "We can make sure you find it, though. The capabilities of Rim—"

"You're talking about running a manip."

Closs didn't answer.

"A manip. On me." A probability manipulation might bring him right down on the missing coolie's doorstep. And it also meant staff, and Rim personnel, and processor time, and *paperwork*.

Met with continuing silence, André tried again. "I don't want that kind of a data trail—"

Closs shook his head. "There won't be one."

Still. André had a bad feeling about this. Too far outside of his usual line of work. Too many ways to get killed, chasing ghosts through the bayou. "I can't take it."

Closs stepped forward and caught his forearm. André paused. The grip was not restraining or sharp; a request rather than a grab. "Do me one favor."

André did not answer. But he also did not pull away.

Closs let him go, first giving his forearm a quick friendly squeeze. "Wait until tomorrow to refuse. Sleep on it."

"I don't need the money, Tim."

Closs smiled, showing whitened teeth. "I know you don't. But the thing is, I need the help."

A hell of an offer. Jefferson Greene's first mate—and, everybody knew, the brains of the Greene's World Rim operation—acknowledging a personal debt. That was the sort of thing careers rose and fell on. And nobody was more aware than André that he wasn't going to stay young forever.

On the other hand, very few people were more aware than André that once he let Rim plant its hooks, he would not be working for himself anymore. Operating under the occasional contract was one thing. Assisting them in conjuring his future—allowing himself to be entangled—well.

André wasn't a superstitious man. But if he wanted to learn from Jean Gris, it would be an unwise thing to let Rim rule his fate. And the whole prospect reminded him uncomfortably of his mother's tactics. Not that Zoë Deschênes could have backed up any threat of ruining his luck.

But Charter Trade could.

"I'll think about it," André said. He stuffed his hands in his jacket pockets. "Don't worry. I can show myself out."

Out in the sun again, he gasped sharply. He dropped his elbows on the railing and put his head down, let the light bake his scalp and neck muscles. The sun picked darker scars out in heat until he shielded his skull with his palms. His blinked-up sunshield helped ameliorate the glare off the water. One more breath, then he shuddered and drew himself up, shoulders square.

He'd wanted to learn. He'd placed a loaded pistol on his tongue and pulled the trigger. That was a commitment.

But instant death was easy. Killing people—painlessly, efficiently—was what he did. *Who* should not matter.

He couldn't take this contract. Because he needed Jean Gris's goodwill, and he wasn't going to get that by assassinating ranid revolutionaries and allowing Rim to run a manip on him. Not when he was already mixed up in learning how to conjure.

It didn't take much imagination to guess that coincidence might proliferate, should one cultivate a conjure man. He who touches pitch besmirches himself.

All he could do was hope Rim would be understanding about finding someone else to take the contract. And that they wouldn't botch it, or, if they did, that the trail of testimony never led back to one André Deschênes.

He pursed his lips as if to whistle. Perhaps that could be his first real experiment in conjuring.

Another blow to the image of the hedge-wise conjuror: Jean Kroc had never been a patient man. Actually, he was rather bad all around at conforming to stereotypes. So by evening, when his new apprentice arrived, he was worrying the hard semiflexible skin from a pulpy fruit the size of his finger joint, a pile of others white and waxy on a rectangular green-glazed plate by his left hand. The fruit's skin was rough, reddish-brown, marked in dimpled hexagons. He picked it off with gnawed thumbnails, trying to keep the pieces as large as possible. A matter of pride, or meticulousness, or just a cheap distraction.

He knew the newcomer was André by the purr of his wet/dry scoot. Jean'd left the front door propped; when André called through it, he didn't bother to get up, just yelled back. "Take off your shoes."

The thumping told him André obeyed. A moment later, bare feet padded from the entry. "Cricket said you wanted me."

Jean smiled, not showing what it cost him. He held up a peeled wax fruit so André could identify it, pinched between finger and thumb. A sticky trickle of nectar crawled across the pad of his hand. He flicked the berry into a long tumbling arc.

André snatched it from the air on its descent, leaning away from spattered juice. He inspected it quickly and popped it into his mouth, then spat the pit into his palm. "When you told me you wanted information, how did you know?"

"Know?" Jean slit another fruit with his nail. The pulp was too tender to squeeze out without pureeing, so he worried at the skin until it flaked. He sucked the juice off his thumb and the pulp off the seed, and laid the shiny dark brown nut on the table beside the bits of skin. "Am I assigned psychic powers?"

André came forward and dropped into the chair across the table. His pit joined Jean's with a subdued click. "Did you know that Rim was going to offer me a contract on a ranid?"

Jean, licking his fingers, smiled. "You said you wouldn't tell me about contracts."

"I'm not taking this one," André answered. "The thing is, Rim wants to run a probability manip to give me a fighting chance to find the coolie. It's affiliated with some froggie terrorist group—"

"Gourami."

"Excuse me?"

Jean pursed his lips, forced to admit that perhaps not *all* the stereotypes failed him. He was enjoying André's slack expression slightly more than was healthy or smart. Although he had to admire the man's gall—well, *admire* was the wrong word. And *respect* wasn't exactly right either. "The ranid's name is Gourami."

"You *know* it?"

"I talked to it last night." Jean ate another wax fruit, letting the pulp burst into fluid as he pressed it to the roof of his mouth with his tongue. The seed felt as slick as it appeared, and he squeezed it out between his lips. For a moment, he turned it on his fingertips, watching the light gloss it. He pretended he didn't notice the way André's shoulders jerked.

"Whoa. Well, I'm glad I said no."

"I'm not. Go back tomorrow. Tell him you'll take it on."

"You realize what you're asking me?"

"Yes," Jean answered, flicking him another fruit. "I'm asking you to lie to Timothy Closs. And buy me some time to operate."

"He'll want me to take the entanglement."

Jean wondered if André knew he was shaking his head like that, a slow oscillation.

"I can lock that off," Jean said. "We'll set up a countervalent field; the entanglement can spend itself on that."

André's attention snapped to him like a shivering compass needle to a magnet. "And I'm better off letting you entangle me?"

"Just a safeguard. Not an entanglement. But take the contract. For me."

André swallowed. "What exactly are you planning, Jean Gris?"

Jean rolled his shoulders up and back. "I'll handle the rest. Just keep Closs thinking the situation is under control."

Jefferson wasn't often the first one into the office, but he was usually among the last ones home. He got a lot of work done in the evening, when things were still and quiet—dark in winter and golden in the summertime. He'd trickle the news, talk to his kids in chat, drink a few cups of coffee or kesha or a martini or two, and plow through business decisions with a ruthless efficiency that got him home in time for supper, just.

Today should have been no different. The to-do list was actually a little shorter than usual; everyone was distracted by the bombings, and as he'd delegated that to Closs it was off his desk until Closs finished the investigation and handed it back. The first item, it looked like, was to return a call to the station. Not the Slide; no problem with that. Lighters came and went, raw materials flowing freely outbound and manufactured goods coming in. The call was from one of his gurus, the Greene's World station chief of the Exigency Corps, Amanda Delarossa. Head god-botherer.

She must have set his code to autoanswer, which was gratifying. She had a chipmunk-cheek of sandwich and a bag of pop lifted to her mouth when her image shifted, and she swallowed hastily and cleared her hands. "Chairman," she said, as soon as she could. "I didn't think you'd call back until tomorrow, sir."

"I like to be responsive," he said. "You seem to think your issue requires immediate attention."

"Immediate awareness," she said. She drank again,

quickly, as if her mouth were dry from swallowing before she was quite ready. "I'm not sure what we could actually do about it at this point. Realistically speaking."

"Intriguing," Jefferson said, because it's what he had trained himself to say when he really meant *get to the fucking point.* "Tell me more."

"Well..." she paused, set her drink aside, and twisted her fingers together, "we've got a massive spike in side effects, and we're not quite sure what to make of it. But some of our best theorists are on it."

"By side effects, you mean..."

"Probability pollution. Weird coincidences. Synchronicities. We track them, you know, and attempt to mitigate. But the problem is, you get a chaotic butterfly effect with even the smallest manipulation. So you patch it up, attempt to introduce a little more randomosity into the system, and it breaks out somewhere else. Rains of toads. God knows what."

"And we're getting more of this?" He rubbed the edge of his desk and thought about Patience, which had been a lovely Earthlike world before the Corps got done with it.

"Some of it, yeah. You have any old coins lying around?"

"Doesn't everybody?" Collector's pieces, talismans, bits of old Earth. Metal from the bones of the homeworld. They had no value as legal tender anymore, but people liked them.

"Next time you think of it, flip one a couple of times," she said. "Anyway, Dr. Gupta thinks it's linked to omelite mining, either due to waste tanglestone escaping into the atmosphere, or a reduction in the worldwide omelite load causing some sort of shift in Greene's World's...equilibrium, for lack of a better word. We're working on it."

"And if you can't get it under control quickly?"

She shrugged, dipping her ear toward one shoulder, and bit her knuckle instead of her supper. "Well, it's not like we can stop exporting tanglestone."

Of course André argued. It didn't matter; Kroc was always going to win. He had the superior bargaining position.

He also had the mojo. And something else that André would need to learn, before Jean would teach him too much. Jean Kroc had the moral unassailability of a god, as was necessary for the power he held.

It was always the way. In premodern societies, those who wielded power beyond oversight were bound by oaths and forms and divine wrath and sacrosanct relationships. In the modern day, there were oaths, and forms... and codes of ethics, to which professionals might more or less loosely adhere.

And divine wrath, of course. There *was* always that.

Jean Kroc's God most certainly did play dice. And Jean was not the only one loading the toss.

Still, he was rather well satisfied with the way the game was going. If André *could* learn, there might even be a chance of—well, not winning. It wasn't the sort of thing one *won*—but making some things a bit better in the short run. As a conjure man, his professional opinion was that that was often the best one could hope for.

At some point in human history, somebody had figured out that you could change the future by staring at it hard enough. The problem with the power of prayer was that it was never exactly quantifiable, though research was suggestive. And then there were the odder aspects of certain studies, where an average taken of ten thousand amateur best guesses turned out to be closer to the truth than any single expert's considered and researched opinion.

In a really profound cosmic irony, it was the failure of A-life consciousness research that finally provided the key. They couldn't make a self-aware computer, but they did find out what the *I* was good for.

The *I* was the evolutionary consequence of the observer effect, the power of luck, the denial of everything ten thousand generations of mothers passed down to ten thousand generations of daughters. Wishing hard enough *did* make a difference. Not a big difference. Not a profound difference. And not a difference every time.

But a few tenths of a percent, a difference almost indistinguishable from experimental error.

It was just that little bit of an edge that let one species thrive when another one perished. Black wings on a should-be-white moth, concealing it against a soot-blackened tree.

The practical application of quantum engineering made it replicable. The technological outgrowth of mojo satchels and washing the car to make it rain. A bit more than an *edge*, these days. Call it a necessity, rather.

People with both the knack for being lucky and the courage to do it right were not, in Jean's experience, common. And they were often opportunists, because their gifts made it possible for them to do very well by living on their wits.

A certain moral flexibility had needed to be shocked out of Jean as well, when he was young.

André Deschênes might do. And if he couldn't be salvaged, well, Jean couldn't exactly leave him wherever he fell. But he'd execute that problem when it became unavoidable.

In the meantime, he had a frog to catch.

After André left, Jean pulled his boots on again. The leftover wax fruit went into the cooler; the peelings into Lucienne's...into Cricket's compost bucket under the sink. If he felt up to it, he'd turn the pile over for her tonight, aerate the rot. It was what he was good for.

The boots sealed over his pantlegs, he made sure he had a light, slung his hip pack around his waist, and locked the door behind him. He'd have been three times through the swamp from sunset to sunset, but twenty years wasn't enough to make him a real creature of the bayou. There were men and women who'd grown up here, who could vanish among the reeds without a ripple, soft as a ranid slipping underwater. Jean knew a few: Old Mike, Sally Feathers. Both born when Greene's World was the sort of place you went to lose the records, both stubborn and self-reliant enough that their names were what they said they were, that they'd never nursed on the crystal teat of a reality skin.

Greene's World was *still* a new enough planet that folks mostly knew each other, and still a wild enough planet that they mostly stayed out of each other's way. Outside of Novo Haven, anyway, where the corporate boys played politics and pretended that instantaneous communication meant they had any idea what was going on in the Core, or any influence that was heard there.

A delusion, Jean admitted with a rueful shake of his head, he was prey to himself.

Reeds cracked where he stepped, the spongy ground oozing water. The sky over the bay was streaked in seashell colors—coral, salmon, dusky clouds like the indigo lip of a mussel shell—by the time he reached the distributary nearest to his minifab, the one where the ranids came to talk.

He crouched on the riverbank, folded his arms

across his knees, and waited. When the evening star—technically, the planet Endymion—shimmered ice-white on the horizon and the last pearlescent light was draining down the darkening sky, a gleaming dart-shape broke the water. One ring of ripple heralded the ranid's arrival, so faint it smoothed before it reached the reeds.

Jean dabbed at the water. His ripples passed over where the ranid's had been, flowing in the opposite direction, and lapped its skin below the eyes. The eyes—great light-gathering half-orbs—blinked. One stem-fingered, four-digited hand reached above the surface, the fingertip pads slightly enlarged, sticky.

Jean reached slowly to lay his waterproof wrist slate in the ranid's grasp. It did not flinch, but rose from the water as if drawn to an anchor. The hand rotated as the eyes came level, both swiveling forward so binocular vision focused on the face of the slate. The other hand emerged from the water as the ranid climbed the bank, crouching between angled knees, its pale ridged throat swelling.

Jean did not hear what it said, but he felt it, the low-frequency words shivering his nape hairs. The ranid was deft with the slate; more literate and practiced than Jean. He thought it might even be the one called "Gourami" by humans who could not replicate its given name.

He waited until it was looking at his mouth. If this was the liaison, it could lipread. "I'm Jean Kroc," he said. "I think we met last night."

The ranid bobbed one fingertip, pausing in what it was doing with the slate. —*Yes.*

It was Gourami, then. He fumbled in his hip pack. The ranid didn't draw back, but waited, curious and impassive, while another star or two slipped out of the

twilight. "I have something for you," he said, careful
to lift his chin and shape the words formally. He might
just have mouthed them, but it seemed to help it
lipread if he put the voice behind them.

Again the pulling gesture, one finger raking the
words in.

"Mojo," he answered. His hand closed on the box,
protective cling-sheeting adhering to his skin. Plastics,
of all things, were imported to Greene's World.
Petroleum was mined here but there was no significant manufacturing.

He pulled the box from the pack, extended his arm,
and opened up his hand. Palm skyward, fingers cupped
slightly, offering the plastic-wrapped object to Gourami.

It was not a gesture a ranid could make. Their arms
did not rotate at the elbow.

Carefully, Gourami lifted the box from his palm.
Still holding the slate, it untwisted the plastic and
peeled it back, but stopped before lifting the lid of the
box. Its head and shoulders canted back slightly. It
wrote a word and turned the slate. —*Mojo?*

"Luck," he answered. The ranids knew about luck,
although Jean could never hope to duplicate their word
for it. The sounds of their language echoed through an
expanded throat that served as bellows, sounding
board, and voice-box all in one, and were meant to be
heard through bone conduction and the vibrations of
water or air on skin and tympanic membrane, not by a
mammal's seashell external ear. They knew about all
sorts of things; theirs was not a material culture, but in
their physical abilities made up for it. They could communicate across half a world, read each other's physical health with pulses of ultrasound. They could build
fires, forge metal if it moved them, though the activity
was even more risky than it might be for a human; a

ranid could not afford to dry out too much, or too often. They built their blast furnaces on rocky beaches, and tended them during short dashes up from the waves.

—*Thank you,* Gourami said, and folded the plastic back into place. It did not care to commit, Jean understood.

"You're welcome." Jean leaned forward, strengthening the connection with the ranid, but careful not to make eye contact. He did not wish it to feel coerced. "I'm going to bring a man to you tomorrow. He'll go with you upriver. Protect you."

—*Safer in the swamp.*

"You'll be in the swamp. He'll stay in the swamp with you."

—*Humen are easy to track.*

"It will be all right. He's being paid to kill you, Gourami. If they think he is chasing you, nobody else will come after."

The ranid's fingers didn't twitch on the slate. They didn't have to. Its stolid froggy regard was enough. The ranid thought it would be safer in the swamp with the savages, trading in its web belt and company housing and advanced medical care and access to connex—all the benefits of Rim technology that the ranids worked for—in return for belts of shells and pearl-and-carnelian necklaces and stories murmured in reedy backwaters through jaws that need not move to make words.

Jean let his lips pull askew, aware the expression would mean nothing to the ranid. He hunkered lower, dropped his chin against his chest. "It's not for you," he said. "It's for him." He paused; the next was hard to say. "And for Lucienne."

The argument with Caetei took longer than the one with Jean Kroc, despite the awkwardness of communicating

with the human. But humen were manageable; all
Gourami had to do was keep saying no. Whereas arguing
with Caetei was like arguing with the tide. And there
was the small matter of Gourami owing se self's life.

—*They killed se mate*, Caetei finally said. Which
was unfair because Gourami had brought back her
body, and owed weal to the human's band. Which
meant, se guessed, in humen terms, her mate, her children, if she had any. Her siblings, though se wasn't
sure how much store humen set by siblings. Their reproductive system was so *invested*, it made everything
about their biology and society peculiar, locked up,
committed.

A humen mate... Gourami flexed fingers in the
muddy channel bottom, where se and Caetei had retired to argue. It would be like having only one endosib, se thought.

What a terrible thing to lose.

Se came back up through the water and found the
human sitting cross-legged on the reedy bank, reading
something on a paper book he'd folded back on itself.
Stories. Humen stories, Gourami thought, mouth watering.

Se lifted a hand from the water, catching the human's eye. He looked up from the book quickly, and se
thought he held his breath. At least the rushy rasping
sound it made through his air passages halted. He
dropped his hands into his lap.

—*Yes*, Gourami gestured.

And the human closed his eyes.

7

HUMEN WERE TERRIBLY STRANGE. THIS WAS NOT A REVE-
lation.

Not just strange because they came in all sorts of pig-
ments, but very few patterns—unless one counted the
rather bland, irregular melanistic speckles displayed by
a few of them. Nor strange because of their stubby su-
pernumerary fingers, their long bodies and stubby legs,
their habit of walking upright on short curved feet with
almost atrophied fingers. Not even strange because
they were endothermic from birth, inefficient though
that seemed for a large terrene animal without any particular evolutionary strategy for coping with extremes
of climate, so that even in temperate areas they hung
themselves in insulating layers or smeared lotions on
their hide to protect it from sunlight.

The mammals that Gourami was familiar with were
small dense-furred darting things, prey to reaverbirds
and redcaps. But humen were big—mostly bigger than

a person, although they had a tremendous dimorphism between their reproductive subcategories, so that some of the small ones were about Gourami's size and some of the big ones more than twice as big as anything but a great-parent—and Gourami understood, from talking with some of the friendlier ones, that on their home-world there were even bigger mammals. Some bigger than a full-grown nessie, which was the biggest living thing Gourami had personally seen.

This particular human was a large one, though not the biggest. His name, according to the humen liaison who had pleaded Gourami's help, was André Deschênes. And despite Jean Kroc's warning that he would be helpless, he paddled better than Gourami had dared beg luck.

Gourami was not in the skiff with André. The humen had sky-eyes, things that saw as well as any winged predator, and anyway se preferred to glide in the skiff's shadow, directing from below. Se had rid self of every bit of Rim equipment; se slate and the other accoutrements of se trade were slagged—carried off by friends or new allies in three directions and scorched over fire. Se would not trade them; humen technology had tracking devices in it, their equivalent of the air-filled metal tongue-bell roped to the harpoon one hunted greatfish with, so that one could swim down the wounded animal by sound. Any person to whom se offered the devices would have been at risk. Se had strapped in place only a knife, a slate of the sort intended for humen offspring, se belt and carrybag, and a (cocked, locked) harpoon crossbow with five extra quarrels.

Se was a "civilized" person, having metamorphosed near Novo Haven and been around humen all se life.

Se had never been without their toys and shelters before, and se kept stroking the crossbow for reassurance.
If the worst happened, at least se could shoot something.

Se mottles were back to a skin-plain pattern, however, which was comforting. Se had been a little worried se would be green for half the season. It had faded
with a gelpaper Caetei had given se; one that Gourami
had let dissolve on se tongue, because se did not care to
stay out of water long enough to adhere it to se shoulder until it melted in the mucus. So se had chosen to
ingest it, though that seemed an oddly reptilian way to
consume medication when one was still perfectly fit,
and permeable.

The water was too fresh. Persons had euryhaline
tendencies, able to tolerate ocean or river water, or the
brackish regions between...but saltless water tended
to osmose into a person's body, which meant a lot of
spitting and urinating as one's body processed it back
out again. It was, anyway, better than becoming waterlogged.

But Jean Kroc had asked, and his reasons had been
good. And so André paddled, and Gourami glided, and
the gray light of dawn pricked through the reeds and
made the surface reflective as they moved upriver, divided, side-by-side.

They were not alone. Caetei and Tetra swam before
and behind, an honor guard masquerading as a reconnaissance team. They were part of the disguise; André
could claim that the persons accompanying him were
hired guides, coolies who had agreed to bring the
hunter through the bayou and help find the renegade.
If they were stopped, seriously, Gourami would have to
disappear. Se genetic material was on file; se could not
submit to a scraping.

Se fingered the box Jean had bestowed. Inside was a waterproofed ampoule, continuing the theme of things-to-be-internalized. It held luck, the human said. Luck being one of their humen words that meant nothing, or meant four hands of things that were all importantly different. For example, they used it to mean *chance*, randomness. And they used it to mean a beneficial break in the same. And they used it to mean a repeated pattern, either for good or ill, that seemed in contravention of randomness. Which Gourami found philosophically opposed rather than allied concepts.

And, even more confusingly, they also used it to mean the *manipulation* of random chance and of probability, and the *ability* to manipulate it. Which is what Gourami would call luck. If se had to try to think in humen words. *And* they had other words that could mean some or one or several or all of these things, and which overlapped other concepts or sets of concepts as well.

The humen mind was quite incomprehensible. As if they did not recognize continuums of individual things, but rather assigned things to lumpish discrete sets and made a game of putting each one into as many sets as possible.

In any case, Gourami was certain from context that it was the last of these definitions that Jean Kroc intended. *Mojo*, that was another word for it. A better word, closer to the skin of the idea, like a bolt-hole one could just squeeze into.

Se could inject the luck, internalize what it offered, accept the contagion. Accept the mojo, choose entanglement, and accede to Jean Kroc's influence over se fate. Just about the time that se was concluding that enfouling self in the humen world—more than se was already—was a poor sort of plan.

Se scratched the underside of the skiff to let the human know se was swimming away, and tucked the re-waterproofed box into its pouch. Se would decide later. Right now, se was going to get something better to eat than could be filtered from the reedy water. A sweet fish, which could be shared with Caetei and Tetra if it was a big one, that would be nice.

And maybe it was technically poaching. But hadn't this been the people's home, the people's river first? And wasn't se already an outlaw?

Fine then.

Upriver se would take the human. To the greatparent-self, if need be. If Jean Kroc thought it important, thought André needed to learn, then so would it be done.

For a human, Jean Kroc was nearly a civilized thing.

The next day, a little after lunchtime, Jefferson Greene went for a walk. The suspended, slat-construction streets and the canals between the barges were almost deserted in the heat of afternoon, and the creak of the city pulling at its moorings and rubbing against its bumpers almost drowned out the distant laughter of a pair of children, though what little breeze there was blew the voices across the water.

It was still enough that the city stank, though Rim's offices were in a desirable spot on Bayside. Upwind of the bulk of Novo Haven, and with a clear view of the pale blue bay and beyond it, the long blue arc of the horizon, broken by the black slashes of drilling platforms silhouetted against the darker blue of the gulf.

Things got caught between the ships, though, ground up and trapped there, and there they rotted. Seaweed, sea animals, algae, the floating bodies of

birds. Nobody was supposed to dump trash or offal in
the bay, of course, but that happened, too—household-
ers frankly more often than the crews of fishing craft.
And when the city hadn't been broken up for storm in
six or twelve months, as happened coming up to the
hot months after a quiet winter, the stench grew op-
pressive.

Jefferson wrinkled his nose and hung over the railing, resting his forearms on the top. He had a slip of
silver and zinc and copper in his right hand, and he
flipped it off his thumb and caught it over and over
and over again. Heads, tails, heads, tails, heads, tails,
heads. The sequence had only broken twice since he
started experimenting the night before.

With a sigh, he folded the coin in his fist and resumed walking, elbows pulled back and hands tucked
into his pockets. The street rasped under his steps, slats
dipping a little. Not too much, and Rim kept its walks
matted with springy white nonskid, so he couldn't
hear his footsteps, just the pivots rubbing against the
office barge. The laughter came again; it must be riding on an air-current coiling one of the other barges,
because there was nothing to Bayside but the butter-
yellow sails of a dark-green pleasure boat, tacking to
windward with silver stickle-backed torpedo shapes
darting through its wake. The sails moved in the
breeze, rippling, but there wasn't enough wind to bell
them out.

A cracked shell lay on the nonskid next to a pinkish
stain. The remnants of some bird's lunch, and
Jefferson swept it into the bay with the instep of his
shoe. Things falling into water made a satisfying
plonk.

The thought made him sick after a second. He
turned and kept walking.

It wasn't that Jefferson didn't trust Closs, exactly. But he did know Closs thought he was an idiot. That Jefferson held a 53 percent share in his grandfather's company, as licensed from Rim, and so Closs had to do what Jefferson told him to do had no bearing on it. Closs would only protect him so far.

You couldn't buy loyalty. Not loyalty of the sort that Anchor Greene had commanded as the head of an explorer's crew and then the patriarch of the initial Greene's World Charter Trade Company, the sort of loyalty—and deference—that Jefferson had been raised to expect.

Anchor Greene had possessed that gift of leadership. And a not insignificant portion of the network of friends and associates that he had assembled was still in place. But Jefferson had never had his grandfather's knack for inspiring loyalty, or for identifying the sorts of people in whom it could be inspired.

He chose to believe that he did not care to trade on his grandfather's name. He had attended school off-planet, by telepresence at a Core university where his name meant as little as any Rimworlder's. Whatever Closs thought of him, he had earned his degree, his grades, his position.

It wasn't cloudy and the sky wasn't growing dark in any dramatic fashion, but the temperature had begun to drop. With the awareness of those who live on the water, Jefferson thought there might be some weather coming.

He'd fire Closs if Timothy wasn't one of his grandfather's protégés. That might be more ill-will than the fragile remainder of Anchor's circle could support without the vibrant presence of the man himself. And Closs knew too much, anyway. Such as, all about the decision to eliminate Lucienne Spivak once Rim's monitoring of her connex, her contacts, and her movements indicated that they had no choice except to silence her.

Tails, heads, tails, heads.

That sailboat had found a wind Jefferson didn't feel. The half-slack sails snapped, cupped and taut, and the little craft scudded over the bay like a symbol of freedom and self-determination. He followed it with his gaze; they were going the same way.

The sight ached under his breastbone, a lifting sensation. It didn't matter, after all, how ugly things had gotten, what mistakes had been made. He'd find a way out of it.

The wheeling gulls followed the sailboat, but after watching it a moment longer Jefferson turned away. Closs wasn't ruthless enough, when it came right down to it. He couldn't see—and do—what needed to be done. And if he didn't manage to catch up with the ranid witness, it would be up to Jefferson to field the contingency plan.

His hands were back in his pockets as he walked downtown, toward the center of the spiderweb of moored vessels that comprised most of Novo Haven. This wasn't something he'd ever want on connex, but there were still people he could call on. And some of them were in town.

André probably shouldn't have admitted it, as a city boy at heart, but he was enjoying the exercise. The skiff slipped through the water like a minnow, his paddle barely rippling the surface, and he only saw the froggies who were his constant silent companions when the tall one—Tetra—showed itself ahead of him to direct his route.

The work was like a meditation. Dip, dip, glide, the occasional brush of reeds against his bow as Tetra led him through a narrow gap, the sun on his shoulders and the nape of his neck beyond the shade of his hat.

He had no illusions that the trip would stay pleasant once it began to be measured in days. Or even possibly past lunchtime. And he wasn't wrong. By afternoon, clouds piled teetering against a stiff breeze from landward, high enough that he could see them over the tops of the arching reeds. Classic thunderheads, and if the breeze failed they would tumble in off the ocean on a wave of low pressure that would make a man's joints pop and groan.

He didn't paddle any faster, though. He struggled toward no shelter, in fact did not even have a destination. The storm would catch him if it caught him, and if not it would slide north and make landfall at Dabrey, where the continental shelf dropped off more steeply and sharp waves pounded crumbling red cliffs.

He was going to get wet sooner or later. Though the timing was inconvenient; his freshwater stores weren't down more than a couple of liters, and with good luck seeming to be at a premium, it would likely rain tonight and then in ten days he'd be down to purifying swamp water in the still.

It was a pessimistic thought. He didn't want to be paddling around a swamp in ten days.

Well, if he wanted out that badly, he could always bring Closs the frog's head on a stick. And forfeit his chance at learning from Kroc.

You paid your money and you picked your poison.

He was thinking about that, the poison and the taste of it, dipping his paddle and gliding, when not just Tetra but Tetra and one of the other two emerged from the water about ten meters upstream. The smaller one—Gourami, he thought, his proposed victim, though both of the little ones were of a size—swam forward and extended its wrist, with the slate.

—*storm coming*

He nodded, leaning away to balance its long-fingered weight clinging to the gunwhale. "Are you certain?"

It flexed its hands, a singular beckoning gesture that he thought was an irritable confirmation.

—*not safe for humen on the water*, it slated. *Follow. Shelter you.*

It slipped back, skull-deep in the channel before he could answer, and stroked away. Awkward and incongruous as they were on land, ranids moved through water with a stroke and glide his clumsy manipulations of the paddle could only mock. He followed, though, paddling harder now that he was not intent on setting a pace he could maintain all day.

The wind died as he passed through the next belt of reed, and now he smelled the storm. Funny to think you could, over the fermented reek of the bayou and the nearby salt of the bay, but the smell of rainwater and ozone was as sharp and strong as that of his own sweat.

No matter how hard he paddled, the froggies were faster. It almost became a kind of game, straining over each stroke, making it long and smooth, leaning into the next one, digging at the water with all his weight. The temperature dropped, cooling the sweat on his neck, and now the sun must be occluded, because its warmth vanished.

The third shape darted past him, green and mottled just beneath the soft brown water. And then he heard something pattering behind.

A hailstorm.

Brilliant.

When the precipitation started to hit, it stung even through his hat. At first that was all; the leading edge of the storm raised goose pimples—a stiff updraft tugging André's brim—and what fell was fat, shocking drops of water. It might have been refreshing after the heat of the day, if it hadn't gusted sideways into his eyes to prick and blind.

But behind him, he could hear the reed canes cracking like twisted straws. Two of the froggies swam backward, legs moving with long sculling strokes and pop-eyes above the water bearing an expression he would have thought worried, if they hadn't looked that way as a matter of course.

The channel grew choppy under his bow, the skiff lurching drunkenly as the wind hit it crosswise. Hailstones rattled around his feet. One smacked sharply above his knee, a blow solid as a fist. The skiff rocked violently to the other side. André grabbed the gunwale left-handed, almost losing his paddle as the little craft pitched.

Another big hailstone glanced off the crown of his hat and left him stunned, shaking off scattered bright flashes. One more struck his shoulder, numbing his arm to the elbow. *If I'm not lucky the next one's going to crack my skull.*

What the hell.

Lucky.

He stared at his left hand, made the fingers close though he could not feel them, lifted the paddle, and dragged it through the water. The skiff rocked forward. André ducked his head against the blinding rain. Luck.

It would be lucky if the big hailstones missed him. It would be lucky if the wind swung round to his back.

It would be lucky if he didn't get brained by a fist-size chunk of falling ice—

He hunched his head between his shoulders, regretting the return of sensation in his arm. Numb was better than prickling flashes of electricity.

A storm was a chaotic system. No way to model the whole thing, not without a more powerful computer than his headset. No *need* to model the whole thing, though. Messing around with weather systems as a whole tended to have long-term repercussions. And nobody could hold that in his head.

Not even Jean Kroc.

Maybe he wouldn't have to. Because the only thing he had to affect was this particular corner of it, this microcell. Just blunt the force, angle it around him— another hailstone rabbit-punched him, and he rocked forward, gagging. All it would take was a series of lucky coincidences and the wit to take advantage of them.

He had the knack. He'd always had the knack. Jean Kroc wouldn't have taken him if he didn't have the knack—

Sideways, swirling, eddies, angles, wind and rain, random chance. Not so random. You could feel it when it clicked, Jean said. Like a wave pushing, like a wind filling your sails. You grabbed it and you rode.

Had it, had it, balanced, fine-line, the wind parting the rain before him, the hail bouncing harmlessly to either side, cold numbing his fingers, stinging his face. He got the paddle in the water and his weight behind it, shoving the skiff forward, the froggies slick shapes in the water, greeny-brown.

One of the ranids popped up out of the water like a prank snake from a can. It hunkered, wincing, head sunk against its shoulders, short neck completely re-

tracted. The hands paddled, wide-webbed, in an unmistakable beckoning gesture.

Solid earth. Land. A little hillock rising between the
reeds, a green bulge rising out of the channeled
swamp, the reeds parting on either side. The ranid
winced and meeped as falling ice struck it, kicked off
with a powerful leap and splashed down five meters
closer to the skiff. The shock of impact nearly sent
André face-first into the water.

Had it. Had it. Riding the edge—

The hailstone that struck him roundly between the
shoulder blades knocked even the thought of breath
away. He held onto the paddle mostly because he was
doubled over it, wheezing, failing, struck again, again.

And then the skiff surged forward, propelled from
behind, strong ranid kicks driving the prow onto the
muddy bank. André spilled forward over the gunwales,
rolled, pushed himself up with the paddle, gasping.
Ooze dripped down his face as he grabbed the skiff and
hauled, and then one of the ranids was beside him—
Gourami, the smallest of the three—helping haul,
flinching at the smack of ice. It pushed, and André
heaved, and the skiff flipped over. As the froggie slithered down the bank, André dropped back into the mud
and writhed under the edge of the skiff, a hailstone
bloodying his mouth before he made it.

He retreated into the shelter, the mud soaking
through his shoulders, and listened to the hail smack
against the hull of the skiff.

It was not going to be a pleasant evening.

8

WHEN MORROW CALLED CLOSS, IT WAS A CAUSE FOR CONcern. When she called him at home and didn't waste time on pleasantries, it was very nearly a cause for panic.

"Cricket Earl Murphy," she said, as Closs toweled his close-cropped curls. He wore another towel wrapped around his waist, water still beaded in his chest hair. No matter where he was, Morrow's calls rang through.

"Who is she?"

"Nobody," Morrow said. She smiled that particular, mysterious smile. One of the things that Closs liked about her was that she wouldn't milk it, though, or make him abase himself for the information. She'd enjoy the superiority of knowing she had his curious attention for a minute, and then she'd share.

She didn't let him down. "She's an archinformist. With no past. Or possibly too much of one."

Closs nodded, running searches. Empty. Empty. Empty. "She doesn't exist."

"But she does. She's fucking André Deschênes. And she's colluding with Jean Kroc."

"I'm not turning up any images. Any information at all."

Morrow's smile transformed her face. She was at home as well, he guessed; tendrils of hair caressed her cheeks, and her face was scrubbed pink between the freckles. The focus was tight on her face, but he thought she was wearing a collarless white shirt. "You wouldn't. It would take a better data miner than her to pull that, and there aren't that many data miners better than Cricket. But I can tell you something about her. You'll need to know it: Spivak managed to dump part of her information to Cricket before she died."

They had what Deschênes had brought back to them. But it was incomplete; Spivak had, they thought, been in the midst of deleting her hard memory when she died. And they hadn't succeeded in cracking the encryption. Which was actually reassuring, because Jefferson's man Kountché had procured copies of everything Security got off Spivak's body and corrupted the originals.

However, if the rest of the data were out there, and in the hands of a competent archinformist, they had problems. And an opportunity, because if this Cricket Murphy cracked the codes, and if Charter Trade could retrieve, collate, and access the files, it was possible that they could uncover the identity of whoever it was in Charter Trade that had given Spivak the information in the first place.

Closs wasn't about to forget that he also had a burrower to contend with. Greene would be starting a witch hunt any day now, if he hadn't already. "We'll need to retrieve her."

Morrow nodded. "There are rules."

Cricket Earl Murphy was *Cricket*, Closs noticed. Not *Murphy*. Morrow would no doubt eventually get around to explaining that, as well. He nodded, to let her know he was ready to hear her conditions.

"Protect her," Morrow said. "Keep her safe. She can be detained, but she's not to be harmed."

"How do I find her?"

Morrow's smile was so irrepressible as to be infectious. It made her brown-flecked eyes seem to glow. "It's easy," she said. "She hasn't changed her appearance. So, unless she's skinned, she looks just like me."

Cricket liked that nobody cared how she looked while she did her job, and that she could work anywhere. Reclining on the second-story deck, for example, crosswise in a broad colorful hammock with her feet up on the railing so she didn't swing on the wind.

Or anyway, that's where she would have been if it hadn't been pelting down hail, chunks of ice big enough to dent the poly of the conservatory roof. Instead she sat inside, her hands folded around a steaming mug, her eyes half-lidded, and with the fraction of her attention that was not otherwise engaged, watched the ice fall.

André was out in that somewhere. She wished him joy.

The undersides of the clouds were gray and flat, smooth-textured. As good a backdrop as any for the images that waltzed across her retinas. She didn't know what she was looking for. Sometimes that was all right, though; you knew it when you found it.

Lucienne's fragment-of-a-file also commanded a third of Cricket's attention. It was tightcoded, biolocked to Cricket's neural pattern. Useless to anybody else unless she extracted it. And yet Lucienne—dying, *murdered*—had felt it was necessary to encrypt it as well. Which argued a high level of sensitivity.

Enough to kill someone over. She'd tried every code key she could think of, every half-remembered joke and lame catchphrase a friendship developed over the years. She had nothing.

She blinked itchy half-forgotten eyes and leaned against the chair-back, wishing her spine would release. If she didn't go in for a massage soon, she'd regret it. André was useless for helping her relax…and she wasn't about to let him put his hands around her neck again anytime soon.

She paused the search and backgrounded the decryption session. As she rose, the thought struck her.

What if it hadn't been Lucienne who encoded the files? Then the code key would be something Lucienne knew, or had memorized, and probably saved to wet memory only, where nobody could hack it. She listened to Cricket, and Cricket had taught her everything she could think of that might help.

There was no way Lucienne could expect Cricket to know such a code. Not unless Lucienne somehow passed it on to her.

Which, of course, she might have. With the recording of her death.

Cricket was going to need more than a cup of kesha to get through this.

She didn't keep any rec drugs at home, other than six different herbal stimulants—two kinds of earth caffeine and four offworld brews—so she was stuck waiting until the hail slacked off. The trip through driving rain, down to the next barge to buy liquor, was long enough for her hands to have started shaking, cold at the center of the palms, when she let herself back into her apartment.

She'd bought harsh, cheap vodka, something intended to numb her brain and her tongue. It came in a fragile disposable. She drained the last of the kesha, touched the heating element off, and popped two bubbles over the empty cup. Even the rough scent was steadying.

She gulped, two mouthfuls, then gagged on the searing third but choked it down. The alcohol made her light-headed, as much from the fumes as from the scouring sensation.

She should be sitting down, lest she wind up on the floor again. Not in the chair; that might tip. She settled cross-legged, leaning against the wall, and decided that was uncomfortable. She stretched out on the floor instead, her head pillowed on a repurposed chair cushion.

And went inside.

The first time, the pain had taken her whole attention—the pain and the awful knowledge, the migraine lights flashing before Lucienne's vision, an aurora of green and violet and shocking pink. Now she tried to look through it, sort the surface thoughts, riffle the images and words and strings of thought flickering through Lucienne's racing, failing mind. She pressed her palms to her closed lids, as if she could press the swelling agony back inside her skull. Her brain might have been herniating into her eye sockets; whoever told her a cerebral aneurysm was a painless killer had obviously never died from one.

It was easier without the distraction of the massive, interrupted download and Jean clutching at her. She could focus; she could feel it, everything, the waves and the pitch of the flashboat, the coronas of color, the scent of the sea. A suprisingly rich environment. A surprisingly rich feed to waste bandwidth on, when you were dying.

It had to be here. Lucienne had hidden it in here somewhere. There was no other reason for all this… detail.

All the way to the end, she rode Lucienne's death down. Again. And she didn't find it.

She opened her eyes and lay, flat-back, staring at the pinkness through her fingers. The vodka came up her throat, burning; she choked it down again. There was more on the counter if she needed the help.

And if she was too drunk to notice what Lucienne had been trying to show her when she found it, that would be stupid. Cricket sighed, gritted her teeth, and went through it one more time.

All those colors. She wondered if there was something fractal, concealed in the water, in the silhouette of the shoreline against moon-streaked indigo. If she subtracted the colors, the shattered light, might she see it then?

Nothing. No help there. Nothing out of place—

—nothing but the colors themselves. Those specific values. Green and violet and shocking pink.

Wavelengths.

Wavelengths were expressed in numbers.

The colors were the key.

She was just slotting them into the decryption protocol when her downstairs alarm starting ripping into the back of her head. *That* was a reflex. She was on her feet and moving, wishing the postmigraine tension headache pinching her upper face were a mask she could peel off and drop aside.

And then she forgot its existence, as she kicked her

flat monitors to manual override and found the place
encircled by half a dozen men and women in Rim
Security uniforms. They'd circumvented the perimeter—they might have managed it even if she hadn't
been distracted, though that was no excuse.

A single flashboat was moored across the channel
she could see from her window, two more uniformed
officers climbing up to the street. Patrol officers
routinely carried chemical accelerant weapons on
Greene's World for animal control and dealing with
the smugglers and activists, who could be violent. The
short arms and tasers strapped to their thighs gave her
pause, nonetheless.

She had Lucienne's unlocked data in her head.

There was no way she was going quietly.

There were options. She could take a hostage, but
Cricket didn't want to shoot some cop who was just doing her job. And that would still leave her trapped in her
house with no way out—they were trying to shut her
connex down now, but her countermeasures were holding—and information she needed to get to Jean Kroc.
She'd had no chance to look over the files, did not yet
know how damaging, or how critical, they might be.

The timing was almost too bad to be coincidental.

That thought cascaded implications, bringing the
stinging pinch of her headache back with a vengeance.
At worst case, that was a very nasty suspicion indeed. It
could be chance and luck and even a bit of conjuring. Or
it could mean somebody had a bug in Cricket's head.

That wasn't a chance she could take. She caught up a
jacket off the back of the chair nearest the sliding door
to the upper deck—it lived there, for just such reasons
as this, and was waterproof, with sealed pockets—and
let herself out under the conservatory roof, next to the
open sundeck. She wasn't wearing shoes: a lucky break.

And as long as she stayed under cover, in the warm moist space, the officers across the channel would be unlikely to spot her. The greenhouse was cramped with plants, ornamentals and flowers rather than the practical vegetables she and Lucienne had grown.

For a moment, she mourned the conservatory. A convenient, sharper ache to distract her as she took a breath and severed her connex. Her sight dimmed, the flicker of attention messages scrolled out of existence, her archive links and news feeds and the conversation boxes of a couple of black chats frequented by archinformists and freelancers vanishing like blown flower petals.

It made her chest hurt when they went, as if her breath had been cut and not the flow of information.

She did it at Jean Kroc's, but this was different. Then, she *knew* when she'd be stepping back online.

The shrilling alarm in her head vanished, but a real sound took its place. A voice, male, baritone. Calm. Counting backward from fifty.

It was as much of a warning as she could offer. She really didn't want to kill anybody. And she'd always thought a countdown was self-explanatory.

There was an air supply in her escape coat, along with some other things. The water four meters below was gray and filthy, churned by the storm. She'd have to hit it straight, or she could break an arm, her back, her neck.

She kicked the channel-side window out and dove through the reaching branches of an Earth-imported ficus. Not even the officers on the street below got a shot at her, or else they were holding their fire.

It was nearly sunset and the afternoon storm had blown inland, trailing wreaths of mist, by the time

Jefferson pushed his chair back and stood. He felt it, too, the pain in stiff muscles and joints provoking a groan as he twisted and stretched. The damn chairs his assistant had ordered were comfortable, but you forgot you were sitting still in them, and then you paid for it. He should set an alarm, something to ding or zap him every half an hour so he'd get up and move around.

The office was quiet. If summer weren't half here already, the sky outside the windows would be the blue-gray of a Rim Security uniform rather than streaky silver still. The storm had left a chill on the air; he bulked his sweater and grew it a high ribbed collar. He hated a cold throat.

He glanced at the silvery coin on the edge of his desk blotter, an English fifty-pence piece from about 5 B.G., but didn't pick it up. He'd tried a few; that was the best one for flipping.

His support staff had received permission to go hours before, so when the light on his panel blinked pink-white, incoming, he activated his headset and took the call himself. His first job had been in his father's office, taking calls. He'd worked his way up; he believed, as his father and grandfather had, that it made him a better boss. And that it built loyalty.

This call was voice only, internal. From the lab. Someone calling from a headset rather than a desk or wall phone.

"Jefferson Greene."

"Hello," the caller said. A woman, pleasant, efficient. Dr. McCarter, he thought. "May I speak to M~ Greene, please? Panel says he's still in the office?"

"This is Greene. Not the only one working late, I see."

She hesitated. "I'm sorry, Chairman. I didn't expect you to answer your own phone."

"They all left me here," he joked, trying to sound vexed. "I've been trying to find the door for the last half an hour."

She laughed, which didn't mean anything. Everyone laughed at the boss's jokes. "Chairman, I've been working on a research project, assisting Dr. Schaffner—"

If Neil Schaffner had brought her in, Jefferson could probably trust her. Schaffner was old school, a college friend of Jefferson's grandfather who had spent enough time relativistic that he'd already outlived the old man by fifty years. Family relationships got a little complicated when near-lightspeed travel got involved.

"The ranid health issue," he said.

"Yes. And I'm a little unclear on what we're going after here—"

"We have intelligence that a rogue splinter group of ELF called GreenWorld has been in contact with illegal biolabs offplanet," he said. "We're concerned for the health of our ranid workers. We're dependent on them for our undersea mining operations. And there are humanitarian reasons."

"Indeed," she said. "How reliable is this...intelligence?"

"Cross-confirmed by three sources. And we know what ELF provided the lab."

"GR-R seven twenty."

The ranid pathogen that Jefferson had arranged for Schaffner to have access to. "Yes."

"They're a coolie-rights organization," she protested, while he paced slowly back and forth, the index and middle fingers of his right hand pressed to the bone behind his ear as if they effected the slightest improvement in his hearing. "Do you believe they'd...introduce a weaponized pathogen to the native population simply to prevent them from working for Rim?"

He cleared his throat. "We don't know," he said. "We can't take the risk that they might. Which is why I need you to tell me first of all, if it *can* be weaponized. And if it can, to tell me how virulent they could make it."

"And to come up with a cure."

"Right," he confirmed. "A cure."

Cricket swam with frantic concentration. The blast would be directed upward; everything was carefully shaped, both to protect bystanders and to prevent her own soft flesh from soaking up the side effects of the demolition. And the water would protect her from gunfire if the Rimmers decided that swimming away constituted a defensible assault upon a peace officer. But that wouldn't prevent somebody with a spear gun from coming after her.

The explosion might, though, so when the water glared barred crimson and the shock wave thumped her solidly in the ribs but did not turn her inside out, she gave herself a half-second's pause to enjoy the relief. The oxygen supply was functioning well; she bit down on the regulator and drew one careful breath, pacing herself. Then she kicked forward again, driving through the water.

She had some way to swim. Her closest safehouse was a mile east; she could not do that underwater on emergency air. But she wanted to put as much distance between herself and that swarm of Rimmers as feasible before she dragged her dripping, disheveled self up onto the street in the middle of the weeknight dinner crowd. Not that people didn't slip off scoots all the time, but it was memorable.

And memorable...was bad.

The closest safehouse was probably a bad idea, too, simply by virtue of being closest. But it was well stocked and pleasanter than the other ones she could get to on foot, which were more along the lines of bolt holes. If she made it there she'd have dry clothes, additional changes of identity—there was one in the escape jacket, but only one, and she didn't want to trust it unless she had to—and something to eat. She'd also have access to an uplink that wasn't connected to the one inside her head.

She missed the connex already. Dead reckoning was a crude way to navigate; the global positioning coverage for Greene's World was riddled with gaps, but it was better than this.

She dove low, grateful the tide was in, and sculled through water still turbid from the storm. The great checkerboard of the channels and barges made squares of light and dark overhead. The undersides of the barges were outlined with safety or running lights, waterproof strings of green or blue or gold, sometimes interrupted with an odd-colored bulb. The water, milky with silt, caught and diffused the glow so that Cricket thought she swam through clouds of rainbows.

The lights weren't the only thing shining. The storm had borne along quantities of warm water. This made Cricket's impromptu nighttime swim more pleasant, but it also meant that her arms and hands were outlined in eddying swirls of minute stinging jellies, though these were too small and immature to so much as raise a welt on even human skin. Shoals of long-bodied fish sharked through them, sweeping up mouthfuls, as innocent of Cricket as Cricket was of anyone who might still be hunting *her*.

Her air ran thin after fifteen minutes. She might

have a breath or three left, but she'd rather save it for another crisis. She let herself float to the surface, almost motionless, arms angled out to stabilize. When her head broke the water she gritted her teeth to breathe slowly, saltwater drooling from her nostrils on ropes of mucus. She dared not cough. There wasn't much water down her throat anyway. It had all gone up her nose. All she could smell was ocean, as if her sinuses had been misted with a spray bottle. It stung the inside of her head, the back of her eyes, grit coating her teeth as she expectorated. A head full of muddy ocean: that was asking for a sinus infection.

If she was lucky enough to live long enough to be spitting out green snot, she decided, she'd endure it cheerfully.

More hazard lights outlined a dangling ladder. Not far. She drifted toward it, the lap of wavelets bumping her shoulder against the crusty waterline of the nearest barge. She heard voices but not close, maybe inside, behind open windows. They didn't seem to notice when she slithered up the rope ladder, though it seemed she banged and thumped with every rung. There was music, too, though, and secondary voices. An attenuated explosion made her shake her head.

They were indoors watching the news.

Like most of Novo Haven would be, if she'd stopped to think about it. There was more than a primary distraction provided by a pretty good boom.

The streets would be half empty.

A disadvantage, too: no crowds for Cricket to get herself lost in. But she wouldn't have to worry about absolute crowds of people remembering a dripping woman with seaweed in her hair.

Sirens sounded. It was a moment before she realized they did not come from the news feed. She tucked herself against the barge's external bulkhead in the shadow of a fire escape. Her jacket had autocamo, unless she turned it off. She blended into the white walls and dappled shadows as if she were part of the wall.

Two flashboats sizzled past, narrow and hissing, both of them in Rimmer livery with the blue-mauve-gold flashing on the prows. What she caught of the news story blamed the blast on terrorists, perhaps the same ones responsible for the destruction of a ranid recruitment center and a security barge earlier in the week. *No group has yet taken responsibility,* Cricket mouthed along with the feed. She raked her hair back with her fingers, trying to make the sodden curls seem intentional, and moved away from the wall.

Her first safehouse was six blocks on, and if she hadn't already been on knife-edge and shaking with adrenaline, she might have missed the nondescript white scoot parked at the dock, the Rimmer plainpaint flashboat half concealed behind the usual gaggle of water taxis. But she was wary and watching, and after putting herself against a low wall—to break her human silhouette—and peering over, she found two other watchers on nearby roofs.

This, too, was closed to her. Which was a quandary. She was cold and disregarded, had no dry clothes, and the cash cards in her pocket might be compromised. If she connexed, they might find her. And if she didn't connex, she had no resources at all.

She could try to get to Jean Kroc, but as Lucienne was dead and Cricket was being hunted, his house would be hotter than anyplace else on Greene's World she might try, short of walking into Rim and snapping the cuffs on herself. Dammit.

Cricket had made a practice of never limiting her options, and here she was with none. She needed a dry place to sit, first off, a warm corner out of the wind, and someplace to finish cracking Lucienne's message and find a way to get it to Jean. Because if Rim got her, she wasn't going to let them do it while she still had that in her head.

She stepped back out of the streetlights and headed for Bayside, away from land—away from where Rim would expect her to run. Toward them; their headquarters. Their strength.

And just the sort of place, among the docks facing open water, to find a nice cabin cruiser to break into for the night.

The first thing Cricket did after reactivating the security system was steam herself pink in the shower. Subverting the cruiser's expert system had consumed a timed forty-two seconds. A strictly mechanical alarm would have withstood her longer.

Thank God for the stupidity of smart machines.

She scrubbed at salt and filth, angling her face this way and that to try and clear her vision with the moisture from the steam. She didn't need her eyes for Lucienne's documents; she flicked through those as fast as she could parse them into hard memory. She didn't slow to consider the content; if she started thinking about what she was ripping, she'd—

She didn't know what she would do. Her hair clutched her fingers as she shoved it back from her temples, working stolen conditioner through. Sand gritted her scalp, wedged her nails. If she didn't grease the rat's-nest up and comb through it before she washed, she'd set the salty tangles into knots.

Three cycles of lather and rinse later, she was still pinching sharp quartz from the strands, but she didn't think she was likely to get any cleaner. And she'd finished the first crash-pass on the data. From here on in, she could read as well in a hammock as in the shower.

Under other circumstances, she would have scorned the clothes she'd swum here wearing. But she didn't have the luxury of fastidiousness, so she borrowed the cruiser owner's bathrobe while she ran shirt and trousers through a cleaning cycle. The jacket wasn't home-washable, but the waterproofing had held up; she hung it in front of a fan. In the morning, with luck, she'd be able to beat the salt crust off and go.

She heated soup—she'd run a DNA scrub through the whole place before she left—and ate it while she listened to the ghost of Lucienne. The implications of even the fragmentary data were profound enough that her spoon was clicking on the mug before she realized she didn't know what soup she'd eaten.

Rim kept secrets from the Core. The Core kept secrets from Rim: no surprises there. One of the stranger benefits of having once been someone else was that the someone she had been *knew* how much was concealed. And sometimes even had a general idea of what not to ask about in order to ensure everyone's comfort and continued peace of mind.

Or, in this case, where exactly to shine the light.

The mere existence of omelite itself was classified. Rim and Core ran the Slides; the technology was un-patented and tightly held, the secret enforced by loy-alty oaths backed with wet viruses. That the stuff occurred naturally—that it was *mined* on Greene's World—was a bit of information that it had taken *Cricket* ten years to unearth, and she was generally un-rivaled when it came to finding things out.

What Lucienne had transmitted, to Cricket's

unscientific but educated eye, was a series of documents regarding mining practices at Charter Trade tanglestone bores. The stuff was innocuous, found laced through crumbly shales that were as often as not also oil-bearing. And it was more precious than any other substance known.

Patterns were Cricket's stock in trade, and as she sorted files, she found patterns emerging. Patterns of injuries, disappearances, safety failures. Strings of shocking accidents, unreported to the Miners' Union or that laughable body, the Rim safety commission, because the victims were not human.

And odder things. Coincidences, sidelong references, sly jokes in e-mails about elves and hauntings. Or of inexplicable happenstance and random chance, déjà vu and double vision. Things got a little weird near the Slides, and near coincidence engineers in general. She'd seen it happen around Jean.

But this seemed more concentrated.

There was more—enough callous safety violations that even Rim's emasculated media might not be able to resist the story. But what really caught her attention was a sine wave pattern of duplicated events; a compressor piston arm breaking, for example, and then three weeks later the replacement breaking in the same place and manner.

Another pattern, and she guessed she knew the cause of this one. A pattern of sabotage.

Which led her to another conclusion; that Lucienne *had* been somehow involved in the recruiting facility bombing.

Cricket stood and carried her mug to the sink, washed it—by hand—dried it and put it away. She left the spoon on the counter; she didn't mean to hide her presence, merely display politeness.

Maybe it would encourage the owners to put in a decent security system.

This—was a quandary. She held in her hands—or her head—a friend's dying bequest. A stolen gift, one tangled up in an uncomfortable moral netting of extremist politics and radical actions. But it was also exactly what Jean Kroc needed: the evidence of cascading coincidence, of disregard for life and limb, of cover-ups and concealment of the environmental cost of the tanglestone mines. And even if Lucienne had painted a target on Cricket with this information, it had cost Lucienne her life. Cricket owed a friend something for that kind of commitment, too. Whatever her life was now, Cricket had made her own mistakes in the past— was still making them, if André Deschênes was any indication—and frankly, she'd class some of them as mistakes only because she got caught.

Cricket had done worse than anything Lucienne and Jean might have committed. The fact that it had almost all been perfectly legal—

—well, that was beside the point, wasn't it?

She would find a way to get the file to Jean. Anything else was cowardice. And then she'd figure out if she had a chance to restart her life just once more, or if the cat had drowned for the last time.

Three explosions in three days, and not even one of them had been Closs's idea. Standing on the ravaged street beside what remained of Cricket Earl Murphy's flat, he contemplated a fourth—more metaphorical than actual. But he considered it a point of honor that when his staff reported a failure, they did so with more shame than trepidation. He didn't care to be feared—at least, not by his allies and subordinates.

That was a crutch for men insecure in their power. Machiavelli's outlook had not been so much simplistic as limited by his times.

There *was* a certain sort of person for whom fear was the most powerful motivator. Closs understood and accepted this, but he considered such people erratic and unpredictable, and they were not the ones with whom he chose to surround himself.

Of course, Machiavelli's prince had not had the luxury of selecting his subjects, and Closs did not have the luxury of selecting his... prince. But then, what soldier did?

He bore that in mind, and kept his temper and his voice level as team leaders and liaisons explained in painful detail exactly what had gone so wrong with the attempt to capture Cricket Earl Murphy, aka Moon Morrow. And truthfully, he couldn't muster much anger.

Legally, in both Core and Rim, the cloned offspring became the parent at the moment of birth. This cheerful legislative dodge effectively discouraged replica cloning except in terminal cases. Given his own close association with Morrow's clone-daughter— the new, legal Moon Morrow—he was reasonably certain that the original was more than a match for Rim security.

It was to his officers' credit that they had come even so close as they had. Especially considering the shoestring haste of the operation.

And now, Closs had to call up his own version of Morrow and explain to her how they had missed. And see if he could get her to explain how somebody got from Earth all the way out to the Rim in... less than two Terran standard years.

He already had a headache.

"Maurice, please."

"What would you do if I ever left this office, Major?" The image was, again, high quality. Maurice wasn't at his desk this time, unless he was running a skin; the background was the bay view through the screens in the staff lounge. Nobody had died in this explosion: the spiral up the fluted edge of Maurice's ear shimmered crimson, fuchsia, silver.

"What can you tell me about experimental or theoretical means of faster-than-light travel?"

"Experimental? There's no such animal, unless I missed an *Astrophysics Monthly*. Theoretical...space warps, tesseracts, what, you want something practical?"

"Let me give you a base assumption. Assume it has been done. How did they do it?"

"Oh, chum the water, Timothy. That'll keep me up nights. Okay, how did they do *what*, exactly? What are my parameters?"

"Get one person from Earth to Greene's World."

"How fast?"

Closs shrugged. "I don't know. A couple of standard."

"Man, you don't come cheap. All right, I'll get back to you. Would you like any more impossible things before breakfast, Major?"

Closs smiled. "*I'll* get back to *you*."

Eventually, the rain stopped and André slithered from the shelter of the overturned skiff. Clotting mud flaked from his shirt, cracking off his skin when he bent his neck. Something was wrong with the shirt now; it didn't flex properly across his shoulders or in the crease of his underarms.

"Lousy damned tech." The point of the smartshirt on a trip such as this was not to have to worry about laundry or carrying extra supplies. If it had stopped processing dirt and perspiration, he couldn't repair it by rinsing in a channel and drying over a branch.

He should have prepared for an equipment failure. It was his own foolishness. But this wasn't his usual venue, and he hadn't exactly had a lot of time to pack.

He tipped the skiff back onto its belly and rummaged in the hull. Fortunately, his supplies had been lashed securely—otherwise he'd be picking everything out of the mud. He pitched his shelter and set it to inflate, assembled the filtration system, and walked the perimeter of his mud spit until he found a bank that wasn't strictly slime and shattered reeds like broken knife blades. He took a leak against a shrub, then picked a gingerly path to the water's edge, keeping his boots on. The jumble of hollow stems looked sharp enough that he wasn't sure even thick soles would protect him.

Bruised and strained muscle twinged as he squatted at the channel's edge. He'd never get *clean* this way, but he didn't have to be crusted.

Babysitting, he thought, rolling his eyes. It wasn't just the coolie that Jean Kroc was getting out of the way. André knew he shouldn't expect more. He was paying the immemorial price of apprenticeship: things concealed, games of trust.

He didn't believe for an instant that Jean was through testing him.

He paused, elbows on thighs for a moment, resting. Sunset was over, the sky still dimming. The smells of rot—some rich, some fetid—rose all around him. The mud was full of flat black-stained particles of decaying leaf; he worked his tongue against his palate, turned his head, and spat. Mud curled over the projecting edges of his boot soles.

Full moons tonight; there'd be enough light to go on by, if he chose to. But if he was hunting a running coolie, he'd camp for the night rather than risking the swamp in darkness. The savages killed people.

And under cover of night, he could have a longer conversation with his tour guides without fear of satellite observation. They would be invisible, as long as they stayed in the moonshadows. Amphibians did not show up as warm spots to a sky eye.

He palmed up water, scrubbed crusty dollops from his eyebrows, and rubbed them from his beard. The mud had dried in little hard berries; they crushed into powder and the powder, wetted, melted instantly back into mud.

That was a good sign that it would dry due to body heat and crack off his shirt if he just kept wearing it. The autofit and self-clean might be able to take care of the rest if he gave them a chance to regenerate.

He washed his face again and rested a few moments longer, contemplating the deep ache in his muscles, the pull of tendons against bones. He was tired—weary—but despite exhaustion and bruises and the sharply tender spot on the back of his head, he was also hungry. And thirsty, but the water purifier could satisfy that want.

He parted reeds and stepped through, surprised to find two of the three ranids crouched beside his cooker, three bright fish speared on twigs turning over it. "Hello, Tetra," he said, making an effort to sound polite and then rolling his eyes at his own silliness. As if they could hear the sound of his voice. "Hello, Caetei."

The short one made a gesture André took as

greeting. The tall one extended a scraped and roasted fish; he pinched the twig between his thumb and first two fingers. He expected bland meat, scorched with the scales burned off. But it smelled of herbs. He sucked flaking flesh from the skeleton, chewing carefully. Gagging on a fish bone out in the bayou would be a hell of a way to die.

Not bad, but it could use some salt.

He'd never actually seen them eat before—not anything more solid than green tea or gruel—and the process was fascinating, if revolting. They hadn't teeth; they were filter feeders. Their wide bony mouths weren't fitted to chew or tear, though the bony frill around the rim of mandible and maxilla could deliver a nasty bite...if you believed the media.

Tetra was processing the filets, using an unlotus leaf spread in a flat dryish spot as a cutting board. It did not so much slice into bites as mince into a paste. The knife was teak-handled, with a blade of some plastic or shock ceramic. The ranid cradled it in a three-fingered, one-thumbed hand. The thumb and the outside two fingers folded around the handle; the first finger extended along the spine of the blade, turning the knife, in essence, into a slicing claw.

A claw that it used with graceful facility. It portioned the minced fish into thirds, scraped each onto another unlotus leaf, and handed the first to Caetei. As it was half rising—to call Gourami from the water, at a guess—André realized he had the means to give the fish the help it needed. He stuck the twig with the nibbled meat on it into the ground and stood as well.

He was turning back, a squeeze tube of salted plum paste in his hand, when he realized that Tetra and Caetei had both frozen in place like run-down clockwork novelties. Caetei was still couched on the ground, fingers spidered over its plate. Tetra was drawn up tall, shivering slightly with the strain of standing erect on its crooked legs. It stared at André, both eyes focused on his chest, pupils contracted. If it had been human, he would have guessed that it was about to go for him.

It was about to go for him. Or it was waiting for him to go for it.

He leaned forward, against the pressure of the regard. Not to make the ranid look down; it wasn't staring him in the eyes. But trying to reassure it, to reach out to it without grabbing or invading its space.

Caetei hunched lower on the ground, a glossy mottled rock.

André actually yelped when something wet touched his hand. The third frog was there, Gourami. It beckoned him closer with two webbed, hooking fingers, and when he hunkered down, it tapped the backs of his knees.

Well, that was plain enough. *Sit.* André dropped onto the reed-covered mud and leaned toward the slate Gourami held out. Backlit letters confronted him.

—*You stood when se stood.*

André nodded, hoping the ranid would understand the gesture. Without retracting the slate, it keyed a next phrase, and a next.

—*Se reacted to threat. Se is a far-swimmer. Se would fight.*

André lifted his gaze from the panel. He didn't want to get into a fight with a ranid in a swamp. "Far-swimmer?" He shaped words carefully.

Gourami's fingers rippled, one of them lumpy and swollen. Whether this was agreement or irritation, André was too human to tell. He turned to Tetra; it was fussing with Gourami's leaf plate as easily as if nothing had happened. It reached out without looking up and brushed the side of its hand against André's. He was already coming to recognize that gesture, the request for attention, like catching someone's eye if one were human.

You couldn't catch another frog's gaze through muddy water, though, could you? It made sense, if you thought about it.

Tetra held out its hand, making a pincher movement. Its webs expanded, as if sucking something that might wriggle away into its grasp. The fingers pointed down; the overall effect was rather like the grab of a crane.

Bemused, André lifted the salted plum paste into the creature's grasp. Startlingly swift and deft, Tetra unscrewed the top and began investigating the contents just as any chef would.

"I'm not sure that's safe," André said, but all three ranids ignored him. He turned back to Gourami and its damaged hand. Its fingers writhed on the slate, as if it was trying to frame a comment. When André reached out to touch, the ranid did not withdraw its hand though it leaned its whole body aside.

André touched gently, stroking tacky, coated skin. There was no heat in the injured flesh, which was odd, because he could feel the sponginess of retained fluid, cushioning the twisted joint. "That needs to be put right," he said, enunciating carefully as Gourami watched his mouth. "It will slow us."

Of course, Tetra wouldn't understand his words—could barely hear his voice. And even if it could lip-read, it wasn't watching André. But the noises he was making must have drawn its attention, because it sealed the tube of plum paste and shuffled over. André scootched back, not wishing to make the mistake of standing again.

Even if his butt was getting soaked.

Tetra reached past him and took Gourami's hand, disentangling the sticky fingers from the case of the slate. Gourami shuddered, eyes staring off at an obtuse angle from each other. André had the bizarre impression that it was staring at its knees. Tetra must have said something, because Gourami flinched dramatically. And Tetra did something sudden and uncomplicated with its hands. A slight nauseating pop followed, and Gourami made a sound André felt more than heard.

These conversations would be easier on the headset, he thought. But who'd let a ranid uplink to their wetware through a slate?

But then it was done, and Tetra went back to fixing Gourami's dinner. It handed the plate to Gourami without ceremony, though Gourami made a little dance of receiving it. It dabbed at the smears of plum paste decorating the minced fish doubtfully.

Tuna tartare, André told himself resolutely, watching Gourami scoop the pasty substance into its mouth between sidelong glances at Tetra. The taller ranid crouched over its own dinner in apparent oblivion. Some sort of courtship ritual? Gourami seemed flustered enough.

André shrugged and applied himself to his own dinner, much improved by the addition of a condiment. As Gourami was wiping the sheen of fat and salt from its leaf with a forefinger, André piled the last sucked fish bones on the ground. "You were going to tell me about far-swimmers," he said, when the motion caught Gourami's attention. Maybe he was getting the hang of this.

The froggie scrubbed its hands together, then wiped them on the underside of the leaf before searching out its slate.

—*One who has earned mating.* It still favored the finger when it typed.

André touched the tip of his tongue to the center of his upper lip and pressed, feeling flesh indent. "But you don't...mate."

—*We don't fuck,* Gourami corrected, stabbing at the keys with vicious satisfaction. —*We have exoparents and endoparents.*

Typing more slowly now. André wondered if he had guessed right, if it had been angry, or just in a hurry. "Fathers and mothers?" André tried. He had some idea how it worked, or thought he did, anyway.

Gourami nearly slapped the *no* key with the side of its palm. —*Exoparents mate. Endoparents bear.*

"What does that have to do with far-swimmers?"

—*You swim from home to mate,* it explained. —*The farther you swim, the stronger those who will mate with you. Exoparents contribute zygotes. Endoparents raise the broods and teach them.*

"Somebody else's children."

This time, it just pointed at the *no* button. —*Your children, humen. Somebody else's genes.*

André gestured around the camp. "You're not a far-swimmer."

—*I was a liaison.*

"So was Tetra asking if you would be its... endoparent?"

The ranid hesitated long enough for André to wonder if he'd crossed some line of taboo. Then it crumpled the leaf in its hand and made a quick oblique gesture that André thought meant no. As if realizing that he didn't understand, it reached for the slate again.

—*not that.* And pushed the slate away, decisively. And then just as decisively, took it back. —*Pay us.*

"...pay you?"

—*We take you through bayou, not for bandweal or clanweal, you owe. Pay us.*

It stared at him, fishy eyes unblinking, focused intently on his chin. The dropped articles were haste, he thought, not ineptness. Alien cultures, and no way of knowing what sort of bargaining Jean Kroc had done to make it accept his protection. "How do I pay?"

—*Tell me a story, André.*

Gourami was good at understanding humen gestures, for a person. Which was not very good at all compared to the complex information that humen could convey with nothing but a rearrangement of their facial muscles. Se thought the long blinking stare was befuddlement, perhaps shock. But se could not be sure.

—*A story?*

—*A narrative. A tale. A fiction.* This new slate came with a built-in thesaurus. All these complicated humen synonyms that weren't, quite.

Se liked it.

André Deschênes stopped and now he was definitely staring. Staring and blinking: for a moment, Gourami almost thought of him as a person. But then he said the most astounding thing se'd ever heard. He spread his stubby hands, paler on the ventral than the dorsal surface, and shook his head.

—*I'm sorry, but I don't know any stories.*

9

CLOSS WAS LATE ENOUGH THE NEXT MORNING THAT JEFferson beat him in, even though Jefferson overslept. Centuries before, virtual commuting had been hailed as the wave of the future. People would eat, sleep, play, work in the same spaces.

Like so many other predictions, it hadn't quite worked out. In Jefferson's opinion, this was because the setup ignored the basic human need for politics. For a community.

People seemed to enjoy the separation, the act of putting on a suit, skinning up, and coming in to the office. And the ones who didn't enjoy it needed the discipline. Leaders and followers, the top dog and the pack animals. It was how it was.

Anyway, Closs's uncharacteristic tardiness was extraordinarily convenient when Jefferson had contingency plans to lay that he didn't really want Closs getting wind of. And that Jefferson preferred to implement in person.

Not that he ever expected to have to use any of this. But it was good to have a fallback position.

The bioengineering labs were on the *Richardson Explorer,* a massive vessel currently moored about thirteen kilometers offshore, using the oldest group of omelite platforms as its base. The labs were too delicate to trust to a barge in Novo Haven, and trying to build a permanent structure bigger than a minifab on land on Greene's World was an exercise in pissing to windward. If unstable earth didn't collapse into sinkholes beneath it, a vast tropical storm would scour it from the surface.

On Greene's World, security meant being able to run.

Jefferson took a helicopter out. He flew himself, because the day was clear and he needed the hours, and it was just as well if Closs couldn't corner his pilot and ask awkward questions. All of Charter Trade's helicopter pilots were ex-military, and all of them revered Timothy Closs.

The clear morning gave Jefferson dazzling light off the water, and he spent the brief flight marveling as he always did at the view through the poly floor panels. The bay itself was brilliant as white spinel, the drop-off to the gulf delineated by the dashed row of drilling platforms.

Any clouds were scudding, cotton-candy things, but Jefferson double-checked the weather report compulsively. Weather blew up unexpectedly in Novo Haven, and cyclone season was upon them. Not that a real howler would come tearing out of the tropics without a week of warnings to get the city out of the way—and Rim's Exigency Corps conjuring like hell to bend its path in the least harmful direction—but savage squalls could arise out of nowhere. And helicopters were inherently delicate creatures, hanging as they did from a single joint.

The flight, for all his caution, was uneventful. The *Richardson Explorer* had cleared her landing deck for him. After setting his chopper in the bull's-eye and powering down, he clambered out of the bubble and met the second mate on deck. "Don't worry," he called, as soon as he was close enough to make himself heard over the sea wind without screaming. "This isn't an inspection tour."

The woman smiled too much, but at least it wasn't that canned fake laughter. "Dr. Schaffner is waiting for you below."

He followed her down. Her role of tour guide could have been played by any ensign, and he amused himself by deciding, as they walked, if he would choose to accept the honor in the spirit in which it was offered, or have a word with the captain about the wasteful use of trained officers.

Maybe a memo, he decided, rather than picking a fight today. And one that didn't mention this particular officer's name: she was trying too hard, but her heart was obviously in the right place.

The forward bioengineering lab was two decks down, still well above the waterline. The second officer rapped on the door, then opened it from a keypad.

"Why knock if you're going to let yourself in?"

She shrugged, lifting the handle. "It's polite to let them know we're coming." And stepped aside to let him precede her.

He followed her into an unpleasant, echoing space. The ceilings were low, metal, ringing back sounds with hard crispness. The long room was crossed at regular intervals by slate-topped tables cluttered with interfaces, isolation hoods, incubators. A centrifuge hulked at one end of the nearest lab bench like an irate stone toad. Other things hummed or dinged; Jefferson winced.

He glanced over his shoulder at the second officer. She shrugged. "The safety officer is always after them to wear ear protection in here."

"I'll see to it," Jefferson said. "Why haven't they requisitioned soundproofing?"

"We were denied, M~ Greene."

He turned. White noise had drowned out her footsteps, but Dr. McCarter's voice carried over the machinery hum. She was a tall woman, broad-shouldered, made taller and broader by high-heeled slides and a white labcoat. She was a startling blue-eyed blond, her hair twisted up at the nape of her neck. Jefferson wondered how much of it was a skin; she didn't affect particularly pretty, but there was something about the eyebrows and eyes that was very...engaging. "*Denied?*"

When she smiled, her cheeks appled. Even when it was as insincere a smile as she used now. "An unnecessary expense, Chairman. If you would come with me? Dr. Schaffner is expecting us. He's just selecting some images for you to look at."

Jefferson glanced around the lab, with special attention to the scraped ceiling. He hurried two steps to catch up, aware of the second officer's understated withdrawal. "Unnecessary?"

"So the lab budget committee informed us. This way, please?" She gestured through a sliding door; he stepped through, and it sealed behind them, cutting the worst of the noise. This was a smaller compartment, the walls upholstered in noise-dampening foam. Dr. Schaffner sat before a wood-topped desk, hunched over an interface. He peered one-eyed through an eyepiece, and lifted one hand in greeting as they came in.

"Hello, Doctor."

"Jeff."

Schaffner got up, rubbing his nose to smooth away the dent from the eyepiece, and blinked a few times to refocus. He stuck out his left hand, and Jefferson shook it while Dr. McCarter stepped back, rounding the desk to the far side.

Schaffner was slab-cheeked, tall, a little stooped, with theatrically busy eyebrows. He continued. "I've picked out some good ones to show you, but I hope you don't think this is going to be easy. Or fast, for that matter."

Jefferson nodded, taking the chair Schaffner gestured him into. He smoothed his hands over the warm wood of the table, considering its contrast to the dinged and whining equipment on the other side of the wall. "What are we talking about here, in terms of fast?"

"Years," Schaffner said. He fielded a significant glance from McCarter and amended, "Years at the earliest, reasonably speaking. If we had a sample of the pathogen to back-engineer, it would be different, of course. But we—"

"—don't. I understand. Hey, Neil, what if you got lucky?"

"How lucky? Lucky enough, we could have you something—for testing, not for use—in a few months, but that's so unlikely I wouldn't want to hang a statistic on it."

"I think the chairman is asking what would happen if he saw to it that we got lucky," McCarter translated, without looking up. She seemed to be scanning files on her headset; Jefferson caught the telltale flicker of her eyes and the micromotion of her fingers. "If I'm not out of place in saying so."

Was her voice cool? Or was she distracted? She seemed not to notice as Jefferson eyed her, briefly. He cleared his throat and said, "How come you can get a hardwood interface, but no ceiling tiles?"

The last directed at Schaffner, who rolled his eyes theatrically. "Because the desk comes from equipment and durable goods, and the tiles come through facilities. Genius, isn't it?"

Jefferson shook his head. "Genius. I'll see if I can get somebody fired for you, Neil. Now, what about these pictures you wanted me to see?"

Schaffner reached for the control, hesitated with his fingertips resting against it. "Was Judith right, about what you were offering?"

Jefferson nodded. "Yes, if you'll take the entanglement. It's painless."

Neil Schaffner looked at him, pale eyes catching light under the silver thatch of his hair. He pushed the start control.

"I'm going to need some ranid volunteers."

It wasn't a great idea to call Moon Morrow for comfort, but somehow Closs found himself doing it anyway. He caught her at lunch, dining from hand-painted china with delicate silver manipulators. The food was bitter greens and some cold, rare, shaved red meat. Bison, probably, unless it was offworld. He didn't imagine that Morrow would eat anything as unsafe as Earth beef, even if it were possible to get.

She wrapped greens in a shred of meat and raised them to her mouth, balancing the bundle on slender tools. He waited until she had swallowed and cleared her palate with a sip of water. He was opening his mouth to request her attention when she fixed him with a glance and interrupted. "There's been another attack, Timothy."

His voice died with the breath that carried it. "Where?"

A transfer icon blipped red in the corner of his display. Expecting a map or a series of still images, he accepted the data stream. And found himself immersed in VR as if dumped into fifty feet of water in a weighted vest—the images rushing past him while he struggled to start breathing, to remember to keep moving the air in and out.

And then the hard-earned combat reflexes took over, and—like a fish dumped overboard—Closs began to swim.

A starship—not a lighter, no, and he still read consoles well enough to see that they were slowing from relativistic; inbound rather than outbound, then. Alarm claxons sounded outside his helmet; he was suited and armed, the powerpack of a beam weapon weighing across his back. This ship had been relativistic for some time; the equipment was not unlike what he'd used when he was active duty.

For a moment, he was afflicted with a powerful sense of déjà vu. He could have been twenty-two and a lieutenant again, a kid fresh from Titan Academy, with more brains and guts than sense. But then the body he rode in moved and he wasn't in charge of it, and he relaxed. This was a game he'd played as a line commander, riding along in the back of a sergeant's or lieutenant's head—sometimes four or twelve at once. The miracle of modern warfare: even the guy at the back knew what was going on at the front, from many angles.

He couldn't imagine what it must have been like when you had nothing to go on but estimated positions, radio reports, and guesswork. What a way to fight a war.

He checked his vehicle's vital stats—PFC Amelie Heaney, age twenty-three (or about 115, nonrelativistic), currently nursing a sprained ankle from training

and a sour stomach from the antifungals she was taking for a welting, cracking case of athlete's foot.

The information might flow faster, but the soldier's
lot never changed. Currently, her heart rate was elevated, her eyes were darting port and starboard and up
and down, and she was only breathing slow and deep
because she was consciously regulating the pattern.
Her squad was six; two were right behind her, three
more detailed to survey a different corridor. Her ship
was the Earth Core Company *True Blue*, and she was
one of twenty-four marines on board, each of them
working out a resettlement stake.

Their normal concern was pirates, though PFC
Heaney had never seen one. She thought they were
pretty romantic, for space scum—striking, pillaging,
and vanishing into the future on a trail of hard-bent
light. But there weren't many; cargo didn't travel by
shipping, which left only the ransom for human lives
to interest an opportunist. So they mostly struck shipping close to its point of origin, while there might still
be somebody alive on the homeworld who cared.

Once they'd passed the halfway point, she'd started
anticipating a quiet trip.

And it had been. Until about ten minutes ago.

And now she was sidling along the *True Blue*'s aft
main corridor, her half-squad guarding her back, a
beam cannon strapped to her right arm, and every
siren on the ship warning of imminent hull breach.
Unless they wanted the ship herself, PFC Heaney
didn't have the first idea what might be going on.

Closs envied her innocence. Because now Morrow
was feeding him schematics, the real-time record of
the ship's nervous system, the sensory motes that
webbed her hull and bulkheads. That knowledge overlaid Heaney's advance, and he wanted to shout at her,

as her own commander must be doing, that the hull ten yards down the corridor was losing integrity, that the corridor would soon be violently open to space.

He multitasked; Morrow threw more feeds at him. He could handle the six half-squad leaders; he made Heaney primary—she was closest to an incipient breach—and watched the other five peripherally, also prioritizing the hull sensorium.

Heaney and her squadmates quit their cautious slide and hustled. Forward, not back, as befitted marines. Their goal was to clear the airproof bulkheads and be on-site when the boarding party came in through the breach. External cameras were showing something weird; not just crawlers ripping the shielding with armored talons, but a night-black macro-fog, a machine made of multiple-component machines—each as big as Closs's fist, and black enough that the object looked at first like a missing patch in the hull of the *True Blue*. It flexed against the hull like a starfish humping a submarine, and sudden white crystals glittered around it.

The snow-globe effect was why Closs knew a split second before Heaney did that the hull had been breached. She found out the hard way; the joints of her vacuum suit stiffened, and the boarding claxons fell silent, though she could still feel their shiver through the magnetic soles of her boots. In the corridor, both behind the half-squad and ahead, airlock shields crashed down, sealing them in.

The rush of expelled air ripped at her suit, but the magnets held, and she was still planted solidly, bringing her weapon to bear, when a knobby matte black tendril curled through the rent in the hull. It groped, twitched, telescoped at the marines with reflexive speed—

Heaney's weapon lashed out silently—no atmosphere to sizzle under its bolt—and was followed a

split-second later by those of her squadmates. There
was a projecting bulkhead on either side of the sealed
airlock and just inside, designed to provide cover; the
squad dove behind it.

Just in time, as the black tendril slammed after
them. It sparked and arced, withdrew, shedding ragged
bits of eviscerated foglets. Some of the component machines stuttered and twitched on the corridor floor.
Heaney kicked one away as it grabbed at her suit; the
armor held. The thing went flying.

She looked up to see the tendril coming apart into
hundreds—thousands—of crawling machines...

Morrow cut the feed. Closs slumped against his desk
chair, rolling his shoulders back. His right hand ached
from clenching on the trigger of Heaney's weapon.
"All of them?" he asked.

Boarding, making sure that the marines and crew
saw the enemy, interacted with them...when the enemy could have just shot a big rock at the *True Blue*.
Starships were impossibly easy to destroy. This didn't
make any sense. He looked at her, image to image,
light-years between them, and waited for her to give
him an answer he could accept.

She shook her head, and failed him. "It took the
ship apart," Morrow said. "Find me a solution, Tim."

Clean, dry, illegally skinned, and wearing stolen
clothes, Cricket spent the next morning and afternoon
hiding in plain sight. It was both easier and harder
than she expected, and quite strange overall, because
she didn't dare connex.

She could surf news through a public terminal, but
she wasn't confident that the false persona she'd
chipped off the stuff in her jump kit would hold up to

a Rim security scan. She had a nasty suspicion that
something had come in with the information that
Lucienne had sent her.

The data was tagged, maybe. And the data was in
her head. And there didn't seem to be much she could
do about it, because Cricket couldn't find the tag, or
beacon, or whatever might be in there.

Which was a problem long-term, if she wanted to
live. Or if she ever wanted to work again. And a problem
immediately, in that activities as simple as hailing a water taxi or paying her lunch tab became infinitely more
complicated when you couldn't just connex the bill. She
had money; her jump identity was supplied. But access-
ing or using it was going to be a real trick.

There *was* somebody she could talk to, if she wanted
to take the chance. André trusted him. But André
trusted Cricket, too, which wasn't exactly a testimonial
to his excellent judgment.

How far she'd fallen, if Nouel Huc was the best she
could do for an ally.

She was waiting at the Zheleznyj Tigr when the
doors opened. She paid at the door, with a dwindling
cash card, and was the first one into the club. Uncool,
but she wanted to beat Huc here.

At least André was unreachable. Huc couldn't ring
him up and spill the beans; whatever Jean Kroc
said about André's motivation, Cricket didn't trust
him either. She didn't trust his ethics or his glib
head full of self-justifying stories and she didn't buy
his motives for wanting to learn to conjure. But
she'd had that fight with Jean, and Jean was as stubborn as they came. It didn't matter how many times
Cricket pointed out that André was the worst kind of
sorcerer's apprentice—the sort that lied and snuck and
eventually betrayed. Jean was sure he could save

André, and if he couldn't save André, that he could
use him.

And Jean was mad enough to see it as a challenge,
too. A test of his dedication, to reclaim the man who
had killed Lucienne.

She wasn't going to make excuses for Jean Kroc. He
knew the parable of the snake as well as she did. He
was just crazy enough to think himself immune.

She picked a round table at the front, near the stage.
Nouel Huc's habitual table, with its red-handkerchief-
hemmed tablecloth and its white waxflowers nodding
sleepily in the vase. The server tried to talk her into another seat, but she tipped her head and said, "I'm expected."

She wasn't pretty enough to be believed, not dressed
like this. But Huc did his own species of business, and
his clients weren't all as natty as André.

"Will you be on M~ Huc's account?" the server
asked, with at least a show of politeness.

Cricket thought of the dwindling balance on her
cash card. "Yes."

Let Huc take it out of her hide. She had enough to
offer that he could stand her the cost of a meal.

Whether the staff of the Zheleznyj Tigr called him,
or whether he was just running early, it was less than a
quarter before she looked up to find his shadow falling
across her. "M~ Huc," she said, placing a hand on the
edge of the table to help her balance to her feet. He
laid a hand on her shoulder and she sat back.

It was a reassuring hand, whether or not he meant it
to be. "I understand we are acquainted?"

She relaxed into the chair as he stepped away,
moved around the table, and sat. She liked the way he
set his elbows on the table, too, wide apart, and leaned
forward between them, not bothering to hide an

amused smile. He wanted her to soak in that warmth, she thought. Soak in it, drown in it. Trust him.

He was better at it than André, and she thought he could probably also beat up her father if he had to. But she really didn't need to go about collecting spare thugs. Not right now.

"Not under any name it's safe for me to use," she said. Her skins were pretty good; they'd hold up even under a parser filter. "But I'm a friend of André Deschênes."

"How close of a friend?"

"Very," she said, calmly.

He nodded. "We've met before. You've changed your hair."

"And everything else," she answered, and he laughed. "I'm in trouble, M~ Huc."

"Call me Nouel," he said, and patted her hand. "You may speak freely here. Though I'm recording."

"Thank you, Nouel." She hesitated, and he stepped in smoothly to fill the silence.

"And what shall I call you?"

Cricket hesitated. There was the name on her false ID, of course, but that was intentionally bland. She wanted something that was less of a lie, at least as much hers as *Cricket*. "Fisher," she said, after consideration. "Like the cat."

"There's a cat named Fisher?"

"No," she said, laughing. "There's a kind of weasel they used to have in the part of Earth where I grew up. They were called fisher cats. They weren't cats. And they didn't fish."

"Ah," he said. He looked up and waved the server over. "I see. And you're not what you pretend to be either. One moment"—as he ordered wine in a lowered tone—"please, continue. Are you a fisher, Fisher?"

"I'm a data miner," she said. "And I have some information I will pay very handsomely to get to Jean Gris."

"And there's a reason you can't deliver the information yourself."

She had her mouth open to answer as the wine came, and held her tongue while Nouel pronounced it acceptable. The server filled their water glasses. They ordered, and as the first course was brought to the table, Cricket reminded herself that it was unwise to let him penetrate her defenses so easily. Formidable charm and a formidable wit did not translate to unassailable honesty.

When she had eaten the first few bites, he smiled and said, "So. You owe Jean Gris money."

Cricket had been waiting for it, and so she managed a cool look, rather than bursting out laughing. "If it pleases you to think so."

"If there are greater risks," Nouel said, with a negligent gesture of his snail pick, "it would be clever of you to inform me of your reasons. It will affect the precautions necessary to see that your message goes through."

"I have several reasons, all of them excellent."

His right hand rolled through the air, two fingers extended as if winding the words from her throat onto a ribbon.

She shook her head. "It would be safer for you not to know."

"M~ Fisher, you have just described my stock-in-trade in its entirety. Perhaps you would be so good as to explain to me exactly what you need, and what you are willing to pay?"

Which was the challenge she would have to meet, of course. She sipped wine, rolling it over her tongue, almost shocked by wood and vanilla. It had been a long time since she'd had wine like this. Part of successfully reinventing one's self, of shedding an old personality, was reinventing *everything*. Likes, dislikes, favorite places, the type of people one associated with. Not just the hair, the clothes, the skin, the postures. To become someone new, you had to swallow it whole, without reservation.

Cricket Earl Murphy wasn't a wine drinker. Maybe Fisher would be, when Fisher became more real. "I have an entire clean established legal persona to offer," she said. "Also, five thousand demarks in cash or cash-equivalent. And a favor from an archinformist. In return, I want a message taken to Jean Gris, and I want assistance in documenting another legal persona, though I'll do the hackwork myself. I just need somebody who can forge the necessary. The problem is that the message I need sent to Jean is all in my head and I need a clean isolated system to download it to, because I think I have a beacon in my head as well, and I can't connex. Jean, by the way, is no doubt being watched. Which is why I don't dare go to him."

"You're offering a lot for some pretty simple requests."

She wasn't going to tell him about Lucienne. If he'd helped André do it, she didn't want to force him into a conflict of interest. "I have proof that Rim is covering up a major ecological disaster in progress," she said baldly, and forked up a mouthful of scallop sashimi and shredded radish. "I'd like to force them to do something about it before they poison Greene's World so badly that Novo Haven goes the way of Patience Station or Port Katherine."

Fifty years after a reactor core excursion, a radius of a hundred miles around the former planetary seat of

Enlil was still uninhabitable. Cricket couldn't be held personally responsible for *that* one, but the long shadow of Port Katherine had been one of the cudgels used to bludgeon her from office... when she had been someone else. She scratched a nail across the table-cloth, feeling the tip catch, bend, and release on each thread. "Nouel?"

He seemed suitably impressed, still staring into his wineglass with his lips pursed out and twisted. He glanced up when she said his name. "You trust me not to go to Rim with this? There'd be a lot of money in it."

"Enough to retire on," she agreed. "And you'd have to."

In an industry where contracts were unenforceable and a deal was still sealed by a handshake, she wasn't exaggerating. If he turned Cricket in, there wasn't an archinformist on the Rim that would give him so much as the time of day or the local acceleration due to gravity.

He scratched his thumb across his chin. His nod did nothing to ease the tightening wire of tension laced across her spine. This was merely embracing danger in a new shape.

"Stay through the play," he said. "Come home with me tonight. We'll set you up. Now sit tight, won't you, and finish your supper? I have to make a couple of calls."

In the morning, the earth shook. This was not uncommon, and Gourami would usually have slept through it, drifting weightlessly for sleeping, anchored by se toefingers in the bottom mud and with eyes and nostrils just protruding from the water. But it was se watch, predawn, while Tetra dreamed, the human slept in his temporary structure, and Caetei swam hunting. And so Gourami was sprawled on slick mud churned up by mudskitters—driven from their tunnels by the previous day's rain—waiting for the human to awaken.

Gourami calculated quickly, decided that they were far enough up the bayou that any water surge would spend itself among the reeds and hillocks before it reached them, and rolled supine to sun se belly. Rustling shook the tent; the human struggling into his clothing, no doubt. Gourami licked eyes to clear the night's grit from them, the warm sun flooding se veins with heat and energy. Se couldn't sun too long, but se could certainly use a little exothermal assistance in digesting last night's excellent meal.

And then the earth shook again, harder and sustained, and Gourami flipped upright and crouched. Se trilled an alarm note. There was a thrash, a splash, Tetra jerking awake, and now thumping inside the tent and some humen noises. A moment later, André flailed out, his boots flopping unsealed. Gourami lurched forward, croaking in dismay, already certain what would follow.

Se did not reach the human in time.

He hit the fallen reeds, which were covered in the layer of wet silt and rotting plant matter the mudskitters had expectorated. He took three staggering, sliding steps, windmilling his arms, and for a moment Gourami almost thought he was going to regain his precarious biped balance. Their mode of locomotion was just falling forward and catching themselves anyway; how hard could it be for them to stop an unintentional falling?

Hard enough, apparently. He went down ugly, all weird angles and wiggling, whatever noise he made audible to a person's ears as a high-pitched yelp, and he hit the mud with a quick green-sounding pop. The earth was still shuddering, a long hard rumble, and Gourami wanted to be in the water so badly se skin itched. Instead, se dragged across the splintery reeds on all fours, scratching palms and ankles, miraculously making it to the fallen human's side without putting a stick through webbing.

The human lay on his back, one leg tucked under him and the other splayed out. He panted heavily. That was good; he was alive. His eyes were screwed up like fish mouths, though, little puckers in a sweating face, and his hands clutched into the mud and reeds, fingers sunk deep. Gourami did not think that was promising.

Se reached out, tentatively, and touched the back of a humen hand. He groaned, and se flinched back, realizing as se did so that the earth had stopped shuddering. Whatever noises he was making weren't words, se didn't think, except occasionally when his mouth moved in the shapes of profanity.

He couldn't read a slate if he didn't open his eyes, and se made a louder, insistent noise. A vibrato thrum, as one would use to summon egglings. Se remembered something about humen bones; they were all hard, calcified, like skulls and jawbones, and like skulls and jawbones they could shatter.

Se tapped his hand again, harder. His eyes opened this time, pupils contracted. Sweat stood out in beads across his scalp and trickled down the furrows alongside his nose; humen did that because they could not secrete mucous, and also when they were in pain or shock. Gourami had seen injured humen before.

Se thought this might be bad.

André blinked, several times, breathing more evenly now, as if consciously controlling each intake and outflow. Could humen do that? They must be able, because Gourami could see the lines that meant concentration or fear or anger—fuzzy creatures, one signal for so many things—and they were easing as he breathed. Se typed quickly, for once using the abbreviations se usually spurned.

—*u need hlp*

He nodded, and mouthed —*I broke it. And my back is cut, I think.*

The reeds, of course. Fingerpads skipped over keys.

—*let tetra look*

Se came beside Gourami, hanging back a little, and touched Gourami's ankle to steady them both. André nodded again, and closed his eyes, waiting, while Tetra and Gourami quickly deflated the shelter and dragged it down beside the injured mammal. Gourami tucked what se could of it under his shoulder and hip on the side that seemed less hurt. He could help, at least. He lifted his hand and reached up into the air when she pushed the fabric under his torso, but rolling his hip up made him squeak.

His hands were already palm-flat, in the mud and on the fabric; when Gourami touched him again and made se hands tumble over and over, he nodded sharply. Se saw a taut flicker cross his face at the same time the muscles in his arms and shoulders tensed, and he levered himself up and over, falling face-first onto the tent. Tetra caught the injured leg before it could fall, but André shuddered anyway, like a dying fish, and went slack and still.

—*breathing*, Gourami said, holding fingers under André's nose to feel the tickle of air moving.

Tetra was looking at the limb. —*This is bad.*

Gourami looked at it, too, and retracted head between shoulders, an instinctive pained flinch. Thick
blood dripped over Tetra's fingers and stained se webs;
something white showed through torn flesh above the
lip of the humen boot. His back was cut up, too, but he
hadn't impaled himself; the bits of reed poking
through his shirt were only slivers.

—*Give him to the humen? They can help.*

—*Make him uplink when he wakes?* Gourami asked.
I will hide. Except.

—*He's bleeding now. How long will it take him to
wake? Will he die before then?*

—*Yes. Those are problems. And also, if we send him
back, Closs will send somebody else.* And, Gourami
thought, sending André back now wouldn't help to
teach him any of the things that Jean Kroc wanted
him taught. And se had promised Jean Kroc.

They had a bargain.

And anyway, André's luck was suddenly, coincidentally, very bad, wasn't it? As if somebody were changing it.

—*We take him to the one-tree-island band. It's not far
and they will hear us if we call,* se said, deciding. And
was surprised when Tetra, a far-swimmer, did not
argue.

Se just said, instead, —*go call them. I will keep his
limb from falling.*

As Gourami wriggled toward the water, the earth
began to shake again.

10

JEFFERSON WOKE TO THE SHRIEK OF AN EMERGENCY CON-
tact alarm and a blue light winking by his bed. He came
up clear-headed and with his hands trembling; his
headset read the coded transmission and dumped epi-
nephrine into his system. A call waited; he swung his
feet to the floor, covers tangled around his ankles, and
scrubbed granules from his eyes. "What the hell is it?"

Amanda Delarossa, the god-botherer. "Chairman,
we have a problem."

He stood, turned off alarm and flasher with a
thought. His wife rolled over and pulled the pillow
over her head. "Fill me in," he said, heading for the
closet. "What's going on?"

"Did you notice the earthquakes?"

"I'm afloat," he said. "I don't hear the tsunami
siren."

"No," she said. "No tsunami. Here"—she hypertexted a link—"look at this."

Once upon a time, humans had bothered to use different terms when they studied of the dynamics of different planets. Now, it was all geology; separate names get unwieldy when you're talking about more than ten or fifteen worlds. The site Dr. Delarossa sent him to was the Greene's World seismic and vulcanology monitoring project, usually quite heavily dotted with recent activity. Jefferson thought it had something to do with the planet's astounding tides, but he wasn't even remotely a scientist.

He knew where his drill platforms were, however, and the three yellow star shapes on the globe that indicated quakes in the last quarter were all centered firmly along the edge of the continental shelf, offshore of Novo Haven, where his omelite wells blossomed. "That's unusual."

"Dr. Gupta has a secure packet for you," Delarossa said. "He's produced a very unsettling hypothesis."

"Send it," Jefferson said. His call-waiting blinked. "Closs is on the other line. I have to go."

In the morning, Cricket went to see a fortune-teller. She knew better, but you couldn't always let that stop you.

Nouel had warned her to lie low before he went out, but she couldn't stand another quarter stuck in a cabin on his barge, trying to get some work done with the clunky manual interface he'd scrounged for her. She couldn't risk connex, even with her hard memory downloaded; whatever was leading Rim to her might not be gone. She'd have to scrub the whole thing and reformat, which she should do anyway, before she installed her new history. So she spent maybe three quarters click-clacking on the keyboard and then got up, found her shoes on their sides under the sofa, and stuffed her feet into them while she skinned. She made herself a blue-eyed blond and about a half-decimeter taller, and used the good stuff—high-grade wearez, implants she wasn't supposed to have. She'd gotten them on Earth, after she ducked out of jail. Or sent her clone to prison in her place, to speak precisely.

She didn't use them often; mere possession was illegal. She'd run light-years to stay out of prison, created a whole new person and betrayed her. Whatever self-knowledge she'd found, it wasn't the sort that left one eager to pay for one's mistakes.

The skin would hide her from just about anything, though. An ordinary cosmetic skin affected the perceptions of the viewer through his headset. *This* was a nanotech hack, and physically altered her fingerprints and retinal scan. She'd have to drop it to get out of Nouel's house and back in: he'd introduced her to his expert system, which expected her to look and smell and scan like herself.

Every plan had its flaw. But sometimes, living in the future was damned cool. Even if she couldn't get a rocket car.

She wandered through a too-warm morning, window-shopping geomancers and fortune readers. No friend of Jean Kroc's could take a storefront tarot reader seriously, but it beat waiting by the door for Nouel to come back.

And she had never been good at waiting for men.

She picked a place at random and pushed through the half-door, which was hung with bells and chimes made of silicate shells so that a layered tinkling surrounded her. Inside, she stood in shadowy coolness; fans moved air across her skin, soothing her nape. She peeled sticky strands from her neck, rubbing fingers smearing sweat rather than relieving her discomfort. "Hello?"

A thin, stooped man came out of the back, his hair a colorless fringe against his weathered forehead. "Early riser," he said. "What's your pleasure, M~?"

"Tell me a story," she said, and took the three-legged stool he gestured her toward.

"Your own or someone else's?"

She shrugged. It didn't matter. One lie was as good as another. "Whatever's more interesting." She extended her hand, in case he wanted it. He ignored it, and instead lit a candle with a gestured flame. Just a neat bit of wearez, but pretty. She wondered where he'd gotten the candle, and if it was the same place Jean Kroc went for his.

There was a mirror on the table, facedown on black silk. The fortune-teller turned it over with a flourish. Cricket was unsurprised to see nothing reflected in it but rippling black.

"Twenty," the fortune-teller said, and Cricket chipped him the cash from an anonymous account. He blinked crystal projection contacts over his irises—checking his balance, she guessed, and not wired for connex or hard memory. A lot of mystics got fussy about things like that, though most not as hardcore as Jean. Others didn't seem to care at all, and some had swallowed as much wire as Cricket had. "It works better if you ask a question."

"It works better if I give you hints, you mean," she said. She folded her arms across her chest and leaned back in her chair, aware how defensive her body language was and not caring at all. "Sorry. You're on your own."

After all, where was the entertainment if she gave it all away? Far more fun to watch him thrash.

A real conjure wouldn't play these games. This wasn't how the mojo worked. It wasn't for parlor tricks.

"You're not a believer?"

"Let's say I'm willing to be convinced." Jean Kroc had convinced her. Lucienne had convinced her—

Oh, hell. She sniffled as he bent over his water-dark mirror, studying the reflection of the flame. It was the only thing that showed there. A pretty good trick, Cricket thought. Probably a skin as well. Still, it was pretty.

Which made it better than half of everything in the world already. Maybe better than two thirds.

"There's a man," he said, after a few quiet moments. She caught the wet flicker of his eyeballs through his lashes as he glanced up to check her reaction. It was as good a starting point as any, and unless she was an orphaned lesbian, likely to provoke some kind of a response.

"Of course there is," she answered, amused. As long as you didn't take it seriously, you could look at these little trips as a cheap sort of psychoanalysis. And it sure beat the stuffing out of talk therapy with an idiot expert system. "Are you going to tell me that he's tall, dark, and dangerous?"

"Actually," the fortune-teller said, sitting back and crossing his own arms in mirror of her own, "I was going to tell you to look out for a frog to kiss. But you seem to have arrived with a narrative intact."

It set her back on her heels, or would have, if she had been standing. Instead, she tossed her hair back and tucked her chin in, and started to laugh. "All right," she said. "You get points for that one. I'll quit giving you a hard time."

"Oh, just be yourself," he said, bending over the mirror again. "I enjoy a challenge."

It was still bullshit, but once they decided they liked each other, he spun her a pretty good story. It even ended happily ever after, though there were trials and tribulations enough in the midgame to make the solution seem earned. Cricket left in a much better mood than when she had arrived, promising to keep an eye out for kissable frogs. She bought a cinnamon-sugar-crusted bagel from a street vendor and ate it steaming warm as she walked back to Nouel's barge, wondering if he would even notice she had gone.

He was waiting for her in the sitting room, with a slender man she knew by reputation, a soft-cheeked archinformist with a coil of neon light up one ear like the stripped half of a DNA helix. They'd never met in the flesh before, but that didn't mean anything to a data miner.

She hadn't known, even, that he lived on Greene's World. But she did know that he worked, almost exclusively, for Timothy Closs. Betrayal was a stone in her belly, and she couldn't shift it just by swallowing, even when she told herself that she'd expected Nouel to hand her her head and had just been too fucking tired to really care.

Sorry, Lucienne.

"Fuck," she said, as the door hissed shut behind her. "I should have gone out looking for that fucking frog prince instead."

André woke mostly dry, mostly clean, and muzzy-headed. Before he opened his eyes, he let himself lie

still, breathing, assessing the place in which he found
himself. He was pin-and-needle prickles from the
waist down, which was both reassuring and unsettling;
if he was badly enough hurt to need a neural block, he
was badly hurt indeed.

Except—

Whatever he was lying on smelled more like compost than a hospital bed. Green and sour-sweet and
heavy, and so when he opened his eyes he wasn't expecting the papery green of trauma wards. It *was*
green, green and fawn, and he jerked reflexively when
he saw the reed-woven roof overhead, thatched with
feathertree leaves.

Whatever numbed him, it wasn't narcotics. His
movement brought sharper pain, an agonizing twist up
his leg that he felt in his eye sockets and across the
bridge of his nose. His hands curled into the bedding
he lay on; a rank scent arose. It was moist and soft, and
it wasn't at all the sort of thing he would normally
sleep on.

The pain was vast. He lay back, balling his fists
against his eyes, and concentrated on breathing. His
leg throbbed; the pain paled and ebbed while he out-
waited it.

He opened his eyes again. Everything was flat—
undetailed, unaugmented—and real. The colors were
off, the sounds muddy. This was a disconnect beyond
merely shutting down his connex. Visual detail was
sparse and undefined: he could not see the fronds of
the feathertree thatch stirring in the breeze. Rather, a
general sense of movement told him what must be
happening, two meters over his head. He caught motion, and some part of his brain extrapolated it into an
image.

Peculiar as all hell. It left him feeling half blind.

And unable to call for rescue. His headset was as useless as a pair of empty seashells strapped to his ears, as useless as his leg and his goose-egged, aching head. He didn't know how long he'd lain unconscious, but it was awhile, if the froggies had managed to throw a shelter over him.

But it was still daylight. Unless it was daylight again.

The leg was splinted uncomfortably, the padded ends of flat restraints pressing André's thigh above the knee. When he stretched even slightly, nauseating ripples of heat rolled up his leg from his shin again. Definitely broken. He grunted and closed his eyes until the pain subsided, then cautiously lifted himself onto his elbow.

The shelter had no walls. By the sun, he guessed it was late morning or early afternoon, and he could see enough mud to know that he was on a different island. If a mud spit in a swamp could be dignified with the term.

This one was larger and dryer and taller, though it still bore signs of periodic submersion. Half a dozen ranids clustered before the reeds, crouched or sprawled, their green and yellow mottles almost invisible against green and yellow leaves.

André couldn't tell them apart. Except maybe the tall one, draped in a net vest hung with old treasures, pierced trophies, jingling shells. That might be Tetra. Beside it huddled a crippled ranid, missing an arm from long ago, one side a ragged mess of scar tissue and proud flesh. André wondered if it had caught up with the wrong end of a nessie.

Another ranid bobbed forward, not as strikingly long and lean-limbed as the one he thought might be Tetra. If he could get a good look at the mottles on its

back he might be able to tell, but for the meantime, as
it extended a slate, he decided to risk it. "Gourami?"

It had to repeat that peculiar hand-puppet-like motion of its body before he realized it was imitating a
human headshake. Pain dropped from his immediate
awareness, replaced by an uncharacteristic spike of
worry. "Is it safe?"

A scritchy-looking affirmative, from its free hand.
André let his breath out slowly, wobbly with dumped
adrenaline. Everything seemed muted, gray. *And what
were you going to do if it wasn't?*

Panic, obviously. He did *not* want to be the one who
explained to Jean Kroc that he had lost Jean's froggie.
And anyway, the frog was...kind of engaging.

Not that he needed to be getting paternalistic about
alien amphibians. Getting soft wasn't a good way to
succeed in André's line of work, or even a good way to
stay alive. He spared a moment to picture Timothy
Closs or Jefferson Greene worrying about a coolie, and
shook his head to clear it.

Getting soft wasn't the way to get ahead in anybody's line of work.

A moment's thought lead him to the obvious conclusion: "Caetei?"

And that was better: this time, it scritched affirma-
tion with one hand, then thrust the slate at him again.
It hurt even more to prop himself on one elbow and accept the device, so he dropped his shoulders back
against the pallet. It was surprisingly comfortable, if a
bit moist. His shirt adhered to his shoulders and his
trousers—with one leg cut away midthigh—adhered
to his buttocks and legs. He didn't think it was all blood
or sweat or swampwater. Whatever the ranids used for
bedding, on the other hand...

—*Good u wake*, the ranid's slate said, as he raised it in front of his eyes. —*Tide rsng*.

They couldn't be too far upriver, then. The New Nile boasted only a shallow gradient, and as far as André knew, if it hadn't been for the mitigating effects of the rushy bayou and the paramangrove, the tides might roll miles up the broad, placid river. But those features existed, and even Greene's World's embarrassment of lunar influences couldn't quite push the ocean through them. The New Nile remained an outflow channel.

The ranids must have moved him out-bayou, closer to the bay, because the tides had been minimal at the overnighting island. The move was good, a smart thing; it would make it easier for a rescue team to reach him.

"Move where?" he asked slowly, enunciating.

He couldn't heads-up the time or a tide chart, but Caetei had no reason to lie to him. That didn't reassure him as he metaphorically picked his way around the fissures in his mind caused by his headset. Even his hard memory was out of service, leaving an unsettling gap. He wondered how much was irretrievably lost. He had backups, of course. He was sane and careful and not as thoroughly paranoid as Jean Kroc, nor the sort to take mad risks. The backups were a vulnerability, of course, the sort that somebody like Cricket could exploit if she knew where to find them, which was why André's were hidden, physical access only, and keycoded.

Unfortunately, that meant he had to get *to* them to get them back.

"I can't move myself," he continued, when Caetei did not reach to answer.

This time it typed quickly. —*We move b4.*

It reached down and tapped a stick by its foot; André, in a moment of disconnect, realized that he was lying not on a pallet as he'd assumed, but on a sort of stretcher. "I need medical help."

—*We take u grtprnt.*

...whatever that was. A witch doctor? Some sort of ranid village elder? A bayou-living human? The froggie equivalent of Sitting Bull?

It sounded very significant. But he needed a doctor more than the answer to a coolie xenocultural exam. "Have you sent someone to bring help? I need an evacuation now. The leg will fester."

Caetei might not know that word, but there was probably some kind of translation protocol in the slate. But Caetei stayed stolid and pulled the slate back. It hung it on its belt and crouched beside the shaft of the stretcher. Three more ranids hopped from the weeds. Tetra was not one of them, and all those who came up wore not vests but web belts strung with tools. André remembered that Tetra had some sort of special status in the group, a dominant reproductive and social role. Which perhaps exempted it from work.

Or perhaps it was just tired, and he was reading too much into things. Other ranids were surrounding them now, more than he had noticed waiting, so that his stretcher—his *litter*—was borne in the midst of a sort of hopping, weaving green honor guard. While Caetei was still looking at him, he asked again, "Where is Gourami?"

But Caetei's hands were full, and it didn't answer.

•

Gourami, it transpired, was already where they were going. It lolled in a shallow backwater, the ridges of its hips and its protruding eyes and nostrils breaking the surface. André didn't see it until the others set his litter down on a pair of cross-braces that must have been prepared in advance. A fair amount of planning had gone into this operation.

Gourami paddled to the bank and stood, water sheeting down its sides. It came up to the litter—now a sort of crude couch—and lifted itself up so it met André's eyes directly. It held its slate alongside its face, and blessedly constructed complete sentences containing entire words, vowels and all. —*Are you feeling better, André?*

"I need medical care," he said, for the tenth or eleventh time.

—*Your bone is set,* the ranid answered. —*Tetra did it, and the greatparent remembered-ahead for you. It will heal. You are safer here. There is too much coincidence surrounding you.*

"Shit," he said. But he wasn't entangled. He hadn't taken Closs up on the offer. He couldn't be...

The hail storm. The bad fall.

Somebody was trying to kill him.

It was a wonderfully clarifying realization. A conjure man was after him. Kroc, or somebody from Rim, or another freelancer: it didn't matter. Somebody was trying to kill him.

Good: a circumstance he knew how to deal with. And one he couldn't do much about right now. On the other hand—*greatparent.* There was a word that made some sense of Caetei's incomprehensible string of consonants. What a greatparent might be was another question, and "remembered-ahead" sounded suspiciously like conjuring. If it wasn't superstition and sorcery. But Gourami was blinking at him intently, nictitating membranes flickering across glossy eyes, and he thought it was waiting for an answer.

"What's a greatparent?" he asked.

Gourami chirrupped. One of the other ranids—not Caetei, he thought, but one that was in the water—picked up the noise and made it again, and again. Like clicking one's tongue to summon a pet, almost. —*old personage,* Gourami typed, with amazing speed, its fingers skipping across the controls of its slate. —*se remembers. I have been telling se new stories, that se may keep them safe.*

A pause, as if Gourami revealed a confidence. —*Someday Tetra may be a greatparent, too,* Gourami finally said, and André thought it wasn't exactly what it might have typed. —*Tetra has many stories: se may grow very old. If se can give up swimming. That is always hard, and some do not.*

Gourami typed more, but André did not see it. Because something was rising from the water, great-backed and amorphous, green and dripping with great strings of algae. Its back was as broad as the islet André sat on, and it seemed to have no limbs, only a glass-clean, mucous-slick fringe about its edges, pulsing softly. And eyes: not two only, but all around the rim, and under them mouths, toothless mouths from which water squirted as it rose. Ballast, and probably food, and maybe respiration . . .

He would have stepped—hopped—back if he were standing. As it was, he startled hard enough to rock his improvised seat.

Gourami held up a marked slate again, as Tetra—he was sure it was Tetra, the only one wearing a decorated vest—trilled to the monstrosity rising from the mud. —*André Deschênes, meet the memorizeur . . .*

The symbols that followed were musical notation, a chord progression overlaid by a quick run of simple notes. A ranid's *real* name, written in the only human language that could handle them.

"Delighted," he said, his hands flexing on the carry poles of the litter where they ran along its sides. "Please, ah. Extend my regards. Or whatever the protocol is."

Gourami bobbled, a movement he was starting to anthropomorphize into laughter. —*Se wants to meet a human*, it typed. —*Se has been told much about you, but has never seen one before. Please, sit up straight so se can look. I am sorry for your pain.*

"It's a *crater*," Greene repeated, and despite temptation, Closs—leaning back in a chair in Greene's office—didn't make the chairman go back and explain it a third time. "The whole damned gulf. The Bay of Novo Haven. That's what Gupta thinks, anyway. The omelite deposits are around the rim—which tells us where we might want to drill inland, by the way, because while the river's backfilled some of it, you can see where the original line would have extended—and that's also where the recent earthquakes are centered."

Greene was dressed with particular care, but his eyes were red-rimmed, pupils pinpricked from too much stimulant. He paced, gesticulating at the screen on his office wall with first one hand and then the other, using a light-wand to outline features on a projected detail map. He paused, tapping the wand on his fingertips, and directed a stare at Closs, as if checking to see if Closs had followed him this time.

"And the probability effects our engineers have been struggling with for the past year?" Closs asked, to make Greene say it out loud, to get it into the discussion.

"Strongest at those sites, yes. And radiating out. But are you seeing the implications, Timothy? Gupta's map suggests that the omelite is the side effect of an explosion."

"An impact? It came from *space*?"

Greene shook his head, hands fanning wide, the tip of the light-stick leaving a dazzled streak across Closs's vision. Something wrong with his connex; there should be antiglare protection. "Gupta thinks the explosion was ground level."

"A tanglestone mine. Blew up. An *alien* tanglestone mine." Closs tried to get his brain and his tongue to wrap around the concepts at the same time. "A *ranid* tanglestone mine? You're telling me they had, what, a technological society? *Industrial mining*?" It was hard to imagine worse news for Charter Trade. Not that Rim had encountered one yet, but there were rules in place for dealing with technological societies.

And they did *not* involve colonizing their planets.

"Omelite mines don't just *blow up*. I'm telling you they had a production facility. Whether it was the ranids or some other alien species, hell, maybe colonists here before us. Maybe there was a dominant land species…it doesn't matter. The omelite is a…a by-product. Of whatever they were doing. Of the explosion."

"There'd be an archaeological record," Closs said, very slowly. "If there had been a technological species on Greene's World."

"There might be. Someplace we can't get to it."

"Spare me the Chinese puzzles, Jeff."

Greene took a breath. Closs tensed: he knew that expression. "I have to tell you something about Greene's World. Something important, that almost nobody knows."

"This is going to keep me up nights."

"And how," Greene said, seeming as if he nerved himself. "When I say it's secret, you should know—I mean a proprietary secret. Covered by your nondisclosure clause. Some of the coincidence engineers and physicists are aware. Dr. Gupta is one of them. Other than that, just my grandfather's descendants. And whoever spilled the story to Lucienne Spivak. Not even my wife. Do you understand?"

There was no end to the things Greene's wife didn't know about him, but this didn't seem the time to mention it. "It's that hot?"

"The hottest. Greene's World is potentially unique in the universe."

And other planets aren't? There was something about Greene that made biting your tongue harder than it might be under other circumstances. "Explain, please."

Greene dropped his chin and looked up at Closs through his lashes. "What do you know about the theoretical phenomenon of forking?"

"Like alternate histories?"

"Sort of. I'm not the guy to explain it well—that would be Gupta—but...There's one multi-universe theory that postulates that the timestream is constantly forking, and rehealing—so things come back together again, and refork, and rejoin. So time is like a braided rope where strands keep getting switched around. Except maybe sometimes, after a really catastrophic event, it forks completely. And never reheals."

"Parallel dimensions."

"Sure."

"So?..."

Green sniffled a bit and rubbed his nose. "So an early survey team postulated that Greene's World is partially forked. By which I mean this, this catastrophe..."—he waved vaguely at the lighted map—"almost shook the planet into another dimension. But not quite. There are two of them, in other words, and they...sort of overlap. A quantum bifurcation. And if whatever caused the catastrophe wasn't destroyed in it—"

"It's on the other branch."

"Yes."

It might be early, but Closs suddenly found the idea of a drink supremely attractive. He stood and went to the stand in the corner, but poured himself a cup of coffee instead. "You just explained where tanglestone comes from."

"It's not my explanation."

"What could...cause something like that?"

Greene winced. "There's a reason we don't put Slide facilities on planets, Tim."

On second thought, maybe it wasn't too early for a little whiskey in his coffee. He added cream on top, stirred it meticulously, and turned back to Greene when he was sure he had his face under control. "A Slide failure."

"A prehistoric one. We theorize."

"Can those aliens get back here?"

A shrug. "The probability storms are getting worse—"

"No shit." The coffee was strong, sweet from the whiskey, scalding hot. Closs drank down half the cup in three slow swallows and wiped his mouth against the side of his hand. "The dimensions are...what, pulling apart?"

"Or remerging, as we consume the omelite. If it's the first, pretty soon, no tanglestone. If it's the second—"

Morrow's aliens. What if they didn't come from…somewhere else, exactly? But right here, right…alongside? He poured and stirred, aware of Greene coming up beside him, holding his own cup.

"If the Slide theory is right, we can *manufacture* omelite."

There wasn't enough whiskey in the inhabited galaxy for this conversation. "By blowing up a planet."

Greene's shoulders rose and fell. "It doesn't have to be an inhabited one."

But what if it did? What if you needed…observers on both sides? What if it only worked if you had, say, the ranids and the mysterious theoretical technologists?

Closs put his coffee cup down again. He rubbed his palms over tight curls and turned to Greene. You looked a man in the eye when you admitted a mistake. "Deschênes has dropped out of contact," he said. "I think we have to prepare ourselves for failure on that front."

Cricket could have run. But she was inside Nouel's house, at the mercy of his expert system, and she hadn't had the foresight—or the equipment—to wire *this* place to blow. So she put her back to the sealed door, folded her arms across her chest, and waited. Nouel stood up and turned to her. "Fisher," he said, shocking her. "I'm sorry; you weren't here, and I couldn't contact you to let you know I was bringing Maurice home. Maurice Sadowski, this is Fisher."

Not even a hesitation to hint that it was a brand-new name. Cricket let her brow crinkle, and her first stuttering panic recede. There was, obviously, more going on here than the evident. She stepped forward and extended her hand, and Maurice stood as well.

"We've met," he said, only a crinkle at the corner of his eye—half smirk, half wink—betraying any amusement at her change of name. "Virtually speaking." His hand was warm, broad-palmed, the grip certain. "I'm not here for Rim."

"Of course, if you were—"

"I would say the same thing." He had a good, flickering smile. "Honey, there's one way I know I can prove I'm on your side. I can tell you what was in the file I gave Lucienne."

She really shouldn't have been so surprised. It had to have come from somewhere. Somewhere close to Closs or Greene, specifically, or somebody who had stumbled across the information. But—

"I don't know what you're talking about," she said.

And Maurice clucked his tongue. "Lucienne took a risk to meet with me," he said. "I took one to meet with you. Take a risk yourself: this is too big not to."

Nouel stood back. Cricket studied Maurice instead, watching his eyes, the corners of his mouth.

Rim, she thought, would just have killed her. The way they had killed Lucienne. They didn't need to talk to her. Unless they somehow thought she could lead them to a bigger fish, but that hadn't been a concern in the past. Quick, ruthless, but not prone to long-term strategy—that was the Charter Trade Company.

"Do you have any proof? Anything we can use to force the media to follow up?"

He glanced at Huc. Huc, jowled head lowered, seemed not to notice. "I purged the file once I transmitted it. You don't keep something like that in your head. I can promise, however, that the tracker didn't come from me, or with that data."

"You say that as if it was good news." Cricket snorted. "It also doesn't help us sell this to Com."

"People love conspiracies." Huc, without raising his head.

"They also," Cricket said calmly, "tend to think they're full of shit. Tell me something, Maurice. What could Lucienne have done with your information that an archinformist couldn't?"

"Give it provenance," he said. He rubbed his palms together, fiddled a gold bracelet. "I could connex it. But not without revealing myself—and we've seen how that works out."

"*Lucienne?*"

Maurice's eyebrow went up. He glanced at Nouel, who was still simulating withdrawal. "Well," he said, "I guess it's okay if I tell you now. Lucienne was an agent."

"Oh, no," Cricket said, gulping against bitter nausea. She hadn't trusted anyone, not since Patience. Not since Moon Morrow's confidential secretary had turned out to be not so confidential, after all. "Core? Not Rim, or Rim wouldn't have killed her. What, infiltrating the insurgents?"

"You are not analyzing the evidence," he said. "Think again."

She did so, paused, staring at the back of her hands. "Holy shit. Unified Earth."

"Yes. Apparently some senator or another actually thinks bringing down a corrupt Charter Trade Corporation might just be a ticket to reelection."

"Earth thinks it can bring legal proceedings against Rim? Against Core?"

"Monopolies," he said, echoing Huc, "make people nervous. You don't know who she was reporting to? You can't get us in contact?"

Cricket shook her head. "I can't." She turned away, folded her hands behind her back, and stared at the wall. Nouel had withdrawn against it and was still waiting with his arms folded. "I've got no authority."

"You've got Lucienne's froggie friends, don't you? What about Jean Gris? Would he know?"

Ah, of course. *That* was the thing she could give Rim that they couldn't get without her.

Assuming Maurice wasn't trustworthy. A big assumption, because if he was, they needed him. On the other hand, Lucienne had been shot immediately after meeting with him. And he was conspicuously healthy. "No," she said. "With Lucienne gone...and anyway, what news feed is going to care what a ranid has to say for itself? We could manufacture a provenance for the documents, if they're authentic."

"They are." No trace of impatience. "There's more I need to tell you, though. There's another thing I find unlikely to be coincidental, and extremely fascinating."

Slowly, Cricket turned her head and stared, not at Maurice but at Nouel. It was thirty seconds at least before he lifted his head, returned her gaze, and shrugged. "You're looking at the wrong man, Fisher."

She rotated on her heels. Maurice had been staring at the back of her neck. "What do you know?"

"I know this," he said, and pulled a flat chip of hard plastic from his pocket. He flipped it at her; she caught it out of the air reflexively, and slapped it onto the back of her left hand. It was an Australian dollar from A.G. 50 or so, when they were still using the old notation: 2048.

Tails. "So what?"

"Do it again."

Heads. Tails. Heads. Tails.

"Trick coin."

"It's not."

She tossed the coin at him. He fumbled the catch, and it rolled off his fingers and under a chair. Cricket almost *heard* Nouel roll his eyes, but nobody went after the coin. "So *what?*" Cricket asked again, though she knew, more or less, so what.

So they were neck-deep in a probability storm, and there was no telling what might happen. And as if to prove her conjecture, what Maurice said next was an almost complete non sequitur.

"So you're a quantum clone of Moon Constancy Morrow." And while she stood there, blinking at him, he continued: "And Closs *almost* knows. He's this close to figuring it out, and when he does, I have no idea what he'll do about it. Also, I wouldn't connex if I were you until we scrub your head completely; the real Moon has ways of finding you when you do that. Which is why I'm absolutely certain it wasn't my data."

"Thank you," she said. Her throat hurt; after a moment she realized that it was because she was dry-swallowing, over and over. "I figured that out."

No, no point in playing it cool at all. And Huc hadn't known either, based on his reflexive step forward and then the cringe that started in his neck and shoulders and traveled his length. "But I'm not a clone. I'm the original. *She's* the clone."

"From what I understand," Maurice said, "I would guess she told Closs the same thing. There's only one problem with that."

"Yes?"

"If it's so, how did *you* get *here?*"

11

WHILE ANDRÉ WAITED ON SHORE, GOURAMI TALKED TO the greatparent. Se voice was deep and grand, a reverberation through the water that tickled Gourami's skin like a caress. The greatparent's attention soothed and opened Gourami's thought, made se pliant and considering and willing, increased se concentration and powers of recollection.

The effect was biochemical. Taken to an extreme, if a person stopped swimming and matured; it was memorizy that made greatparents the center of people's culture and history.

Because greatparents could remember *everything*. Everything they had experienced, every story they were told. So younger persons—adults and farswimmers, not the presentient egglings—told greatparents their stories, and some of the ones that did not get eaten or killed in accidents or while defending their bandweal became greatparents in their turn, and memorizy other things. Old persons did not die. They either swam until they stopped, or they were killed somehow.

Gourami tried to explain this to André, on the slate, while se spoke with the greatparent, but soon gave up and left the human on the bank.

—*They're like living databases?* he had asked at one point, and se was forced to admit that this was close to the truth. Except not exactly, of course. Because the humen remembering-machines did not tell stories. Or make patterns. Or make sense of things. Or comfort the afflicted.

Or soothe the young and fragile with the weight of their experience and wisdom and accumulated centuries of knowledge.

The remembering-machines could talk like greatparents, across vast distances. But greatparents also had the knack of changing luck, for which they used the same coiled organs with which they generated bioelectricity. Like some of the small swimming things, greatparents could defend themselves with shock if their bands and clans did not succeed in keeping danger at bay. It was a talent that only developed with the final metamorphosis. Adults and far-swimmers were expected to run from danger, or fight it.

Coming to a particular point in se narrative, se dug in se beltpouch and pulled out Jean Kroc's watertight case, explaining what he had wanted done with the device inside. Conversation with a greatparent was so easy: they understood, and explained back, sometimes more than one understood oneself. Though *this* greatparent was one of the youngest—se had stopped swimming since the humen came—se was also interpersonally gifted.

Gourami found se challenging and reassuring by turns.

—*The human wanted to entangle you?*

—*He did.* Gourami basked in the ambient calm and well-being. The sort of inclusion that se had not felt since se went to live among humen.

It had been a sacrifice. But having adventures and bringing home new stories was one way to make one-self worthy. Even if, sitting in shallow water with the greatparent floating beside se, Gourami could not imagine how se would ever become what this person so effortlessly was.

Oh, but se wanted it.

Of course, as Tetra and Caetei had hinted, first se had to admit that want, and take the first steps.

—*You did well in not accepting the entanglement. As you grow, you will not wish to be bound to the humen.*

—*No.* They were erratic and inconsistent, and their political structures seemed to be applied with very lit-tle consideration for bandweal or anything but individ-ual gain. Gourami suspected it had something to do with their method of reproduction, which seemed very...competitive. Probably everything could be traced back to that: their hierarchies, their violence, their jealousies. Their survival strategies were very dif-ferent from those of people.

They were climbers, not schoolers.

—*The Company humen are . dangerous,* Gourami added. Which of course the greatparent knew already, but it bore reinforcing. An opinion expressed was a step toward consensus. —*We do not wish to be bound to the rebel humen, but we wish their assistance in opposing the Company humen.*

The greatparent thrummed, stroking Gourami's

forelimbs with se fringe, draping a curtain of tendrils over se shoulders and back. No sting and no shock, just the comfort, the calm of the womb, of being enclosed in and protected by another. It was a memory that lingered in every person, peace from the eggling's first seasons in an endoparent's care.

The greatparent continued, —*Many of the others do not care to have any humen here.*

Gourami thought of how fast rumor could swim, and of the attempts on se own life. Se thought of one-armed, so-scarred Parrot, whom se knew from the drill platforms in other days and whom se had become reacquainted with after se and Tetra and Caetei had brought André, unconscious, to the one-tree-island band. Se thought of Tetra's harpoon gun, which se had been at pains to conceal from André. Of se own crossbow. And what a person might do with a weapon like that.

—*Will it be fighting? Tetra and se followers? Will they do more?* There was already skirmishing, and Gourami knew at least some of the greatparents were involved. It was only they that had the skills to make their luck. They rooted deep, sent down trunks into the sediment, and brought up the oils the humen dug for, too.

The greatparent bobbed placidly in the shallows. Water slopped over Gourami's back, refreshing se mucous; cool mud squelched under se handfingers.

—*There will be a war,* the greatparent said. Loud enough that the echoes would carry wide, to many ears, when se could have murmured it against Gourami's skin, under the curtain of tendrils draped between them. —*You will swim with Tetra and the others, when the time comes. You will bear a weapon.*

Gourami's throat swelled. Se would. Se would do it. The greatparent had decided. Had foreseen.

It was not an unalloyed tribulation. There would be adventure, risk. Glory. Status to be won.

Stories.

—*You must tell the persons who work for the humen, they must stop. They must come away, come home. You must be the messenger, as you were between people and the humen.*

—*And there is no way of avoiding it?* Gourami asked. Not an argument: se was incapable of argument, huddled against the greatparent's fringe as se was. But a question, a fair question to ask.

—*The humen could become peaceable.* The greatparent's tone, murmured softly now, indicated heavy irony. Not a likely outcome, no. —*Speaking of Tetra, se thinks well of you,* se said, changing the subject entirely. Although of course it didn't call Tetra by that name, but the one that could not be translated, or spoken by humen. —*When are you going to start making your vest?*

Seductive, yes. Gourami croaked harshly, in pain. Se knew—se *knew*—what the humen would do. Could do. Not so many who came home to the clans knew the humen culture as se did. Not so many had studied it.

—*I must tell you some humen stories, greatparent,* se said. Not arguing. Telling was not arguing. Just providing information that the greatparent might not already have. That, also, was permissible. —*They will destroy us if we try to fight.*

Jean rather thought Ziyi Zhou was expecting him. Her door swung open as he came up the gangplank, and she was dressed for company. "No," she said, before he could open his mouth.

He stopped, one foot on planks, one on a strip of tarpaper nailed crosswise to the gangway. "I haven't asked yet."

"What are you doing with André Deschênes?"

Jean closed his eyes and let an extended hand fall back to his side. "I have uses for him."

When he looked up again, Ziyi was slowly shaking her head. "That's like keeping a nessie in your bathtub, Jean. You're not actually planning to train him?"

"He's too gifted to leave wandering loose," Jean said. "He's more of a threat untrained than trained."

"There's another solution to that."

"Maybe," he suggested, quietly, "we should take this conversation inside."

She bit her lip but stood aside, and he walked past her into the cool, dim living room. Unlike Jean, Ziyi didn't isolate herself from technology. Which was the reason he was here.

She shut the door and immediately said, "You took him as a *pupil*?"

"I think I can straighten him out." Not waiting to be asked, Jean settled himself on a soft burgundy sofa. "But it'll get ugly, Ziyi. Soon."

"I turned him down, you know," she said. "Do you want lemonade?"

"Make it a double."

When she came back from the kitchen, she had two glasses in her hands. She poured the lemonade from one to the other, to assure him that it was unadulterated, and held both out for him to pick from. He chose the glass to port and waited until after she tasted hers to drink.

"He killed *Lucienne*." Not stridently, but the stress

was there under her voice, a suppressed whine. "Jean, how could you?"

"We're holding this planet together with our teeth and fingernails. We're going to need him, and the ranids, and everybody else we can find with an ounce of talent."

"I hope I'm not included in that we."

"You can't be blind to the toxic level of coincidence lately. Unless you've stopped tugging God's coat-sleeve."

She rolled lemonade over her tongue, resting the tall glass on one palm and steadying it with the opposite fingertips. "I've noticed," she said. A tactical retreat. "It's the worst I've ever seen. But...Deschênes. I've been tracking his probabilities."

"Divination? That's about as useful as casting tarot cards."

"Which I happen to know you keep a set of."

He snorted. "What did you find?"

"Deschênes's line crosses yours. Practically winds around Closs's. And crossed Lucienne's, before it ended."

Jean threw one arm over the back of the sofa. "He's not entangled. Your readings are no better than guesses."

But she shook her head, rolling the glass between her palms, and he swallowed. He was not used to being taken by surprise, and even before she spoke he knew he'd just walked into a doozy.

"He is now." You could have cut cake with her smile. "I know his baker."

He set the lemonade down on the arm of the sofa and leaned forward, elbows on his knees. "Oral application? You might as well throw darts."

She lowered her gaze, redolent of false modesty. "Two months of trying," she said.

"Damn. I never want to hear another *word* about my ethics—"

"Jean," she said, suddenly serious, her expression smoothing. "I just wanted to let you know I wasn't going to weep if anything happened."

"Don't cry for him," Jean said. "Cry for me. Look, I need your help. Before she died, Lucienne sent some data to her friend Cricket. The packet was interrupted. Cricket got the data out—"

"How bad?"

"Bad enough. It would help if we had the rest."

She seemed to contract, elbows pressed to her sides, chin dropping. "I already said no once."

"Rim has it," Jean said. "If it's anywhere. I've got the best archinformist in the business"—if we can get her head fixed, he did not add—"and I've got André Deschênes, though I have to go fetch him back first. And I have Nouel Huc."

"That's already two people more than can keep a secret."

"It doesn't have to be kept for long. If we can get this information, Ziyi, we can bring down Rim."

"*Rim?*"

"Charter Trade on Greene's World at the very least. Get Jefferson Greene the hell out of there. We've got them dead to rights on environmental and safety issues. But we need to find out who contacted Lucienne. And we need to establish a provenance for the data before the media will touch it. We have a witness—"

"Shouldn't that be enough?"

"It's a ranid," he admitted, and Ziyi winced.

"Oh, hell, Jean . . ."

"For Lucienne?" he asked. "If you won't do it for me?"

"What do you need?"

"I need this data broken out," he said, extending a chip across the gap between the two of them. She leaned forward to take it, manicured nails brushing his fingertips. The opposite of Lucienne. "It'll need to be combined with whatever we bring back. Careful—there might be mines in there. Don't stick it in your head."

"Wouldn't dream of it, Dad." She turned the chip over curiously, rolling it across her fingertips. "This isn't an original?"

"Not on a bet."

She nodded, considering. "Mines?"

"I'm told that Rim was locating the person who had it whenever she connexed. Even after a biometrics swap."

"*Damn.* That's vicious."

He nodded. Of course, it probably wasn't the data, but it didn't hurt to install caution. "That's Rim. I'll bring you the rest when we have it. Start thinking, would you, about how we're going to get hold of somebody who will push the story."

"Jean, darling," she said, setting the chip down on the table beside her. "I know perfectly well why you came to me. You don't have to dissemble. But he won't take it unless you make it good. It's his career and his life, too, taking on Rim."

Her lover—via connex, anyway; a decades-long-relationship that she had told Jean had started in university and that would never result in a meeting in the flesh unless they *both* went relativistic and met in the middle—was Bryson Pace, a minor newsnet legend.

Ziyi's mojo got bent to make sure she knew everyone. Jean had no idea when she had time to earn a living.

"I know," Jean said. "I'll make sure it's unimpeachable."

"And what about Deschênes? If it doesn't work out, your plan to . . . whatever it is you think you can do."

"If it doesn't work out," Jean relied, "I'll shoot the son of a bitch myself. Just give me the chance to find out if I can help him turn into a human being."

Her eyes widened, all perfect feral innocence.

"Ziyi."

"All right," she said. "All right. I'll stop trying to kill him, Jean. For now."

A sensible man would take off into the bayou and stay there until it blew over, whatever *it* turned out to be. A sensible man would have stayed home in the first place. Would never have taken on Closs and Greene.

Would be spending a lot of time in front of the sim-stim, pretending to be alive because it was easier than getting out of his damned chair and doing the real thing.

At least Jean had the option of taking off into the bayou temporarily, if not for good.

The tide was in: his house was temporarily on an island, and the channel where Lucienne had usually met Caetei was under several feet of brackish water. Instead, he loaded a pack up—he wasn't planning on coming back, now that Cricket was hunted, and there was nothing in the house that mattered. He poled his skiff past reeds tattered by the hail storm, heading inland through laced waterways. An electronic chime hung from the stern of the skiff, emitting an intermittent ping.

If Caetei wished to speak, se would find him. If Caetei was still alive and at liberty. A big if, when he'd heard nothing from any of the renegades since the night before. Whatever he'd told Ziyi about his

well-established conspiracy, it could all have come
down on his head.

Discomfortingly, it was not Caetei who answered his
call. When he had been poling for about four quarters,
a green head broke brown water. It was scarred terribly, though, and the ranid swam crooked in the channel, an effect of having only one arm. Jean winced in
sympathy, as he did each time he saw Parrot.

At first he'd tried to conceal the compassion, as he
would for a human, but the ranids reacted to the injury
of another with patting and cuddling and a head-
ducked empathy.

Parrot was inconvenient in another way. Gourami
had Jean's slate, and he hadn't had time to obtain another. And Parrot was not a liaison: it could not lip-
read human speech.

Jean hoped that neither Gourami nor Caetei had
come to collect him due to an inconvenience, the sort
of thing that made a funny story later. But it was something to tell himself, not something he could believe.

In his belt, between layers of hide, he had a second
chip. A holographic playback device in a waterproof
carryall lay stuffed into his bum bag. There were
greatparents in the bayou; maybe Ziyi could help, and
maybe...

Maybe a few hundred amorphous amphibians that
were little more than giant, highly specialized, floating, quantum-connected brains could do it better. At
the very least, if he gave it to the greatparents, he
didn't have to worry about Cricket's headworm alerting whomever had put it there in the first place.

The lack of connex had to be driving Cricket crazy.
She could barely spend an afternoon at his house—at
what had been his house—without jittering like a to-
bacco smoker denied a fix.

But everybody was entitled to a few bad habits, he guessed. He had a share of his own.

Parrot bobbed beside the skiff, swimming crookedly. It wriggled in the water, spun about, and grabbed the gunwale in one spreading, webbed hand, tugging the boat in a new direction as it frog-kicked. Jean swung his pole around, pushing the skiff after. Seeing that it was understood, Parrot dropped off the bow and sculled forward, moving gracefully enough though it swam on a diagonal. They cut through the water silently, swiftly, gold-limned brown ripples folding out behind them like the ribs of opening fans.

He was still poling determinedly two quarters later, when the first of the helicopters went over.

Cricket ought to be worried about liking Maurice Sadowski too much. It was a dangerous habit to get into, liking people. But it was hard not to like the man who had arranged for her to be sitting in Nouel Huc's living room, her feet tucked under her on scratchy fabric, while she watched him lie to Timothy Closs.

She was off-camera, the expert system handling the uplink instructed to ignore her existence, with Nouel sitting cross-legged and gnomelike on the divan opposite. They could see each other, and they could see Closs, but Closs could not see them.

Magic.

"So tell me more about Moon Morrow," Closs said in the presumed privacy of a coded connection. "What have you learned about this cloning process?"

Maurice picked at the luminous coils in his ear, caught himself, and fussed with a nub in the couch fabric instead. "Well, I can tell you that the situation is being misrepresented. There's no way Cricket Murphy can be Morrow—the original Morrow—because to have been here for fifteen years, even if she sent the clone to jail in her place...quantum clones wouldn't survive Sliding any better than anybody else."

Closs couldn't see her, but that didn't keep Cricket from breathing like there was a snake in the room. This was the person who had ordered Lucienne's death, the one who would do the same to her and Jean—and Maurice, too, and that poor frog—if he could. She studied him, the cropped hair, the hazel eyes lighter than his skin.

André, she reminded herself sternly, bore just as much responsibility for Lucienne's death as Closs did. André was the one who had pulled the trigger.

Her palm itched. She wasn't sure if she wanted to touch him, or strike him so hard his head would spin around. She wasn't sure either if she wanted to hit André more, or Closs.

"So if she's not Morrow," Closs said, "she's the clone? Legally inconvenient. For Morrow. Although that doesn't tell us how she got here."

And that was it, wasn't it? Her nails weren't sharp enough to cut her flesh. Unfortunately. Because she couldn't argue with Maurice's logic, and it was kind of stunning.

"She is the clone," Maurice said. "I'm convinced of that. Which means, legally, she's Moon Morrow, and legally, Moon Morrow does not exist. She's not a *person*, Tim."

"And dead from having Slid here."

"There's a theoretical answer." Another day, Cricket might have admired how smoothly Maurice interrupted Closs. "When you create a quantum clone, you don't have to create it in the same place. It's easy enough to reconstruct your parent body..."

"On the other end of a Slide," Closs finished. He stared at his steepled fingers, blinking, for long minutes. "What's to stop anyone using that as an instantaneous method of transportation?"

"Nothing," Maurice said promptly. "As long as you don't mind duplicates of people piling up all over the galaxy. Or you're willing to indulge in a little flexibility with regard to your definition of the word *murder*. If I'm right about how this works, when word of the technology leaks—"

"When."

"—information always leaks, Tim. It'll mean the end of interstellar travel by ship. Adjust your portfolio accordingly."

Maurice glanced down at his hands—a mistake, Cricket thought. That always made it look like you were lying even if you weren't. He cleared his throat and continued, "Did you get anything out of the Spivak file?"

Thank you, Maurice. But of course he cared as much as she did. If Closs cracked it—assuming Maurice was telling the truth, and boy wasn't she getting tired already of caveating her every thought with that clause—then Maurice was as dead as Lucienne.

"We're working on it." Closs's steepled fingers interlaced and dropped together. He looked up, as if glancing over Maurice's shoulder: something on a wall screen, or his headset, or somebody had come into his office. "No luck identifying a code key yet. Also, I need to see if you can dig up some information for me on what Jeff's up to."

"Chairman Greene? You mean, my notional employer?"

"Tell him all about me if that's how you feel about

it," Closs said. "He's up to something, and whatever it is, I have a feeling it's a dealbreaker."

"Ethics?"

"I think," Closs said, "I think I shouldn't offer too many leading comments. Just see if there are any currency transfers, unexplained visitors in the middle of the night. You know what to look for."

"I do," Maurice said.

"You're the best in the business, after all." Cricket's chin snapped up at that comment, but of course—Closs didn't know she was there. "Anything else?"

Maurice nodded. "You wanted to know if we should blame GreenWorld for the recruitment barge explosion."

"It doesn't matter so much now, with Spivak dead."

"It might," Maurice said. "I don't think it was them. Mostly a gut feeling, but if they needed a conjure man, and if we're right about Spivak being the replacement for Tavish...well, why would they need anybody but Kroc?"

"It could have *been* Kroc."

"Explosions aren't his style," Maurice said. "Too random. Too much collateral damage. I think we're looking for somebody else. And there's another piece of evidence."

"You turned up something about Angley?"

Maurice smiled. It wasn't a nice smile. "You might want to double-check and see if she's really dead, Tim. Because I found a pattern of credits to her accounts that match incidents of sabotage and news leaks. She might be your girl."

"She faked her death?" Closs did not seem to change expression when he was startled—if he *was* startled. He did, however, get up from behind his desk and begin slowly to pace.

"I'm not prepared to commit to that," Maurice answered.

Cricket fidgeted. Across the room, Nouel sat like a statue, but his eyes were unfocused. Cricket suspected he was a few hundred light-years away.

"But you're suspicious."

"I'm always suspicious," Maurice answered with a flick of his forefinger against his forehead, as if he were tweaking a nonexistent hat. "Cheerio, boss. Unless you have something else for me?"

"No," Closs said. "Thanks. Closs out." His image snapped one-dimensional and went out.

Maurice sat back on his chair. "Fuck," he said. "I think we are going to have to hack Rim."

"Not with a bug in my head, we aren't hacking anything. My motherself is a nasty piece of work." It was actually a sort of lightning relief to realize she wasn't exactly who she thought she was. A chance at denial, at a new life, free of guilt.

She hadn't done those things.

Except she had, hadn't she? If she was honest? If she accepted responsibility? She hadn't served the jail time. But legally, she was Moon Morrow.

She caught herself nibbling her nail, and made herself stop.

"Fisher—" Maurice said, and when she looked up she realized he was staring at her. He blinked three times once she met his eyes, and then smiled at her. Cricket realized he'd had her filtered, too, so that his reactions to her presence wouldn't give anything away to Closs. "Sorry," he said. "You know, I can go in and look for what she left."

She let her hands fall to her sides and stood, pacing like Closs. Time to decide. Not about who she was, what she owed.

She wasn't Moon Morrow. She was Moon Morrow. She wasn't sure any of it lessened the burden of guilt. Moon Morrow had forked herself in two. But Cricket was a graft on the same root.

That could wait. About Maurice and Huc. Time to pick a side. "If we find it, can we use it to hack into Morrow's head?"

Maurice smiled like he was sucking ice chips. "Nouel. Can I isolate your entertainment system? Take it offline for a while?"

"What are you going to do with it?"

"It should have enough memory to download whatever Fisher's got in her head," he said. "And then we can pick it over on a code level."

"How long will that take?" Nouel sounded more curious than unwilling.

"If we're lucky, an hour. If we're not lucky or there's nothing to find, a month."

Cricket knocked the back of her hand against a chair arm for attention. "What about me?"

"We purge your system and start over from the ground up," Nouel said. "We can't use your backups."

She scratched her thigh. "I want to start clean. Fresh licenses."

"Big deal," Maurice said, with a respectful half-nod. "Can we do this?"

Do I trust you? Cricket wondered. Nouel trusted him. And André trusted Nouel.

And Cricket did not for a minute trust André. But sometimes you had to commit.

"All right," she said, into the silence in her head.

Maurice tipped his head, his earwire shifted red-green-scarlet. "Excellent. Come on over here, darling, and we'll see about getting your pretty head scrubbed clean."

"And then," Nouel said, "we have an awful lot of work to do."

André didn't hear, at first, what caused the frogs to cringe and scatter. The enormous creature they had gathered around submerged abruptly, trailed by ropy stings of algae and bubbles. Mud swirled through viscid water.

André's shin shot white heat to his groin as he struggled upright, trying not to think about what he'd do if the ranids left him there. There wasn't anything within reach from which to improvise a crutch. His lacerated back, a minor irritation beside the pain in his leg, flared when he turned, craning to see what was behind him.

He heard the thumping of rotating blades, and knew. *Bastards.* There was nothing he could do to avoid them. And they'd used him, hadn't they?

Like a Judas goat.

But then a green-yellow shape trailing slimy greener strings of algae and waterweed charged up the bank in one tremendous leap. Gourami crouched beside André, long arms pulling him out of the stretcher. André knew enough about froggy physiology to know that it must have hurt the ranid when it ducked under his arm and lifted. He felt its protective mucous coating skid and tear, and felt its astonishing strength as it shoved him upright.

And then they were staggering down the bank, toward the water, as three helicopters swept over in formation. No gunfire, not yet, but they were low, bending reeds until they snapped against one another like the sticks of a rattled fan. At least there was no dust, though bits of hurled plant matter whirled around them. André coughed and shielded his eyes.

Gourami staggered, slid. What surprised André most was its silence. A human would have grunted, whimpered, made some small sound of distress. He felt its joints pop through the contact; alien as its strength might be, he was still nearly twice its mass. But it just got under him and heaved.

André helped as he could, using the ranid as a crutch and trying to limit the weight he put on it. It hopped and he hobbled, and the thump of retreating, turning, returning choppers shattered the steaming, insect-stirred stillness.

The bank here, at least, wasn't covered in wooden knives of broken reeds. André opened his mouth to ask what was going on, closed it again in red frustration. Even if he could get Gourami's attention and make himself understood, distracting it might get them both killed. And it had no fast way to answer him; he didn't think either of them wanted to spare the time to type lengthy explanations.

He stumbled gamely along, thought about crawling, decided it would be faster to hop. The splint wouldn't help him bear any weight; he didn't dare put the broken leg down. Muscle spasm locked it, anyway. He gritted his teeth and, with intermittent success, tried not to let it drag.

Gourami seemed to be headed for the water, though. Which was smart; less than a meter would protect them from propellant weapons. Less than a meter, and they would be safe.

Pity he couldn't breathe it. He hoped Gourami remembered that.

There were some reeds standing along the bank.

André patted Gourami's arm as he'd seen the ranids do for attention, and gestured.

Its head didn't turn, but its eyes swiveled. *Then* it croaked, a deep rolling resonant sound.

He wasn't sure if he'd expected it to drag him the length of the bank, across the stinking mudflat, or if he thought it would leave him precariously balanced on one leg while it bounded down to the stems and tore them loose. Instead, it croaked again, urgently, and another weed-dotted head lifted from the water, followed by a lean body strung about with nets.

Tetra.

The second ranid lurched from the water, through splintering plants, and up the bank. Something chattered in the near distance; gunfire, and André sucked in his gut, as if that would make the slightest difference. The old atavism didn't care, though—and the bullets were aimed somewhere else. He didn't even see the muzzle flash.

Tetra caught them still ten meters from the water, and so did the second wave of choppers. The downdraft was like a strong hand pushing André down. Bullets smacked around them now, and Tetra—slick, tender-fleshed—dove under his other arm. Gourami and Tetra grasped André each by one elbow, and leaped.

His arms snapped against his shoulder sockets; he would have yelped in pain if he'd had the air to do more than huff. His head jerked back on his neck, whiplash and insulted muscle, but the hurt was nothing to when they hit the water.

It knocked the air from him and spasmed his diaphragm; as if expecting it, Tetra punched him in the back. He gasped, kickstarted, and the ranid shoved a broken reed into his hand. One quick desperate breath,

that was all, and they were under, muddy water gritty
in his eyes. Tetra's long fingers enfolded his hands,
molding them around the reed. He held on somehow,
as the ranids pulled him under, turned him bodily, and
rolled him onto his back. The water in his ears
thrummed with cries and argument. He didn't understand a note of it, but it beat against his skin until he
felt like a sounding chamber, resonating with anger
and distress.

But he guessed what Tetra and Gourami meant him
to do, and stuffed the end of the reed pipe into his
mouth and sucked.

No air.

He might have panicked as the ranids dragged him
deeper, but he was too goddamned tired for hysterics.
He puffed out, felt whatever was in the reed give
way, and blew harder. The air in his lungs was used up
anyway.

The plug shot from the reed like a blow-dart.

The next breath came laden with dust and fiber-
glass-sharp broken plant. And sweet, sweet moisture-
drenched air.

André gasped like a fish, breathed out through his
nose because it was faster, dragged at air again. The
water was tepid, too close to body temperature to knife
shocks of pain through his wounds. But he knew; infection was inevitable, amoebosis likely.

He couldn't think about that now. He breathed, and
let the ranids pull him. Long pulsing strokes kept them
moving. André concentrated on breathing, and wished
he could ask where they were taking him.

12

GOURAMI SPENT FAR TOO LONG THINKING ABOUT WHAT TO
do with the human. But se couldn't have left him to be
shot. Se had brought him to the village. Se had
brought him to the greatparent's attention. Se had left
him stranded on the bank.

Se hadn't expected Tetra to be the one to help.
Se hadn't expected Tetra to crouch beside se, hunkered under the overhang of a bank of reed bound together by cutthroat weed and broken at the root by the
hail.

—*They are hunting the greatparent,* Tetra said,
bleakly, as the killing machines made another pass.
Gourami flinched, but Tetra laid a hand on se
thigh. —*And they are hunting us. Watch what happens.*

They crouched low, lifting the human from the water so he could breathe and see. He huddled, quiet despite what must be enormous pain, floating between

them. The tide was in. Gourami caught self rattling fingers against the reeds and stopped, an act of will.

And bore witness.

The helicopters came over, gunning, churning the water where the greatparent lay submerged. The bullets could not reach it, and the people stayed out of sight, under cover, under water. But then the explosions began, and Gourami, unwitting, would have started forward if Tetra had not restrained se. Reflex. Programming.

The elder was in danger. Egglings were expendable, but the old were the memory of the race.

Others did not have a far-swimmer to caution them. Some rushed forward heedlessly; they would not be herded by bullets, and some of those were cut down. The water grew violet; it all tasted of blood, like a hunter's kill. Gourami ducked and shivered, rocking back and forth against Tetra's touch. Se could not pull free, se could not stay where se was.

Se had to help, and se distress rolled up se throat in ringing harmonics, quickly damped. Tetra took the human's hand and put it on Gourami's other arm. The human's weird irises ringed with white. He held on, as if he meant to do it gently, but he only had one leg to tread water with, and he bobbed up and down, tugging skin.

The first wave of defenders schooled wherever the humen cared to drive them. Vibrations through the water heralded the phalanxes of scoots, roaring up the channels. But it wasn't the scoots themselves that made Gourami cringe; it was the billowing net each pair dragged between.

The throb of engines was confusing. Se thrashed and warbled—*go to them, go to them*—but Tetra, far-swimmer, less programmed for clanweal, would not let go. Tetra and the human held on, bruising, breaking tender skin, and dragged Gourami farther into their fragile shelter, where the bank was undercut.

The scoots were not moving as fast as they could. They zigged and zagged in unison, keeping the nets untangled, scooping up persons willy-nilly. Gourami saw the captured persons struggling to hold one another up, despite the entangling nets, pushing one another's noses above water.

Se could not watch. Se could not look away. Se trembled.

If Gourami had been a far-swimmer, if se own reproduction had become important to bandweal, it might have been easier to abide. Se might have maintained Tetra's presence of mind. But se was a young adult, and not carrying egglings. Se thought of the greatparent, of the babies, of the village.

Se bore witness, and moaned low chords of agony.

These were not se sibs, at least, which made the slaughter and seizure not less terrible, but less compelling. Se had no ties by blood or water here. Except Caetei.

Where was Caetei?

Although the humen were well armed, the persons were not helpless. The second wave of defenders consisted of far-swimmers as much as adults, and many of these had taken the time to arm.

Se tugged the crossbow from se web belt. Tetra, gently, lifted it from se hands, chirruping.

Gourami saw the attack in slashes of action through the reeds. The humen had apparently not expected automatic-weapons fire. Several jerked from their scoots, which cut off as they were meant to when the rider fell. Persons, no longer dragged through the water, struggled free of the nets, bleeding from abrasions and holding wrenched limbs awkwardly. One scoot pilot, insufficiently attentive or lacking adequate reflexes, lost control when his partner's vehicle stalled. The net swung him into a channel bank. A person Gourami did not know impaled him with a reed spear as he struggled up the bank.

Smoke and fire pillared from one hillock; Gourami's view of the target was obscured by mats of overhanging reed, but se heard the roar and felt the heat as a helicopter died screaming. Another scoot passed so close Gourami felt the wash, and André flinched against se. He made some whining humen sound; Gourami did not turn her head to see if it was a curse or a cheer.

Gunfire scattered ground to air and air to ground. André yanked again, and se was about to shake him away, send him surging back through the water, but then Tetra tugged, too—Caetei, where was Caetei?— and the violet water churned. A great black thundering belly lowered, flattening the reed shelter against their heads, and Gourami caught confused glimpses of hanging cables, of humen thrashing awkwardly through water, dragging steel rings wired to drawn nets. Another circling chopper died, but then the remaining ones were hovering over the heart of the village, where the netted ranids and the submerged greatparent were.

Something sizzled—a chopper returning fire—the rocket trail a long tumorous arch of smoke, cracked with flame. A flattening boom shook bits of plant on Gourami's head. Se did not flinch.

There were no more losses among the humen machines.

Tetra and André were still pulling at Gourami. Se turned to the human and saw the shapes his mouth

was making, how they resolved into words. Tetra
might be croaking something. Gourami could not hear
it over the explosions.

—*We have to go,* the human said. He jerked his paw
up. —*We have to run.*

Gourami did not understand, but the human was
confident—and projecting urgency—and Tetra dragged
at se other arm. Se let self be moved, pulled through
the swamp, bobbing low, slinking from tussock to tussock. They made short dashes underwater, only as long
as the human could hold its breath. Tetra was really
the only one directing, the only one swimming. André
was almost dead weight, and Gourami could only think
of Caetei, and the greatparent, of the egglings and
adults they were abandoning.

A few other persons ran with them; they caught
glimpses of far-swimmers, and of one adult so full of
egglings se would have sloshed, risking rupture, if se
climbed out of the water. The others, the young adults,
had run inward.

Into the trap.

The thrumming, the straining thunder of choppers,
the sound of explosions took a long time to soften behind them. They sheltered under vegetation when the
choppers passed over, hanging nets dripping water,
squirming with green bodies. André finally floated behind Gourami, clinging to se back, his hands over se
eyes to force them retracted and closed. It helped when
Tetra led.

Se still kept wanting to turn back and look for
Caetei.

They had not been running long when both André's
and—he presumed—Tetra's instincts were proven

brutally correct. The explosion flattened all three of them, the compression shock wave through the water thankfully attenuated by distance and topography, or they would have been dynamited like fish. It took both André and Tetra to keep Gourami moving. The froggie was like a sleepwalker; it would paddle despondently as long as somebody directed, but if not provoked and cajoled, it began drifting aimlessly. André wished he could talk to Tetra, ask questions, anything. But there was no means of conversation; damaged Gourami had the slate, and André was not sure Tetra knew how to use it even if it was so inclined.

At first, André thought Gourami might be physically injured. But when they had struggled far enough from the devastated village that Tetra allowed them to rest (not far enough that André felt safe, but he didn't think he'd feel safe anywhere in the bayou) and André beached himself on the cleanest, least-muddy bank he could find, Gourami crawled up, too, and seemed remarkably unharmed. It sprawled alongside him, ribbiting repeatedly, sawing like a distressed insect. André sat up long enough to glance it over.

No lumps he could see, except the ones that were meant to be there. No twisted bits, no oozing wounds.

Did froggies suffer posttraumatic stress? They must; he was looking at the evidence.

If he'd had the sense to secure one of the abandoned scoots during the massacre—or if he could somehow either drag himself back or explain to Tetra what he needed—then he might make it to Novo Haven before fever in his wounds incapacitated him.

But that would mean leaving Gourami helpless.

When it had risked its life coming back for him. When he had promised Jean Kroc he would look out for it.

Still, it was his life. And dying of gangrene in a swamp wasn't as enticing as a single bullet through the brain.

He was unwilling to sell himself too cheaply.

He knuckled silt from his eyes and regretted it. He'd probably added more mud than he'd wiped away. If he could see himself, he'd be nothing but flaking clots; he felt cracked and itchy already.

Tetra had remained in the water. It swam back and forth restlessly, periodically submerging or darting out of sight, but always reemerging. André forced himself not to watch. It was too unnerving.

Beside him, Gourami also did not seem to be calming. Its distress, if anything, was growing; it shielded its eyes with its hands and curled tight.

At a loss, André reached out and laid a hand on it, as he might anyone.

The response was immediate and striking. Gourami breathed more slowly, scrunched eyes opening. It peeked between webbed digits without flinching.

"Gourami?"

It was looking at him when he spoke. It shuddered, a sort of releasing gesture, and leaned into his palm. He'd been thinking of pulling his hand back, but he left it there, although he knew he might be hurting the froggie.

Sometimes, you took your chances that you were doing more good than harm.

The froggie stared at him, silent, pouch taut and still against its throat. It extended its wrist, the one with the slate on it, and calmly, decisively, typed. André felt the muscle and tendon gliding under its slick skin.

—We have to go back.

He wasn't about to argue, anyway.

André had never seen so many dead things. He was used to clean death, quick, in comprehensible quantities.

This was unfathomable.

The water he moved through was thick with dead ranids, and parts of dead ranids; the only reason it didn't run red was that ranid blood, though violet when oxygenated, was otherwise nearly clear. Once the water diluted it, the color faded, and the river pushed what remained to the sea.

Tetra and Gourami moved away from him as they came within sight of the massacre. André hauled himself up on the bank, slithering like a snake, and tried not to think about his pain.

He tried even harder not to think about what was in the water saturating his open wounds.

He felt fretful, useless. He lay on the bank and watched as Gourami and Tetra worked among the dead, among the drifting chunks, and was sickly glad he could not help them.

They dragged the dead between them, weighted them down and sank them in the mud. Over each one, Tetra made some gestures; André could not tell if words were spoken. Every so often, fingers plucking deliriously through the water as if it tickled fish, Gourami scooped something up and swallowed it, sometimes with a glance at Tetra that André would have said was guilty, if Gourami were human.

Tetra, for its part, seemed unconcerned. André, on the other hand, was reasonably certain that this was one funeral custom he didn't want a better look at.

He lay back and dozed in a not-too-muddy spot. He'd exhausted himself with the flight, and with the return. He'd salvage a scoot when his leg throbbed less, when he was rested.

But the splashing kept him awake. And a ranid somewhere was ribbiting, wasn't it? Something was, anyway—a terrible cringing sound that made him want to cover his ears. He did, but he could still hear it, and it occurred to him that it must be a ranid crying somewhere. There was a quality to it that itched at him, demanding action, like the cries of kittens or of terrified children.

André opened his eyes. The body of a ranid floated past on the retreating tide, wreathed in gray loops of intestine, fish tugging at the drifting innards. Surely it couldn't be making that sound. Surely *it* couldn't still be dying.

André called out, but maybe he couldn't make his voice carry or maybe ranids did not care to hear him. He clawed through mud for a rock to throw, anything to get their attention. When he rooted one up, it was slimed and muddy. He chucked it overhand; it plunked into the swamp a few meters from Gourami.

Gourami turned at the sound, and as quickly turned back again. André could not keep its attention. As soon as he stopped shouting, he heard the noise again. He pressed his hand to his mouth. His breath tickled his fingers.

He was the person making it.

Jefferson did not like to look at the cages. They were spacious and comfortable, the floors and walls moistened membrane, misters running intermittently for the comfort of the subjects who would soon be installed. A regular vacation spot, Jefferson told himself. He made a note to have the data trail amended so it would seem that Dr. McCarter had been the requisitioning authority for this equipment. An overstep of her authority, but the other option was Schaffner, and he was an old family friend.

Besides, it wasn't as if anybody would ever check. Nothing was going to go wrong.

He checked his headset. Schaffner was just out of sight behind a bank of equipment that blocked the view of the processing floor. Jefferson didn't particularly want to walk out there among the sedated ranids; he contented himself with sending a quick ping.

Schaffner responded immediately, and Jefferson opened the connection. "How are the facilities, Neil?"

Schaffner's image straightened; he dusted off his hands. Jefferson was willing to bet that the real one hadn't so much as looked up from whatever subject he was examining. "It's fine, thanks. These specimens are a little the worse for wear."

Jefferson smoothed a hand over a cool work surface, slick steel and slightly gritty black slate. The lab was new, sound-absorbent tiles making it pleasant. "Best we could do on short notice." There was no point in picking a fight with Schaffner. A ping interrupted before either of them could speak again. "That's Tim. Gotta go."

It was Tim in a fury, too. That was evident as soon as Jefferson opened a screen. "Just what the hell do you think you're trying to pull?"

"Tim? What are you talking about?" Jefferson arranged his icon in the most open pose he could manage, and waited.

"Your attack on the ranid village at"—a flashed

map image, grid coordinates blinking—"using Rim security forces."

"A retaliatory raid," Jefferson said. "We have intelligence that that particular native colony was the staging ground for the recent terrorist attacks. We've retained prisoners for questioning. We have reason to believe that one of their elders may be responsible for the conjured explosion at the recruiting station."

"You've started a war."

"We've acknowledged one," Jefferson answered. "Bring it up at the next board meeting if you're unhappy. See you there."

He closed the session before Closs could answer, and set his messaging to *away*.

Jean smelled the carnage before he saw it. The bayou had its own range of odors, from sweetly rotten to musky-cold, briny or gassy or sulfuric. But this was a battlefield reek of cold burned gunpowder, spilled bowels, and shed blood. Ranid blood, more redolent of sugar than iron, relied upon cooperatively bonding haemerythrin as an oxygen-carrying agent.

They bled fuchsia.

He let his skiff glide silently for a while, poling only when it threatened to drift to a stop or run aground. There was silence ahead, and he feared it.

A body floated by—a far-swimmer, still tangled in se nets. Jean wondered where this one had come from, originally, bringing with it the freight of its stories and its genes. After a moment's consideration, he captured the dead froggie with a weighted rope and drew it close, alongside the skiff. Freshly killed, he thought; there was no sign of small crustaceans colonizing the wounds, so it could not have been dead for more than a couple of hours.

And yet, everything was silent.

Considering, he lashed it alongside the skiff, and poled on.

When he came out from among the reeds, he was braced for the worst. Jean Kroc had seen slaughter before. He had been on-planet when the Hogarth's World Charter Trade Company had seen fit to put down a worker uprising there. Hoggie was surface-dry; most of the water was pumped from deep wells. In some of the newer homesteads, though, they were just drilled and capped, and operated with a hand-pump. Half the residents were transportees or the children of transportees; no one cared too much for their creature comforts.

Jean Kroc knew of three people who had been crushed to death—suffocated—when they and dozens of others had climbed into the well-shaft to escape the automatic-weapons fire.

Jean hadn't been one of the civilians hiding in the well.

He'd been one of the militia holding the guns.

Not too long after, he'd found ways to get the money to emigrate. By the time he'd left, he'd had to. A soldier's pay wasn't the price of an emigration stake, even to a manpower-hungry world like Greene's. And Jean Kroc hadn't always been a conjure man. So he'd done what he thought he had to, and he'd gotten the funds to leave.

Jefferson Greene was not the worst rich man on the Rim. Jean Kroc had worked for the worst rich man on the Rim. For three years, before he'd wriggled loose.

But that was light-years and the best part of a

century ago. It was just the smell of blood—even ranid blood—bringing back visceral, garish memories.

When he found where the greatparent had died, two froggies Jean knew were singing over it. And André Deschênes was passed out, fevered, on the bank.

When André awoke in the hospital, imperfectly washed and still gritty in the crevices, the first thing he did was call Jean Kroc a fool. "Rim is trying to kill me. Did you hang a target on the door?"

Jean rolled his shoulders in that way he had. "What makes you so sure it was Rim? Anyway, the hospital has a licensed coincidence engineer on duty. And I have been keeping an eye on you. Just in case."

"Thanks," André said, not bothering to conceal his sarcasm. An IV protruded from the back of his hand. He felt no pain; not even in his cast and elevated leg, despite an elaborate arrangement of screws and inflatable appliances that told him a little bit about the complexity of the surgery he'd missed while unconscious. His skin was cool where he pressed the back of his other hand to his cheek. "Good of you to care. Where's Cricket?"

A sideways flicker of his eyes. Jean didn't so much change the subject as refuse to allow André to change it. "Besides, I know who's been gunning for you."

"So do—"

"Not Rim."

It was awkward to lift his head, to try to get a look at Jean while his leg was lifted in the air. His lacerated back didn't hurt at all, but he could feel the cool resilience of a gel dressing laid on the mattress under him. He wondered how much glue and how many stitches it had taken to put him back together again, and whether they'd managed to match his skin tone with the stem culture or if he'd have tan spots he'd have to have corrected. Mottled like a frog, which would have made him laugh if it didn't make his eyes sting.

Jean rose from the green-and-white hospital chair and touched the control to inflate André's pillow slightly. André leaned back, let his neck relax. But he didn't let his guard down. "Who, then?"

"None of your damned business."

André jerked forward; the lack of pain tended to make him forget that he was incapacitated. He felt incredibly pleasant, actually; floating, but not disassociated. And so comfortable. It was hard to sustain the irritation, even when Jean put a hand on his shoulder and eased him back, one more time. "It's my business when it's my life at risk."

"I handled it," Jean said. "You're my apprentice; you're my problem. You worry about it when I say you do."

A shock of cold water, that. He hadn't gone to anyone else to fight his battles in fifteen years. And it was humiliating, infantilizing; *now* André's cheeks burned. He glared and bit his tongue. "Whatever you say."

Jean stepped back. His smile creased his prickled cheeks. "I know you're just mouthing that, but I appreciate the effort." He pulled a talker out of his pocket, the kind used by kids too young to be wetwired yet, pushed in the earbud, and clicked the activator. "Hello, yes, he's awake," he said, and paused to listen. "Why don't you come on in?"

"Cricket?" André asked.

But Jean shook him off, and moved toward the door. "I'll be back. Don't worry, you're safe here."

The door hissed open, shut, open again. André bit

down on his tongue, stopping the words before they got out, and was glad. It wasn't Cricket.

It was Maryanne. And she wasn't alone.

She came through the door first, but she was a scout, not the leader. And a meter behind her sailed a taller, older woman, straight as a mast, her broad shoulders and chin already set with disapproval. Zoë Deschênes.

Fucking Zoë.

She was cheaply dressed, under her dignity, and André flinched from it. "What are *you* doing here?"

"The doctor," Zoë said, calmly, "says you shouldn't even have a limp. How are you feeling?"

"I asked what you were doing here," he said. She already had him on the run. *Already.*

"I'd ask the same," she said. "But I know it. I wouldn't be here——"

"You shouldn't be."

She bulled over him. "I wouldn't be here if you...weren't. You stupid *bastard.* If Mother could see you——"

"She can't," André snapped back, despite himself, so sharp. Under his skin, like that. Instantaneously.

Maryanne stood back against the wall and twisted her fists in her skirt. Chin tucked, eyes downcast. She was a cousin on his father's side, not the same thing as being one of Zoë Asceline Deschênes's children at all.

Of course Zoë could push his buttons. Her mother had installed them.

She didn't smile; if she'd broken his defenses, he thought he'd snapped through hers just as completely. "You are such a bitch, André. Such a bitch. Such a *child.*"

He drew a breath, restored by it. "And you're here to call me names?"

The frown deepened. And then she did smile, lips

furling up to reveal broad white teeth. "No. And I shouldn't have done that." She paused. "I'm surprised you kept the name. When you were walking out on everything else."

"Not fair." He waved the back of his hand at Maryanne. "I was there for the family."

"Don't you bring me into this, André."

"You brought her!" He made his hands lie flat on the sheet, when he wanted to point at his sister, wave them wildly. He made himself look steadily at Zoë. Too much like *her* mother. Even the name. As if the elder Zoë had been able to imprint her personality on her firstborn child. "I'm surprised you came to see me here. Or not surprised, come to think of it. Did you visit to gloat, or to rub my nose in my crimes?"

"I came because I don't want to see you floating dead in the street," she said. "And because if Mother were alive, she'd have come for you. Even now."

"You're like a reefcrawler," he said. His fingers plucked the cool, slick bedding; he forced himself to stop. "You don't want me near you when I'm strong. But maybe if I'm easy prey, you'll come see what you pick off my carcass, is that it?"

Zoë hadn't moved from her spot near the door. She folded her arms over her chest; the cheap fabric of her blouse pulled taut. "Is that what you think of me?"

"I think you're a charlatan," he said. "I think you're a con artist. You wouldn't know real conjuring if it sent you a birthday wish. You tell people what they want to hear, you keep them trapped in their fantasies, and you skim off whatever you can. You're a profiteer, Zoë. Just like Mother was."

She stared for a minute, her knuckles paling where her fingers laced over her arms. "An *ethics* lecture?"

"Leave me the hell alone."

"Oh, I don't think so." A thoughtful purse of her lips punctuated the slow rocking of her head. He was in for it. Good; that would make it easier.

Angry was better than shamed.

But she surprised him. She nodded, and unfolded her arms, and came to him. She didn't sit on the bed; instead, she dragged over the chair that Jean had used and perched on the edge. On a smaller woman, it would have looked delicate. On her, it gave the impression of hunger. "You think you're better?"

"I'm not in the gutter lying to people," he said. "I'm not that."

He'd almost forgot Maryanne was in the room until she snorted. He glanced over; she was looking at him now. She shook her head and looked down.

"You're right," Zoë said, and patted his hand before she stood. "You're in a much better class of gutter now."

The door whisked shut behind them both while he still lay, stunned, chewing on his tongue.

Where the hell did she get off being embarrassed by him?

13

THEY LET ANDRÉ GO HOME IN TEN DAYS; IT WAS TWENTY-
four before he was on his feet. He spent the interim flat
on his back, at the mercy of a pair of home-care atten-
dants whose visits never seemed to coincide with when
he needed them.

He was fortunate; by the time doctors and diagnos-
tics pronounced him fit for weight-bearing exercise
and swapped him into a walking cast, he was free of
pain and just waiting for the new bone to harden.

Not quite a miracle cure. But pretty effective.

Cricket didn't call him during his recovery, and after
a while, he stopped asking Jean if he knew where she
was. Jean didn't answer, and André figured that was a
good an indicator as any that Cricket had found out
more than she wanted to. Sometimes people couldn't
handle the truth.

He had a long time for thinking, though, between
Jean's lessons (mostly theoretical, at this point) and it

occurred to him one morning as he struggled off the sofa and into the motorized cart that some truths were not of the nature that people could be expected to handle. He wished he could say it was some sort of a spiritual revelation, but mostly it was the wisdom born of nightmares.

You think you're fine. You think you got through it all right. And then you wake up sure the cold sweat on your face is blood, so real you can taste it.

It was just as well Cricket wasn't talking to him. He wasn't sure, anymore, what he had to offer.

It was almost a relief when Jean came for him, the day after he was allowed to walk again, and told him to pack a bag.

Gourami glided forward alone in the ocean, and thought, *I'm a far-swimmer now.*

Tetra had gone another way. Every capable person that Gourami and Tetra had found in the aftermath of the massacre had swum, bearing reports to other bands, other clans, other greatparents as well. The greatparents would share information, of course, but this way many of them would have different perspectives.

Younger adults had traveled upriver or along the coast. It should have been far-swimmers who braved the open water, but there were not enough. So the older and stronger young adults had swum.

Including those who were pregnant. As Gourami had become.

So now they were far-swimmers. But not far-swimmers such as the bands had often seen. One did not take on egglings when one meant to journey.

Gourami had not considered the consequences when

se first saw an eggling thrashing in bloodied water and realized what the birds were feeding on, among the dead. Se acted on instinct, in hope and terror; se netted the fearful eggling in handfingers and swallowed it. The shock of water stretching se virgin brood pouch was like pain. Gourami reeled.

And then seen and rescued another, another, another—

So many endoparents had jettisoned their broods in frantic hope of the young surviving. So many—and Gourami, no matter how se searched, even to examining the brood pouches of the dead, could save only a few.

And they could not live on their own. Gourami saw other young adults collecting egglings, one—Parrot— despite old crippling wounds, another with a broken forelimb lashed to se chest. None of them had any way of knowing which egglings were exosibs. They mostly could not even identify the endosibs. The young were all sizes, from first-hatched to almost-budded.

Gourami worried that the eldest would eat the youngest; they were not old enough to know better yet. And that happened sometimes when there was trauma or hunger.

So se must keep them well fed. Which was not a simple matter when one was swimming in open water.

The warm surface of the ocean coursed over Gourami's back, buoying. When se could not fish, se filter-fed, shunting much of the greens and chlorophyll into the pouch-water for the proper development of the egglings. They needed to establish their skin flora before they could live on their own. Although Gourami's crossbow dragged, se was glad to have it. With a coil of humen twine, it made fishing much easier. Sometimes great schools of silver-flashing jackharley or gray-gill surrounded Gourami, and se could shoot one without breaking stroke.

Se could not rest. Se sucked the flesh from the bones of the catch without stopping. There were larger predators in open water, and they knew the scent of blood. The fish-bones, se ground between jaw-plates until they powdered. Se enriched the pouch-water with it, so the egglings would grow strong, flexible skeletons.

This was especially important for the two egglings who were just budding, absorbing their tails and developing limbs.

Fortunately, the fish were plentiful. So the egglings thrived—except for three that Gourami lost and mourned and ate in the first week. Probably all the dead had been shocked or hurt beyond surviving at one-tree-island.

Only Gourami grew thin.

When Gourami reached the floating colony at two-half-moon-reef, se at first could not remember how to stop swimming. Se butted against the outer bladders, long muscles still twitching. The bladders floated lightly, taut, and Gourami bumped and bumped again.

But then there was splashing, the water slapping se flanks, someone touching, stroking a back Gourami had not known was sunburned until soft hands smoothed mucous over raw flesh. Strong hands lifted and led se, their owners patting and exclaiming as they brought se before the greatparent, who floated like an enormous stinging jelly in the midst of the colony. Se

had heard the news, of course; Gourami had swum farther than many others.

But that was not the same as touching a survivor.

Cricket—Fisher—was starting to prefer her new
name. Especially the way Nouel said it, with a little
twinkle, as if it were a joke shared. As he said it now,
sliding a drink across the desk to rest beside her hand.

"Fisher—" He waited for her to look up and smile.
She appreciated the training. "Company's here."

She appreciated the warning, too. She pushed herself upright on his couch. In the back of her head,
Maurice—present only in spirit—felt the shift in
her attention away from the code they were double-
teaming, and pinged.

She pinged back. *All clear; your data.*

The inside of her head was a changed place. When
she'd scrubbed her headset and reformatted, she'd
cleaned everything. Flashed the bios, sealed the old
data and wiped it, reformatted, and sent Nouel out to
purchase a new drive, memory, and parser off the shelf
from a shop chosen at random. Her hardware felt
chromed, and in the spirit of reinvention she'd done
the same kind of purge and start over with the soft-
ware. Over the course of years, one layered up clutter.
Dozens of half-used programs and heaps of old files
lurked in the corners of one's mind: three or four different messengers or mailers, newsfeeds about things
she used to care about, security codes to a house she
hadn't lived in since she was twelve.

All gone now.

"Fisher," Nouel repeated, "that company. Still need
a minute? How goes the war?"

She shrugged. Just under a month, and she was

already Nouel Huc's biggest fan. Except when she was Maurice Sadowski's. Because Nouel could definitely beat up Cricket's father. And Maurice could run him into the gutter. And the really shocking thing was that she honestly believed either one of them would do it for her.

Even though neither one of them wanted to fuck her. Nouel, as far as she could tell, was perfectly happy with his long-distance love.

Anyway, she had no glib answers for his questions. "They've incinerated Lucienne's body," she said. "Maurice thinks that if they managed to download her—I don't know if we have any way to get that information out of André—"

"Who is in the living room—"

"Yes, I caught that. Thank you. Maurice thinks they'd have it on an isolated system. No connex. So hacking into it, unlikely to happen. Even for him."

"Well," Jean said, from the doorway, "then we'll just have to break in. I've talked to Ziyi Zhou. She can get us coverage in the Core media if we can deliver the goods."

She'd been braced, she realized. Ready with an emotional death grip on herself, ready to greet André Deschênes with a chill and perfect facade. She almost didn't register what Jean said; she was too busy staring at the door.

André limped in, fifteen pounds thinner, one leg awkward in a green and blue walking cast, leaning on an orthopedic cane. He smiled when he saw her, a sweet childish expression that caught at her composure, fuzzed up its surface like burr-prickles snagging in silk. She couldn't answer in kind; she looked at him, and saw somebody she used to like.

She licked her lips, looked back at Jean, and said,

"That doesn't help us if we can't back it up, Jean Gris. If I'm legally Moon Morrow"—in the corner of her vision, André performed a perfect theatrical double take—"then I have access to Rim corporate secrets. If I can prove in court that I'm the new original. But I'll bet you my bottom demark that my motherself has signed a nondisclosure agreement—"

"That matters?"

Maurice, listening over Cricket's feed, seemed about to pop an icon into the room and explain. But Cricket beat him to it. "Technically, she has no rights," Cricket said. "*If* I can prove I'm her quantum clone. When you sign the paperwork, you sign your identity over to the childself." Cricket didn't tell them that she remembered signing it, thumbprint and retinal scan and an old-fashioned ink pen, a thing you only used for wills and marriages and adoptions.

Ten thousand years of literacy as a species, and there was still something about signing your name that *felt* like a contract.

"Draconian," André said, the first word out of his mouth.

Cricket almost looked at him, but stopped herself in time. "Keeps people from cloning themselves for fun, now doesn't it? Anyway, if we're going that route, I need to file papers. And then Rim will be after me for real. André—"

"André is retired," André said.

"—is not their only gun."

"Oh," he said. This time, she did look at him, and found him lip-pursed, eyes half lidded, as if studying his arrogance from an interior angle. "You have a point."

"The information has to come from somewhere, people." Maurice, rezzing in the center of the room, threw up his hands. Cricket hid a smile; she'd been making herself bets on how long he could stay away.

André leaned around his image, looked Cricket in the eye, and said, "I'll testify."

The silence was palpable. Cricket heard her heart beat in her ears. The meta-visual clutter of her over-hauled headset, even pruned, was suddenly unbear-able. She shut it down, all of it, and focused on the three men and the one icon.

Nouel got up and crossed the room. He poured a fin-ger of straw-colored liquor into a squat tumbler and knocked it back. The next one, he tried to hand to André, but he might as well have been pushing it on a mannequin. For André, it seemed as if there was no one in the room but Cricket.

"It will mean jail time," Cricket said. United Earth didn't have the death penalty, except for treason.

"Maybe life," Nouel added. "On Greene's World. Where Charter Trade can get to you."

And that *was* a death sentence.

Jean took the untouched glass from Nouel's hand and brought it to Cricket, who did accept. She let the rim rest against her teeth, the smooth glass warm from Jean's skin, and watched André breathe and think. He still hadn't dropped his gaze from hers when he shrugged and said, "Life? What else am I doing with it?"

Cricket set the glass aside, watching it click on a checkerboard side table. When she looked up, André was still staring. She crossed to him, put her hand lightly against his chest, and balanced up to kiss him on the corner of the mouth. Warm flesh, dry lips, the small curls of his beard.

"This doesn't make me a better man than I was yes-terday," he said.

Cricket shrugged and stepped back. He loved her, and she didn't love him, but that didn't mean they had to be assholes about it. "See you in hell," she said cheerfully, and leaned her shoulder against his arm.

Maurice would report to work in person the next day. He would bring Closs the final bombshell that they had been saving—the news that Lucienne Spivak had not been merely a local activist, but an agent of Unified Earth, a government agitator working for the Bureau of Extraterrestrial Affairs. That she had been operating on Greene's World under several identities, one of which was that of Lisa Anne Angley, who had faked her own death in the process of facilitating a coincidentally engineered explosion on board the ranid recruiting ship.

That she had, with the aid of ranid extremists, escaped underwater before the ship blew up. That she had been instrumental in the deaths of several men.

André listened impassively as Maurice laid out the information he would deliver. Only when the archinformist was done did he speak, shifting uncomfortably on the sofa where he reclined, his healing leg propped on cushions.

"Is that true?"

"Tolerably," Jean said, when Maurice didn't answer. Cricket gave him such a look, and he shrugged. "I knew who she was working for. Unified Earth would just *love* a legal excuse to get the omelite monopoly away from Jeff Greene. As you can imagine."

We were friends, Cricket almost said. But she hadn't told Lucienne who she had used to be either. Did that make *her* less a friend?

People had secrets. You lived with it or you didn't.

André said it again, as if he needed to fix it in his

head. "I assassinated a government agent for Jefferson Greene."

"Still time to change your mind," Nouel said, hands folded together so the sinews in their backs stood out. It was obvious what he thought the best course was, and Cricket was a little startled by his loyalty.

André shook his head. "Keep talking."

It was at its heart Cricket's plan, and she thought it was a good one. Judging by their expressions, the men didn't disagree. Jean let a faint smile deepen the lines between the corners of his nose and the corners of his mouth, and Nouel was giving Cricket that querying eyebrow. Maurice might be a bit less sanguine, but as it was his neck first on the block, Cricket couldn't blame him. They would need an inside man.

There were two choices. Him, or André. And André was needed elsewhere.

To his credit, though Maurice went pale and tight-faced when Cricket made her suggestions, his only reply was a nod.

"Maurice goes inside," Cricket reiterated, wishing she could just flash-highlight the relevant text. Not with Jean in the conversation. She could *talk* much faster than she could *speak*, and with much greater information density. *Words are hell.* "The rest of us, except André, come in from the outside on a data run, and get intentionally messy. Carefully. While we distract Charter Trade's security, André waits on his scoot for Maurice's transmission. Maurice recovers what he can off the internal systems and makes a handoff to André. André ferries the data personally to Ziyi Zhou and stays with her until she sends it to Earth."

"And we vanish into the night like ninja," Maurice said, and embarrassed himself with a karate chop.

She glanced around the room one more time, saw

tight concentration, nodding. "Maurice told us something else," she said, looking to Nouel for permission to continue.

Maurice took it as an invitation. "The god-botherers have a theory," he said, "that the ranids used to have a technological civilization. That they possibly abandoned it by choice. It gives us another point of leverage against Charter Trade, if I can pull out some proof. Proof, even that Greene suspects and hasn't reported it."

For once, it was Jean looking most puzzled. André's relief was almost palpable. Cricket took pity on them both. "You know the rule about planetary colonies."

"Only on worlds where the natives are prespace," Jean said.

Cricket nodded. She knew this through her motherself. It had been her *job*. "There isn't a rule for worlds that have *chosen* barbarism. Nobody ever thought of that. If Charter Trade is suppressing that information, the scandal could last years."

"Oh," Jean said. And then, quite unnecessarily, he added, "Damn. I wish Lucienne were here."

Cricket snapped away. She hadn't forgiven André, not exactly. And she wasn't going to let him see her cry.

Her hand caught her discarded glass on the edge of the table. It sailed into the air; she fumbled after it, felt her fingers glance off. Nobody else was close enough to catch.

They stood and watched it fall.

It landed upright on the floor and did not shatter. A narrow column of liquor followed it down, splashed inside, spat a thread up to catch the light, and fell into concentric ripples in the cradle of the glass. Not a drop spilled.

"Wow," Cricket said. "That was convenient."

It was Jean Kroc who murmured, "Oh, *shit*."

14

THE PROBABILITY STORM SIMMERED THROUGH THE NIGHT, and Jean refused to let anyone travel. "Why put yourself in the way of coincidence?" he said.

Later, as Jean was helping Nouel make up the red-upholstered couches for him and André to sleep on, Cricket asked, "Can't you do something about it?" Cricket already had the guest room; Jean watched André visibly consider asking if he could share it and then, just as visibly, let go.

The first answer on his tongue was sharper than she warranted. He turned it around until he found a kinder way to phrase it; this couldn't be easy on her either. "No. Because mucking with probability now is not the best, er, possible idea."

Her mouth made an O. She looked at her feet and nodded. "Stupid question," she said. But it hadn't been, really. Just a human one, and he patted her on the arm. She moved as if he hadn't touched her, but bent and pulled a sheet taut. Where her fingers dented the fabric, three of them went right through.

As luck would have it.

She looked up, startled.

"It would have happened sooner or later. Nothing to do," he said, "but sit tight and wait it out."

As it played out, none of them slept much. Nouel fired up the living room system; they got news on three walls, seven feet high. Cricket reported that Maurice had retired his connection, ostensibly to sleep. The rest of them piled onto the chairs and couches and settled in under blankets, despite the lingering warmth of the night. Jean imagined that the other three were also following newsdrips, feeds, and real-time chats.

Jean was suddenly, unsentimentally grateful that he'd left that behind. He rested his head against the back of the couch and just watched the walls, captions on and the sound turned down. Occasionally, Cricket or Nouel read out a headline. André said almost nothing.

It was a night of news worth staying up for, Cricket's unspilled cup being the least of it. Broadcast stories included a roster of biblical exigencies: the death by burning of an elderly woman alone in a locked room; the spontaneous appearance of a young man in evening dress—speaking no known language—in the middle of Troutbrook Street; a rash of mysterious objects appearing in public places while no one happened to be looking. A refrigeration unit, a piece of garden statuary, a half-ton pile of whitefish.

There was another seaquake.

A mining platform burned.

Those did not worry Jean as much as the teleporting objects. "Apports," he said, drawing his knees to his chest. A sinkhole seemed to have opened in his stomach. He pressed both fists into his flesh, but his voice

would not be steadied. "Oh, that's very bad news indeed."

"Apports?" Nouel asked. He lay on the floor on his
stomach, his chin propped on his hands. His eyes were
closed; whether he was shutting out the news or
watching a scroll on his headset, Jean was not quite
sure.

"There is a statistically small, but nonzero, chance
that any given object will not be where you left it,"
Jean said. "It has to do with timestreams forking and
healing. It's how the Slide works."

André said, "Oh."

"The Exigency Corps hasn't issued a warning—"

"Nouel," Cricket said, "they didn't on Patience either." She also sat on the floor, her back to the sofa,
next to André's unbroken leg. He kept glancing down
at her as if he wanted to ruffle her hair, but his hands
stayed on the couch. *Her* fingers plucked at the fringe
of the rug; she didn't seem to notice that she was in-
ducing it to shift color with each stroke. She looked up,
across the room. Jean looked back. "How bad is this going to get?"

"I don't know," he said. And then, because it seemed
like a bad time to lie, he added, "worse." He turned his
attention to Nouel. "May I use your screen? I need to
make an interplanetary call."

That was worth it for the looks Cricket and André
gave both him, and each other. He expected he could
produce superior expressions in a moment, and yet he
felt a profound reluctance.

They had planned this. He had been a party to it.
He had allowed Lucienne to choose, although he had
not been in accord with her choosing. But her death
had been part of the game, and he'd let her play it the
way she'd intended.

They all had debts to pay. Lucienne had her own reasons, and he'd never asked what they might be.

It didn't make it any easier to enter the code and call her, though, half a galaxy away.

André had killed her. He'd laid her limp body out, turned her head, slid a cable into the access port for her headset. He'd combed his fingers through her sweat-damp, sea-salt hair, pushing aside tendrils that had snapped off too short for the braid. He'd lifted her body in his arms, held her like a sleeping child, and sunk her in hundreds of feet of water, where she'd become entangled. He'd watched the sea close over her as the weight of the water he'd piped into her lungs carried her down.

Lucienne Spivak smiled at him and said, "André. Nice to finally meet you face to face, even if it is by transmission. I hope you're well?"

"Oh, fuck," Cricket said, and ran for the bathroom.

André tried to struggle to his feet, whether to follow Cricket or meet standing the woman he'd murdered, he wasn't sure. He heaved and fell back, and then Jean was beside him, hand on his shoulder, and he didn't try again. He couldn't settle back on the cushions either, though, so he leaned forward and disregarded the twinge from his propped foot. "How did you—"

Not the most politic of questions. Perhaps he got some consideration for shock. Lucienne smiled, and said blandly, "You killed me. No game."

Cricket had just emerged from the bathroom, wiping her mouth on her hand. André thought she might slump to the floor, from the way she was heeling over, but she braced herself on the doorframe and rolled her shoulders back. "How *could* you?" she said. "How could you let me think you were dead? How could you, how could you let me feel your death? We were friends."

André had heard children say the word that way, with total conviction and total betrayal. Friends. As if it were the only thing that mattered in the world.

"Sweetheart," Lucienne said gently, "that wasn't me."

André blinked. He reached out a hand to Cricket; without seeming to look, she came and sat beside him, settling into the couch under the curve of his arm. She leaned against him, and it was all sun-warmth and bittersweet longing. Even when Lucienne winked at him like a rabbit punch, the sweet hurt, the emptiness that was Cricket curled against him for the last time, did not fade. If anything, it sharpened.

You don't *always* know, when you touch somebody for the last time. But sometimes you can tell. Sometimes, you get a chance to appreciate it in all its spiky glory. "It was you," Cricket said. "We were friends, and—"

"You lied to each other."

"We didn't tell each other everything," Cricket said. "That's not the same."

Lucienne swallowed. André saw the ringlike shadows move under her skin. "The person you knew was my daughterself," she said, quietly. "She—I—followed you to Greene's World when you fled prosecution on Earth. And you turned out quite different from the Moon Morrow I've been hunting since she got out of prison, I might add." She lowered her eyes. "I hope you don't think your motherself has your scruples."

André squeezed her, lightly, with the embracing arm. She didn't quite shake him off, but the stiffness in her shoulders told him he wouldn't get another warning. "I remember," Cricket said. "I changed."

"You thought you were Morrow."

"I—"

"Posthypnotic suggestion," Lucienne said. "She had a pretty clever plan; to send you on ahead, avoid the prison sentence that way, and use you to solidify a hold over Charter Trade."

"But I didn't go to Charter Trade."

"No," Lucienne said. "You went to ground. You didn't do what Morrow would have. You developed a conscience."

"She didn't?" This time, Cricket snugged against André's side by herself. He let her, and didn't try to hold onto her.

"You grew up somewhat. You came to an understanding about Patience, among other things."

"If I'm her," Cricket said, "then how can I have changed when she didn't?"

Jean cleared his throat. André had been so focused on Cricket, and on Lucienne—who, he was thankful, was not staring at him with that particular expectant expression—that he had almost forgotten that Jean and Nouel were in the room. "It could have gone either way," he said, with a self-effacing shrug.

Nouel cleared his throat, leaned forward, and said, "Doesn't this all seem a little coincidental to you?"

Cricket frowned. "Don't be silly, I can't possibly be entangled. I've never ever worked for Rim—" Her eyes widened.

"What?" André's plan had been to stay silent. He should have remembered that plans never survived contact.

Cricket stood, stepped away, and turned back long enough to give him an accusing look. He spread his hands. The couch was too hot and too moist against his back. He wished he could just stand up and follow her.

She tweaked her hair behind her shoulders, and looked back at Lucienne. "When they ... made me. But Morrow must have hidden that? I mean, if everybody knew——"

"I work for Unified Earth," Lucienne said. "I'm sorry, Cricket. Lucienne was my quantum clone, as you were Morrow's. There's ... an awareness that we have. When you were scared or hurt, she could find you. We knew Morrow wouldn't let you get too far out of sight. So you were our ticket for taking the whole filthy Greene's World Charter Trade cabal down."

"But you had Maurice."

"Not then." She tilted her head. "There's another issue; there has to be enough of a public scandal to discredit Rim before UE wades in. When Morrow did what she did, she was our problem. Us going after her could look vindictive."

Oh, André thought. And that had nothing to do with it, of course. "So you're telling us to trust the government?"

"I'm asking you to consider the alternatives. Also, we needed people who could testify. Personally. We needed a bulletproof case."

"You've got it." Cricket turned her head and looked at André. Looked through André, the brown flecks swimming in her tea-colored eyes. "Don't you?"

There are moments, he understood, when your life changed in front of your eyes. Sometimes you knew it. You pulled a trigger. You kissed a girl.

Other times, you only caught it in the receding view.

He could walk away now. He didn't have to go to the

wall for them. Jean and Lucienne had just admitted they'd set him up.

He deserved it. But Cricket didn't, and they'd fucking *conjured* her. And convinced her that he'd killed her best friend. He *had* killed her best friend.

That was something of an unpatchable betrayal.

And *she* was still standing there.

And he didn't, he realized, have to decide right now.

"That's why you took me on?" He stared past Cricket, at Jean Kroc, and Jean Kroc nodded. He'd been expecting the question; he didn't have to pause to think.

"Son of a bitch," André said. "I thought it was my talent."

"No," Jean said. "All the talent in forty worlds doesn't make you not a killer, André."

And there it was, held up for him. Something he could look at square, through the filter of the mud and the violet blood and the scent of sugar and the poor damned froggies stupidly trying to bury their dead. "No," he said, with Jean and Cricket and Nouel all looking at him, and the projected image of Lucienne carefully looking away. "I guess it doesn't. So why did you take me on?"

Jean shrugged. He got up, came over to André, and helped him to his feet. André balanced unsteadily, and Jean brought him his crutch. He leaned on it and watched, as Jean stepped back, as Cricket silently withdrew to sit again, this time beside Nouel and not looking at Lucienne at all.

Jean cleared his throat, drawing André's attention again. "Because you're not the only killer in the room."

Nouel lifted one finger, breaking a waiting silence.

"Maurice has just been called into work," he said. "We're on a little early, friends."

By the fourth quarter, Closs knew he was looking at the end of the world. He'd spent the evening in crisis management, but for each one he passed off to a capable subordinate or handed down the chain of command with a resolution plan, two more bloomed in its place. His office became a virtual situation room, the view through the tall windows obscured by projections, icons showing his night-shift troubleshooters working, heads down, eyes moving restlessly.

They even made it through the seaquake; disaster response had protocols in place to handle those, and Novo Haven did not suffer a tsunami. But Closs knew by then that things were going to hell, and he didn't think this failure would be the last one.

When the first drilling platform went—it could have been terrorism, or coincidence run riot, or both— he knew it was time. He told his executary to wake everybody up, to call them in. He didn't bother sending a message to Jefferson Greene. Either his own people would do it, he was already working on a problem and hadn't bothered to inform Closs, or he would find out in the morning. In any case, Closs was not in the mood for a fight, and it was still easier to get forgiveness.

He had already given the order to break the city up when the alert came in warning of a freak storm brewing in the gulf. The first IM from Amanda Delarossa was only half a minute behind, marked *critical*.

Can't reach Greene. Taking the Slide offline, it read. *Executive decision. Major probability correction under way. Hang on to your ass.*

He called her. It went through on a heartbeat; whether she'd been waiting for the call, hoping for Greene, or whether she was just sitting in her ready room staring at the cup of coffee in front of her, waiting for the storm to blow over so there was something for her to do, he wasn't sure. *"Offline?"*

"The whole oyster," she said. "It's powering down now. We'll have in-system communications, but you should expect a slight lightspeed lag."

Her eyes were slightly unfocused, as if she were watching a countdown; she was, because she popped it up on his display, too.

"Starting about—" The image flickered. Hiccuped. Came back midword. "—ow."

It lasted less than a second. A flutter. The lag was so slight that it could seem like a thoughtful hesitation in speech. It was only what it signified that made Closs feel as if he'd plunged his hands in ice-water to the elbows.

They were cut off. Cut off from Earth, cut off from Core, alone in the measureless cosmologic sea. "There's a theory," Amanda said, "that if they'd done this on Patience when things went squirrelly, they might have saved the station."

"If they'd jettisoned the antimatter, they might have saved the station, too," Closs said. "So I take it you can't give me any help with this storm?" He popped up a weather map, in case she'd missed the warning. A vast swirl of angry clouds confronted them, the twisted meeting of three low-pressure fronts—two warm, one unseasonably cold—feeding into one another.

"Damn," Amanda said. "Is that an *eye?*"

Closs nodded. "An extratropical cyclone. We've got maybe fifty, sixty quarters before it hits." Normally, Novo Haven had two or three days to respond to

cyclone threat. The usual recourse was to disperse the
city, run before the winds, rely on the god-botherers to
send the storms on as harmless a path as possible, and
return when the threat had passed. Sometimes, years
went by without a drill. Some years, they fled two or
three times.

They'd been having a run of good luck, Closs
thought bitterly.

"No," Amanda said. "I can't do anything for you.
I'm sorry, Major." She looked up, then, startled from
her chair fast enough that the coffee wobbled on
her table. "Shit, I think I have a more immediate
problem—"

"Amanda—"

"*Oh, shit!*"

Closs remembered hearing somewhere that those
were the most common last words spoken by those who
died in accidents. He had no idea from whence the data
came. It didn't comfort him; there was no merciful fuzz
of static and wipe of black this time.

Amanda's words were followed by a thump that
would have deafened Closs if he'd been hearing it with
his ears instead of his brain. A whoosh, and then nothing: absolute silence. There was a split-second of
blackness as the power failed, before emergency lights
kicked in.

Amanda had been using an external mote rather
than a headset projection, sending him her real-time
image. So he glimpsed the empty, shattered ready
room, the twisted remains of the bulkheads and ceiling, plumes of escaping, frozen air in the weak green
glow of what emergency lighting remained unbroken.

And through the torn-open floor, the silverfish flash
of a spaceship whose design he did not recognize, turning as it looped away.

"Shit," Closs said. It was thirty seconds before he could bring himself to break the connection, though there wasn't a chance in hell that anybody was alive in there. Finally, he blinked it away, though, and started composing another emergency alert message in his head. If anybody *had* made it off the station—if anybody *did* make it off the station—they would need to keep the landing lanes open and lit for the lighters as long as possible, and volunteers in cutters would need to stay behind to evacuate the crews.

This time, he *did* send an instant message to Greene, highest priority. And wasn't surprised by the *unavailable* tag that popped back. He spun on the ball of his foot and began to pace, fielding the requests for clarification and direction as they flooded in.

Outside, the cyclone alarm climbed the night.

Jefferson passed over the Y-15 omelite rig and landed on the *Richardson Explorer* only a few quarters after midnight. The sky was already louring, the moon-glow only permeating a few threadbare places in the overcast.

On the rig, work continued under floods despite the hour. They had to meet rising quotas. From his vantage overhead, he got a good view of the workers, as purposeful and mindless as colony insects. The *Explorer*, however, was still and dark. She rocked gently in the chop; Greene checked his weather eye before beginning his descent. There was one hell of a storm blowing up to the south; he'd have to finish here quickly and beat feet back to Novo Haven, unless he wanted to spend the next day tossed on the ship.

This time, the only people waiting for his chopper were the crew members who secured it—a much more efficient use of manpower. Jefferson thanked the nearest one and headed below, refusing an escort. By now, he thought he'd better be able to find his own way down to the labs.

They opened to his ident, and he stepped inside after overriding the interior monitors—with McCarter's code, not his own. The lights were out; he heard only soft chirping. The surviving research subjects: the controls.

They would have to be sacrificed as well.

Jefferson had kept himself well apprised of the layout of the lab and its contents over the course of the previous few weeks. There was a time, he understood, when his desperate plan would have had no hope of success. A time before exigency engineering; a time before a thorough understanding of biomanufacturing.

But Schaffner had called him that afternoon, and told him that stage one of the project was partially successful. A single pathogen had been engineered. Whether it bore sufficient similarity to the rumored one, he couldn't assure the chairman without a sample, of course. But it was a start, and others would follow.

Jefferson knew where the vials were kept. The inside pocket of his flight jacket was lined with therm. From it, he pulled a padded titanium box thirty centimeters long. Six vials fit into it, nested side by side. He closed it and sealed it, and took one last look around the lab.

A fire would not be obvious, given the ongoing festival of sabotage. But it would be inhumane to leave the animals to burn. Jefferson crossed to their cages—half of them empty now—and felt the thrill of their noises up his spine. They went subsonic as he approached, the sneaking creatures, and crowded the glass, as if trying to see what he was doing.

The emergency purge button was under several layers of glass and fail-safes. He used McCarter's code again, and lifted the bubble with his sleeve wrapped over his fingertips. He pushed it down. There was a hiss of gas.

One of the frogs was still signing weakly against the glass when he turned away. He didn't look back; it would be with its friends soon enough.

15

THE CYCLONE SIRENS BEGAN TO WAIL IN THE SWELTERING dark hours of morning; Cricket almost overturned the chair she had been sitting curled in, her knees cupped in her hands. She stumbled but caught herself. "Crap. Just the siren."

André nudged her thigh with his elbow from his spot on the sofa. She glared, then shook herself and settled. He meant to be comforting. She could tell by his eyebrows. He *was* trying.

"We'll have to speed up our schedule," Nouel said, leaving Cricket grateful that he'd filled the silence. "Inside of two hours, we'll have to resort to a commando raid at sea, and I don't think——"

"Right," André said. "I'm on my way." Cricket helped him up; his palm was cool and sweating. She wanted to pull away from the contact. It nauseated her to see him nervous. Human.

"I won't be able to help you," Jean said, and André

waved it aside with the back of his hand. "The probability storm."

"Careful—" Lucienne's icon said, as wide-eyed as if blind to any irony.

Cricket wondered. Lucienne had been her best friend. Lucienne would have slipped Cricket a sideways glance as she said it, and Cricket would have been meant to understand that the comment had its barbs.

This Lucienne was not her friend. Nothing had changed; André had still killed the Lucienne Cricket cared for.

Why would you choose to die—really die—even if your motherself survived? It didn't mean that *you* were any less dead.

Cricket couldn't imagine dying for Moon Morrow. But then, maybe she was just the sort of person who couldn't imagine dying for anyone. Or the sort nobody should be dying for.

André shifted his cane to the other side and wiped his hand on his trousers. Cricket stepped back. By the time he summoned up his bulletproof smile, she couldn't look at it. "I'll come back. I promise."

Don't come back for me. But she nodded, drymouthed, and touched the back of his hand. "Try not to get killed."

And there was no more irony in it when she said it than when Lucienne had.

Less than sixty seconds later, he was out in his scoot, pulling away from the dock. He'd paused to put the top up. Cricket didn't watch him from the window, other than one quick glance when the headlamp flashed on.

She was definitely way too jumpy.

Nouel cleared his throat and said, "Message from Maurice." Cricket, despite her promise to herself to calm the hell down, shied from a sudden flash of memory: if everyone here except the impeccable Nouel had been better dressed before they started looking shopworn, this could be any UE situation room.

Nouel gave her a curious look and kept talking, once he had Jean's attention. "He's not quite at the office. Says they expect to be clear for breakup within two hours; the outermost barges on Bayside are already moving out. He says to tell André that he's not going to be able to transmit once he's in. They'll notice the bandwidth if they're locked down, and protocol is to lock down."

Cricket flinched. "I'll call him."

"Also, he wants me to pass a message to you, Jean."

"Go for it," Jean said.

Half a second later, just as Lucienne was looking as if she was about to interject a comment, her image flicked off like a closed fan. And half—no, *most* of Cricket's network dropped out of connection. Routes she used daily were truncated, chats—she'd had to find new ones, in the person of her reincarnation, and start working her way up again—were empty, and archives she'd been mining for fifteen years were nonexistent. Most of the data holds were gone.

"Jean—" she said, and then bit the rest of the sentence back as Maurice's icon resolved in the center of the room. But Jean turned to her, and she had the answer ready. "Earth's down. No, wait. *We're* down. We're off the fucking Slide."

"No connex," Jean said. And Maurice interjected, "Not quite none. I'm here. They shut down the station."

"There's a massive probability correction under way," Jean said. "A storm of coincidence."

"There's more than that," Maurice said. "I think the planet is forking."

"Forking?" Everybody was looking at Cricket, which was how she knew she must have said it.

There was no way she could have felt Nouel's house rocking on the swells yet, even if a storm was coming, but still she groped backward, sat down where André had been sitting. The dark red cloth of Nouel's sofa was soft against her palms, though the nap caught her skin. "The *fucking planet* is cloning itself? Planets—" She bounced up again. She stalked toward him, and she thought if he were present in the flesh, she might have hit him. "—don't just fucking *mitose*."

She heard herself, and stopped abruptly. "Maurice. Sorry."

He blinked at her. She saw him shudder, the kind of bone-deep flex your body makes when a chill grabs you by the nape. "Okay. You're Moon Morrow's clone daughter."

"Touché. You were saying when I went orbital?"

"There's not time to explain," he said. "Some of our scientists"—Cricket tried not to think about how easily he referred to Charter Trade as *we*—"think that the source of the omelite is a prehistoric explosion. Caused by the ranids' attempts to build a Slide on-world."

"So they had a fairly high-tech civilization," Jean said, but not as if he understood the tiny, shuddering epiphany that hovered at the edge of Cricket's mind. "You mentioned that before. And they lost it in the disaster?"

"The planet...forked," Maurice said. "Split. Incompletely. Got stuck halfway. I dunno, I'm not a physicist and I'm not a conjure. If we had six-dimensional eyes maybe we could see the other half of it. And on this side..."

"They took the technology apart," Cricket said.

"Right? They didn't lose it. They decided not to use it. And Rim is covering it up?"

Maurice nodded.

"Wow," Cricket said. "And we haven't got any way at all to get that information to Lucienne?"

A stupid question; she knew it when she asked it. But sometimes, you still had to ask. "I'll call André," she said.

He picked up immediately. "Deschênes." And listened impassively as she outlined the situation. She felt him looking at her, as if he were across the table, and not out in the prestorm calm.

"Right," he said, after a moment's consideration. "Tell Maurice I'll meet him inside."

If André had had the engine power to manage it, he would have been seeing a redshift. The scoot was full throttle as he zipped under folding sidewalks and between water taxis, threading the needle over and over without so much as a hard rub. He was in his element, and for a moment he could forget. Enough concentration, enough adrenaline, and the thick feel of water full of churned mud and blood dropped off his skin, the noises of the wounded and the grieving fell away from his ears.

If only he could spend the rest of his life running, he thought he'd be just fine.

At this hour, the streets should have been empty, but the claxons had ended that. People and devices scurried about, making ready; sidewalks were scrolled up, rolled up, and stowed, lines cast off, the city made ready to scatter under floodlights and the occasional arcing searchlight of an observing helicopter. The Bayside barges were already peeling away, their white and yellow and sea-green hulls turned shadowy in moonlight, the water curling phosphorescent from their bows. It was an eerie sight—a hundred outbound barges with their running lights red to port and green to starboard, moving in a purposeful ballet.

All channels led from Novo Haven.

In addition to the shipping lanes, three of the inbound lighter channels blinked red-blue-orange rather than their usual green, cleared for outbound surface traffic, though lighters were still coming in on the remaining two, trailing their cargo pods behind them. Tenders hurried to them; enough of the city had broken up that André got clear glimpses of the action through the moving lines of outbound cruisers, which stopped being "barges" as soon as they were no longer moored. His was not the only one- or two-man craft skittering through the larger vessels: escort boats, last-minute errands, and people playing the odds that they could make it home or to a loved one's residence rather than sheltering in place.

He caught up with the Charter Trade flagship before she was unmoored, just as black water rippled with carnelian and ivory moon-paths and the broken green and red streaks of reflected running lights was opening up beyond her. Her sidewalks were stowed, her engines warming, the anchors rising at her bow and stern. It was a magic moment, if he'd been in the mood to appreciate it; the instant when an office building became a ship of the open seas once more, when an *it* became a *her*.

He hailed a crew member, and got a winch sent down to haul the scoot on deck. It weighed under a hundred kilos empty; they'd just lash it along the rail and forget it. Climbing the Jacob's ladder in a cast wasn't something he'd want to do twice, and he tried not to think about what the way down would be like.

He'd have to get this done before the wind picked up.

I hope Maurice is ready for me, he thought, and swung himself onto the deck with some assistance from the woman running the winch.

Jean sat down kitty-corner to Cricket and leaned his elbow on his knees. "Do you really think hacking into Greene's system is going to make much difference?"

Her eyes were closed, her head leaned against the sofa back and propped on cushions. "Maybe yes," she said, her lips barely shaping the words. "Maybe no. It all depends on the luck of the draw. But I've been running clumsy, unsuccessful incursions at them for the past two weeks. They should think of me as a part of the scenery by now."

"Oh." He sat back, feeling useless. She must have heard him shift, because he looked up and saw the shining crescents of half-open eyes through veiling lashes. She regarded him for a moment, and he was struck by how her displayed slender throat, her open slightly moving hands, should have seemed vulnerable but instead gave the impression of a lean, dozing predator.

"Jean, I realize you feel useless. Would it help to talk?"

He shrugged and glanced over his shoulder for Nouel. Their host was still out of earshot, topside, making ready to get under way. "Lucienne," Jean said.

Cricket closed her eyes again, her face a convincing counterfeit of serenity except where her eyelid fluttered on the right-hand side. "That's not her, back on Earth."

"No, it's not." And of course it wasn't fair to talk to Cricket about this, when she felt the loss as acutely as he did. "She thought of herself as expendable."

"She wasn't," Cricket said, after she'd been quiet long enough that he thought she wouldn't answer. And then she fell silent again, until without opening her eyes or otherwise shifting, she reached out and fumbled up Jean's hand by memory. "Damn. Who's going to pick the tomatoes?"

Jean squeezed her fingers and didn't remind her that they'd be underwater by morning. She didn't respond. A moment later, he stood and went to help Nouel cast off, leaving Cricket behind.

The water tasted like a coming storm, and the air was full of anticipated electricity. Along the horizon, behind the moving streams of humen ships, a shadow rose as if the edge of the bright night sky was rolling up like a blind, revealing the darkness behind.

Gourami waited in the shallows at the edge of the humen city, and felt se sibs move around se and the egglings move within. The latter swam easy, well fed and content. The former were more restless, their few vocalizations soft with wrath. No person had many words to say. The discussions were over. The decisions had been reached.

The far-swimmers and the young adults had argued it, and the greatparents had decided. Tolerance had extended as far as it might. The humen and their technology were no different—no safer—than the Other Ones. And the greatparents said that persons had driven out the Other Ones, when they would not relinquish the technology that had nearly destroyed the world.

Persons were not humen; they would not make war here as the humen had upon the one-tree-island-band. They would make their own kind of war. Directed, and precise.

It had worked before. It would work again.

The greatparents remembered ahead.

The humen craft continued running before the gathering storm. The breeze was from seaward, and freshening. Gourami felt it tickle when se bobbed high in the warm water. On each side, before and behind, others waited—sibs and bandmates and clanmates and persons to whom se was totally unrelated. Every one who could reach the humen city in time, who had been within the range of the swimmers and the greatparent summoning.

Se caressed the crossbow stock. Some person—se did not hear who—gave the order. It thrummed through the water, the first coherent word loudly spoken in hours.

—*advance*

The ship shuddered as she got under way, as if she were coming unstuck from the water. Between the cane and the walking cast, André rode over it with only a stumble. The ship boasted enough displacement and a deep enough keel that the interfering wakes of other vessels did no more than shiver her. André made sure of his balance with the cane anyway.

He didn't want to talk to Closs, but he needed an excuse to be there. And then, he had to argue his way in. Fortunately, Closs's position and paranoia warranted a living assistant rather than just an executary. She knew

him, and he managed to convince her that the matter
was urgent enough to interrupt Closs midcrisis. "It has
bearing," André said, leaning heavily on his prop. He
managed not to sigh in relief as she eyed his battered
self and nodded reluctantly.

He showed himself in past security, which was de-
fanged by the bracelet she issued. No help from the expert system today; the ship was busy, unnecessary
niceties shut down. Closs must have alerted the executary to detect André anyway, because the door eased
open at his approach.

André stepped inside, and from the hushed, almost
deserted corridor, found himself in a war room. Closs
stood, spurning his desk and his chair, pacing slowly
with his arms folded. As André came forward he raised
a hand, one finger lifted, eyes focused on the middle
distance and tracking rapidly. André swung his casted
leg in time with his cane and Closs's pacing, and
stopped two meters from the near end of the arc the
major wore in the carpet.

No more than thirty seconds passed before Closs
glanced up, connection cut, and said, "Is it worse than
thousands dead and downed communications?"

"No," André answered. "But it's not *much* better."

"Thirty seconds," Closs said flatly, André's heart
bloomed with joy that he had never developed a reputation for melodrama.

"Jefferson Greene is going to provoke a ranid uprising, if he hasn't already. He destroyed one village that
I know of. Took captives."

Closs tipped his head back and let it loll for a moment, then took one deep breath and reassembled his
facade. "I know," he said. "How do *you*?"

André thumped his cane on the deck. "You sent me

into the middle of his damned massacre. Hunting your renegade. He's out of control, Tim."

There was a pause. Then Closs said, "Thanks. It's going to have to wait. Look, why don't you ride out the storm here? There's a skeleton staff in the galley. Go down, get fed. Are you armed?"

A loaded question. "Never without," André answered.

Closs half smiled, then glanced away. It was a dismissal. André turned for the door—

—and almost walked into Maurice, who had a mug of coffee in each hand. He dodged André neatly, making André feel like a lumbering beast on his cane, and set one cup on Closs's desk. The major, focused on the voices in his head, nodded thanks.

It seemed to be his only delivery, because—the other cup still steaming in his left hand—he followed André back out, without a word until the door was closed behind them. Then he said, "Going to the mess?"

"If I can find it."

Maurice sipped his coffee left-handed. "I'll show you the way. Maurice Sadowski." He held out the right hand.

"André Deschênes," André said, and took it. He was expecting the handoff then, but he pulled his hand back empty.

"Come on. We'd better eat before it gets too rough."

André hesitated a half-step, and Maurice hurried to walk beside him. They made idle conversation through the corridor and down the lift.

The mess wasn't busy, but a few crew and employees ate with haste and concentration at small tables. "Who would I see to volunteer?" André asked. They queued for food, André stumping awkwardly on his cane.

Maurice gave it an eloquent glance.

"I didn't mean as a deckhand," André snapped. Maurice grinned, and dropped a packet of chocolate pudding on his tray.

"It's full of calcium," he said, as André was about to lift it and replace it on the rack. But it was a glimpse of a black glossy data chit underneath that made André return it to the tray.

"Do you always mother strangers?"

"Always," Maurice said. André snorted, and they flashed their cards at the cash register on the way out, pausing a moment to let it total the food. Maurice led André to an empty table. It rocked slightly when André set his food down: on gimbals. He'd have to watch his knees if they hit any discernable chop.

André palmed the chit and slipped it into a pocket as he moved the pudding off his tray. "I was raised right the first time." He heard the glib words roll off his tongue and stopped speaking abruptly.

A perfect piece of luck, it turned out. Because he heard the flutter in the background noise of the mess, and started to his feet before he consciously registered the source of the problem. He dropped his fork on the tray, where it clinked dully, and let his hand drop to hover beside the butt of the short arm concealed under the hem of his tunic.

There were five Rimmers near the main entrance, and three more at the back door, all uniformed. They didn't look hungry.

"André?"

He didn't need to answer. Maurice had turned to follow his gaze, and as two members of the first team came forward, he lunged to his feet. The table rocked, creaking on its gimbals. He glanced over his shoulder. André, aware of their surroundings, already knew what he would see. There were two more armed women and a man behind them, blocking escape through the kitchens.

Should have seen it coming. Should have seen it coming when Closs asked him if he was armed, if he'd been operating at anything resembling normal capacity.

The one André took for a leader stepped forward and indicated his ID. "Dayvid Kountché," he said. "Please come with us quietly, and you'll be treated well."

"Certainly, Officer," André said, but what he tight-beamed Maurice was: "Well, I guess the time for subtlety is over."

Maurice just gave him a wide-eyed stare. Brave enough in his own way, but not exactly an action hero. It was on André.

And then Maurice cocked his head, a funny sideways kind of gesture like acquiescence. André was cc'd on the message Maurice snap-sent Cricket: *Fisher, now would not be a bad time.*

Cricket's agreement flashed green over both of them, and as Maurice shouted—squalled, really—and grabbed the edge of the table, snapping it up hard, the ship's lights and engine sizzled and died. A split second's silence broke on a startled scream; the dinner trays went up and out and over, and whatever had been on them spattered Kountché and the floor around him.

The link was still up. "André, *go*," Maurice called down it, and threw himself at Kountché. They went sprawling, elbows and fists and grunting, a shot that ricocheted at least once. One shot, and then a woman shouting at whomever to put the gun up.

At least one of the Rimmers had a brain. There was one of André and one of Maurice, and eleven of them, and a couple dozen bystanders. The odds were not in the cops' favor.

Nor were they in Maurice's. And there wasn't a damned thing André could do to help him. Harder choice than he would have expected, but he dove for the darkened galley, his pistol in his hand. André had an advantage: the only person in the room he minded shooting was lying on the floor.

His augments at least let him see where the tables were in the dark. But the Rimmers had that, too, and the ones by the galley must have seen him moving, because one stepped in and dealt him a stunning blow on the point of the shoulder with the butt of her gun.

So they wanted him alive.

André had no such scruples; without turning, he leveled his pistol in her face point-blank and pulled the trigger. The pistol took caseless ammo; he had a good thirty rounds. Her jerk backward was more dying reflex than recoil; her blood and bone still splattered him. The smell of iron made his gorge rise, acid stinging his sinuses. *Shit.*

The second one was also too close to control him with a gun. It kept her alive; André broke her forearm with his cane as he went by. The third would have shot him, but André heard the *tap tap* of a jamming gun.

He could run on the cast, after a fashion, swinging himself along with the cane. But it wasn't pretty, and it wouldn't help him long.

Skeleton staff, Closs had said. He hoped to hell there was a ladder up to the main deck in the back of the galley. They had to bring food in somehow, right? So, logically . . .

He laid down two shots over his shoulder to discourage pursuit. Something crunched. It sounded like bone. "Maurice?"

"*Go!*" said the voice in his head, and then a burst of pain and static ended the transmission hard. He winced. Maurice might have been knocked unconscious.

But in André's professional opinion that wasn't the case.

And the shocking thing—as he found the damned ladder, broke the security lock, ducked a badly aimed shot, and hot-wired the box—was that it hurt.

It wasn't supposed to hurt. Maurice wasn't anybody. Wasn't anybody to André, and also wasn't anybody in particular.

And he'd died so André could get out.

Fucking waste of a man's life, was what that was.

He paused inside the door at the top of the ladder— you called it a ladder on a ship, but it was really a flight of stairs—and listened hard. Somebody out there, yes. And noise like the outside.

Lucky breaks, bad and good. His own luck; tonight, there was nobody pulling his chain.

Waste of a man's life, to trade it for somebody like André.

Except André had nothing to do with it, did he? He could have been a paper airplane, flying from hand to hand. All that mattered was the information written on his wings.

André zorched the lock, was ready when the door snapped open. The Rimmers on the other side were not.

André shot them both.

Nonfatally.

They were just doing their jobs.

There was no way he was getting the scoot unloaded. He was going to have to jump, and swim for it until he could hijack a small craft from somebody.

Through choppy wake-slashed seas, in the teeth of an onrushing storm. Weighed down with his walking cast.

A thump of thunder rattled his teeth, so close he felt it as a blow.

Okay, so maybe he was paying for that luck after all.

Maurice spoke; Cricket snapped the Rim ship's breakers and sent her into darkness, drifting. And into real, immediate danger of collision with the escaping vessels on either side of her and behind. And then Cricket had to duck, hard and fast, as Rim's security protocols found her and grabbed, hard. She dumped herself out of the system, flicked a trailing edge of code out of their grasp like a coattail, and hoped like hell they hadn't gotten a trace on her. There was transmitted pain, buffered by dampers; someone hit him, hard, again and again and again.

"Maurice?"

Sharp silence, and nothing. He might have dropped the connect, but it felt open—open, with nothing on the other side. His absence pushed over her like a buffeting wave, knocked her under, dragged her down. Not again, not again, not again.

The tail. Oh, hell, there it was. A trace on her signal, like phosphorescence curling in a wake. She dropped channel fast, and, oh God, Maurice. Maurice!

Mouth open, she spasmed, gasped, expecting lungs full of weighty pain, blackness, and dark water. The warm night air—her own continued existence— shocked her as much as brightness would have if she'd been drowning, and somehow kicked herself into daylight again before the black water could suck her down.

She lay on the couch and gasped, chest heaving, lank hair stuck across her face. Two minutes at least before she could move, before she could think of anything more than air in, air out, heaving as if she'd beached. Then elbows against the back of the sofa, hands on the lip, shoving herself to her feet.

"Jean!" Two more breaths, sucked deep enough to hurt, a stitch in her side as if she'd been running. "Jean! Nouel!" Scrambling barefoot over rug and parawood deck. They'd come for Maurice and André. That meant, that meant—

"They're on to us, they're—"

She burst through the hatch yelling and drew up so short she went to her knees. Hard on the wooden decking, toes bent under. The pain washed her vision, but couldn't eradicate what she'd seen.

Jean and Nouel lay facedown on the deck, hands on their necks, legs spread wide. A man in Charter Trade green stood over each, both four steps back with their rifles nestled to their shoulders and angled down to cover the prone men.

Cricket herself stared down the barrels of two more leveled guns.

On her knees seemed like a safe place to stay. Slowly, she raised her hands. Jean's head was turned; he looked right at her. She didn't meet his eyes, and saw by the flinch along his jaw that he understood why.

At least she had the comfort of knowing she'd been wrong to suspect Maurice.

Maurice.

She would have pressed her fists against her teeth if she'd dared lower her hands. No more. Please no more people dying in my head.

"Cricket Earl Murphy," said a fifth man, who held only a handgun and who wasn't pointing it at anyone,

"you are under arrest for sedition, terrorism, conspiracy to commit murder, conspiracy to commit terrorism, data trespass—"

In a moment, she thought with outlandish slow-
motion lucidity, he would order her down on her stomach and kick her legs wide to make it difficult for her
to rise. Then he would either handcuff all three of
them and bring them in for a show trial, or he would
order his men to fire two bullets into the back of each
of their heads and leave their bodies on the drifting
barge. The storm would handle the cleanup; sometimes people—and boats—didn't make it back when
the city ran before a storm.

"Please lie down," the officer said. In the silence of
a cocking rifle, the salt storm-wind lifting her hair,
Cricket breathed a prayer. Along the horizon, rising
clouds walked on insect legs of lightning. The crack
that followed might have been gunfire, or thunder.

16

IMAGINE A SINGLE PHOTON, THE SMALLEST INDEX OF LIGHT. The human eye is an optical instrument sensitive enough to detect that single photon. It is attuned to the subatomic level. But if we could register that sensitivity consciously, the flash and flicker, the background noise of the cosmos, would render our visual acuity useless. It would drown out more vital stimuli—such as the presence of a hungry leopard.

So our nervous systems take care of it. Neural filters prevent our conscious minds from responding to single-photon events. We can see the subatomic but we are prevented from noticing it.

There exists a classic experiment in which a point-source light projected through a pair of slits forms an interference pattern on a screen set behind them. The existence of this pattern would indicate that the light travels in a wave. Except in that it persists even when the light is emitted in single quanta, one photon at a time.

If either slit is covered, the light—whether it is projected as a beam or as individual photons—will pass through the remaining slit, and the backstop will show only a single bright peak with areas of increasing shadow on the sides, rather than the contrasting light and dark bars of the first stage of the experiment.

Even when emitted as a single particle, in other words, light also behaves as a wave. The cat is both dead and alive.

But if a detector is placed at each of the two slits, so that the experimenter is aware through which slit it has passed, then no interference pattern emerges. The bars of light and dark vanish.

Until the particle is detected, it isn't *perhaps* everywhere—it *is* everywhere. When it may pass through either slit, it passes through both. The wave propagates both ways.

But if a method exists, the wave—collapses. The universe is forced to choose.

Unlike the infamous cat in the box, this is not a thought-problem.

This is experimental fact.

The speculation arises when we consider why. According to Bohr and Heisenberg's Copenhagen interpretation of quantum theory, the individual photon passes through both slits simultaneously and produces the striped pattern by interfering with itself. In other words, it simultaneously follows both possible paths. The "many worlds" formulation additionally suggests that the particle not only travels through both slits, but that it takes every possible path to get there, and that it is detected at every possible destination—in mutually unobservable worlds. But as long as no one notices where it's going, and how it gets there—the fork heals itself again.

Until the box is opened, the cat *is* both dead and alive.

And no matter how the photon gets where it gets, in each particular instance, we see all the outcomes at once.

A bullet splashed Jean Kroc's skull open on the deck. A Rim security officer fell like a toppled tree as Jean twisted impossibly and shattered his right knee. The bullet missed; the bullet severed Jean's spine. Jean went quietly, head lowered. Jean went for the rail. Jean took a rifle-butt in the ribs. Jean ripped a weapon from the hands of the guard who stooped to handcuff him. There was no shot.

There were three.

Lightning struck the superstructure of Nouel's barge. There was no spark. Cricket lunged from a runner's crouch between the riflemen. She went down on her face and awaited the twist of the cuffs. She jumped backward and out, over the rail with a kick-slither, plunged along the side of the boat feetfirst, headfirst, executing a gainer. She tangled on the rail and dashed her brains on the lip of the deck as she fell. She slid on wet wood and hit the bay flat, broke her spine, and drowned. The water closed over her.

They cuffed her and pushed her to her feet.

The forward edge of the rain—thin still, barely misting—washed Jean's and Nouel's blood down the deck, minicurrents rippling around and over chips of bone. *Ogod, ogod, ogod.*

Jean, shoulders drawn back by the cuffs, had half a second to turn and catch her eye, lift his chin in disdain of their captors before they herded him away. Cricket, neck snapped in the fall, was drowning, her flaccid body swung against the side of the boat by the lapping waves.

Nouel ran for it. Nouel ran below. Nouel got shot trying. Nouel, wincing, on his stomach, wiped his data and prayed.

André—got lucky.

Freakishly, unnaturally lucky. There were no more Rimmers. There were two. There were four. He walked between bullets like a wire-dancer; he shot one opponent and disarmed the other with a swing of his heavy cane; he danced across the deck and lifted himself over the rail.

He slid in blood and landed hard on his casted leg.

Even luck has its limits.

And anything that can go wrong—

—already has.

He screamed; they were far enough from the disintegrating remains of Novo Haven that the storm claxon was not loud enough to cover the sound. He gritted his teeth and made no sound at all. The cane had gone flying, and so he crawled. The cane lay by his hand, and he levered himself to his feet, his knee grinding sweet agony when he tried it with his weight.

As he was dragging himself to the rail, as he was lifting himself to his feet, as he was bleeding from a wound to the chest, the thigh, the throat—

—all the ranids in the world came frothing over the rail.

Jean smacked hard and sharp into the water between barges, headfirst, dove deep. Was cut by a propeller, was broken by the fall. Knifed to the surface and kicked. Snorted water that tasted of oil, that he imagined tasted of Cricket's blood. Of course, it did not—she was not bleeding, she bled on the deck he had left, she surfaced ten feet off, she surfaced beside him and a sniper blew her white face red.

Then he tasted blood for real.

Down, down, only a few feet of water would shred a hypersonic bullet like soft cheese. Down, kick, down, die, down, live, down, swim, *swim*.

André could have shot at the frogs, but in no set of choices did he do so.

He never raised the pistol; he lowered it again; he tasted violet ranid blood thick in his mouth and gagged, his steady gun-hand shivering. He could have shot.

He could have.

He remembered Gourami and Tetra sinking their dead, remembered them searching the fallen for Caetei.

He lowered the gun, he turned it and surrendered it to the nearest ranid, he slipped it into his holster. And sometimes they killed him—what was one more strange human in the dark?—and sometimes they didn't. But he never pulled the trigger.

He walked in among them; he limped; he stumped; he helped them drag him. There followed silence; there followed screaming.

The ranids made no sound.

There was a craft—a scoot, a dinghy, a flashboat. Sometimes, corporations being what they were, its codes were still set to one of the factory standards. There was a froggie, a pair of frogs. He knew this frog, one of the frogs, knew its worried eyes and its long vague mouth, though it seemed teardrop-shaped and fat under the bandoleers. "Ziyi Zhou," he said to Gourami, over and over again, a thousand voices, one choice. "I have to get to Zhou."

For Timothy Closs, it was a long and shattered night. The barge drifted broadside into shipping and met an outbound ferry full of evacuees amidships; the engineers restarted the engines in time; an electrical fire started in the machine room and she burned to the waterline while the fleeing city parted around her in two floodlit streams.

The saboteurs—including Deschênes, including *Maurice,* fuck, *fuck*—were captured. They escaped. They were killed, singly or in combination. They waves broke in interference patterns, the probabilities greater or lesser, bright bars and dark, fuzzing at the edges. Some futures grew almost inescapable, some diverged on random looping paths from a single freakish chance. A barge exploded, Jefferson Greene's chopper crashed in the storm, one of the lighters overshot the landing zone in the storm and crashed through two dozen still-moored barges.

The ranid army arrived, and arrived, and arrived. All Rim's defenders fell. They drove back the boarders with few casualties. Rim held the center of the ship by force of arms; staff escaped in helicopters; staff went to ground to wait out the battle.

Sometimes, Closs was one of the ones that made it out.

There were times for subtlety and concealment. For the Jean Krocs who escaped the raid on Nouel's boat, this was not the time for either. A transfinite number tried sneaking; an insignificantly smaller transfinite number failed. The few who succeeded were too late.

But some of the Jeans chose to run, to steal fast boats moored alongside fleeing barges or knock a pilot from an idling flashboat. They put their heads down and the throttle on full; they cut the night with roaring engines and wakes that rose like shimmering curtains on either side and fell behind. They died on the bay and they died in the bayou—in collisions, in malfunctions, when their roaring boats hit snags, when they missed a turn of the narrow channel and were crushed under a somersaulting craft.

But some of them won through. And of those, some did not break a leg or an arm or their neck clambering through trees with no moonlight to aid them, as the storm sealed up the brilliant night.

Every single one that made it into the humming embrace of the hollow tree remembered to lock the door.

And then there was no choice. Because half a glance at his instruments told him that his intent—to shut the system down and hunker until nature took its course—might be a worse disaster than anything else. Here in the calm, shut away from the storm and the cascading effects of other's choices, he could think. Could even experiment, one of him risking, the others observing.

There wasn't time, he all thought, for much of that.

The world was trapped midchoice. Stuck.

Middecision. Midfork. He would have to push it through. Have to fix it, observe it, make it real. Lock down the path that the world would follow.

There was a problem with that. *He* was probably safe. He was the observer now. But he wasn't the only one who had died that night.

Or who hadn't.

He sat down in his chair. He pulled the virtual-reality helmet over his head, positioned the keyboards, worked his hands into the gloves by feel. He flexed his fingers and the interface lit up, sharp relief.

The timestreams normally ran through his interface in a smooth braided strand, like weavable water. Loops might curve off, but they arched back, and the whole had a kind of flowing inevitability.

What he saw now was a cataract. Loops and coils and rivulets bounced wildly, intersecting, splashing. Some were fatter—more probable timestreams—and some were bare hair-threads, finely shining wires.

Jean just paused for a moment and blinked, boggled. And then he took a deep breath—the VR mask pushed against his nose—and assumed his avatar.

He wore a ten-legged spider for this work. Not a biological spider, but a delicate creature of silver and cobalt glass, its legs adorned with pinchers and combs and feather-fine barbs. He scampered across the surface of the virtual timestreams, testing them with palps and toetips, the movements of the spider controlled by the fine twitches of his gloved hands.

Normally, he was meticulous and hesitant over this work. He'd dip a limb in the timestream, let it flow over the sensing hair, sample and test and inspect weave after weave for the intersection of most advantage.

Now, he plunged and grabbed and shoved. He moved through a storm of time like a dancer dodging whirling blades, captured renegade threads that slithered, slick and willful, through his grasp. The thicker streams were muscular as snakes, the thinner sharp as wire. And they could dissolve into water, or fork into a fistful of writhing medusa strands, at a touch.

He chose the thickest one, the hardest to bend, and

bestrode it. His legs darted about him, three or four shaping and sustaining that base timeline, the rest snagging any stream that wandered close and edging it back into the channel. He tried to pick—to snip the threads that ended in disaster and reinforce the ones that led to tolerable futures. But he didn't know, half the time, what he was grabbing, and there was so much—

He juggled cold silver fire. It tasted of death and diesel and explosions, of spilled blood and the salt of storm. It sang to him like flicked crystal.

He bound and wound and twisted tight, sharp, and sweet.

Winning.

And tried not to wince each time he grabbed one thread and integrated it, and watched another one snuff out, vanished to a fading afterimage of silver, and the one he'd chosen smelled of char.

André dragged himself from the cockpit of the flash-boat, or he walked, or the froggies helped him up the ladder. Ziyi Zhou sometimes came out to meet him, and sometimes helped him up the ladder. André's cast was soaked and dripping, inflated plastic squishing water out the top of the boot with each pained step. Sometimes, Zhou even turned him away.

"I can't reach him," she said, or "Not in this storm," as he commended the data Maurice and Lucienne had died for into her hands. Or she raised a disapproving eyebrow at him as he retained it, unwilling to let the chit out of his hands. Or she said, "Come with me," and took his elbow, and supported him inside.

There were locks and codes and pass-pads, and a concealed space in the bow of her barge. And a small

soothingly lit compartment with a plain virtual interface, just a helmet and a touchpad. Very stark, calm
light on brushed steel, a screen on the wall above the
panel that showed a soothing abstract seascape, moving
gently.

André felt a faint misgiving as she seated herself
and smoothed her hair back, or he felt nothing but the
euphoria of adrenaline, or nothing but drained and
tired. "Someone brought down the transfer station,"
some of her said. "I heard it's an alien invasion."

"Aliens." or "That can't be true." or just numb silence.

And whatever he said, some of her answered, "We
have to do it on the ham radio."

And some of the Andrés that heard her answered,
"Brought *down* the station? Destroyed it?"

"I don't know." Her hands moved over the touchpad; the pattern varied. "You want a concrete answer
in *this*?"

Outside, worlds away, another André Deschênes
died in agony when a ranid insurgent put the bolt of a
spear-gun through his abdomen. Other Andrés felt it,
and winced. "Probability storm?"

Some of her laughed, some of her called him ignorant, some explained what that meant. And that those
who worked with wave states called it a *correction*.

And that she'd never even heard of one like this.

The barge pitched and yawed as the wind picked up;
André felt its conflicting shivers through his many
feet. All the Ziyis at their consoles downloaded the
chit, burned a copy of the data, and handed the original back to André. Then the current one pulled the
helm on over her head and composed herself. "Calling
Bryson now," she said. "We'll see if I get through."

She placed her hand on the smooth dome of the touchpad, and exploded into flames.

From the inside, head and chest and the white-hot fire eating her as if her bones themselves were phosphorus, the flames tunneling through, burning to the extremities. André reached for her, somehow thinking he could yank the headset off, pull her clear. But the heat licked his fingers, and a thick column of oily grease rolled from her chair.

And André felt himself collapsing. Narrowing, narrowing, crashing in, clenching down.

The man who grabbed Ziyi Zhou's shoulder would likely die. Unless, on some other timeline, he was already dead. Unless he were about to vanish from possibility, like a photon detected passing through the other slit.

Knees like gelatin, eyes watering from the smoke, André backed out of the hold, the data chit folded in his left hand.

Cricket—this Cricket, of all the Crickets that could have been—was still alive when she finally met Timothy Closs, in an improvised meeting room aboard an evacuation ship, running before the storm. They'd brought her in by chopper, a ride harrowing enough that she planned never to leave the surface again. She didn't know if Closs had come in the same way, or if he'd been here all along.

Judging by the state of his hair and a tear in the sleeve of his jacket that was still repairing itself, he'd probably been in the fighting, which she knew about because she'd been eavesdropping in the helicopter.

Despite it all, though, it was morning, and the world was unsplintered, though the storm defeated any glimpse of rallying dawn. Cricket was wet to the skin. Her blouse—saturated with salt spray—had given up the ghost and hung against her body in sodden, lifeless folds. She shivered, and with her hands fixed behind her, couldn't even hug herself for warmth.

She drew her shoulders back, though, and set herself on her heels, refusing to tilt her head and stare up at him. He wasn't tall, but it didn't take much to be taller than she.

He studied her for a moment, though, and didn't step too close. He was a fit, compact, older man. He frowned, his hands clasped behind his back as if in unconscious mimicry of her own less-voluntary pose. Any minute, she thought, he'd cock his head and say something like *You've been a great deal of trouble.*

But what *do* you say in a situation like that, if you don't have the scripts to fall back on?

He surprised her. A thoughtful regard, straight-on, and then he turned away. "Major?" she asked his back, her teeth rattling.

"Get this woman a blanket," he said. "And something hot to drink. With sugar and caffeine in it."

They did, and eased her restraints, resealing the plastic cuffs in front of her instead of behind so she could sit and manage the cup. When she was halfway comfortable, her hair and clothes soaking the dry blanket—garish Charter Trade green—they wrapped around her shoulders, he leaned back against the edge of a table, folded his arms across his chest, and gave her another considering look.

The silence in the room let the sound of the storm seep through. Beyond the shutters, wind wailed and hail and rain slashed the sides of the vessel. She hoped they didn't run into a waterspout. On the other hand, that wouldn't matter much to her if they were planning an execution.

"I hope you're proud of yourself," he said.

The gesture of her chin included the storm, his torn sleeve, the restraints on her wrists. She cupped both hands around the mug of cocoa that warmed her palms. "I hope you don't think I had anything to do with this."

"Enough to go forward on," he said. "Unless you want to tell me a little about what your plans are."

Oh, what the hell. Either André had gotten away or he hadn't; if he had, Ziyi had the information already. If he hadn't, maybe she could scare Closs into doing something stupid. "We know," she said. "We know that the omelite is the by-product of a Slide explosion; we know about the exploitation of the ranid workers; we know that Greene's World is undergoing a major ecological catastrophe due to unregulated tanglestone mining; and we know that the ranids had a technological society and willingly relinquished it. And we're telling the Core, Major."

"You're bluffing." Calm, but that crease between his brows was deepening. "You can't prove any of that."

She sipped the cocoa. It was she who cocked her head. "Lucienne Spivak was a Unified Earth security agent, Closs. You killed a uniform. And André Deschênes will testify to it." *Please, André. Please have gotten away.*

Closs was good. He didn't flinch. He didn't close his eyes. His fingers didn't tighten on his biceps. She couldn't be sure.

But then he licked dry lips, just a pink flicker, and she covered a smile. *Owned.* "It'll spend years in court," he said.

She finished her cocoa. "Kiss enough frogs, get a

prince. Do you want to stand trial for my murder or kidnapping, too?"

"You're not free to go," he said. He glanced at the door; his executary must have summoned her keepers, because the panel slid back a moment later. "We have a stateroom for you, M~ Murphy. I'm afraid it's not luxurious."

Inside his hollowed tree, Jean was accustomed to silence. And so a teakettle moaning startled him, jerked him out of head-held exhaustion. He let his hands fall to the control panel and pushed himself up. The short cord on his VR helmet snapped him back into the chair. He bruised the backs of his thighs and cursed, too exhausted to stand again.

He concentrated, lifted his hands, and tugged the helmet forward from the bottom rim. The dimly lit chamber was bright enough to make him squint.

Helmetless, he heard the sound more clearly.

It was the wind.

The unnamed extratropical storm had made landfall, and his tree was thrashing, chafing, rasping branch on branch. Each collision shivered through the heartwood beneath his feet. When he laid his hand on the console again, it trembled against his fingertips like a racing pulse.

Two deep breaths and he forced himself shakily to his feet, clutching the crudely welded edge of the console. He used the toilet, leaning one forearm against the wall for support. There was a concealed locker full of high-calorie food; he rummaged out two logs of vitamin-enriched dried fruit and a preserved salami, which he hacked chunks off with his knife while coffee brewed.

Not dead. His left arm was numb where it didn't sting or burn or prickle. He could use it if he looked at what he was doing, but the fine motor control was almost nonexistent. He shrugged his jacket down, rolled the sleeve up, and found a stun-gun burn on his upper arm. He couldn't remember how or where he'd gotten it, or under what circumstances.

Which Jean was he? And had the others scattered, their diverse worlds irretrievably diverged, or had they all collapsed into him?

And did it, in any practical consideration, matter?

A first-aid kit lived in one of the storage cabinets. He sat down at the console again, too tired to clean the wound, and sliced off another piece of a fruit bar.

The coffee dripped from the filter. His console pinged an incoming call.

That should only come for one person. "Lucienne," he said, sliding down in his chair. "I'm alive."

"That's good," she said. "Because everybody on Greene's Station isn't. And either André didn't make it to Zhou, or something happened once he got there. No data."

"Ping him," Jean said. There was a sterile tube of condensed milk in the cabinet. If he got up, he could get coffee, add the milk. Warmth, sugar, caffeine, protein, fat. It would help.

"The Slide," Lucienne said. "It's down. I can only reach you because of your tech. Listen carefully."

The coffee was too far away. And Lucienne's voice was . . . coldly terrified. "I'm not doing anything else."

It still took her five minutes to make him believe— that to all appearances an alien attack force had taken down the transfer station, that the entire planet was floating in the dark, alone, unconnexed. "Zhou's out of contact," Lucienne finished. "You are sitting at the only live console on Greene's World, Jean."

He slumped in the chair and regarded the backs of his hands, stiff and vaulted as dead spiders. "Shit." He could just about turn his head to look at her face on the screen. She bit her thumbnail as she studied him.

"Jean, go make yourself some coffee."

"It's made," he said, but heaved himself out of the chair. "What do you want to do?"

"Put me in touch with André. If he's alive. Have you heard from Cricket?"

"I don't know if she's..." Jean fixed coffee, pretending distraction. "We had one hell of a probability correction. A probability *collapse*. I saw her dead. I don't know if she still is. She might be off connex even if she lived. I have no idea what it's like out there; I'm pinned down under a storm. I think I forced the fork to completion, though. I think we're split."

"No more omelite," Lucienne said. "Well. That's going to change things. Open a channel to André."

"And if I connex this thing and they find me through it?"

"Slide to Earth. You need to take your machine down anyway, don't you?"

He nodded. Because to keep it live was to take the risk of breaking the planet again. "*Clone* myself? I don't have a matter transmitter here, Lucienne."

She laced her fingers behind her neck, under the hair. It hurt to look at her; he stared down at the oily surface of the coffee. "You don't need one. I can get one on this end. Just send the data; we'll tune your daughterself in." Her fingers waved beside her ear. "What, are you chicken?"

"It won't be—"

"You aren't you. You aren't the you you were this

morning. Your consciousness provides a semblance of continuity, but if you've had an exigency incident, you've been an infinite number of people between then and now. There is no free will. It's all an illusion. Besides"—she smiled—"I came to you. Are you too much of a sissy to come to me?"

Rather than answer, Jean put the mug to his mouth and drank deeply, scorching his palate and tongue. When he'd had a moment, he said, "You set that up."

"No." Lucienne smiled, and if she'd been standing by him, she would have touched his arm. "It's just a goddamned coincidence. Find out what you can about Cricket, Maurice, and Nouel, while you're at it?"

17

GREENE STEPPED THROUGH THE DOORWAY, WIPED HIS forelock out of his eyes, and stood dripping on the worn-out carpet. "Nice fucking evacuation, Tim."

Closs thought of half a dozen schoolyard taunts—*next time you start a war, check to make sure we have an army first*—and remembered himself in time not to engage. He settled for parade rest and an impassive expression. "We lost," he said, and waited for the emotions to cross Jeff's face.

He was only slightly disappointed. Greene attempted to counterfeit innocence, but only managed to look angry. "The hell you say."

I should have stayed in the service. "I had a conversation with M~ Morrow while you were... wherever you went, Jeff. Core knows that the ranids are posttech, or if they don't, they will as soon as connex is back up. We have no rights to this world. We lost. It's all over but the jail time. Assuming we survive what looks like a

fucking alien invasion, Jeff. *If* the alien ships Slide
back from wherever they just Slid off to and have another go at us. Have you paused to think about that?"

The silence dragged a little. Closs expected Greene
to squirm, thrash, deny. Instead, he slipped both hands
into his suit pockets and pushed them forward, ruining
the line as the autofit stretched cartoonishly. He bit his
lower lip, and then looked up at Closs and said, "The
information being out doesn't matter if the froggies
don't exist."

"I wish you wouldn't use that word. They're ranids.
What do you mean, 'don't exist'?"

"Because it's so much less racist to call them 'froggies' in Latin? I mean, I have a bioweapon, Tim. We
can get rid of the little bastards for good."

"...and the aliens?"

"The aliens are ranids from the other fork, right?
Well, let me tell you something else you probably
haven't been paying enough attention to notice, Major.
The omelite wells are pumping sludge."

"Sludge?"

"All of them." Greene waited three beats. "We're
out of business. And your alien invasion? I'm willing to
bet it isn't coming back."

The humen argued while Gourami struggled to understand them. Se dared not press against the glass; instead se hunkered back in the darkness, se new net-vest
making an irregular outline, licked by the rain and the
wind.

Se companions hadn't found the captives, or any
sign, on the fleeing barge that the Company humen
used as a village-heart. They had taken Caetei, and se
would not leave Caetei in their dry, rough hands. So se

had attached self to the humen leader's helicopter as it fled the overrun barge. And se clung there, water sloshing in se brood pouch, se hand and toefingers wrapped in a deathgrip on wet metal until bone ran with traced flame and digits cramped in claws.

Se still shook from the flight. The storm, though it tugged se and would have tumbled self from the deck of this new ship if it could, was just a storm—rain and wind, safe enough if one were far from shore. Se'd already swum through the chop to reach here. Se could not have risked being spotted hanging on the skid of the arriving helicopter, and so se had dropped into the ocean and swum aboard.

The storm was se friend. There were almost no humen on deck, and when they emerged, they did so briefly. Se could endure the pitch and surge of the ship as it rode heavy seas. A bullet would have been harder to survive, and self had no illusions how the humen would feel about a stowaway person now.

But se could not leave while the humen leaders were arguing. Not when they were arguing about people, and when they were arguing also about the Other Ones. And Gourami struggled to read their lips through the rain-streaked glass. The light-colored one seemed to be defending an idea or an argument, waving away the dark-colored one's objections. He pulled something from his pocket, a box that he opened to show one two three four five six silver tubes. He lined them up on the table and tapped the one on the end with his fingernail. They sat there, silent and small and inoffensive, frosting faintly on the outsides unless that was a smear of condensation on the glass.

Sometimes, Gourami caught the outline of words on the humen mouths. *Mortality rate. Effective. All age morphs. Unethical. Retrovirus.*

Genocide.

The dark one said that last, and Gourami, shaking, pained and frozen in brewing horror, was pierced by hope for a moment as the pale one drew back. The human stared at each other, a contest of wills rather than support and assent. All Gourami heard was the rush of wind, the creak of the ship as it pitched and yawed.

I'm not going to jail for a bunch of frogs, the pinkish one said. It looked down and away from the other, at an angle, and Gourami saw what its lips shaped, clearly. *We can't lose this planet, Tim. And Core won't protect us if there's no tanglestone.*

Fight him, Gourami willed, leaning one hand foolishly on the glass, the rain slashing se back like whips. As if se could press close to the human, influence him somehow. As if he would understand the words se thought at him so fiercely. As if it would matter at all.

Se was not a greatparent. Se did not have the skill of making luck.

For Christ's sake, the one called Tim said. He turned his back on the pink one, and that let Gourami see what he said clearly. *I don't want to know what you do.*

At first, Cricket tried to sleep. Her connex was damped—she'd get nothing as long as she was on this boat—and she could only play so much solitaire.

But she might as well try to fly to the moons, or swim to the bottom of the ocean, or turn back time. Actually, she thought—composed on her narrow cot, staring at the bulkhead where it curved in over her head—she'd have a better chance, statistically speaking, of any of those. She felt the ship move ponderously in the heaving ocean, its massive length and heavy keel a match for the fury of the cyclone—at least for now.

She'd left the windowless compartment lit, preferring to see anything that might come at her in the night. And because it made the creaks and shudders of the storm-tossed vessel easier to bear—if the light was on, it was just a ship being driven by the storm. In the dark, she would have been a rag tossed and shaken in the teeth of a beast.

When the door whirred open, she came to her feet. She was not expecting a crouched and shivering ranid, water pooling beneath it on the deck. "Don't come in!" she said. "The door's locked from the outside."

The ranid—a far-swimmer, with the net-vest knotted about it like you saw on dramas, and pregnant, which they never were in the media—gestured at Cricket impatiently. She moved forward, shuffling and sore but not slow by any means, and stepped over the guard slumped against the wall. She didn't ask if he was dead or unconscious.

All the corridors were abandoned, which did not surprise Cricket. The ship seemed to be running a skeleton crew, and they'd be needed to keep her together in the face of the cyclone. The ranid led her along its own backtrail of dripped water, but paused as they entered an aft ladderway. It drew Cricket into the shelter behind the ladder with the light grip of slimy twig-fingers, and held up a child's waterproof slate. —*Cricket Murphy*, it keyed. —*Humen call me Gourami. We must destroy this ship.*

"There are people on it!" Cricket whispered, leaning forward so her face would show in the light of the screen. "The lifeboats won't make it through this."

The ranid hesitated. Then it turned the slate away from her and bent over it, fingers moving with precise rapidity. When it raised the slate to Cricket's eye level. —*Must. ?Tim? And ?Jeff? have virus to kill ranid people. All of us. We cannot let them. Please. I need your help.*

"We stay with the ship or I die, Gourami. And—if we sink the ship, how do you keep the, the virus"—*shit, Rim is using bioweapons on the natives? Fuck me raw*—"from getting into the water?"

—*Fire,* the frog typed impatiently, goggling up at Cricket with beseeching eyes.—*Virus is sealed in tubes, in refrigerated box. Help me sabotage the ship. And then we swim. It is only a storm.*

"I can't!" Panic, tightening her throat, her heart thumping like an angry fist.

—*You will hold onto my vest,* Gourami typed. — *I will swim for you. All you need to do is breathe. And stay warm.*

Easier said than done.

Cricket swallowed acid. "It's not easy to burn a metal ship," she said. "I don't suppose you packed a bomb?"

The ranid shook its head, ducking apologetically. — *Must,* it typed, and Cricket thought if it were a human it would have been weeping in frustration.

How many people were on this ship? Closs and Greene. And thirty crew members? Fifty? "How do you know they have this virus? How do you know they'll use it?"

It had to be a misunderstanding. A mistake. It was the sort of thing a villain in a brainimation might do. And Cricket held on to that self-delusion for almost a minute, until Gourami's careful explanation and word-for-word account of what it had seen chipped away at her disbelief, and left her leaning against the bulkhead, gasping.

"He said that."

—*Yes.*

"And Closs didn't stop him."

—*Closs said he did not want to know anything about.*

"Oh, fuck me running," Cricket said. Thirty people.

Thirty.

Maybe fifty at the outside.

How many had she killed on Patience?

Was it different if you went in knowing you had made the *decision* to kill? Was it different if you did it in self-defense? In defense of another? In defense of a species?

Or was it still just murder, like what André had done to Lucienne, like what Closs had done to Maurice?

Like what Gourami had done to the guard?

"All right," Cricket said. "If you don't have a bomb, we have to get to the hydrogen compression tanks."

—*Cricket?*

Cricket sighed exasperation. Bad enough to be here, doing this. Worse to have to stop and think about it. "Come on. Come *on*."

The storm was going to kill him, and André thought he should probably be more upset about that than he was. But there was a certain element of justice in it, if you believed in such things, and he was pretty fucking tired. Ziyi's barge would never survive the cyclone in the confines of the harbor, and André could not run before the storm without her codes—even assuming the electrical system had survived her death. Fire systems had extinguished her corpse; belowdecks, the surfaces were covered in a mixture of greasy soot and foam. He could not contact Nouel or Cricket—or Lucienne, for that matter—and he had no means of reaching Jean. The data that Maurice had died for was in his hands, and he had no way to get it where it would do any good.

So he stood on the bridge, behind the barge's tall glass windows, and sipped liquor that Ziyi was never going to get around to drinking, and watched the green and red running lights stream away on either side. He had the stolen flashboat and nowhere to go in it.

He could run to Jean's minifab. It would be watertight. If the storm didn't wash it away. He could head for a refugee ship; there were always one or two, among the last vessels to clear the bay. They would be waiting for fishers straggling home from the bayou, for the crews of the last lighters to touch down.

Charter Trade ran the refugee ships. Charter Trade was going to be looking for André Deschênes. *If* he could make it through the rising wind, the falling rain.

The choices paralyzed him. He understood some of what had happened—the probability storm, the sharp brief moment where every choice had been made, where every potentiality had become real. But that was over now. When he chose, he was choosing. He was collapsing a wave.

And every choice could be the wrong choice. And then he'd be like Cricket—like Moon—with the blood of a world on his hands.

Or he could stay here, on this ship that had no chance of moving, and wait for the storm.

The anchor cables were already groaning, the waves breaking over the rail. It would not be long.

He finished the drink and dropped the glass on the floor. It didn't break but rolled down the pitching deck to clink against the useless navigation pane. He should have thrown it against the bulkhead. In a moment, the barge rocked, the deck slanted the other way. The glass slid instead of rolling.

André brought his heel down sharply and cracked the glass under his cast. It shattered, skipping down the deck, and he grabbed the wheel so that he would not fall.

And then his headset blinked live with an instant

message, and he accepted hastily and then laughed out
loud. Because it was—of all the mad possibilities—
from Jean Kroc. Typed, obviously, bereft of mood or
context modifiers, containing nothing but the words.

André, follow my beacon. It will bring you in.

André ran before the wind, hunkered under the flashboat's canopy, skipping across whitecaps like a spun
stone. It would have been easy to get lost among the
reeds and the narrow channels in the dark and the
slashing rain. But Jean's beacon came with a map.

He followed it, and tried not to think of the bayou
and the unburied bodies sunk in its storm-churned
mire. Faster would have been better, but he was pushing his reflexes and the autopilot's, and if he ran
aground there was no one to rescue him. And now he
had a reason to live—half a reason to live, anyway—
because he traded messages with Jean while he traveled, and Jean told him a lot of things.

"Will you do the time?" Jean asked, outright.

The chit André carried could be whatever tiny payback he could offer for Cricket and Nouel, whether
they were alive or dead. Dead, most likely; he didn't
like to fool himself with false hope and denial.

He'd made some mistakes.

It still might be all right.

"I'll testify," he said. And plugged Maurice's chip
into the flashboat's playback so he could upload the
data to Jean as he drove, in case he didn't make it in.

The storm covered any sound of the flashboat's engine
as André doused the lights and motored in near-
darkness to within sight of the mooring, relying on his

augments to find his way. The craft Jean had liberated
at Nouel's barge wasn't the only boat tied up by the
paramangrove roots. Not surprising, given the beacon;
somebody in Rim must have gotten lucky. Through the
coded channel, André said, "Jean, you have company
on the way, if it's not there yet."

"Thanks," Jean said. "I can see them on the motes.
They're unlikely to find their way in——shit."

"What?"

"Well," Jean said, reluctantly. "They appear to have
brought equipment. And some of it looks like it might
go boom."

"Am I going to need this boat again?" André fought
it into the shelter of a paramangrove, wincing as the
wind blew it hard against the roots and something
crunched.

"Anything's possible." André waited; Jean caved.
"But we'll probably be dead. Or gone out the back
door."

"You have a back door?"

"Every good fox has a back door, André. Can you
handle the company? There seem to be about six of
them. No, seven."

"And one in the boats," André said. "Sure. I can
handle that."

He checked his pistol.

He had five bullets left.

The trees looked easy, but not with his leg in that
cast. André popped the bubble on the flashboat to get a
little more room and hauled himself up on the gunwale. The boat tipped somewhat, but he extended his
broken leg across the beam, and it didn't rock more
than once. There was an underdash light, dim and
greenish. Rain lashed his scalp and trickled down his
back as he bent forward to struggle with the straps on

the cast. The boat was already shipping water. He didn't expect to see it again—but then, he didn't really expect to come back.

The bones were at least partially healed. If it had been a less complicated break, he would have been walking unassisted after three weeks. As he opened the clamshell halves of the cast, he told himself that his orthopod was being unnecessarily conservative.

His body heat evaporated in cool moisture, as if someone lifted a warm cloth from his skin and left only shreds of vapor behind. The flashboat had a first-aid kit; he dressed the calf in gauze where hardware broke the skin, and wound it with waterproof bandaging, trying to ignore how the shank had wasted. He'd be fine without the cast.

If the leg would hold his weight. If he could stop thinking about the fall that awaited him if he slipped, in the rain and the dark. If it wasn't for the red memory of bone and blood and incapacitating pain.

Meticulously, André removed his other shoe. He placed it beside the cast in the flashboat, then checked to be sure his gun was securely in place. He thought about programming the autopilot to rev the engines to life after a five-minute delay—as a distraction—but either he'd be dead by then or he'd be better off with the Rimmers not knowing there was anybody home but them and Jean Kroc. The beacon was enough of a clue that somebody was coming.

The boat gave one more good wobble when he stood. He stabilized it; the effort sent a spike of pure white electricity up his leg.

This wasn't going to be any fun at all.

The bark of the paramangrove was slick, but he managed to wriggle and slide into a low branch, kicking off from the spreading roots with his uninjured leg. From there, he could all but walk up the branches, though he limited himself to more of a painstaking sidle.

Before his adventure in the swamp, he would have skipped along the branches as if trotting along a sidewalk, sidling effortlessly from shadow to shadow. Now he stopped and calculated each step, lifting his good leg up first so he could heave the rest of him after, one hand always on a branch or the trunk of the paramangrove.

Good joke, that. André alone knew of three different worlds that had species called something like paramangrove, neomangrove, whatever. He guessed it didn't matter, though, if you never got off the ground.

The rain and wind shipped about him, and farther from the trunk, branches lashed. He felt the vibrations through the soles of his feet; they thundered and thumped and itched in his healing bone until he felt like the bridge of a violin. He crept along the branches hunched, trying to present as small a silhouette as possible to the wind.

The guard by the boats was just as well ignored. He couldn't spare a bullet, and the sounds of a scuffle would just alert the others. Assuming that André could win that argument in his current weakened state.

That was the most worrying question of all.

Well, he'd heal. Or he'd have more to worry about than a shattered limb.

"Jean, you still there?"

"Like a bog tick. And so are my friends by the door."

"Do you have any weapons?"

"If they don't blow the place apart around me, I can defend myself when they enter. But if they take the probability engine offline, then we've lost anyway. It's our only way to get to Lucienne. I sent the data on ahead."

The conversation was silent on André's end; he willed his conversation into the headset. Jean, without implants, answered verbally.

"Good. Right," André said. "Uplink me a schematic of the opposition, please?"

Jean did it, and André paused and considered. There were three on the branch, two covering, two—not counting the one at the boat—serving as a picket. And the most dangerous weapon on site wasn't his sidearm, or that of any of the Rimmers.

It was the bundle of explosives that Jean had correctly identified, and that they were affixing to the trunk of one of the largest and most stately trees. It was a small enough package that he was reasonably certain it contained one of two or three shock-resistant high explosives, which would have to be triggered by a small quantity of more volatile explosive. If they had any sense, the Rimmers wouldn't try to hook up the detonator—and the timer—to the bomb until it was secure. Then they'd place a blast shield over it, to shape the charge, and retreat.

"You don't have any booby traps?"

"What do you want, killer robot squirrels? They already disarmed the weapon I had covering the door. You distract them enough for me to get this door open without getting my face blown off, and you'll have all the help you're crying out for."

The officers had lit their work area with IR floods clamped to nearby tree limbs; these suited André's augments fine.

"Yeah," André said. "It'd be nice." He wanted some elevation on the Rimmers, but not too much. And with his leg fragile and the wind threatening to sweep him from his slick-wet perch with every painstaking motion, he was asking for a noisy slip. Eventually, though, he found a limb he could straddle, a lateral branch crossing it at a forty-five-degree angle about a half-meter higher. It didn't point in quite the right direction, but it would do.

The wind wasn't going to help either. The labyrinth of branches made its gusts chaotic; it blew cold down his neck and rain into his eyes. And not only would he have to watch all those flickering leaves and try to outsmart the wind, he was shooting some twenty meters with a handgun. At night, amid trees that creaked and shifted and moaned as they rubbed together, on branches that thumped branches, sending showers of fat droplets through the canopy.

It was a crazy, impossible shot.

"Jean," he said. "I need a little luck."

"That's still an extraordinarily bad idea."

"If it wasn't important—"

Jean's silence implied much. As did the slow deliberation with which he said, "By which we prove ourselves no more capable, under pressure, of picking the hard and risky path than any Charter Trade exec."

"Excuse me?"

"Never mind," Jean said. André heard clicking. Was Jean actually using a keyboard? "It's all right because we're the good guys, right? Consider it done. Look, just disable the charge and get inside the door, okay? Don't worry about anything but speed."

Oh, the implications in that demand. André steadied his hands on the cross branch and sighted, timing the whip of leaves, the sway of branches, the movement of the officer as he finished setting the charge against the door and turned to receive the detonator from his assistant. Waiting the moment. The gale still rose, the rain stinging hard. The limb the Rimmers stood on was as broad as a sidewalk, and it would take

André at least five seconds to reach it, probably another
second and a half to get to the door. If nobody shot him
along the way. If he didn't rebreak his leg. If . . .

The moment came, a lull, a luff, as if the storm
drew a breath.

André caressed the trigger.

Loud as the end of the world, loud even over the
roar of the storm through the trees, the gun wrenched
in his hand. One shot.

The officer who had had the detonator in his hands—

—had no hands. He toppled backward, blood trailing like strewn confetti. The other two cleared the
branch so fast that André couldn't tell if they dove
aside or had been blown clear.

It didn't matter. He moved. Clipped the pistol into
its magnetic holster, dropped three meters, caught
himself on rough slimed wood, and swung. His shoulder wrenched, his left hand tore. His hot, bloody palm
skidded on rain-cold bark. A weapon barked, and
something drew a line of fire along his hip and thigh.

Flailing, swearing, André swung and fell to the
lower branch, managing to take most of the shock on
his good leg. The branch didn't even dip under his
weight. Blood oozed from the gunshot wound, made
treacherous footing deadly. He went to one knee.

Luck. He felt the hiss of a bullet pass him, never
even heard the report. The wind that had saved him
frayed the sound. Leaving handprints in blood, André
scrambled forward, crouched like a froggie. There was
light ahead, suddenly, an oblong shape. He dove toward it, heard this gunshot, all right, as Jean unloaded
the shotgun over his head. Once, twice, three times in
under two seconds. Cold rain rivuleted André's scalp,
dripped from his eyebrows. Jean might have two more
rounds, or five. André couldn't clearly see the gun.

He fell inside the door. Jean grabbed him by the collar, backing up, and hauled his feet inside.

Blood smeared everything as André pushed himself to his feet. It was dark, opaque as milk. For a moment, he stared at it, stunned. "How bad?" Jean asked.

André shook his head. "Not bad." And then he poked the wound in his leg to be sure, and hissed. No, not bad. "Stings like a bastard. You said you had a back way out?"

Jean handed him the shotgun. "Watch the door. Stay back."

The officers might have another detonator. André and Jean shared a look; they didn't need to share the words. André hauled himself up. "Lucienne?"

"She's on the VR," Jean said. "I don't really have screens."

The temptation to turn and see what Jean was doing, to ogle his bizarre hand-shopped console with its scorch marks and its rainbowed, heat-discolored metal, was unbearable. André folded his hands on the shotgun and watched the door. Five minutes, seven. "Can you see what they're doing out there?"

"Bringing up another detonator," Jean said. "Come here, plug into this thing. We'll download your head to Lucienne."

"She's already got the stuff from Maurice?" André dug inside his shirt, found it in the pocket next to his skin. "God, got a chair? My leg—"

He'd have gnawed it off, given half a reason. It couldn't hurt more. Jean rose, silently, and gestured him into the chair. "I got it to her. She wants your hard memory, too. Anything you have on Closs."

"It's all wet memory." But he could dump some of it to hard. Most of it. As he settled himself and surrendered the shotgun back to Jean, he was already transferring. A matter of microseconds, once he set the pull variables. It wouldn't get everything. It might get enough. "There's no back door, is there, Jean? This is my fucking testimony."

"Would I lie?" Jean said. He glanced at the door. André couldn't hear what was going on out there, but the Rimmers had to have brought the fresh detonator up by now. "Put the headset on."

You'd lie and lie again, André thought. Neither he nor Jean had had the time to get the device off the outside of the door. It was still stuck there, a deadly limpet mine.

He closed the VR set over his eyes and looked into Lucienne's. "Hello, M~ Spivak."

"Dump," she said.

"Dumping," he replied. He slotted the chit, gave her the unsorted contents of his head, all the information Maurice had died for, and Cricket, probably, and Nouel. Everything that he and Jean were going to die for now.

All his secrets.

André Deschênes felt naked, and full of a numinous truth. It took under ninety seconds. He felt nothing.

Lucienne had been looking aside, perhaps conversing with someone on another connection. But she glanced back and smiled when he was done, a wide, red-lipped, flashing smile. "I won't be able to get you a suspended sentence, André," she said. "But this might take off some time."

"That's all right," he said. "That's not what I did it for."

She winked and cut the connection.

The chamber door blew in.

André lifted his head in a plain white room. "I'm dead," he said.

"No," Jean answered. "*You're* on Earth. Feel the gravity."

He lifted one foot, the other. There was no wound on his hip. His leg didn't ache. His palm wasn't torn. Blood, fatigue, and rainwater did not blur his sight.

"How?"

Jean smiled, bristled face sparkling like mica in the unforgiving light. "Same way Cricket got to Novo Haven." He paused, but another voice filled his silence as the door whisked aside.

"You're dead, M~ Deschênes," Lucienne Spivak said. She wore a butter-colored jumpsuit a little paler and more golden than her skin, her black hair dressed up and sparkling with jeweled feather-pins. "Charter Trade officers killed you on Greene's World, approximately seventeen seconds ago. I realize this comes as something of a shock."

André Deschênes is dead. Long live whoever the hell I am. "Cricket?"

"We haven't heard," she said. "There's no connex yet. I'm sorry."

She was talking to André, but she was looking at Jean. And Jean was looking back at her.

"I'm not him," Jean said.

Lucienne came three more steps, leaned in, turned her head and kissed him lightly on the cheek. "I'm not her either. You'd better know that from the top."

André turned his back and walked away. There was bound to be someone in the area who could find him a shower and cot. And he couldn't stomach standing there and watching them stare at each other anymore.

And he wanted a nap before somebody came to arrest him.

They were well clear of the explosion by the time the hydrogen tanks that Cricket had rigged went off. They

heard it through the storm, and Cricket saw the column of flame, and some of the burning wreckage
when it fell. None of it came close to them, though—
Gourami was already swimming strongly away, and
the lights of the cruiser had already been out of sight.

Cricket, at least, was praying they'd cooked off the
virus rather than releasing it into the ocean. She didn't
know if ranids prayed, and it didn't seem like a good
time to ask. Wind whipped her; rain hammered her; the
tall seas tossed them both. Cricket put her whole will
into her hands, knotted in Gourami's harness, and the
ranid kept her head above water. She lost feeling in her
fingers; she thought she might lose use of both hands.
Water blinded her. Slammed her. Spun them like flotsam, like dancers, like foam on the curve of a wave.

The ocean under the storm was warm, warm as the
bayou in sunlight. If it had been cold she would have
died, rattling teeth, hard shivers, and then the calm
chill of sleep in the dark dark ocean.

But it was warm, and Gourami kept her head above
water. And Cricket lived.

The storm passed in fifty quarters. Dehydration was
the worst enemy, though Cricket got some moisture from
whitefish that Gourami hunted. She missed the storm,
when the sun baked her. In the storm, she'd been able to
catch rainwater in her open mouth, a little. She let her
hair fall over her face to protect her skin as much as possible. Gourami hid them both under festoons of algae.
They floated without moving when a nessie as long as
the sunken cruiser glided past, its gray back just another
long gliding wave . . . rolling in the wrong direction.

When it was gone, Gourami ducked underwater,
and croaked over and over, calling, calling again.

They drifted a day and a half before the search volunteer ranids found them, a coast guard cutter gliding behind them. Of the ship Cricket had destroyed, there were no other survivors.

There was no contact with Earth; neither Closs nor Greene were there to demand her arrest and detention. When she was released from the hospital, she went free.

Some nine months later, the first liner arrived. And with it, the capacity for communication with Rim and Core were reestablished. It would take several years to repair and reconstruct the transfer station, but there were still more ships outbound to Greene's World, and they could form the framework for a temporary system. The planet wasn't dead.

The first thing Cricket did when she had connex was call Lucienne. She was sitting in a white cane chair on the outside deck of a little bar in Landward, waiting for Nouel, nursing a seabreeze that had cost a mint. Grapefruit juice wasn't cheap, anymore.

It was meant to be a brief call; it had already been on the news that the Greene's World Charter Trade Corporation was disbanded. Lucienne said there was no need for Cricket to testify. André Deschênes and Jean Kroc had served.

"Do you want to talk to André, Cricket? He's awaiting sentencing, but I can get a call through." She smiled. "He'll do less time than Morrow. They're not letting *her* out again."

Cricket paused, and considered tangled emotions. She interlaced her fingers and rolled her neck to crack it. "Call me Fisher," she said. "It's what I go by now. And no. Not really."

Lucienne nodded. "Do you still see the ranid called Gourami?"

"Sometimes," Cricket admitted. "Se's busy parenting. Thirty-six egglings. Apparently, none of them are related. 'Gourami's family.' They were on the news."

"André said he wonders if you will take it something from him."

So Cricket knew that Lucienne had André in another chat. And that was fine; it was good to know he was doing all right.

"What sort of something?"

"Payment on a debt. A story, he says."

A story. Gourami had told her a lot of stories while they drifted. And Cricket had told Gourami a few.

And they had stayed in touch, though Gourami was a parent and a far-swimmer now, honored among se kin.

Yes. Cricket could take Gourami a story. But she wanted to know something before she said yes. "Is it a good story or a sad story? I mean, how does it end, Lucienne?"

Lucienne's eyes defocused briefly, her chin dropping. When she looked back, she shrugged. "He says he doesn't know. He's not sure yet. But he'll let you know when he finds out, if you want."

Cricket picked at the arm of the chair with a fingernail. Nouel was coming up the sidewalk, his hat cocked against the glare, a walking stick swinging in his left hand.

"He can call," Cricket said, and waved Nouel over. When he caught her eye, she reached for her drink. He was wearing a big grin; he'd been talking to his girlfriend. "When he knows how it ends."

About the Author

ELIZABETH BEAR was born on the same day as Frodo and Bilbo Baggins, but in a different year. This, coupled with her childhood tendency to read the dictionary for fun, has led inevitably to penury, intransigence, and the writing of speculative fiction. Her hobbies include incompetent archery, practicing guitar, and reading biographies of Elizabethan playmenders.

She is the recipient of the John W. Campbell Award for best New Writer and the author of over a dozen published or forthcoming novels, including the *Locus* Award–winning Jenny Casey trilogy and the Philip K. Dick Award–nominated *Carnival*. A native New Englander, she spent seven years near Las Vegas, but now lives in Connecticut with a presumptuous cat.

Be sure not to miss

DUST

by

Elizabeth Bear

This is the first book of a thrilling new space opera trilogy that combines elements of *Ghormenghast* and Zelazny's *Amber* novels with *Upstairs, Downstairs*—all set on a vast generation ship orbiting a doomend star.

Coming in spring of 2008.

Turn the page for a special preview

DUST

Coming in Spring 2008

AT THE CORNER OF THE WINDOW, A WAXEN SPIDER SPUN.

Rien's trained eye saw the spider, the way her spinning caught the light. But Rien did not move her rag to break the threads and sweep the cobweb down. She pressed to the wall between that window and the door and held her breath, praying like the spider that no eye would fall on her, as Lady Ariane Conn and her knights brought the naked prisoner from Engine in.

Rien knew the prisoner was of noble blood by her chains. They writhed at her wrists in quicksilver loops of nanotech. In terms of energy, costlier than rubies and more rare, but forestalling any untoward transformations.

The girl was tall, almost sexless in her slenderness, and anything but sensual, though she was naked except for streaks of indigo blood, and dirt, and manacles. Her bony face was square, and tired sweat stuck her dirt-brown hair to her cheeks and shoulders. The only breadth on her, other than across the jaw and cheekbones, was in the wiry muscles of her shoulders and her chest. Even her bare feet were narrow and elegant.

Rien could not see her hands through the twisting chains, but judged they must be the same. Nobody would waste chains like that on a Mean when cheap extruded would serve. And then there was the way she bore herself—strong, shameless steps that swept the nanotech across the floor behind her like silken swags—and the buttermilk blue of her complexion.

Furthermore, the prisoner was escorted in by a half-dozen soldiers with beam weapons slung across ablative armor carapaces, faces concealed under closed and tinted masks. The girl—no older than Rien, though far more imposing—was Family.

Rien drew back among the other upstairs maids, twisting her polishing cloth between her hands, but started when Head's hand fell on her. Rein craned her neck around, catching a comforting glimpse of Head's craggy profile, the long furrows beside hir nose, and whispered. "Will there be war?"

Head squeezed. The pain was a comfort. "When isn't there? Don't worry, girl. We're beneath soldiers. It never touches *us.*"

Rien's mouth made an O. "Who's *she* then?"

Head's hand slid down Rien's sloping shoulder and brushed her elbow when it dropped. "That's Perceval. They'll want her well-fed once she's in her cell."

The chained girl's eyes swept the room like searchlights. Rien lowered her gaze when the stare seared over her.

Head cleared hir throat. "You can do it."

Care for the prisoner. Not a job for an upstairs maid. Not a job for a mere girl. "But—"

"Hush," said Head.

And Rien had run out of words, anyway. For when the girl Perceval passed, back still straight as a dangled rope, chin lifted, and eyes wide, Rien saw what she had not seen before.

From long gashes between her shoulder blades, two azure ropes of blood groped down her back, across her spine. They writhed when they touched each other, like columns of searching ants.

Fruitlessly. The wings they sought had been severed at the root. And if Rien were to judge by the Lord's daughter Ariane striding beside the captive, her unblade bumping her thigh, the maiming would be permanent.

That sword's name was Innocence, and it was very old.

Rien raised her hand to her mouth and bit at the skin across the bones as the mangled angel was led through the hall, down the stair, and away.

At first, Perceval thought the tickle in the hollow of her collarbone was the links of a silver necklace she always wore, kinking where they draped over bone. Then, as she came awake, she remembered that she was a prisoner of the House of Rule, and they had taken her necklace along with her clothes, and so it must be a trailing strand of hair.

But she turned her head, and nothing slid across her nape and shoulders. They'd shaved her head—one more humiliation, and not remotely the worst.

Perceval's arms were chained over her head, and as her shifting weight fell against them, sensation briefly returned. The chains were not cold and hard, but had stretch and give, like oiled silk. Fighting them was like fighting the River, like a child wrestling adult power.

But she must fight anyway.

She bent her elbows, dragged at the bonds, tugged the sheets of nano that chained her feet to the floor. It hurt, though her weight was halved now; though her shoulders were shorn as naked as her scalp. They set the gravity high, here. Her muscles hardened reflexively across her shoulders and her deep-keeled breast, and where translucent blood-warmed membrane should have cupped air, instead she felt the clean-cut rounds of bone twist in her new-scabbed wounds.

The tickle at her throat was a forlorn tendril of blood, still groping for the severed wing.

At least there was light here, light from a high window, falling warm and dusty across her scalp and shoulders. Perceval knew it was only to taunt, like the breeze that ghosted between the bars, but she found it a small mercy anyway. If she were to die here, at least she would die within sight of the sun, its strength soaking her bones.

She wrapped her fingers around the sheets of nano, straining to close numb hands, working her fists to move the blood inside. Sensation came back to her in pins and needles, bursts of static along chastened nerves. The effort broke her scabs, and more blood ran from her wounds, dripping along her spine, outlining a buttock's curve. The blood was hotter than the sunlight.

She would not weep for her wings. She would not weep here at all. Not for anything.

She pulled at her chains again, and again, and stopped only when she heard the echo of a footstep on the stair.

Rien came down the spiraling polycarbonate steps, one elbow brushing the wall for balance as she steadied a tray on her hands. Sunlight falling through the stairs cast her shadow on the welded floor seven stories below. Her shoes tinkled on the high-impact plastic, the sound ringing back from roof and walls.

The prisoner would know that she was coming, which of course was the design.

At the bottom of the stair was an arched doorway into a short passage. There was no door, nor any need of one; no one who could escape nano-chains would be forestalled by anything as fragile as a material barrier. Rien passed the locked and trapped controls and stepped through into the spacious, well-lit dungeon.

Perceval hung in her bonds like a marionette from a rack, head lolling and fingers limp. She did not stir when Rien entered, but Rien thought she saw the quick gleam of a flickering eye. "I've brought food," she said, and set the tray on a folding stand beside the door.

The food was quinoa porridge, steamed and sweetened with honey and soy milk, and a jug of peppermint tisane. Simple fare, but nourishing: the same breakfast Rien had partaken of, though colder now. Rien picked up the bowl, a transparent plastic spoon, and an absorbent shock-wove napkin, and crossed the chamber to where the prisoner hung, silhouetted by falling light. "Lift up your head," Rien said, trying to sound stern. "I know that you're awake."

Fortunately, the bowl was durable. Because when the prisoner lifted up her head, and blinked eyes the same color and transparency as the peppermint tea, and said "Hello, Rien," Rien dropped it.

Some of the milk and porridge splashed out when Rien dropped the bowl. It spattered Perceval's ankle, and her chains writhed toward it, defensively. But once they tasted the spill, they withdrew again. Nonplussed, Perceval could not help thinking.

"I'm sorry," she said. "I did not mean to startle you. Was that for me, Rien?"

The girl stammered, staring. She was small, fine-boned, with delicate features and a wild froth of frizzy black hair chopped off shoulder-long and clipped back with jeweled plastic spiders that spun a transparent hairnet between them, something cheap and pretty.

She looked nothing like her mother. But then, who did?

"It is for you," she managed, bending down to pick up the bowl. It hadn't overturned.

She picked the spoon off the floor as well, and scrubbed it on the hem of her tan blouse. As if a little dirt from the dungeon floor could discomfit Perceval, now.

When Rien looked up again, Perceval spread her hands in a gesture of helplessness. She could not feed herself with her hands bound up in chains, the strain dripped fire down her neck and shoulders, which hurt even more, ridiculously, than the missing wings. *Ariane Conn*, Perceval promised herself, feeling a little ridiculous. She could say the name a thousand times, but it would not free her, nor put her in a place where she could fight Lady Ariane.

Except here, unlooked-for, was the child Rien, sent to serve Perceval in her captivity, apparently in all innocence. An Engineer's miracle. Perceval arched up on the balls of her feet to ease her arms and shoulders as Rien fussed with the spoon.

Maybe Perceval had a friend in Rule, after all.

"I will feed you," Rien said, as if noticing Perceval's gesture. She spooned porridge and held it up, so Perceval had only to push her chin forward to take it.

Of course the stuff might be drugged, but they had her in nano-chains. If they wanted to poison her—or kill her, or interrogate her—there were easier means.

And Perceval had no doubt those means would be used.

Even such a small motion as eating made her want to gasp in pain, though she schooled herself to let only a little air hiss from her nose. Rien noticed, however, and after Perceval had her mouthful, Rien walked around her to examine her back.

Mere nudity could not make Perceval naked, but standing spread-eagled while a servant of the House of Rule gawked at her stumps was true humiliation. She lifted her chin anyway, and chewed the porridge before she swallowed it. The stewed grains popped between her teeth. She could taste the flowers in the honey. Thyme and lavender, she thought.

A mercy, that Rien did not touch her. But she did say, as if she would like to touch, "So why is it that your wounds aren't healed?"

Perceval shuddered, as if Rien's words had been a hand brushed across the fine shaved stubble on her nape.

Her wounds weren't healed because she could not bear to heal them. She could not bear to admit that she would never fly again. And that was the darkest kind of foolishness.

She did not need to close her eyes to heal herself. She just reached into the symbiotic web that interleaved her brain, pumped through her veins, and laced her flesh and muscle, willing the wounds to heal. There was a prickle and itch; she felt the scabs writhing, the cells growing, the wounds sealing closed. She let the chains take her weight again, though the pain was dizzying. Healing exhausted her.

Rien still stood behind. Perceval could picture her, mouth agape, watching the scars knit where the unblade had bitten deep. She wondered if she could actually feel the heat of the girl's palm hovering near her freckled back, or if she only imagined that Rien would want to touch and barely restrained herself.

In any case, now Perceval needed food more than before.

"The porridge," she said, and Rien gasped an apology, scampering around to raise the spoon and bowl again.

Perceval ate it all, and drank the tea. And as Rien was leaving, Perceval stood up strong and stretched against her chains. If she had wings, they would have fanned for balance—

Instead, the tender healed skin broke, and blood trickled in quill-thin streams down her back once more.

Rien ascended the stairs again, shaking. The empty bowl rattled on the plastic tray, and her feet clicked on the transparent steps. The echo—through strangely silent halls—could have been the reverberation of Perceval's voice, as if the prisoner called after her: Rien, Rien, Rien.

When Rien came into the kitchen with the dirty bowl, Roger was there with Head, being trained to supervise the scrubbers. He was skinny and dark—a beaky, random-jointed man with a cleft chin, in counterpoint to Head's stocky muscularity. Head glanced up as Rien came in, and with a flick of fingers gestured her closer. Rien leaned past Roger to slide the dishes into the scrubbers. Pink and frothy, they reached up to cushion and coat each item as it dropped from Rien's hand.

Head stepped closer and pinched Rien's cheek to make her smile. "Why the worryface, Rien?"

Strange that sie should tease, when Head's own expression was taut. But that was Head. Sie had been castellan and householder to the Conn family since Tristen and Aefre were crawling babes, to hear hir tell it. Rule might have grown up around hir.

Head had no need to enforce hir authority through blows or remonstrations. And Rien, who was without family, could think of none she trusted more. "Head, she knew my name."

Head tched, and touched Roger's elbow to draw his attention to a place where the scrubbers were working over the same spot again and again, caught in a feedback loop. "They say demons know all sorts of things," Head said, without a glance at Rien. "And if what crawls out of Engine is not demons, why, there are no demons in the world."

Rien snorted, and that *did* net her a jaundiced look. "You have opinions, Miss Rien?"

"No, Head."

But Head smiled, a quick flicker of lips, and Rien smiled back before she dropped her eyes to the scuffed toes of her shoes. Then Head dipped a hand into hir pocket and extended the closed fist to Rien.

What sie laid in Rien's cupped palms, though, was no gift, but a crumpled length of black crepe. "While you were in the dungeon, the Commodore struck Lady Ariane because of the prisoner," Head said. "And the princess sent for a sharpening stone. You'll want to be ready with that."

At the sound of footsteps, Rien backed into the shadows of the portrait hall, wringing her rag between her hands. It was slightly greasy, aromatic of lemon oil.

If she closed her eyes and crowded the wall, she could

convince herself that she smelled only that, and not the acrid machine-oil scent of noble blood. She could convince herself that the burled gold-and-black ironwood frame of the Commodore's portrait—of the *old* Commodore's portrait, now—was deep enough to hide her, even as it shadowed the image of Alasdair I within.

There was no black sash across it yet, though the confrontation had been a long time coming. Rien had the sash looped through her belt in the back, freshly pressed, and she had a hammer in her apron pocket also, and sixteen long framing nails.

Eight of the other eighteen portraits in the hall were already crossed by mementos of mortality: those of the Princes Royal Tristen, Seth, Finn, Niall, Gunther, and Barnhard, and the Princesses Royal Aefre and Avia. Nine smiled or frowned from the wall, unmarked: Benedick, Ariane, Ardath, Dylan, Edmund, Geoffrey, Allan, Chelsea, and Oliver.

Three more were turned to the wall, frames nailed down.

Rien had never heard their names.

The blood smell wasn't fading, no matter what lies she recited. And the footsteps were growing closer. Crisp footsteps: a woman's hard small boots, and the shimmering of silver spurs. Rien forced her eyes open, untwisted the rag in her hands, and began rubbing the scrolled edge of the frame, work smoothing the tremble from her fingers.

No gilt to concern her, just oil-finished wood, with a deep luster developed by centuries of polishing. Like the spider in the window, whose web had already been cleaned away when Rien went to see, she wouldn't look up, wouldn't pause, wouldn't seek notice.

Not until the jingling spurs drew closer. Then she put her back to the painting, lowered her eyes—closed her eyes, the truth be told—twisted that sorry rag in her hands again, and bowed so low she felt it in her knees.

The footsteps paused.

Rien held her breath, so she wouldn't sneeze on the odor of gardenias and death.

"Girl."

"My Lady?"

"Your rag," the Princess Ariane said, her spurs ringing like dropped holocrystals at the slight shift of her weight. Rien knew she was extending her hand. She risked a peek to find it, and laid her greasy yellow chamois across the princess's calloused palm.

Lady Ariane Conn of the House of Rule could never be mistaken for a Mean. Her hair was black-auburn, her eyes peridot. Her collarbones made a lovely line over the curve of her velveted ceramic mail, and her cheek would have been smooth as buttermilk had the plum-dark outline of a gauntlet's fingers not been haloed in yellow upon it—pricks of scab night-colored against the bruising where sharp edges had caught her.

As she repaired herself, the scabs writhed.

Lady Ariane laid the flat of her unblade on Rien's chamois and wiped first one side, then the other. She scrubbed a bit where forte joined hilt, angled it into the light for inspection, picked with a thumbnail—careful of the edge—and scrubbed again. The blood she wiped was scarlet, not cobalt. The unblade had already absorbed whatever virtue had been in it.

At last, satisfied, she handed the rag back, then sheathed Innocence almost without steadying the scabbard.

"Will there be anything else, my Lady?"

Her lips pursed, and then she smiled. It closed her more swollen eye, but she did not wince. "The Commodore is dead," she answered. "Stop polishing the old bastard's picture and hang up the crepe."

Rien tried to look only at the princess's hands, at the pale celadon flush coloring her skin. Had she consumed the old Commodore's blood already? Were his memories prickling through hers, coloring whatever it was that she saw through those modified eyes? Rien knew the House of Rule did not see or think as the Mean did. Their sight, their brains, their hearing was as altered as their blood.

Before she turned away, Rien cleared her throat.

"Yes?" the princess said.

"I'm ... Lady, it is I who is caring for the prisoner."

Silence. Rien sneaked a look through her lashes, but Lady Ariane gave her no help, only waiting impatiently with one hand on the hilt of her unblade.

Rien took a breath and tried again. "Lady, she knew my name."

"And what is your name, girl?"

"Rien."

Rien thought the princess tilted her head, as if surprised. And then her smile broadened, the swelling around her eye already diminishing as the bruise faded across her cheek. "Fear not, Rien. I'll eat her in the morning. And then after that, she can't very well bother you again."

PRAISE FOR LESLIE CAINE'S DOMESTIC BLISS
MYSTERY SERIES

FATAL FENG SHUI

"I love this series. Leslie Caine has a knack for cracking-good plotting and character development, with a touch of humor, and for giving readers something beyond standard cozy fare. She integrates the story with bits and pieces of design wisdom without getting the plot too far off-track. . . . All-in-all, it's a fun series cozy fans should give a whirl." —*Mystery News*

"This is Nancy Drew all grown up, armed with a tape measure and fabric swatches." —*Rocky Mountain News*

"Caine, a certified interior decorator, adds helpful decorating tips to her well-constructed mystery, making this a stylish, satisfying cozy." —*Publishers Weekly*

KILLED BY CLUTTER

"Sympathy for the hoarder's obsession and compassion for the elderly add appeal to the puzzle."
—*Booknews* from The Poisoned Pen

"Erin Gilbert is someone I'd like to hire." —*Deadly Pleasures*

MANOR OF DEATH

"A blueprint for murder." —*Mystery Scene*

"Caine delivers another top-notch Domestic Bliss whodunit. . . . Everyone in Maple Hills has something to hide, and that 'something' has to do with the decades-old death of Abby, the young girl who is rumored to haunt the Victorian mansion next door to interior designer Erin Gilbert. Can Erin unravel the truth before she becomes the next victim? Nifty decorating tips complete the package." —*Publishers Weekly*

"*Manor of Death* by Leslie Caine is a blueprint for murder as the third Domestic Bliss mystery unfolds.... Tips abound in this delightful package."
—*Mystery Lovers Bookshop News*

FALSE PREMISES

"*False Premises* is a pleasant mystery that readers caught up in the current redecorating craze will not want to miss." —*Mystery Reader*

"Replete with interior decorating, antique furnishings, not to mention floor plan and clothing critiques."
—*I Love a Mystery*

"Humor is never in short supply in this fun, engaging mystery, which is certain to delight fans of cozies."
—*Romantic Times*

DEATH BY INFERIOR DESIGN

"What a delight! A mystery within a mystery, a winning heroine, a yummy love interest, some laugh-out-loud lines ... and as if that weren't enough, some terrifically useful decorating tips."
—Cynthia Baxter, author of *Dead Canaries Don't Sing*

"Mystery lovers who love *Trading Spaces* will adore *Death by Inferior Design*, a tale of dueling designers. In this stylish debut, Leslie Caine paints a winsome heroine with family woes, furnishes a well-upholstered murder, and accessorizes with well-patterned wit and a finishing touch of romance. Open the door, step inside, and enjoy!" —Deborah Donnelly

"Leslie Caine deftly merges hate-fueled homicide with household hints in her 'how-to/whodunit' mystery."
—Mary Daheim

"Witty and smart, with home decorating tips to die for!"
—Sarah Graves, best-selling author of the *Home Repair Is Homicide* series

"Leslie Caine's *Death by Inferior Design* sparkles with charm, design lore, and a sleuth with a great mantra. Cozy fans will embrace the Domestic Bliss series."
—Carolyn Hart, Agatha, Anthony, and Macavity awards winner

"*Trading Spaces* meets *Murder, She Wrote*! Talk about extreme makeovers! Dueling designers Gilbert and Sullivan might want to kill each other, but no one expected anyone to try it. Who will hang the trendiest curtains? Who will choose the poshest paint? Who will come out alive? I'm not tellin'." —Parnell Hall

"Interior designer/sleuth Erin Gilbert is wonderfully appealing and reading all the lovely details of her latest decorating job will make you feel like you've stumbled across the deadly side of HGTV."
—Jerrilyn Farmer, bestselling author of the Madeline Bean mysteries

Also by Leslie Caine

Death by Inferior Design
False Premises
Manor of Death
Killed by Clutter
Fatal Feng Shui

a domestic
bliss mystery

POISONED
BY
GILT

Leslie Caine

A DELL BOOK

POISONED BY GILT
A Dell Book / July 2008

Published by
Bantam Dell
A Division of Random House, Inc.
New York, New York

This is a work of fiction. Names, characters, places, and incidents
either are the product of the author's imagination or are used fictitiously.
Any resemblance to actual persons, living or dead,
events, or locales is entirely coincidental.

Dell is a registered trademark of Random House, Inc., and the colophon
is a trademark of Random House, Inc.

ISBN 978-0-440-33600-6

Printed in the United States of America
Published simultaneously in Canada

www.bantamdell.com

OPM 10 9 8 7 6 5 4 3 2 1

Dedicated with love to Francine Mathews,
who has been an invaluable resource to me in
my writing and an even more invaluable friend

**POISONED
BY
GILT**

chapter 1

Steve Sullivan's handsome face grew pale upon answering our office phone. I had no clue who was calling, and he seemed to be deliberately avoiding my gaze. I tried to distract myself by focusing my attention on the cozy sitting area we'd created on the far side of our long, rectangular office. The fabric on our luxurious new sofa — Thai silk jacquard in a bronze-gold tone, scattered with the pale outline of rust-colored leaves — beautifully complemented the luscious red-brown hues of the exposed-brick wall behind it.

But as the seconds dragged by and Sullivan remained

on the phone, my imagination ran wild. Was the landlord of this building suddenly giving Sullivan and Gilbert Designs the boot? Had a loved one died? Was the IRS going to audit us?

In any case, the phone call had come at a particularly bad time. I'd just worked up the nerve to tell Sullivan something excruciatingly difficult. Now, based on his reaction to the news on the other end of the line, I braced myself for news of a different sort.

He raked his hand through his light brown hair—yet another bad sign—and finally said, "Sure, Richard. We'll be here for at least the next half hour. See you then." He hung up and rose from his red leather office chair. His brow was furrowed, and he clenched his jaw tightly as he strode over to the Palladian-style window.

"Was that Richard Thayers calling about the Earth Love contest?"

"Yeah. Bad news."

"But . . . his appointment as contest judge wasn't even official until yesterday. Did he *already* decide that Burke's house didn't win?"

"It's worse than that." Steve stuffed his hands into the pockets of his black jeans. "Richard is withdrawing as judge for 'personal reasons.' He's also citing our client for possible rule violations. They're going to have to launch a full investigation. Might even turn the whole thing over to the police."

"What!? That's ridiculous! You and I have been to Burke's house fifty times since we first got the rule book from Earth Love! We went over everything with him with a fine-toothed comb. His house sailed through all the judging for the previous rounds. How could he *possibly* have cheated?"

Sullivan remained silent and turned his back to me. I couldn't begin to guess what he was thinking, which was unusual. In the past two years, we'd gone from bitter rivals to business partners. Along the way, we'd endured more than our fair share of trauma, which has a way of revealing a person's true nature very quickly. Fortunately, the first six months in the life of our new business had been relatively smooth—not silk, maybe, but top-grade linen. Our personal relationship, on the other hand, was, as ever, about as smooth as jagged glass. We were constantly plagued by bad timing and bad luck. Steve's last two phone conversations with his "mentor," Richard Thayers, were the perfect example. I'd yet to even meet the former teacher whom Sullivan so greatly admired. But last night, Richard's call to Sullivan's cell phone had interrupted my hopes for the perfect ending to what, until then, had finally, *finally* been Steve Sullivan's and my perfect date. And now, the phone had rung just as I'd worked up the courage to suggest to Sullivan that maybe tonight we should pick up where we'd left off the night before.

Sullivan continued to stare out the window, fixated on its majestic view of the Rockies. I decided to scrap my heartfelt but memorized speech. Time for Plan B, which was to turn brazen hussy—*cute* brazen hussy, I hoped—and simply blurt out: "So, Sullivan. My bed or yours tonight?"

"So, Sullivan. Are we being investigated, too, or what?" (Somewhere a chicken was squawking, just for me.)

"Sure hope not," he mumbled in the window's direction.

I struggled to string together the meager clues that

Sullivan had given me to this point. The Earth Love contest for energy-efficient homes meant much more to Sullivan than it did to me. He was acting as if this award would be his crowning professional achievement, whereas *I* felt that the contest's lucrative cash prize went to the homeowner, not the interior designer, for good reason. But the finalist judge, Richard Thayers, had been Steve Sullivan's favorite professor at the Art Institute of Colorado, which he'd attended a dozen years ago. Sullivan claimed that Thayers taught him everything he knew, and he was both anxious and ecstatic at the thought that Thayers might choose *our* design from the three finalists for "Best Green Home in Crestview, Colorado."

Still trying to pry some answers out of Sullivan, I asked, "By 'stepping down for personal reasons,' does Richard mean the fact that he's your mentor? Didn't he tell you earlier that the contest sponsors were fine with that?"

"Look, Gilbert." He turned and glowered at me. "You'll have to grill *him*, all right? I already told you what little I know."

My heart sank. Wasn't it only last night that his dreamy hazel eyes were staring into mine with loving tenderness? He could never keep things in perspective, and minor problems often turned us into adversaries. But all I said was: "You're obviously only giving me *part* of Richard's message, though. What exactly did he say?"

"I wasn't *recording* him, Gilbert."

"That's a pity, Sullivan," I snapped. "Because if you *had* been using a tape recorder, you could hit the rewind button. Clear back to our date last night. When you were calling me 'Erin' as if you liked me."

"You're the one who made the rule that we were to stick with 'Gilbert' and 'Sullivan' when we're at work!"

"I'm objecting to your tone of voice when you say my name! Call me . . . Princess Dagweeb, for all I care! Last night, when you took my hand and asked me if I minded if we skip dessert, I thought . . ." Damn! My throat was getting tight with emotion. No way was I going to start crying.

"That *is* what I meant," he said gently. He crossed the room, but stopped short of rounding my desk. "And, believe me, I was sure it was going to be a two-second phone conversation when Richard interrupted us last night, or I'd have let it keep ringing. But he was acting weird. The first thing he said was: 'Why the hell didn't you tell me Burke Stratton was your damned client?' Then he accused me of teaming up against him with his 'worst enemy.' "

That caught my attention. "Why would he have a problem with Burke?"

"That's just it." He spread his arms and grumbled, "I still don't know. Richard wouldn't tell me. Just claims the guy wrecked his life . . . says if I'm smart, I'll stay the hell away from Burke before he finds a way to wipe out Sullivan and Gilbert Designs."

I nodded, starting to understand. The thought of having his life ruined in a business arrangement would have been a painful déjà vu for Sullivan; a few years ago he'd been conned by a corrupt business partner and had lost nearly everything he owned.

"Having Richard freak out at me was the very last thing I wanted to happen last night," he continued. "By the time he calmed down and I got off the phone, it was too late for me to call Burke and get the story from him."

He scowled at me. "And *you* were acting so crushed that I didn't know—"

"You left the table, Sullivan! One second you're holding my hand, smiling at me, happy because your long-lost friend, Richard Thayers, is on the phone, and the next you're striding out the door!"

"One of the men I admire most was yelling in my ear, accusing me of betraying him!"

"I didn't know that! All you had to do was whisper to me, 'Something's wrong,' or 'He's upset.' Or you could have explained when you returned to the table. Instead, you were distracted and abrupt, and you completely gave me the brush-off when I asked what Richard had said."

"Yeah." Sullivan sighed and ran his fingers through his hair a second time. "Guess that wasn't one of my better moments." He added with a charming smile, "Although, again, *you* made the rule about not talking business after hours."

"*Again*, I couldn't read your mind," I explained gently. "All I knew was, you chose to take a phone call during our date, and then you were in a funk. Put yourself in my shoes."

He gave me an exaggerated wince. "I would, but high heels make my calves look too big."

"Don't try to joke your way out of this," I said, though I was already having a hard time keeping a straight face.

"Erin." The man had a gift for saying my name in a way that could instantly make me melt. He finally came around my desk and leaned toward me, filling me with relief at the thought that, *for once*, we were going to avert a potentially disastrous argument. "I promise you that—"

The door burst open. In walked a man in smudgy gray pants and a ratty forest green sweater that I'm pretty sure was on backwards. He had a sizable bald spot amidst his wild, unkempt hair, and a large red nose that hinted at a drinking problem. But at that moment, he could have been Santa Claus himself and I still would have hated him, as well as each and every one of his reindeer. To make matters much worse, Steve's eyes had just lit up as though the man *were* Santa.

"Good to see you, Richard," Sullivan said, striding toward him.

"Likewise, S.S.," he returned, giving him a bear hug. "Ridiculous that we live in the same town now," he said in a raspy voice, "yet we hardly ever see each other. And I feel terrible about the circumstances."

"No kidding." There was an awkward pause, then Sullivan said, "You got here pretty quick."

"I was just around the corner when we hung up, and I found a space right away. Before I forget...did you get my e-mail about my night class?"

"Tonight at CU, right? Okay if I drop in?"

"Absolutely. That's a great idea! It's in room one-ten of the history building. We can go hit a pub afterwards... grab a sandwich and a brewski."

"Sounds good."

Richard and Sullivan continued to make arrangements, but all I could think was: *So much for our picking up where we left off last night.* How had the two men gone from face-paling angst and accusations of betrayal to chatting about night classes and beers?

Remembering belatedly that I was still in the room, Steve clapped his mentor on the back and turned toward me. "Richard Thayers, this is Erin Gilbert. Erin, Richard."

I rose for a moment, and we exchanged "Nice to meet you's" and shook hands over my desk. I hoped that his pleasantry was less insincere than mine. I hadn't set the bar especially high.

"Have a seat," Sullivan suggested, giving Richard a pat on the back. The three of us moved from our desks to the cozy nook near the window. We always allowed our visitors to sit first, and then, if it was available, Sullivan would grab the leather smoking chair and I would grab the yellow slipper chair. Today I strode directly to Sullivan's smoking chair and plopped myself down before our guest could. I hated to act so petulant, but it was the best I could do. At least I was keeping my mouth shut. Part of me wanted to scream at Thayers: Do you realize you're wrecking my love life?!

Sullivan took my usual seat. Once Richard had settled into place on the sofa, I said, "Steve tells me that you're stepping down as Earth Love's finalist judge."

He nodded grimly. "It's the responsible thing to do." He sighed. "Too bad. I read the reports from the initial-rounds' judges and saw the photographs. Burke Stratton's interior was by far the best. Not surprisingly." He winked at Sullivan.

"Thanks," Sullivan said. "Got to say that I agree with you. Though I'm far from impartial. But I also have to admit, Darren Campesio's architectural design is interesting and really energy-efficient."

"That's the one that's partially built into the hillside, right? So that the place is part cave? À la Batman?"

He was mocking the house, sight unseen. Annoyed, I chimed in, "The design compensates for the windowless portion fairly well. The space makes great use of skylights and mirrors."

Richard looked at me with wide eyes, then blinked a couple of times, as if puzzled. "Ah. Glad to hear it."

"And the interior for the third finalist has a lot to be said for it, too," I added.

"She means Margot Troy's place," Sullivan explained unnecessarily—assuming Richard could subtract two from three. "But Erin's biased. She designed Margot's kitchen a couple years back."

"Did she?" Richard asked, again raising his bushy eyebrows. "Too bad you guys didn't just stick to working on Margot's house." He shook his head. "When I agreed to judge, I didn't know Burke Stratton was even in the competition, let alone a finalist."

Sullivan was nodding as though he was following Richard's thread, but I remained on the outskirts. "And you're biased against Burke, so you recused yourself?" I prompted.

Richard nodded and, in a gesture eerily reminiscent of Sullivan's, dragged a hand through his messy, patchy hair. "The two of us have a problematic relationship. I can't begin to be impartial toward that pompous peacock." Shifting his gaze to Sullivan, he said, "If I were you, I'd disassociate with Stratton A.S.A.P."

"Because you think he cheated somehow?" I asked.

"Oh, he most definitely cheated," Richard said with a snort. "There's no doubt about that."

"How so?"

"Evidence, my dear. Evidence." He chuckled. I battled the urge to fire off a sarcastic reply. Before I could ask: *What* evidence? he continued, "Sorry to be so vague. But when word of what Burke is *really* up to gets out, no one will want to have their names associated with him or his residence."

Sullivan and I exchanged glances. Why was Richard paying us a personal visit if he wasn't going to pass along any helpful information? And why was Sullivan now giving me the evil eye if he'd just told me that I would have to "grill Richard" myself? "I'm sorry, Richard," I said, "but I'm confused. You didn't know till last night Burke was in the contest. His house passed the inspections for the previous rounds with flying colors. Yet this afternoon, you've found such a major violation that you've suggested it may be a criminal matter. How did you get from point A to point F so quickly?"

Richard stiffened and all but sneered at me. "As I believe I already told you, Miss Gilbert, I can't go into the details. I'm sorry." He rose, faced Steve, and only then forced a smile. "Well. I've wasted enough of your time." Steve, too, got to his feet as Richard continued, "I just wanted to apologize, face-to-face, for jumping down your throat last night."

"Hey. That's all right."

"No, it isn't. I leapt to some ridiculous conclusions. I'm not always rational when it comes to Burke Stratton. The man is bad news. If you continue to work with him, you'll regret it. But that's your decision. And this has been a hell of a lousy way to resume our friendship, S.S."

"Yeah. Cruddy circumstances." The men shook hands. "Thanks for stopping by."

"Technically, since I'm the finalist judge till they accept my resignation, I *shouldn't* have said a word about this. But I felt you deserved the heads-up. It was the least I could do, really." He gave me a thin smile. "Sorry that I'm forced to be so cryptic, Miss Gilbert."

Not knowing what else to say, I muttered, "Thank you. Drive carefully."

The moment the door closed behind Richard,

Sullivan dropped into his desk chair, shot me a look of disgust, and snapped, "*That* was awkward."

"Yes, it was. And I'm sorry, but truth be told, my questions seemed completely reasonable to me."

"He'd just gotten through telling us that he shouldn't even have been talking to us in the first place! That he wasn't at liberty to discuss any details!"

"No, he hadn't, Sullivan. He must have told *you* that over the phone. All he said at first in *my* presence was that he was sorry to be so vague."

"It's the same thing!"

"No, it isn't. Apologizing for being vague is not at all the same as being ethically or perhaps legally under a gag order."

He made no comment and returned to his work—rifling through several pictures of formal dining room sets in order to whittle down the selection process to the best two or three for our client. His every motion was made with extra zeal and noise. I reclaimed my seat at my desk, which was at a right angle to his, and tried to get back to work, too. I gave up within only a minute or two.

"Why are you angry at me, Sullivan? Could you please explain to me what's going on here?"

"I don't know what Richard knows, Gilbert. But I do know he always tells it like it is. *Always*. So we need to listen." He paused, still so edgy I didn't dare interrupt. "I wanted you two to like each other. He's a great motivator... has such great vision. He believed in me when no one else did, including myself. There was a time when just having him look over my shoulder at a project I was struggling with would suddenly help me to find the answers. Somehow, it feels like the exact opposite is happening. As though he's looking over my shoulder right now, and I'm suddenly see-ing all our flaws."

My heart leapt to my throat. "Our *flaws*? You don't mean in our relationship, do you?"

He ignored me. A silent *yes*!

I stared at him in profile. "Are you having second thoughts about our decision not to see other people?"

He lifted his hands in exasperation. "Damn it, Gilbert! I happily quit seeing other women because nobody mea-sured up to you. But when I'm with you, I'm not measur-ing up to *your* standards, and—"

"That's not true," I cried, but he was talking over me.

"I'm always screwing up. It's always wrong! You were right before. We shouldn't date."

His words seemed to hang in the air. I swiveled in my chair to face my monitor and hide my expression from him. "Oh. I see."

The phone rang.

"I didn't mean 'we shouldn't' as in 'we won't.' Just that . . . you were right that it's not working."

"No, that's fine."

"The words just slipped out. I didn't mean to hurt your feelings, Erin."

"I'll get over it." Just like I could dive face-first through the window and probably survive. Two years of harboring a crush on this one man had just crushed *me*. Despite my overwhelming urge to cry, I picked up the phone.

Sullivan had risen and was now leaning on my desk. He whispered, "But I didn't mean that the way it sounded."

I was too upset to listen. I cleared my throat and said, "Sullivan and Gilbert Designs" into the phone.

"I don't want to stop seeing you."

A woman was speaking. I asked her: "Can you please hold?" and pressed the button without waiting for her response.

"Who is that?" Sullivan asked.

"I don't know. A soon-to-be-former client, most likely." I sighed and looked up at him, suddenly feeling a horrid pang that made it hurt to breathe. If only he weren't so close to being everything I wanted, and yet never within reach. "We can't do this now."

"I don't want to do this at all."

"Oh, Steve." I massaged my temples, willing myself not to lose my composure. "I don't know if you mean 'do this' as in breaking up or as in being together. But *I* just meant that this isn't a good time for us to talk about it."

"No kidding. It's a train wreck. Look. Let me cover our last two appointments this afternoon alone, while you see if you can get us caught up here. Okay? Meet me tonight at Richard's class. Please."

I nodded as I clicked back on the line and said, "This is Erin Gilbert. I'm sorry to keep you waiting." Silence. "Hello?" Nobody was there. Sullivan pushed out the door.

"It *is* a train wreck," I muttered to myself.

The phone rang again, and I answered immediately.

"Erin, it's Burke," he said. His typically gentle voice was tinged with desperation. "I need your help."

Had he already been told about the charges Thayers had made against him? "Why? What's wrong?"

"Some idiot with an ax to grind has put me under investigation for false claims of rule violations. Turns out the finalist judge is this guy named Richard Thayers, who hates my guts. He did some work for me four years ago, and it was all such garbage, I refused to pay. It had to be him who made these ridiculous charges. But I don't know for sure. Nobody at Earth Love would tell me."

"Should I—"

"At any rate," he interrupted, his words gushing out in a semitirade, "I'm telling you, Erin, *promising* you even, that the claims are totally bogus. But my status as a finalist is now pending. Worst part is, there'll be some sort of trial. It'll be covered in the *Crestview Sentinel*. My name will be dragged through the mud."

"I'm so sorry, Burke. That's terrible."

"I need you and Steve to testify. I'll get Jeremy Greene, my architect, to testify as well. Once I find out what the charges *are*. Earth Love won't tell me *that*, yet, either. They said I'll have to call back tomorrow morning, after they've had a chance to read through the reports."

"I'll do what I can, Burke, but—" I stopped. This wasn't the time to explain about Sullivan's possible conflict of interest. Burke was our client, and we'd been paid to be on his side.

"But what?"

"Steve's not here, and we'll need to talk this over. All three of us. Let's aim for sometime tomorrow, after you've learned exactly what you're up against. Or Friday, if that works better."

The other line was flashing with an incoming call. I set a tentative time to meet at the office in the morning, said a hasty good-bye to Burke, and answered the new call. "Erin, this is Margot Troy," a woman's voice huffed. "Did you realize you hung up on me?"

"Was that you on the phone just now?"

"A minute or two ago, yes. You tried to put me on hold."

"I'm really sorry, Margot."

"You've got too many clients. This is the reason I didn't hire you to spruce up for the open house last Saturday. Today I'd decided I wanted to hire you *again*, for a second small job, but now I won't. In any case, it was nice seeing you at the Earth Love open house, and best of luck to Burke."

"That's very kind of you, Margot. And I'm—"

"True," she interrupted, "but it's also just basic manners. You should have thought to wish me well, for old times' sake. But you're obviously too busy even to answer my phone call."

"Margot, I am so—"

She hung up. "Sorry," I said to myself.

Margot Troy. My *former* client from hell. I found both her and her home fascinating, though. The woman was filthy rich, yet believed so strongly in recycling that she'd built and furnished her home entirely from secondhand or salvaged materials. I couldn't work for her until the contest was over, in any case, but I needed to repair this new rift. Tomorrow, maybe. If Sullivan and I had any free time.

Thinking about Steve's and my schedules reminded me that I didn't know what time Richard's class was. Had either of them mentioned it? And what on earth was going on between Richard and Burke?

More importantly, were things over between Steve and me? Were these walls thick enough that I could let out a scream without causing anybody to call 911?

I took a calming breath and counted to ten. Okay. I could still breathe. And count. All was not completely lost. On most days, I love my job. I truly do. Just not this particular day.

chapter 2

We cannot continue to abuse Earth's resources, and we must all do our part. Reducing wastefulness can be as simple and painless as using fewer paper napkins and rethinking the type of wall and window treatments we use.

—Audrey Munroe

DOMESTIC BLISS

This is what my life's work is all about, I thought as I shed my coat and marveled at the delectable ambience of my home's foyer. The space itself was perfect: Currier and Ives, *Architectural Digest*, welcome-to-my-lovely-life perfect. The earthy tones and textural depths of the pearl gray plaster walls were divine, as was the sparkling chandelier, with its soul-cheering wash of light. And the three white calla lilies in the crystal vase atop the charming antique table. But what was making my heart soar at the moment was the breathtaking view of the parlor through the French doors.

Never had I been forced to work quite so hard on a room, and especially not on one which already had such great bones—high ceilings, hand-carved trim, and antique wide-plank floorboards. I helped my landlady with interior design in lieu of paying rent, and it was as Sisyphean a task as I'd ever known. This room had gone from a storage room for mismatched furniture to an arts-and-crafts rumpus room and back more times than I could count. Even so, my eventual triumphant design had been worth every exasperating moment: I had achieved bliss. I hung my coat in the closet and entered my new favorite space.

From the mouthwatering reds and blues of the Oriental carpeting to the hint of peach in the medallion on the marvelous coved ceiling, every item in this room was beautiful on its own—and seemed even *more* extraordinary when seen as one piece of the whole composition. Within these four celery-toned walls, the textures, shapes, and lines were in such harmony that the space was nothing less than sublime. Even Hildi, my cat, looked like a scenic prop as she sat curled into a black, satiny oval shape on Audrey's gold brocade wing chair. Best of all was that Audrey, the epitome of a recalcitrant and skeptical home owner, now loved this room every bit as much as I did.

Just around the corner, in stark contrast, the den had a willy-nilly mishmash of furnishings. And around the *other* corner, the walls of the dining room were undergoing yet another of Audrey's experiments in, well, something or other. She used her house as a testing laboratory for possible segments on her local, Martha Stewart–like TV show, *Domestic Bliss with Audrey Munroe.*

I greeted my kitty and sighed at the joy of being embraced by my warm surroundings. But my thoughts quickly returned to my latest spat with Sullivan. Then it hit me: If we ever got our act together, I would have to move out of Audrey's fabulous house. Could that be part of what was driving my interminable attraction to him? Was I unconsciously drawn to him and our perpetual pattern of limbo, because it delayed me from having to grow up? From getting my own place and moving forward with my life?

With sagging spirits, I made my way to the kitchen, where I could hear Audrey working at the chopping board. With Audrey at the helm, anything could be getting chopped, from carrots to strands of—

I lost my train of thought as a ghastly alteration to the dining room ceiling commanded my full attention. Were those cherubs?! And was this some kind of a fresco? She'd painted a pink-and-yellow-hued baby, with its torso on the ceiling and lower half on the wall. A second baby was sitting on that one's shoulder, and a third was apparently clinging to his ankle for dear life. I looked again and corrected myself: *her* ankle.

Audrey must have heard my footsteps, because she joined me in the dining room. "Erin! You're home early!"

"Yes, but not for long. I'm grabbing something to eat, then meeting Sullivan at CU. We're going to a community class together." Like metal paper clips to a magnet, my vision was drawn once again to the ceiling. "Audrey, I have to ask. What's with the pudgy babies in the corner? You're not thinking of going all Sistine Chapel in here, are you?"

"Are the cherubs too much?"

"That depends. If you're thinking of continuing to *live* here, as opposed to turning the place into a museum or a church, then yes."

She sighed. "That's what I thought, too. I was going to apply a decoupage of some sort, but then decided I shouldn't be using up paper products. With all your emphasis on green home designs lately, you've raised my social consciousness."

But apparently not your *taste,* I thought sourly.

"I couldn't help but think about all those poor trees being cut down just to be ground up into wallpaper."

"There's a wide array of fabrics and sea grasses available for wall treatments nowadays."

"Maybe so, but last year, I did a show segment on using paint to *mimic* wallpaper. That surely has to be an even greener alternative. In terms of conservation, I mean, not literally the color green. So, I was going to paint a nice pink rose up there. Unfortunately, it started to look like a baby's derriere. Then I started to think about you and Steve, and what adorable babies the two of you would have, and next thing you know, voilà!"

"Eww! I'm never going to allow Sullivan into our dining room again!" Panicked, I scanned all the walls and the ceiling. "Thank God. No storks." I shook my head in exasperation. "This grandmother thing must be getting to your head!" Some six months ago, she'd been thrilled to welcome her first grandchild, and her eldest son had just announced that he and his wife, too, were expecting—but they all lived hundreds of miles away. Locally, I seemed to be the next best thing to a blood relative.

"*You* were the one who admitted your biological clock was going off."

"That was just a moment of weakness, inspired by two glasses of Beaujolais on an empty stomach." I brushed past her into the kitchen and headed straight for the refrigerator. I had a leftover serving of pasta with pesto in there that was perfect for a quick dinner. "Besides, you know how it is with Steve and me. You'll be working on a second coat, with every inch of the dining room filled with bouncing babies, before we'll have fully committed to our relationship. *If* we ever do."

She studied my features, her own expression crestfallen. "Oh, Erin. You're saying you two are back to an 'if' state now? Last night, the vibes you two were giving off when he came to pick you up were so strong that... well, frankly, I wasn't even expecting you to come home till this morning."

Time for a subject change. "Seriously, Audrey, using paint to emulate wallpaper is an excellent idea. But let's nix the cherubs. I'm going to suggest in the strongest possible terms: No naked people or mammals of any kind."

"All right. Would *clothed* bunnies be okay?"

"No." I put my pasta into the microwave and began to throw together a salad, stealing some of the mushrooms and scallions that she'd just been chopping. "Didn't your show's expert last year talk about painting vertical stripes? That's a must when you're mimicking wallpaper. Also, surely he or she mentioned how you should start the process by creating stencils."

"I don't remember." Audrey crossed her arms and leaned against the door casing that trimmed the dining room entrance. Thankfully, that lovely section of white decorative wood had gone unscathed by Audrey's paintbrush. "Although, now that you mention it, I do remember something about stripes and stencils. But I wanted to use some free-form drawings."

"Free-form is just not a smart way to go about creating faux wallpaper. Use chalk plumb lines and masking tape, and create vertical painted lines as your first step. Or, better yet, allow *me* to create them for you. That's going to make things *much* easier than painting freehand on these huge walls. And it'll force you to get the scale right. Then, I'll help you cut out two or three stencils for the basic shapes of flowers. You can add free-form filigree and leaves, and shadings on the flowers."

She clicked her tongue. "You are such a fuddy-duddy, Erin."

"I'm not a fuddy-duddy. I'm a designer. Selecting wall treatments is a huge part of my job. I know what I'm talking about, Audrey."

She threw up her hands. "Fine, fine. I'll take your advice . . . on the condition that you'll take mine."

With visions of her asking me to paint angels sitting on clouds, I braced myself and asked: "Which *is* . . . ?"

"Regarding your love life. Stop driving me up the wall!"

"The one with the cherubs?"

"You and Steve remind me of the amateur ballerinas I used to work with. You're so concerned about not stepping on each other's toes that you're always trip-ping on your *own* feet. Erin, there's no such thing as the perfect mate or the perfect relationship for any of us. We all have warts. Stop waiting for a guarantee, and trust that, whatever the future brings, you'll be able to handle it."

"It's really *Steve* who needs to learn that particular lesson, Audrey," I grumbled.

"Interesting. That's exactly what Steve said about *you,* when I gave *him* that very same piece of advice yesterday."

Stunned, I gaped at her. She swept out of the room.

chapter 3

The steel gray sky of a typical winter late afternoon had turned black and starless by the time I followed the brick walkway at Crestview University. A chill wind whistled through the bare tree branches, and I struggled to keep my footing on the icy patches that glittered in the yellow light of the street lamps. I made my way to the ivy-covered sandstone building and wrestled with its heavy door.

"Let me get that, miss," a man called from behind me. "Thank you."

He followed me inside. He was wearing a dark wool

beanie and a sheepskin coat, and he was nice-looking—
in his late twenties or early thirties. He gave me a once-
over and a broad grin, then said, "My pleasure," as
though he really meant it. It was a testament to just how
badly my day had gone that I flashed a grateful smile.

The warmth from his flattery lasted two seconds, until
I recognized Richard's raspy voice emanating from the
open doorway directly ahead of us. The class session was
in full swing. I'd guessed wrong on the time, although I
wouldn't have *had* to guess if Sullivan had bothered to
answer the message I'd left on his cell phone a couple of
hours ago. I dashed across the hall and slipped into the
room, quickly finding Sullivan. A young woman was blatantly ogling him, and I was only too happy to slip into
the empty seat between them. He gave me a you're-
unforgivably-late arched eyebrow. I gave him an I'd've-
been-on-time-if-you'd-returned-my-call shrug.

I took in the worn-out room at a glance—fifty black,
threadbare seats in five tiered rows where fewer than
twenty of us now sat at semiattention. Redesigning our
surroundings in the blink of an eye, I gave Richard a
more enticing stage that curved into the center aisle.
Then I swapped the dreadful overhead fluorescents and
acoustic ceiling tiles in favor of a lovely blue-lit coved
ceiling, and livened the textures and colors throughout
the space.

The three of us—Sullivan to my right, his ogler to my
left, and me, the monkey in the middle—were by far the
youngest people in the room. I took off my gloves and
Sullivan allowed me to shed my coat unassisted, which
was unlike him. He looked tired and miserable, even in
my peripheral vision.

I studied the jet black hair of the woman seated directly in front of me. Her precise, sharp-cut bob was identical to that of—she turned around and fired a glance at me with narrowed eyes—Margot Troy!

Come to think of it, her presence here made sense. Margot would have been drawn to the name of the course—Going Green. Could she have known in advance that Richard was going to be the finalist judge for the green home contest? If so, her being his student certainly tipped the scales in her direction.

I struggled to focus on Richard's lecture. Did Margot know that he'd stepped down as judge? If she was here primarily to suck up to him, this latest development wasn't going to sit well.

Margot raised her hand. "I'm sorry, Richard," she said in a saccharine voice. "I couldn't hear what you said just now. Could you please repeat your observation? The one about conservation being our moral obligation?"

Richard repeated a hoary cliché about our being the children of our beloved Mother Earth and it being our duty to love, honor, and protect her and her precious, diminishing resources. After several minutes of his droning on and on with variations on that same theme, I began to suspect that Richard's lecture was the real cause of the furrows on Sullivan's brow; Sullivan probably hated that his one-time idol was regurgitating the homilies of countless conservationists instead of dazzling us with his own vision.

The girl seated beside me struggled to peer around me at Sullivan. She was clicking the spring on her pen repeatedly, probably trying to annoy me into changing seats. Fat chance. She looked twenty at the most. I had almost ten years on her, Sullivan had fourteen, and we had amassed a world of shared experience in our relatively short time together.

Richard finally began discussing something personal—his sideline business producing and selling nontoxic products for households, including paints and wood-finishing sealants. A middle-aged woman said timidly, "But your products cost so much more than the products at the home-improvement stores."

"In terms of money, sure," Richard countered. "But think about the cost to the environment. Think about how the toxins in all those products are permanently polluting the earth. And once the air and water are gone, we won't survive. Mankind will simply cease to exist."

"Oh, get over yourself, Thayers," a man yelled from the back of the room. I turned. It was the man in the sheepskin coat who'd held the door for me.

"Matthew Hayes," Richard intoned wearily as he eyed the handsome young man. "Figured you'd show up here eventually to disrupt things."

"Oh, I'm not here to disrupt. I want you to teach me. Teach me something I don't know, Mr. Thayers. Something that I haven't heard a zillion times before. Teach me how I can use responsible products and still make money. Just don't focus on the so-called earth-friendly products that *you* personally profit from!"

Several classroom members had slouched down in their seats. Others were stealing tense glances at Richard and his heckler. Was it just a coincidence that on the same day, this man whom Sullivan so admired had made two such ardent enemies? Or had Burke Stratton *sent* Matthew Hayes here?

"Don't force me to call security, Matthew."

"Please, don't throw me out, Master Thayers. *Teach*

me how I'm supposed to make my own profit when you antipollutants fanatics are picketing outside my business." He stood up, the color rising in his cheeks. "When protestors block customers from my door, while handing out fliers, printed on your oh-so-ecologically-responsible paper, urging people to *boycott* my company! Teach us how big business is bad! Yet *they're* the only ones who can keep their profit margins low! *They* can survive despite your boycotts. All of which just *happens* to help sales for all *your* touchy-feely products!"

An elderly man at the end of our row rose on wobbly legs and called to the man behind us, "Sir? I paid good money to be here and to listen to Professor Thayers. And I'll thank you to either sit there quietly or leave!"

Matthew Hayes plopped himself back down into his chair and crossed his arms. "Dude, sorry to break this to you, but if you paid more than a dime for this class, you got ripped off." Again he snorted with forced laughter. "You actually believe Thayer's nonsense, don't you?"

"Class," Richard said in an authoritarian voice, "this is simply a personal vendetta that Mr. Hayes has against me. Don't give this misguided man the time of day. He skirts the law with his use of ivory and rain forest wood."

"Untrue! I use recycled materials only, and you know it! If any of my materials were illegal, the SEC would shut me down."

"This is not the time or the place," Richard said. "If you want to have a private discussion, you—"

"Yeah, right. Admit it, Thayers. You just can't handle anyone with a different mind-set from your own."

"What mind-set?" Margot remarked over her shoulder. "Do you even *have* a mind?"

I began to wonder if this had all been staged—if Richard, the "great motivator," had hired Hayes to liven up the class with a debate. I stole a glance at Steve. He was glaring at the heckler.

Hayes again got to his feet. "Come on, Thayers. If your product is so safe and earth-friendly, put your mouth where your money is. *Drink* it."

Richard grabbed a quart-sized can of paint. He smirked at Matthew. "This is gold paint, which, as you must know, is normally the most toxic of all paints, because of its metallic content. You want me to drink this in front of you to prove it's safe?"

"Absolutely!" the heckler fired back at Richard. "Go ahead! Drink your paint. If it's so safe, why not?"

"No! Don't be crazy, Professor Thayers," a woman student cried, echoing my thoughts exactly.

"He just wants to make you look foolish and desperate," another woman said.

"No, no." Richard calmly held up his hand. "He's right. About this one thing, I mean. I'm happy to prove to this...earth-eroding miscreant that every word I say about my products, and our duty to the planet, is the truth." He pulled out a Swiss Army knife from the pocket of his baggy slacks and started to pry open the can.

I looked at Sullivan, who was aghast as he watched his mentor. "Stop him!" I whispered harshly.

"How?" he whispered back.

"Take the cans away from him!"

"I'm sure he knows what he's doing." To my ear, however, Sullivan had never sounded less sure of himself.

"He'll be fine, Erin," Margot said under her breath, turning toward us.

"Wait, Mr. Thayers." I shot to my feet. "Can't you just

point out that there's a big difference in calling something nontoxic versus edible? Or potable, in this case? I mean, just because it won't kill you to eat a cup of mud doesn't mean it won't make you sick. Furthermore—"

I broke off. My words were falling on deaf ears. Richard set down the lid and held the gold paint high with both hands as though he were a priest lifting the Holy Cup at Mass. With his wild eyes and hair, however, he looked more like the quintessential mad scientist. All around me, his students were shrieking or laughing as if this were a grand staged event.

Richard Thayers took three or four deep gulps from his can of paint. Disgusted, I sank into my chair.

"Ah. Not bad," Richard said, wiping his lips on a paper towel that he'd produced from behind the dais. He coughed a little, set down the can, and gave his heckler a triumphant smile. But I was certain that I glimpsed a hint of fear in his eyes.

Richard glanced at his watch. "Thank you for your attendance tonight." He cleared his throat. "Class is dismissed."

"Are you okay, Professor Thayers?" an elderly woman's frail voice behind me asked.

"Just fine. Thank you. And thank you all for coming tonight. We'll see you here next week. For our final session." He gave a wan smile, then focused on packing up his things.

"This is really not as big of a deal as it seems," Margot said quietly, again rotating in her seat to face us. Her expression and voice sounded sincere, her dark brown eyes directly meeting my gaze. Margot had the kind of patrician features and style that screamed old money. I guessed her to be in her late forties, but she'd had "work done," so it was hard to tell. "I've taken his class three years running, and he does this every year."

"Really?" I asked, still appalled and feeling a little sick to my own stomach. "He drinks gold paint every year?"

"Oh, yes. The first time he did it, everyone panicked. Half the class was about to call nine-one-one on our cell phones till he convinced us not to. Word's starting to get around, though," she grumbled, eyeing Matthew Hayes. "Obviously."

"Matthew Hayes couldn't have known. If he was aware that Richard drank paint every year, why would he goad him into doing so? He'd only be playing into Richard's hand."

"True. Well. In any case, no worries." She grinned at me and stood up. She whispered, "I need to go pay our illustrious instructor some compliments now. It probably won't help me win the contest, but it certainly won't hurt."

"Too late for that, Ms. Troy," Steve said. "He stepped down today. He knows one of the finalists and couldn't be impartial."

"Oh, but he—" She gave Richard, then me, a confused glance, but a moment later focused on Sullivan with a steely resolve. "That could only be *your* client. Otherwise, *you* wouldn't know before I did. I'm one of only three finalists, for heaven's sake. What happened?"

"We really don't know anything beyond the fact that he stepped down, Margot," I said.

"Peachy," Margot growled. "Just peachy." She narrowed her eyes at the doe-eyed girl beside me, who was blatantly listening. "I'm sorry, young lady, does our conversation concern you?"

"Um, no, er. I was just . . . worried about Mr. Thayers."

"Well, as you've already heard, you needn't bother." Margot gathered her things and swept out of the room.

Steve laid his hand on top of mine and gave my fingers a brief squeeze. To my chagrin, that was enough physical contact to get my pulse racing, especially when our gazes locked. He looked sad. "I'd better go talk to him," Steve muttered, then rose.

"I'll meet you outside," I told him. He caressed my shoulder for an instant as he walked behind me, then brushed past the girl beside me as though she—despite her doleful gaze—were invisible. My karma would no doubt give me a head-whack for the glee that brought me. The girl rushed out the back door as Sullivan strode down the stairs.

Meanwhile, Matthew Hayes came partway down the stairs and stopped at the end of my long row of seats. He stood, arms akimbo, giving Richard the evil eye. Oblivious, Richard finished packing his half dozen quart-sized cans and a pair of spiral notebooks into a filthy canvas bag, which he slung over one shoulder. He looked up and smiled at Sullivan.

"Hey, S.S. Thanks for coming tonight. I'd meant to have you say a few words to the class. But then we were so rudely interrupted."

"Oh, puh-lease," Matthew growled.

"Enough, Hayes," Richard snarled at him. "Show's over!"

Matthew gave him a withering look and stood his ground.

Richard's face was discolored and damp with perspiration. Steve was studying Richard's features intently, and seemed to be seeing the same thing I was.

"'Fraid I'm going to have to take a rain check on that

beer," Richard told Sullivan. "Turns out, I've got to dash over to a client's house tonight." He patted Steve on the back. "Next time, okay?"

I hoped that Steve would stick with him, suggest that he might need to have his stomach pumped, and insist on driving him to an urgent care clinic. Steve looked up at me as if to seek my opinion, and I pointed with my chin at Richard. He seemed to get the message as he turned to leave with him.

Matthew Hayes was now heading out the back door, and I quickened my step to catch up to him. I wanted to find out if he'd been hired by Burke to harass Richard.

"Matthew?" I called just as he was leaving.

He turned around. "Yeah?" His brow was furrowed. He clearly expected me to bicker with him.

"Hi." I gave him a shamefully flirtatious smile. "My name is Erin. That instructor is a piece of work, isn't he?" Realizing only then that I'd spoken too quickly and too loudly, I looked behind me. To my horror, Steve was standing in the other doorway, glaring at me. Damn it! Why couldn't I have held my stupid tongue for two seconds!?

"Yeah," Matthew was saying. "You can say *that* again." *Not bloody likely.*

Sullivan stormed out the opposite door, calling, "Richard. Wait up."

I forced a smile and turned back to Matthew. "Don't get me wrong. I'm into saving the environment. I love our planet just as much as anyone. It's just that you need to save yourself, too. You can go so overboard that you turn everyone else off."

"Exactly." He studied my features and gave me another appreciative smile. "You're Erin *Gilbert,* aren't you? I think I saw an article about you in the *Sentinel* a while back."

"You did?" I was smiling, but was cursing on the inside. I was going to be forced to drop my camaraderie routine immediately. No way would I smear my reputation as an earth-friendly designer, just to ply an annoying heckler for information about his relationship with my client.

"Yeah. You're a designer, right?"

"Of interiors. Yes."

Matthew stood aside to allow me to pass through the doorway first. As I brushed past him, he grumbled, "I hate that guy. But I thought he'd be smarter than to drink paint. Yeesh!"

"So you haven't heard that he drinks from a can every year? That's what one of the other students told me a minute ago."

"Actually, yeah, I heard something to that effect, but I figured it was just a rumor. That's what gave me the idea." He grinned at me. "You know, Erin, we're in different areas of the same field. You've even ordered some furniture from me. At least once."

I finally made the mental connection. "Oh, that's right. Of course. Matthew Hayes. You're the 'M.H.' in M.H. Custom Furniture."

He nodded, eyeing me. "And you're the designer for one of the finalists for the green home contest."

"That's right. Do you know my client, Burke Stratton?"

"Not personally. I see that he's in for a big-deal prize, though. Yet more greenbacks for the green home owner. Huzzah."

"I haven't heard anything about any boycott of your store in almost a year. Is that really still going on?"

"Nah. Tonight was just a preventative measure. See, every year, Crestview holds this community course, and for Thayers's final class, he hands out fliers, along with his list of supposed abusers. M.H. Furniture is always one of 'em. He gets his students so psyched up, they think it's *their* idea to picket."

"Even though *he's* the one handing out the fliers?"

"Exactly. So this year, I'm cutting them off at the pass." He wiggled his eyebrows. "Clever, right?"

"But *you* don't consider your furniture production ecologically irresponsible?"

He spread his arms. "I admit that I use toxic varnishes. And paints. And I use *salvaged* materials that are illegal to import in the raw form. What are we supposed to do? Never rework ivory? Hell, by the time I get ahold of it, the elephant's already been dead for fifty years. That makes *me* the bad guy, according to Thayers?"

I didn't reply, but the truth was, I could see both sides of the issue. It was such a small step to go from salvaging ivory to importing tusks. Yet Audrey had recently procured an antique piano with ivory keys, so, with an only moderately ruffled conscience, I now had ivory in my own house.

We entered the lobby, where I saw no sign of Sullivan or Richard. I slowed my pace and glanced back. The two men were coming out of the men's room. Richard's color was considerably better, and his shoulders looked less hunched. I breathed a sigh of relief. Steve, however, developed a hitch in his step when he spotted Matthew still standing beside me.

"How did you get on his list of ecological violators in the first place?" I asked Matthew quietly.

He honed in on Richard with laserlike eyes. "I had the guts to argue with the pompous jackass at a conference a couple years back. He's been riding me ever since."

"I see."

"The funny thing is that the guy's a *hypocrite!*" Matthew raised his voice to make sure Richard could overhear as he neared. "He's really not that much into the environment. He's just fooled a lot of people into thinking he is. He only pretends to be green, because that's been his bread and butter for years. Richard Thayers is about as green as my rear end."

"Strange," Richard asked him as he and Sullivan walked past us. "Did you hear a noise just now? It sounded like a lot of hot air being let out of a balloon."

Matthew retorted, "*You* should know."

We left the building. It was freezing outside, but Richard wiped dots of perspiration from his brow. Matthew horse-laughed. "What's the matter, Thayers? Feeling a little ill from your *non*toxic product?"

I gritted my teeth at the way Matthew was taunting him. "Can I give you a ride someplace?" I asked Richard, thinking he might accept help from a woman more easily than from his former student.

"No. I'm fine," he barked, and headed quickly into the parking lot. He walked with his weight forward, as if he was once again in physical pain.

"I'm Matthew Hayes, of M.H. Custom Furniture," Matthew said to Steve, and held out his hand. "Are you Steve Sullivan?"

Sullivan clenched his fists as he faced Matthew, who appeared to be oblivious to Steve's hostile demeanor, per-

haps due to the dim light of the street lamp. "Yeah." He
hesitated, then shook Matthew's hand.

"I was telling Miss Gilbert that I read the article about
you two in the paper."

Sullivan shrugged. "They must have been short on
news items that day."

We all turned as Richard drove off in an old Volvo station wagon. Steve and I waved, but he didn't acknowledge us.

"So, Erin," Matthew said, "could I take you to dinner?"

"I ate before class. But thanks anyway."

"You *did*?" Sullivan asked in a snarky voice. "You
weren't planning to join Richard and me after class?"

"It sounded like you were planning on catching up on
old times, and I didn't want to be a third wheel."

"I *said* I wanted you and Richard to like each other."

"Ouch. Sorry," Matthew interrupted, holding up his
palms. "I didn't realize you two were a couple."

"It's all right," Steve said. "Erin does her own thing."
He turned away and strode toward his van.

I felt both hurt and affronted. "It was nice meeting
you, Matthew," I said automatically, although it was far
from true.

"You, too. Stop by my store sometime." He slipped a
business card into my hand. "My workshop's in the back,
so I'm pretty much there twenty-four seven."

"I'll do that," I called over my shoulder as I trotted
across the lot, only to see Sullivan pulling away. I let myself into my own Sullivan and Gilbert Designs van,
grabbed my cell phone, and pressed Sullivan's number
on my speed dial.

"Yeah?" he answered a moment later.

"Hi, Steve. It's me. Doing my own thing. And calling *you*."

"What did you expect, Erin? You *had* to flirt with the guy who was harassing Richard? You had to hang out with him in the lobby? To rub things in Richard's face? And mine?"

"Jeez, Sullivan! Give me a little credit! I was trying to find out if Burke Stratton had set up tonight's confrontation! We've run into terrible luck where our clients are concerned, so I was worried about Richard's *health*." I paused. When Sullivan said nothing, I added, "Despite what Margot Troy said, it really looked to me like something went wrong when Richard drank the paint this time. *That's* why I deliberately struck up a conversation with his heckler. So I could ask if he knew Burke Stratton. He claims he doesn't."

Steve remained silent. He pulled his van over ahead of me, just a short distance from the parking lot.

I waited.

"I . . . didn't put that together," he finally said quietly.

"So I gathered. And by the way? Even though I *did*, in fact, have dinner before class, I would have *claimed* to have eaten, just to get away from Matthew Hayes."

Another long pause. "You don't have to worry about Richard's health. He told me he'd gotten the mix wrong, is all."

"The mix?"

"He . . . cheats a little every year." Steve's voice was deflated. "He dilutes the product he's planning on drinking. He says it was too thick this time . . . that he didn't add enough water. So he was feeling a little nauseated. But he took an antacid, and he assured me he's fine now."

"Good. I'm glad."

"Erin? I was a real jerk just now. I should've known you wouldn't..."

"Flirt with your mentor's arch rival, just because I'm such a habitual slut?"

"I was going to put things more tactfully than that. And I know you're not a slut. I'm sorry."

I crossed my fingers and said suggestively, "You want to try and make it up to me?"

"I'm dying to. Believe me. But..."

He let his voice trail off. Oh, for crying out loud! He'd loused up, he admitted as much, and yet *he* was sticking a "but" into our making-up-again conversation?! How fair was that?!

"Erin, I just think I need to call it a day. Before I...put my foot in my mouth again. Let's start fresh tomorrow."

I said nothing.

With a smile in his voice, he teased, "I'll bring you flowers and peel you some grapes."

"Grapes?"

"Yeah. I think there's some line in *Cleopatra* about grape peeling. By her love slave. If I'm not mistaken."

I chuckled. "Well, I like the sound of that love slave thing."

"I was hoping you would. So I'll see you tomorrow?"

"I guess so. At work. Yippee."

"Doesn't really feel like work, when you're around."

My heart made a little flutter that felt like a joyful leap, but he said, "Night, Erin," and hung up before I could reply.

The next morning, as I strolled from my parking space toward our office, the view of crystalline blue sky against snowcapped mountains made me fall in love with Colorado all over again, even though I'd lived here for almost three years. On such a morning, it was easy to find inspiration for my work—the lavender colors of the white crested mountains, the azure sky, the deep forest greens of the pine trees.

I felt almost giddy as I let myself inside through the carved oak door, smiling at the brushed-nickel faceplate that read *Sullivan and Gilbert Designs.* I was so lucky! I lived in one of the most beautiful areas in existence, I was working in the career that I loved with the man I—

Perish that thought! I was getting way ahead of myself. Sullivan and I had only recently figured out how to work together without letting our differences boil over—and cost us clients. None of the famed couples in happily-ever-after fairy tales had to navigate running a two-person business together. If I was going to let myself start believing that Sullivan and I could manage that feat, I had to ignore an enormous amount of evidence to the contrary.

After a few minutes of stalling, I gradually got to work. By the time my drawings of Burke's sunroom had captured my full attention, I had resolved that my business-hours focus needed to stay squarely on the job. I simply could *not* be daydreaming about my love life, or lack thereof, when the object of those dreams would, in mere minutes, be occupying the only other desk in the room.

As if on cue, Sullivan stepped through the doorway, his cheeks adorably flushed from the cold. My heart instantly began its familiar thrumming. He hung his black wool coat next to mine on the antique brass coat rack. He carried nary a flower nor a grape, peeled or otherwise. Disappointment was already clutching at my throat.

Maybe if I sat in a closet for long enough, my emotions

and my intellect would eventually introduce themselves to each other.

"Hey, Gilbert," he said as he strode toward his desk. "There was a traffic snarl-up on Main Street this morning. Really slowed me down."

"Was it caused by construction?"

"Maybe. The police had it detoured. Around Aspen Street." He gave me a sly smile, then turned back toward the door. "Almost forgot." He reached into his coat pocket and removed what looked like a tiny white paper cup for a catsup dispenser from a fast-food chain. "This is for you, m' lady."

Inside the cup was a single red grape, which he had somehow managed to carve into the shape of a rose. "Oh!" I cried, gently removing the grape from the cup. "This is amazing!"

He grinned at me and said, "Glad you like it. You'd be surprised how many grapes I had to search through till I... found one that was shaped like a flower." He'd grown distracted as he spoke and was now peering at the drawing behind me.

Holding his miniature fruit sculpture up to the light, I cried, "I love it, Steve! I shall cherish this until it turns into a raisin rose!"

I had just decided to risk having a customer walk in on us while I kissed him, but I hesitated. For some reason, he was glowering at my artwork. "You're redoing Burke's solarium?" he snarled.

"A little. I was thinking we could check out the salvage yard again for some metal to remake into benches. Maybe from some old iron security bars. Why? You don't like it?"

"Jeez, Gilbert! I thought you'd be willing to take

Richard's advice for at least twenty-four hours! He says we should back off from working for Stratton!"

"I'm not going to do that!" I dropped my carved grape back into its catsup cup. "If this was anybody but Richard Thayers talking, you would never have given a suggestion like that a second thought!"

"But it *was* Thayers! Somebody whose opinion I know I can trust. So your point is utterly—"

He broke off at the sound of someone opening our door. I had to stop myself from cursing out loud at the sight of the blue uniform. A police officer entered the studio, followed by a second officer.

"Morning," the first man said with a solemn nod. "I'm Officer Dantley. This is Officer Riggs."

Steve rose and shook their hands. "Steve Sullivan. And this is my partner, Erin Gilbert." His features were drawn, and I knew he had every bit as bad a feeling about this visit as I did.

Officer Riggs nodded at me. "We met last year, Ms. Gilbert."

"That's right. At the benefit." I had a good friend, Linda Delgardio, who was on the Crestview police force.

"We've been told you both were in a class at CU last night taught by Richard Thayers. True?"

"Yes," Steve managed, his voice uncharacteristically low. "He was a mentor of mine. He taught some of my classes at the Art Institute of Colorado when he was living in Denver."

"We've got some bad news for you," the second officer said. "Richard Thayers died early this morning."

chapter 4

O h, no," I moaned. Steve just gaped at the officers.

"He was poisoned," Officer Dantley said. "At least according to the preliminary tox screens. He drank something that he apparently didn't realize was extremely poisonous."

The color drained from Steve's face. I rounded my desk and grabbed his arm. He appeared to be too shocked to say anything. I resisted the urge to embrace him and instead asked the policemen, "You mean the gold paint from last night's class?"

"That's what it appears to be," Dantley replied. "The autopsy won't be ready for another day or two."

"According to our information," Riggs interjected, "he's done that drinking-paint act more than once. This time it caught up with him."

"That's what a former client of mine in his class said last night," I muttered.

"Margot Troy?" Officer Riggs asked.

I nodded.

"Professor Thayers had her name circled on his class roster," Riggs explained. "We spoke with her earlier this morning. She told us about your being there."

Sullivan pulled away from my grasp and leaned back onto his desk, gripping the edge so firmly that his knuckles turned white. I wished that the policemen could give him a minute or two to collect himself.

"Mr. Thayers was obviously feeling ill after drinking the paint yesterday," I said. "Did he get himself to a doctor?"

Riggs shook his head. "That's where we think he was heading last night. But he pulled over. Apparently too sick to keep driving. Unfortunately, he pulled into a small side street. Nobody saw him there. Or if they did, they didn't realize he was in distress."

"He died in his car?" I asked.

"'Bout halfway between the campus and the hospital," he answered with a grim nod. "A jogger found him in the early hours of the morning."

"He was murdered," Steve insisted. "Someone must have switched labels on the can . . . fooled him into *thinking* it was his own nontoxic paint, when he was actually drinking a toxic product from some other manufacturer. That's the only reasonable explanation."

"We're investigating that possibility, Mr. Sullivan," Dantley said sternly. "Although it could also have been a careless accident, made in the production line. Or maybe a deliberate act on his own part."

"Suicide, you mean? No way!" Sullivan fired back.

"Mr. Thayers had a half dozen of his environmentally friendly products in his book bag," Officer Riggs explained, "which he apparently brought to class with him. First thing the lab did was test all six cans, and they all had exactly what the label said. 'Cept the gold paint."

"He always drinks that one product," Sullivan said. "It's the most impressive, because it's metallic. Yet he says it also thins out with water the best."

There was a pause as both policemen peered at Steve. "So . . . you knew he added water," Officer Dantley stated. "Did you share that information with anyone else?"

"No. Not counting Erin. And I only heard about it after the fact. When Richard told me."

"For this to have been murder, the killer had to be real familiar with Mr. Thayers's routines," Riggs said.

"We need to interview you two separately," Dantley said, giving his partner a piercing glare. He had a more authoritative manner than Riggs, which led me to believe he was his superior officer. "Miss Gilbert, would you mind coming with me?"

"Uh, no, that's fine." I cast a longing glance at Sullivan, hating to leave him reeling from the news, as I followed the policeman through the inner door that led to the lobby and stairs.

The main entrance to our three-story office building had a rarely used alcove—rarely used because it was poorly lit, stark, and unappealing. Dantley and I took seats on the marble slab of a bench as I recounted for him the short history of my dealings with Richard Thayers. That led to a lengthy discussion about what little I knew of Richard's relationship with Burke Stratton.

Eventually, we returned to the matter of who could have been highly familiar with Richard's lesson plans. "Margot Troy told me she'd taken the class two other times," I said. "I don't know if anyone else in the class was a repeat."

He made a notation in his pad. "Anyone in the class strike you as acting suspicious?"

"A local furniture maker named Matthew Hayes was heckling Thayers, as I'm sure Margot already told you."

"Yeah. She did." Dantley held my gaze for an uncomfortably long time. "She *also* said the two of you came in together last night."

I was surprised and a little offended. How had Margot even noticed our entrance directly behind her? And why had she reported such trivia to the police so quickly? "We weren't together. He held the door for me. We just happened to arrive at the same time. That's all."

"So you didn't talk to him, other than maybe to thank him for getting the door?"

"Not exactly, no." My seat on the marble bench felt intolerably uncomfortable, so I tried to reposition myself, then noticed Dantley raise an eyebrow and scribble something in his pad. "I chatted with him *after* class. I was curious about the statements he'd made to Richard."

"Can you recall the exact conversation?"

I took a calming breath and tried to quell the feeling that I was being investigated as a murder suspect. Nobody was pointing a finger at me. Officer Dantley was merely being thorough. Margot, too, must have felt this anxious during *her* sudden early-morning police interrogation. I repeated what Matthew and I had said to each other last night as best I could, omitting Sullivan's and my brief quarrel in Matthew's presence. Afterward, Dantley flipped back through his notes.

"What's your personal take on Burke Stratton?"

"I'm not sure what you mean by 'personal take.' He's been our client at Sullivan and Gilbert Designs for around six months. He's trying to win the Earth Love green home contest. He's a nice guy. Thanks to this contest, he's on the verge of getting major recognition for his house, and we're helping him."

"Who's 'we'?"

"Steve Sullivan and myself."

"Got any idea what caused the rift between Thayers and Stratton?"

"All I know is that Burke said he'd hired Richard four years ago and fired him because he felt his work was shoddy."

"Had to have been pretty bad, right? Their parting of the ways, I mean. You said that Thayers warned you he might damage your professional lives."

"Yes."

He studied my features, waiting, but I had nothing to add.

"Your partner might be able to fill us in a little better." Dantley shut his notepad and tucked it into a jacket pocket. "Wait here, please." He returned to my office, and I promptly rose. No way would I stay seated on this uncomfortable bench like a disobedient child waiting for the principal's punishment; I wanted to know what was happening in my own office.

After a minute or two, both officers emerged, and

Riggs said, "Thank you, Ms. Gilbert. Please call the station house if you think of anything important you'd like to add. We'll be in touch."

Dantley tipped his cap, and they left.

I rushed back into my office, deeply concerned about Steve. He was staring at the drawing I'd been working on for Burke. To my dismay, he tore the drawing off my easel and crumpled it.

"Steve? Do you want to talk about it?"

"It?" he snapped.

"About Richard." I couldn't keep my discouragement from my voice. *Was this how it was always going to be between us? One door opens a crack only to have another one slam shut in my face?* My rose-shaped grape was still sitting in its little cup on the corner of my desk. It seemed to be shriveling before my very eyes.

"No. Talking won't help. Only getting the bastard who did this to him will. Seeing him get locked up with the key thrown away. That's all I care about at this point."

"So when you crumpled Burke's plans for the solarium just now . . . you think he did it?"

"Yeah, actually, I do. I think he hated Richard. I think it was the last straw for Burke when he found out Richard was cutting him out of the competition. And I think he killed him."

"Burke wasn't there last night. And the two of them have been estranged since before Richard started teaching that class. So, even if he *had* learned somehow about Richard's drinking his products, he couldn't have realized that it was always gold paint."

"You don't know that." His hazel eyes were once again burning with anger. I had to turn away. I slunk toward my desk. Some defeatist part of my brain whined that this thing between Sullivan and me was just too hard. Not meant to be. Not worth it. "They were probably friendly at one time," he said.

"True."

"This is my fault," he muttered, staring at the red and black oil painting against the exposed brick wall behind his desk.

"No, it isn't!" I leaned forward on my desk. "Steve. Please. Don't bludgeon yourself like this!"

"I should have insisted on taking him to the hospital. I knew something was wrong." His fists were clenched. He tossed the mangled floor plan into the steel trash can.

"But he told you he was feeling better. And that appeared to be the truth."

"I should've seen through that. My god, the man drank poisonous paint right in front of me! And I let him walk out and try to make his own way to the hospital. All because I was so wrapped up in you and that Matthew Hayes joker."

"Oh, Steve! You can't seriously be blaming yourself for not reading Richard's mind, can you?"

He was grinding his teeth, avoiding my eyes. "I know in my gut that Burke's guilty."

"But... Burke's a successful M.D. He's well respected in the community. All this green design stuff he does is just a sideline for him. He doesn't need the winnings. And he's already won community service awards, so he's got whatever respect and status he could want."

He sighed. "Maybe that was the problem, Erin." He was finally calming down a little, thank goodness. "Maybe he couldn't stand to lose his lofty status. His reputation was going to get damaged, thanks to Richard. He's got his pride on the line."

"So you think he decided to murder the contest judge? Seriously?"

"Image is everything for some people. He loses his self-image, he's dead. He killed to protect it."

"I guess there have been worse reasons to take someone's life. But...he might be innocent." My heart ached for poor Steve. I felt strongly that he was being much too hasty to condemn Burke, but at the moment, he needed my support, not my critique. "We have to honor our contract with Burke, but I think it's best if I handle all our interactions myself, for the time being," I suggested gently. "Okay?"

Sullivan sighed again, his shoulders sagging. "Why the hell didn't I insist on taking Richard to a doctor? What was I thinking?"

He'd already answered that question. He'd been thinking that I was flirting with Matthew Hayes. "I know this is harsh, but the fact is, Richard was the only person who could have known for sure how sick he was feeling. His pride got in the way of asking for help, even when his life depended on it."

Steve gave me an anguished gaze. "I've got to get out of here for a while. Clear my head." He grabbed his coat and headed out the door without a backward glance.

I sank miserably into my chair. Why had I argued with him? Just once, couldn't I have said what I'd really been feeling? Thrown my arms around him and told him how much I cared?

Even as I asked myself those questions, an answer niggled at me. I'd been afraid to test his reaction. It would have been unbearably painful for me if Sullivan had pushed me away and blamed me for distracting him from Richard's plight last night.

A minute or two later, the door opened, and I whirled around, hoping Steve had already returned. Instead it was Burke Stratton. I remembered we had an appointment this morning and as usual, he was right on time. His face looked ashen, though his complexion was always quite pale. He was a bookish man in his early forties with Nordic coloring—blond with gentle blue eyes behind his thick wire-framed oval lenses.

With no preamble and without removing his parka, Burke asked, "Did you hear what happened to Richard Thayers?" He winced immediately and held up a palm. "Never mind. You *must* have." He dropped into the Sheraton chair in front of my desk. "I bumped into Steve just now. He wouldn't talk to me. He barely even looked at me."

"He's upset."

"The two of them were friends?"

"Yes. Thayers used to be his favorite professor, and they'd kept in touch over the years." I peered at him, thinking how ironic it would have been if Richard *had* made it to the emergency room last night, and if Burke— his arch enemy—had been there. "How did you hear about his death so quickly? Were you at the hospital when they found him?"

He shook his head. "I phoned Earth Love first thing this morning, trying to get a handle on when they're going to hold my hearing. The receptionist was in tears."

"I wonder how *they* found out."

"The police. Richard probably had a business card in

his wallet." He searched my eyes. "Is this going to be a problem?"

"Pardon?"

"Steve Sullivan. And his friendship with Richard Thayers. The way he looked at me ... the glare on his face ... it was as if he thought *I* had killed the guy."

"I'm sure that's not true," I lied. "He glares all the time when he's thinking. It's one of his standard facial expressions."

Burke stared at the maple flooring by his feet. "If somebody actually murdered Richard, it wasn't me, Erin. I'm a doctor, for God's sake. I *save* lives. Or at least, I *used* to, and will again. I've been doing medical research the past few years."

"You have? I thought you worked at the hospital."

"I do. But in the lab. I used to be a pediatrician, but when my son died, I needed to take a break from patient care."

"Your son died? Oh, how horrible! I'm so sorry to hear that!"

He nodded. "Almost four years ago. Before I moved here from Denver. Childhood leukemia. I thought I'd mentioned that when you were looking at the pictures in my house."

"No. You'd just said it was your ex-wife and your son. I assumed your wife had full custody." It had been a reasonable conclusion; I'd seen for myself already that he had no boy's bedroom or toys in his home, just a Raggedy Andy doll in the corner of the master bedroom.

"I wish that was all there was to it. Then Caleb would still be alive." He was battling such sorrow that my heart ached for the poor man. "But in any case, Erin, I swear. I could never take a life. I'm not a killer. I don't have it in me."

"I'm so sorry. I've dealt with a couple of clients over the years who've lost a child, and I know there's no greater loss."

He nodded, wringing his gloved hands. "There's nothing more painful. If I could have switched places with my son, died instead of him, I would have gladly done so. Your hopes are gone. You lose your future. Gone."

"I'm so sorry," I repeated quietly.

"Thanks." He squared his shoulders and looked at me. "That's what led to my rift with Richard. Now he's suddenly dead."

"Your falling out with Richard was related to your son's illness?"

He closed his eyes and nodded, swallowing hard. "Truth, Erin? Richard had good cause to hate me. We'd hired him to help us rid the house of carcinogens. Caleb died anyway, of course. We all knew it was going to happen. But...I stiffed Richard on the invoice. He presented it to me the day I got back from intensive care, when they told me Caleb wasn't ever coming home. I was crazed. I...took it out on him. Called him a con man."

"And was he?"

"No. He did what we hired him to do. He'd told my wife and me up front that there was nothing he could do to reverse the cancer...but we all *hoped* he could slow it down. He taught us what we should have done originally with our interior paints, and so on. He lowered the radon emissions in our basement and garage. Hooked us up with a dietitian." He shrugged. "About a year ago, I paid him what I owed. I tried to apologize, but he wouldn't listen to me." He frowned and added under his breath, "Though he cashed my check."

"You told me yesterday you fired him for his shoddy work."

"That was just the easiest explanation. And was partly true. I *did* fire him...but I only claimed it was shoddy because I needed to blame him...blame *somebody* for my loss. And he *does* hate me."

"Why did he hate you, though? Anybody in his position would have understood how..." I let my voice fade as the color rose in Burke's cheeks. "Oh. Did you damage his reputation afterwards?"

He averted his eyes and said, "At the time, I felt I was justified in telling people he was a fraud, you know? Then, once I returned to my senses, I told myself my behavior was understandable. I'd lost my only child. My marriage was in ruins. Who wouldn't need to lash out? But after a year went by...things finally dawned on me. Right around the time I was building my house in Crestview. That's when I discovered that I'd managed to hire the same architect as Thayers, so—"

"Jeremy Greene was Richard's architect?"

"Yeah. Of Greene Home Architecture. Guess the name appealed to both Richard and me. Anyway. It finally hit me that personal tragedy doesn't give anyone the right to verbally abuse others. What I'd done to Richard was just like if *I'd* lost a terminal young patient, and the parents had sued me or made me into a scapegoat for not being able to perform a miracle. Yet..." He paused and hung his head. "I hate having to talk about this. But. For the first few weeks after Caleb's death, I really went out of my way to spread the word that Stratton's products weren't actually reducing carcinogens. I'm a doctor, so people think I know what I'm talking about on all health-related subjects. I've since felt horrible about my behavior. Ironically, last night, it occurred to me that maybe this whole thing with Richard becoming my judge was paving the way out for me...for Richard to get even, or for me to get him to accept my apology and put it behind us. But now that's never going to happen." He closed his eyes. "Instead, this just brings some of those feelings back to mind. Of holding my dead son in—"

He couldn't continue. I retrieved an unopened bottle of water from my desk, handed it to him, grabbed a tissue for myself, then slid the box over toward him. He availed himself of both. I could only imagine the paralysis he must have felt as not only a grieving parent, but a children's physician as well. After a lengthy pause, he rubbed his forehead and said, "Enough of this subject. But... do you know how it happened? The receptionist said Thayers had been poisoned."

"He drank what he thought was his own nontoxic product, but the cans had apparently been switched and relabeled."

He gaped at me, incredulous. "What product was it? Paint? Varnish?"

"It was a can of gold paint."

"Gold paint! Oh...crap!" He sank his face into his hands. "My God. I'm being set up."

"What do you mean?"

He took a few seconds to collect himself. He rose and paced. His eyes remained wide with fright, and he kept clenching and unclenching his fists. "Do you remember the cans of generic paint we had on display in my garage for the green-home open space last weekend? How I'd selected gold, because it was more toxic than nonmetallic colors?"

"Yes." We'd put a display together for the open house—the dos and don'ts of home building. I put two and two together. "Someone took the paint can out of your garage?" I asked incredulously. "The 'don't' can was stolen?"

"Right. I'd noticed it was gone, but I figured it just got mislaid someplace. Or that the cleaning crew I hired after the open house had put it away in the wrong spot."

"The police didn't say anything about fingerprints."

"That doesn't mean they didn't find any." He hugged himself, even though he was still wearing his heavy parka. He sighed, looking weary and defeated. "Maybe it'd be best if I went to the police station myself to tell them this. Instead of waiting for them to come to me."

My heart ached for the poor man. "That might be wise. And . . . I'd get a lawyer, if I were you."

He gave me a grim smile and headed toward the door.

"I'm so sorry about all of this, Burke. I'll try to help in any way I can."

"Thanks, Erin. I appreciate that. I just hope it isn't going to cause friction between you and Steve."

"I'm sure it won't," I lied again.

Fifteen minutes later, Steve returned. "Burke was here," I told him. "For our scheduled meeting this morning. He says he ran into you."

"Yeah. Erin? We need to cut him loose. I can't give him the kind of service he deserves."

"Like I said before, I'll handle our interactions for the both of us, but I don't think I can drop him as a client.

Not after what he told me. He says his only child died of leukemia. He'd hired Richard to try to help extend his son's life. But when he died, Burke was so grief-stricken that he took things out on Richard. He went so far as to lie about Richard's products and skills. He'd tried to apologize later, but Richard wanted nothing to do with him."

"He's lying. That doesn't sound like Richard."

I held my tongue, wondering how well Steve could possibly know his professor, considering their limited contact during this past decade. "Steve, maybe you should take the day off."

"Maybe I should," he said. And just like that, he left.

chapter 5

*T*he afternoon was hectic, to say the least, with my covering work for both of us, and I found myself deeply annoyed at myself for having suggested Sullivan take the day off. The more I reflected on our conversation with Richard, the more skeptical I was about Richard's claiming not to have known that Burke was in the contest. I also wondered if Richard had known that Burke had hired his architect to design his potentially award-winning house.

Despite being pressed for time, I ran a computer search in the local online newspaper for any articles linking Jeremy Greene and Richard Thayers. To my surprise, a short article had been published six months ago reporting that Richard had sued Jeremy because of the "structurally inadequate" design of his foundation. I found it odd that Richard was holding the architect, not the builder, accountable for the problem. No subsequent articles had been published, so perhaps the matter had still been pending when Richard died.

A fabric-shopping expedition at the end of the day happened to place me in the vicinity of Jeremy Greene's architecture studio. If nothing else, I wanted to know if his being the architect for both Richard's and Burke's homes had really been a mere coincidence. And from a purely business standpoint, considering the nature of the lawsuit, I wanted to know if my client's foundation was going to collapse.

Jeremy's office was in a boxy redbrick structure in South Crestview, sadly lacking in architectural interest. Jeremy had done little to enhance his one-size-fits-all office space or to show off his skills, other than putting his truly excellent basswood models on display. I wondered idly if he'd consider hiring Sullivan and Gillbert Designs to jazz up his space.

He was poring over blueprints at his drawing table when I arrived. Jeremy was about my age (twenty-nine, which reminded me that I was due for celebrating my next birthday in the Bahamas). With his eager grin and sparkling eyes, he was more cute than handsome—baby-faced with a weak chin and a receding light brown hairline.

He pushed back from his work when I asked if he had a minute to talk and said convincingly that he appreciated the chance to take a break. I sat down on a wheeled swivel chair identical to his own, and silently observed that the chocolate brown vinyl flooring was the perfect surface for propelling oneself around the space on these caster-wheel chairs. This, however, was an acutely inappropriate time to share such inanities, so we somberly exchanged a few words about our sadness and dismay at Richard's untimely death. I then told Jeremy how I'd only recently learned that he'd designed both Richard's and Burke's homes.

He nodded and indulged in a proud smile. "Modesty aside, those are the two best straw-bale homes in Colorado. Did Burke tell you that we used much of the same floor plan?"

"No. He told me he didn't know at first that you were Richard's designer."

"The name didn't come up for a while, when I was first showing Burke the design. It never occurred to me that they'd know each other. Small world."

So it *was* a coincidence—but then, the world of the ecologically superfocused in the town of Crestview, Colorado, truly was small. "I guess it's no wonder that Richard felt he had to withdraw. He was going to be judging a house which was so close in design to his own."

He shrugged. "Mostly in basic structure ... rooflines, floor plans. And they both use straw-bale construction, of course. But in terms of aesthetics and energy efficiency, Burke's house had Richard's beat hands down."

"I wonder if that made Richard envious. I mean, that was the heart and soul of Richard's business ... green designs and so forth. And yet here's this physician who has built a house that looks like his, but is another ten or fifteen percent more energy-efficient."

"More like twenty-one percent, actually."

"Wow."

"But Richard knew that was just the nature of these things. A lot of breakthroughs have occurred in the last couple of years. You can't possibly keep up with them."

"So Richard didn't get angry about his house not being as energy-efficient as it might have been?"

Jeremy studied my features for a moment and replied cautiously, "He didn't complain to me about it."

I feigned nonchalance and asked, "So he only complained about his home's foundation?"

Jeremy's features turned stony, and he stayed silent.

"I read about the lawsuit. Was that ever resolved?"

"Yeah. I mean, I haven't heard anything more about it, so he probably dropped the suit. Or his lawyer did, based on lack of evidence."

Nice evasion, I said to myself. "The newspaper reported that he was getting cracks in his basement walls from an expansive-soil problem. Why did he blame you and not the builder?" When Jeremy didn't answer me right away, I pressed, "Surely as a conservationist himself, Richard wouldn't be objecting to the amount of fly ash in the concrete, right?" Fly ash was a by-product of coal furnaces that could be mixed into cement instead of being merely discarded, an excellent practice that I knew Jeremy always recommended.

"No, Richard knew the problem had nothing to do with fly ash; it was caused by improper construction. But the builder shifted the blame onto me, claiming he'd built the foundation wall according to my exact specs. Richard believed him, for some reason. And, anyway, all they needed to do was underpin the support wall. As far as I know, that's what they did, finally, and then the house was fine."

"Jeez. So your design was fine, but the builder screwed up, you told them how to fix it, but you *still* got sued? That must have made you furious!"

He shrugged. "Things like that are the price you pay for running your own business. Once Sullivan and Gilbert Designs has been around for six or seven years like I have, you'll run into lawsuits, too. If you haven't already."

He wasn't telling me the full story. Richard would have had no cause to sue his architect over a construction problem that had been easily remedied. I tried in vain to read his expression. "I guess that's probably true. Unfortunately."

"Why are you asking about this, Erin? You're not playing amateur sleuth, are you?"

"I'm just watching out for the interests of my client. Burke Stratton would freak if it turns out his foundation is crumbling. He's put his heart and soul into that place."

"Yeah. He sure has." Jeremy sounded bitter. He rolled his chair back into position at his drawing table. "It was good seeing you, Erin. But I've got to get back to work."

"Thanks for taking the time to talk," I said in a breezy voice. "Take care."

I left. When the time was right, I was going to have to discuss my concerns about Jeremy's design with Steve, and then with Burke. If there was a serious flaw in the design or construction of Burke's home, he would most likely have to follow in Richard's footsteps and hire a lawyer.

Furthermore, if Richard had uncovered a major flaw that was going to topple "the two best straw-bale homes in Colorado," Jeremy could have been driven to desperate measures—possibly murder—to protect himself. I considered calling Linda Delgardio, my friend on the police force. She never took kindly to my voicing theories regarding police investigations, though.

As I walked back to my car, my heart leapt at the tones of my cell phone. I hoped it was Sullivan. Instead, a friend from the Pilates studio I belonged to was organizing a last-minute girls' night out. I hesitated before agreeing to join them. I knew how much pain Sullivan was in, and although it felt disloyal of me, I needed a dose of fun and a temporary escape. Sadly, Steve's problems were still going to be there tomorrow, and by all appearances, the only thing he wanted from me right now was some space.

The next morning, Sullivan was in the office when I arrived a few minutes after eight. He'd already completed a presentation board for a major remodel we were bidding on next week, and he'd redone the sunroom drawing of mine that he'd crumpled. "You must have gotten here at six," I said.

"Closer to five. Couldn't sleep."

He was avoiding my gaze. "Since you've already got us caught up, how 'bout I take you to breakfast?"

"No. I want to just...keep working. Stay focused on the job. Thanks, though."

Did he mean he wanted to concentrate his energies on work for merely this one morning, or for the foreseeable future? "We'd planned on going to that concert in Denver tonight. Should we bag it?"

"Yeah. I'm not...I just can't right now, Gilbert. I've got too much on my plate already."

"I understand."

"Good. Thanks."

"Just don't push me away. I'm on your side."

He ignored me and went on. "By the way, I crossed paths with the woman who cleans the office. She threw out the grape I gave you."

"Oh, no! I meant to take that home last night."

He still wouldn't look me directly in the eye. "Was that drawing okay?" he asked solemnly.

"Which drawing?"

"My alterations to Burke's solarium. I figured when you said there were iron pieces you wanted to use for building the bench, you meant the grating we got at the salvage yard for him last week."

"Yes, that is exactly what I was thinking. It's fine, Sullivan. Thanks." The drawing he did, especially the in-set showing the bench he'd designed, was much better than fine, actually. But it was difficult to praise someone who was actively shutting the door in my face.

Fortunately, I was able to get lost in my work that morning until some ninety minutes later, when a portly middle-aged man stepped through the door. He was dressed in low-riding jeans, a flannel shirt, and a denim jacket. He scanned our posh surroundings as he dried his construction boots on the mat with the enthusiasm of a child trying to build up a charge of static electricity. He gave me an affable grin. "Hello, there." His voice was halfway to a shout. "Have I got the right place? Is this Gilbert and Sullivan Designs?"

"Sullivan and Gilbert Designs, actually," Steve quickly corrected, rising.

"Ah. Come to think of it, there's probably a sign on the door. Should've read it." He opened the door, craned his neck to peer at our nameplate, then shut the door again. "Which one's Gilbert and which one's Sullivan?"

"I'm Erin Gilbert."

"Steve Sullivan." Steve stepped forward with proffered hand. "And you are . . . ?"

"Name's Walter Emory," the visitor said, his voice still booming as he pumped Steve's hand. His name sounded familiar to me, but I couldn't place it. "Pleased to meet you. I'll probably be seeing you two quite a bit in the next week or two."

As he shook my hand, the name clicked. "You're the original founder of Earth Love, aren't you?" I remarked. He was also the head of World's Watchdogs, a much more controversial association, as I recalled.

He beamed at me. "That's right. Here to act as the new judge for the contest. Earth Love felt it'd be best to move forward quickly . . . then maybe to set up some sort of memorial fund in Richard's memory."

Sullivan peered at him. "You're heading up World's Watchdogs now, right?"

Walter Emory chuckled. "I can tell by the way you're both looking at me that you've heard the rumors that we have some dangerous ecoterrorist members. Rest assured, those are just rumors. No basis in fact. I haven't done anything the Feds consider a crime since I was a wild teenager." He had an endearing twinkle in his eye. "Quite a ways back, as you can see." The man had to be pushing sixty.

Sullivan took a seat in the leather chair facing him, and I sat down in my usual spot. "Richard was a friend of mine, too," Sullivan said. "How'd you meet him?"

"He worked as my consultant while I was forming

Earth Love. We met over the Internet, something like ten or fifteen years ago. I was still in Juneau at the time."

"I hear it's beautiful up there," I remarked.

"Sure is. My parents were hippies and raised me in Alaska. A commune, actually." He chuckled. "We never had a TV. Took me till I was in my late twenties to discover that most folks in the lower forty-eight figured getting a piece of the good life was all that mattered, and natural resources be damned. Now someone's killed one of the world's true guardian angels. All I've heard about his death is he was teaching a conservation class and poisoned himself with paint, thinking it was nontoxic."

"That's about the extent of our knowledge, too," Sullivan said. "Someone replaced his can with a toxic one. He was murdered."

"And earlier that same day, he'd filed charges against your client to boot him from the competition. True?"

"We don't know if those two things are related," I interjected firmly. "What we do know is that Burke Stratton would like to clear his name as quickly as possible." I exchanged glances with Sullivan, realizing too late that I must have sounded cold and even heartless to him.

"I should have figured out this could happen," Walter muttered. "To recognize that there'd be some problems, at the very least."

"Pardon?" I asked, confused.

"Never mind. Just thinking out loud. I should have advised Richard not to agree to be judge. Hindsight's always twenty-twenty, as they say."

"Judging the contest might not have had anything to do with his death," I said, pressing my point. "For all we know, the police might be on the verge of arresting some bitter ex-employee or jealous lover."

"Did Richard say anything to you about Burke Stratton?" Sullivan asked, ignoring me.

Walter shook his head. "Name means nothing to me. You two must know him pretty well, though. You think he's nuts enough to kill a man just because he caught him cheating in a contest?"

"Not in my opinion," I answered quickly.

Walter fixed his gaze on Sullivan, who had merely clenched his jaw. "You disagree?"

"They'd had a major blowup a few years ago."

"Ah. Sure. Sure."

Walter shifted his attention to me as if expecting a re-buttal, but no way was I going to get into a big disagree-ment right now. It was disconcerting that Walter's energies appeared to be much more focused on investi-gating Richard's death than on judging the contest. "Have you had a chance to examine whatever reports Richard filed with Earth Love about Stratton's viola-tions?" I asked.

He rolled his eyes. "What there is of them. He cited Stratton for tampering with his meters and with his water allocations. But he doesn't list any of the actual evidence that led him to those conclusions. Guess he figured he'd be presenting that at the hearing."

"When's that going to take place?" I asked.

"Soon as possible. We're hoping for Monday, if that works out for Dr. Stratton."

"Is that going to be enough time?" Sullivan asked. "You're going to need the police to release whatever evi-dence Richard had collected, and then examine it your-self."

Walter lifted his palms. "Vanished. If it ever existed in the first place."

"Wait." Sullivan gaped at him. "You mean, all of Richard's belongings have been searched in the past twenty-four hours, and you're already certain Richard's evidence against Burke can't be found?"

"According to the officer I spoke with this morning, Richard had all the files from Earth Love with him in his car. Not a single report regarding Dr. Stratton's violations, though. His latest notes in his journals were examined. Nothing about Stratton. The contents of his desk and file cabinets were inventoried. Under the circumstances, we're just going to have to go with what little we've got. If more information turns up, we'll hold a second hearing and reexamine the issue."

"Why hold a hearing at all?" Sullivan grumbled. "You're obviously going to clear him."

"Earth Love's trying to follow their own contest guidelines as best they can, I guess," Walter replied. He patted his thighs twice, then rose. "Good meeting you both. Thanks for chatting with me. I'll be seeing you again, I'm sure."

I got up and shook Walter's hand. I thanked him for stepping in to help out with the contest, then offered a few words of condolence for the loss of his friend. Sullivan shook his hand as well.

Just a few seconds after Walter had closed the door, Sullivan turned to me. "That proves it, as far as I'm concerned. The evidence that Burke was cheating had to have been stolen from Richard. And only Burke would benefit from its sudden disappearance."

More likely there was no evidence in the first place, I thought glumly. "Burke isn't necessarily the only one who'd have benefited. I had an interesting conversation with Jeremy Greene yesterday evening. There's something fishy going on with him. Did you know that several months ago, Richard was suing him for an inadequate design of his foundation?"

"Whose foundation?"

"Richard's. Jeremy was his architect for the house that he built five years ago."

"Huh. That's . . ." He let his voice trail off.

"Jeremy said it was the builder who loused up and nothing was wrong with his design. The strange thing is, though, that Richard was suing Jeremy, not the builder. In any case, I'm worried about Burke's basement now."

Steve paced. "Jeremy stood to lose invaluable publicity for his design, if Richard kicked Burke out of the contest," he said thoughtfully. "Still, though, Burke was the only one who would have been publicly accused of cheating when Richard's evidence was presented in the newspapers."

I considered arguing the point, but held my tongue.

He started to collect his things, including his portfolio case. "I've got to head to Jennifer's house."

"Jennifer Fairfax? Our presentation for her isn't till noon, is it?"

"No, she moved it up. She wanted me to show her our design, then take her to the Denver Design Center this morning."

"Really? When did she suddenly decide all of that?" *And why was I being cut out of the equation?*

"Uh, yesterday. I ran into her downtown. She said she was free all morning and wanted to move our presentation up. I figured the least I could do after you covered for me all day yesterday was to do it solo and free up your lunch hour today."

"Great," I said in a monotone. "Thanks."

He did a double take. "You don't have a problem with this, do you? I'm just taking her to the Design Center, not the Brown Palace."

My *problem* was that Jennifer Fairfax was a gorgeous divorcée who blatantly flirted with Sullivan every chance she got. And should I point out that he hadn't as much as mentioned the change to *my* schedule till now, after I'd pried the information out of him? If this had been a simple case of a client changing an appointment, he wouldn't be acting so defensive.

Apparently it wasn't just *Burke* who had a potentially crumbling foundation. I forced a smile. "No problem. Have fun."

chapter 6

You can't help but take special pride in home-improvement projects when you've done them yourself. On the other hand, if you're all thumbs, you can take pride in being smart enough to hire good help.

—Audrey Munroe

DOMESTIC BLISS

"I'm really not sure about this base color, Erin." Audrey crinkled her nose and stood with her hands on her hips by the dining room table, peering at my handiwork. "It's a little too beige."

I took a deep, calming breath and counted to ten. Truth be told, I hadn't been pleased with the beige myself, but this *was* Audrey's house, after all, so I'd proceeded after checking with her repeatedly about the color—back when it would have been a snap to repaint. "That's because it *is* beige."

"Oh, I know. But this is a linen beige. I think I'd have preferred a lemon beige."

"Lemon versus linen. Interesting difference in enunciation." I was babbling, trying not to lose my temper. She'd made up both of those names. The nicely descriptive name of the muted yellow that she *should* have allowed me to use was "buttermilk."

Audrey, meanwhile, was rifling through my books of paint chips. She paused and studied one. "Here." She tapped it with her fingernail. "This is perfect."

With a sigh, I set down my little one-inch roller. Just three feet remained unpainted on my final stripe in the entire room. I wiped off my hands and joined her. She was leaning against the buffet. We'd moved all the furniture to the center of the room and, on Audrey's insistence, had draped drop cloths over it in an unnecessary step of caution. If only she'd taken this much care with her paint selections.

I glanced at the paint chip. Buttermilk. "That's the one I recommended when we first started." That color would brighten this sometimes too dark northern-exposure room. It would also make a lovely contrast with the forest green upholstery of her chairs.

"Is it?" She held it up to the sunlight. "Oh, so it is. Excellent recommendation, Erin. I should have listened."

"Thank you." I started to put away the paint for the accent stripes.

"No, wait. I love the navy blue and the lilac stripes you painted. *Those* colors are perfect."

I continued to tap down the lid with my hammer. All paint cans seem to have an amazing resistance to being properly resealed. At least by *me*, that is. "They're painted on top of the beige, Audrey."

"What are you saying?"

"That it might be time to hire a professional painter. And that, in any case, it's time to call it a night."

She winced. "In other words, all the stripes have to be redone, too? Oh, dear. I should have said something much sooner."

"It's all right, Audrey."

She surveyed the room, turning a slow circle. "You know what, Erin? I was wrong. This beige is just fine. Let's keep it as is."

"No. We can change color schemes completely, or rethink the faux wallpaper, but keeping this paint is the one option that's off the table."

"I mean it," Audrey protested. "It's fine. I *like* the beige."

"You don't call anything 'fine,' Audrey. You're not one to settle. And there is no way I'm going to let you change your . . . spots now."

"But I don't want you to be angry at me."

"I'm not. And in any case, right now, I'm working as your designer, and I've got to handle this situation the same way I would at any other client's house. No designer worth her salt wants her client to cave merely for the sake of not causing trouble. We would much rather redo something five times than do it just once but leave the client less than thrilled with the results."

"You're sure?"

"Absolutely. And especially in this case, because I agree with you. That buttermilk color will not only set off the design, but it will also complement the yellow tones in your kitchen."

"Which is precisely what you told me at the start. I'm sorry."

"It's really all right, Audrey. But I do think it's best at this point to hire a professional. For painting the base color only; I'll still do the stripes. This way we'll have a nice clean—and wonderful—canvas for painting the faux wallpaper design, and I won't feel like I need to rush things, which is when painting mistakes happen."

"If that's really what you want."

"Just don't let the pros talk you into hiring them for painting the stripes and the roses. I really want to do that myself."

"Deal." She peered at me and to my surprise, gave me a hug, which was a little out of character for her. Afterwards she held my gaze for a moment. "This isn't exactly the way you wanted to be spending your Friday night, is it?"

An understatement. Right around now, Sullivan and I should have finished a romantic dinner in Denver and been walking hand in hand in Larimer Square to the concert venue. "It's not how you'd like to be spending yours, either, I'm sure."

"Well, but my heart isn't invested in any one man, so it's different. I've got my little black book at the ready anytime I choose to access it."

"Good for you."

"If you want to consider dating considerably older men, I can let you borrow it."

I laughed. "Thanks. I'll keep that in mind."

I resumed putting away the painting supplies. Even

the striped beige was a massive improvement in this room, and I'd be happy to live with it for the next few months—or however long it would be until Audrey was motivated to hire a painter.

My thoughts promptly wandered to Sullivan. He'd been highly distracted when he returned from his trip to Denver with Jennifer Fairfax this afternoon. He'd said only that she'd really liked our presentation board, but wanted to be "really hands-on with our final decisions." It had taken every ounce of my self-restraint to refrain from asking whether or not he was sure that "our final decisions" were exclusively where she wanted to be "really hands-on."

Audrey was never much help when it came to preparation or cleanup, but she did help me move the buffet back into place to hide the one missing stripe segment. As we inspected its placement, she said, "I'm joking about your dating other men. You and Steve are meant for each other. I have a sixth sense about these things."

"Then why have you been married four times?"

She gave me a dirty look but said evenly, "My powers are only effective when used to match *other* couples."

"Ah. Well, I think your powers are a tad out of focus this time, I'm afraid. Unless I'm wildly off base, Steve's recently decided that his life is complicated enough as it is, and he's going to start dating our glamorous divorcée client who's been chasing him for weeks. And even if *they* don't date, there's always going to be some other single woman or unhappy not-single woman chasing after him."

"Maybe so. But ultimately he's going to make the smart choice and choose you. I'm absolutely certain."

"Well, thanks, Audrey. I'm touched by your loyalty. But frankly, your pronouncement would have been more reassuring if you hadn't also insisted you were 'absolutely certain' about the beige."

"In any case, the moral of this particular story is: Trust what the experts tell you. And, Erin, you are the expert with paint and interior design . . . but *I* am the expert at matchmaking."

chapter 7

On Monday afternoon, Burke rose from his seat on a pale green sofa as I entered the lobby of the Earth Love headquarters, where we were scheduled to meet for his hearing. He gave me a nervous smile and pushed his wire-rim glasses into place. "Thanks for doing this, Erin." His gaze lingered past my shoulder to the doors, and I knew he was hoping that Sullivan had come as well. Burke didn't ask me about him, so I didn't volunteer the information that I had no idea where Sullivan was, but that he would almost surely not be joining us. The last time Sullivan and I had spoken, two hours ago, he was with our hands-on client, Jennifer Fairfax, and I'd reiterated that he should let me handle this hearing.

A receptionist escorted us to a small auditorium-style room, where Walter Emory and two Earth Love executives were seated at a long table on the stage. Walter spotted us and beckoned for us to grab a seat in the front row. We did so and waited, Burke a one-man band of jitters. Some fifteen minutes later, Walter said, "Let's get started." By then about thirty people were in the audience, and because it was cold outside and yet none of them had been wearing coats, I figured they must have been Earth Love employees. As best I could tell, there was only one newspaper reporter in attendance, although there were camera crews from all the local TV stations.

An environmental engineer at Earth Love led things off, sitting witness-style in a chair on the opposite side of the stage from Walter and his two de facto judges. She spoke about the predicted range of meter readings for the types of heating, cooling, and passive solar systems in the house. She said that all findings were consistent with her expectations.

Next, Burke was called upon to take his turn on the hot seat. He said that he absolutely did not tamper with his meters or misrepresent the source of the water for his nonpotable water usage. (Apparently Richard had accused Burke of diverting water from a nearby brook to water his lawn. Earth Love required that only "gray water"—runoff or recycled water from one's own property—could be used.) Burke went on to say that I was here on his behalf and would be happy to testify as well.

Walter conferred very briefly with his cohorts and said that wouldn't be necessary. He then dismissed the charges against Burke, pending the discovery of significant evidence to the contrary of his ruling, and announced that the awards banquet would be held a week from Saturday, at which time the contest winner would be announced.

That was it for Burke's hearing, which was about as undramatic as it could be. The newspaper reporter asked Burke for his reaction, and he replied, "I'm glad this formality is behind me. I knew all along that I'd never done anything wrong." The reporter nodded, thanked him, and headed over to interview Walter Emory. Only one of the TV reporters bothered to approach, asking Burke if he felt that this hearing had something to do with Richard's death. Burke answered simply: "No," and walked away. The reporter stammered for a moment, but let him go. The rest of the crews packed up quickly, their reporters grumbling that this story was too dull to air. Clearly, Burke's fears that he was going to be dragged through the mud were not coming to pass.

He and I had parked on opposite sides of the building, which wrapped around a large courtyard. As we parted company in the lobby, he said, "It's awful that Thayers wound up dying so suddenly. I know that under the circumstances this sounds petty, but I would have liked to at least defend myself against whatever evidence he felt he had against me. This way it's like . . . having to show your grades to the professor to get an A in the class, when you already knew you had a perfect score." He shook his head, and added, "Or rather, you show 'em to the dean, after the professor's died. So you wind up feeling ridiculous and selfish for caring that you got an A in the first place."

"Maybe so, but ultimately what matters is that you *earned* your perfect score."

"I guess that's how I have to look at it." He smiled a little, said, "Thanks again, Erin," and headed out a door to the side parking lot. I crossed the slate floor, which I knew had been built from salvaged roof tiles, and headed out toward my van. Today's perfunctory proceedings, without so much as a mention of Richard's death, felt heartless and empty, as though we were a gaggle of geese merely reforming our V formation a few seconds after one of our own had been gunned down. On the other hand, maybe we were worse than geese. Wasn't there a Jack London story about a goose staying by its wounded mate's side until death claimed them both?

As I made my weary trek across the parking lot, I decided that neither extreme was correct, as is so often the case. Walter should have said a few words about Richard's death and how none of us wanted to be there under these sad circumstances, yet the underlying principles driving this contest were so important to Richard and to the world that I knew he would have wanted us to soldier on.

I was jarred from my reverie by the sight of Sullivan emerging from his van a few rows down from my own van. I hurried over to him, glad that he couldn't read my mind at that moment; I was picturing myself in the role of the goose, rushing to her wounded gander's side. "Hi. There's no need to go in. They already exonerated Burke."

"They did?" He sounded disappointed.

"Of course. There was no evidence. Why? Did you find something incriminating?"

"Not really. But I'm still going to go talk to the judges."

"Why?"

"Someone needs to stand up on Richard's behalf. May as well be me."

"No, it shouldn't be you! For one thing, you've got a conflict of interest regarding our client. For another thing, like I said, it's too late. The decision has already been reached." To my immense relief, beyond Sullivan's shoulder, I could see the string of news vans heading down the access road; the last thing I wanted was for this disagreement about the innocence of our client to end up on the ten o'clock news.

"If I don't speak up for him, Richard comes out looking like a crazy old fool," he countered. "Like he drank poisonous, metallic paint just so he could freak out his class, and he made wild, baseless accusations against a finalist. He deserves better than that."

"I see your point, Steve. I do. And I feel for your loss. With all my heart, I wish things were different. But the problem is, you and I are supposed to be supporting our *paying* client right now, not testifying against him . . . when you have no proof that he did a single thing wrong."

"That can't be helped. My loyalties are with Richard. Nobody else is going to speak for him. He was a good man and he deserves to have his side of the story told. Furthermore, I'm keeping an eye on our client from here on out in order to gather murder evidence, just like you would if our positions were reversed."

"I wouldn't be testifying behind our client's back!"

"And *I* wouldn't be buying his sob story. He hired Richard to rid his former household of carcinogens. His son died anyway. I think he blames Richard and finally took his revenge."

"Some four years later? And on that very same day, he tells me that he was wrong for how he treated Richard?" Despite my best efforts, my anger was only rising. "You know, Sullivan, maybe we should look at what we actually *know* instead of speculating. We *know* that Richard went berserk and was making wild, baseless accusations toward *you* when he found out Burke was a finalist in the contest. Why is it hard for you to believe that Richard also made wild, baseless accusations toward *Burke*?"

Sullivan met my gaze, but his expression never softened. We both knew I'd made an excellent point. He turned away, calling over his shoulder, "I've got to go say my piece before the judges scatter. I'll see you later."

"When?"

He ignored me and entered the building.

Though neither he nor anyone else could hear me, I retorted, "You'd make a lousy goose, Sullivan!" If *I* was mortally wounded, he'd desert me to go honk at the hunter. Then we'd both get shot and die alone.

While tightening my coat collar, I employed my tried-and-true calming tricks—I counted to ten and uttered my silent confidence-and-optimism mantra. Individually, we'd both been through rougher times than this. We would survive. With a heavy dose of luck, so would Sullivan and Gilbert Designs. But one thing was now abundantly clear to me: The aftereffects of Richard's death were going to weigh heavily on us until the killer was behind bars. Richard's murder needed to be solved as quickly as possible. I was in the position to possibly glean some insider information, which I could pass along to the police. I also had some free time, because Sullivan obviously intended to work on the Fairfax assignment alone. I could start by speaking with the two other finalists: Margot Troy and Darren Campesio.

I had some fences to mend with Margot, so I dialed her number on my cell phone. She was as brusque as

ever and gave me the impression that she was surprised it
took me this long to call and arrange a meeting. (One of
the hardest parts of running a business that lives and dies
on referrals is having to eat crow when, if anything, you
should be the one serving it.)

I arrived at her place some fifteen minutes later. It was
a two-story, three-bedroom house, featuring the earth-
tone-colored stucco that had become very popular for
Colorado residences built in the last decade. Unlike
Darren's underground home or Burke's straw-bale structure, Margot's house looked to the unpracticed eye like
any other home in Crestview. Yet she had maximized
every inch to harness passive and active solar energy. The
external walls were two inches thicker than standard
homes to allow for extra insulation, and the foundation
and attic used an ingenious system of energy-efficient
heating and cooling. But truth be told, I found such
house construction details about as interesting as a
popcorn-textured ceiling. What really got me excited
about Margot's house were its furnishings. (Well, that
and the kitchen, which I'd designed for her two years
ago.) A visit to her home was like going to a new exhibi-
tion at a first-rate museum; there was always something
delightful to look at, but at the same time, there was also
that museumlike look-but-don't-touch aura, which always kept me from feeling at ease. Homes have a way of
taking on the personalities of their owners, and Margot's
aura was made of barbed wire.

She invited me inside. We got off to a great start while
Margot took me on a tour to show me her favorite acqui-
sitions of the past several months. Despite her wealth,
Margot loved to frequent rummage sales and consign-
ment shops, and she studied the classified section of the

newspaper every day with the fervor of a sports-gambling addict watching the point spread. Brilliantly, however, she'd made a rule for herself: Every time she purchased an item for her home, she had to donate a comparable item to charity. This policy forced her to avoid clutter—the garage-sale aficionado's downfall—and to be extremely judicious with her purchases. Her taste wasn't all that similar to mine—she had a fondness for Danish modern that I didn't share—but her eye was superb when it came to selecting accent pieces that could make a given room. I raved about the yellow-and-sage painted metal chandelier in her enclosed back porch. Its lemon-bough motif would have looked ridiculous in, say, her formal living room, but in this airy, outdoorsy space, it was divine. Likewise, she'd hung a delightfully delicate mahogany étagère on one wall in her ultraelegant living room and placed three of the prettiest teacups on it that I'd ever seen. She'd also found a stunning ceramic statue of lovers embracing at an antiques store in London, which she'd set on the mantel in her parlor. This was the room where, I gathered, my tour ended, because she told me to have a seat. I avoided her Danish chaise and opted for the floral sofa, which she'd picked up a couple of years ago at an estate sale.

"Margot, I wanted to apologize in person for—"

"That's the least of anyone's concerns now. How is Burke taking Richard's death? With his typical intensity, I assume?"

"You know Burke Stratton personally?"

"We used to date. About a year ago. But it didn't last long. He dumped me once he found out we were cocompetitors in the green home contest."

This was a surprising and unsettling development. For

one thing, Margot tended to be guarded about discussing her love life, and for another, Burke had never given me any indication that he even knew Margot, let alone had once dated her. "Why would that bother him?"

"Oh, it was mostly an excuse. Frankly, his shock at finding out I was a fellow contestant seemed staged to me. But ostensibly it was because he believed we were going to feel too bad if one of us won. What it really came down to is that it was obvious to both of us that his architect and I were much better suited for each other."

"You're dating Jeremy Greene?" I tried not to sound quite as surprised as I actually was, both at the news and at her willingness to share this intimate information. He was some fifteen years younger than she was, though to be fair, I wouldn't have given that a second thought if their ages had been reversed.

She beamed at me. "Yes, I am. Ever since Burke set me free. Isn't Jeremy wonderful?"

I didn't know Jeremy well, and yesterday's conversation regarding Richard's lawsuit had left me suspicious of the man, so I merely replied, "That's great, Margot. I'm glad you're happy."

"I am. But let's get back to the business at hand. Knowing how you're always wanting to make citizen's arrests," she sniffed, "I'm sure you want to hear all about what I may have noticed that night . . . if anyone was hovering nearby the poisonous paint before you arrived, for example."

"Did you see something suspicious?"

"No, but I do know for a fact that Richard Thayers never locked his car. And he used that old Volvo of his like a storage locker on wheels. He'd have been driving around for weeks with that paint in his backseat. It would have been easy as pie for anyone to swap cans."

"Who besides you knew that out of the half dozen products, he was going to drink the gold paint?"

"I have no earthly idea. But like I told you in class, it had gotten to be fairly common knowledge among us ecologically responsible people."

Which wasn't all that big a community. And it certainly included Jeremy Greene.

"Did you know *Richard* personally?"

She gave me one of her patented stares, in which she lowered her chin and peered into my eyes as though she were looking over the top of invisible reading glasses. "I told you I've taken classes from him for three years running now."

I hoped she'd elaborate, but when she didn't, I felt stuck. As a client, she tended to get annoyed and to clam up whenever she felt she was being pressed too hard to voice her opinions. She'd likely explode if I asked how she'd gotten so familiar with her ex-teacher's personal driving habits. So why had she volunteered the information about her dating Jeremy Greene? I had a feeling that I was being played, and that she was feeding me specific information she wanted me to know, but I couldn't begin to decipher why.

She was fidgeting with a tissue, winding it into a paper rope.

"Is everything all right, Margot? You seem a little on edge."

"Yes, I'm fine."

She still didn't elaborate and seemed to have no intention of doing so in the near future. "I should get going, Margot. I just wanted to apologize to you again for my shoddy phone manners the other day. The house is looking great. Best of luck with the contest."

"Thank you. Although I must say, I had a much better chance of winning with Richard than with Walter Emory. They were both fruitcakes, but Walter's even nuttier." She clicked her tongue. "If you're looking for suspects, I hope you remember to put *him* on your list."

"What motive would he have? He and Richard were friends."

"And friends sometimes turn into the worst enemies."

Feeling frustrated by the limited information I'd gathered from Margot, I hoped things would go better with Darren Campesio. First, though, I dropped off the drawings of the sunroom at Burke's very ordinary-looking house. His boxy two-story home was painted a buttery yellow with a charcoal gray roof of photovoltaic tiles — utterly unremarkable. But he had an attractive front porch, and I'd convinced him to add dollhouselike shutters, which added visual interest and really perked up his exterior. He wasn't home, so I left the drawings between his inner and outer doors. It seemed wasteful to drive the quarter mile or so to Darren's house, and anyway, I didn't have an appointment with him, so I decided that I'd walk along the hiking trail behind the properties. This way I could mention to Darren that I was in the area and was curious to see another state-of-the-art green home.

There was a large piece of property separating Burke's and Darren's properties. Months ago, Burke had warned Sullivan and me that the home owner, Asia McClure, was a major character — and not in a good way. With that in mind, I couldn't help but wince at the sight of the towering white windmill behind Darren's house. Burke, I knew, was in the process of building an even bigger one, and that couldn't possibly make Asia happy. As much as I believed in alternative energy sources, I wouldn't want to have two enormous towers on either side of my home. Zoning laws inside the city limits prevented home owners from building such tall, unsightly structures, but Burke and Darren were governed by the much more relaxed county regulations.

Burke had also said that Asia was an amazing gardener. She had a split-rail fence surrounding her property, except for the small pond situated halfway between Burke's and her homes. There was an opening between two evergreens next to her back fence, and I couldn't resist taking a closer peek at her property.

The siding was a pale gray with liberal use of white trim and instantly brought to mind the old farmhouses of my childhood in upstate New York. I loved the large overhangs that shaded the windows, as well as her large New England gray-painted deck and lattices on the south-facing side. There were cheerful dormers above the roof for the deck. The architecture style appeared to borrow from the old-fashioned bungalows that had been so popular in the 1920s. I grinned at the place as I pictured warm, cozy bedrooms upstairs and inviting public spaces on the main floor.

"What do you think you're doing!" a shrill voice shrieked at me.

I let out a cry of surprise and jumped back.

Doing a fast step-march across the lawn toward me was a short woman in a big sun hat, fastened with a red checkerboard ribbon beneath her chin. The woman was built like a bear cub, with short stocky legs and arms, and fierce, beady eyes that were focused on me.

"Sorry, ma'am. Your property caught my eye from the footpath, and I—"

"Look what you did!" She pointed to a spot just to the right of my feet. "You stepped on my flower!"

I looked down and saw the dried-up stem of a daisy that had apparently grown out through the rails of the fence and had snapped off near its roots. "I'm sorry."

"That's my private property! You destroyed it!"

"It wasn't intentional. I must have brushed against it with my leg."

"I didn't say it was intentional. But my plant is equally ruined either way."

"Um, all I can say is I'm sorry. At least it was long past its bloom, right?"

She was glaring at me. Maybe I'd hit a sore spot with my mention of its being past its bloom.

"What were you doing, leaning over my fence and ogling my house? Why didn't you stay on the path, where you belong? That's the middle of the path right there." She stabbed her finger at the path three times. "You're a skinny thing. Wasn't it wide enough for you? You think you need to tread on my flower beds?"

"I was simply admiring your lovely home. From *outside* your fence. I truly didn't mean to come anywhere near your flower bed." *Your* dormant *flower bed with its* dried-out *flowers*, I added to myself. "I couldn't resist taking a look at your house. I'm naturally drawn to nice homes. I'm an interior designer. Burke Stratton is my client."

She put her hands on her hips and glowered at me. "Aha! You mean you're a decorator for his granola-crunching, tree-hugging, it's-not-easy-being-green contest. With that contest judge who got knocked off. Though he probably deserved it."

Surprised, I asked, "Did you know Richard Thayers?"

"I heard through the grapevine that he was one of those...ecoterrorists. Like the people who burned the ski lodge in Vail years ago."

"Where did you hear that? About Richard, I mean?"

"Around. I belong to some groups who happen to believe in the power of corporate America, not in maniacs like that crazy paint-drinking professor." She pursed her lips and eyed me up and down. "Whereas *you* are obviously one of those liberals who flock to Crestview like it's their mother ship calling them home. You recommend those big ugly windmills to your clients, and you ruin *my* life! You don't even respect private property!"

Any further discussion was obviously going to be pointless. I turned away and headed for the path. "I think I'll get back to work now. Pardon me if I caused you or your flower any permanent damage."

I could feel those steely eyes boring holes into the back of my head as I continued to Darren Campesio's home. I took the well-trod minipath along his property line, being careful not to brush against Asia's fence, and rounded to his house. Richard was right when he'd mocked Darren's house as being "part cave." Seen from the rear, the only indication that there was a house here was the circular smokestack protruding from the highest point of a round hill. I knew from photographs and drawings that the snow-covered bumps in the hill were actually skylights. I'd never been inside his house and was dying to do so now.

I made my way to his front door and used his brass

knocker. From this angle, the house looked like an ordinary yellow-brick ranch, albeit one with unusually hilly landscaping and a windmill in its backyard.

Darren came to the door. Burke had told me he was a retired military man, and he certainly looked the part: muscularly built and wearing camouflage clothes, in his sixties or seventies. "Can I help you?" he said, giving me a disdainful visual once-over. Clearly, I hadn't passed my first inspection.

"My name is Erin Gilbert. I'm working on the design of Burke Stratton's house, and—"

"I know who you are. I remember seeing you at Burke's during the open house."

His own open house had been at the exact same time as Burke's, so that was odd. "You were at Burke's?"

He gave a slight shrug. "It was my best chance to see what the competition was up to. Nothing illegal about that. I checked." He lifted his pointy chin. "Unlike your client, I'm making an effort to follow the rules."

"My client was exonerated by Earth Love this morning. He hasn't cheated."

"Why are you here?"

"I just wondered if you were willing to talk about the contest with me."

"Why would I want to do that?"

"I'm trying to help Burke, if I can. I want to clarify some things about his past relationship with the deceased, Richard Thayers, the judge of the competition."

"In other words, you're part designer, part private investigator?" He snorted.

"I guess you could say that."

"You're also part fool if you think I'm going to allow you to pick up any energy conservation tricks by letting you inside. The guy's already copying my new windmill! Isn't that bad enough?"

"I have no intention of picking up tips at this late date. Besides, didn't you say that *you* were examining Burke's house just last week?"

"Good day, Miss Gilbert." He shut the door.

Baffled by his belligerent behavior, I walked back the way I'd come, passing Asia's property by staying dead center on the path and not so much as taking a sideways glance at the trees behind her backyard.

At Burke's back door, I glanced behind me and did a double take. "Talk about the pot calling the kettle black," I muttered to myself. Darren had followed me partway down the path and was now watching me through huge binoculars. Annoyed, I plastered on a phony smile and waved. He shifted his lenses to the tree, as though he were merely bird watching.

Burke had gotten home just then and followed my vision to his nosy neighbor. Burke stood in front of me protectively. "Hey!" Burke yelled, gesturing emphatically for him to get back. "Go mind your own business, would you?"

"That's exactly what I'm doing," Darren shouted back. "Everyone knows you're under investigation! I'm not letting a cheater steal the contest!"

"A, I was already found innocent by the judges, and B, get a life!"

Darren said nothing and walked back toward his house.

"Can you believe that guy?" Burke muttered, shaking his head.

"Neither of your immediate neighbors was especially friendly to me."

"I could have predicted that. Let's just say that this isn't exactly *Mr. Rogers' Neighborhood.* What were you talking to them about?"

"I was trying to get a feel for whether or not they had a motive for killing Richard and if they could have taken the paint can from your garage."

He gave me a grateful smile. "I'm so glad I have someone on my side. Now if I could just get the police to believe me when I say I'm innocent."

The next morning, there was a chill in the air, and the western sky had that pearly gray color that foretold snow. Sullivan and I arrived at our parking spaces at the same time and walked in together, chatting about the predicted snowstorm that evening. A business card was on the floor when Sullivan opened the door. I picked it up, expecting to see a card that a rep had slipped through our mail slot.

"What's that?" Sullivan asked.

I stared at the card in surprise, wondering why someone had splattered red ink on our Sullivan and Gilbert card. An instant later I realized the card had deliberately been altered. The red ink was supposed to resemble drops of blood. "Oh, damn it," I muttered as I flipped it over.

"What?"

I held it out so Sullivan could see. On the back, handwritten in block letters, were two words: YOU'RE NEXT!

chapter 8

*S*ullivan and I decided to call my police officer friend, Linda Delgardio, immediately. She said she'd come to our office as soon as she could and arrived about twenty minutes later. Linda was a warm, pretty, vivacious woman, and when she was off duty, she had a droll and infectious sense of humor. Right now, however, she was all business. "Someone could have picked up one of your cards almost anywhere?" she asked as she sealed the doctored one into an evidence bag.

"'Fraid so," Sullivan replied.

"Do you have any way of telling how long this

particular card has been circulating? Did you make a new print run of cards, for example, at some point?"

Sullivan shook his head. "We just made the one big printing more than six months ago. And we gave a hundred or so of them away at the open house for the green home contest, over a week ago."

"We set stacks of them in several rooms at Burke Stratton's house," I explained, "and Margot Troy gave them away at her place, as well."

"She did?" Linda and Steve asked in unison.

"I designed her kitchen a couple of years ago, and she told me she was willing to help me advertise."

"That was nice of her," Sullivan said.

"Is it possible to lift fingerprints from the card?" I asked Linda.

"I'll take it to the lab, of course, and we'll hope for the best. Realistically, I don't see much chance. It's likely whoever did this only handled your card by its edges." She shrugged. "But sometimes we get lucky."

"I've got to say, I don't feel especially comforted by the thought that we might 'get lucky,'" I said. "This is serious. It can only be a threat from the killer."

"Not necessarily," Linda replied. "It could simply be a prank. Murder always brings out the nutcases in the community. Some people seem to crave the thrill of making veiled threats."

"People who just happened to know that Richard Thayers was a friend of mine?" Sullivan countered skeptically.

"The papers carried that article about your work on Burke Stratton's house and its being a finalist in the Green Design contest," she countered. "And Thayers was announced all over the local media as the judge."

"But still," I objected, "why would we get singled out? Why not one of the contestants, for example?"

"There's really no way to answer that question, Erin," Linda replied. "But then, it doesn't have to make sense to us, just to whoever wrote 'you're next' on your business card."

"Come to think of it, there's our link to the Earth Love Web sites," Sullivan said. "And to Richard Thayers's site."

"You added links to our Web pages?" I asked, annoyed. I never once failed to notify *him* when I made significant changes or additions to our site. I fired up my computer.

"Sure. And they linked to ours. For mutually beneficial business referrals."

I pulled up our Web site and the "Links" page, and Linda looked over my shoulder. Sullivan had added several sites to our list. "I don't even know who half of these people are," I grumbled. "I doubt that we'll get any business from them at all."

"It doesn't hurt."

"Actually, it might, if it established a connection between us and Richard Thayers in the mind of some homicidal maniac." As I scanned the list of links, I gaped at one of them. "M.H. Custom Furniture?" I asked in amazement. "You linked to Matthew Hayes?"

"I did?" He sounded equally surprised and rushed next to Linda to peer over my opposite shoulder. "Jeez, I did! I'm taking *that* one down. I must have added that a couple of months ago, when we ordered the dresser from him. For that client on Sable Road."

"Matthew Hayes is the guy who heckled Richard Thayers the night he drank the paint," I explained to Linda.

She nodded. I could tell by her demeanor that she'd

already recognized the name. "The link to Richard Thayers's site could be the connection, all right, which encouraged some random jerk to target you." Linda peered at the screen.

"I guess," I muttered.

"Or it *is* the killer trying to scare us," Sullivan said, "and he or she is out for Erin."

"Excuse me?" I bristled. "*Your* name is on the card, too, you know."

"That *is* a possibility, Erin," Linda said, touching my shoulder. "The article mentioned the assistance you gave us in solving the murder cases last year." She held my gaze and said evenly, "It's hard to know how the killer took that news."

I sighed. "That was just a throwaway line...the reporter insisted it would beef up the human-interest angle."

"Nevertheless. Who have you been in contact with who had a possible motive for killing Mr. Thayers?" Linda asked me.

"What do you mean?"

"Come on. I know you, Erin. There's no way you haven't been asking questions. You seem to be incapable of removing yourself from any murder investigation in town."

"That's a little harsh."

"Yeah, yeah." She flipped open her notepad. "Sorry to offend. Just give me the names."

That was a simple enough question to answer. "Burke Stratton, of course. Margot Troy. And Darren Campesio."

"The three finalists," Linda said.

"Right."

She waited for a second or two, then studied my features when I didn't continue. "That's all? You haven't spoken to Jeremy Greene, Stratton's architect, about the murder?"

"I've talked to him since then, yes."

"But not about Thayers? Even though there was an article about them in the paper a few months ago? About Jeremy Greene and Thayers having a legal squabble concerning the design of his house?"

"Well, sure. Thayers's name came up. For one thing, I wanted to ask if our client's basement is similar to Thayers's since his was apparently substandard."

"And *is* it?" Sullivan asked, which, come to think of it, was a darned good question that Jeremy hadn't actually answered sufficiently.

"Meaning he's on the list," Linda said before I could answer Sullivan, making a notation in her pad.

"Also, Erin was flirting with Matthew Hayes," Sullivan said. I glared at him, but he continued casually, "After Richard's final class."

Linda looked at me expectantly, pen poised.

"I was making conversation, not flirting," I said to Linda. "But it's possible that Matthew's guilty, and if so, he would certainly know that our business is connected to Richard. But now you've got the complete list. Definitely." I paused. "Well, not counting Asia McClure. She lives in the house right between Burke's and Darren's. But as far as I know, she has no connection to Richard Thayers, other than an obvious grudge against environmentalists."

Linda scribbled in her pad and then put the pad in her pocket. "Okay," she said with an officious nod. "Take care. I'll keep you posted as best I can."

"Thanks, Linda."

"No problem. Let me know right away if you get any more threats." I could read frustration in her every little gesture. She detested my connection to yet another murder case. I'm sure *I* detested my entanglement even more.

Sullivan released a sigh the instant Linda left. "She's right. You're an incorrigible snoop."

"Thanks so much."

"I didn't mean it as a knock against you. I am, too. Occupational hazard. We have to have an intense curiosity about what makes people tick, and we enjoy poking around in people's homes. Otherwise we wouldn't be in this business."

"That's true, I suppose," I said, relieved that this wasn't going to turn into a quarrel.

"It's the killer who made this personal . . . who's threatening *us* now. All the more reason to get the bastard before he gets us. We need to focus."

"On the investigation, you mean?"

"Yeah. It's great of you to try to gather information about who killed Richard. Even though I think you'll eventually draw the same conclusions I have about our client. Which reminds me . . . I'm sorry about how I acted at Earth Love. It was too late for me to testify, by the way, so I just had an informal chat with Walter about Richard and my suspicions about Burke. Nothing I said changed his opinion in the least. We were already on the same page."

He paused and looked at me with an anguished expression. "But Gilbert . . . right now, I feel like I've got so much bottled-up rage in me. I've got to make sure this killer pays for what he . . . or *she* did. That's just how it is."

"I know. I understand how you feel."

He leaned back against my desktop. "So what have you found out so far?"

"Not much. Like I told Linda, I talked to those people, and while nobody dropped any huge clues in my lap, nobody struck me as being incapable of the crime. Darren Campesio is a belligerent kook who seems to equate the green home contest with Homeland Security. And my exchange with Asia McClure, Darren's and Burke's neighbor, was also pretty nasty."

"She has a bad relationship with Burke, right? Hates the windmill he's erecting?"

"Right. She grew especially hostile once she gathered I'm pro-conservation. She acts as though ecology is a personal affront to her. And she was so unpleasant that she might have doctored our card, just as a mean practical joke."

"A practical joke?"

"To harass me. It might be a payback for my having stepped on her flower when I walked up to her property line."

"You stepped on a flower? How ghastly!"

"Yeah. According to Asia's reaction, I should have been handcuffed and dragged off to jail on the spot, even though the daisy was already dead. Heaven only knows what she'd have done to me if I'd killed a live one."

Sullivan grabbed his coat.

"Where are you going?"

"We. We're paying a visit to your grouchy friend."

"Asia?"

"Yep. We'll test her reaction when we tell her we got her message and want to talk about it."

My hunch was that knocking on Asia McClure's door

would be seen by her as an act of aggression. But the fact that Steve was both asking me to do something with him and taking a proactive role was too appealing to resist. I snatched my purse and my coat.

"Be sure to drive dead-center down Asia's driveway," I said as Sullivan signaled to turn onto Asia's property. "The woman completely flipped out when I brushed against her dead flowers. If you get too close to her junipers, she'll consider it a declaration of war."

"Let's not assume the worst."

"That's not an assumption, Sullivan, but rather an informed assessment. I'm telling you now: Do not expect sweetness and light from Asia McClure."

"Okay, but she's not the Antichrist either, surely. Let's just give this our best shot." He winked at me, then shut off the engine.

I shook my head in dismay. "You're thinking you're going to charm her in spite of everything I just told you." We got out and walked along the path. "No offense, Sullivan, but I'm thinking you've met your match."

"We'll see. In any case, I stand forewarned." He gave me what had to be the world's sexiest grin and jabbed at the doorbell.

Moments later, Asia pulled the door open, but kept a grip on both the knob and the doorjamb. Her scowl made her look like a stone gargoyle. "Well, well. It's the decorators. Did you forget the address for your client?"

"No, not at all," Sullivan said with a chuckle. "We're simply following up on your message. The one that you dropped through our mail slot."

"I didn't *give* you any message. Why would I want to

contact you? I have no interest in hiring a decorator. I like what I like, and I don't need to pay someone to tell me what my tastes are."

"Good for you." Despite his words, Sullivan's confidence was already visibly faltering.

"If someone gave you a message and told you to come here today," Asia continued, "it wasn't me. Or else you made a mistake. Which is more likely."

"Also, I wanted to apologize one more time," I blurted out, sensing that Asia was about to close her door in our faces. "I remember how gorgeous your gardens were last August, when we first started working at Burke's house. You're truly an extraordinary gardener, Ms. McClure."

She crossed her arms and regarded me coolly. "That's because I love flowers. And I love to garden. I like to cultivate beautiful things. It's not hard to get skilled at something you love to do. Though the pests are a problem."

"You mean the aphids and caterpillars?" Sullivan asked.

She shook her head. "My ecomaniac neighbors. Which includes your client. The fool is erecting a windmill now! All because that bigger fool, Darren Campesio, has one, so Dr. Stratton wants a taller one in his own yard. It's going to cast a shadow across my flower beds! Instead of my view of the Rockies, I'll be looking at a damned oversized beanie-cap propeller! He should move it to his *front* lawn, so it blocks his own door and not *my* mountain views! Plus, who knows how much noise the thing's going to make?"

"They're virtually silent, and they produce no noxious fumes," I assured her.

"Regardless, it's a huge butt-ugly metal contraption that I'll be seeing every day! And speaking of noxious fumes, our pond stinks, thanks to Stratton and his hippie food."

"Hippie food?" Sullivan repeated.

"Shrimp and algae and green glop! This is infuriating! I buy my house for the views and the peace and quiet, and now I'm getting a polluted pond and whirling blades over my head on both sides!"

"We'll see what we can do about Burke's windmill," Sullivan cajoled. "We might be able to keep the height reasonable and reposition it so it's as unobtrusive to your property as possible."

"Better yet, tell him to take his windmill and stick it where the sun don't shine! It's all the fault of this blasted contest! That's what made both of those men go crazy, trying to eke out more and more energy savings, all of which are now at *my* expense! They're stealing my happiness! If your client wants a green home, far as I'm concerned, he should just paint the blasted thing chartreuse."

Sullivan chuckled.

"That wasn't funny," she snapped at him.

Sullivan looked at me in frustration. Just as she was shutting the door, I cried, "Wait. We're here because someone wrote a veiled death threat on one of our business cards and stuck it through our mail slot at some point last night."

"Really? Well, it wasn't me." She made a derisive noise. "How juvenile. Although you both should have been mature enough to come straight out and ask me, so maybe you're getting what you deserve." She started to close the door in our faces.

Sullivan stopped the door. "Ms. McClure, please. Hear me out. Richard Thayers was my mentor. He meant a great deal to me. Do you have any idea who killed him?"

"No, I do not." She slammed her door shut.

We walked back to the van in silence. As he slipped behind the steering wheel, Sullivan muttered, "Thanks for not saying 'I told you so.'"

"You're welcome."

I caught a look of deep sadness on his features as I glanced at his profile.

"They'll catch the person who did this, Steve. Richard's death is not going to go unpunished."

He gave me a small smile of gratitude, but said nothing.

The weather rapidly deteriorated that afternoon. Sleet was falling as reports of a major snowstorm rolled in. By two P.M., we decided it was best to reschedule our late-afternoon appointments, which all our clients readily agreed to. By two-thirty, we'd decided to head home.

"Steve?" I asked, gathering my nerve as we put on our coats. "How about coming to my house? We can make ourselves some hot cider or cocoa, put some logs on the fireplace, and just unwind a little."

To my horror, he actually winced. "Uh, thanks, Gilbert. I'd better get home, though, in case this storm's as bad as it's threatening to be right now."

I stopped myself from asking if having to spend the night at my house would be such a terrible hardship, and instead said, "Suit yourself," with a shrug. "See you to-morrow." He fumbled with getting the key in the lock, which struck me as an intentional diversion to avoid my gaze. I brushed past him.

"Yeah. See ya, Gilbert."

I knew at that moment what it felt like to harbor un-substantiated certainty of another person's guilt. Sullivan had to be seeing another woman behind my back. At least the heavy sleet made it easy to dash away from him with my head down. It also masked the tears pricking at my eyes.

The drive home was slow and slippery, and I was very glad to arrive in one piece. Four hours later, Audrey arrived, having had a much harder time getting home from the studio in Denver. She was shaking, so I suggested either peppermint schnapps in her hot chocolate or rum in her cider. She opted for both and mixed them together, calling the concoction a "hot choc-o-cider pepperum." To no one's surprise, she soon discovered that the names were a better combination than the flavors, and she dumped it down the drain in favor of a port wine.

The three of us—Audrey, Hildi, and I—settled into the parlor, as Audrey held court and described her harrowing drive in detail. What was normally a forty-five minute drive had taken her nearly five hours, and she'd seen so many fender benders that her recap turned out to be surprisingly lengthy.

We were just starting to discuss our options for dinner when an enormous crash shook the house. Hildi tore out of the room and up the stairs. I felt like following her. Was this noisy attack on my home related to the death threat?

"What on earth was that?" Audrey paled, shrinking into her wing chair.

"I don't know. It sounded like a bomb going off in our

kitchen." I gripped the back and the arm of the Ultrasuede sofa. If I could have managed the feat, I'd have burrowed between the cushions.

"Where did Hildi go?"

"She ran upstairs, probably to hide under my bed."

"Sensible," Audrey replied. "Maybe we should go join her."

"I think we'd better go look at the kitchen. Something large must have hit it."

"You first. I'll be right behind you, though."

We rose, and wordlessly shuffled through the dining room toward the kitchen. A stiff breeze blew toward us, which could only mean that a wall or window was missing. The damage greeted us as soon as we neared the entrance. "Oh, my god," Audrey said as we surveyed the broken tree limbs and the knee-high pile of debris.

"It's the cottonwood tree. A branch broke off." Although I held my tongue, I'd warned her last year that cottonwoods were notorious for losing huge branches in storms, and that hers had been planted too close to the house for comfort. "It took out half your kitchen," I said, stunned. The lovely black granite countertops were cracked. The island and cooktop were crushed, the sink smashed. Water burbled through the pipes somewhere underneath the trunklike tree limb. "I'm going to run downstairs and shut off your water main."

She nodded. Tears brimmed in her eyes.

"Audrey, I am so, so sorry this happened."

Again, she nodded, still unable to speak. I turned and jogged down the stairs. The least I could do was keep her kitchen from flooding. Yet I had the desperate feeling that there was little else I'd be able to do to shore up her spirits, now that her gorgeous, sparkling kitchen lay in ruins.

It took me a while to squeeze past all of Audrey's suitcases and boxes of art supplies and shut off the main. Afterwards, I raced back up the stairs, expecting to see Audrey sobbing. Instead, she was on the phone, calmly making arrangements. She thanked whoever was on the line and hung up. "I've called a tree company," she declared. "They'll cut up the branch and haul it out of here. Next I'll call my insurance agent and get him up to speed."

"Okay. I'll call my favorite contractor, and we'll see how soon he can get here to board up the damage." I sighed. "Again, Audrey, I'm so sorry."

"Oh, well," she said cheerfully. "The house is fully insured. The refrigerator's fine, so we didn't lose any food. And now that the branch has knocked out half the room, it's the perfect time for me to bump that wall out and build the breakfast nook I've always wanted."

chapter 9

DOMESTIC BLISS

After donning parkas and fastening an old wool blanket as best we could across the gap in the wall, followed by several minutes of phone calls to the insurance company and contractors, Audrey and I were able to find humor in the sudden intrusion of half a tree in our kitchen. As we inspected the damage, I remarked, "You never said anything about wanting a breakfast nook before."

"Well...I do *now*. And I live with an interior designer who can help me plan an even nicer kitchen. How perfect is *that*?"

I chuckled. "Gee, thanks, Audrey. It's nice to know that I can help you turn this disaster into something positive."

"Yes, indeed. We can bring the kitchen up to green-home standards this way."

I hesitated. "Actually, Audrey, we can—and will—get the most energy-efficient appliances on the market, for anything that's sustained considerable damage. But Energy Star guidelines went into effect in 1993, so that's when efficiency standards took a quantum leap. There's nothing in here more than five years old."

"Well, not counting the two of us."

I grinned. "Right. I just meant that they'd be worth considering replacing if they were ten-plus years old, because of energy efficiency. And we'll do whatever else you'd like to do in addition to that. But the truth about green homes is that the greenest home is the one that's already built."

"Maybe so, but this home is missing one wall and a sizable portion of its roof."

"True. But when you apply that same axiom to a remodel, it's the one that uses the fewest new materials."

"Oh, I see." She scanned the damaged roof, window, and wall. "In that case, we'll concentrate on rebuilding only the damaged areas and building the breakfast nook there." She pointed to the corner where there were cracks in the walls from the heaviest part of the branch. "Are you saying that we'd be better off continuing the heart-of-pine floorboards rather than going with bamboo or cork throughout?"

"Almost definitely, just because there's such a small percentage of the pine that's likely to have been damaged. By the same token, we should order replacement cabinetry from the same manufacturer, instead of all new cabinets throughout. We just need to ensure that they use formaldehyde-free materials for the shelves and drawers...maybe wheatboard or strawboard, if that's an option."

She nodded and scanned the ceiling. "You know, I've always wanted a skylight over my sink. And we can make a combination greenhouse/breakfast nook with lots of windows."

"That'd be wonderful. That's what's known as day-lighting—when we reduce our power use by taking advantage of daylight." I stopped, realizing she was well familiar with the term and didn't need a lecture from me. But as I scanned the room, I made a mental inventory. We could use individually controlled task lighting so we wouldn't waste electricity illuminating more space than we'd need, and we'd install fluorescent bulbs. We'd add insulation when we rebuilt the wall, and all the new windows would have high-performance glazing. Plus we'd make sure we could create cross breezes through the new kitchen. "Since the sink's a goner, we can consider getting rid of the garbage disposal and installing a recycling center in one cabinet."

"I could live without a disposal," Audrey said thoughtfully.

"And we could construct the greenhouse to have an external door. We can heat the room exclusively with passive solar energy and close it off at night. That way, too, we can do wonders with the floor...put down heat-absorbing slate. I'm sure I can find nice tiles at the reclamation yard."

"Hildi will love a nice sunny room with a warm floor."

"She will. It'll be like her own private sauna."

"I can't wait. I'm so glad this happened!"

"You *are*?"

"Yes. Work with me, here, Erin. This is how I avoid needing mood-enhancing drugs."

"In that case, this storm damage is a stroke of good luck. Just not for the tree."

"Well, no. But this was an act of nature, so it must have been its time." A chilly breeze swept through the room. "Let's seal off this room once we get my dishes and cookware moved into the dining room. I've got that thick roll of plastic in the storage room of the basement, and some duct tape. Good thing you didn't quite finish painting the dining room. Now we'll be able to tape the plastic to the walls without worrying about damaging the paint."

"Yet another positive take on this."

"And I've got the perfect architect in mind. We'll be killing two stones at once when I hire him to work for us."

I chuckled a little at her deliberate botching of the two-birds cliché. "Really? Who?"

"Jeremy Greene."

"Audrey! I consider him a key suspect in Richard Thayers's death!"

"Precisely! And what better way to get information out of him than by hiring him?"

chapter **10**

The next morning, it was strange and upsetting for me to enter the dining room and realize that we would be using this cramped, claustrophobic room as our makeshift kitchen for weeks to come. The space was the typical clutter catastrophe that normally caused people to solicit my services. Last night, I'd urged Audrey to put everything in storage except those few items that she knew we would need for the short term. Yet she must have dragged armloads of stuff into the room the minute I'd gone to bed. Two full sets of plates, including her fine china, were stacked in the corners. We were now equipped to serve a dinner party of sixteen, provided the dinner guests ignored the fact that we had no oven or cooktop, and that seven of the eight chairs at the table were either filled or blocked by the complete contents of her sizable pantry. Cans, pasta boxes, cereal boxes, and spices were piled everywhere, and cookware, utensils, and glasses sat on every flat surface.

Audrey had at least stuck with my directive to reserve her sidebar for her essential small appliances, which would temporarily serve as our only means to cook indoors. There I'd placed her coffeemaker (which was already doing its thing, thanks to the timer), her toaster, hot plate, and electric frying pan. The microwave was too large for the sidebar, but rested on the ice chest next to the designated temporary home for the refrigerator. Unfortunately, she'd also brought out the pasta maker, the bread maker—which hadn't been used once in the two years that I'd lived with her—two mixers, the ice cream maker, and the blender. I was betting that the waffle iron was around here somewhere.

I heard Audrey open the front door, no doubt to retrieve the newspaper. She shuffled into the room in her robe and snow boots, her nose buried in the paper. I watched her nervously. She was taking her life into her hands, given the numerous opportunities to trip over something. Once she'd arrived safely, I considered quipping that she'd missed the opportunity to use the chandelier as storage hooks, but I didn't want to give her any ideas and instead simply gave her a cheery, "Good morning."

"Morning, Erin." She poured herself a cup of coffee. "We got an even foot of snow yesterday. Maplewood's been plowed, so you'll be able to drive to work. You're going to want to read the front-page story first, though." She handed me the A section of the *Sentinel*.

My vision was drawn to a photograph of Richard Thayers at a rally, holding a placard that read *World's Watchdogs*. The banner headline was "Ecoterrorism Connection?"

"Oh, jeez. Sullivan's going to be on the rampage." With considerable effort, I angled myself past the stacks and boxes and into a chair to read the rest.

"Did you see the paper this morning?" Sullivan promptly asked when I arrived at the office. "The *Sentinel* printed nonsensical speculation by a batch of talk-radio airheads, claiming Richard was an ecoterrorist. And so some *rational* person got fed up and decided to strike back by committing first-degree murder."

"I did see it." I hung up my coat and scarf, and made my way to my desk chair. "They must have been talking to someone in the same social circles as Asia McClure, because she suggested the same possibility to me the other day."

"Yeah, well, that woman's a crabapple with legs. The story is total crap. No way was Richard an ecoterrorist."

"The papers never said that he was, you realize . . . only that the killer could have assumed he was a member of World's Watchdogs, because he was photographed at their rally."

"Watchdogs has nothing to do with ecoterrorism, either. It was a misguided splinter group of theirs that claimed responsibility for a handful of ecoterrorist acts."

"I know." That doesn't mean the killer knew that, though, I said to myself.

Sullivan remained tightly wound. "I called Walter Emory and asked him to drop by to discuss this. *He* cares as much about finding Richard's killer as I do."

That last remark stung me immeasurably. I couldn't decide if objecting would make things better or worse, but after a few seconds, I reluctantly let it pass. "What time did he—"

The little brass bell above the door jingled as someone opened it. Speak of the devil, I thought, as Walter stepped inside, wearing the same coat and baggy pants he'd worn on his last visit, although he'd added a hat with Elmer Fudd earflaps to his ensemble.

"Morning, Walter," I said.

"Morning." He beamed at me. "Fine day, isn't it?" he nearly shouted.

"If you like gray, dreary, and cold," Sullivan replied.

"When you get to be my age, any day you can get out of bed counts as a fine morning." He removed his hat and coat, but kept hold of both instead of using our coat tree.

"I've been worried about the story on the front page of the *Sentinel* today," Sullivan said. "Did you read it?"

"Yeah, I did."

"Do you think there's any substance to the claim that Richard could have been killed by an antiecoterrorist?"

"Kind of doubt it." Walter lowered himself into the chair that was stationed halfway between our desks and laid his coat and hat over his knees. "Don't you? I mean, killing somebody for being a zealot when it comes to the environment doesn't make a whole lot of sense."

"Yeah," Sullivan said, "but there've been less sensible motives that have driven people to murder."

Walter crossed his arms and regarded him for a moment. "You see, Steve, here's the way I look at it. Of the two of us, Richard Thayers and myself, I'm the one with the national reputation for lobbying to save our planet. So if anyone's going to be a target of pro-pollution vigilantes, it's going to be me, not him."

"But whoever killed Richard Thayers probably *isn't* someone who's focused in on the national news," I interposed. "It's more likely someone with a personal ax to grind. Maybe someone who's just thinking locally, about a perceived slight, or because his own business failed." Someone like Matthew Hayes, I mused in silence.

"Ah. You mean someone who's got his or her self-interest at heart, but who is spurred on by a big hatred of environmentalists."

"Maybe," I replied with a shrug.

"Well, I guess that's always possible."

"Aren't you nervous?" Sullivan asked Walter.

"About?"

"About your own safety. If this is the work of someone who detests your organization and all that it stands for, don't you worry that you might have put yourself in the crosshairs?"

Walter sat staring into space for a moment, his eyes widening. "Hmm. In other words, I could be next in line."

"I didn't mean to scare you," Sullivan said. "In fact, Erin and I got the message 'You're next' on our own business card . . . with red paint splattered on it. We're in the crosshairs ourselves."

"So you're just spreading the joy around, eh?" Walter replied, giving me a jovial wink. In that moment, my appreciation for the man doubled.

"I'm sure nothing will happen, Walter," I said. "For all we know, Richard's murder might have nothing to do with the contest, or his interest in conservation. But a little precaution and vigilance wouldn't hurt."

"Just keep your eyes open," Sullivan added.

"Right. I will." He grinned at me. "Thanks for your concern, Erin. And don't worry. I'm nearly done with my judging. Just one more impromptu visit to each of the finalists' homes, to see if catching them off guard makes any difference. Then I'm putting this sorry affair to bed, once and for all."

"Good," I said. "I'm glad for everyone's sake that this is almost over with, so we can move on."

"Yeah. Not counting *Richard*," Sullivan growled.

I winced, chagrined at my own insensitivity.

"Oh, now, Erin didn't mean it like that." Walter got to his feet and struggled back into his coat, shuffling his hat between his hands. "Anybody can see she doesn't have a mean bone in her body." He gave me a nod, and said, "I've got to shove off." He grinned at Sullivan. "It's been good for me to see for myself that part of Richard lives on through his students. I'll keep you posted on the contest."

Walter's visit seemed to put Sullivan into a funk. Maybe he took offense to Walter's taking my side, or maybe he was still mired in angst over his recent loss, but once again he seemed to need some space. I wondered, though, if all this "space" he needed wasn't steadily pushing me right out of his life. I started working on Audrey's new kitchen, calculating that with all the extra hours Sullivan was putting into our work, I could squeeze in an hour or even two for my personal project without falling behind.

Audrey called on my cell phone at half past eleven

with a cheering suggestion. "You should drop by to see Jeremy Greene during lunch and tell him about the design ideas we were discussing last night. He came by the house a couple of hours ago and said he'd get right to work."

"This is a small project, Audrey. You don't really need an architect," I told her for the third time.

"Oh, I know. I realize you could do this for me. But I'd really like to get the chance to know Mr. Greene a little better." (This was the second time she'd given me this explanation; the first time she'd offered me the lame excuse that I was "too busy," which wasn't the case.) "And, frankly, I'm surprised you're not jumping at the chance to have him around here yourself."

"Why would I want a murder suspect hanging around my house?" In my peripheral vision, I saw Sullivan pivot from his drawing and gape at me. "The reasonable question is why do *you* want one nearby? Plus, the man's being sued for malpractice."

"Irregardless, I want to help you smoke out the murderer."

"So you're spending money on an architect who's a possible murder suspect just because you're curious to see if he's stupid enough to say something incriminating?"

"Something like that, yes. My insurance man just promised me a generous check, so I can afford Mr. Greene's services. One of the best things about being wealthy and single is that nobody can tell me what to do with my own money."

"Point taken. But I hope you'll get a discount if he winds up finishing the job from the Crestview jail while serving a life sentence for murder."

"I'll see if he'll put that clause in our contract. Take care, dear, and I'll talk to you later."

I said good-bye and hung up. Sullivan was still staring at me. "Audrey hired an architect?"

"Yes. A tree branch crashed through our kitchen roof last night, so she decided to expand."

"And to 'Go Greene' with an *e* on the end?" ("Go Greene" was Jeremy's advertising slogan.)

"Exactly. I tried to talk her out of it, but she's stubborn." But then again, as the look of concern on Steve's face reminded me, so was I. Prideful, as well. Maybe I'd rushed to the wrong conclusion yesterday about his seeing someone else. In any case, I couldn't very well expect Sullivan to wear his heart on his sleeve for me while I was keeping *mine* locked away in a vault. "And, by the way, I want this murder to be solved, too. Because I care about you."

Our gazes met as Sullivan seemed on the verge of saying something, but then he turned back to his computer screen.

Margot Troy was sitting on Jeremy's desk with Jeremy standing right beside her when I arrived at his office a few minutes after noon. He straightened his collar as he sat down in his chair. It was all too obvious that I'd interrupted an embrace. "Hello, Jeremy. Hi, Margot."

"Erin!" she exclaimed, atypically happily. "What are you doing here?"

"Audrey hired Jeremy to work on some passive solar lighting for our kitchen. I wanted to discuss some ideas with him."

"Oh, what fun!" Margot said. "What's she thinking about doing? A full remodel?"

"No, just repairing some major damage from last night's storm, and adding a sitting area. She insists she doesn't want to increase my workload by having me design it myself."

"I wonder if she's considering building a solarium," Margot said. "That might be really nice. She can grow her own spices and even some vegetables."

I grinned. "That's precisely what Audrey and I decided we wanted to do last night. We'll put a second kitchen table out there."

"Wonderful! Are you going to attach a glass ceiling and walls to—"

Jeremy cleared his throat, obviously not appreciating her discussing design ideas with his de facto client.

Margot took the hint and said, "Well, must hop." She collected her purse and donned her coat. "See you later, hon." She gave him a quick peck on the cheek and left.

"So what's up, Erin?" Jeremy asked, gesturing for me to sit in the same chair as I'd taken the last time. He scratched at some stubble. Perhaps he was trying to grow a beard to compensate for his weak chin.

"I drew some quick sketches for Audrey's new kitchen. She asked me to show them to you."

"Fine. I'll take a look." He didn't mask his irritation very well.

"Thanks for humoring me."

He caught my cold gaze, and at least had the decency to blush a little. "You know how it goes. Too much input from the home owners can really screw up my plans."

"Audrey and I are the ones who'll be living with the

final results. That's why it's important to take our opinions into consideration."

He peered at me. "Did you show these drawings to Audrey?"

"I described them to her, and she approves."

He frowned and slowly pushed back from his light table. "Well, then, I guess I should look at them right now."

"Only if you actually want this job."

"Ouch."

So much for Walter's assertion that my bones were never mean. "Sorry. I'm a bit stressed," I said.

"Still worrying about Richard Thayers?" he asked.

"Yes. I'd like to know that the killer will be brought to justice sooner, rather than later."

He unfurled my drawings and looked at the first one. "Nope. You've got this ceiling too high. That's going to trap the hot air and warm the room like nobody's business."

"That's why there's a ceiling fan in the next drawing."

"Really?" He chuckled. "A *designer* who doesn't cringe at ceiling fans? What's next? Futons?" I had no response, and a moment later he said, "The cabinets look good."

"Thanks."

He rolled the plans back up. "I can work with this. I'll get back to you both next week, and we'll go over my initial ideas."

"Thanks, Jeremy." I glanced over at a blueprint spread on his desk. It was of Burke's house. "Are you doing some more work for Burke?"

A flash of panic registered in his eyes. "No. I was just

going over them with an eye for what I can adopt in my current projects."

"So there are no problems with his foundation or anything?"

"Why do you ask?"

"No reason."

"The foundation's fine. Now if you'll excuse me, I've got to prepare for an appointment at one. See you later, Erin."

Later that day, I stewed over Jeremy's reaction as I drove to Burke's house for an appointment to discuss his sunroom. Maybe my paranoia had kicked into high gear prematurely, but I was now very worried that whatever went wrong in the design of Richard's foundation had also gone wrong with Burke's.

I needed to take a look down there for myself. There was no sense in alarming Burke unless it was clear that something was amiss.

Burke said he'd already reviewed my drawings for his solarium, and he approved the changes before we'd even had the chance to sit down, or even to leave his small but tasteful foyer. Sullivan and I had played up the rustic French country charm in this entrance. Sunny yellow paint warmed the plaster walls, and we'd designed a pair of arched sculpture nooks into the thick straw-bale construction on either side of the front door. The gold-hued slate floor added to the charm in the space, which served as a wonderful welcome to Burke's quaint, comfortable home. We'd emphasized a homey, kick-off-your-shoes-and-stay-awhile atmosphere throughout the home. The entire house now had the feel of an unpretentious and cozy old-world cottage that Sullivan and I — and Burke — utterly adored.

I gestured toward the glass inner door and asked, "Do you mind if I take a quick look in your basement before I go?"

"No, but why?"

"Just curious. Jeremy happened to be looking at your blueprints when I stopped into his office to talk about someone else's house."

"Why would that—" He broke off as the doorbell rang.

To my surprise, it was Asia at the door. She beamed ominously at us. Skulking behind her was Darren Campesio. Asia said, "Good day, Burke. And Erin."

"Hi, Asia," Burke said warily. His gaze shifted to Darren. "Darren," he muttered with a nod.

Darren held up a palm and said, "I got no idea why I'm here. Asia dragged me over, claiming she didn't want to have to repeat herself."

"May we come in?" she asked. She hoisted a big shopping bag to chin level. "I brought some visual aids with me."

"Visual aids?" Burke asked as he gestured for her to come in.

"Yes," she said matter-of-factly. I stepped back as Asia and Darren entered the close quarters. "I thought you'd be interested in seeing my plans for my new exterior decorating."

"Exterior decorating? I . . . don't follow."

She stationed herself in a corner of the small foyer, turned, and set down the bag by her feet. Eyeing Burke with a malicious grin, she said, "I've got some inventive home-improvement ideas that I'm going to install between the trees and the fence that divides our properties. I've drawn a sketch of their precise locations." She thrust the sheet of paper at Burke, and I peered over his shoulder at what resembled a child's treasure map. "Wherever you see little X's behind all of my evergreens, there will be one of these." She removed a pink plastic flamingo from her sack. "People are always sticking such things in their front lawns, but that would be too respectful of your rights. I'll hang *my* flamingos from the tree branches. If I were to put them in the ground, you could simply replace the split-rail with a cedar picket fence, which would block your view of them completely. We can't have that, now, can we?"

"You're out of your mind!" Darren said with a laugh. "No wonder you're named after a third-world continent!"

Burke and I both gave Darren a long look, though Asia ignored his offensive and inane comment. "Asia, be reasonable," Burke pleaded. "I'd remove the windmill if I could, but that would be the least green thing I could possibly do—ordering a whole batch of customized materials for a big construction project and then scrapping them."

As if he'd never spoken, Asia continued, "This way, with my pink flamingos wired into place on the tree branches, they will forever grace your property, looking down at you from above the fence. And furthermore, I'm stocking the pond with carp."

"Carp? But... they'll eat the shrimp larvae that I'm going to raise in the spring! And they'll—"

"I'm putting them in *my* half of the pond." She put her hands on her hips. "Which is my right. The same way you put shrimp in *your* half of the pond."

"But my *shrimp* aren't going to eat your *carp*!"

"Rules of natural selectivity." She turned one of her hands aloft and dipped slightly to that side. She looked like the proverbial little teapot just waiting to be tipped over and poured out. "As a big-deal environmentalist, I would think you'd be all in favor of such a thing. You people do advocate letting nature take its natural course, don't you?"

"At the moment, I'm more interested in not having my food source get destroyed by you!"

"Oh, please. Food source? You showed me those shrimp last spring. They're no bigger than insect larvae! That's why they call them 'shrimps' to begin with."

Darren chuckled. "*Asia* doesn't like *shrimp!*"

Burke glared at him, and Asia quickly told Darren, "Oh, don't worry. I have plans for your property border, too. *Big* plans. Consider it payback for the my-windmill-is-bigger-than-yours competition."

"But your view of the mountains isn't blocked by my windmill! I'm on the east side!"

"Even so, I don't like the thought of my property being flanked by *your* windmill, either. What if a big blast of wind knocks over your tower, and it crashes into my fence?"

"The weather moves from west to east! It's Burke's windmill you've got to worry about crashing into your house, not mine!"

"An earthquake, then. Regardless, you were the one who started this whole ridiculous business of windmills in the first place." She pulled out a white inflatable toy, still in its bag. "Now, these inflatable Santas and snowmen are going to look a little out of place among my trees year-round, but it *is* my property, after all. So I can do as I please."

Burke and Darren were turning red. Burke kept fidgeting with his glasses, and I half expected him to rip them off his face and chuck them at his neighbor's face.

"To top it all off, I've decided to get more with the times, so I'm going to be using an iPod from now on when I garden. That's going to become a necessity, because I'm taking up a second hobby. Along with raising carp, I'll be collecting these!" She brought out a ghastly violet-colored wind chime. "Since both of you have such an interest in wind, I know how much you'll appreciate being able to monitor the wind just by listening. I'm thinking a hundred chimes should do the trick."

"Asia," Burke moaned, "this is a ridiculous overreaction."

"Oh, and I'm installing colored lights along our fence line, Darren. It'll look just like Mardi Gras, year-round. Won't that be nice? And, with all those wind chimes going at once, it'll sound like one, too." She turned to glare at Burke. "And smell like one, thanks to your stinky shrimp hatchery. Unless my carp do the trick."

"I'm merely trying to develop personal food sources from the pond."

"You make enough money to buy groceries!"

"That's not the point. It's about sustainability. About not taking more than we put in."

She looked him over from head to toe. "You're a doctor. If you're that obsessive about maintaining our resources, why don't you reduce the earth's population by letting your patients die?"

"I don't expect people like you to understand," he growled.

"No, Dr. Stratton. Because people like *me* are sane! Whereas *you* and that dead judge of yours are both loony." She forced a smile. "You've got one week from to-day to take your windmills down, or my exterior decorating goes up. Good day, gentlemen. And Erin." She gathered up her bag of goodies and left, leaving Burke and Darren staring in stunned silence.

"Would carp really eat shrimp larvae?" I asked Burke.

"Probably." He sighed. "Maybe she's bluffing."

"She isn't," Darren replied. "She hates conservationists. Told me so herself. I spotted her lugging an orange cooler toward the pond this morning. I asked what was in it, and all she said was, 'You'll find out soon enough.' Damn it, we have a right to put up windmills! We have to stop her! Or at last retaliate!"

"How? She hates everything and everyone. It makes her unflappable." Burke paused and added thoughtfully, "Except...she does love flowers."

"Yeah, of course she does," Darren grumbled. "But that's only because they're the only life form that doesn't actively shrink from her presence."

Burke chuckled, and as the two men smiled at each other, they seemed to share a moment of friendship. Darren was the first one who looked away.

"There's another possible course of action," I said. "Acknowledge her point and take down your windmills."

"I can't allow someone to bully me into giving up on my plans," Burke retorted. "The windmill's already been paid for."

"Mine, too. Plus mine's already fully installed. The thing cost me a fortune. I'll get reimbursed twofold when I win the contest, though."

"Unless *I* win," Burke said.

"That's never going to happen."

Burke snorted.

Darren shot him a furious glare, then opened the door. "Never!" He slammed the door.

Burke shook his head and sighed, his shoulders sagging. I didn't know what to say. Both of Burke's neighbors struck me as being borderline emotionally disturbed. Asia could have felt that poisoning a conservationist was mere poetic justice. Darren had so much emotional investment in this contest that if he'd had an encounter with Richard, he might have killed Richard over a disparaging remark about his house.

And for that matter, Asia or Darren might be so malicious that one of them had taken the paint from Burke's garage and swapped it with Richard's—just to frame Burke Stratton for the crime.

chapter 11

The next morning, Sullivan, looking a little out of sorts, entered our office carrying a stack of notebooks, which he shuffled from arm to arm as he hung up his coat. I was on the tail end of a phone conversation and nodded to him in greeting, but he paid me no attention. As I hung up, he dropped a stack of nine obviously well-used spiral notebooks onto his desk. He eased into his leather desk chair, eyeing the stack all the while.

"Okay, I'll go first. What's up with the notebooks?"

He glanced at me. "Turns out, they're my inheritance. From Richard's estate. He left specific instructions in his will that I was to get the contents of the top drawer in his file cabinet." He gestured at the notebooks. "That's what was in there. Richard's lawyer had to call the police, and they just now called me and said I could come in and claim them."

"That's . . . surprising. You and Richard hadn't been in touch in years."

"I know. He must have changed his will in the week or two before he died."

"Are they notes from his classes?"

"A couple of them are. Mostly they're just . . . ideas that he's had. For environmental projects and things. I've only had the chance to skim through them so far."

"He didn't leave you any instructions about them, did he? Telling you what he wanted you to do with his notes?"

"No. I wasn't expecting to get anything at all, of course. And it just feels strange . . . reading Richard's words, now that he's dead."

"Have the police examined them yet?"

He nodded, paging through the notebook on top of the stack. "That's where I got them, just now. From Detective O'Reilly. Your favorite," he said sarcastically.

I shuddered and made a comical grimace, and he grinned and said, "He asked about you."

"He did?"

"Of course. The guy's obviously got a big crush on you."

"Oh, please! He does not! He treats me with nothing short of contempt!"

"Just calling 'em like I see 'em."

"Have you had your vision checked lately?"

Sullivan ignored my remark and sighed as he flipped

through a notebook. "When O'Reilly handed the notebooks over to me, he said, 'Most of this stuff is better than sleeping pills.' A lot of the notes do seem to be pretty random. But there could be a clue in here someplace, and if so, I'm going to find it."

As the day wore on, Sullivan was only halfway present. He made a reasonable showing when we visited with clients, but he spent every other moment with his nose in one of Richard's notebooks. I tried hard not to get annoyed, but my patience had worn thin when he told me to drive—even though he'd insisted we take his van—to all our joint appointments just so he could continue to read Richard's notebooks.

"Huh. This is interesting," he muttered as I swung into the left lane. We were navigating heavy traffic on our return trip from a client who lived halfway between Crestview and Denver.

"What?"

"Richard wrote down Margot Troy's address and phone number and circled it."

"In what context?"

"Can't tell. There are a couple of businesses on the same page. They sound like investment firms."

"Maybe her name's just there because he was going to judge her house for the Earth Love contest."

"No, these notes are from long before then. Five years ago." He flipped back and forth through a couple of pages as he scanned Richard's angular handwriting. "Yeah. Looks like Margot might have been an investor in some business venture of Richard's. That was right around when he was first starting to market his eco products." He paused. "I noticed she called him Richard in class. Her fellow classmates were all calling him Professor Thayers. He paused. "Would Margot be home this time of day?"

"I have no idea."

He glanced at his watch. "Let's give it a shot, just in case."

Far be it from me to object to investigating a surprising link to a murder victim. Truth be told, because Margot worked out of her home—she had a computer-consulting business—I knew she was quite likely to be home. "This whole thing keeps getting more and more strange," I remarked.

"Yeah."

"Richard had prior relationships with two of the three finalists chosen by the committee. It's odd that he dropped out as judge for Burke, when he must have already known Margot Troy was also a finalist."

"Which implies he knew he *could* be impartial toward her," Sullivan replied defensively. "In any case, he wouldn't need a second reason, so why mention it as he was stepping down?"

"Margot skirted the question when I asked if she knew him personally."

"Maybe she just didn't want to gossip about their relationship."

"It's not gossip when you're talking about yourself." I glanced at him when we stopped at a red light. His brow was creased, and he tilted the page at an angle. When he continued to stare at one spot, I asked, "What?"

"Looks like the two of them might have dated or something."

"He writes about his *romances*?"

"He doodles."

"You mean things like Margot plus Richard enclosed in a heart?"

"Not exactly, no."

As he flipped the page, I caught a glance of what looked like a drawing of a naked woman. It hit me then how little I knew about Richard's personal history. "Was Richard ever married?"

"For thirty years. His wife died several years ago. Heart disease." He switched notebooks. Even from the briefest of glances, it was obvious that this particular notebook was the most recent; the paper edges were much cleaner, and a sizable portion appeared to have been unused. Sullivan thumbed through the pages to find the last journal entry.

"Not to be unduly pessimistic, but I don't know how forthcoming Margot's going to be. Like I said, she's already dodged my questions about Richard. And when the police examined the notebooks, they must have picked up on Margot and Richard's relationship, too."

"True. But we might have an easier time getting information out of her than the police could."

"How so? The police have a legitimate reason to ask. Whereas, if you're planning on questioning her about obscene doodles in Richard's notebook, I can guarantee Margot's going to throw us out on our ears."

He looked up from his reading material. For the moment, I'd captured his full attention. "Good point. Now that you mention it, you'd be better off solo. You can . . . make girl talk with her. You know. Get her chatting about former lovers and stuff."

"Oh, sure, Steve," I said with a sarcastic laugh. "That'll be a snap. I do that with all my clients. Especially the ones who are as friendly and low-key as Margot. We like to have giggle-fests and pillow fights in our underwear."

Sullivan grinned. "Sounds great to me. Tell you what. I'll be a good soldier and keep an eye on you through the window."

I had to smile. It was nice that he was teasing me, at least. We pulled into the driveway, and he ducked into the backseat, quickly reabsorbed by his reading. I went to Margot's door, half hoping she wasn't home, while trying to think of a viable excuse to draw us into this girly conversation that Sullivan was expecting of us. She opened the door, sporting her usual frosty expression. "Erin. This is a surprise."

I could only think: *For you and me both. Wanna have a pillow fight and talk about boys?* "I was in the neighborhood and, well, I just wanted to stop by to see if you'd already handled that quick design job you mentioned last week."

"I mentioned a design job?"

"Yes, you did." I could feel my cheeks warming. It sounded as if I was desperate for work and had come begging. I wished a better excuse had come to mind. "That time you called but I put you on hold, you'd mentioned having reconsidered hiring me."

"Oh, heavens, Erin." She arched an eyebrow. "I'd forgotten all about that. You know how I am."

"I see. Well, since I'm here, maybe we could chat for a few minutes."

She eyed me suspiciously, but then stepped aside. "Come on in."

This felt awkward and downright embarrassing. At least I'd been granted entry. Sullivan owed me, big time. She led me to what was, hands down, the nicest room in the house, if I did say so myself: her kitchen. Margot held fast to the rule that everything must be secondhand or salvaged, and so even her modern, energy-efficient appliances had been purchased either at scratch-and-dent sales or from homes in forfeiture. I sat down on one of her cognac leather barstools. I'd found them at an ill-fated downtown restaurant. I ran my hands appreciatively over the counter—a lovely green made from recycled glass. The backsplash, too, was a light green, also produced from recycled glass.

"Would you like a cup of tea?"

"I'd love some. Thank you."

She already had water steaming in her kettle. As she prepared two cups of peppermint tea, I said lightly, "I suppose Richard's going to have lots of friends and loved ones at the service tomorrow."

"Probably so."

"You're going, aren't you?"

"Yes."

I waited a beat in the hopes that she'd mention that they'd once been friends, but she merely pursed her lips and started bobbing the tea bags in the cups with so much energy that the hot water almost sloshed over the rims. I sighed. "Did you and Richard know each other before you first took a class from him?"

She drained the last drops from a tea bag by squeezing it, then cursed and dropped the teabag, shoved the cup at me, and ran cold water over her burned hand. "Why do you ask? Did Richard say something to you about me?"

"No."

She gingerly dried her hand, flung the second tea bag into the sink, and sat down beside me with her own cup, her lips pursed all the while. Knowing what a recycling queen Margot was, I felt honored to have been granted my own unused tea bag, but she was so on edge, I elected to keep that thought to myself.

"Burke said something, then?" She fixed a piercing glare on me as she studied my features. "Because I know I didn't say anything."

Now I was stuck, and my tea was so hot I could only take the smallest of sips as a means for stalling. "Steve found your name and address in one of Richard's old notebooks, which Richard left to him in his will."

"I see." She frowned and took a sip of tea. "The police gave the notes to Steve. And he told you. So much for *my* privacy."

"We won't share that information with anyone else."

She rolled her eyes. "Well, I suppose I might as well tell you the truth. Let's just say that my financial dealings with Mr. Thayers provided me with an unexpected, and substantial, tax write-off. His heart was in the right place, but idea men like Richard Thayers tend to dismiss marketing as part of the equation for successfully launching a business."

"Do you mean that Richard's products didn't sell?"

She snorted. "It was a disaster. I basically lost every dime of my investment…in air purifiers." I waited through some lengthy sips of tea for her to continue. "He learned his lesson, though. That's why he started teaching continuing-ed classes at CU. That way, he could sell his zero-off-gassing products to his students."

"He had his own private, captive audience."

"Not unlike professors who teach exclusively from textbooks they write themselves." She took one more sip of tea and made a face, then glanced at her watch. "I hate to be rude, Erin, but I have a conference call."

"Oh. Okay." I took a couple of quick sips of tea, realizing I'd be deserting most of it. "I'll let myself out, then."

"Thanks for dropping by. Don't worry. There will always be the wannabes, like Richard Thayers, who can't quite figure out the inside joke."

She swept out of the room, and I let myself out her front door, utterly perplexed by her parting words. I got back into the driver's seat of Sullivan's van and shut the door.

"That was quick," he said.

"And strange. You were right. She was an investor in Richard's air purifiers and lost her entire investment. But I couldn't find a graceful way to ask if they were once a couple, as well."

"Did she seem resentful toward Richard?" Sullivan asked.

"Not at all. Although . . . she was very reluctant to tell me about it. Maybe they'd had a secret agreement that he'd compensate for her lost revenue by judging this contest and selecting her home."

"No way! Richard wouldn't have done anything so underhanded."

I kept my expression placid and said nothing. Sullivan appeared determined to believe that Richard Thayers hadn't changed in more than a decade since they'd known each other well. Yet I was sorely tempted to ask if, back then, Richard would have swallowed paint in front of his students or accused Steve of "teaming up with an enemy" merely because he'd been hired for a design job. I dearly wanted to be there for Steve in his time of need, but it was difficult when the Richard Thayers whom Sullivan admired greatly and defended vehemently was so strikingly different from the odd and unimpressive man Thayers seemed to *me* to have become.

Sullivan returned to the passenger seat after we'd pulled away from the curb and promptly resumed reading. "Are you learning any brilliant ideas from Richard?" I asked.

"Sure. Always."

We were silent for several minutes. Sullivan seemed to be stewing about something. At length he said, "I can't help but wonder about these notes. Why he gave them to me."

"It is a little strange. I guess it must be because you were his favorite student, and he wanted you to carry on in his footsteps."

"Maybe."

We'd joined a long string of cars at an intersection, all of us waiting to turn left in heavy traffic. His brow remained deeply creased, and I battled the urge to reach over and smooth it. Finally, I asked, "What's wrong?"

"There's a disturbing passage in here. It might explain why the police aren't working full-steam on the case."

"Read it to me."

Just as I was finally able to make the left turn, he cleared his throat and read, " 'I can't help but wonder if there's truth in what they're quietly saying about me . . . that I'm a fraud, just in it for the money. Sometimes it all seems so pointless. Even if I never drive or fly anywhere again for the rest of my life, I still wouldn't spare the ozone as much damage as one burning oil well in the Middle East causes. The world would be better off without me.' "

He stopped.

I asked softly, driving on, "You don't think he was talking about suicide, do you?"

He started flipping pages. "Not until you consider what he also wrote a few days later."

"Go on."

" 'I get a thrill from shocking my students when I drink the gilt. The way the girls shriek! Just for that moment, I imagine what it'd be like to actually poison myself in front of a full classroom. I should just do that and get it all over with. Let's face it. That's precisely what I deserve.' "

There was a long, awkward pause. "I don't know what to say," I finally stammered. "But it seems strange that the police would release something like that to you, if they'd read it and considered it solid evidence."

"You're forgetting, Erin," he said dejectedly. "It's not evidence of a murder, but rather a motive for suicide. So they probably don't need to keep it in their possession. I'm sure they just made a photocopy."

We had reached our lot. I pulled into his parking space and turned toward him. He'd shut the notebook and was now staring straight ahead, his expression glum. I put my hand on his shoulder, hoping some words of wisdom or reassurance would occur to me, but he pulled away from me and got out of the van.

At least he waited for me between our vans, though, as opposed to storming off someplace by himself. "It wasn't suicide, Gilbert."

"Okay," I murmured.

"No, I'm positive. He was just having a weak moment when he wrote that stuff. He would never have invited me to that particular class, or seemed so surprised by the consistency of the paint, if he was planning on killing himself."

"So we'll solve this thing ourselves, if we have to."

He gave me a grateful smile, which I struggled to return. I didn't know Richard enough to say one way or the other, but I was inwardly panic-stricken by my own suspicions.

What if Richard had asked Sullivan to the lecture as part of his plan for framing Burke Stratton to take the murder rap for his suicide?

I started to head toward our office, but Sullivan hesitated, staring at the asphalt near my van. He headed toward the front tire. "What's wrong?" I asked. "I don't have a flat, do I?"

"Not yet. But you'd better be careful as you leave. There's some broken glass."

With a sinking feeling, I quickly rounded the front of my van. "Jeez! One of my headlights is smashed!"

Sullivan joined me, cursing. We both knew this couldn't have been an accident; my space was at a right angle to the side of a building, which made front-end fender benders impossible.

Something was protruding from the ring of jagged glass that rimmed the cavity of my headlight. It looked like a business card. "Uh-oh."

"Another anonymous message?" Sullivan asked me, while I extracted it with my gloved fingers.

Indeed, it was a second red-splattered Sullivan and Gilbert card. I flipped it over quickly, expecting to see a second death threat. This time, there was only a crude drawing of a smiley face.

chapter 12

It was strange how ominous a childish little sketch could seem. Sullivan wanted to go with me to the police, but that seemed like a waste of his time, so he reluctantly agreed to let me go alone, provided I made good on my promise to keep him informed.

Linda Delgardio took my statement. After I'd given her what little information I could, I asked how the investigation was going. With a slight shrug, she replied, "It's still considered an open case, at least."

The phrase "at least" clearly spelled doom. My heart

sank, for Sullivan's sake. "You're ready to conclude it was suicide, aren't you?"

She peered at me, weighing her words. "There is some talk that it'll eventually get ruled a suicide."

"Were Burke's fingerprints found on the can of gold paint?"

"I'm not at liberty to say, Erin." She touched my hand, her demeanor both gentle and sad at once. "You know that."

"That's okay. I already know the answer. Burke told me himself that a paint can that had gone missing from his garage had to be the one that Richard drank from, so Burke's fingerprints would have been all over the can itself . . . just not on Richard's company's label. The killer would have stuck the label itself onto the can later. And Sullivan read the section of Richard's notes to me where he was speculating about drinking a toxic product. So I'm sure Detective O'Reilly and lots of your colleagues have concluded this was Richard's last act of vengeance . . . trying to make Burke take the fall for an act of suicide."

Linda pursed her lips.

"I know how much you hate it when I play amateur sleuth, but for what it's worth, Sullivan swears Richard would never commit suicide."

"How well did Steve really know his former teacher, though?" Linda asked rhetorically. "Plus, we located several people who toured Burke's place at that open house the Sunday before Mr. Thayers's death. One middle-aged couple picked out Richard Thayers's photograph from a number of random pictures and said that he was there that day."

"Uh-oh. So it *is* looking like Richard could have taken that can himself." Something was bugging me, though, and an instant later, I made the connection. "Richard told us he'd only found out last Tuesday that Burke's home was in the contest, let alone a finalist. Those were his exact words. But if he'd really been there the previous Sunday, he *must* have known Burke was a finalist. Which either means he was lying to Sullivan, or that the couple who picked out Richard's photograph was mistaken."

Linda held my gaze for a long moment before replying. "Sometimes witnesses see photographs of victims or suspects, and their minds can play tricks on them and give them a false memory. You were there that weekend. Did you ever see Thayers? Or any of the suspects?"

I shook my head. "Hundreds of people came through Burke's house that weekend. I hadn't met Richard, yet, so we could have crossed paths without my noticing."

She nodded. She was chewing on her lip, which she sometimes did when she was lost in thought. After another lengthy pause, she said, "You mentioned the name Asia McClure to me. Have you had any more dealings with her recently?"

"Yes. And not pleasant ones. It's an understatement to say that she is *not* a conservationist. She says she spotted *me* at the open house, so *she* certainly could have swiped the paint can. But she's not really a suspect, is she? Did she even *know* Richard Thayers?"

"Not personally," Linda replied. "But a few months ago her political group, Consumers for Common Sense, had quite a skirmish with his World's Watchdogs group. Things got ugly and both Asia and Richard were arrested." She studied me, then said, "By the way, I'm only telling you this because that story will be in tomorrow's paper anyway. Our public information officer was asked about it in a press briefing just this morning."

"Asia is combative enough to resort to extremes. She might have felt that Richard deserved to be tricked into making himself ill by drinking toxins. She's currently on the warpath about Burke's building a windmill and ruining her view. Maybe that's related somehow to Richard, since he was a vocal advocate of renewable energy."

I paused, trying to put my thoughts in order. "Maybe Richard *was* at the open house, but didn't want to admit it, because Earth Love had specifically stated he wasn't allowed to attend the finalists' open houses. Asia and Richard could have crossed paths that day and gotten into an altercation afterwards. Maybe he saw her spraying pesticides and confronted her."

"Using a pesticide? In January?" Linda asked skeptically.

"Or something similar." I considered alternative scenarios, and remembered something about Asia's house that had barely registered with me at the time. "Last week, during that stretch of warm weather, her back porch had what looked like a fresh coat of paint. Maybe she was painting that weekend, and Richard gave her a lecture about poisoning the environment with noxious off-gases."

"That's what lawyers call sheer conjecture, Erin."

"Sure, but it makes sense. For one thing, Richard's attending the open house could explain how he could have found Burke's violations so quickly. One of those violations had to do with nonpotable-water usage, so he would have been examining the small pond that's bisected by Asia's property line. Asia watches her property like a hawk. And, frankly, it's much more believable that

Richard *did* read the articles in which the finalists were announced, though he claimed he didn't learn their names till the very night it was publicly announced that he was judging. I know *I* would be reading everything I could about a contest I was about to judge. Wouldn't you?"

She sighed. "I really shouldn't be discussing my theories with you, Erin. But do *you* think an argument between Asia and Thayers would be motive for her to poison Richard Thayers?"

I shrugged. "In a boxing match, she'd hit below the belt at every opportunity. And she's my top suspect for doctoring my business cards."

"I'll have a talk with her."

"Thanks. I'd appreciate that." I paused, still pondering the scenario of Richard's having kept an eye on Burke's property. "You know, if Richard *was* skulking around on Burke's property, he could have run into Darren Campesio at some point, too. Darren told me he went to Burke's open house, and I've seen him watching over Burke's property with binoculars. He runs around in combat fatigues, like he's part of some covert surveillance operation."

She studied my features. "You're not going to suggest that Mr. Campesio killed Thayers because he thought Thayers was trespassing, are you?"

"No, but Darren's an odd guy. He could have confronted Richard, learned that he was the contest judge, and gotten into an argument with him about rule violations. Richard seemed singularly unimpressed with Darren's house when we spoke about it the afternoon before he died."

Linda said nothing, but she shook her head slightly as if every bit as confounded by the behavior of Burke's neighbors as I was. She shoved back from the table. "Erin, I'll see if I can learn who's doing this with your business cards and smashed your headlight. And I'll talk to Ms. McClure and Mr. Campesio. But..."

"Don't hold my breath?"

"The simplest explanation is usually the right one. In other words, it's likeliest that Richard committed suicide. But we'll do our best."

"You personally don't think it was suicide, though, do you?"

"I wouldn't be surprised either way."

In all honesty, neither would I, but Sullivan would never forgive me for saying that to a police officer. I thanked her and left, then called Sullivan from my van in the parking lot. I gave him a severely edited version of my conversation with Linda. He sounded skeptical when I finished by insisting, "That's really all we discussed."

"You sound too perky, which usually means you're not telling me something. They think it was suicide, don't they?"

"Yes."

He sounded utterly discouraged as he said good-bye.

As I drove home, I found myself bothered by something Linda had said. It was next to impossible to remember seeing someone in passing among the steady stream of visitors. And yet, I did remember some man watching me long enough to catch my attention.

At a red light, I used a designer's trick and shut my eyes momentarily to recall the room at that moment. It took me less than a second, but sure enough, I pulled up a clear mental picture. I was now almost positive that my ogler had been Matthew Hayes.

Audrey wasn't home by dinnertime, which meant she was either working late or on a date. With no functioning kitchen, it was easier to microwave a frozen dinner for myself than to prepare a healthier meal. I ate at my computer in the messy, cluttered den, trolling the Internet for possible connections between Burke Stratton and Matthew Hayes. The possibility of their having met at Burke's open house and discovering that they had a common enemy was weighing heavily on me. I could find no clues or connections, but I *did* find a photograph of a desk on the M.H. Custom Furniture Web site that would be stunning in Burke's study. This was why it was a good thing I was a designer and not a police officer; I was forever getting distracted by lovely furniture. I could see myself having to bite my lip rather than make unforgivable statements like: "It's terrible that your friend is dead, but that table his head is resting on is absolutely fabulous!"

I surrendered to my urge and called Burke to describe the desk. He went to the Web page showing the piece while we were still on the phone. "You're right!" he said. "I love it!"

"So do I. But you recognize the name of the company, don't you?"

He paused. "No. Not at all. Should I?"

"It's Matthew Hayes's company. He was the one who was heckling Richard Thayers the night he drank the toxic paint."

"Shoot! No, I missed the connection completely." He paused. "What should I do?"

"It's really up to you, Burke. This particular desk in the photo is tiger maple, which is not from the rain forest, and it's entirely custom-made. We can request that he use environmentally friendly varnish and locally processed pine, and so on. But you should know that he *does* use banned materials, although he claims they're recycled only."

Another long pause. "What would *you* do?"

"I'm not sure, to be honest. We've bought from him in the past, before we knew about his questionable ethics."

"Okay. Well, just...go ahead and order it from him, but make it very clear that I'll only accept the desk on the condition that I can return it if I discover that he's abused any trade regulations."

"Will do."

He thanked me and hung up.

Late Friday morning, Richard Thayers's family finally held a service in Crestview for him. It was a dreary affair at the small, drafty shelter of a local park that Richard had reputedly frequented. The gray, overcast sky seemed to suck all the color from the surrounding landscape. Sullivan gave one of several eulogies—as did Walter Emory—but kept his speech impersonal, sharing only how he tried to keep in mind the lessons Professor Thayers had taught him every day in his own job. Margot was there but ducked out quickly afterwards, and she was the only mourner I recognized.

Sullivan seemed so determined to hide behind a stoic mask that, at the gathering immediately following the service, he treated his own parents as mere acquaintances—

thanking them for coming down all the way from their new retirement condo in the mountains two hours away.

His mom spoke to me privately and said, "Even as a little boy, he could never stand to let anyone see him cry."

"That doesn't surprise me."

She searched my eyes. "How are things between the two of you?"

"Good." Trying to evade the issue, I said, "Business has been excellent, really, and it looks like it'll continue strong this year... knock on wood."

"I mean, how are things personally? Romantically?"

I fought off a sigh. This hardly seemed the time or the place for such a question, not to mention that she should be asking her son that question, not me. "Frankly, I think he's seeing someone else."

"Don't let that stop you, Erin."

I glanced around and spotted Sullivan on the opposite side of the parking lot. He couldn't overhear us from that distance. "I'm letting the need to keep our *business* relationship strong stop me."

"Hmm. Steve gave me the same excuse when I asked him that question."

"Probably because it's not merely an excuse. Running a two-person business and trying to date is kind of like... making out in a canoe. It's hard to stay afloat."

"Clever analogy. But you two are meant for each other. Take care, Erin." She and Sullivan's father gave me parting hugs, then called another good-bye to Sullivan, standing by his van.

He and I made our way toward each other as his parents drove away. He gave me a sheepish smile. "I saw you talking to my mom. She can talk your ear off sometimes."

I touched his hand and said, "Let's leave the van here, and I'll buy you a cup of coffee someplace."

To my surprise, he took my hand and laced his fingers through mine. "Deal."

We strolled over the lovely wood bridge that spanned Crestview Creek. After a minute or two, I gathered my nerve and said, "So tell me more about the real Richard Thayers."

"He was a great teacher and a true role model. Like I just got through saying at the service." He released his grasp and stuck his hand in his coat pocket. "And you've already made it clear you weren't impressed by him."

"But I didn't know him. So enlighten me. Tell me about your favorite experience in his classroom."

Sullivan thought for a moment, then smiled a little. "That had to have been the day he brought a frog into the classroom to demonstrate design ergonomics."

"Using a frog?" I asked with a smile.

"Like I said before, he was a nonconformist. He'd built this mazelike foam-board house with a clear plastic roof. In the center of the house is a sunken goldfish bowl, half full of water. Then he sets the frog inside the outer wall. And the frog just sits there. So Richard asks: 'Why doesn't the frog move?' The students are calling out answers all at once: 'The walls are too narrow.' 'The ceiling's too low,' and so on, and Richard is making adjustments to the enclosure and nodding. This rapid interchange of ideas is happening, and he asks us things like: 'What would make this even better for the frog?' We keep firing ideas at him, but, ultimately, the frog still isn't moving, even after Richard has removed all the inner walls. We're throwing out suggestions—maybe it's too hot in there, or too cold, or the walls should have been green or the floor covered with silt. Finally, one girl says, 'How would we know? It's just a stupid frog!' So Richard points at her and says, 'Whose fault is that? The frog's?' And I interrupt and say to him, 'It's *yours*, because we didn't get the chance to re-search habitats for frogs.' And he grins and says, 'Exactly, S.S. When you're building a home, you've got to build it with the occupant's needs in mind. You can't expect your client to always be able to tell you what those needs are. *You've* got to be able to know what options to present. In short, you've got to be smarter than the frog."

Although my first thought was how resentful our clients would be to hear themselves likened to frogs, I said, "Wow. He sounds like a wonderful, engaging teacher."

We reached the coffee shop, where eight aluminum tables were crammed into a space big enough for only six, ordered coffees, and found seats. Sullivan told me several more anecdotes about Richard, both as a teacher and as a sounding board for Sullivan's environmentally minded designs. He then said, "Now that some time's gone by, I'm ready and able to work with Burke again."

"You are?"

"Yes."

"Okay . . . but why do you want to? Are you starting to doubt his guilt?"

"Not really. But I'll be better able to keep tabs on him when I'm part of his inner circle."

"You're going to work for the person you think killed your friend? Do you really think that's wise?"

He shrugged. "I can handle it." He checked the dis-play on his cell phone. "Jeez. Look at the time!"

I glanced at my watch and silently agreed that it was much later than I'd have guessed. We hurried back to the van. As he moved toward me, I thought he was just going to unlock my door, but to my total surprise, he took me in his arms and kissed me tenderly. As our embrace ended reluctantly, he whispered, "Thank you," then opened the door for me.

My head was spinning, but as Sullivan drove us toward the office, I remembered reading an article in a women's magazine, addressing what they'd termed "funeral passion." Apparently, attending funerals encourages us to confront our own mortality, thereby inspiring false feelings of passion.

I had to stop reading women's magazines.

As we neared the office, Sullivan said he had something to do, and dropped me off at my van. Although I didn't call him on it, judging by his caginess, his "something to do" had to be with Ms. Hands-on. Just like that, my mood did one of its flip-flops. I avoided looking at him as I got out of his van and into mine.

Feeling miserable, I drove to M.H. Custom Furniture and went into Matthew's store. He was there alone. I forced a smile. "Hi, Matthew."

He smirked at me. "Well, well. Erin Gilbert. This is a surprise. Fraternizing with the enemy?"

"I don't consider you a personal enemy."

"Just an enemy of the environment."

I shrugged at the element of truth in that statement.

He grinned. "You're going to love the article in tomorrow's paper, about how I'm giving a discount to all card-carrying members of Consumers for Common Sense."

"I heard about that group yesterday, for the first time. I met the woman who founded it, in fact."

"Asia McClure," he said with a nod. "She's the one who suggested the discount."

"What's this 'common sense' that they've apparently got and the rest of us lack?"

"We object to environmental extremists. We're for sensible fair exchange on the open market. We don't want the government or anyone else telling us what we should or should not buy."

"Isn't it self-defeating for any business owner in Crestview to actively come out *against* conservation?"

"I'm not against conservation. Just against this notion that we've got to criminalize selling products made from rare and exotic materials. It's basic supply and demand. When the supply is low, the demand and the price go up. Nobody is ever banned from selling antiques, or rare coins."

"It's not the same thing. One's a fixed entity. The other is trying to preserve diminishing resources."

"Oh, we'll have wiped the human race off the planet long before anyone will notice or care that the mahogany trees are gone, too. Anyway, what brings you to my offensive little corner of the world? Other than to debate global policies, I mean."

"As it happens, I'm on a mission from one of my clients. Burke Stratton."

"Mr. Green Machine himself? That's ironic."

"There's a corner desk you make that would be perfect for him. Provided you use a zero-off-gassing finish on it, of course."

"Of course," he replied. "So Gilbert and Sullivan isn't boycotting my company?"

"Not yet."

"Glad to hear it." He grinned. "I'm grateful for your hypocrisy."

"Oh, from everything I've read you're in complete

compliance with the trade laws. You're simply trying to change them through legal means. Am I giving you too much credit?"

"No, that's absolutely true."

"You're sure? Because it's not too late for me to boycott you."

He held up his palms and gave me a sincere-looking smile. "Honest, Erin. I might not be the planet's best steward, but I'm nowhere near its worst, and I never will be."

"That's nice to hear, Matthew. For one thing, this sale will be contingent on your practices remaining true to the tests. If Burke discovers you are, in fact, violating import agreements, he's going to demand a refund."

"I can't see that happening anytime soon," he said cryptically.

My cell phone rang. It was Sullivan. I excused myself and walked to the far side of the store to answer quietly.

"I'm at Burke's. You'd better come out here right away," Steve said.

So he *wasn't* with Jennifer Hands-on Fairfax. Maybe I'd jumped to conclusions. Maybe he wasn't seeing her, after all. Part of me wanted to leap for joy, but the somberness in his voice kept me grounded. "What's wrong?"

"I know why Richard disqualified Burke." Before offering any additional explanation, he hung up.

I finished placing my order with Matthew and left. Some fifteen or twenty minutes later, Sullivan was waiting for me in his van when I pulled into Burke's driveway. "Is Burke here?"

He shook his head. "The garage is empty. That's the first thing I checked."

"You're here by yourself?"

He spread his arms. "It was the only way I could search for evidence in private."

"Evidence that he was cheating on the contest, or that he killed Richard?"

"Could be both."

Sullivan walked me down along the small creek that formed the water source for the pond. He pointed at the ground. "Look carefully along the underbrush."

At first I didn't see anything, but when I told him that, he said, "Look harder."

"Uh-oh." I stared in disbelief. "Are those power cables?"

"Yep. I traced them back. They lead from Asia's to Burke's property. Burke has been siphoning power from Asia McClure. His home isn't truly self-sustaining, after all."

I stared at the cable, still not quite believing my eyes. It was impossible to believe that nobody had noticed this—that Sullivan and I hadn't noticed it—during the full six months and more since Burke had first entered the Earth Love contest. Finally, I muttered, "This is just...unbelievable."

"It's what Richard must have meant when he talked about what our client was 'really doing.' Let's face it, Gilbert. Burke has a double motive for killing Richard."

"You think he would have killed Richard just to save himself from getting booted out of this contest?"

"By the time you consider their past relationship, yes."

"According to Burke, he was trying to resolve their problems."

"He was lying."

"How do you know? Did you find anything in his notes about their troubles?"

"No, I didn't. But I knew Richard. He didn't pull all this out of a hat. If he complained about someone, that person had a problem. Period. So Burke did something to him."

"Or maybe Richard never forgave Burke for the vile things that he said when his son died!"

"I just can't believe that," Sullivan said. "I'm reporting this to Earth Love."

"Absolutely. But maybe there's another explanation. Maybe he wasn't siphoning power with the cable, but rather—"

A twig snapped behind us. I turned quickly. Burke was standing there, glowering at us. "What cable?" he demanded. "What are you talking about?"

I felt more than saw Sullivan tense up, and I knew that he was inwardly seething at Burke's presence. "Sorry to be sneaking around on your property, Burke," Sullivan said, his voice clipped. I doubted Burke would detect the source of his discomfiture, at least. "It's my doing, not Erin's. I wanted the chance to double-check in privacy whatever Richard Thayers had found on your property that wasn't kosher."

"But I haven't done anything wrong!" Burke protested. "What *cable* are you—"

He drew closer and looked at the ground by our feet. He'd obviously spotted the black cable for himself.

"It's a power line from Asia's house to yours."

"It can't be!"

"Burke," Sullivan said, "this cable runs between your and Asia's properties. It's located at the back corners of both of your yards, where the power company is likeliest to have installed their power lines. It looks like it's a splice, which taps into her power supply and feeds into yours."

"But . . . I didn't put it there."

"Somebody did. And it's going to be really hard to believe that anyone other than you would have installed and buried the cable without your knowledge."

"But . . . that's exactly what happened!" He gaped at the coax cable, as if willing it to vanish. "Maybe Richard set me up."

"He wouldn't have done that," Sullivan insisted. "He wouldn't have any reason to do that. He'd already said he was stepping down."

"Burke?" I interjected. "We're going to have to report this to Walter Emory and see what he says about it."

"I'm being set up! If not by Richard, then by *somebody*! By Darren or Asia, maybe."

"That would have taken a lot of nerve," I said, "not to mention electrical know-how."

"Asia's a major nutcase, but she's also a genius. And Darren's held several jobs, including repairing computers for IBM. Either one of them could have done this."

"But they're both fanatics about watching out in the neighborhood. Unless they were working in cahoots, one would have caught the guilty other in the act."

"Or it was done at night, or when one of them was out of town. In any case, there's no way I did this myself. So go ahead and call Walter. I've got to find out who's doing this to me!" He looked at us, wild-eyed, and grabbed his head. "I'm being framed *again*!"

chapter 13

The three of us—Burke, Sullivan, and I—went inside to talk things out. Sullivan was obviously loath to admit that Burke's claims of his innocence were very convincing, but at least he was attentive and cordial toward our client. Sullivan got ahold of Walter Emory and convinced him to meet us at Burke's house immediately. "It's time for Earth Love to hire a private investigator," Sullivan urged Walter over the phone. "Someone who can test for fingerprints."

Burke said to me, "I'll have someone cover for me at the lab," as he dialed a number on his cell phone.

While we waited, Burke paced and fidgeted incessantly with his glasses, muttering that he couldn't believe this was happening. He continued to offer various scenarios as to how someone could have gotten away with it. He even suggested, "Maybe it was Margot Troy. I think she still resents me for breaking up with her. I don't think her ego could withstand my winning the contest right after dumping her."

"Margot doesn't live anywhere near here," I replied. "She couldn't have run those wires without being seen by anyone at the three houses with views of the footpath."

"She could have easily done it with her boyfriend's help, though," he fired back.

"You think Jeremy would have sabotaged a house of his own design?" Sullivan asked.

He shrugged. "If he's nuts enough about his girlfriend. Guys will do all sorts of crazy things for their ladies."

"Not *that* crazy," Sullivan retorted.

"The thing is, Jeremy and I have been butting heads lately," Burke countered. "I got real concerned about my basement after reading about Richard's lawsuit, and Jeremy keeps trying to blow me off. What if he realized he's backed the wrong horse? That my house is falling to pieces, thanks to his faulty design? He could have decided to cut his losses...shift the blame for losing the contest onto me by making it look like I was cheating, and help his wealthy girlfriend to win."

Steve gaped at Burke for a moment, then shifted his gaze to me, and I knew at once that Steve's certainty that Burke was guilty had been shaken. Either Asia or Darren was angry enough about Burke's windmill that one of them could have tried to sabotage his chances in the contest, and now Burke had just given us plausible motives for Margot or Jeremy to frame him, as well.

"Discovering this cable might give you exactly what you wanted," I said to Burke, patting him on the shoulder. "This is your chance to answer Richard's charges against you."

Burke sighed. "Yeah. I guess that's *one* good thing to come of it. As long as the judges believe me when I say I didn't hook the damned thing up myself. What do you think my chances are of that happening?"

Sullivan cleared his throat. "You've got Erin and me to vouch for you. You're our client, so Earth Love will know we have a vested interest, but it can't hurt."

Burke said, "Thanks, man," and gave him a friendly jab on his arm.

I gave Sullivan a grateful smile, which he didn't acknowledge. It killed him, I knew, to have to admit to himself that his mentor's intense rage at Burke might very well have been completely misplaced. Which in turn meant Sullivan's suspicions about our beleaguered client might have been misplaced, as well.

Walter, accompanied by another man, arrived about an hour after Sullivan had called him. Walter had been somber at the service earlier, but his usual cheery demeanor had since been restored. "So, my friends," he said. "Another power tap line, eh? Don't you hate it when this happens?" He chuckled at his silly sarcasm, then introduced his companion as Earth Love's security chief and investigator, Bob Jones.

"I didn't do this," Burke immediately implored. "Someone is framing me."

"That's what the last guy said," the investigator replied. Walter chuckled and nodded.

"*What* last guy?" Burke asked, his voice desperate.

"I've judged more than twenty of these contests across the country in the last few years," Walter replied. "This is the third time a power line was run from an external source."

"That's . . . appalling!" Burke said. "But this is the first time the home owner was set up."

"Second time, actually," Jones said.

"Yeah," Walter explained. "We had a really jealous maniac over in Dallas. Eating too much tofu, you ask me." He drew air circles around his ear. "That's when Earth Love started the policy that all semifinalists had to provide their fingerprints."

"That guy had the ugliest kids I've ever seen," Jones muttered.

"Okay. So there's precedence, at least," Burke said. "Provided *you* can be open-minded about my innocence."

"Oh, sure," Walter replied with a wink. "I'm always open-minded."

"Even when your friend and colleague was murdered?" Burke asked incredulously. "And withdrew from judging because of me?"

"Let's examine the evidence, shall we?" Walter said evenly. "Fear not, my friends. We'll get to the bottom of this."

Sullivan and I explained that we had to get back to work. Burke merely shrugged his shoulders when we said goodbye to him, saying that he was resigned to his fate. The moment we were alone, I asked Sullivan, "So are you starting to have doubts about Burke having killed Richard?"

"Some," he grumbled. "Right now, we both have to concentrate on getting caught up at work."

All told, our remaining meetings for the day didn't go well. One carpenter had put a nail through a pipe, and another client had changed her mind completely, causing us to start over from scratch. At home afterwards, Audrey and I were both cranky. We snapped at each other as we ate our microwaved dinners. Feeling exhausted and discouraged, I went to bed early, calling it another exciting Friday night. But the phone at my bedside rang a few minutes after eleven P.M., awakening me from a deep slumber.

"Erin, are you awake?" the caller asked.

"I am now." I tried to rouse myself. Hildi was meowing in protest, and I agreed with the sentiment. "Who is this?"

"It's Burke Stratton."

"Burke? What's wrong?"

"Nothing. Nothing at all. Sorry to be calling you so late, but I just got home and listened to a phone message from Walter Emory. I'm going to be cleared!"

"Cleared?"

"Eventually. It was Margot Troy!"

"You're . . ." I stopped, shaking off my brain fog enough to realize that he wasn't talking about the murder, but rather, the running of the illegal power line. "That doesn't make any sense."

"Maybe not, but her fingerprints were found on the cable itself and on my meter box. And there's no way for them to have gotten there innocently."

"That's great news." I yawned. "I'm glad to hear that they're getting this resolved."

"Me, too. Sorry for waking you. Sleep well." He hung up.

I returned the phone to its cradle, now wide awake and with the sinking feeling that I was going to stay that way for quite a while to come. For Margot Troy to have pulled such a stupid, ugly stunt, she must have hated Burke. Maybe she'd framed him for Richard's murder, too.

The following morning, I called Steve Sullivan to tell him what Burke had reported to me the night before. "Jeez, that's weird," Sullivan grumbled. "Seems way out of character for her."

"Yeah, it is. But like Burke told me last night, there's no other viable explanation for her prints being on his electric meter." I hesitated, then said, "I'll be setting myself up for more than one major tongue-lashing, but I've got to know what's behind this. I'm going over to her house and asking her point-blank what's going on."

"Let me know what she says."

To my pleasant surprise, Margot quickly agreed to have me come over, so I went directly there from my house, and we took seats on her living room sofa. Wasting no time on small talk, which I knew Margot appreciated, I asked, "Did you hear from Walter Emory about what happened yesterday?"

"About my fingerprints being on Burke's meter, you mean? I heard, obviously, but I was merely checking out my competition's power consumption. Nothing sordid was going on."

She was avoiding my gaze. "Margot, things just aren't adding up for me."

"What do you mean?"

"For one thing, I can't imagine you really being so interested in your competition's electrical usage that you went sneaking around his house, checking his meter readings. You could have asked someone at Earth Love to tell you what his consumption rates were. It wasn't privileged information or anything."

"I had my reasons, Erin."

"*What* reasons?"

She sighed and pursed her lips, but I was determined to wait her out. Eventually she frowned and said, "I couldn't ask Earth Love about Burke's meter readings without possibly tipping my hand about...my concerns. Jeremy has more riding on this contest than anyone else."

"How so?"

"Having his design win this contest could finally give him the respect for his work that he's deserved and craved for years now."

"I can see that being true. But...he'd have had a lot easier time explaining his fingerprints on Burke's power meter than you would. He's the architect, after all, and he's working on the sunroom design even as we speak. Why did you take it upon yourself to check it out?"

"Because...I needed to see for myself if the energy consumption was really as low as Jeremy was bragging about. I didn't believe him. And, as it turned out, with good reason."

She was now fidgeting so badly that I half expected her to start digging the upholstery tacks out of her vintage linen sofa. Only one explanation came to mind. "Do you suspect *Jeremy* ran those auxiliary power lines?" I asked.

She winced and answered dejectedly, "The latest figures that Jeremy bragged to me about were impossible.

Unless Burke's windmill was operational, that is. After I saw for myself that the windmill hasn't been fully installed, I confronted Jeremy and he confessed to me privately. But please don't repeat that to anyone."

"He had to know the engineers at Earth Love were going to realize the numbers were impossible. In fact, he's incredibly lucky that the engineer who spoke at Burke's hearing didn't pick up on the discrepancy."

Margot nodded. "That's why Jeremy waited till the last minute to hook everything up . . . on the very day Richard Thayers was officially named judge. The final round was only supposed to last a week. Jeremy gambled that it would be just long enough to make Burke's meter readings first-rate, but not unduly suspicious. And Jeremy never would have felt forced to hook it up in the first place, except that things kept going wrong with the installation of Burke's windmill."

"And so . . . Jeremy siphoned power from Burke's next-door neighbor?"

She nodded. "When it was clear the windmill wasn't going to be operational in time, Jeremy calculated that, even so, the tower and the blades would be in place. So he ran the cable, planning on hooking it up the minute the shell of the windmill was in place. That way, he could siphon power but make it look like the windmill was producing it. Except the supplier botched the job and had to backorder most of the tower and the blades. Jeremy knew by then that he'd get caught in the act if he pulled out the cable, so he waited till the last minute to hook it up, thinking it would boost Burke's chances of winning, but not lead to his getting the boot. In retrospect, he knows full well how stupid that was, but he was desperate."

"Was Burke in on the deception?"

"I asked Jeremy that, and he says no."

"Do you believe him?"

"Yes. Jeremy would have no reason to take full responsibility. It would speak better for him if he'd merely been acting on his client's behalf."

I took a moment to digest the information. "Margot, this is too serious for you to keep quiet. This could easily turn into a criminal investigation. A man is dead! Right after he was publicly seeking answers to those very improprieties at Burke's house! You've got to tell the police about this."

She pursed her lips, and her eyes misted over. After a long pause, she gritted her teeth and said defiantly, "Who's to say I didn't?"

"*Did* you?"

"Jeremy would kill me if he knew this, but yes, I told them."

"I haven't heard any news about his being arrested."

"I doubt he was. Burke called me right after you did this morning, and apparently he'd already told the police he didn't want to press charges against Jeremy. Burke wanted to know if I was the snitch who'd turned him in. I lied and said no. But I don't know what will happen with whatever home owners he was pilfering power from. Maybe they'll have Jeremy arrested, I don't know. *They* were the ones who were actually getting ripped off."

If Asia McClure failed to prosecute to the fullest extent of the law, I'd be shocked. And suspicious about her motives. "What about the utility company? Are they pressing charges?"

"They've been getting paid and didn't know there was a problem. Frankly, the greatest damage at the moment is to my and Jeremy's relationship. He hasn't called me since the Earth Love people first talked to him about this yesterday, and he hasn't been answering any of my—" She broke off at a soft thump against an outer wall of her house. "What was that?"

"I don't know, but—"

I'd been about to say it was probably nothing, but she leapt to her feet and raced out the back door, grabbing something from the kitchen cabinet en route. I followed a few paces behind her and grew alarmed when I heard her cry: "Stop right there! I'm armed and dangerous!"

I rounded the corner after her, petrified that she'd grabbed a gun. She'd shouted at Walter Emory and the investigator, Bob Jones. "Whoa," Walter said, as Bob and I gaped at her. "We're just running an unscheduled inspection of the finalists' meters to make sure everything's copacetic. No need for the pepper spray. Or mace. Or whatever you've got there."

"You were right the first time." Margot put the little bottle into her pocket. "You scared me."

"Likewise, ma'am," Walter replied with a chuckle.

"You're not going to find any cable splices or whatever at my house. I'm a very capable watchdog." She hesitated. "I mean in reference to a Doberman. *Not* to your ecology group, World's Watchdogs."

"So I gathered."

"Everything checks out fine," Jones said to Walter.

Walter grinned at me. "Hi, Erin." He feigned wiping sweat from his brow. "This is just not my day for stealth. Second time in one day."

"Did you have trouble at Burke's house?" I asked.

"No, but I sure did at Mr. Campesio's. Scared me so bad I decided to save Burke's house for later. Campesio came popping out at me, wearing this guerrilla-warfare outfit. I half expected him to shoot me on the spot."

"Not with me there, he wouldn't," Jones immediately stated.

"Oh, right," Walter said amiably. "Forgot I was traveling with a security officer. It's like having my own bodyguard."

"You got it," Jones said, puffing out his chest.

Walter rolled his eyes and gave me a wink. I'm sure we all noticed that Bob hadn't exactly leapt in front of Walter, prepared to take a shot of pepper spray for him from Margot.

Margot lifted a sculpted eyebrow. "In *my* case, you should have knocked on the door. I don't appreciate surprises."

"Have you already told them about Jeremy?" I asked her, pretending it was an innocent question.

"Erin!" Margot snarled.

"Yeah, she did," Walter quickly replied. "We talked to Mr. Greene last night. He admitted he was the one who hooked up the power line. Said it was all his own idea. It made sense," Walter added with a shrug.

"And it fit the evidence," Bob said. "It explained why the only place on the power cable where Ms. Troy's fingerprints were found was right where it hooked into the box . . . not where the power lines were coupled together."

"You were trying to unhook the line," Walter asked her gently, "weren't you, Ms. Troy?"

"Without risking electrocution, yes," she said. "And unless Burke or Darren has been tampering with *my* lines, you're not going to find anything wrong here."

"Good thing," Walter said.

"As long as we're all here," Margot said, lifting her

chin, "just tell me my status now. Have I been disqualified?"

"No, Ms. Troy. We discussed this with management at Earth Love first thing this morning, and we're convinced that Jeremy acted alone. You've been absolved. As has Burke Stratton, and, of course, Darren Campesio."

"That's great, but..." I hesitated as Margot's piercing gaze shifted toward me. "Sorry, Margot, but isn't there also a rule about getting disqualified if you willfully ignore knowledge of rule-breaking by another party?"

"She didn't," Walter quickly interjected. "Mr. Sullivan wasn't the first I'd heard from yesterday regarding this matter. Ms. Troy beat him to it. She called me right after the memorial service."

"I'd only just found out myself two days ago, when Jeremy came to me privately and confessed. I said I'd give him some time to work things out for himself, but yesterday, when he'd still done nothing, I finally took matters into my own hands."

"Coincidentally, right when Sullivan had found the pirated power line?" I asked her as gently as I could.

"Coincidences *do* happen, Erin," she replied in a haughty voice.

"One piece of important information that should make you both happy," Walter said, "is that I'm nearly done. Just have to check to make sure all my *i*'s are dotted and my *t*'s are crossed, and I'll be ready to make my final decision. Monday or Tuesday at the latest."

"That's wonderful," Margot said, finally boasting a sincere-looking smile. "I can't tell you how much I'll enjoy having this whole contest ordeal come to an end."

"Yeah," Walter said, chuckling again "I think we're safe in saying that goes for all of us."

On Monday morning, Sullivan and I pulled into Burke's driveway for a scheduled meeting. "I just wish I could figure out how Margot knew I'd discovered the bogus power line," Sullivan grumbled. After my phone call on Saturday morning, we hadn't spoken again all weekend, but during our drive I'd filled him in on every last detail of my conversation with Margot.

"Maybe she paid someone to keep an eye on Burke's house. In any case, that wasn't the part that bothers me. It's that Jeremy hooked the splice up in the first place."

He said nothing. I knew I'd given him that reply at least twice. We made our way to Burke's door, and Sullivan rang the doorbell.

After waiting a reasonable period, he knocked and again pushed the doorbell button. Sullivan said, "He's not here."

"We'd better check the garage," I muttered, already heading around the house to peer through the window in the door by the backyard. "He's never late for an appointment."

Sullivan followed in my footsteps. Just as I rounded the corner, I froze. Some twenty feet ahead of me, I saw what looked for all the world like a man lying prostrate on the ground. He wore an Elmer Fudd hunter's cap.

Sullivan pulled up short, followed my gaze, and muttered a curse under his breath. An instant later, he was running toward the body. I followed, cringing.

Sullivan knelt beside Walter Emory's lifeless body. His clothing was drenched in bright crimson. There were two bullet holes in his jacket.

chapter 14

Steve checked *Walter's body frantically for vital signs* as a wave of sorrow and despair washed over me. Though I knew it was too late, I dropped to my knees, grabbed Walter's lifeless hand, and cried, "Walter?!"

"He's dead," Steve said quietly.

I released my grip and got to my feet. "What is going on?! Why is Walter even here? On Saturday he said that he'd nearly completed his judging."

"I'm calling nine-one-one," Steve said, already punching the numbers into his cell phone.

Snow was beginning to fall. The crystalline white flakes were starting to land on Walter's face. I couldn't stand the sight; it seemed inhuman and degrading to leave him in the elements like this. Sullivan must have shared my reaction, because even as he solemnly spoke to the dispatcher—reporting a murder and giving the address—he was removing his coat.

"Wait," I said. "There's a blanket in the van. I'll get it."

He nodded, and I dashed to the van, eager to get away for even a few seconds to clear my head. The instant the macabre scene was out of sight behind Burke's house, a sense of bitter rage overtook me. In the space of two weeks, Sullivan had lost his mentor, and now Walter Emory, an eminently decent human being, was dead, too. I wanted to throw a tantrum and rail about the unfairness of it all.

I threw open the back door to the van, grabbed the navy blue fleece blanket, and slammed the door shut. I turned and tried to take a few slow, deep breaths, willing myself not to fall apart.

A car was parked across the street. It looked just like Burke's forest green hybrid. The vehicle was facing the wrong direction and partially in the ditch.

I took a step toward the car, then remembered that Sullivan was waiting for the blanket. I strode back to him. The snow was already starting to accumulate. This was the Colorado champagne powder that was a skier's delight. Right now, though, it just felt like so much salt, pouring onto an open wound.

Sullivan shook his head at me and lowered his cell phone. "The dispatcher told me we shouldn't drape anything over Walter. We'd be lousing up the evidence."

"So we're just supposed to leave him like this? Getting covered in snow like a . . . park bench?"

Sullivan gave me a defeated shrug, listened to his phone for a moment, then explained to the dispatcher that we hadn't entered the house and couldn't say for certain whether or not it was vacant.

When he paused, I told him, "I'll be out front." I tossed the blanket back into the van and stared across the street. The vehicle was still there. My heart was pounding as I approached the car. Was Burke the second victim? My feet seemed to be moving of their own accord, bringing me to the car window against my will.

It was indeed Burke's Toyota.

His car was far enough off the side of the road that Sullivan and I must have driven past without even seeing it. Burke sat behind the wheel, motionless.

"Burke?" My heart was in my throat. He didn't answer.

With the various patterns of shadow and light on the windshield, I couldn't see if Burke's eyes were open or shut. He certainly appeared to be unharmed, though. As I started around the car to the driver-side door, I could see that he was alive. He was pale, with dots of perspiration on his brow. He was gripping his steering wheel hard with both hands, and his engine was turned off.

He looked at me for a moment, turned the key in the ignition to activate the power, then rolled down the window. "Did you call the police?" he asked.

"Sullivan's on the phone now with nine-one-one. What on earth are you doing, Burke?" I had to consciously keep my voice below the level of a shriek.

"I don't know. I . . . kind of panicked."

"When?"

"When I found Walter's body. In my backyard."

Again, I willed my voice to stay reasonably calm, although I wanted to grab the man by his lapels. "So you found him dead, and you didn't call the police?"

He shook his head. "I was going to run away. All I could think was: I've got to get out of here! I mean, I couldn't believe it! This is such a nightmare. A second murder. This time at my own house!"

"But if you're innocent, nothing makes you look guilty faster than running."

"Worked out okay for O.J. Simpson."

"You're not a celebrity."

He searched my eyes, his own nearly bulging out of their sockets. "Erin. I'm screwed. The police are going to assume I did this! I know I'm still tops on their list for Thayers's murder."

"Was anybody else here? Do you have an alibi?"

"No."

"Did you see anyone? Hear any cars in your driveway? Anything?"

He shook his head. "I thought I heard the doorbell while I was in the shower. But when I shut off the water, it was quiet. I figured I must have been hearing things. Then I heard a bang a minute or two later. I assumed it was someone's old pickup truck backfiring."

"When did you spot Walter Emory?"

"Um, I happened to look out my back door. In the kitchen." He still seemed to be out of sorts and was struggling to concentrate. "When I came downstairs. I thought someone was lying in my backyard. And then I started to put things together... and I realized that had been a gunshot earlier. I ran out and tried to do CPR on him, but it was too late. That's when, I dunno, I just... went a little nuts. I got into my car and started to head out of town. Then I got ahold of myself and came back. But this is as far as I could force myself to come. Erin, they're going to arrest me on the spot."

The distant sound of sirens was growing louder. "That's the police. They'll be here any second. You've got to come back with me to the house. Right now! Tell them the whole story."

"They'll arrest me!"

"Burke. You have no choice but to take that chance."

His eyes were vacant, his face and his lips pale. He still wasn't budging from his car. The sirens sounded like they were just around the bend. He stared through the windshield with a glassy expression.

"Look at me, Burke. You've got to come with me now and explain things to the police."

He nodded numbly and emerged from his car. "This has been the worst nightmare. Why does this keep happening?"

I had no answers for him. Two black-and-white police cars pulled into Burke's driveway just as we were making our way up his walkway. A pair of officers emerged from each car, and we were promptly ordered: "Hold it right there!"

While Burke explained that this was his house and that he'd discovered the body in his backyard, a third vehicle, a tan four-door sedan, pulled in and parked at the base of the driveway. I gritted my teeth at the sight of the driver—Detective O'Reilly. He was my least-favorite officer. He glowered at me as if to make certain I knew that *I* was his least-favorite Crestview citizen. And to think that Sullivan had the ridiculous notion that O'Reilly had a crush on me!

He drew a steady bead on me. "Miss Gilbert."

"Detective O'Reilly."

"Come with me," he ordered, and pulled me away from Burke, marching me through the freshly fallen snow in the front yard. "Sergeant Holcombe," he called to the closest policeman. "Keep an eye on her. I'll question her myself in a few minutes."

O'Reilly and the three remaining uniformed officers spoke to Burke. I could only hear snippets of the conversation. Understandably, they were taking tremendous exception to his decision to bolt without calling them. I waited, shivering in the cold. At length, O'Reilly ordered one of the others to come with him to the backyard to see what Sullivan had to say, and for two other officers to take Burke to the station house and get his statement.

That left just me and the officer who'd been assigned to watch me in the front yard. He was obviously a body builder—his uniform seemed ready to burst at the seams, à la Hulk Hogan. After a few minutes of silence he said, "This was a shooting death?"

"Yes. Of someone I knew. He was judging this eco-built home of my client for a contest."

"Hnnh," he muttered, then we fell into a silence again. Finally, O'Reilly returned. He was talking on his radio. With a jerk of his chin, O'Reilly indicated that the other officer should go to the backyard.

O'Reilly completed his radio conversation and sauntered over to me. "What does this make now, Miss Gilbert?" he asked. "Three, four times someone's been murdered at your client's house? If things didn't always manage to shake out otherwise, I'd swear you were a serial killer. I don't even know what to say to you at this point."

It felt humiliating to have to endure his remarks. "You

usually don't *say* all that much to me. You ask me questions and act as if my every answer is a lie. You make me feel as though it was *my* fault for being the one to find some poor person has been murdered. Well, I'm not asking for any of this to happen! What am I supposed to do?"

"Have you considered relocating to Denver?"

"No. Have you considered switching to the Denver police department?"

He glared at me. "It *has* crossed my mind of late, yes."

I said nothing.

"Let's proceed," he commanded. "Take me through your morning, till the time you arrived. And then be sure and explain precisely why, with a dead body splayed in front of you, you decided on your own to go traipsing down the road toward Stratton's car and speak with him about the murder."

"It wasn't like that!" My knees were shaking and I dearly wanted to sit down someplace before they buckled.

"Like what?"

"Like I decided to take a little stroll and have a chat with my client! When I first went up to the car, I wasn't even sure if he was dead or alive! He was scared and didn't know what to do, so I convinced him to come back with me and talk to you people!"

"You're doing this backwards, Miss Gilbert. Let's get to that chronologically. *Then* you can offer up all your excuses for talking to our prime suspect before we had the chance to interrogate him ourselves. All right?"

"Is there any way I can request a different detective to question me?"

"Sure. You can request it. Won't do any good, though."

"Are you this snide and nasty all the time, or just when you're on the job?"

"Nah. Only when I'm working. Being around murderers and other criminals tends to bring out the worst in me." He waited a moment, sighed, then said gently, "Let's go sit in my car. You look about ready to collapse."

A couple of hours later, Steve and I were finally allowed to leave. We promptly got into an argument regarding Burke's innocence. "Okay, Sullivan," I finally told him. "I admit Burke's behavior today was really bizarre. Even though he knew he'd be accused, he should have contacted the police immediately."

"Right."

"But... that's just it. This is all so incriminating, I have to think he's telling the truth."

"Either that, or he somehow found himself with no options and grew desperate. He killed Walter after finding out that Walter uncovered the evidence that was going to convict him of Richard's murder. Then he concocted this whole story once he realized he wasn't going to be able to escape."

"Then why stay in his car? Why not return home and act shocked at our having discovered Walter's body in his backyard?"

"I don't know. I'm not a killer. I can't begin to imagine a killer's thought patterns."

"You don't know that he *is* a killer! Just last Friday, you admitted you had some doubts whether or not he was guilty. We need to presume his innocence here," I stated firmly.

"Why?" Sullivan asked, smacking the steering wheel

with his hand for emphasis. "We're not jury members. I think we should presume that we'll live longer if we stay the hell away from Burke Stratton!"

"In other words, you've changed your mind about gleaning inside information from Burke that might help the police to convict Richard's killer."

Sullivan said nothing, but his jaw muscles were working overtime. Finally he replied, "No. But we're watching each other's backs really carefully from here on out. Neither of us ever comes into this neighborhood without the other."

"I can live with that."

"I sure as hell *hope* so," he replied.

The next day, Burke called my cell phone. "Well," he said, "at least I haven't been arrested yet. But it's obviously just a matter of time. Someone's framing me so well that *I* half suspect I'm guilty, even though I'm the one person I know for a fact is innocent!"

"Hang in there," I muttered, not knowing what else to say.

"I need help. I can't just sit back and assume the police are going to sort out the truth. They're going to go with the simplest scenario. And that's with me as the killer!"

I winced at the wording and held my tongue. Hadn't Linda Delgardio just recently said something about the simplest answers usually being the correct ones?

"Do you know of any great private investigators in Crestview?"

"No, I'm sorry, I don't."

"I'll...look in the yellow pages." He paused. "Are you

coming to Earth Love this afternoon?" When I hesitated, confused, he continued, "They're holding a meeting for the finalists at four P.M. Undoubtedly to inform us that the contest has been canceled."

"Nobody notified me about the meeting, and I—"

"Please come, Erin. I'm going to be treated like a pariah, and I'd really like to know at least one person is there who's on my side."

"Sullivan and I have a client appointment. But we'll try our best to reschedule. I'll meet you there, if I can swing it."

"This competition has become totally bogus," Darren grumbled. He and I were the first to arrive for the meeting at Earth Love, and we were waiting in a conference room at their headquarters. "First off, nobody is going to have such a death wish that they'd be willing to become the new judge. And even if they do, it's an unfair competition because the judges keep dying!"

I gave him my most withering stare. I'd developed an intense dislike for Darren and could all too easily envision him as a crackpot capable of murdering two men. "This *has* been a terrific inconvenience to all of us," I said dryly. "It was really inconsiderate of both Richard and Walter."

"I didn't mean to sound heartless."

Intent on ignoring him, I scanned the hallway through the glass wall. Maybe I could excuse myself and track down the receptionist; she'd shown us in and then promptly left, muttering something about a coffee cart. The same pair of executives who'd conferred with Walter at Burke's hearing had also left, saying they'd return in a few minutes. I smiled as Sullivan neared, ushered in by a second receptionist.

"In any case," Darren continued, "Margot Troy and I should just throw in the towel at this point."

"You think Burke will win?" I asked just as Sullivan entered the room.

"Of course. He has an emotional advantage because he's been implicated, so the new judge will be scared to pick anyone else."

Sullivan said, "Hey, Gilbert. I didn't miss everything again, did I?"

"No, we're the first ones here."

"Earth Love's running of this meeting is a disorganized mess," Darren added. "Not exactly big news, right?" He cupped his hands over his mouth and cried sarcastically, "Stop the presses!"

Sullivan's posture stiffened beside me, and I silently willed: Go ahead, Sullivan. Pop Darren one, right in his lantern jaw.

Burke arrived next. His eyes were bloodshot, and his blond hair had a cowlick that stuck straight up like the flag on a mailbox.

"I'm grateful you're both here," Burke said. "Thank you."

"It was the least we could do," I replied, just as Sullivan was muttering, "No problem."

"I half expected to read in today's headline you were in jail," Darren said to Burke.

Burke stared at him with empty, exhausted eyes. "I'm the police's chief suspect. And I didn't do it. I'm innocent."

"Good luck with that," Darren said.

"Your sympathy is overwhelming," Burke growled.

Darren shrugged. "Hey. It's not like you're the only one the police are investigating."

"You, too?"

He nodded grimly. "Let's just say that they don't take kindly to the fact that my Magnum is missing from my gun collection."

"You've got a gun collection?" Sullivan asked him, just as the harried receptionist returned, pushing a cart containing a coffee urn, a pitcher of water, and a box of sugar cookies.

"Got my own shooting range, in the back room," Darren continued proudly. "One of the advantages of having an underground house." He glared at Burke. "Apparently, though, I've got to do a better job of keeping the place locked up when I'm not home."

"The gun wasn't stolen at the open house, was it?" I asked. Maybe the thief had stolen both the gun and the gold paint at roughly the same time.

Darren shook his head. "On the following Monday. I had everything locked in the glass case through the weekend. Though I sure wish now I hadn't let half of Crestview see that I own firearms. I'd figured I could show them off without having some bleeding-heart liberal contest judge see 'em. The finalist judge wasn't supposed to *attend* the open houses, you know. Not that it stopped Richard Thayers."

"He was there?" I asked in alarm.

"Yes. As I told the police," he answered, nodding. "Course, I never saw him come inside, just spotted him over by the pond."

"That must have been when he discovered that illegal cable my idiotic architect ran!" Burke exclaimed.

A full battalion of Earth Love executives, from what

looked like the CEO down to first-level managers, swept into the room, Margot Troy in their midst. She took a seat across from Burke. Her fingers were so fidgety that they looked like spider legs. The two female managers sat down as well, taking all of the remaining seats in the room and forcing the three men to remain standing.

One of the more regal-looking men, wearing a sports jacket and seated at the head of the elongated oval table, introduced himself as Preston Wilcott. He glanced at a three-by-five note card and stated, "We've decided, under these tragic circumstances, that we're going to cancel the green home contest. No winner will be declared. We will instead start a fund for outstanding ecological contributions to society. The fund will be named for both Walter Emory and Richard Thayers." He paused, scanned the crowd's faces, then continued, "We deeply regret the events that have transpired and our inevitable decision to cancel the contest. All of us at Earth Love recognize the considerable effort that each of you has—"

"Please, let's not be too hasty," Margot interrupted. "I believe I have a suggestion that will fill everyone's needs."

Mr. Wilcott peered over his reading glasses at her. "I hardly think that's possible at this juncture, Ms. Troy. The loss of two colleagues can never be recompensed."

"No, of course not. But there is one person, a local celebrity, who can restore the dignity and stature to this contest that it so richly deserves."

"A celebrity?" he repeated.

"Yes. We are fortunate to have a strong connection to a TV host whose show specializes in homes and lifestyles."

Uh-oh. I knew exactly what was coming next, and it was a terrible idea. Margot grinned at me, and I shook my head violently at her. She looked puzzled for a moment, but then returned her gaze to Mr. Wilcott and announced, "I propose that we ask Audrey Munroe, of *Domestic Bliss with Audrey Munroe* on Channel Four, to judge the Earth Love green home contest."

"I'd like to go on record saying I'm opposed to that idea," I promptly interjected. Margot glared at me, and I glared right back at her.

Mr. Wilcott allowed everyone to discuss the idea for several minutes, at which time Sullivan and I both said that we could be putting Audrey Munroe in danger—a notion that Margot, Darren, and a couple of employees countered by stating that there was no harm in asking Audrey, who could simply decline if she felt in any way jeopardized.

At length, Wilcott took a quick straw poll of his employees in the room, which turned out to be unanimous in Audrey's favor. He sighed and stared into space for what felt like several minutes. Finally, he said, "To desert the contest feels like an admission of Earth Love's culpability for two murders. That is abjectly unfair. Furthermore, if we complete the contest successfully, we might be able to spare not just ourselves but the very *concept* of green design from becoming the butt of late-night talk show jokes. Both Richard Thayers and Walter Emory devoted their careers to the noble cause of saving our planet. Regrettably, it seems they've also sacrificed their lives to that cause. They deserve better than to become a punch line for their efforts. So, I'm willing to continue the contest *only* if Ms. Munroe agrees to be the judge. Otherwise..."

"Then that's what will happen," Margot stated firmly. "I'll convince her." She lifted her chin. "We've met more than once at charity functions," she added, giving me a sideways glance, "and *she* is a wonderful, generous person."

"All right, then. Let's adjourn. Please ask Ms. Munroe to contact me personally. Assuming she's amenable, we'll attempt to carry on."

"Thank you, Mr. Wilcott."

He gave her a thin smile, weariness and sorrow weighing heavily on his features. The Earth Love employees left en masse.

Margot promptly turned to me and hissed, "Once again, Erin, you disappoint me." She swept from the room.

Burke grimaced as he watched her. Then he shook his head and gave me a sympathetic smile. "Typical Margot self-centeredness. That's the reason I recognized early on that the two of us were a bad match."

Darren guffawed. "You just don't know how to handle ladies with money, my friend." He winked, then left, calling, "Ms. Troy! Wait up. Let me get that door for you!"

Exhausted and discouraged, I arrived at home a couple of hours later. I was eager to curl up on my favorite sofa with Hildi and shake off the stress of the day.

Hildi promptly greeted me with a rub against my legs when I stepped into the parlor. I swept her up and cuddled her, just as Audrey entered the room from the dining room-cum-temporary kitchen.

"Erin, you're never going to believe what I've just decided to do," she said with a huge smile on her face.

I must have unconsciously squeezed Hildi, because she hissed and scampered from my arms. "Please don't tell me you're the new judge of Earth Love's contest."

"I'm the new judge!" She arched an eyebrow and gave me a disapproving once-over, apparently having gathered the tenor of my last statement. "Aren't you going to thank me?"

"Why would I be thankful? You're deliberately putting yourself in harm's way! Did you forget all about my telling you that the first two judges were murdered, for heaven's sake?"

"How many times have I asked you to keep yourself out of danger, but you haven't listened? This is very hypocritical of you, Erin."

"You're right. I'm a hypocrite. Be that as it may, you really, really need to reconsider."

"I've thought this through enough times already. I told them that come hell or high water, I was only going to spend the remainder of this week on the contest. I'm simply going to pick up right where their last judge left off."

"And by that you mean shot dead on somebody's lawn?"

"Of course not! I'm not in any danger. The fact that two contest judges have died doesn't mean that they were killed *because* they were judges. The previous victims had prior relationships with each other and with the finalists. I don't. And while I certainly am correctly considered an environmentalist and a conservationist, those are far from my most noted characteristics."

"Which would be more along the order of...oh, I don't know. Maybe rashness and stubbornness."

Ignoring me, she continued, "The contest will be over once and for all by this Saturday. I assure you, Erin, I do not have a death wish. I simply believe in what Earth Love is trying to do for the world, and I want to help them accomplish their goals. My biggest fear is just that I'll be partial and unable to judge your client's house as harshly as everyone else's. But when I thought about it more, I realized I'm up to the task. *You* will understand, after all, that I absolutely cannot show favoritism. Won't you, Erin?"

"I don't know," I snapped, aware that I was sounding a bit like a petulant brat, but not caring. "I wasn't listening. Just like *you* haven't been listening to *me*."

"Pardon, Erin?" She winked. "My thoughts must have wandered. I'm afraid I didn't hear a word you just said."

chapter 15

"An old Mexican proverb (although I could be wrong about its derivation) warns us that, unless you know where you've been, you can't possibly know where you're going. Perhaps that's why we sometimes feel so lost."

—Audrey Munroe

DOMESTIC BLISS

"You know what bothers me, Erin?" Audrey asked, breaking the silence that had only recently blessed us as I settled into my book and she had momentarily taken up her latest project—a quilt for her second grandchild.

"Is there only one answer to your question?" I asked, a little testy, not wanting to leave the company of my book's characters.

"We no longer treasure anything."

Uh-oh. *That*, if I'd ever heard one, was a precursor for one of Audrey's patented rants. I'd be lucky to get back to my reading within the hour. Time for preemptive measures. "That's not true. I treasure your friendship. And I treasure this book that I'm reading." Laying it on thick, I continued,

"Most of all, I treasure these quiet evenings at home. They're so restorative for me that, without them, I couldn't possibly keep going during hard times. Such as the day I had today, when I was feeling so down in the dumps from Walter's death, coming so soon after Richard's. So thank you, Audrey, for this gift of refuge and respite that you've given me."

"I mean in general," she replied, not batting an eye at my obsequious speech. "As a society. We've turned ourselves into a nation of disposables. Disposable income. Disposable toilet-bowl brushes. Disposable relationships. When does it end?"

"That's a question I was just now asking myself," I muttered, cradling the book in my hands.

"Take this quilt, for example. I'm making it for my second grandchild's crib. And every single scrap of cloth that's going into it has particular relevance for the baby. Each piece of fabric was worn by one of the baby's relatives."

"That's sweet."

"More importantly, it's an heirloom in the making. How can we hope to teach our culture to treasure its ancestry if we don't teach the new members of our own families to treasure their grandparents and great-grandparents?"

"That's an excellent point, Audrey, although I hope you were teaching your sons to treasure *their* grandparents. Back before you became one yourself."

"I'm not saying that mothers should teach their daughters and sons how to cross-stitch their family tree, mind you." I reluctantly shut my book, realizing that when she was willing to ignore my snide remarks, there was no stopping her. "Although, come to think of it, that's an excellent idea to present in a future broadcast. There's been a resurgence of sewing circles, you know. Probably because we *have* lost so much of our heritage lately. I'm going to suggest to my audience that they consider introducing some of the classics of the past— cross-stitched family trees that are handed down to the next generation, along with the skills to continue them. Coiled rag rugs, made from outgrown hand-me-downs. And, of course, quilts like this one."

As she spoke, she spread out her patchwork fabric, and a pink petal on her cornflower pattern caught my eye. I leaned forward. "Hey. That pink fabric looks familiar. This isn't from my pink blouse, is it? I've been missing that blouse for months now!"

"Didn't I tell you about that?" Audrey asked, blushing to match the hue of the pirated fabric. "I had an accident involving some India ink when I was working on Japanese painting techniques."

"And how did *my* blouse get involved?"

"I don't recall the precise sequence of events. But it brings to mind something I've been meaning to tell you for a while now." She looked impishly at me. "Pink isn't really one of your colors, Erin."

"Audrey!"

"I'll replace the blouse, the next time we go shopping. But you really should look at a deeper red. Magenta, maybe."

"Speaking of fabric stains," I snapped, "isn't this going to be a problematic baby gift? Handmade quilts aren't really all that washable, are they? Don't they need to be hand washed?"

"Well, yes, but—"

"And I'm sure you don't think a new mom has time to do frequent hand washings, do you? I mean, you know a baby's blanket is only going to go for two or three days tops between washings. That's going to cause a whole lot of wear and tear on all of those heirloom fabrics of yours."

"Not to mention on your pink blouse," she said under her breath.

"It's not as if your mother's wedding dress, for example, was intended to be washed twenty or thirty times inside of two months."

"Good point. Fortunately, however, I'm way ahead of you. Quilts of this size make wonderful wall hangings for a baby's room. My son and his wife can wrap little Audrey in it when they're coming home from the hospital. Then they can capture the moment in photographs and frame some of them. Those photographs, along with the quilt itself, will make a wonderful matched set to hang on a wall of the nursery. It will look lovely. And, many years from now, when Audrey is old enough to appreciate some family history, she will have a memento. One which can be handed down through the ages. Which is why, incidentally, I'm also creating a chart that lists where each piece of fabric comes from. Including your pink blouse, from her auntie Erin."

I felt touched and said, "It's amazing that you can recall the source of that many different fabric swatches."

"Yes, well...I'm taking creative license whenever necessary." She pointed at a particular section of her quilt. "This parallelogram is from a striped shirt that somehow wound up in a lost-and-found basket in my laundry room when the boys were little. But it now belonged to Cousin Jason, twice removed."

"Actually, I take back everything I said, Audrey. A baby blanket quilt is a lovely idea. In fact, I hope you're making one of those for your grandson Colin, as well."

"I am indeed." She went back to her stitching, but then paused and looked at me. "You look a little tired. I suppose I should quit talking and leave you to your reading."

"Thanks." I opened my book to the bookmark.

"An Agatha Christie?"

"Yes."

She craned her neck and studied the cover. "I read that one."

"Yes, I know. I borrowed it from you."

"Is there anything new happening between you and Steve?"

I gritted my teeth. "Audrey, please! Do I have to go to my room in order to read in peace?"

She glared at me, but mimed locking her lips with a key and didn't answer. Her silence lasted all of thirty seconds, till she grumbled, "The butler did it, by the way."

"I'm sure the murder was well justified," I retorted, knowing she was kidding. "He was probably provoked by someone giving away the ending to the book he was reading."

chapter 16

Around mid-morning the following day, Burke's voice rang out over the answering machine: "You two are going to want to see Asia's exterior decorating as soon as possible." Sullivan had pressed the message button in my presence, so we heard his gloomy tone simultaneously.

"Come to think of it," I said, "it's been a week since Asia gave Burke and Darren a week's notice to take down their windmills, or else. She must have gone ahead and hung those plastic flamingos in the trees that border their joint property line, like she said she would."

"Along with all of those hundreds of noisy wind chimes."

The image of plastic flamingos in evergreens was a much-needed touch of silliness, and I smiled. Sullivan was also grinning as we caught each other's gaze. "I wonder if she's put plastic penguins on ice skates on the pond, too. That would be a nice finishing touch."

"We shouldn't laugh," Sullivan said, although he was chuckling as he spoke.

"No, we shouldn't. Burke's obviously upset."

"Poor guy," Sullivan said sarcastically, clearly enjoying the notion of Burke's discomfiture.

"I'm sure he's worried that the ugly lawn and tree ornaments so close to his house will have an adverse affect on the contest judge."

"On *Audrey*, you mean," Sullivan said. "Or did you manage to talk her out of it last night?"

"I wish. I think she's secretly too enraptured at the thought of helping me to ferret out the killer to say no. Plus I'm sure it was immensely flattering to her to be singled out as the one and only person who could help keep the contest going."

"Low self-esteem has never seemed to be an issue with Audrey."

"Don't make snide remarks about Audrey!"

"Sorry, but it's true."

"I know, but that doesn't mean it's all right to say so."

Sullivan glanced at his watch. "We've got some free time before our next appointment. Want to head over there right now?"

"You sound almost cheerful. I thought you were positive Burke was a murderer."

"He's a smart man...a doctor. Doesn't make sense

he'd be so stupid as to shoot Walter in his own backyard. So, yeah, some of my doubts have returned."

"Good, because I'm still positive he's innocent. Let's go see what Ms. Crabapple has done to him."

Asia had allowed the front yard's property line to remain undisturbed. Burke led us to the side yard, which bordered the pond, where the three of us stood staring at Burke's property in unabashed awe. The only thing to be said for the riot of bright, cheap plastic excess was that it was infinitely more pleasant than the crime-scene tape that had cordoned off Burke's *back*yard two days ago.

"Kind of like being transported to a tourist trap in Florida," Burke said, "without our snow and ice, that is."

"More like what the artist Christo would do if someone dared him to work with only tacky toys instead of brightly colored fabric," I said. "Or maybe a yard sale at a dollar store."

Between her line of trees and her three-rail fence, Asia had installed what looked like the type of mesh that golf courses used on their driving ranges. Hers was twelve feet high and extended from the front post of her side yard to the pond. A second mesh began at the other side of the pond and ran to the back corner of the fence. She hadn't stopped at flamingos and wind chimes, although she'd used plenty of those. Her rule of thumb seemed to be that if it was cheap, garishly colored, and plastic, it was on her fence. She'd stuck a toilet bowl brush on the mesh, along with combs, an inflatable rooster, a backscratcher, horseshoes, an inflatable Santa with at least four of his reindeer, and several oversized bubble wands. Virtually every square inch had something ugly and gaudy hanging from it.

"She's trying to get your goat by displaying so many nonrecyclable plastic products," Sullivan surmised, stating the obvious.

"And she complains about my windmill ruining her view," Burke said. "This is one hell of an eyesore, for her, too."

"Cutting off her nose to spite her face," Sullivan agreed.

"Her pond decorations are almost pretty," I remarked quietly. Both men glared at me. "Well, they are. It's kind of like a floating conga line of bath toys." She had strung all sorts of children's floating devices together, from neon green frogs to electric blue dinosaurs. Together they formed a straight line atop the iced-over pond, and appeared to delineate the halfway point between the two properties.

"She didn't secure it very well," Sullivan said. "She just used tent stakes. The next windstorm we have, that string of toys could get wrapped around some bush in the next county."

"I think it's a safety hazard," Burke said. "It's going to lure kids to try to jump onto the ice, and it won't support them. We should take the toys down, don't you think?"

Burke was obviously looking for a viable excuse to do just that, but he did have a point. "I'm going to take a closer look at the pond," I said.

I made my way down the slight incline and started walking along the water's edge toward Asia's house. Something caught my eye in the shallow water ahead of me, about halfway to the starting point of Asia's colorful contraption.

"That's odd," I said over my shoulder. "There's something in the water—between the ice and the bank."

"Probably a dead carp," Burke retorted.

It didn't look like a fish to me; it was dark and shiny and metallic-looking. My heart started to race. I found a long stick. After a few failed attempts, I managed to snag the object in the pond and drag it to the shore. By then both Burke and Sullivan had joined me and could see it, too.

"My god," Sullivan said.

Sullivan grabbed it with his gloved hand as Burke watched, looking horrified. It was a handgun.

The police finally allowed Sullivan and me to leave Burke's by the time I'd rescheduled all of my client appointments. In less than an hour, Audrey would have me chauffeur her to the finalists' homes. Sullivan and I had agreed that, if there was even a remote chance that my presence might help to keep Audrey safe and sound, my time would be well spent.

Matthew Hayes called and asked me to stop by his store at my convenience. Sullivan was with a client in a neighboring town, so I made the short drive to Matthew's store and found a space. His siding looked especially pretty in the bright sunlight. It was a chalky blue-green, like the copper patina of the Statue of Liberty.

Inside, a young man with long hair and droopy eyelids greeted me with a lazy, "Hey, how goes it?" When I asked for Matthew, he said, "Oh, yeah. He's in the workshop. Go on back." I thanked him and headed through a tangerine-colored door. There was a marked drop in temperature between the two spaces, but for me, the scent of fresh-cut lumber was made all the more delightful by the crisp air.

I found Matthew using a lathe, carving what appeared to be a pedestal for a table out of a six-by-six piece of yellow oak. As I approached, he spotted me, smiled, and shut off the motor, the spinning piece of wood gradually slowing to a stop. Beneath a light coating of sawdust, he was wearing jeans, a mustard-colored T-shirt, and a black backward-facing baseball cap.

He promptly removed his safety goggles. "Morning, Erin. Wasn't expecting to see you quite so soon. You must have dropped everything and run right over here, eh? It wasn't anything urgent, you know."

"Sure, but I had some free time."

He wiped the sawdust from his hands and sturdy-looking forearms. He truly was a nice-looking guy. Too bad he was also a major jerk. "I wanted to show you the desk you ordered. It's almost good to go. Just wanted to give you the chance to inspect it before I invested a whole lot of time in the sanding and finishing work." As he led me toward the desk, he put his hand on my back, which annoyed me. "I used the boards from the local lumberyard, just like you and Dr. Stratton wanted, so I was stuck with pine. There was only so much I could do with the pine, you understand."

"Of course. But it's a lot better for the environment when materials are being processed and used all from within the same small geographic area."

"Maybe so, but it's bad for the craftsmanship. I can do wonders with mahogany."

"From the rain forest. But Burke would never have supported that. You'll just have to use a dark stain."

"One that has zero off-gassing. Yippee. Might as well

hand me a mahogany crayon. Anyways." He gestured at a desk against the wall. "Here you go."

Matthew was so arrogant and short-sighted that I wanted to hate the desk. But I couldn't. He'd made wonderful use of the knotty pine and incorporated the whorls into his overall designs. The rhomboid shape of the desk would hug the corner of Burke's bedroom. I loved the lines, the cabriole flair in the legs, the playful echo of those gentle curves in the front piece and drawers. "It's beautiful."

He shrugged, but there was no small measure of pride in his smile. "It's okay. It'll look much nicer as I continue to sand it between coats of finish. 'Course, if your client would quit obsessing about off-gassing, I could use the best varnish on the market...make this pine look like rare wood."

"Right, Matthew. You *could* do just that. But if you'd change your attitude and promote your skill at using woods from your own backyard, you'd turn a big profit by appealing to the major green contingency in this town."

"Exotic woods are what *sell*." He pointed at a lovely armoire a few feet away from us. "I can charge three times more for that piece of case furniture because nobody can get it at some 'Cheap Furniture R Us' chain store."

I walked over to the armoire and opened a drawer. "Nor could you buy this quality dovetail joinery from a discount factory."

"True, but believe me, exotics are what set my work apart from other furniture designers."

"Maybe that's because those *other* designers have a conscience."

He smirked. "You know, Erin, it's easy for you to be high and mighty. If your customer requests something that contributes to pygmy hippos dying in Botswana, you can just tell yourself: 'The customer is always right. It's his big money and his fat butt that's going to sit on it.' Meanwhile, the American furniture business is a sixty-five-billion-dollar industry, with killer international competition. As a craftsman working for myself, I'm either a cut above, or I'm cut off at the knees."

"So that's why you took it so personally when Richard Thayers called attention to things like this ivory inlay?" I asked, testing his reaction.

"Yeah. Of course I took it personally. He was threatening my livelihood! If my sales slip, I go under, and I'm out of work. Period. And those ecology groups are ruthless."

"Groups like World's Watchdogs, you mean? The one Walter Emory founded?"

"Yeah. I had a couple of run-ins with Emory. He and Richard were taking turns harassing me for a while. But it stinks that somebody offed the guy."

My vision was drawn to a chest of drawers that looked to be made out of rain forest wood. "I couldn't help but notice that this wood is merbau."

"Very good. You know your woods."

"I always recognize this deep red, gold-flecked color. But I steer my customers away from it whenever possible because of the damage its harvesting is doing to the rain forests in Indonesia."

"I got it from a legal dealer."

"Within the United States, the dealer was legit, sure," I retorted. "But it's doubtful that the original *exporter* of the lumber was legal."

He made a derisive noise. "I'll bet if your partner, Steve-o, were to present you with a diamond one of these days, you wouldn't ask about *its* exporter, or anything about its origin. More blood's been shed for diamond mining than for *conflict-wood foresting*, as World's Watchdogs calls it."

"And I'll bet if you were to have a customer ask you to surround the mirror of a dressing table with a hundred diamonds that you had to purchase yourself on the black market, you wouldn't hesitate."

"You got that right. Now, *that* is something I could make a bundle on. If you can talk one of your rich customers into buying it from me, I'll split the profit right down the middle."

I started to turn away in disgust and spotted a green label on a can on the shelf along the adjacent wall. I crossed the room to investigate. Surprised, I turned back to look at him and exclaimed, "You have one of Richard's Earth-Friendly Wood Finish products."

"Just bought them yesterday," he said with a shrug that looked like a forced attempt at indifference. "I knew you'd want to use a nontoxic product."

"There are others on the market. Why did you choose to help out Richard's business? I thought you resented his sales tactics in his class."

"It seemed like the decent thing to do, now that the guy's dead."

And buying Richard's products was an easy way to gain access to his labels, then glue one onto the can of toxic paint that Richard had been tricked into drinking.

chapter 17

Some ninety minutes later, I found myself negotiating congested traffic while driving Audrey's Mercedes. Impatient and annoyed, I snapped, "I should never have agreed to do this. I shouldn't be showing you Burke's home. It's a huge conflict of interest."

"No offense, dear, but you're just the interior designer. The architect and the creators of the products that Burke uses are much more responsible for his low energy consumption than you are."

"First off, Sullivan and I were the people who sat down with Burke and Jeremy and chose his e-rated materials. We also helped him design some of the specific features of his kitchen and bathrooms that made them so environmentally friendly and functional, such as the ventilation and exhaust systems. In the second place, you and I are obviously going to be speaking to each other as we drive between the finalists' homes, and that conversation could unconsciously affect your overall opinion."

"I'm my own person and always have been. I intend to pretend that you're simply here as my driver, and that Burke's house was designed exclusively by Steve Sullivan."

"That'd be ironic," I muttered.

"Is there a problem there?"

"Sullivan suspects Burke is the murderer."

"He does? And do you agree?"

"Not at all."

She fell silent for several seconds, then remarked, "That's probably making interactions between you two and your client awkward."

"To say the least."

"Well, then. Let's talk about something else for a while. Which of the three houses do *you* like the best?" Audrey asked.

"I'm not going to answer that!" I had to slam on the brakes and honk as the driver of an SUV tried to make a sharp turn without relinquishing her grasp on her cell phone.

We remained silent until I parked on the street beyond any view from Margot's windows. "We're here."

"This is Margot Troy's house, right?" she asked. "You're not even going to get as close as her driveway? Why are you being so paranoid?"

"To avoid an embarrassing situation."

"Oh, come join me. I'll just claim that you're acting as my bodyguard."

I shook my head. "No, Audrey. Margot's angry at me for not wanting you as contest judge. I don't want to give her any ammunition for claiming that I'm brainwashing you."

"All right, then. I'll be back as soon as I can." She started to get out, then hesitated. "When she comes to the door and sees that there's no car in her driveway, should I tell her I walked here? Or are we pretending that I'm environmentally conscious enough to have taken the bus?"

"Say that you wanted to make note of your initial reaction as you approached slowly from the street."

"Oh. Okay. That's very clever of you, Erin." She gave me a wink and headed down the driveway.

I spent the time returning phone calls on my cell and working out some designs in my head for current customers. One of our new clients had chosen Brazilian cherry hardwood floors for her remodel. We would have that gorgeous, rich wood running from the front door throughout her kitchen and dining room. In my mind's eye, however, I could see Matthew Hayes smirking at me. Brazilian cherry was hardly earth-friendly or politically correct. He had made some excellent points about how easy it was for me to merely mention green alternatives when ultimately, I had to let the customer decide.

After thirty minutes or so, Audrey returned. "Interesting woman, that Margot. She's very pushy, isn't she?" Before I had time to formulate a tactful reply, Audrey asked, "Do you think she's guilty?"

"I hope not, but I have to admit, she's close to the top of my list of suspects."

"Who's at the very top?"

"Matthew Hayes. Of M.H. Custom Furniture."

"Oh, yes. There've been some articles in the *Sentinel* about him and his politically incorrect beliefs. At least he speaks his mind and sticks to his guns."

"I guess that's a positive. Unless he *fired* one of those guns recently."

"Indeed. So where are we heading next?"

"Well, Darren Campesio and Burke Stratton are neighbors, although they both have something like ten-acre spreads."

"Good. One-stop viewing. And we can park in an actual driveway. *Burke* obviously won't mind that we're traveling together."

I waited, hoping she'd volunteer her reaction to the home she'd just seen, but she remained silent. A minute or two later she asked, "Where is Steve right now?"

"He wants to meet us at Burke's house." I glanced at the dashboard clock. "Actually, we'll arrive about twenty minutes ahead of him. So we'll go to Darren's house first."

"My. You're really timing this down to the minute."

"We're trying to keep up appearances to show Burke that we're a team. That's difficult when I'm trying to help Burke clear his name, and Sullivan's trying to trip him up into divulging some major clue that'll convict him."

"Is that the only source of conflict between you and Steve?"

"Pardon?"

"I have the feeling that something else is bothering you."

"Not really."

We lapsed into silence, probably because Audrey

didn't want to talk about Margot's house, and I didn't want to talk about Sullivan. We parked at Burke's, intending to take the path to Darren's property. Burke, however, came running up to us from his backyard. His smile looked plastered into place, his brow was dotted with perspiration, and his eyes were nothing short of panic-stricken. "Erin! Ms. Munroe! You're here early!"

I pointed with my chin at the minipath that led to the trail behind the homes. "We were going to go to Darren's first, actually, so that Steve could meet us here at four."

He gave me a peculiar look that involved a quick head shake and a grimace, then focused his attention on Audrey, grabbing her hand and panting, "It's such an honor to meet you in person, Ms. Munroe."

"Why, thank you, Dr. Stratton."

He gracefully turned their handshake into his taking her arm and pivoting, saying all the while, "There's no need to wait. You're here now, and I'm afraid you won't enjoy even a short walk at this hour. The wind's really kicking up, and the temperature is dropping."

Audrey peered at me. There was no chance that she'd missed Burke's all-too-obvious ploy to prevent her from cutting across his backyard to the footpath. I didn't know what his motive was—maybe his windmill construction had taken a bad turn, or maybe he didn't want her to see some new monstrosity that Asia had placed near the pond or along her fence.

"I can survive," she said. "I wore sensible shoes. Isn't Mr. Campesio's house just one house down from yours?"

"Yes, but the melting snow has made the path muddy and slippery in some places." Burke shot me a desperate look as it belatedly hit me that he needed my help.

"Of course," I said. "I should have thought of that my-self. Burke and I will show you his house now, and then we'll drive to Darren's. All right, Audrey?"

"Certainly. You've got possession of my car keys, after all, which they say is nine tenths of the law." She gave me the patient smile that I knew meant to step lightly. She patted Burke's hand, which was still on her arm. "Let's see this lovely home of yours, shall we, Dr. Stratton?"

"Please call me Burke," he said with a grateful smile. He was still obviously anxious about something. He began a rambling dissertation on the thickness of his external walls and the benefits of straw-bale construction. I'd heard him give this lecture countless times during the open house. Back then he'd sounded like a tour guide at a museum. Now he sounded like an amateur actor with stage fright. He botched the presentation of the foyer and living room so completely that Audrey walked straight through them with barely a glance around.

The three of us entered the kitchen. "We installed three layers of . . . I mean, triple-paned windows, with, um, with . . ." He paled and looked ready to pass out when Audrey wandered toward the glass door that faced the backyard. "Ms. Munroe? The windows over *here* have superefficient e-coatings. They're like Superman. The Superman of glass."

Audrey arched an eyebrow and held her tongue. I surreptitiously scanned the yard, but could see nothing wrong.

"But, I, uh, guess you can read about all of the, um, our choices that make, in construction, I mean, in the spec sheets that Earth Love gave you, that make this house such a green winner."

"That's true," I jumped in. "We *are* talking about the

Domestic Bliss Goddess herself, after all. Audrey, you don't need me to point out the inner door of the foyer, which serves as an air lock to reduce the air exchange as people enter and exit. Or the environmental benefits of the bamboo flooring in the living room, and the sea grass area rugs. And I'm sure you also already noticed the cork kitchen floor. You've done dozens of shows on sustainable building materials, so you know how earth-friendly those materials are. But aren't they gorgeous?"

"Yes, they are," she agreed with an appreciative smile.

"Now feast your eyes on the kitchen."

"Stunning," she replied.

"And I bet you know how environmentally sound it is to use these kitchen cabinets made from highly compacted sawdust—waste products from less responsible building practices—that are then veneered with cypress, chosen because of its sustainability and durability. The same reasoning went into selecting the concrete countertops. Burke wouldn't settle for merely reusing a granite slab from someone else's old kitchen. He's taken a waste product—fly ash—and recycled it into a new, functional, and fabulous surface. And, of course, every appliance is a modern miracle of energy efficiency." I had taken a cue from Burke and grabbed Audrey's arm, slowly leading her away from the back door. We approached everyone's favorite conversation piece—the small window built into the stucco surface of the wall, which showed the straw composition within.

"But before we allow you to inspect the kitchen at your leisure, notice the reveal here."

Audrey smiled at it and said, "Yes, that's honest-to-God straw, all right."

I did a double take at the reveal. Was it my imagination, or had the straws shifted a little? "I wanted to create a minidiorama inside the glass," I said, "with a wolf collapsing as he tried to blow it down. I thought it was whimsical, but I got voted down."

Audrey chuckled. "You know what else might have been fun? You could put a needle in it, so you'd have the proverbial needle in a—" She stopped. "Oh, wait. That's a haystack, not a straw-stack." She tapped her cheek, lost in thought. "A plastic drinking straw or two might have been humorous."

"I try to stay away from plastic products," Burke said, with his characteristic lack of humor.

As Audrey inspected every square inch of the kitchen, she was at least as inquisitive on her own as any home owner I'd spoken to at the open house. She grilled us about the large component of conservationism that went into Sullivan's and my every decision. As we continued our dry, detail-intensive tour, I couldn't find any way to momentarily shake Audrey so that Burke and I could have a private word. While Audrey was examining Burke's bookshelves in the den, Burke finally managed to whisper, "My backyard stinks to high heaven. Asia's prank, no doubt."

Sullivan arrived just then, and I promptly said, "Hi, Steve. Why don't you show Audrey the second floor? I've got a couple of questions for Burke about the sunroom."

He knew me well enough to play along. He launched into a monologue about where Burke had gotten the salvaged lumber for the stairs as they climbed to the second floor.

I had just turned to ask Burke what was going on when

he looked out a kitchen window and snarled, "There she is now." He marched out the back door, and I followed.

"Asia! What the hell have you done?"

Before she could answer, I spotted something that gave him his answer. "Look over there, Burke." I pointed at a hose starting to appear in the melting snow. The hose snaked around the pond and halfway across his yard.

"Oh, jeez! I'd just gotten home myself when you and Audrey arrived. I didn't see it." There was no spigot, but he chinked the hose to stop the water flow, making a face as he dragged it back toward Asia. "Is this a shunt from your sewer line?!" he cried.

She shrugged. "Call it a payback for your siphoning electricity off my power line."

"You want a payback, do you?"

Burke was so livid he was scaring me, but Asia merely clicked her tongue. "Oh, honestly! You're the big-deal conservationist. I'd think you'd appreciate all this free water." She shook her head. "There's just no pleasing some people."

"Appreciate it?! You seriously think I'll buy that you've done me some kind of a favor?! My house smells like a skunky swamp, thanks to you! Right when Audrey Munroe is here!"

"Oh, was that today?" Asia said, the picture of innocence. She turned her gaze to the windmill and murmured, "I'm so terribly sorry. I'd forgotten. Just as *you* seem to have forgotten all about stealing my power."

"You manipulative little—" He broke off just as he heard the door open. We both turned and saw Audrey approaching. Burke continued: "—annoying person, you."

"Burke," Audrey called, "we heard a funny noise and went downstairs. Your basement is flooding."

"Oh, my god!" Burke exclaimed, and ran inside.

"Is that her?" Asia asked. She looked at Audrey and said in an ironic monotone, "Our own local minor celebrity, right here in our little corner of the world. Why, I'm practically starstruck at the very notion."

chapter 18

urke turned off the main breaker to prevent any possibility of an electric current being carried in his floodwater, then returned to the fence and watched as Asia dragged the hose away from his property. Afterwards, Audrey and I followed him as far as the bottom step of the basement stair. There was enough ambient light from the window wells and the open door behind us to see how shallow the water was—less than an inch deep. I started to roll up my sleeves, intending to help the two men bail out the basement, but Sullivan, who'd already removed his shoes and socks and stepped into the water, said, "It's okay, Erin. This really isn't bad. Why don't you go ahead and accompany Audrey to Darren's house?"

Burke had been wearing soft-soled shoes and strode right through the water without hesitation. He was red-faced and his jaw and fists were clenched. He set his anger aside long enough to say, "That's a good idea, Erin. It was nice meeting you, Audrey. Thank you for stepping in as judge. But stepping into floodwater would be above and beyond the call of duty." He'd come as close to making a joke as I'd ever heard, but he couldn't muster any semblance of a smile to help pull it off.

"My pleasure, Dr. Stratton. We'll meet again soon. Hopefully under better, and drier, circumstances."

He nodded. "You can go, too, Steve. This won't take very long for me to clean up, and my . . . annoying neighbor has already shut off the source of the water."

"Thanks," Sullivan said, "but I've got some time. Let me give you a hand."

I started to turn, then did a double take at a crack in the foundation at the west wall. It unnerved me. Two whole sections of the wall had shifted such that one portion was indented by a full inch. Water was seeping through that seam.

Audrey was studying my features and surely must have registered my alarm. In any case, she couldn't have missed the crack in the wall, and with the home's structural problems accentuated by sewer water, Burke's chances of winning were now zilch. "Let's drive next door, shall we?" I suggested to her.

I got behind the wheel and made a show of preparing to drive away, but then announced, "Oh, gosh. There's something I need to mention to Sullivan before I go. I'll be right back."

Sullivan was waiting for me by the door and let me in before I could knock. "We need to tell Burke to get a structural engineer or soil engineer out here," I said quietly.

"Yeah. I'll tell him that. But we should also discuss this mess with Jeremy Greene. In person. I'd like to see his reaction. Burke's foundation must have the same design flaws that Richard was suing over. Jeremy should be forced to pay restitution to Richard's estate."

"Fine, but remember that—"

He held up his hand. "I know. Burke's our client. And it's his house. I'll recommend an engineer right now." He turned and headed back to the basement without waiting for my reply.

As I returned to Audrey's car, I pondered whether or not Burke's bad relationship with Asia or his defective foundation could be connected to the murders. If both Richard Thayers and, later, Walter Emory had threatened to expose Jeremy's seriously flawed designs, could Jeremy have been deluded into believing that killing both men would save his career? Certainly *Burke* now had cause to be driven into a murderous rage, but at Asia and Jeremy, not Richard or Walter.

I got back behind the wheel. Audrey was jotting some notes on her pad, which she returned to her handbag when I started the engine.

"Once again, Erin, you did a truly remarkable job on that house."

"Thank you, Audrey." I turned onto the road.

"I'm simply stating the obvious, but you're welcome. I only hope your work isn't going to go for naught."

"What do you mean?"

"Just that Dr. Stratton's house appears to have been

built on a sinkhole or something, judging by the cracks in the basement."

I winced, but if she noticed she didn't let on. She mused, "None of the questions on my score sheets ask me to rank the home's durability or its prospects in the event of a geological disaster. But clearly that's an oversight on Earth Love's part. It hardly matters how energy-efficient your refrigerator is, for example, if you've built your house on top of quicksand. I can't rave to Earth Love about Dr. Stratton's house's wonderful green design and ignore the tiny issue of the entire place *collapsing*."

"It's just one little crack." *So far.*

"So is the San Andreas fault line, but I wouldn't build my house directly on top of it."

I pulled into Darren's driveway. Her eyes widened as we swung around in his circular driveway. "Now *this* place, on the other hand, looks like it could survive a nuclear explosion."

"I've seen lots of photos, but I've never been inside, and I'm dying to see it. Mind if I tag along?"

"Of course not, my dear. *You're* the one who's been so worried about Burke's competitors crying foul."

That was back when I thought he had a good chance of winning, I thought. Before I saw Burke's basement. "I've changed my mind. Everyone was there when Margot nominated you for this job. Darren will just have to deal with it."

I let Audrey lead the way and stood slightly behind her as she used his brass doorknocker. Darren wore a big smile as he swung open the door. The smile faded a little when he saw me, but Audrey hastened to explain that we'd been carpooling and she'd asked me to join her.

He mumbled a welcome at me, but only regained his enthusiasm when he returned his gaze to Audrey. "I'm so glad you're doing this," he said to her. "Thank you for volunteering your time. I'm Darren Campesio."

"Audrey Munroe."

"I've heard about your show. I don't own a television, I'm afraid, but I'm sure I would enjoy watching you, if I could." He pulled the door shut behind me so quickly that it nearly closed on my heel. "Let me take you on the dime tour." He grabbed Audrey's arm and turned his back on me. Apparently he'd decided to handle my joining his cozy twosome by pretending not to see me. "But first, can I get you some refreshments? Tea? Juice? Coffee? Cinnamon toast?"

"No, thank you," Audrey said graciously. "Erin? Would you like anything?"

I was tempted to ask for a slice of watermelon just to be obnoxious—it would have been no more incongruous than the cinnamon toast—but I took the high road and said, "No, but thanks for offering, Darren."

He gave me a perfunctory nod, then launched into a well-rehearsed spiel about the wondrous benefits of underground living. If anything, though, the front rooms of the house were surprisingly unexceptional and had the feel of any other modest home. The furnishings were what I'd term rustic-western-cabin: plaid upholstery, lots of antlers and metal doodads shaped like caveman drawings of bears, and low clunky butcher-block tables, which, not surprisingly, Darren had made himself. The back rooms, which were actually underground, featured light tunnels, which worked with mirrors and lenses, not unlike periscopes, and looked like portholes. No room was completely shut off from sunlight, and he'd positioned mirrors wisely—although their frames were adorned with deer antlers. In my opinion, antlers as décor is a stylistic choice in which a little goes a long, long way. The loftlike upstairs, with its three bedrooms all in a row separated by two three-quarter baths, reminded me of a Motel 6 layout. In fact, I suspected he'd gotten all his artwork from one of those hotel art "no paintings over sixty dollars" sales that were periodically advertised on late-night TV.

However, tacky décor aside, his home was remarkably fuel-efficient. He heated the entire house using his wood-stove, and cooked with it as well. So little wood was required that he only needed to burn branches that he gathered from his own trees. He had an outstanding water collection system, which used charcoal filters of his own design. The energy from his windmill and his solar panels heated a hot-water tank and was stored in fuel cells to provide him with electricity year-round. He had a garden in the courtyard in front of his house where he grew and canned enough fruits and vegetables for him "to live off of forever, if I had to!" (He was a vegetarian because it was "better for the ecology.") His home was one hundred percent self-sustaining. Ugly, yes, but very green. Not unlike an avocado kitchen from the seventies.

"I'm impressed," Audrey acknowledged as Darren returned us to the front door at the end of the tour.

"Thought you would be," he said with a wink. "Do you have any questions?"

"I do," I said immediately. "Where is this shooting gallery of yours? Is that through the one door you didn't open, off your den?"

"Er, yes."

"I'd like to see that room, if I may," Audrey stated.

"Ah, well, that room isn't really...in good viewing shape."

"Oh, I can overlook a little dust and clutter, or what have you," Audrey replied. When he gave no response, merely shifting his weight from foot to foot, she added, "I'm under a directive to inspect all rooms, Darren."

"Well, then. We can't have you ignore a directive, now, can we?"

He ushered us back into the den, which was a more cavelike version of the same mountain-man motif. He removed a small keychain from a pocket in his olive drab khakis, unlocked the door, and flipped a switch, which gradually illuminated a long, narrow, windowless room. We stepped inside. I generally avoid horror movies, but this room reminded me of the trailers for any number of gruesome films, and it was all I could do not to bolt out of there in order to restore my normal breathing pattern.

Directly in front of us was a half wall with a swinging door that divided the room into two sections. We stood in the small, square shooting portion, with a long, narrow target hall on the other side of the half wall. Darren patted the dividing wall's two-foot-wide ledge. "Got this from a restaurant downtown that the owner was remodeling. Used to be part of his bar. I fortified it with two-by-fours. I stock it with ammunition and some odds and ends from my military days. It's perfect, don't you think?"

He grinned at Audrey, who merely shifted her gaze to me without reply. The salvaged bar was certainly the nicest feature of the room. Then again, it was also essentially the *only* feature.

Beside the door next to me hung a sturdy-looking gun case, which held three rifles and two handguns, with unused brackets for several more weapons. At the far wall opposite the entrance, three targets—black torsos on white cardboard—had been lined up on easels. Black drapes behind the targets completely hid the back wall. The floor consisted of strips of carpet over hard-packed dirt, and the two long walls were cinderblocks. The low ceiling—less than eight feet—was made of particle board left unpainted, which supported four or five unadorned low-wattage light fixtures.

"I love what you've done with this space, Darren," Audrey deadpanned.

He chuckled. "Some folks get claustrophobic the instant they walk through the door. But don't worry." He pointed at the wall behind the targets. "Hidden behind those black drapes is an emergency exit, in case there's ever a fire blocking my front door. It lets you out on the other side of the hill."

"That could be problematic if someone's entering through the back door when you're in here target practicing," Audrey remarked. "You wouldn't even be able to *see* the person behind the drapes."

He gave her a full-wattage smile. "I've got three deadbolts on that door, and the door itself is solid steel." He pointed at a ceiling fixture in the center of the room. "There's a red light and an alarm that goes off in here whenever anyone opens the back door."

"Can you hear that alarm from inside the rest of your house when this door is closed?" I asked, indicating the very solid-looking door behind us.

"Er, no."

"So...the gun wasn't *stolen* during your open house, but someone could have sneaked behind your drapes then and unlocked the deadbolts, and returned later to steal your gun. You wouldn't have been able to hear them enter."

"Yeah, the police pointed that out to me," he snapped. "In retrospect, I should have taken down the drapes temporarily and checked to make sure the deadbolts were still locked after the open house. I kept my gun case locked tight, at least, but the thief must've used one of those little battery-operated power tools. Cut right through the latch. I had to replace the whole damned case."

"What a shame," I said evenly, angry that he'd been so irresponsible with his firearms. Provided this whole thing wasn't a cover story for his having shot Walter himself, that is.

"Well, I'll tell you what. I'd like to see the joker try to steal weapons from me a second time. *This* time I'll have more'n one surprise up my sleeve."

He straightened his shoulders and returned his attention to Audrey. His lingering gaze was more than a little daffy-looking. "You've seen every room, so I guess we're done for today. Unless, of course, you'd like to do some target shooting. I've only got two sets of earmuffs to protect your hearing, though, so Erin would have to wait outside for us."

"No, but thanks for offering," she said. "I think I've seen quite enough for one day, but I'll probably need a fellow-up visit."

"Any time, Ms. Munroe. Any time."

He locked the door behind us and once again escorted us to the foyer. "Thanks, Darren," she said, shaking his hand. "It's been a pleasure meeting you and seeing your house."

"The pleasure's all mine," he said with a wink and a lecherous smile.

He was still watching Audrey from his doorway with a lovesick expression on his face as I turned the car around and drove away. "I don't know what you thought of his house, but you sure made a big impression on *him*. I'd say the man's totally smitten."

"And the two of us have so very much in common," she joked. "Ain't love grand?"

Just as she dropped me off at work Audrey informed me that she was meeting with Jeremy at home at six P.M. I was determined to be there, as well. Ironically, Sullivan was waiting there impatiently for me, determined to head straight to Jeremy Greene's office and confront him about his client's inadequate foundation.

"Burke's basement is falling apart," Sullivan announced the moment we strode into Jeremy's office. "You used the same crappy design as on Richard's house."

"There's nothing wrong with my design!" Jeremy cried.

"I already advised Burke to contact an engineer," Sullivan said. "I'm betting he'll disagree."

Jeremy grimaced and pressed the heels of both hands to his temples. "I . . . cut some corners I shouldn't have, in retrospect."

"That's an enormous understatement," I said.

"We can still save the house. I'm sure of it. And Audrey Munroe doesn't need to know about the cracks in the basement walls."

"She already discovered it on her own earlier this afternoon," I informed him.

His eyes widened. "But . . . she wasn't too concerned, though, right? I mean, it was just a little crack. It could have happened to anyone's basement."

"It's much worse than a little crack," I said.

"But . . . it's only the one wall, right?"

"So far," Sullivan replied, "but that's kind of like leaving only one door unlocked in your car. We've recommended that Burke get someone out there immediately to make sure the house is still safe to live in."

"It is. It has to be. The place passed all its building inspections. Everything was done to code."

"The same was true of Richard's house," I said, "yet he felt forced to sue you."

"It was a bogus claim! I told you that!"

"You blamed the builder. But you must have used a different builder on Burke's place, when Richard's builder did such a lousy job. Right?"

"Sure, but . . ." He stopped and sighed. He couldn't very well blame a *second* builder for his bad design. "We can't let this get out. If the community finds out about yet another bad foundation, they'll blame it on straw-bale construction. It'll set the industry back fifty years."

"So you're concerned not for your own hide, but for the reputation of straw-bale homes?" Sullivan said skeptically.

"For both, obviously. My business could be ruined."

"If it's any consolation, it's highly doubtful that this will set green construction back," I said. "Although your method of using adobe bricks to build the foundation will likely be banned."

"Again, the inspector gave me a green light."

"My hunch is they'll tighten their standards after this incident," I replied.

"And that I'm going to lose the contest," he grumbled.

"Technically, it's *Burke* who'll lose the contest."

Jeremy shook his head. "I designed the house for free,

in exchange for claiming all the proceeds from the contest myself."

Sullivan's and my jaws both dropped. "Why did you gamble your entire fee on the possibility of your winning the contest?" I asked. "It was such a long shot."

He sighed. "You have to remember, this contest was first announced four years ago. Its sole purpose was to motivate architects, builders, and home owners into constructing self-sustaining homes. I put my heart and soul into this design. If I win, I prove that I'm the best green designer in possibly the greenest town in the country. I could make my career, just like that."

"Which is why you cheated," Sullivan stated. "By running that power line tapping into Asia's electricity?"

He pursed his lips and glared at Sullivan. "You don't seriously expect me to confess to anything, do you? This contest is important to your careers, too, you know. I would think you'd be on my side."

"Not when you resort to breaking the law," Sullivan said.

"I didn't necessarily commit any crimes."

"Stealing power from a neighbor is a crime, Jeremy," I countered.

He muttered, "That damned Asia! If she hadn't flooded Burke's property, nobody would have noticed the crack in the basement wall! All I needed was another week or two, and the contest would've been over, and I'd've won the damned thing! In any case, I didn't have anything to do with the judges' deaths. The killer's probably that guy who owns the furniture place."

"Matthew Hayes? Of M.H. Custom Furniture?"

He nodded. "I saw his truck at Burke's house the same morning Walter was shot. I should have told the police that, but I didn't want to have to explain why I was there myself."

Sullivan said, "Because you were there trying to get rid of the illegal power-line tap, before you could get caught?"

"Jeremy, my god! You're withholding evidence and impeding an investigation for a capital crime!"

He sighed. "You're right. This has gotten out of hand. Not letting some bastard get away with murder is more important than my damned career." He hesitated. "I guess."

"It *is*, Jeremy. He's already killed twice. You can't risk thinking he'll stop there."

"Right." He fished Detective O'Reilly's card out of a drawer. "I'll get this over with right now."

I watched him dial and heard O'Reilly's gruff tones on the other end as Jeremy told him about spotting Matthew's van at Burke's house the day of the murder. Stunned by what we'd learned, Sullivan and I left without another word.

"I'm starting to think you're right," Sullivan said as we drove to our office. "It's looking more and more like Hayes or Greene killed Richard. Do you trust Jeremy enough to call the cops?"

"I know he's at least actually talking to O'Reilly. I recognized his voice."

"Do you think Matthew Hayes is the killer?"

"It's certainly very possible." I needed to have another chat with Matthew. I could claim I was merely checking up on Burke's desk. As long as I didn't mention anything about why he might have been in Burke's driveway the day of the shooting, I might be able to get a feel for whether he'd been there for legitimate reasons. "Steve?

Why don't you drop me off on Thirtieth Street, near the mall. I'll take RTD back. I need to check on a client."

"*Which* client?"

"Suzanne Langley. I told her I'd come pick up the wallpaper samples today and get the paper ordered."

"Okay. She does live nearby. So I guess I can trust you."

"Of course you can. We're partners. We've got to trust each other."

"Good. Because if I didn't know better, I'd think that Matthew Hayes's shop is right on the way to Suzanne's house, and it'd be just like you to try to pry information out of him." He gave me a smug grin.

I was annoyed at his obvious delight in outsmarting me. "Just because I was planning a little side trip doesn't mean that you can't trust me."

"Except that it does." He continued past the intersection where I'd wanted him to leave me.

"But one of us needs to return phone calls and keep things in order at the office. We haven't exactly been working at full steam the last couple of weeks."

"Hey, it's more important that I babysit you than stay in our office. After all, we're partners."

"But we won't *have* an office or a partnership if we keep ignoring our business. Be reasonable, Sullivan! I can get Matthew to talk if I'm on my own. He'll clam up if you're there, listening to our every word."

"Fine. I'll stay in the car. And you can beep me with your cell phone if you need help."

"Will do," I replied.

"You should have just told me the truth about where you were going."

"Are *you* always forthcoming with the truth to *me?*"

Sullivan said nothing. His jaw muscles were working. I'd hit a sore spot, and we both knew it. The atmosphere was suddenly so charged, it felt like the van windows could explode at any moment. I couldn't stand to address the real issue between us, but I also couldn't endure this tension in silence. "You don't have to be so patronizing, Sullivan! I'm simply going to enter Matthew's place of business and ask a few questions, not stage a shootout, for heaven's sake!"

"Regardless, we agreed to watch each other's backs. I'm holding up my end, even if you're unwilling to hold up yours."

Once again, *I* was the one who had let *him* down. We arrived in the parking lot. "Thanks for driving," I snarled as I opened the passenger door.

"Don't mention it."

"I won't ever again."

"All the better," he said.

"What does 'all the better' even mean? You're just making sure you get in the last word! As if we're still in grade school! This is sure one heck of a healthy, mature partnership we've got going for ourselves." He'd begun to scribble something on his notepad, but I got out of the van and slammed my door shut without asking him about it.

Just as I'd taken a step toward the store, Sullivan tapped on his windshield and, despite my better judgment, I turned to see why. He held up a sign in the window. In a nod to a Gilbert and Sullivan lyric from *Pirates of Penzance,* he'd written:

We are the very model of a modern, MAJOR partnership.

Surprised that Sullivan had been the one to lighten

the situation, I couldn't help but giggle. Sullivan winked at me, and my steps felt infinitely lighter as I walked away.

My amusement faded when I entered Matthew's shop and remembered it was quite possible that he was a double murderer. He was alone, reading the newspaper, and glanced up at me with a hopeful-for-a-sale glint in his eye that quickly faded when he saw it was just me.

"Afternoon, Erin."

"Hi, Matthew. I was in the area and thought I'd check on the progress with Burke's desk."

"Should be ready by the end of the week."

"Great."

"Will the contest still be going on by then?"

"I'm not sure. Why?"

He frowned and muttered, "Nobody seems to know."

"Who else have you asked?"

"Burke, actually. I was hoping to make a deal with him . . . to give him a discount in exchange for his pointing out the desk to the judge to prove that I *can* do green designs."

That could explain Jeremy's having spotted his truck at Burke's on Monday morning. "Did you go to Burke's house, or call him on the phone?"

"Why do you ask?"

"Just curious. I wondered if you felt compelled to visit Burke in person. After all, you've pretty much burned your bridges with conservationists . . . and contest judges."

He made a derisive noise. "No comment, Officer Gilbert." He held my gaze. "I don't suppose you'd be willing to talk me up to Audrey Munroe, would you? I'd love to do a segment on her show about local furniture makers."

I wasn't about to say straight out that he'd be one of the

last people I wanted to help. "An appearance on her show can really boost sales."

"Lucky you to be living with her."

"Yes, I am lucky. But the publicity is the least of my good fortune. She's a terrific person."

"I'm sure she is."

Which is why I couldn't bear it if someone killed her! "As was Walter. Between you and me, Richard struck me as being a bit of a loon."

He chuckled. "It's nice to hear you say that. The papers are making him out to be a fallen saint."

"Either way, he didn't deserve his fate."

"No. He didn't," Matthew admitted. "Just because the guy was such a stupid show-off as to drink his own paint doesn't mean someone should've taken advantage and poisoned him."

"You don't feel guilty for egging him on?"

"Actually, I do. But I'm also angry. Some bastard turned me into his henchman."

"*His?* Do you know for certain that the killer was a man?"

Matthew shrugged. "No idea." He leered at me. "But now that you mention it, poisoning someone does seem more like something a woman would do."

chapter 19

The phone was ringing when we returned to the office. It was Burke. He was upset about his conversation with the structural engineer. I put him on speakerphone so that we could have a three-way conversation. Apparently, the engineer had asked Burke over the phone to describe the crack and had surmised that he was right to be concerned about it. Burke had pressed him further, and the engineer had said that, yes, it was possible that a whole new basement might need to be built.

"I can't do that," Burke shouted at us. "I mean, sure, it

can be done physically—the whole house can be jacked up and a new basement can be built underneath it, but that would be almost as expensive as building a whole new house from scratch!"

"The engineer hasn't even seen the house yet," I said reassuringly. "He only told you it was possible that you might need a new foundation, right? So he was giving you the worst-case scenario because you asked him to do so."

"This has got to be the all-time biggest irony," Burke replied. "Here I've been thinking I'd struck this shrewd deal, saving thousands of dollars, by agreeing to give my architect all of the proceeds from an energy-efficiency contest in exchange for designing my house. I figured that he'd work his butt off to make my house the best in the city. Instead, he does such shoddy work that the entire place is going to sink into the muck!"

"It's not anywhere near that bad," Sullivan said.

"I'm sorely tempted now to just surrender to Asia and tear down my windmill. Hell, I should just give her my entire property and make a clean start in some other city. Some other state, even. Let her be the one to sink with the ship. It was her flooding me with sewer water that sped up the whole process in the first place." He chuckled bitterly. "Hey, global warming might even be my friend. It might dry out this basin my house was built in."

"If it's any consolation," Sullivan said, "I doubt there's any way Audrey is going to be able to overlook the seepage in the basement and award your home with first place."

"That's supposed to *console* me?" Burke growled.

"Only in that Jeremy won't be earning all that prize money now."

"Yeah. The incompetent boob who caused my misfortunes now has to share in them. I'll start doing my happy dance any day now."

"Speaking of Jeremy, I need to run home. He's meeting with Audrey to discuss his plans for the kitchen remodel right about now, and I want to sit in on their meeting."

"Hurry Erin out of there, Steve," Burke said. "Jeremy's a quack. Maybe Erin can stop him from taking advantage of Ms. Munroe."

I was relieved to discover that Audrey was alone in the dining room; I'd gotten home ahead of Jeremy's visit. "Something smells good," I said.

"It's lamb stew, heavy on the basil," she explained. "A good thing about the whole kitchen-tree fiasco is that it's encouraged me to use my Crock-Pot more often."

"Wonderful. I'm looking forward to it already. Have you heard anything from Jeremy Greene?"

"No, why?"

"Things haven't been going well for him at Burke's."

"That crack in the basement is looking like his fault?"

"Yes, and now I have serious doubts about the caliber of Jeremy's work in general."

"Do you think I made a mistake by hiring him?"

"Yes."

The doorbell rang. "Shoot. Well, that's him now. I suppose we could just ignore that and tell him we've moved away."

"It's your call. I'm willing to act irresponsibly if that's what *you* want to do."

"Fine." She headed toward the foyer. "Let's see if his

design is so wonderful that it changes your mind about him."

"I hope so," I replied, although I suspected I'd see a pig fly over Audrey's demolished kitchen first.

I stood sentinel in the parlor as Audrey and Jeremy made small talk. She hung up his coat in the foyer closet and then started to walk past me, saying, "Let's sit down in the . . . parlor."

"Good evening, Erin," he said with great cheer, which was in striking contrast to the mood he'd been in when we parted company a few short hours ago. He held up his rolled-up cylinder of oversized papers. "I've got the blueprints right here, and this is my all-time best work. You'll love it, Audrey."

"Excellent. Let's all have a seat." She gestured at the sofa.

Jeremy hesitated as he eyed the small oval glass coffee table. "I could use more room to spread out the drawings." He glanced around. "Dining room table, maybe?" He strode as far as the entrance to the dining room, caught sight of how the kitchen contents had monopolized that space, and said, "On second thought, the coffee table's fine." He unrolled his set of four drawings. "Now, these are just preliminaries, of course. I didn't want to start ringing up the charges on you till you had the chance to give your approval."

With the briefest of glances, I was irate. "You're doubling the room's floor space?" I asked.

Looking at Audrey, he replied, "I want to move back your west and south walls, so that we can give you both a bigger kitchen and a bigger dining room. As you can—"

Audrey flipped through the drawings and said, "It looks to me like you'd be gutting my entire kitchen."

"Yes, but in return, you'd have a professional-style kitchen, suitable to prepare feasts for the queen."

"I can do that now. Or rather, I used to be able to, before half of a cottonwood tree took up residence in my kitchen. Erin has enlightened me about how building green means reusing what you've already got wherever possible. All I want is a separate solarium, big enough for a small eating area."

"You'd just be wasting my talents that way," he stated flatly.

"But we'd be wasting all of my perfectly good cabinetry *your* way. All that needs to be replaced is the sink cabinet and the island. And the countertops, of course."

She looked at him pointedly, but he said nothing and looked right back at her. Apparently he hoped to win a staring contest with Audrey. The guy did not know how to pick his battles.

Jeremy sighed and shifted his attention to me. "Erin, could you and I have a word in private?"

"Certainly." I rose. "Let's step into the den."

Before I'd even had the chance to shut the door behind us, Jeremy uttered the same curse word three times. "I knew you'd turn her against me," he snapped at me. "You had no intention of actually hiring me in the first place! I did all this work for you for nothing!"

"Jeremy, I told you when I went to your office the other day that we just wanted you to add a solarium for us!"

"And I came up with a better plan. Obviously your scope is too narrow to see that."

"Obviously your vision is too hard-wired for you to listen to your clients."

"I sure hope you're not planning on getting any more

referrals from Margot. We're back together, you know. *She* can appreciate a good design when she sees one."

I followed him as he marched back into the parlor and gathered up his things. His cheeks burned a deep magenta as he said to Audrey, "I'll let myself out, Ms. Munroe. Thanks anyway."

"I'm sorry you were unwilling to listen to Erin. What she says goes for both of us. Frankly, I'm surprised you took it upon yourself to assume otherwise."

Jeremy gaped at her for a moment, then pivoted on his heel and left without another word.

"Well, that didn't go especially well," Audrey said. "I had hoped to pick up some clues from him, but all I learned is that he has the temper of a crabby old man and the attention span of a teenager. On the plus side, he didn't kill me on the spot for telling him off."

She wandered into the dining room, and I followed to see if I could help get dinner on the table. Or, to be more accurate, on our laps; the surface of the table was obscured beneath all the dishes and cookware.

"What time is your stew going to be ready?" I asked. "Will I have time to run to the store for some dinner rolls?"

"I think so. Let me look at the recipe..."

She glanced at her watch. "Hmm. This takes longer than I thought. I'd better turn it all the way up." She cranked the dial on the Crock-Pot as far as it would go. She looked again at the recipe. "Oh, that's much better. Now it'll be ready by...nine-thirty tonight."

"On the bright side, I have plenty of time to get to the store."

"Several times over," she said.

"How very stylish of us to eat late. This officially turns us into metro-singles, you realize."

"Good of you to put a positive spin on my bad planning. By the way, you're now in full charge of the kitchen remodel. Whatever you say goes."

"Wonderful!" My mind's eye was instantly agog at the colors and textures and lines I could integrate, all the while maximizing the sunlight from the solarium and skylight. I'd recently spotted cinnamon-colored tiles in the salvage yard that would make a divine backsplash. It would look stunning against her cherry cabinets, and the reddish hue would complement the slate floor in the solarium.

"I want you to re-create Margot's kitchen, except with my cabinetry."

"Ah."

"And I want less green in the recycled glass backsplash. I probably want to go with cement countertops. Or maybe granite. We have to start from scratch with the countertops, no matter what, so you can take me around to the kitchen design stores, and I'll tell you what I want when I see it."

"I wouldn't have it any other way, Audrey."

"Which is what makes you so good at your job. You don't impose your taste on your clients, you merely steer your clients toward the very best in *their* tastes."

"Thank you, Audrey! That's exactly what I try to achieve every day at my job."

"Let's hope you succeed here. And quickly. The longer I have to cook with this Crock-Pot, the longer we're going to be eating dinner at midnight and living like bats."

I snatched up my purse. "I'll run out to Safeway now."

"You might want to wait another minute, just in case Jeremy is still out there, fuming in his car about how this is all your fault."

"Oh, I'm sure he's long gone."

"Unless he's a homicidal maniac who can't shake things like this off."

I set my purse back down. "No rush."

"I was thinking about the murders as I was making dinner . . . stewing over the stew, as it were, and it seems to me that several people had a motive for killing Richard Thayers. So what you should be thinking about is: Who had a motive to kill poor Walter Emory? After all, yes, he was Mr. Thayers's friend and he took over as contest judge, but other than that, they had nothing in common. Sullivan was *also* Richard's friend. Where's the connection between the two men that resulted in two deaths?"

"That's a very good question, Audrey."

"I know it is. I'm starting to think like you." She gave me a sly grin. "Which reminds me, you should invite your Mr. Sullivan over for a late dinner tonight."

"Here?" I said, gesturing at our surroundings.

"Force of habit. Invite him for an after-dinner brandy, then, perhaps."

I snatched up my purse and left the room, saying over my shoulder, "I'll think about it," although we both knew I wouldn't.

I was alone at the office the following morning. Sullivan was working with Ms. Hands-on yet again, so I was startled when the door banged open, but relaxed when I saw it was Margot Troy—and that she was unarmed. Even so, I found myself sitting up straighter at my desk; Margot had an aura of authority about her that made you want to improve your posture in her presence. "Oh, good. I was hoping I'd catch you alone here," she said without preamble.

"Oh?"

She peered into my eyes as though she was trying to find a wandering contact lens for me. "Who do you think the killer is?"

"I really don't know." In actuality, Matthew Hayes was my biggest suspect, Jeremy Greene was number two, and Darren, Asia, and Margot herself were tied for third place.

"I think it's Darren Campesio. Darren has a few screws loose. Having given up on me, he's now taken to asking Audrey Munroe out. We spoke on the phone yesterday afternoon, and she told me so herself. You have to keep an eye out for her. I think Darren's a sexist pig who would do anything to avoid losing the contest to a woman."

"So he resorts to murdering the judges? And kills two *men*?"

"I know. It's far-fetched. But stranger things have happened. Besides, there's probably a hidden motive or two in his bag of tricks. The man's house is a step away from being a survivalist camp. I'll bet he wants to start his own army next."

"He hasn't really struck me as being antigovernment."

"He's into a zero-impact lifestyle," she replied. "He wants to force that choice onto everyone, and that's where I draw the line. He's a Nazi conservationist."

"I guess you've got to admire him for the level of commitment and passion he has in his beliefs."

"No, I think he needs to be locked up for everyone's safety."

"You seriously think he's dangerous?"

"Yes, I do. I'm urging Jeremy to stay away from him. And you should really think long and hard about keeping watch over Audrey when she's with him. Darren Campesio is wacky."

"I'll keep that in mind."

"Do. I like Audrey, and I'd hate to see her get killed just because *you* thought Darren was perfectly harmless."

I held her gaze, waiting for the other shoe to drop. At length, she said, "Jeremy told me about how the two of you summarily dismissed him from his job last night."

Here it comes, I thought, nodding at her. She was going to try to convince me to change her mind and rehire her boyfriend. It would take a lot for me to want to defend myself in something that was none of her business.

"He's a talented architect," she went on, "but he needs to learn to work better with people. And he didn't have anything to do with either man's death. Neither did I, so we're pretty much down to Darren, Burke, or that young man with the beef against Richard in class. And I know Burke well enough to be certain he's not a killer. Richard's heckler had no reason to kill Walter Emory, so there you go. It's Darren. Have a good day."

Sullivan returned to our office not fifteen minutes after Margot had left. "How's it going?" he asked.

"Not bad. I'm not making as much progress with the

bookkeeping as I'd have liked. But I had an interesting visit with Margot Troy just now."

"Oh?"

"She's of the theory that Darren Campesio is the killer, and that we should be protecting Audrey from him."

"Why does she suspect him?"

"Process of elimination. She *knows* she, Jeremy, and Burke are innocent, and—"

"Burke?"

"They dated for a while and she says he's not a killer. The only other person she considers a suspect is Matthew Hayes, who, as she said, had no motive to kill Walter."

Sullivan seemed lost in thought as he took a seat at his desk. "Interesting."

"That she suspects Darren?"

"I actually find it more intriguing that she dismisses Hayes as a suspect because she assumes he had no motive to kill Walter Emory. I've been making the same mistake. But the last couple days I've been talking to some of Matthew's business associates and doing computer research. Turns out Walter had been trying to convince the Crestview town council to shut down Matthew's workshop."

"On what grounds?"

"Importing and using illegal materials."

"Was he able to establish the fact that Matthew was actually *guilty* of that?"

"Not to anyone's knowledge. Anyone that *I* could find to ask, I mean. But Walter had recently made some inroads."

"With the city government, you mean?"

He nodded. "They were going to at least block any

efforts of Matthew's to expand the store. Which would have been a thorn in Matthew's side."

"But not enough to motivate two murders."

He shrugged. "That's what I'm thinking, but who knows? Another interesting fact is that Walter swore out a complaint against Matthew for damaging his car. Walter had a little hybrid. Matthew smacked into it with his SUV at a stoplight last year, and Walter was sure it was no accident."

"What became of Walter's . . . complaint?"

"Lawsuit was still pending," Sullivan replied with a shrug.

Not unlike Richard's lawsuit against Jeremy, I thought, shaking my head at this new entanglement.

**Sullivan and I worked with separate clients that afternoon, and afterwards, I returned to the office and finally got us caught up on our bookkeeping. Next month it would be his turn to do the bookkeeping, which was our least favorite activity.

When it was time to go home, I dashed toward my car. The temperature had once again dropped significantly, and the sky seemed heavy with snow. I hesitated when I spotted a man on the sidewalk ahead, weaving his way toward me. He appeared to be seriously inebriated. A moment later, I realized it was Burke.

I paused at my van and said, "Burke? Are you all right?"

He took a deliberately broad stance, as if to get his balance on a swaying surface. "Oh, hey, Erin, good see you."

Yep. Drunk as a skunk. Even the frames of his glasses were askew on his nose. "Can I give you a ride home?"

"Me? Naw. My car's here someplace. Dunno. Parking lot, I think. Don't ya worry your pretty little head about it. I'll find it. I know it's around here someplace." He tried to walk backward as he spoke, which was painful to watch. He could barely walk forward without stumbling. "See ya, Erin."

"No, wait. You can't drive home like this. You're drunk."

"Just a little. I'll be fine."

I unlocked my van. "Get in. I'll take you home."

"But... my car."

"It'll be safe for the night wherever it is. The worst that will happen is you'll have a parking ticket to pay tomorrow. But at least you and everyone else on the road will be safe."

"I'm pretty sure I'm just fine to drive."

"Let's test that. How do you say 'Alabama' backward?"

"Umm... it'd end in 'la.'" As he was pondering the question, which was the first thing that had popped into my head to offer as a distraction, I guided him into my passenger seat. "Too bad the word's not Alamama," he said. "That'd be cool to say."

"Yes. It sounds like a way to describe a pasta dish just the way your mother made it. À la Mama."

He stared at me with blank eyes. Granted, the line was far short of hilarious, but it at least warranted a tiny smile. The guy didn't seem to have a funny bone, even when intoxicated.

"Were you downtown celebrating with friends?" I asked him as the light at the intersection turned green.

He shook his head. "Just memories. Lots of those. This is the anniversary of my son's death."

I instantly felt guilty for having silently sniped at his lack of humor. "I'm so sorry."

"I toast myself for surviving another year with no future and nothing to look forward to."

"Your job is fulfilling though, surely?"

"Fulfilling? I guess so. It's sure not the life I'd envisioned when I watched my only son being born. When I held him in my arms for the first time." Burke's voice was getting softer, and he closed his eyes. Next time I looked at him, he was asleep with his head forward and his chin pressed to his chest.

Just as I made the turn onto Burke's dead-end street, he jerked awake. The lights from an oncoming car appeared to frighten him. He made an odd sound and suddenly grabbed the wheel. We veered toward the oncoming car.

"Burke!" I screamed. "What the hell are you doing?!"

I slammed on the brakes and barely managed to miss the other car. We jackknifed around on the icy road.

Thankfully, we came to a complete stop. "You could have gotten us killed!"

He was staring at me with goggle eyes, now wide awake. "I'm sorry, Erin. I don't know what happened. I just... instinct'ly grabbed the wheel when I woke up."

"Were you trying to kill yourself? And take me and some other innocent driver with you?"

"No. The opposite. I had a dream I was driving and fell asleep at the wheel. So I just... Thank God nobody was hurt!"

The other driver had stormed out of his car and was approaching us. It was Darren. I shouldn't be surprised, I realized; there were so few houses on this street.

"Darren!" I cried, rolling down my window. "You didn't go into the ditch, did you?"

"Jeez, Erin! Are you all right?" He ignored my question, but now that I looked for myself, I could see that he'd managed to pull off the road safely. "What happened? You nearly swerved right into me!"

"I know. Sorry about that."

He sniffed the air. "Have you been drinking?"

"No. That's Burke's breath that you smell."

"My son died four years ago today," Burke said to Darren.

"Too bad."

"Yeah. Thanks."

"I'll help you get him inside the house," Darren said, all business. He returned to his own vehicle. I drove up Burke's long driveway and Darren followed. He parked behind me and quickly got out and strode over to Burke's door. As Burke fumbled with the latch, Darren opened the door and said firmly, "Come on, buddy. Let's go."

He grabbed Burke's arm, but Burke shook him off, saying, "I can handle it from here. I can walk just fine. No need to make a big deal out of it."

"Okay, then," he said, standing back to let Burke pass. He glared at me as I rounded the car. "Erin, you're going to have to wait here and call a cab. You nearly crashed into me. I'm not so sure you should be driving."

"It wasn't my fault, Darren."

"Well, it sure wasn't mine. You came into my lane."

"I grabbed the wheel when I woke up. I was disoriented," Burke admitted.

Darren rocked on his heels. "Ah. Now I get the picture."

"I got an idea," Burke stammered. "Why don't you both go and just leave me alone?"

"You're depressed," Darren said flatly. "Maybe I'd better stick around your place, Burke. Make you some coffee. I was going to head into town and run some errands, but it can wait till morning."

"That's really nice of you, Darren," I told him honestly.

"Hey, that's not *right* by me. You can't stay over. I'm fine."

"What's going on?" Asia cried, trotting along Burke's driveway from the road. "I heard a big squeal of brakes. Did somebody get run over?"

"No," Darren said. "Erin and I just had a near collision. That's all. No big deal."

"Burke?" I asked gently. "Are you sure you're all right?"

"Yeah. Jeez! I just had a couple drinks! Go home. All of you!"

"Fine. I'll see you later." Darren gave me a little wave, then got in his car and left, heading back toward town and away from his house.

Asia clicked her tongue and whispered to me, "Are you sure Burke is actually drunk, not faking it?"

"Why would he fake being drunk?"

She chuckled and shouted at Burke, who'd reached his front steps, "Someone must have nearly caught you in the act, hey, Burke?"

He turned around and gave her a chilling glare, then he unlocked his door, walked inside the house, and shut the door. Oddly, if I hadn't smelled the alcohol on him and seen how he'd been staggering earlier, I actually would have sworn the man was completely sober at that moment.

Asia was watching him. She turned toward me and looked me up and down. "Were you partying with Burke, or did you just happen to bump into him like that?"

"We bumped into each other downtown."

"That's what I figured. He's up to something."

"He's drunk."

Asia shook her head. "He never drinks to excess. He says it releases the demons in him."

"Well, he did this time." And the demons emerged, all right. A shiver ran up my spine at the thought of how close he'd come to getting us into a serious car accident.

"Ha! I wonder what the true story behind *that* one is."

"What do you mean?"

"Oh, that's right. You're just the drop-in worker bee for him. You haven't lived next door to him for nearly four years. I forget that you don't know him all that well." She turned and started to walk back toward her house.

"Wait. Enlighten me."

"Whenever Burke gets in trouble, he always hauls out the grieving-father card."

"Oh?" I asked skeptically.

"Oh, yes," she chided. "Just last month my car broke down and he gave me a ride home, way over the speed limit. A female officer pulled him over." She rolled her eyes. "You should have seen him pulling out the violins to play his 'Poor, Poor Me' tune. He was practically sobbing the whole time he was talking to the lady cop. Right up until she downgraded the ticket to a warning and let him go. He laughed all the way home." She harrumphed. "The man's absolutely shameless."

chapter 20

*T*he next morning, I couldn't help but notice the dark circles under Sullivan's eyes. He hadn't shaved, nor had he combed his hair. He was working at an easel near his desk, putting the finishing touches on the dining room design for a first-time client.

I stared at the powder blue shirt he wore over his black T-shirt. He had a smear of lipstick on his collar!

"What?" he said.

I averted my gaze. "Nothing. You look like you tied one on with Burke last night. That's all."

"Burke?"

My heart was racing. Had Sullivan come straight to work from the woman's house? Was there any other explanation? How clichéd could this get? "Yeah. I had to drive him home last night. I bumped into him downtown. He seemed to be drunk."

"What do you mean, *seemed* to be? You think he might've been pretending, so he could score a ride home?"

Unwilling to look again at Sullivan and his telltale collar, I stared at my computer screen. "No, Asia McClure accused him of faking it. He'd told me he drank too much because it was the anniversary of his son's death. But then she claimed he did stuff like that, played the sympathy card, whenever he got in a jam. She seemed so sure of herself that I did some computer research last night and found Caleb Stratton's obit. He died four years ago yesterday, just like Burke said."

"Why were you talking to Asia last night?"

Who the hell cared!? "Um . . . Burke nodded out for a while, and when he awoke, he was disoriented and kind of grabbed the wheel from me. The tires squealed right by Asia's driveway. She came running out to scold everyone."

"Damn it, Erin!" He tossed his colored pencil into the tray and shot to his feet. "You *deserved* a scolding!"

I gaped at him.

"Either Burke's a two-time murderer, or he's being framed as one! Either way, it's stupid and risky for you to be alone with him at night!"

"The man was drunk! What was I supposed to do? Let him drive that way?"

"You should have called him a cab!"

"With my car right there? That would have been ridiculous!"

"It makes a lot more sense than driving a murder suspect around, alone, late at night!"

"He is our client, and I'm certain he's innocent. Furthermore, if you care so much about me and my personal safety, why don't you *show* it, instead of yelling at me all the time! Not to mention having the gall to come into work with lipstick on your collar!"

His jaw dropped. He tugged at his collar, then mumbled, "Sorry." He yanked off his outer shirt, examined the collar a second time, and draped the garment over the back of his chair. "That'll teach me not to let my laundry go this long." He gave me a sheepish smile, his gaze barely flickering in my direction, let alone meeting mine. "I think I ran into a friend the last time I happened to be wearing this shirt. She must have given me a peck on the cheek." He eased himself into his chair with the weariness of a long-distance runner who'd just lost his race.

Stunned into silence, I stared at him. He really did look defeated—and guilty. Much as I wanted to believe him, I had too good of an eye for color for my own good. The lipstick was the same copper shade that Hands-on Fairfax favored.

The silence was palpable. I needed to get out of here. I stood. "Um . . . that structural engineer Burke hired was supposed to be there first thing this morning. I want to drop by and speak to him myself."

Sullivan nodded. "I'll come with you." He paused. "Notice that I'm not shouting."

His voice was gentle, reminding me of why I was so drawn to him. That reminder only made me feel all the more miserable. His suggestion defeated most of the purpose behind my hasty exit, but he was my business partner, and I had to act like a professional. Regardless of how badly my heart was aching.

A small pickup truck drove out just as we neared Burke's driveway. Jeremy stood outside, as he had apparently been speaking to its driver. He waited for us as we rounded the mailbox and parked.

"I take it that was the engineer," Sullivan said to Jeremy as we emerged from the van. "Did he already give Burke a preliminary report?"

"No, he collected the data and told Burke he'll get back to him first thing Monday. He and I spoke at length just now, though. I said I'd relay the gist to Burke myself." Jeremy rubbed his face, which was pale and drawn. He'd shaved his scraggly beard and was wearing off-white Dockers, which matched the color of his wan face. "You two might as well listen in. That way you can all have a piece of me at once."

Sullivan and I exchanged glances as Jeremy trudged ahead of us. All that remained to be seen was how badly Burke was going to handle the engineer's dire prognosis for this house. I already grieved for all our wasted work. We had managed to wring every last cubic inch of visual interest, cozy warmth, and sparkling appeal out of what had started out as a ponderous, drab, and boxlike space.

"Burke?" Jeremy called as he ushered us inside. A moment later, Burke appeared at the doorway to the kitchen. "Gilbert and Sullivan stopped by. I offered to have them join us as I fill you in. That all right with you?"

"Uh...yeah. Sure. I was just making myself some coffee. Anyone else want some?" He was dressed in a sweatshirt and jeans, his eyes bloodshot. He certainly looked like someone with a hangover.

We all declined. He poured his cup and then headed to his kitchen table. We'd all taken so much pride in describing to visitors how we'd commissioned the Crestview Lumberyard to make the boards for this circular table from the lodgepole pine that had once stood in this very spot. Jeremy remained standing, but the moment the three of us were seated, he said, "Okay, Burke. 'Fraid I got some real bad news."

"Ah, jeez." Burke shoved his cup to the center of the table, then balled his fists. "Go on."

"As you started to suspect a few months ago, the foundation just wasn't built right. Or at least it wasn't for the movement in the underlying soil. Your house is kind of like the tower of Pisa . . . starting to lean."

"Damn it, Jeremy! How did the inspectors fail to notice that the foundation was this bad?"

"You're right. The structural inspection should have caught it. But it looked fine. It was just . . . bad luck."

"No, it was bad design work on your part," Burke growled. He slammed his fist on the table. His full coffee cup sloshed with the vibrations.

I hoped this lovely little table wasn't going to get wrecked. I signaled Sullivan with my eyes, and he reached behind him and grabbed a cloth napkin from the built-in sideboard.

"You said you'd take care of the soil inspection for me," Burke continued, "and you obviously didn't. So you now owe me a million dollars."

"A million dollars?!"

Steve grabbed Burke's cup in anticipation of future table poundings.

"That's just for starters. Make it two, come to think of it. You deserve to pay an additional million for punitive damages. But the good news is, for two mil, you can have this place, lock, stock, and barrel. She's all yours."

"There's no reason to overreact," Jeremy said meekly.

"Oh, no? You wouldn't call the fact that my house is toppling over a reason to get upset?"

"It will be years before you can even tell there's a problem." Jeremy forced a smile, but dots of perspiration were forming on his brow.

"You mean, not counting the cracks and seepage in the walls of my basement?"

"Okay, fine," Jeremy countered, beginning to pace. "Yes, the basement doesn't look great. But it's just a basement. You're living here alone, and not even really using it for anything. Except for your pool table. We'll move it upstairs. Into your den. It'll be nicer there anyway."

Now *that* was beyond stupid. We'd maximized every inch of the den to keep that small space from becoming cavelike. We'd designed the built-in shelves for the specific sizes of his medical journals, textbooks, and chess trophies. It was Burke's favorite room.

"Oh, will it?" Burke pounded the table once again. "And will we build levelers into the table legs? So that as the house leans, we can keep jacking up one side?"

Jeremy waited patiently through Burke's sarcastic remarks. "The engineer says we can shore up the supports on the case-ons," Jeremy pleaded, "and we'll build a retaining wall. With any luck whatsoever, your house here will last as long as forty years, with no additional damage. That's really not all that bad, when you think about it."

Burke turned his desperate eyes to Sullivan and me

and asked, "If I put this place on the market tomorrow, do you think I could break even?"

Sullivan frowned and shook his head. "You'd be obligated to report the problem to prospective buyers."

Burke grabbed his head with both hands and said nothing. Finally he sat up. "Well, Jeremy. Thanks for telling me. You'll be looking forward to hearing from my lawyer, I'm sure."

"I...guess I'd better go."

Although Sullivan slid the coffee cup back over to him, Burke stayed seated in stunned silence for several seconds after Jeremy had closed the front door behind him.

"I'm really sorry about all of this, Burke," I said.

He shrugged. "Must be my karma. Or maybe I really screwed some people over in a past life. And now I just can't catch a break." He shook his head. "At least Asia will be happy now."

"How so?" Sullivan asked.

"There's no reason for me to finish installing the windmill. The house won't even be standing by the time it pays for itself."

That afternoon, Matthew Hayes phoned while Sullivan was engaged in an "emergency meeting" with Jennifer Fairfax. The desk was finished. I arranged to come in and pay for it now, so he could deliver it tomorrow— Saturday morning. It worried me a little that Burke might want to refuse delivery, considering the fiasco with his house.

A much bigger worry, though, was that Sullivan and I had argued about his sudden appointment with Ms.

Fairfax. I'd very reasonably pointed out that if something had gone so wrong with her home that he had deemed this appointment an emergency, we should both attend. He had *un*reasonably countered that he needed to handle this alone. Fed up, I asked, "Why? Are you two having a fling?" And as he stormed out the door, he had yelled, "Erin, please! I've got enough troubles on my mind without you acting jealous!"

When I arrived at Matthew's store, the strung-out sales clerk was talking in agitated tones on his cell phone. He did a double take at me as I approached, then said, "Here's someone," into his phone, flipped his phone shut, and headed toward me.

Unable to imagine an enjoyable outcome after that greeting, I took a tiny step back.

"You were here before," he said to me. "Listen, dude, I gotta split. When Matthew gets back, tell him I had an emergency."

"But, wait! Where's Matthew?"

"He'll be right back," he answered over his shoulder. He charged through the door.

"Okay, then," I murmured to myself. Well, I could wait five minutes for Matthew. At which time I would be sure to get his employee's name to nominate him for a good-service award.

The phone behind the counter rang. I took a moment to consider what I'd want a customer to do if this was my store, but decided to answer it anyway, in case Matthew was calling. "M.H. Custom Furniture," I said cautiously.

"Yeah," a man said. "How late are you open?"

"Six P.M." I answered, reasonably certain that was accurate. I tensed. A large and extremely scruffy-looking man had chosen that moment to enter the store. I wondered if this was who the flake had been talking to on his cell phone before bolting. Maybe he was here to rob the place.

"Okay. Thanks," the caller said.

"You're welcome," I replied, briefly toying with the notion of asking him to send the police. This was one scary-looking customer/robber. He was at least six feet seven and three hundred pounds, wearing grubby gray sweats, and unshaven except for his lumpy scalp. He'd have looked equally fitting in an Oakland Raiders uniform or prison garb. I hung up.

"Hey. Is your boss here?" His voice was deep enough to make the floorboards rumble.

"Matthew stepped out. But he'll be back any second. Literally." I chewed on my lip. Should I tell him that I didn't work here and didn't know how to work the cash register? As far as I was concerned, he was welcome to take the whole thing with him.

"Just want to know where I can unload the copper." He gave me a wink.

My sense of relief at his wink was enormous. It meant that the man wasn't a robber. Well, actually, it meant that he'd probably stolen the copper, but wasn't here to rob *me*. I was never again going to have such a golden opportunity to check into Matthew's business ethics. I found myself able to grin as the large man held my gaze. "Is this the kind of shipment that fell off a truck, by any chance?"

He laughed. "You got it, lady."

"The loading dock is right around back."

"Can I get around the building on the left side, or the right?"

Beats me was not going to be a good answer. Whereas getting myself outside where I could hightail it to my car would be advantageous. "I'll come out and show you."

"Suit yourself."

He led the way outside, not bothering to slow the door from swinging back at me. With my chances no worse than fifty-fifty, I indicated with my chin that we should go to the left. "So, where did you get this copper . . . really?"

He eyed me. "Where do ya think?"

"I've heard about people stripping copper out of houses that have been foreclosed . . . ripping out the copper pipes and even the electrical wires."

He chuckled. "Good guess. You're not as naïve as you look."

I silently wondered if I should consider that a compliment.

"But, for the record, Matthew and I work on a strictly no-ask-no-tell basis. For all our dealings."

"Are *you* the one who gets him the ivory for his inlays?"

"Could be." He looked at the concrete dock. Luckily, I'd chosen the right path for him to drive down; the other side was barricaded. "I'll go move my truck. You can unlock the back door."

"I don't actually have access to Matthew's keys. But he's probably returned to the store by now. My name's Erin Smith," I lied. "What's yours?"

He narrowed his eyes. "That's one of those no-ask-no-tell business dealings I was explaining a moment ago." He held out his hand. "That'll be nine hundred. Cash only."

"Erin!" Matthew's voice boomed at me. He was marching toward us, his gaze smoldering. "What the hell are you doing?"

That was an excellent question. Moments ago I'd been so frightened that I was willing to hand over a cash register, and now I was standing behind a building with this shady character! What kind of a moron was I?! "Here's the man with the money, right here," I said, gesturing toward Matthew.

"What are you doing back here?!" Matthew asked me again.

"Showing your supplier where to unload your materials."

Matthew clenched his jaw and shot us both a furious glare, which he allowed to linger on the big man. "You've been here a dozen times. You know where the loading dock is. What's up, Lee?"

He grinned. "I'm just having a little fun, teasing your new employee. That's all."

"She doesn't work here! She's a decorator!"

Designer, actually, but this wasn't a good time to quibble. I edged away, planning on running for all I was worth.

"She sure acted like she was. When I got here, she was standing behind your—"

"Hey, Matthew," a familiar voice called. I whirled around, immensely relieved to see Sullivan heading toward us. He waggled his thumb over his shoulder. "Did you know that there's nobody inside, minding your store?"

"Your clerk said he had an emergency and took off," I explained. "So I answered your phone. And by the way, if you can just deliver Burke's desk for us tomorrow, that'd be great. You can send us the bill."

While I was talking, I grabbed Steve's arm and started to head with him toward my van.

"I don't know what you think you found out just now,"

Matthew called after me, "but it's all perfectly legal. I'm simply buying some used copper."

"I'm sure," I called back lightly, my heart still pounding.

"What were you talking to her about?" I heard Matthew ask Lee under his breath.

"Nothing," came the low reply.

We passed Lee's large, unmarked white van. I whispered to Sullivan, "Get that license plate."

Sullivan keyed the license plate number into his cell phone. His van was parked right next to mine. He grumbled at me, "I am not even going to ask what the hell you thought you were doing just now."

"Good, because I already know I made a stupid mistake, and we need to get out of here."

We'd barely pulled out of the parking lot in our separate vans before my cell phone rang. It was Sullivan. I could see him on the phone in my mirror. "What were you doing just now?" he asked in lieu of a greeting.

"First off, thank you for not shouting." *This* time I probably deserved it. "But you said you weren't going to ask me that."

"Changed my mind. Answer the question."

"Originally, I was just going to pay for the desk. That big guy confused me with an employee, but that isn't important now. What matters is that I found out Matthew's company is buying stolen goods this very minute, so we should get the police over there pronto."

"That was a supplier you and Matthew were talking to?"

"Yes, and he admitted he'd stripped the copper wiring and pipes from a house."

"Jeez. I read someplace that World's Watchdogs was

trying to call people's attention to that very crime. Copper is now five times more expensive than it was a decade ago."

"At least copper is being recycled this way. Stolen, yes, but recycled nevertheless."

"I'll call Officer Delgardio," Sullivan said. "Maybe I should double back. Matthew might send that van owner packing before he buys the stuff. He's got to figure you were going to blow the whistle on him."

"No, Sullivan. If Linda wants your help making an arrest, she'll ask for it."

He let out a bark of laughter. *"You're* telling *me* something like that? To stay out of police business?"

"Because it's impossible to say what those guys will do next. I caught them red-handed. Luckily, you arrived in the nick of time."

"Yeah. I was there because we got our wires crossed. I spoke to Matthew yesterday, and I thought *I* was going to pay for the desk, not you. We seem to be on a different page. Once again."

"Tell that to Jennifer Fairfax," I blurted out. "Miss Hands-on."

There was a pause long enough for me to feel like my heart was now in my throat. "What are you talking about?" he asked finally.

I pulled into our small parking lot and into my space. "I recognized her shade of lipstick this morning. Are you going to tell me you're not seeing her?"

His phone clicked off, and he pulled into the space beside me. I got out of my car, just as he was coming around the side. "I know full well she's after you, Sullivan. It couldn't be more obvious."

"That isn't my fault, Gilbert. Nothing's going to come

of it because I told her I was in—" He broke off, looked away, and said, "—a really bad place right now."

Stunned, as he'd obviously been on the verge of saying something very different, I managed to mutter, "Oh. Good." Had he been on the verge of using the "L" word? Or was he merely going to say that he was involved with me? Or interested in someone else?

"Give me Delgardio's number," he demanded irritably. He was avoiding my gaze. It wasn't *his* fault how *Jennifer* behaved, after all. She did tend to kiss people's cheeks when she greeted them. The lipstick on his collar could have meant nothing.

I brought up Linda's work number on my phone and held it out to him. He almost yanked the phone from my grasp, then turned his back on me.

I tried to take stock of the situation. This morning, I'd freaked out because of his collar, accusing him of not showing me he cared and constantly yelling at me. Yet two weeks ago he'd given me a rose carved from a grape. That was both creative and endearing. Now I'd held him accountable for someone else's flirtatious behavior, idiotically put myself in real physical danger, and backed him into such a corner that he hadn't dared to even yell at me—even though shouting was probably justified.

While I raked myself over the coals, Sullivan calmly explained the situation at Matthew's store to Linda. If I had to guess what he was thinking about me, it would be that we should admit defeat and stop trying to date, once and for all. It was probably high time one of us grabbed the reins and admitted that was the wisest move for both our sakes.

Sullivan said, "Okay, thanks," and snapped my phone shut. He tossed me my phone. "She says to tell you hi, and that if you go back to Matthew's store she'll never speak to you again."

"Is it too late to tell her 'hi' back?"

Sullivan stared at the asphalt a foot or two ahead of where I was standing. He sighed. "Erin, I really think—" He broke off and finally sighed.

"What?" I prompted.

He searched my features, his eyes pleading.

Just say it, I silently urged. Say we need to stop dating so that *I* don't have to. Because I can't.

"I really think I can handle the job at Suzanne's on my own today. So you might as well go home and oversee the demo work on Audrey's kitchen."

"Okay. Thanks."

I stepped aside and watched as he got back in his van and drove away. He didn't look back at me even once.

chapter **21**

Later that afternoon, my first remodel-related task in my own home turned out to be getting Audrey out of the house. The exasperation etched on the foreman's face, along with the limited progress his crew had made with the demolition, had made my role abundantly clear. I convinced her to accompany me to the salvage yard to see if they had gotten in any useful items or materials for the remodel. They hadn't, actually, but Audrey was a shopaholic when it came to any and all household items, so she cheerfully purchased a used eight-by-ten red heavy-duty plastic mat for the garage floor. She hoped to use it in her potting shed someday. Provided she ever actually built one.

By the time we returned, the workmen had left for the day. Audrey and I unloaded the mat, which linked together like a toddler's jigsaw puzzle. As we were stacking the pieces in the back corner of the garage—it was going to take me a few days to convince her that the practical way to store a garage mat was to spread it across the garage floor—I suggested that she guard herself against micromanaging the workmen. She took my lecture reasonably well, though that usually meant my words went in one ear and out the other.

We'd been home about twenty minutes when a motion outside the window caught my eye. I rose and looked out.

"Is something the matter?" Audrey asked, looking up from the newspaper to peer at me over the rim of her reading glasses.

"No, I just—" I broke off. Was that a man trying to hide behind the blue spruce in our side yard?

"What is it?" Audrey rushed to the window. She gasped when, sure enough, a man peeked out and then ducked back behind the tree. "Good Lord! A trespasser! And he's wearing combat fatigues! I'm calling nine-one-one!" She dashed to the phone.

"It's Darren Campesio!" I cried.

Audrey froze with the receiver in her hand. "*Darren?* From the contest? Are you sure?"

He was now darting toward another tree. I pointed with my chin, and Audrey spotted him. "You're right." She returned the phone to its cradle. "That *is* Darren! My neighbors are going to think this is a drug bust or something!"

"Or that he's a burglar. And they'll call the police."

"Getting arrested would serve him right. Honestly!"

She threw open the door and marched outside. "Darren Campesio! You come out from behind my evergreens this minute and explain yourself!" I snatched the phone receiver and dashed onto the front walk to stand beside her, wishing the phone were Margot's pepper spray.

After a second or two, Darren rounded the tree. "I was just trying to protect you by keeping an eye on the house."

"Nonsense! We have an unlisted phone number—how did you even know where we lived?"

"I found your address on the Internet. It's really very simple, you know."

"Did you think you'd be able to learn whom I've chosen as the contest winner by spying on me?" Audrey asked.

"No."

"Then why are you here?" I asked him.

He hemmed and hawed for a while, then finally said, "The truth is, I was doing some . . . reconnaissance work for personal reasons."

"Which are?" I asked.

"I'd really rather not say."

"Explain yourself or I'm going to report you for trespassing," Audrey demanded. I held up the phone to reinforce her words.

Darren looked from her to me, then sighed. "I was trying to keep track of when you come and go. And to make sure nobody else was living here."

"Pardon?" Audrey said.

"I was . . . trying to get a look at your bedroom to see if both sides of the bed were being used."

"Oh, for heaven's sake! *This* is your way of finding out if I'm available? All you had to do was look at the 'Goings On Around the Town' column in next Friday's *Sentinel.* I'm allowing myself to be auctioned off for charity."

"You are? How much are you expecting to sell yourself for?"

"A king's ransom. Although it's a single date with me that's being auctioned." She turned to me. "Oh, and by the way, Erin, I put your name down, too."

"You didn't!"

She shrugged. "It's for a good cause."

Darren was now grinning at us.

"We'll discuss this later," I snapped at Audrey. "This is really not a good way of impressing a woman, Mr. Campesio."

He donned a sheepish smile and turned to Audrey. "Sorry about that, Ms. Munroe. But, now that you mention it, I *am* also curious to find out if the contest is over."

"Yes, Darren, I *have* made my decision, and you can wait till tomorrow night for my announcement at the Earth Love awards ceremony."

"Did Burke win?" he asked me in conspiratorial tones.

"I don't know who won, Darren."

He nodded and then turned hopeful eyes to Audrey. "Do you have a date to the event, Ms. Munroe?"

"I just told you, I'm announcing the winner. I can't very well turn that into a date with one of the three finalists, now, *can* I?"

"You don't think that would look good?"

"No, I do not. And next time you want to ask me on a date or to glean some information, don't dress up like a duck hunter and stalk me." She stormed into the house.

"Really, Darren," I said. "You've gone way too far."

He shrugged and kicked at a piece of ice on the ground like a petulant little boy.

"I'll call the police if you ever stake out our house again."

"Fine. I won't do it again."

I went back inside the house, leaving Darren in the front yard, staring down at his combat boots. Audrey had settled back into her wing chair with the newspaper. She muttered, "This has been my first chance to read today's paper, I've been so busy."

"Were you serious about putting my name in for the auction?"

She lowered the newspaper. "It truly is a good cause, Erin. And I *truly* meant to discuss it with you first. It slipped my mind."

She was one of the least forgetful people I'd ever met. "I'm sorry, Audrey, but I can't go along with you this time. You've got to withdraw my name. Or I will."

"I'm sorry, Erin, but it's too late for that. I'm afraid you're stuck."

Before I could come up with a reply, the doorbell rang. Although she made a show of annoyance, Audrey struck me as eager for an interruption. She went to the door and swung it open. It was Darren, camouflage cap in his hands. "Good afternoon, Ms. Munroe. I was wondering if you would please give me the pleasure of your companionship, for dinner and a movie, sometime next week or the following week."

"No, but thank you for asking."

"Next month?"

"I don't think so. In all honesty, Mr. Campesio, the two of us don't have a single thing in common."

"You'll just have to get together with me, so we can find out if that's true. I'll be clipping that 'Around Town' column, Ms. Munroe. And then I'll be seeing you at this charity auction. If you won't agree to date me in person, I'll just have to be the highest bidder. Good evening, ladies." He nodded politely, then went on his way.

Audrey held her composure until he was out of sight, then grabbed my arm, squeezing way too tight, and said, "How much money do you have in savings, Erin?"

"I don't know off the—"

"It doesn't matter. I'll pay you back. You have got to promise me you'll outbid Darren Campesio!"

"Gee, Audrey. No offense, but you're really not my type. And, I can't very well agree to bid on *you* while you've forced me into being auctioned myself. So, I'm afraid I'll only be able to bid—"

"Oh, fine! I'll get you out of it. Honestly, Erin! You're acting like a big baby."

I chuckled, but Audrey was in such a foul mood that she brushed past me without as much as a smile. "See if I ever offer *you* access to my little black book again."

On Saturday morning, Sullivan called. He said he'd just spoken to Burke, who wanted us both to meet him at Asia's house around noon. Apparently he needed two witness signatures for his formal agreement to dismantle his windmill in exchange for Asia's removing the gaudy bazaar of items along their joint property line. He promised our visit shouldn't take more than ten minutes.

Sullivan picked me up, and we made it there right on time, at noon. There was no sign of Burke's car as we pulled up near Asia's driveway. "I wonder why Burke chose us for this strange task," I said as we waited.

"I asked him that. He didn't know anyone else who'd met Asia McClure and could still tolerate her company."

"That's probably true. Although I doubt he looked all that hard."

He shut off the engine. "We'll have to wait here. Burke felt strongly that all three of us should arrive together."

Burke was fifteen minutes late, which was very unusual for him. I'd been just about to call him on his cell phone when he drove into Asia's driveway and waved. We pulled in after him.

"Sorry I'm late," he said as we emerged from our vehicles. "Especially since this is a weekend. Let's get this over with fast, so I won't take up any more of your time, okay?"

"Lead the way," Sullivan said, gesturing to the door.

Asia must have seen us approach, because she opened the door as we were still starting to make our way up her steps. "What are you doing here? Is this an energy-consumption intervention or something?"

Ignoring her remark, Burke said, "I asked Erin and Steve to meet me here and act as mediators." He paused, but when she said nothing, he pulled a trifolded sheet of paper out of his inner jacket pocket and held it out to her. "I typed up a friendly little proposal. It says that I will take down the windmill from my property in exchange for your removing any and all obstacles from the border between our properties. Including those in the pond and the webbing itself."

"Let me read it for myself. Wait here." She went into her house and shut the door.

"Was your desk delivered this morning, Burke?" I asked.

"I hope so. Matthew said he'd deliver it no later than ten, but I had to take off before nine. I left a note telling them to remove its packaging and recycle the materials, and to leave the desk on the porch."

"Out in the open?" I asked in alarm.

"Why not?" Burke replied. "The sky's clear as a bell, and my house is in the middle of nowhere."

That was true, but the idea of a custom-made desk left on someone's porch still made me nervous. Obviously Burke didn't share my concerns, however, and it was his property. "We should inspect the desk, since we're here," I said to Steve.

Burke rolled his eyes. "The three of us could probably head over there right now, move it into place, write a couple of letters, and return, all before Asia will open her door again."

But Asia came outside right then. "Fine. I signed it. Just add your initials to my handwritten codicil, and you've got a deal."

Burke puzzled over her handwriting for a few moments, then said to us, "We have until noon next Saturday to take down our windmill and our fence, respectively." He initialed the document. "Which is fine by me. I can have workers here Monday morning to dismantle the windmill."

"In which case I'll get the fence down on Tuesday," Asia replied.

"Great. I'm glad we could—" She shut her door.

"Always such a pleasant woman," Sullivan remarked.

We walked to our cars. Burke was grinning. "I'm sure she'll be ecstatic when she finds out I sold my windmill to Darren Campesio. *And* that I talked him into building a third."

"You did?" I couldn't help but grin as well.

He laughed and nodded. "She can do what she wants to Darren's fence. It isn't visible from my property, and I'm sure Darren won't mind." He rubbed his hands together. "So, want to follow me and take a quick look at the desk?"

"Absolutely."

He led the way.

We arrived a minute or two later and followed him up the walkway. The three of us stood on his front porch, unabashedly admiring the gorgeous hand-crafted desk.

"It's a thing of beauty," Steve said. He sometimes designed furniture himself, and I had known this desk would be totally to his taste.

"Wow!" Burke said. "I like this even better than the one you showed me on Matthew's Web site." He pulled out one of the drawers on the side, and then slid it back into place. "It's great. You can open and close these drawers with one finger."

"It really is amazing," I said. "Let me show you the joinery, Steve." I tried to open the kneehole drawer. "Huh. This one drawer seems to be a little stuck," I muttered.

"Let me take a look," Sullivan said.

I tugged hard on the drawer. It slid open. A bracket had been fastened to the bottom of the drawer, and just in front of it, a ball-like object attached to a string was vibrating. The action of my tugging the drawer open must have dislodged the ball from where it was wedged. But why was it there in the first place?

My brain took forever to make the connection, but Burke's reactions were faster. He yelled, "It's a grenade!"

chapter **22**

The bracket had kept the safety clamped down, and my opening the drawer had pulled the grenade loose! The next thing I knew, Burke was pushing me off his porch and into the snowbank. He dove on top of me, his glasses flying off his face in the process.

"Steve!" I yelled, twisting around and struggling to get out from under Burke. "Run!"

Despite my warning, I watched in horror as he reached into the desk. "No!" I yelled. But he grabbed the grenade and yanked it free from the string. He threw the grenade onto the ice that covered the pond. It skittered to a stop as it caught on the chain of water toys that Asia had strung together. An instant later, it exploded.

Although I automatically ducked and covered my head, the blast was small and just distant enough that nothing hit any of us. A few seconds afterwards, I was staring at the pond, which had been instantly cleared of ice in spectacular fashion.

Steve looked pale and shocked. He jumped off the porch and helped me to my feet, leaving Burke to scramble to his feet by himself. "Are you all right, Erin?"

"I'm fine. Probably a little bruised is all."

"That was really quick thinking, Steve," Burke said as he retrieved his glasses. "Thank you!"

Asia came running toward the pond. She gaped at the pond, the ice now blown to bits and the water toys in fragments. She put her hands on her hips and cried, "I just got through telling you I'd take this stuff down! You didn't need to blow it up!"

"I didn't mean to," Burke said. "Somebody just tried to kill me with a grenade!"

"But they missed and hit the pond?"

"No. I'll explain later."

"Fine. You can explain when you're reimbursing me for all the toys you just destroyed!" She spun on her heel and marched back toward her house. "Along with any dead fish!"

"I'll just give her five bucks and call it even," Burke muttered.

My heart was still pounding. "Thank you, Steve." I had such a strong desire to throw myself into his arms that I didn't dare even meet his gaze.

"Cripes!" Burke cried, looking at the desk. "Matthew Hayes booby-trapped my desk so he could kill me! Or else someone rigged the thing while it was sitting out on my front porch."

"We have to call the police to investigate," Steve said.

"I'm sure as hell not moving that thing into my house until a bomb squad examines it." Burke eyed the desk suspiciously as he fished his cell phone out of his pocket. "I'm going to call the police right now."

Sullivan and I exchanged glances. "Here we go again," he said under his breath. Another police report meant spending our Saturday waiting around and answering the same predictable questions over and over again. "Erin and I were on our way to lunch." He removed a business card from his wallet. "Just give the police one of these and tell them how they can reach us as witnesses."

"Will do," Burke said, pocketing the card. He then said into the phone, "Yeah, hi. My name is Dr. Burke Stratton. Someone tried to kill me just now with a grenade. It was hooked up to explode when I opened my desk."

That will get their attention, I thought, as Steve and I strode purposefully to his van. Though we let it go unsaid, neither of us wanted to give the dispatcher the chance to instruct Burke to keep us there until the police arrived. The call would probably go directly to Detective O'Reilly's desk, and he would not appreciate our leaving the scene. Yet there wasn't one iota of information we could tell the investigators that Burke couldn't tell them as well.

"Now someone's trying to bomb us," Sullivan muttered the instant we were in the van.

"Who knew interior design was such a dangerous profession?"

We both laughed. "This explains our high insurance premiums." He pulled onto the road. As our nervous levity evaporated, he said, "I hope Burke didn't plant the grenade himself."

"No way. He was standing right there beside us. He could have gotten killed himself!"

"True. Unless he wanted to divert suspicion from himself... assuming the calculated risk of injury."

Refusing to let this conversation devolve into yet another argument, I squeezed his arm and said, "Thank you for saving our lives. So where are you taking me for lunch?"

He smiled at me. "I was hoping you hadn't already made lunch plans. Since we're stuck going to that hokey awards ceremony on a Saturday night, let's pull all the stops and go to the Lookout."

"Yum!" And whee! In no time flat, my day had gone from a grenade nearly exploding in my face to an unplanned meal with Steve at my favorite restaurant. Now if we could somehow just get our romance back on track, the trauma of the day would be well worthwhile.

That evening, the big event that would draw this ill-fated contest to an end was finally at hand. I was wearing the old standby—a little black silk dress and stilettos—as I mingled at the Earth Love rotunda in their courtyard. The bar was strictly nonalcoholic—a selection of sodas and mineral waters were on tap and served in glass tumblers. The catering staff bustled around with trays of appetizers—all organic and vegetarian—and stacks of small white ceramic plates were stacked at the ready. The only disposable items were the off-white paper napkins, made from recycled paper, and the unadorned toothpicks jabbed into the appetizers.

The building itself was a sparkling glass geodesic dome. It was also a greenhouse, and so well designed that the vegetation inside was almost self-sustaining. The lines and angles of the dome itself were compelling, but keeping all that glass clean seemed a nightmare task.

Steve and I had enjoyed a wonderful lunch before the day took another nosedive: Detective O'Reilly called first Steve's cell, then mine. O'Reilly had vindictively separated the two of us, then held us hostage at the police station all afternoon. For my part, most of the time was spent alone in a tiny interview room, where I knew officers could watch me through the one-way glass mirror. I knew O'Reilly wanted me to complain so he could snap at me for leaving the scene, so I'd been the picture of patience and spent three hours accomplishing nothing.

Sullivan was waiting for me afterwards, but by then we were both in foul moods, and had to rush home to get dressed and drive to the ceremony separately.

I vowed not to waste even more time thinking about it now. I had to focus on working the room, something of a job requirement in my occupation. After my horrid afternoon, that was a tall order, especially considering that the strongest ingredient in my beverage was its lemon twist, and there were some two or three hundred attendees in this particular room.

Burke Stratton spotted me, waved, and headed toward me. He looked handsome in his black tailored suit and red silk tie. Every few people he brushed past stopped him for a friendly exchange, wishing him luck, of which he would need plenty in order to win. Luck, plus a better basement, I mused wryly.

"Hi, Erin. Did things go okay for you at the police station?" Burke asked solicitously.

So he'd heard that the police had insisted that I come in. "Fine."

"Did you learn anything?"

"Nothing about possible suspects or motives, no. Just that Detective O'Reilly's first name is Phil."

"That's . . . not exactly useful information to me."

"Nor to me." The subject had come up when I objected to how O'Reilly had shaken his head and said, "Erin, Erin." I promptly asked him what *his* first name was, and, when he answered, tried to demonstrate how condescending he'd been. But O'Reilly had acted pleasantly surprised by my question. It had crossed my mind that Sullivan might be right about the detective's having a crush on me after all. But the notion was quickly proved wrong by O'Reilly's harsh treatment of me from there on.

Burke's sigh brought me out of my reverie. "Do I have a snowball's chance in hell of winning this contest?"

"Oh, sure." Just no *better* of a chance than that, I silently added. "Audrey can be unpredictable."

"Enough to award a house that we all know will be a pile of rubble inside of ten years?"

"I doubt it."

He grimaced and scanned the room. "Figures Earth Love would be so health-conscious that they wouldn't serve alcohol."

I finally located Steve, who was chatting with a bevy of women across the room. He looked gorgeous in a wool pinstripe suit, obviously hand-tailored. He grinned in my direction and started to make his way toward me. Just then I also spotted Jennifer Fairfax standing by the door, scanning the room. She, too, was dressed to the nines, her blond hair in an attractive updo, wearing a shimmering coppery dress that looked great on her. She spotted Steve, and I could tell by simple triangulation that she was going to reach him before he'd reach me.

Fortunately, there was a sudden buzz in the room, giving me the perfect excuse to turn my back so I wouldn't have to witness their rendezvous. Audrey, I saw, was approaching the stage, along with the top executives of Earth Love.

A lengthy introduction required our clapping every twenty seconds or so as one after another Earth Love affiliate or employee was thanked for their contribution. Audrey finally took the microphone. She gave a gracious prelude, thanking Earth Love effusively and speaking glowingly of Richard and Walter's reputations and impact on the field of conservation. Though my cheeks were burning, I was determined to remain focused on the stage and not to turn and look at Sullivan with Miss Manicured Hands-on.

To one side of me, I saw Darren Campesio, wearing a tan corduroy suit, a green tie, and a cocky smile, edge closer to the stage. He gave Audrey a little wave when she glanced toward him, and she quickly looked away. She wasn't looking in Burke's and my direction either, and although I hadn't located Margot, it was very easy to surmise that she'd won the competition.

"All three homes had wonderful features," Audrey continued, "and all of the home owners and designers are to be congratulated for jobs so very well done. After giving the matter considerable thought, I felt that one house was my favorite and best fulfilled all judging categories. The winner of the first annual Thayers-Emory

Green Home Award given by Earth Love is Margot Troy."

Over the applause, Darren's grunt of disgust was so loud it could easily have been heard halfway across the room. Margot, standing a few yards away, emitted a little gasp, followed by a cry of delight. Jeremy kissed her and whispered something in her ear, then joined in the applause. She climbed the steps to the stage, where she gleefully accepted the three-by-five-foot check, along with a small green glass trophy, no doubt made from recycled bottles.

Red-faced and wearing a furious glare, Darren made his way over to Burke and me. "Mine's better," he promptly said. "I've got the better efficiency ratings and comfort and everything."

"Ah, give it a rest," Burke said. "Your house looks like the top of a hollowed-out toadstool. You know it. I know it. Audrey knows it. Nobody in their right mind would want to live there."

"And *your* house is turning into a moldy toadstool. You'd better do something about your drainage issues, or it's going to smell like one, too, my friend."

Burke shot him a glare, but held his tongue.

I was still dying to turn around; Sullivan and Jennifer had to be behind me, chatting each other up by now. "Were you home around lunchtime today, Darren?" I asked to distract myself.

"Er, I think so. Why?"

"I'm just surprised you didn't hear the explosion on Burke's property. That's all."

"Explosion?" he asked, his tawny cheeks coloring a reddish brown. "Did your septic tank explode?"

"A grenade went off," Burke explained. "It does seem real odd that you didn't hear the blast."

"Yeah. Huh. I must have been inside my shooting range. Once those doors are shut, you can't hear much of anything." He looked past my shoulder, then said good evening to someone behind me—Sullivan, I realized with a lump in my throat.

"Good evening, everyone," Sullivan said. My pulse was instantly racing. I inched away from him. I was still determined not to look around for Hands-on. "You're discussing the grenade, I gather," he continued. "It had been jerry-rigged inside a desk, which had been recently delivered to Burke's front porch. The police were theorizing that it could have come from your private cache, Darren."

"You have hand grenades in your house?" Burke asked Darren in alarm.

"Not any more. The police confiscated them after the shooting. Walter Emory's, I mean. So I guess maybe someone took one of my grenades at the same time they stole my guns."

"Guns?" I repeated in alarm. "More than one was stolen?"

"Aw, jeez," Burke moaned. "I moved out to the sub-urbs of Crestview for the quiet, peaceful lifestyle. *Not* for the easy access to firearms and grenades!"

"Hey! It wasn't *me* who blew up your pond, buddy!"

"So you *did* know about the explosion," I said.

Darren winced, realizing his gaffe.

"Why did you lie about hearing the blast?" Sullivan asked.

"I didn't want to get involved. It wasn't my fault some-one broke into my home and took my personal property. I'm not going to be made responsible. And...I didn't want to ruin my chances with Ms. Munroe." He glared at me. "I knew you'd tell her about it being my grenade if I'd charged over there while you were still at Burke's house."

"You even knew we were there when it exploded?" Steve asked, balling his fists.

"Yeah. I came outside when Burke and Asia were shouting back and forth."

"You figured nobody got killed, so you just went back inside your house," Burke said with disgust.

"Which is no less than what you'd have done if our situations were reversed."

"Not true. I'd have run to the scene to see if you or anyone else needed medical assistance," Burke retorted. He returned his attention to Sullivan and me. "Thank you for all the hard work you've put into my home. I appreciate it. I'm sorry that it's proven to be...gilding an ice castle, but I appreciate it. I'm going home." He glared at Darren. "Before it turns into a rotting toadstool."

"I'm sorry about how things turned out for you, Burke," I said.

He mustered a smile, and Sullivan thanked him and even shook his hand.

Unable to resist a moment longer, I glanced behind me, but couldn't see Hands-on anywhere. Sullivan said, "Jennifer Fairfax was in the area and dropped by. She said to say hello."

"Oh? Did she leave already?" I tried to hide my glee.

"Yeah. She just wanted to wish us luck and took off when Audrey made her announcement."

Darren, too, mumbled something about leaving and started to shuffle off. He stopped and gazed into my eyes. "Erin? There's really no reason for you to mention to Audrey about it being *my* grenade that exploded near you, is there?"

"A reason? No, but we talk about almost everything, so I wouldn't count on the subject not coming up."

"This is why I'm a confirmed bachelor." He stormed away.

Steve grinned at me, and I said to him, "And speaking for Audrey and all of womankind...what an excellent decision on Mr. Campesio's part."

He chuckled and our gazes locked. I hesitated for just an instant, but reasoned that we'd both narrowly missed being injured or killed by a grenade today, and in comparison, how bad could a conversational bomb be? "As long as we're on the topic of confirmed bachelors, are *you* one?"

"A confirmed bachelor, you mean?" he asked, a playful sparkle in his eyes.

"That's right." I wasn't going to turn this into a joke and let him get away with a nonanswer.

"No, Erin, I'm not." He brushed his fingertips down the length of my arm and then took my hand in his. "In fact, back before Richard was killed and everything went to—"

"Erin!" a woman behind me said.

Annoyed that we were being interrupted at such a time, I whirled around. It was Margot. She looked ecstatic, crossing the floor toward me with her usual grand composure and grace. Standing a short distance behind her, Jeremy, on the other hand, looked decidedly gloomy. I could see why—this was an enormous setback for him, and might result in his having to shut the doors of Greene Home Architecture.

"Hello, Steve."

"Congratulations, Margot," he said, and gave her a peck on the cheek.

I took my cue from him and congratulated her, as

well. She thanked us both, then said, "You were obviously deep in conversation. I'm so sorry to interrupt."

"That's all right, Margot," Steve said graciously. "Erin and I can talk anytime."

Except that we never seem to actually do so.

"Erin, I just wanted to say how very grateful I am for your contributions to my kitchen design. For all we know, that's what made the difference in your own client not winning."

"That and the crumbling foundation," I remarked.

"Oh, yes. Poor Jeremy." She glanced back at him, and Jeremy quickly mustered a smile. He grabbed his cell phone and began to talk into it, or at least, to pretend that he was. He made what looked like a hasty apology to Margot, and then left the room, still speaking into his phone.

"I'm giving him the proceeds from the contest to help him stay afloat," Margot told me in conspiratorial tones, "but there's only so much I can do. He's had nothing to do with the design of my house." She sighed and searched my features. "How's your investigation coming along, Erin?"

"You mean the police investigation into the murders?"

"Of course. Everyone knows you have a skill for solving these things. And now that I've won the contest and the money, it's extra important to me that you succeed. I'm surely next on the hit list."

"Hit list?"

"After Richard and Walter. Granted, they were judges, not contestants, but maybe the link was their roles as public figureheads for ecology. Now that my green home has gotten such prestigious recognition, someone might try to take me out of the limelight."

"I don't know what to say, Margot. I wish you could

just be happy that you got this tremendous honor, which you deserved."

"Life can be so unfair," she replied. "All you have to do is think about poor Richard and Walter, if you have any doubts about that."

"That's true," Steve said sadly.

She nodded. Her mood had darkened considerably, and there were no vestiges of the confidence she'd exhibited as she crossed the floor just moments ago. "If I get killed tomorrow, it'll be too late to worry. Or to ask you to keep an eye out for me."

"That much I can do," I replied. "For whatever it's worth."

"Thanks."

"You're welcome. And congratulations again."

She grimaced a little and said again, "Thanks."

An Earth Love representative called for her to come join him for some more interviews, and she plastered her smile back into place as she joined a group of people across the room.

At last, I was able to return my attention to Steve. He appeared to be lost in thought. "You were saying?" I asked gently.

"Hmm?" He looked at a spot behind me. I turned. My heart sank. Jennifer Fairfax was still here, after all, apparently waiting for us to finish our conversation. She was gazing at Steve with unabashed desire. No self-respecting woman would be that publicly brazen with her emotions if her affections were completely unrequited. I whirled around and glared at him.

He averted his gaze. "I lost my train of thought completely. Sorry, Gilbert."

"No problem, Sullivan." I turned a little. Audrey was

watching us, but she quickly looked away. "I need to go thank Audrey. See you Monday."

I walked away without giving him much of a chance to respond.

Audrey greeted me with a hug. "You look a little upset. It isn't because of my decision, is it?"

"No, of course not. I'd have chosen Margot's house, too. I just wanted to thank you for stepping in and saving the day. I'm relieved this contest is over."

"I'm sure that's true for all of us. Well, not counting Mr. Campesio and Dr. Stratton."

I glanced back at Margot, thinking that she, at least, was not feeling especially relieved at the moment. I stiffened as I saw Sullivan heading toward me. I whirled around to face Audrey once again. She caught my expression, looked behind him to where Hands-on was standing, and said, "Oh, *now* I get the picture."

"Good evening, Audrey," Sullivan said, exuding charm.

"Hello, Mr. Sullivan," she replied coldly.

"Steve," he corrected, sounding both hurt and surprised. "I wanted to thank you before I left."

"There's no need, Mr. Sullivan. And I'm leaving, too. Time, as they say, flies. Next thing you know, it's later than you think." She grabbed my arm. "Let's go home, Erin." She narrowed her eyes at Sullivan. "Nobody appreciates stragglers."

At nine o'clock Monday morning, Margot was waiting by our office door. Surprised, I greeted her and asked if everything was all right.

"Can I come in?"

"Of course," I said, unlocking the door and holding it for her. "Can I take your coat?"

She ignored the question and began to pace while I flipped on our lights and hung up my own coat. "They're trying to ruin me," Margot said. "I should have known this would happen."

"Who is?"

"The press. The public. It's all your client's fault."

"Do you mean Burke?"

"Who else? He's the only one with enough of a grudge to tell the media. They must have interviewed him. This morning's paper said they got the information from 'unnamed sources.' I won that contest fair and square. My choice of modes for transportation has nothing to do with my house."

"True. Although all I've ever seen you drive is that SUV-style hybrid. Doesn't everyone know it gets excellent gas mileage? For an SUV?"

"My car isn't the problem. It's my plane. I have my own private jet for when I travel. And Burke's the only person I can think of who knows I have a private jet *and* who would have been all too happy to blab about it. Haven't you read this morning's newspaper?"

I sat down at my desk. Margot continued to pace. There was no point in suggesting Margot have a seat; she'd sit if she wanted to. "Not yet. I take it they disclosed that you had a private jet in the article?"

"Worse. In a sidebar. Sidebars are the only part of a newspaper story that actually get read." She sank into the Sheraton chair in front of me. "The headline of the side story was: 'How Green Is Hypocrisy?' "

"Ouch. How often do you use your plane?"

"Why?"

"Just curious."

"Every couple of weeks. I enjoy the occasional foray to my condo in Telluride."

"I didn't know you had a second home."

"I do. I keep thinking of hiring you and Mr. Sullivan to redecorate the place. The original owner had it covered in monkeys."

"Monkeys?"

"Everywhere you look. The wallpaper, the artwork, the bric-a-brac. It's tasteful enough, I suppose. If you like monkeys."

"Would our transportation be provided?" I couldn't help but ask.

"In my jet, you mean, obviously. I don't suppose you meant my paying for your gas for you to drive the eight hours each way. Even though a car ride causes less than a tenth of the carbon emissions of a flight. See how easy it is to compromise one's ideals?" She sighed. "I give huge amounts of money to environmental causes. I don't even get to declare that as a tax deduction, because saving the earth is considered political, or some such nonsense. You don't see the *Crestview Sentinel* doing a sidebar on my donations, though, do you?"

"No."

"Well, of course *you* don't. Since you didn't see the original story either."

"I'd be happy to discuss getting rid of your monkeys with Steve, if you'd like." Now *there* was a sentence I never could have imagined myself saying.

"Yes, I would. Thank you." She rose. "Although I am just not making that drive twice a month. So we may need to wait to see if I get so much flack about my jet that I'll want to sell my monkey depository."

"Cheer up, Margot. You won a contest that you deserved to win, and you worked hard for the honor."

"*And* I lost my boyfriend."

"You and Jeremy broke up?"

She nodded. "He came over to my house yesterday. He said our lives were heading in such opposite directions, he just couldn't take it anymore. That he wanted to be the one I could look up to for a change. So he had a lot of rebuilding to do."

"Maybe he means that."

"And maybe my monkeys will fly me to and from Telluride," she grumbled as she let herself out my door.

"On the bright side," I called after her, "you're no longer going to be the queen of ecology. So that will keep you off the hit list you were worried about last night."

"Hooray for me," she said over her shoulder as the door swung shut behind her.

Not five minutes had passed before someone threw the door open so hard it banged against its stop. Matthew stepped inside. His cheeks were red, his eyes blazing, and he seemed to be staring directly at my neck as he came toward me, breathing heavily with his hands balled into fists.

I sat up and braced myself. I had no place to run. I could flip my chair over and use it to shield me. Should I try to call 911? Would it be too late when they arrived?

He shook a piece of paper, clenched in his fist, at me. "I now have a police record, thanks to you, bitch!"

"What do you mean?"

"They arrested me in connection with stolen merchandise!"

"When?"

"Saturday!"

"Morning? How did you deliver the desk to Burke?"

"I had Mike do it. My employee. And thanks so much for your concern!"

"Your being under arrest at the time might have been the best thing that's happened to you, Matthew. The desk was booby-trapped with a grenade. This way you might have an alibi."

"I know! The police grilled me about that Saturday night! I had nothing to do with the damned grenade, and no idea how the damn thing got there!"

He was leaning into my face close enough for me to smell his sour breath.

"If that's—"

"It was put there after Mike delivered it. So I don't give a rat's ass about the grenade! I just care about trying to keep myself out of jail and my business afloat despite these lame-ass charges!"

I mustered some courage and said, "This is *my* office, Matthew. Get out of my face before I call the police on you again!"

He snarled at me, but took a step back. "I'll get you for this, Erin! You'll be sorry for reporting me!"

To my immense relief, he turned and left, slamming the door again behind him.

chapter 23

*S*ullivan arrived at the office half an hour later. By
then, all was quiet, no shrieking former clients
or furniture makers barging through the door to vent at
me. I had calmed down enough to decide that Matthew
was just voicing empty threats in my direction—if he'd
been the killer, his words would have served no purpose.

I'd vowed not to say a word to Steve about Jennifer
Fairfax's presence at the awards presentation Saturday
night. Or to ask if they'd spent Sunday together.

With his hair adorably tousled and his coat collar up,

he looked ridiculously handsome. I sighed and shook my head.

"What?" He removed his coat and hung it up. "Did I miss an appointment already or something?"

"No, just some whining and shouting. Margot's upset that the *Sentinel* ran a sidebar on the front page about her private jet...not exactly a solar-powered vehicle. And Matthew Hayes is probably going to get a heavy fine for buying stolen merchandise. Personally, I doubt he'll do jail time for that. In any case, he blames me."

"He should look in the mirror. *He's* the one who broke the law."

"That's exactly what I told him."

"Good. Did he thank you for showing him the light?"

"Of course. And then we burst into a rousing rendition of 'Amazing Grace' together."

He chuckled. "Sorry I missed that."

My heart was racing. Something was wrong with the way Sullivan was acting. The tone of his voice was fine, but he wasn't quite looking at me. He and I felt out of step somehow, and it now seemed impossible to keep my promise to myself.

"Guess you should have gotten up earlier, then," I said.

He ignored my remark. He raked his fingers through his hair. His eyes were glassy, and his hands were shaking a little.

"What's the matter? Did Jennifer Fairfax keep you up late last night?"

"No, Erin."

"Something's going on between you two, Steve. I saw the way she was looking at you Saturday night."

He set his jaw and stared at the top of his desk.

"Tell me something, Sullivan. How is it that you can find yourself standing two feet away from a grenade that's ready to explode, and calmly pick it up and throw it into a pond, but you can't sit ten feet away from me and tell me the truth about your feelings?"

"Because I'd rather lose my right arm than lose you." He spoke through clenched teeth.

"*Lose* me? By telling me the *truth*?"

Sullivan winced, but otherwise remained motionless.

"Oh, God. I'm right about you and Jennifer." I sank my head into my hands. "Just when I'd have given anything to be wrong."

"Erin. It was just—"

"Just what?!" I shouted. I was suddenly so irate that I felt utterly out of control. "Just a mistake? Just a one-night stand? Just sex? What are you going to say? That it was meaningless and you were thinking of me the whole time?"

"I *was*, actually," he answered in a choked voice. "Not that it makes it any more forgivable."

"No, it doesn't." I got to my feet. This felt unreal. How could this be happening? How could I feel stabbed in the heart like this? *Because I'd believed all along that he was my soul mate.* "You knew full well that I didn't want you making love to Jennifer Fairfax and imagining it was me! I wanted it to *be* me!"

"I know, Erin. That's what I want, too. I'd go back in time and change it if—"

"Are you in love with her?"

"No!"

"It sure looks like she's in love with you, though."

"She thinks she is. But I told Jen Saturday night that—"

"Don't say her name! I know who you're talking about!"

"It was a one-night stand. Right after Richard died. When we ran into each other downtown. I was out of my head, Erin. And I know it was wrong of me, but I was so mad at you. For not... knowing things that I hadn't told you. And there she was, all of a sudden, throwing herself at me..."

"Yet you went on seeing her time after time, working with her one-on-one as your private client! What's this going to do to our business? To our word-of-mouth referrals? Don't you realize she'll tell her friends about this?"

"She won't, Erin. I told her before and afterwards that it could never happen again, and she said it was fine. That she, too, was a consenting adult. That she was just looking for a good time, and that it meant nothing to her, either."

"Here's a news flash, Sullivan. Women lie. It's less painful than admitting to someone's face that he's just broken your heart."

"Have you ever gotten your breath knocked out so bad you can't get your breath again? And for a split second you feel like you're going to die from the pain?"

"Yes, Sullivan, I have! That's what I'm feeling right now!"

"That's the way I felt when I heard Richard died," he continued, ignoring my remark. "When I felt like it was my fault." The phone started to ring. I stared at it. "Don't answer that," he said. He went over to the phone jack on the wall and disconnected the wire.

I headed for the door. "I've got to go."

"Please, listen to me, Erin. These last few weeks... months, even, I'd gotten so wrapped up in you, in us, it was all I could think about. Wanting to be with you, to make love to you. Then Richard called out of the blue. It just felt... connected somehow. I got this fantasy stuck in my head where he'd be my best man at our wedding. You two would hit it off, and we'd introduce him to Audrey, and the four of us would be these fast friends, for the rest of our lives. It was crazy and stupid. Then, just when I realize it's actually happening, that you want me, too, Richard calls, totally whacked-out. And you two meet, and you hate each other. Then he gets murdered right in front of me, and it was too damned stupid to take him to the emergency room. And—what's-her-name comes on to me like gangbusters. I was in a state of shock. Couldn't figure out how it all went so wrong. I started thinking... maybe I was wrong about you and me."

Although I'd listened to his long confession as best I could, part of me was silently arguing with his every statement. "I've endured my own share of rough times, damn it all! You don't see me hopping into the sack with the first client who comes on to me!" I grabbed my coat.

"Erin, please." He came toward me. "I don't deserve you. I know that. Don't let this be the last straw for you. I'm begging you to forgive me. I hope I can make you understand. It was a mistake that I regret. But I told you the truth. All of it. I thought that's what you wanted."

"I wanted the truth to be different."

"So did I. So *do* I." He stood in front of me, blocking my path to the door. "Right after the awards ceremony I told... her that I was in love with you. I love you, Erin."

"What am I supposed to say to that now? That you've got one hell of a way of showing it?"

He looked stricken. "How about that you understand that I made a mistake? And that you can find it in your heart to forgive me someday? Can't you focus on the fact that I love you? Not on the screwup I made when I was out of my head?"

"Not right now, I sure can't. This is all too much to sort out at once, Sullivan."

"I understand. All I can do now is apologize and promise nothing like this will ever happen again."

"I have to go." I left, and this time, he didn't try to stop me.

I ran to my van, got behind the wheel and sobbed for a few minutes, but afterwards I didn't feel any better. I needed to talk to a girlfriend right now. And although I had several closer friends, it was Linda Delgardio whose advice I most craved. Maybe because her relationship with her husband was the one that I most admired of all my friends.

She answered her cell phone by saying, "Hi, Erin. What's up?"

"Are you on duty right now?" My voice sounded utterly pathetic to my own ears.

"Not for another two hours." Her voice was rife with alarm. "What's wrong? Please tell me you're not being held at gunpoint, so I can keep breathing."

"No, I'm fine. Rather, I'm not in physical danger. It's about Sullivan. We broke up. He slept with a client."

Silence. "Was this right after his friend was killed?"

"Are you psychic, or something? He didn't talk about that during a police interview, did he?"

"No, Erin. It's just . . . something that's been known to happen. A reaction to being confronted with one's own mortality. But never mind that now. Do you want to come over?"

"No, I want to know what to do! I want to be somebody

else … anybody but me! He just said he loved me, but now I can't believe him. We agreed a while ago that we weren't going to see anybody else. I thought I could trust him, but I obviously can't. I'm feeling so … I don't even know how to describe it. Like I'm getting pulled every which way."

Linda was silent for several seconds. "Where are you right now?" she asked gently.

"In my van. In my parking space."

"If he came after you right now, what would you do?"

"I don't know."

"Do you love him?"

"I don't want to answer that question. The man just told me he cheated on me!"

"I thought you hadn't even slept with him yet."

"I haven't. Why? Should that make a difference?"

"It would to me."

I reconsidered. It wasn't as if we were engaged, or married. I wanted an operator's guide to this situation. Or just a step-by-step guide to surviving the next five minutes. "What would you do if you were me?"

"That depends. Do I still get to be a cop, and carry a loaded service revolver?"

"No, you're an interior designer. And he's your business partner. Linda, he said all the right things that I've been dying for him to say, but at the worst possible time. He broke my heart." I sighed. "I can't take this. It's just not worth the pain."

"Sure it is."

"Jim's never cheated on you, though, has he?"

"Not since we were engaged, no, but we've had plenty of fights and other people who caught his eye, or caught mine. Plenty of times over the years one of has done something stupid or claimed that this was the last straw, that it's over between us. But we just . . . muddle through them somehow. If you really want my advice, Erin, it's to go treat yourself to a massage, or whatever helps you relax. Me, I'd go to a shooting range, but that probably wouldn't be the ticket for you. Just let your heart heal. See how this feels in another day, then a week, then a month. Give yourself a chance to gain some perspective."

I took a deep breath and let it out. "I can do that."

"Good. So are you okay to drive? You can come here. I can make you some comfort food. Chicken soup. Hot chocolate, maybe?"

I hesitated. The phrase "the last straw" kept ringing in my ears, and now a strange image came to my mind's eye. I kept seeing the reveal in Burke's wall, showing the straw bales. All those broken and bent pieces—were they really just the result of the shifting foundation? Maybe it was just a coincidence, or a product of my utter confusion, but something nagged at me.

"Thanks, but I don't think so."

"What are you going to do instead?"

"Go to the shooting range. Aim at any targets that remind me of Sullivan."

She laughed. "Now, *there's* a plan."

I couldn't muster a smile, but at least I was breathing. And talking. Maybe even thinking. Things could be worse. "On another subject entirely, when the police investigated the scene of the shooting at Burke's house, you didn't find any loose pieces of straw, did you?"

"Not that I'm aware of. Why?"

"It's just . . . he's got construction problems, with the concrete in his foundation. The shifting could be causing problems with his straw-bale walls."

"So the house could be . . . leaking straw?"

"I'm just thinking out loud. Anyway, thanks so much for your advice. I feel a little better now."

"Any time. And, Erin, Jimmy and I were talking about having you over for dinner. Tonight's a little hectic, but what about tomorrow? I don't get off till late, but . . ." She was obviously making this up as she went along.

"I'd love to. Thanks. But why don't we try for next week, okay?"

"That'd probably work even better. So. Are you going to be all right?"

"Eventually. I'll give you a call tomorrow or the day after."

"Take care, Erin. And don't do anything rash."

"Now, when do I *ever* do anything rash?"

She chuckled and we said good-bye and hung up.

I repaired my makeup as best I could, then backed out of my parking space. Linda would be furious with me, but a growing suspicion was starting to get a stranglehold on me. I couldn't get the image of all those damaged straws in Burke's wall reveal out of my mind.

There was a simple way of finding out if anything strange was going on at Burke's house. Many months ago he'd shown us where he hid the key to his front door, for times when we needed to let our crews into his home while he was at work. As long as Burke was at work right now, it would be simple enough for me to let myself in, remove the screws holding the glass in place, and investigate to see if the straws were getting mangled by Burke—or maybe Jeremy—using that access into his thick walls as a hiding space.

I arrived at Burke's house and peered through his garage window. His car was gone. Good. It would only

take me five or ten minutes to prove or disprove my latest
shot-in-the-dark theory, and then I could scoot out of
here with no one the wiser. If, God forbid, Burke caught
me red-handed, I could tell him I was afraid that the
shifting straws could indicate that his house was becoming even more unsafe and that I wanted to take a second
look before calling the structural engineer again. It was a
weak story, but then again, I had red, puffy eyes; every
man I'd ever met hated to belabor any point made by a
woman who'd recently been crying. Men were always
afraid emotions would get stuck to them like white cat
hairs on black velvet.

I stuck a screwdriver in my pocket, raced up Burke's
porch steps, and removed the cap from his lamp. I could
hear his spare key clink inside as I did so. I slid the false
bottom out of the cap, retrieved the key, and set the lamp
cap in the middle of the porch where I couldn't possibly
overlook it. This was undoubtedly a wild-goose chase—a
by-product of my inability to think straight—and the last
thing I wanted to do was accidentally run off with Burke's
key.

I let myself inside, locked the deadbolt behind me,
and entered the living room. The warm air smelled of
cinnamon toast. Burke must have only recently left home
for work after eating breakfast. "Burke?" I called, just to
be cautious, though the jig would have pretty much been
up already if he'd answered.

The desk had been removed from the front porch, I
suddenly realized. Was it in his bedroom, or had the police taken it for fingerprint evidence?

"Focus!" I commanded myself.

I strode boldly into the kitchen and to the reveal on
the east wall next to Burke's table and chairs. I got a sink-

ing feeling of futility as I looked at it. What had I been thinking? This was straw. Of *course* the pieces would get broken along the wall! It was pressed right up against the glass, after all.

Then again, I thought, unscrewing the fasteners, it *was* only the lower third of the visible straws that appeared to be pressed downward, as though something had been jammed between them and the drywall. Plus, this spot was in full view of anyone who happened to be standing near the glass back door. Which was very likely where Walter Emory had been when he made his unannounced inspection of the property, in the final moments of his life.

A chill ran up my spine as I continued working to remove the eight screws that held the frame for the window in place, my mind racing. This would make such an inconvenient—and small—hiding spot. Yet Burke had been excessively concerned about privacy these past few months. He'd complained to me before the open house about how nosy strangers could be—always poking into his closets and cabinets. That thought alone had almost driven him to withdraw from the contest. If he'd wanted to keep some papers well hidden in his house, this would do the trick.

I finally removed the last screw and removed the glass—frame and all—from the wall. Sure enough, the lower portion of the frame had hidden the top half inch of what looked like a bright yellow plastic folder, which had been jammed between the straw bale and the Sheetrock. I cursed at the sight.

It took quite a bit of effort, but millimeter by millimeter I managed to pry the thin folder from behind the wall.

I sent up a quick prayer that its contents would be innocent in nature—stock certificates or savings bonds.

My hands shook as I unfastened the clasp on the
folder and emptied it onto the kitchen counter. Two
items were inside the folder—a photograph and a dozen
or so typed pages stapled together. The photograph
showed Burke holding a beautiful towheaded boy as they
both beamed into the camera. At once the portrait
tugged at my tear ducts and filled me with fear. The implications of why he'd stashed the picture in a hiding
place with what appeared to be a scientific report were
dreadful.

I scanned the report about data findings for an air-
purification system called the CleenAir 2000 System.
The document had been compiled by Dr. Burke Stratton
and listed the results of various airborne particles, which
I recognized as carcinogens. According to the time
stamps and the graphics, the particle counts had increased, rather than decreased, as the samples were
taken.

"Damn it, Erin," a quiet voice behind me said.

I gasped and whirled around. I tried to speak, but I was
too frightened. No words would come.

Burke had managed to unlock the front door and tiptoe inside without my hearing a sound.

He shook his head. "I knew I was in trouble when I
saw the Sullivan and Gilbert van in my driveway. I was
hoping it would be Steve."

He aimed a gun straight at me.

chapter 24

I *didn't want to do it, Erin,*" Burke said. *He looked to be* on the verge of tears, and the hand holding the gun shook. "I *save* lives. I don't take them. But...Thayers killed my son. That idiot invention of his not only didn't work, it made the air quality worse! Caleb was breathing in more carcinogens. And I'd put my son's life in his hands."

Now he was openly crying. His face was the picture of a man in agony. "My wife was against it all along. She wanted to keep Caleb in the hospital in the final stages of his chemo. It wipes out the patient's immune system. But

Richard promised me his air purifier was as good as anything they could do at the hospital."

Burke's eyes were staring into mine desperately, as if begging for my understanding. His plaintive demeanor, when combined with the gun aimed at my chest, made a physical oxymoron that was both surreal and terrifying. I'd trusted him! I'd fought with Sullivan over him, insisted on his innocence! He was guilty all along!

"I believed Richard," he went on. "I had to. There was no time for more testing. We would be able to keep Caleb home, you see? In his own bedroom. Patients do better there. Especially when they've got skilled caregivers. It's a proven fact. I told my wife I knew best, as a doctor."

Burke was openly sobbing. He'd lowered the gun, but kept it trained on me. The irony of the situation hit me full force. I was going to die, all because I'd believed in Burke and refused to listen to Sullivan. Just two days ago, Steve warned me that Burke could have boody-trapped his own desk to make himself look innocent.

"That decision took months off my son's life, Erin," Burke continued. "It turned me into an accomplice in my own little boy's death. I tried so hard to live with that. But I couldn't. Richard Thayers took everything from me. My son. My self-image as a healer. My wife. My home, because I couldn't stand to live in that house after Caleb was gone. My job."

"Because you went into research?"

He shook his head. "I was fired months ago. I was putting too much time into my own research on that damned CleenAir flimflam contraption that killed my son."

"I'm so sorry, Burke."

He nodded and said in a cracked voice. "I know you are. And it's...there's no justice in this world. This is a place where beautiful, innocent little children get sick and die. And it doesn't matter how well they're loved. But, Erin, it shouldn't also be a place where a father who loves his son more than anything else gets conned into having a hand in hastening his child's death. That's just too much."

"It was still wrong, what you did, Burke," I said in a near whisper, my throat too swollen with pent-up emotion to speak.

He made a derisive noise. "I should have sued, right? Brought Thayers to court on charges of criminal negligence and so on?"

I managed a small nod.

"I didn't want a dollar figure attached to Caleb's life. To have judges and lawyers and doctors calculating how much money parents deserve for some bastard shortening their dying son's life. Besides, Richard made it clear that the product was still in Beta testing. Though he *also* claimed that it was this state-of-the-art product that would eventually revolutionize air quality in the home. *I* was the one who wanted to partner with him—turn it into a legitimate business that could allow patients with weak autoimmune systems to convalesce at home. If I had sued Thayers, I would've been publicly humiliating myself. The press would have played me as the arrogant doctor who tried to play God. The fool who defied prevailing wisdom about patient care and trusted the snake-oil salesman with his own son's life."

Not knowing if it would help or hurt my cause of getting out of here alive, I decided I had to at least go down fighting. I said sternly, "So you took revenge instead and tricked Richard into poisoning himself."

"Yes."

"Did it make you feel any better? Did it restore your sense of justice in any way?"

"No. No, Erin, it didn't." He swiped at his tears, then pointed the gun at me again. "I rented lab space by myself at a private facility. When I began the research on CleenAir, I expected only to find that his product was ineffective. Once I found out that the damned filtering material was emitting *more* harmful particles into the environment, I had no choice. I could not let that man continue to live."

"He didn't do it intentionally, though. I can't believe he knew how bad his system was and still sold it to you."

"That's irrelevant, Erin! It was *his* responsibility to do the kind of testing that *I* did myself! My own work was just...too late to save my son from Thayers."

"And Walter Emory? What was his crime? What did *he* have to do with your son's death?"

"Nothing. Not a thing." He sighed and shook his head. "It was your partner's fault! Steve Sullivan knew right away what I'd done. You should have seen the hatred in his eyes when I bumped into him the morning that Richard died! I knew he was never going to let the police drop it. And...I guess I panicked. I wanted to scare him off...Sending him those threatening business cards to frighten him into thinking it was a serial killer. But, jeez! Not even a live grenade scares that guy! I got your van confused with his when I kicked in the headlight. I was going to plant another threat in his van on the anniversary of Caleb's death, but you spotted me first, so I acted even drunker than I was."

"But Steve had nothing to do with Walter's coming here, Burke!"

"I couldn't sleep," he continued as if I hadn't spoken. "Steve didn't know...*nobody* knew that Thayers had done a terrible thing, much worse than what I'd done in making him pay for it. So I kept the data hidden right there." He gestured wildly at the opening in the wall behind me. "One morning, I was taking it out. I wanted to think through how I could make the information public without incriminating myself. Turns out Walter Emory was standing at the back door, watching me. I was so startled that I dropped the folder. The report and the photograph of Caleb went sliding across the floor toward him. I knew right away it was all over. That he'd seen the photograph of me holding my child, and that he'd spotted 'CleenAir' on the cover sheet and recognized the name as Thayers's invention. He knew I'd done it. He had the same expression of horror on his face that you had a minute ago."

"You had a gun in your hand at the time?" I asked incredulously.

He shook his head. "In the kitchen with me. The weapons I stole from Darren had always been my Plan B. In case my plan for poisoning Thayers failed. I sneaked over there during the open house, just long enough to unlock the back door to his shooting gallery." He released a bitter laugh. "The idiot never even checks his doors before going to bed." He shook his head a second time. "That morning, when Emory surprised me with an unexpected inspection, I'd been...contemplating suicide. But then I saw that look on Emory's face. Nobody was ever going to understand! I grabbed a pistol, and he tried to run, but I shot him. I killed an innocent man."

He straightened his shoulders, his expression looking frighteningly determined. He aimed the gun at me with more resolve, as though he'd steeled himself. "This is how my life has been, ever since Richard Thayers entered it, Erin. I can't get a break." He gestured at me. "Now, the only person who believed in me is the one who finds the evidence that will put me in a prison. So I have no choice."

"No! You have to stop this now, Burke! You said it yourself. You *save lives*. You don't take them."

He was gritting his teeth. My words were having no effect.

"Turn around, Erin. This will be easier for both of us if you're not looking at me."

"I'm not going to turn my back on you, Burke. Anyway, there's no way you can get away with this."

"I'll say it was an accident. That you were here when you shouldn't have been, and I thought you were a burglar."

"That won't work. No jury in the country would believe that!"

"I'll think of something. I always do. Turn around, damn it!"

"You know Caleb wouldn't want you to kill me." I held Caleb's picture in front of me like a shield.

"Oh, God!" Burke started sobbing again. He pointed the gun at his own temple. "Get out of here, Erin. Get out of my house."

"Give me the gun, and I'll give you Caleb's picture. Then I'll go."

"No. Just leave it on the countertop. This is the only way this can end."

"You're going to get a sympathetic jury, Burke. You

can plead temporary insanity for Walter's shooting, and they'll wonder if they'd have done any differently in Richard's death. It might not even be murder, because of intent. You can claim you only wanted to make him sick, and then everything snowballed."

"Maybe Caleb will be waiting for me on the other side," he said quietly.

He did something to the gun with his thumb to remove the safety, then again pressed the gun barrel against his temple.

"No! Stop!" I pleaded.

He shut his eyes.

I sprang forward, tackling him, my shoulder hitting him in the chest just as the gun went off. We crashed to the floor with such a jarring force that a shock wave of pain raced through me. For an instant, I thought I'd been shot, but quickly realized my breath had merely been knocked out of me when I'd landed on top of him. The gun had gone flying behind him and crashed against the back door.

I fought against my body's instincts to curl up and struggle for air. Expecting Burke to be lifeless, I pushed myself away and grabbed at a kitchen chair to help me scramble to my feet, all the while desperately gasping for air.

Burke was still alive. His head was bleeding, but he pressed his palm to the top of his head, over a gaping wound.

"Oh, jeez!" he cried. "I just grazed my cranium! Leave it to me to miss!"

I staggered toward the gun. Just then, the front door flew open and a woman's voice yelled, "Police!" Linda

Delgardio barged inside, her weapon drawn. She gaped at me.

I could only stare back at her, a sense of relief flooding through me. It was short-lived, however, as I shifted my gaze to Burke. He still had one hand pressed against his head wound, but he'd also grabbed the photograph. He curled into a ball on the kitchen floor, holding the picture against his chest as he wept uncontrollably, looking for all the world like a scared little boy.

chapter 25

epilogue

On Valentine's Day, why wait for someone else to give you flowers? Buy them yourself! If your special someone brings you a bouquet, all the better. A second room in your home will be graced, and you'll feel all the more loved.

—Audrey Munroe

I awoke on February 14 to the sound of power saws and nail guns. The kitchen remodel was in full swing. Audrey had taped this morning's show, and had tried to convince me to take the day off and go to a spa with her. I had waffled and said no, but was still mulling the possibility of calling in sick, not only because a spa on Valentine's Day sounded like the all-time best treat imaginable, but because I simply did not feel up to facing Sullivan today, of all days.

By the time I'd showered, dressed, and come downstairs, the construction noises had stopped and the carpenters were laughing. This meant that Audrey had brought them their daily coffee and doughnuts (although she'd probably cut them into heart shapes and chosen ones with pink icing), and that she was now entertaining them with one of her many stories. Judging by the volume of their laughter, this had to be one of her more ribald tales from her ballet days.

The coffeepot was dry, so I got the coffeemaker going again and cleared my chair at the dining room table. This was a daily exercise, because the clutter seemed to behave like silt and refill whatever troughs I managed to scoop away. Finally, I sat down with the morning newspaper and a steaming cup of coffee. Hildi pranced into the room and gave me my first valentine by leaping onto my lap and rubbing against me affectionately as she settled down.

I stroked her silky fur as I scanned the paper. There was only the briefest of stories about Burke's impending trial—various legal experts opining about whether or not it would have to be moved from Crestview in order to get him an impartial jury. The discussion was premature at best, because any trial was months in the future; only a week had passed since his arrest.

Audrey chuckled as she closed the kitchen door behind her. The sturdy exterior door was a temporary feature which we'd installed upon my suggestion. Audrey had needed it there for noise abatement, though she'd insisted on easy access to the construction. The door featured a large glazed window and would be moved to the sunroom/breakfast nook during the last step of the remodel.

"Morning, Erin." She grabbed her notebook and pen

from the top of a stack of recipe books and sat down at the head of the table beside me. "I heard all the latest from the carpenters. Just like Joe predicted, his daughter Laurie brought home a dog from the Humane Society. Laurie was doing community service volunteer work there, if you remember. And now Susan is going nuts, having to housebreak a two-year-old dog, while Laurie and Sammie are at school and he's here on the job." She paused. "Oh, and Scott's sister is expecting again."

"I take it there's nothing major going on in Bill's life?"

"He's trying to decide between a used Chevy and a Toyota 4Runner. I told him to talk to my car dealer first and mention my name to see if he could get a better deal."

I managed a small smile and a nod. "It's great that you're on such good terms with all the workmen."

"It makes the whole experience so much more pleasant for everyone. Plus, it's just human nature that they'll want to do a better job for home owners who've treated them with the respect that they deserve."

She made some notations in her notebook. "I'm putting a show together on tips for remodeling. Getting to know all the subcontractors and their staffs is one. And saving little jars is another."

"Little jars?"

"Yes. To serve as containers for small quantities of every color of paint in your house. That has saved me so much time and hassle over the years, I can't even tell you. This way, whenever I get a nick or mark on my walls or trim, I can simply grab a jar, shake it to stir the paint quickly, and then I can dab fresh paint over the mark with a fingertip. Compare that to having to haul out a big paint can and a screwdriver to open it with, along with a stir stick, putting out newspapers, finding a paint-brush, et cetera."

"That's a brilliant suggestion, Audrey." Hildi leapt off my lap.

"Thank you." Audrey beamed at me. "Do you have any more tips like that one for the show?"

Hildi was headed in the direction of her food dish and managed to knock over a cut-crystal bud vase just then.

"How about passing along my kitchen-remodel sug-gestion to keep only the barest necessities in your living space and put everything else in storage?"

"Oh, absolutely. My do-as-I-say lifestyle is one of the many reasons my show is filmed in a studio and not in my house." She closed her notebook. "We can talk about this later. But right now, Erin, I have a confession to make."

"Uh-oh." I braced myself.

"I know this is going to make you angry, but I felt so strongly about it that I went ahead and butted into your personal business. I asked Mr. Sullivan to handle work without you today."

"Audrey! You can't keep—"

She held up a palm. "You're right. It was wrong of me. I promise not to do anything remotely like this again, if I can possibly help it. But this is Valentine's Day. You're both so miserable just on ordinary days now. On a holiday specifically made for lovers . . . well, the thought was simply too grim for me to sit back and do nothing."

I leaned forward and reached around some empty Tupperware bowls to put my hand on top of hers. "I appreciate what you're trying to do, Audrey. I do. But this isn't something you can fix. We have to work this out between us. It may or may not end with our being together, but either way, it's going to take time."

She put her hand on top of mine. "I understand that, Erin. But sometimes things are too overwhelming for us to carry on with business as usual. This is one of those times. You have the stress of coping with two murders and a suicide attempt, on top of Mr. Sullivan's stupid transgression. All the while you're seeing him every day and trying to hold your business together. *Then* you compound all of that with *today's* expectations and baggage?"

Just hearing my litany of woes listed aloud like this was depressing me. I pulled my hand away and began to rock myself slightly in my seat.

"I'm not taking no as an answer, Erin. I went ahead and made reservations for us at the spa for the full four-hour treatment. That, by the way, is always my biggest tip for a really special treat for your Valentine's Day. One of my ex-hubbies—I don't remember which one—taught me that. We'd treat each other to massages and facials."

"That's a great idea for anyone who can afford it."

"Oh, it's adjustable for any budget. You give your significant other a card, and inside the card you place a handmade coupon: Good for the person's favorite meal or activity, or what have you. The point is really just to give your loved one a little TLC. Which is exactly what you need today, Erin."

"You're right, Audrey. And thank you."

"You're welcome. Does this mean you forgive me for butting in?"

I managed what could very well have been my first smile in more than a week. "Yes. Especially considering that *this* is the last time you're butting in like this. Provided you *can possibly help it,* which doesn't sound all that promising to me, by the way. What time is our reservation?

"One P.M."

"That late?" I asked. "Too bad you didn't make your confession to me last night. I'd have stayed in bed for another hour."

The doorbell rang, and Audrey winced. "Oops. The second half of my confession is here early, so I'll make this quick. Mr. Sullivan and I talked at length, and we both decided that his taking you to dinner or even lunch on Valentine's Day was too much pressure with things so raw."

I sprang to my feet. "So he's taking me to breakfast!?"

"Just to coffee. I really should have stopped you from making yourself a cup here. More than one cup makes you so edgy." The doorbell rang a second time.

I started cursing.

"Count to ten, dear, and try to remember that although I have my annoying traits, I have plenty of endearing ones to counterbalance them."

"But you just got through saying how it was too much for me to be seeing Sullivan today, which is true! Then you go and . . . and—"

The doorbell rang a third time.

"You should really go answer that. He's probably brought you flowers. You can't just leave him standing there."

I growled, but turned and headed to the front door. Sullivan was my business partner, after all. However bad things were for us romantically, I still hoped we could keep Sullivan and Gilbert Designs together.

I swept open the door. Sullivan stood on the porch holding a spectacular array of exotic flowers—red amaryllis and anthuriums, white calatheas, calla lilies, and Oriental lilies—in a red-tinted glass vase. He gave me a shy smile. "Morning. I was afraid you wouldn't answer." He held out the bouquet to me. "These are for you. Happy Middle-of-February Day."

"They're beautiful. Thank you." I sighed and asked if he'd like to come inside for a moment. I was experiencing the usual agony of seeing him, being this close to him as he stepped through the door. Every time we were in the same room together now, my insides felt like they were being squeezed. I pressed myself against the foyer wall to give myself some distance. "It figures you wouldn't be so predictable as to bring roses."

"That's not entirely true. There's more."

"Oh, Steve. I'm sorry, but I don't *want* more. I already feel like I'm recovering from getting trapped in an avalanche. I'm just trying to get my feet back under me."

"I know. I feel that way, too. Can you put the flowers down, please?"

I sighed but complied, putting the bouquet on the coffee table in the parlor. I stood there admiring them for a moment, struggling to get my heartbeat and my nerves back to normal. I wondered for a moment if it was possible that, beneath his suave exterior, Sullivan was as nervous as I was.

When I turned around, Sullivan hadn't followed me. He was still standing in the foyer, now holding a red envelope in one hand and a tiny white paper cup in the other. I grinned. "You carved another grape into a rose?"

"Not quite." He stepped toward me and handed me the paper container, saying, "Actually, *this* time I kept trying to carve a rose into the shape of a grape, but that's surprisingly difficult to do."

I peered into the cup and then removed a tiny ceramic rose. It was pale pink and impossibly delicate, not much bigger than my fingertip. "Oh, Steve. This is so cute!"

"Plus, it should last longer than the grape-shaped rose. Or the rose-shaped grape, for that matter." He handed me the envelope. "Here. Open this now."

I obliged him. The front of the card was a picture of a perfect red rose, and the inside was blank except for Steve's brief handwritten note:

> Dearest Erin,
> Forgive me.
> Love always,
> Steve

I met his gaze. "I won't belabor the point," he said gently, "but I *am* going to keep asking your forgiveness periodically. Sooner or later, *one* of us will cave, and it isn't going to be me." He gave me a sexy smile. "But for now, I'm just hoping you'll agree to get a cup of coffee—or maybe a hot chocolate and a bagel—at the place on the corner. Just in honor of Middle-of-February Day. No pressure."

"That sounds nice." I put the ceramic rose and the card on the table next to the flowers. Audrey would read the card the instant we were gone and would be dying to know what I'd said in return, but I had no intention of answering. If I had my way, my very own compulsive meddler would suffer in suspense for a long, long time.

Steve helped me with my coat and we left the house. We seemed destined to walk to the coffee shop in silence, but for once I didn't mind at all. I let my hand brush against his, and before long I'd laced my fingers through his. We continued our short journey, hand in hand, our steps in perfect harmony.

about the author

LESLIE CAINE was once taken hostage at gunpoint and finds that writing about crimes is infinitely more enjoyable than taking part in them. Leslie is a certified interior decorator and lives in Colorado with her husband and a cocker spaniel. She is at work on her next Domestic Bliss mystery.

If you enjoyed Leslie Caine's
POISONED BY GILT,
you won't want to miss any
of the wonderful mysteries in the
Domestic Bliss series.
Look for them at your favorite bookseller.

And read on for an exciting early look at the next
Domestic Bliss mystery,

HOLLY AND HOMICIDE

*a domestic
bliss mystery*

by
Leslie Caine

Coming in fall 2009

Holly and Homicide
on sale fall 2009

chapter 1

The article about a grave robbery caught my attention.
It was a short piece on the second page of the *Snowcap
Village Gazette*, which quoted the haughty wisecrack
of the local sheriff: "Probably another case of yuppie
skiers robbing us of our ancestry, like the way they're
turning the Goodwin Estate into the Wendell Barton
B and B." My heart began to race, and I thought: Here
we go again. A picturesque December morning in the
ski town of Snowcap, Colorado, had just turned a lot
colder.

Sullivan handed me a cup of decaf. Although he'd
pulled on a pair of jeans and a black T-shirt before
heading downstairs to the kitchen of the aforemen-
tioned Goodwin Estate, he slipped back under the covers beside me, his own cup in hand. "Thanks, sweetie."
I took a tentative sip. Perfection. "Did you see the story
about the grave robbery in this week's *Gazette*?"

"Yeah. Annoying potshot about the inn. Sheriff
Mackey sounds like a major jerk."

"No kidding." Wendell Barton, who owned the

town's new ski lodge, was only *one* of the partners who'd purchased this fabulous Victorian mansion from Henry Goodwin, who was a direct descendant of its original owner. "I suppose by 'yuppie skiers' turning this place into a Wendell Barton B and B, he means you and me."

"Not if he's ever seen you try to ski," Sullivan teased.

I considered swatting him, but his coffee cup was too full, and I didn't want to risk a spill on our divine burgundy silk duvet. I settled for narrowing my eyes at him. He laughed and kissed my forehead.

I felt the warm glow that I'd grown so wonderfully accustomed to during the past nine months, since Sullivan and I began dating in earnest. "I'm getting better at skiing, you know. You said so yourself."

"You are. Absolutely. If you make good use of our last three weeks here, you might even be able to stop without grabbing on to a tree."

His snide remark called for a comeback, but the grave robbery preoccupied me. Why would somebody steal a man's bones? I took a couple sips of coffee and reread the article.

"I'm sure the incident at the cemetery was just a prank," Sullivan said. "Drunken frat boys on a ski trip, blowing off some steam, maybe."

"The timing's really weird, if that's all it was. Why dig through snow and frozen ground, just for a dumb joke? You'd think they'd have dug two inches down and decided to go TP some trees instead."

"Yeah, but it *has* to be a prank. What *sensible* motive could there possibly be? It's idiotic to dig up a random fifty-year-old grave. Wasn't there a really common name on the tombstone?"

"R. Garcia, and the cemetery records are inadequate, so they don't even know how to track down Garcia's relatives." I let my imagination gnaw on the conundrum for several seconds. "Maybe that's why this particular grave was chosen...so as to ruffle the fewest feathers. I hope I'm just being paranoid, but I think this was done by one of the hundred or so townspeople trying to prevent the Snowcap Inn from opening."

Sullivan took a sip of coffee, appearing to ponder my words. "No way."

"All I know is, every time Henry Goodwin or anyone else puts up a sign about the Snowcap Inn, someone covers it in graffiti."

"Still. That's a gigantic leap...from scribbling four-letter words on a sign to digging up a grave and maybe planting someone's remains here, don't you think?"

How could I answer that? His point was valid, but my counterargument was a combination of women's intuition and past experience. A string of terrible past experiences, to be more precise. The police department in Crestview—our hometown some forty miles away—had undoubtedly been on the verge of assigning a homicide task force to follow me around. In the last three years, client after client had dragged me into a string of bad luck so long that Job himself might have offered me a sympathetic shoulder. But my gloomy run of catastrophes had magically lifted on Valentine's Day, when Steve and I finally gave in to our mutual attraction. Since then, we'd become the proverbial happy couple. And yet even as a young child, I'd known there was no such thing as happily *ever* after. We were long overdue for a stumbling block.

I tried to employ my "confidence and optimism" mantra, but it was too late. With my penchant for finding dead bodies, I had an unshakable certainty that "R. Garcia" was sure to turn up in my van or in my laundry basket and our idyllic job would devolve into a disaster. The rambling three-story Goodwin Estate had been built eighty years ago, as commissioned by the current owner's grandfather—the founder of Snowcap Village—but in these last couple of months, it had come to represent how far I'd grown in my career and in my life. Now the grand home, with its cupolas, curved turrets, festive stained-glass accent sidelights, and transoms, and all its countless handcrafted details, was somehow going to turn dark and ugly. And so was my life.

"Erin? You're shaking. Are you cold?"

"A little."

He set down his coffee cup and pulled me close. "Let me warm you up again." He kissed me tenderly, and just like that, my fears melted away.

An hour later, I trotted down the stairs. Our bedroom was on the third floor of Henry's house—soon to be the Snowcap Inn. When the inn officially opened on Christmas Eve, Henry, too, would live elsewhere; he planned to rent a condo in town for a year, and then, once his mayoral duties officially ended, to travel. As I entered the central hall, which would be converted into the hotel lobby, I spotted Sullivan's notepad on the newly built receptionist's desk. He'd probably left his pad there by mistake, since it contained measurements for the perfect Christmas tree to grace this space. Several minutes ago, Sullivan and

Henry had headed out to cut down one of the large spruce trees on Henry's enormous parcel of land.

When I entered the kitchen through the double doors, a tall, angular, fortyish woman was peering into the knotty-pine cabinets and compiling an inventory of kitchenware. I waited till she'd completed her count of serving spoons, then said, "Hi. I'm Erin Gilbert, an interior designer here at the inn."

She peered at me a little too imperiously for my liking. I got the feeling that she was tabulating the cost of my Icelandic cardigan (a gift from Steve) and designer slacks. She was wearing a crisp white shirt with pleats and piping, black pants, and loafers. She had limp brown hair in a blunt cut just above the nape of her long neck. She would have been pretty except for her permanent-looking scowl. "Mikara Woolf. Manager-to-be of the Snowcap Inn." Her voice was confident yet flat.

"Ah, great. Henry Goodwin said that you'd be starting sometime this week. My partner, Steve Sullivan, is here, too, and he—"

"Yeah, he's out back with Henry. Something about Christmas decorations...chopping down a tree or looking for the lights. Quite a hunk, that Mr. Sullivan." She raised an eyebrow. "You two are sleeping together, right? And you're not married?"

I bristled. "Um, much as I hate to get us off on the wrong foot, frankly, I don't see why you're asking."

She gave me a slight smile. "Oh, I realize it's none of my business...even though you *did* give me my answer just now. I'm simply checking the accuracy of the local rumor mill. I'm a native. Ten years ago, before Snowcap Village was turned into the new mini-Vail, everybody in this town knew one another. Till Wendell Barton bought the mountain...along with every*thing* and every*one* else."

"If small-town life means everyone discussing who's sleeping with whom, there's something to be said for tourist towns and anonymity."

She crossed her arms and gave me another visual once-over. "Spoken like a city girl. Where are you from originally? New York? Philadelphia?"

"No, I grew up in the suburbs. Of the Albany area." She cocked an eyebrow as if she doubted me, and I conceded, "But I went to college and trained in New York."

She smirked and nodded. "Another Easterner. Figured as much."

I found myself adding defensively, "Steve's a native Coloradoan."

"Yeah, I figured that out, too."

"Huh. I'll have to remind him to stop wearing his Colorado Native sweatshirt so often."

To her credit, she laughed. Maybe she wasn't quite as standoffish as all that. "Guess I'm coming off as a little judgmental. My apologies. It's been a rough week. You wouldn't believe the flack I'm getting from my sister and my former neighbors for accepting this job. People think I've sold my soul to the devil by agreeing to work here...considering it now belongs to Barton."

"Oh, for heaven's sake! *Henry Goodwin* has the final say in everything regarding the remodel, not Wendell Barton. Furthermore, it *doesn't* belong to Wendell. He's just one of three partners, including Audrey Munroe, my landlady back in Crestview. She's got more integrity than anyone I know. She's not about to cede full control to Barton, or to anyone else, for that matter."

"I assume you mean Audrey Munroe of the *Domestic Bliss* television show." Mikara gave me a smug smile. "Did you know she's currently dating Wendell Barton?"

"What?!" Apparently the small-town gossip express was way ahead of me.

"Angie, my sister, spotted them together at the Nines last Saturday night."

Much as I wanted to deny the accuracy of Mikara's information, there had definitely been some sparks between Wendell and Audrey when I'd last seen Audrey—at an inn meeting on Friday afternoon. Steve and I had gone back to Crestview immediately afterwards. During the remodel, we had full use of any of the eight mostly finished guest bedrooms, which we'd designed ourselves. That allowed us to make the ninety-minute commute to Crestview only when we so chose—which generally meant on weekends, so that I could be with Hildi, my adorable black cat, who was happier at home.

Truth be told, I disliked Wendell Barton, a real-estate mogul who'd struck me as a blowhard. I'd yet to find a Snowcap resident who had a single nice thing to say about the man. Then again, from the sound of things, Mikara hadn't found any residents to say anything nice about *me*, either, so maybe this town was snooty about all non-natives.

"In another week or two, Wendell's going to have Ms. Domestic Bliss in his sweaty palm," Mikara continued, "and next thing you know, he'll flatten that gazebo you just built out back and erect a half dozen condos in its place."

"If you're so negative about the Snowcap Inn's future, why did you take this job?"

"I'm a pragmatist." She shrugged. "The inn is paying me really well. Especially compared to the pittance I used to make at the art gallery."

I heard the back door open, followed by the stomping of snow boots on the mat and the rumbling tones of Steve's voice. I couldn't help but smile. All the seasonal beauty that surrounded us—the blanket of pure white snow, the glittering stars, the red sashes and green boughs on all the storefronts, the charming cabins, town homes, and quaint shops in Snowcap Village—was only encouraging my lovesickness.

The two men entered the kitchen. Henry, soon to be the former owner of this large estate, was a tall, lanky man in his mid-forties who looked like he'd stepped out of an L.L.Bean ad. He'd been born with a silver spoon in his mouth, although he'd apparently traded that spoon for a camper's spork. Aside from his current duties as mayor, he hadn't held an actual job in his life. He'd invested his father's sizable fortune well, and now spent his time pursuing women and the great outdoors.

Steve's face lit up when our eyes met, and Henry smiled broadly at the sight of Mikara. "I'm glad you're here, Mikki," he said to her. "Just in time for you to butter up Angie." Henry waggled his thumb in the direction of the back door. "She's here now, doing the inspection on the new gazebo."

"Wait," I said to Mikara, instantly anxious. "Your sister is the building inspector?"

"It's a small town," she replied with a shrug.

"But you just told me she doesn't want the inn to open!"

"She'll be reasonable, though, won't she, Mikki?" Henry asked.

"Sure. She won't cause trouble...as long as you don't have any violations. She'll be a total stickler for detail. Don't go expecting her to cut you any slack, is all I'm saying."

Henry stared at her. "But...the city codes are chock-full of minutiae that could be used to nitpick us indefinitely! You're the manager. And her sister. She'll show some family loyalty, surely...right?"

"If that's why you hired me, Henry, you misjudged my sister by a mile!"

Henry massaged his forehead in a silent confirmation that he *had* hired Mikara for political reasons. "Good thing it's just the gazebo, then. We can tear it down if we have to. Everything inside the inn—the plumbing and electrical work—has already passed."

Sullivan grimaced. "But...wasn't Angie the one who took tap-water samples last Friday?"

"Probably," Mikara said with a nod. "She does some contract work for the health inspectors, too."

Henry paled a little at this news but seemed to visibly steel himself a moment later. "So, Mikki, you wanted to make this a live-in position, right? Did you pick out a bedroom yet?"

"Not yet. Why? Does my bedroom have to be located in the basement?"

He laughed heartily and winked in Sullivan's and my direction. "Such a kidder. No. Just not the master bedroom."

"Ah, yes," she said with a sigh. "I remember that room well."

Henry winced slightly at the remark, an unmistakable implication that the two had once been lovers.

"I'm sure you plan on charging hundreds a night for that room," she added.

"During the ski season, absolutely we will. It's a huge space. Erin, Steve, and Audrey Munroe, my co-investor, are using the third-floor bedrooms until we open on Christmas Eve. Gilbert and Sullivan Designs is refurbishing this place from top to bottom, literally."

I gave Sullivan a quick grin, which he answered with a wink; we were actually Sullivan & Gilbert Designs, but clients inevitably got it wrong.

"The bedrooms just need Christmas decorations and whatnot," Henry continued, "then they're all set to be rented out. So...I was hoping you'd consider moving into my old office on the main floor."

"Fine. That makes sense," she said with a grim nod. "You wouldn't want to confuse the guests by having me mingle with them after hours. Otherwise, everyone might have a hard time setting boundaries between the paying guests and the hired help."

He clicked his tongue. "Come on! You're not the hired help. You're the *manager*. I need you to lead the troops. My contract only gives me control of the daily operations of this joint for another ten months. As of next October first, I'm entrusting the operations and procedures of the Goodwin Estate entirely to you. To be honest, I wouldn't have sold if I hadn't known you were going to be here, watching my back."

Although I personally found his mini-speech quite

persuasive, Mikara glared at him and put her hands on her narrow hips. "You should never have sold this place to Wendell Barton and a couple of in-name-only partners, even so."

"They're hardly puppets, Mikki. Audrey Munroe and Chiffon Walters each own thirty percent of the inn now. And this town has got to accept that fact... and learn how to maintain its community ties even while embracing the seasonal tourist trade."

"But Chiffon's just a mindless bimbo who happened to record a couple of hit pop songs some five years ago. And promptly bought a huge condo next to Wendell's mountain. She's no match for Barton!"

"That's not true! Chiffon's got a great head on her shoulders. Barton's powerless unless she or Audrey sides with him. And I trust both of them implicitly." He added pointedly, "I set things up that way specifically so Barton could never tear down this house and put a hundred condos in its place."

"Better get ready for the bulldozer, then," Mikara said with a snort. "Your Ms. Munroe and Mr. Barton are the new hot couple... or as hot as anyone in their sixties can be, that is. Angie saw them necking at the Nines."

Henry's jaw dropped open.

I needed to make my allegiance to Audrey clear before one more remark was made about her. "If Wendell's dating Audrey strictly to win her vote, his plan will backfire."

"Right," Steve added. "Audrey has a mind of her own."

"So does *every* woman"—she glanced at Henry, then added sadly—"right up until she falls in love."

There was an uncomfortable amount of truth in Mikara's remark. We women *do* have a tendency to adopt our lovers' viewpoints.

Sullivan glanced at me, and I felt my cheeks grow warm. "Erin, did you see my notepad?" he whispered. "I measured the—"

"It's on the desk in the lobby."

He nodded.

The doorbell rang. "That's probably Angie," Henry said. "I asked her to give us the results of her inspection right away. Let's all treat her with respect, regardless of what she says."

"Oh, darn," Mikara muttered. "Now I won't be able to spit in my sister's eye, like usual."

Ignoring her, Henry strode into the lobby. Moments later, a blonder, younger version of Mikara entered the kitchen, followed by Henry. Mikara forced a smile. "Hey, Angie," she said. "You've got the work done already?"

"Yeah. But there's a big problem."

Why am I not surprised? I thought. Henry scowled and did a double take at Angie, but Mikara merely sighed and introduced Angie to me.

"Nice to meet you, Angie," I said with a big smile.

"Hi, Angie," Sullivan said, giving her a charming smile. "Good to see you again." She barely looked at him.

"I can't believe there was anything wrong with the gazebo construction," Henry said. "You know what a great job Ben Orlin always does."

"There's nothing wrong with the gazebo. But there's too much lead in your tap water. I can't approve this residence being converted into a motel."

"Fortunately," Henry promptly countered, "you don't *have* to. We intend to use the house as a bed-and-breakfast inn."

"Right," Angie said with a sneer. "That's even worse. You'll have to get restaurant approval. Cooking meals and serving tap water rife with these poisons is out of the question."

"We use the city water here. Same as everyone else."

"Yeah. It's got nothing to do with the water supply. You've got bad pipes. You'll have to replace them all."

Sullivan and I exchanged puzzled glances. Contaminants could be removed with filters, which would be much easier and less expensive than replacing the pipes. We needed to wait until Angie left to tell Henry that, though; my hunch was that otherwise, Angie would find some arcane ruling that prohibited water filtering.

"Our pipes are copper, not lead!" Henry shouted.

"Must be the solder in all the joints," she said with a shrug. "Or else maybe they're copper-coated lead pipes."

"Oh, come off it!" Henry shouted. "You're making this stuff up, and we both know it! Now, what's it going to take to get you to give the water here a passing grade?"

"Are you offering me a bribe, Mr. Goodwin?"

"No, I'm just—"

"Good, because that would be a federal crime, and you're in enough trouble already. What with your lead contaminants and your faulty front steps."

"Front steps?"

She gave him a sly grin. "I must have forgotten

to tell you. They're too steep for a business... and particularly for a business that's going to have geriatrics and little children going up and down them all the time."

"Toddlers and geriatric guests can use the back door and our handicap access."

"*Or* you can follow the law and rebuild them to meet the city codes, so they can use your *front* steps."

"Angie!" Mikara cried. "Quit busting Henry's chops!"

She glowered at Mikara. "Hey, sis. You know, it's like what you said to me when you left the house this morning: 'I'm just trying to do my job.'" She used a lilting voice and fluttered her eyes derisively, mocking her sister.

"You're being a brat, Angela!" Mikara stomped her foot.

"And you're being a weasel!" Angie shot her sister a furious glare, then softened her expression slightly and said to Henry, "The bottom line is, there are unacceptable levels of lead in the water supply. Fix it, or else you're not going to be able to convert this place into a bed and breakfast."

"But we're opening on Christmas Eve! In three weeks!"

"Then you'd better *get the lead out*, hadn't you," she said. "Plus, have the entire concrete stoop demolished and rebuilt to code." She tore off a pink copy from her clipboard and handed it to him. "Here's your official notice. Pity your violations will probably delay your opening. But take heart, *Mayor Goodwin*. There's always *next* Christmas."

She strode toward the front door, glanced back over

her shoulder, and said with a haughty smile, "Good seeing you, Henry."

"Be real careful on the steps," he snarled. "We wouldn't want you to fall and crack your head open."

Sullivan and I exchanged glances.

Steve Sullivan - Erin Gifford - Partners

Richard Thayer - Withdrawing as Judge
  for Earth Love contest - Steve's
  mentor. Was Steve's favorite Prof. a
  → dating / Art Institute - Didn't know
    a Prof.

Burke Stratton was their client. Says
  "   "   wrecked his life, was an M.D.

Margot Troy - 3rd place - dated Burke

Burke says Richard "hates his guts."
  Wants Erin + Steve to "testify" once he
  knows what "charges" are
  → didn't hire G + S to do. Was a "client"
    from hell.

Hildi - cat (Erin's)

Matthew Hayes - M.H. Custom furniture

Riggs + Dantley - police

Richard Thayer - died. drank paint from a
  can. wasn't nuts.

Margot - dating Jeremy Greene
  Walter Emory - suspect in Richard's death
    one of the judges
    belligerent kook.

Darren Campesio → Burke's neighbor

Casia McClure → had windmill behind
  Gardner   his house
  → retired military

Linda del gardeo - Erin's friend + a cop

Jeremy Greene - Stratton's architect

Asia McClure - lives in a house between
  Burke's + Darren's.

Audrey - Erin's Roommate

Jennifer Fairfax client of G + S

Bob Jones - EBAT + Libes security Chief

SUSANNE LANGLEY - A client